·The Three Heretics

Scott Hale

THE THREE HERETICS

Copyright © 2016 Scott Hale
Cover art by Natasha MacKenzie
Map by Jacquelyn Graff
Edited by Jacqueline Kibby

First Edition: October 2016

ISBN-13: 978-0-9964489-2-5

BOOKS BY SCOTT HALE

The Bones of the Earth series

The Bones of the Earth (Book 1)

The Three Heretics (Book 2)

The Blood of Before (Book .1)

The Cults of the Worm (Book 3)

The Agony of After (Book .2)

The Eight Apostates (Book 4)

Novels

In Sheep's Skin

The Body Is a Cruel Mistress (Coming Soon)

KEY

1. CALDERA
2. ALLUVIA
3. TRAESK
4. RIME
5. ELD
6. LACUNA
7. GEHARRA
8. NORA
9. ELDRUS
10. NYXIS
11. ISLAOS
12. HROTHAS
13. BEDLAM
14. GALLOWS
15. CATHEDRA
16. PENANCE
17. CADENCE

18. NACHTLA
19. LYNN
20. TRIST
21. MARWAIDD
22. RHYFEL
23. ANGHEUAWL
24. COMMUNION
25. SKYGGE
26. FORMUE
27. BRANN
28. HVLAV
29. KRES
30. THE DISMAL STICKS
31. GARDEN OF SLEEP
32. DEN OF UNKINDNESS
33. SKELETON'S KEEP
34. SCAVENGER'S TOWER

 CORRUPTED   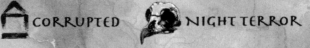 NIGHT TERROR

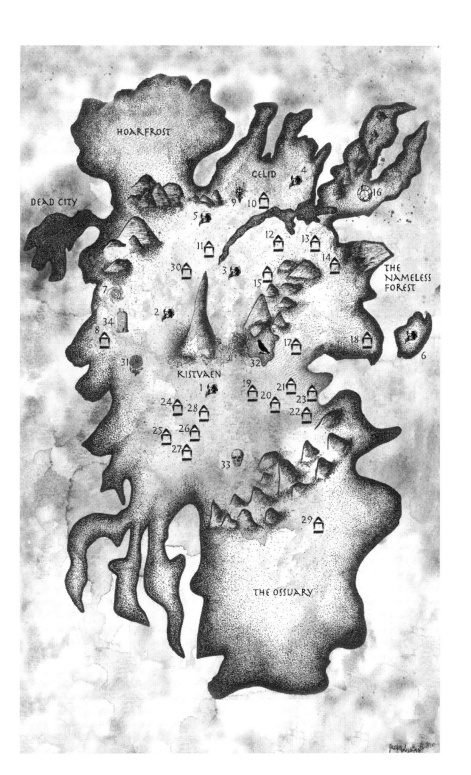

HOARFROST

GELID

DEAD CITY

THE
NAMELESS
FOREST

KISTVAEN

THE OSSUARY

PART ONE

THE BLOOD IN US ALL

CHAPTER I

Carrion birds wheeled overhead, cawing and clawing and laying claim to the bodies on the forest floor below.

Startled awake, Edgar stared from the ground at the winged death that darkened the skies. He turned over, shedding the feathers that had fallen onto him, and pulled a sword from the dead man nearby.

The birds hissed, barbed tongues flicking inside their black beaks. United by hunger, they swarmed and dove into the sea of leaves.

Edgar scurried backward, up and over the second corpse—a fly-ridden horse. From there, using the beast's bruised flesh as his bulwark, he watched the creatures descend.

Their massive claws clamped down on the nearest branches and rocks. Out of their scaled breasts, mouths unraveled, extended, and started chomping at the air. From their riotous hunger, the branches and rocks began to snap and crack. The twenty-pound scavengers lifted off, back into the air, and rushed forward.

Edgar gripped the sword, closed his eyes, and hoped that when they opened again, the birds would be lying dead before him, just like the man had been.

A talon dug into his flesh and tore a chunk of it away. His eyes snapped open to the whirlwind of claws and dripping jaws that surged before him.

Crying out, he gave the sword a desperate swing. The blade cut through the feathery maelstrom, splitting stomachs and nicking necks. Edgar stumbled backward as he hacked at the birds, while those he'd grounded crawled after him, their torso mouths fully protracted, looking like intestines. With teeth.

The carrion birds circled him, their hunger second to their sadism. They came in twos and threes, tearing off pieces of Edgar's skin in passing as he stabbed at them and cursed their cruelty. Blood streamed down his face, beaded down his armor. He screamed, drove his sword through a bird mid-flight, and impaled it into the earth.

A few minutes into the bloody ordeal, and Edgar was already exhausted. His movements were pained, sluggish and worn by the journey he couldn't remember, and handicapped by the training he had never received. He cut another bird from the sky, and crushed its skull underfoot. His arm had grown heavy, the Corruption that colored it enflamed by the violence.

He turned to flee, outnumbered and overrun, but the beaks, by fours and fives now, kept him in his place.

Tears streaming down his face, Edgar dropped to his knees, curled into a ball, and accepted what was to come.

The carrion birds descended, their black wings like curtains closing around him. So close, he could smell and feel the unholy creatures. They smelled of the grave, the ravenous escapees from Death's great cage, and burned hotter than the sun under which they slaughtered.

Again, Edgar closed his eyes. Splotches of pain, like paint, were splattered across his lids. This time, he was certain they wouldn't open again.

A bell chimed in the distance, somewhere beyond this fog of suffering.

One eye open, Edgar watched the carrion birds crash into the ground. There, each of them writhed in shared agony. The mouths in their breasts twisted and stretched to their ripping limits.

When the bell hit its loudest tones, the mouths snapped back and clamped down over the birds' own heads. Blood and skin leaked from the pale appendages as the birds feasted on themselves.

The carrion birds were neck-deep before they stopped moving.

Edgar struggled to his feet, fighting to stay conscious. Before him, the forest swayed peacefully, indifferent to the massacre that wetted its soil.

As he bent down to grab the sword, he caught sight of something in the distance: a ragged shadow, small and jittery, ducking into the foliage.

A second bell rang throughout the killing grounds. The shadow vanished, and when it did, it took with it the piercing din.

Edgar didn't have to be a physician to know he didn't have long before he bled out. He went to the ground and rooted through the plants around the cannibalized birds. Hiss, Twist, and Dark—he passed over the flowers. Numb, Dawn, and Dream—he clutched, crushed, and chewed. His body warmed, deadened, and drifted, but it wouldn't be enough to see him through the night.

He grunted like a ghoul, and crawled like one, too, towards the grass that shimmered silver and sang of salvation.

The hurt inside him had coalesced into a suffocating knot around his chest. Edgar blinked the tears from his eyes, and reached for and ripped out the Anansi growths he'd spotted along a tree. The small nests of webbing pricked his fingertips as he pulled them apart and shoved them into his wounds. His neck, arms, legs, and sides stung as the webs coated the cuts and gouges and pulled them together; any bacteria or disease the birds had been carrying would be left to prosper, but at least he wouldn't be dead before the hour's end.

He stepped over the birds, minding those that still twitched with intent. He went to the corpse of the man and the horse. Although he didn't recognize them, he knew they had been the ones to bring him here. He grabbed a pouch full of water, then searched them for food. When he found it, he shoveled the bread and meat into his mouth, in much the same way the birds would have done to him, had the shadow not intervened.

As Edgar chewed the meat and sucked water, he studied the man's stomach. There was a slit from where a sword—Edgar's sword, most likely—had split him. Edgar wondered why he had killed the man and if the man had deserved it. He glanced at the horse and worried its demise may have been his doing, too.

His family would be proud; of all the qualities to inherit from his mother and father, murderousness was not one he, nor anybody else, had expected.

He couldn't stay here, of that much he was certain, for the stench of death would call forth from all corners and crevices the skittering and starving.

Edgar gathered provisions—food and drink, dagger and blankets, flowers and Anansi growths—and stowed them in the bag he had lifted from the horse. He considered the forest, which gave no hint as to his whereabouts. He noticed a depression between the trees, where the horse's hooves had stomped out a path, and followed it, for he believed it would surely lead him out of this terrible place.

It did not.

The further he went, the deeper he plunged into the forest, traveling in maddening circles over familiar sites. He crossed the same stream twice, passed the same felled tree thrice. A gathering of stones like an altar mocked him on his fifth visit. A cave yawned in boredom as he studied it for the tenth time.

He wiped the sweat from his brow. When he thought he could sweat no more, he felt its familiar sting at the edges of his eyes.

Living in Eldrus hadn't prepared him for such a harsh climate. In fact, living in Eldrus hadn't prepared him for much of anything at all; he was weak, ignorant. He swung his sword in such a way because that's how he had seen his brother do it. He knew of the qualities of curatives because he spied his sister mixing them. All that he brought with him to this wooded seclusion was kindness and blood; the former of no use, the latter almost run dry.

The Gray Arbor, Elsa's Rest, and Keldon's Retreat. The Darkwood, Sun Spot, and Sorrow's Garden. Edgar thought of the many forests of the North, and knew by where he stood this wasn't any of them; the landscape was senseless, endless. Distant hills disappeared when approached, and waters flowed opposite one another on the same plot. In the blink of an eye, massive clouds would form and shower the land in rain that never reached the ground. In some places, the temperature would plummet, and in these pockets plants stood frigid in a forever winter. Even the wildlife was mysteriously absent, and yet he could feel their presence all around him, like they were stalking him. This forest was nowhere, and everywhere; a combination of all things expected, respected, and feared.

The twelfth time Edgar came upon the cave he called it quits. He searched it, front to back, and, to his relief, found nothing awaiting him.

The sword dropped first, and then his body. He hit the stone hard, more fatigued than he had ever been. He was at a loss, at an impasse, at the very moment that would decide the moments to come.

He went through the bag he had been carrying. A chain slithered out of it, to the side. He grabbed it, and held it up. It was an identification tag, the same given to traders as proof of their profession. The metal was worn, bloodstained, and read: Jack Abney, Cathedra. Had this been the corpse's name? Edgar's finger found the loop of a second tag. He lifted it and saw engraved across its plate: Alex Greene, Islaos.

More identification tags followed, of both men and women, from the Heartland towns, the Southern Cradle outposts, and the city of Geharra itself. The corpse had lived a hundred lives before Edgar had robbed him of his last.

Edgar wondered what the man had called himself to slip past the gates; what promises he had made to those Edgar trusted the most to see Edgar drugged and delivered here.

"I bet you thought I could make you rich," Edgar said. He dropped the tags. "I bet—" he scanned his surroundings, "—you set your ransom and asked them to meet you here."

Radiating warmth and madness, he mumbled, "But where is here?"

The answer came quicker than he expected, and in the form of universal dread. Ahead, where the trees were intertwined, sunlight glinted and gleamed.

Edgar squinted, stood up, and followed the winking refraction coming through that crowded place.

In the cropping, behind the bark, vermillion veins fed in and out of the trees. The growths bulged as a thick, brooding liquid coursed through their crystalline tubing.

"Oh no." Edgar put his hand to his mouth. "Oh no, no, no."

He retreated to the cave, took up his sword, and sat there until nightfall, where he chewed on his lip and jumped at every sound, and wondered if god would truly damn him if he were to kill himself; for from the Nameless Forest, there was no other escape.

CHAPTER II

Fifty Days Ago

The city of Eldrus stood in Edgar's peripheral, taunting him to turn around and have a look at all its disappointments. He ignored the city, just as so many had told him to do, and kept his attention on Ghostgrave. Despite its name, the keep did not want for life; at any time of the day or night, one could look through any window, walk down any corridor, or climb up any tower and find one of the many distinguished persons that stayed here, or the servants that served them.

"Little brother, what are you doing out here all alone?" a voice called out from behind Edgar.

He glanced over his shoulder. The pavilion upon which he stood was congested with people today. It was a popular place for dignitaries to come and spread rumors, while at the same time enjoying the dismal sight of the city, which the pavilion overlooked. It wasn't a haunt he expected his brother Vincent to frequent, and yet there he was, cutting through the crowd, practically chewing on the gossip he seemed so eager to share.

"Not much," Edgar said. He strolled over to the white, ivy-laced balcony that stood a good forty feet above the ground and took a seat at one of the benches beside it. "Going somewhere?"

Vincent grinned as the incessant wind tugged at his black robes. He joined Edgar at the balcony and settled in on the bench beside him. Nodding at Eldrus, he said, "If that heart of yours bleeds any more, we'll have to find you a new one."

Edgar rolled his eyes. "What good are we to them if we don't even listen to what they have to say?"

"What good are we to them if we give them everything they want?" Vincent smiled victoriously.

"There's a difference between wants and needs."

"Do they know that?" Vincent touched the family seal that had been burnt into his bracelet. "Enough is never enough."

Edgar stared at Eldrus. The city sat in the palm of the five spires that surrounded it, and behind the great ashen walls that guarded it. Tens of thousands moved through the obsidian sprawl on a daily basis, between home and work, crime and casualty. Eldrus was massive, a world all its own; a city capable of providing anything, and yet it gave so many nothing.

Edgar wanted to debate social responsibility with his brother, but he knew he would sound foolish, so instead he said, "Why are you happy?"

Vincent smiled, patted his knees with excitement, and stood up. "We got one," he said, laughing. His eyes widened as he shouted, "A Night Terror. We got one."

Edgar was reluctant to follow his brother through the headstone-gray corridors of Ghostgrave; Vincent wasn't a cruel man, but his curiosity often begot cruelties.

Who am I to judge? Edgar nodded at all the irrelevant dignitaries that passed him by. *I've been dying to talk to a Night Terror ever since Horace told me about them.*

Vincent twirled around like a girl after her first dance and said, "What should we ask it?"

"Why not start with why they're so determined to murder us all?" Edgar could think of a thousand other questions to ask the creature, but only if he were alone with it, where no one could listen to him, or judge him.

"My lords," a calming voice called out.

Edgar and Vincent turned around, going red like the boys they had been and were supposed to have outgrown.

Archivist Amon stood a few feet away, half-hidden behind one of the many pillars that lined the hallway. He shook his head, having clearly heard everything the two had said to one another.

"Why not invite the whole keep?" the Archivist teased. He walked toward them. The buckle on the book he held clapped against the cover. The book was titled *The Disciples of the Deep*, and it was a novel he had been writing for as long as Edgar could remember. "I'm coming with you."

If there ever were a ghost in Ghostgrave, Archivist Amon could have surely been it; he was thin and pale. When he moved, he did so in silence, without any effort, as though no feet carried him beneath his heavy robes. His age and lineage were often the matter of speculation.

He had no known birthright that would justify his place on the royal council, and yet no justification could be made to remove him from it. His knowledge of the Old World was invaluable. Edgar's father trusted him above most others, and if the old man was good enough for the king, then he was good for everyone else as well.

Amon leaned into Vincent. "How did you come about this poor creature?"

"Patrol found him wounded against the wall. He broke his leg coming over." Victor steered them around the corner, through a doorway, and down the staircase that would lead them to the bowels of Ghostgrave. "I think we can all figure out what it had in mind."

Two guards stood by the dungeon door, their faces not much different than the cracked cobblestone wall which divided the entryway from the rest of the cells. On the workbench beside the door, a card game was in session. The winnings, which consisted of teeth and nails from the keep's prisoners, were piled sloppily on a three-legged chair.

The guards nodded at the Archivist, and bowed to the brothers. With an overflowing key ring, the smaller of the two men undid the lock to the door and stepped aside.

Edgar, Vincent, and Amon went through. Prison cells and the despondent criminals inside awaited them. Spit, blood, and a bubbly pink mixture of the two were hurled back and forth across the dungeon, as the inmates tried to soil these esteemed men.

Edgar covered his nose, the smell of sweat and feces turning his stomach. Naked bodies with welted flesh pressed against the bars. These people begged, in between threats of violence, for a pardon. Repulsion quickly replaced Edgar's feelings of pity; he hated himself for it.

The dungeon ended in a rotund space that contained several cells to hold prisoners of importance.

"My lords," the guards here whispered, rising from their tables and chairs to bow. "Archivist," they added, as Amon stared at them.

"It's just over here," a portly guard by the name of Brennan said. "We patched it up." To Amon, he said, "It's not in pain anymore."

Edgar and Vincent exchanged glances; what was the relationship between the guard and Amon?

Brennan led them to the northernmost cell. He lifted an ancient key from his soiled pocket. With two hands and half the cuss words available to him, he unlocked the door and kicked it open.

On the other side, a Night Terror sat on the floor, manacled at the wrists and ankles. The short chains that held his body to the wall rattled as he shifted to see his visitors.

"I can't believe it," Edgar said.

He and Vincent stepped back, shocked by the creature's face as it leaned into the light.

The Night Terror wore the skull of a large eel as a mask. All the scales and flesh had been stripped away. Two hateful eyes shone behind the bones, as the brothers knelt and looked on with intrigue.

"I can't believe it," Edgar repeated.

"Is that a mask? Is it somehow attached?" Vincent started forward, hands outstretched as though to touch the Terror. "Can we take it off?"

Amon propped himself up against the cell's cobblestone wall. "Do you know what will happen?"

Vincent shook his head and, with Edgar, rose to his feet.

"Then maybe you should stick to words for now."

"Will you tell Father?" Edgar asked. He tried to tame the thoughts running through his head. "Do you think it understands us?"

"I'm sure your father already knows," Amon said. "And I expect it understands us better than we understand ourselves."

The Night Terror grunted. Its right arm, free of Corruption, tugged on the shackles.

"What do you think?" Vincent chewed on his thumbnail. "What do you think, Edgar?"

"I want to know why they hunt us, where they came from, what we did to deserve..." The words spilled over Edgar's trembling lips. So many considered the Night Terrors savages for their actions against humanity, and yet he couldn't help but feel in his most honest moments they were somehow justified.

"Where they're from? The Nameless Forest, Edgar," Vincent scoffed. "Let's not waste time on that." He paused. "I have to see what's under the mask. Brennan, my tools please."

The Archivist stopped the guard. In the booming voice that had often frightened them as children, he said, "Another time, my lords. If you spend too much time in the presence of demons, you will become a demon yourself."

Vincent groaned. "Did you get that from your book?"

Amon flipped over the book, the worn-down cover of *The Disciples of the Deep* facing him. "No, but I rather like the line. Come—" He waved them out of the cell, his attention never wavering from the Night Terror. "—It's been through enough. Let's be better than the beasts that hunt us."

CHAPTER III

In the nightmare haze that followed the Trauma, the world reformed itself. Those that remained crawled out of the chaos and cruor and, once again, gave themselves to subjugation. The weak went to their knees, the strong to their feet, and kingdoms were cast in the forms of Old. All that changed became as it had been, and all lessons learned were lost on those left alive.

Time passed, and on the hottest night of the year, the capital city of – courted tragedy. A maiden, the king's own daughter, who was known for her beauty and wit, was taken. No note had been left, nor ransom made known. No one knew anything, and it seemed nothing could be done to bring the young woman home.

Then the stories started.

Stretching from the eastern shore to the midland marshes, the Nameless Forest sat shrouded in rumor and myth. Around it, several villages had been established with the intention of collecting the rare, vein-like roots found on the trees. It was here, in the outskirts populated by the destitute and desperate, that the maiden was seen, bound by rope and to the man of violence at her side. But by the time the stories had reached the young woman's father, it was too late to respond. The Nameless Forest had called to the maiden and her captor, and when they answered, it swallowed them whole.

They never emerged. There were only the tales of woe none could know, and yet were told as truth. Five sons, the maiden gave to the man five sons. Born of rape and fed on hate, the boys grew quickly. When they came of age, they divided the Forest into five wards, ruling as kings over the outcasts that had congregated there.

Edgar didn't sleep, because he feared what he would find when he woke. As the first light of day broke across the cerulean sky, he wondered where the night had gone.

His stomach voiced its hunger in all the ways it knew. After a while, he gave it the rest of the food from the dead man, mostly so no creature could find him by its growling. He stared at the Nameless Forest, so vast and unyielding, and considered the niceties of death.

"I won't do it," Edgar said, as though anyone or anything here actually cared. He rose, sword in hand. He glanced at the blade and gasped.

"Holy Child!" He dropped the weapon, jumping as it clanged against the cave floor. He leaned over, all sweat and consternation, and watched as Old World images were reflected on the metal.

"How is this possible?" He watched a helicopter disappear over a cityscape horizon, into the murky swathe of dusk that colored his blade orange.

He ground his teeth as the cityscape crumbled into dust. "I have to get out of here."

He slowly reached for the sword and grasped it. The images fled at his touch, into the silvery depths of the steel.

Edgar gathered his belongings and left the cave with newfound purpose. He had heard many terrible stories about the Nameless Forest, and this gave him hope; if the place were truly larger on the inside than on the outside, then that meant the explorer who had discovered this had escaped.

Similarly, if the philosophers who insisted the place to be a living lobotomy of time and reality were right, then that meant they had noted the disturbance and returned to tell of their findings. Better yet, if the tales told of children becoming fanged beasts and blood raining from the sky weren't true, then he had even less to worry about.

All in all, it was a pathetic hope, and Edgar knew this. It was the kind of hope tailored by naivety, but for now, for now it would do.

With no stars or landmarks to guide him, Edgar decided on one direction and followed it religiously. The sun had worked itself into his skin; no amount of shade would see it freed. His mouth burned as though a fire had been built inside it. The best he could do was guzzle the water from his pouch, but all that managed was to soothe the ache in the desert his lips had become. He sighed, turned inward, and marched onward.

How did I get here? The question echoed through Edgar's mind while he searched for missing memories. As he pushed past trees and bushes, he moved from childhood to adolescence.

It's all here, he thought, arriving at the memory of the Night Terror in the dungeon. *Except for how I got here.* It seemed too generic, too cliché, his conveniently inconvenient amnesia. *No, this place wants me to forget for a reason*, he decided, slipping into a copse. *But it doesn't matter. If I'm wrong, I'm wrong, and I'll be dead by dawn, no matter how hard I try.*

Edgar emerged from the copse, onto a road paved with white satin. He stumbled backward, careful not to let his feet touch the fabric, afraid that he might spring a trap. The road twisted through the trees, like a snow-covered snake slithering toward a kill.

He gripped the hilt of his sword and followed beside the road. Blood drops dotted the winding ribbon, and they turned his stomach.

He trailed the pale path to a hill. At its crest, he found a woman in white sitting atop a rock. She wore a bloodied dress. It was from the ends of her garb that the road had been formed, so that all who followed it would find her.

Edgar approached slowly, afraid to startle the woman. She had a blank look on her face as she stared off into the windswept distance.

"My lady?" he said softly. He noticed a bit of worn beauty beyond the long, dark hair that whipped about her head. "Are you okay?"

The woman in white's gaze slid to the side. Edgar saw, in those large, black pupils, himself, and hate.

She made a subtle gesture with her fingers. From her bodice to her skirt, all the blood that stained her dress came to life.

Edgar tripped over his feet going backward. The crimson streams poured off the dress and onto the white road.

He ran alongside it, and they followed. As the stinking fluid pooled, he drew his sword. The blood puddle began to rise out of the satin, became solid. Hands rose out of the puddle, followed by arms, a shoulder, and a head.

A shape in blood pushed itself free of the wicked weave and stood on two dripping legs before Edgar.

The wayward royalty swung his sword at the blood-borne body. The blade passed through, slinging a wave of red onto the greenery.

The creature grabbed Edgar before he could make another pass.

He punched the blood beast as hard as he could, in its featureless face and churning gut. But the shape could not, would not be stopped.

It wrapped itself around him and, together, in a bloody embrace, the two sank into satin and white nothingness.

CHAPTER IV

Forty-Two Days Ago

Edgar sank into his chair, while Vincent and Lena argued over him. He looked across the dinner table to the twins, Auster and Audra, for moral support, but they were ensnared in a political debate with the oldest sibling, Horace.

He sighed, and stuffed some food into his mouth. Even his father, King Sovn, and his mother, Queen Magdalena, were too busy talking to each other to see that he, the youngest here of them all, had no one.

The royal family of Eldrus seldom ate dinner together, even when they were eating dinner together.

"What are you going on about?" The force behind Vincent's words projected a few berries from his mouth onto the table.

Lena scowled; it was an expression she had mastered, and the only one which she seemed to possess. "You shouldn't have to ask."

Vincent laughed, stabbing his fork into the mutton on his plate. "Oh, I see," he said, cutting off a piece of the meat. He prodded it with his fork and pointed the hunk at his sister, almost hitting Edgar's nose as he did so. "Well, then I apologize for all transgressions I've made, haven't made, and will make in the unforgettable past and unknowable future."

Edgar batted the fork away. "Will you two shut up?"

"Such violence," Lena goaded, her scowl curving into a smile. "Vincent—" she returned to her victim, "—when will you stop wasting your time on experiments and do something useful for once?"

"Do something useful? Does that include the servant girls?" Edgar added, with a stupid grin on his face; he was, after all, a part of their conflict now.

"Mother Abbess, Holy Child," Vincent said, shaking his head. "I've been relegated to outcast. When you've discovered a new fault of mine, sweet Lena, let me know." At this point, he became very animated. "I'm already aware of the burden that is my great intelligence, and even greater libido."

"Edgar, if you would, cut out his tongue," Lena pleaded. "No one will mind, and no one will miss it. Not even the servant girls."

Edgar smiled at his sister. "Especially not the servant girls." He liked being in her good graces, even if it wouldn't last for long.

"Servant boys it is, then," Vincent said, not missing a beat. "I can adapt, unlike you two."

Lena lifted a cup to her mouth. "What's that supposed to mean?"

Vincent's eyes glinted. "You shouldn't have to ask."

A creak disturbed the room as the dining room doors opened, and more courses were carried in by the servants.

Edgar twisted his mouth at the various shades and shapes of excess that were offered to each of his family members. He waved away the sauces, meats, and fruits, and avoided desserts entirely. He sensed the unsaid offense taken by the servants from his dismissal, but he didn't care. He did it for them, and for those who would better benefit from leftovers than their vomit.

"How goes your work at the suffer centers?" Horace asked Edgar.

"The 'food banks' could be better," he said, correcting his brother.

Auster's spoon clinked against his bowl as he stirred the spiced slush inside it.

In a voice deader than the dead's, he said, "I heard there are more beatings than bread being given out in those places."

"We need more men to keep the peace, and more food to keep everyone calm." Edgar's face went red. "A good deal goes a long way. It all adds up."

Lena looked past Edgar. "It all adds up, but to what?" She wasn't speaking to him, but their father, King Sovn. "Let the people run the suffer centers. The last time we tried, they accused us of poisoning the food to thin out the poor. Which, granted, is not the worst idea in the—"

"It would take a considerable amount of effort to disguise the taste," Audra said, her words wispy syllables.

Edgar looked at the twenty-one-year-old, and smiled a pathetic smile that told the girl now was not the time to prove to the others her talents as a botanist.

The twenty-one-year-old girl looked back, the heat of pride draining from her face, and asked with wide and welling eyes, "When?"

King Sovn muttered behind his clasped hands, "My children would have this city reduced to skeletons."

Edgar turned to his father. It comforted him to see that the king smirked when he spoke.

King Sovn, sovereign of Eldrus and the Heartland, Blood Drinker and Heart Eater, and all those other titles and profanities that often followed his name was, despite these things, an average man. He was neither large, nor small, nor was he grossly scarred or excessively scrubbed. He did not strike his wife, nor his children, and because he was neither violent nor villainous, the privileged felt judged in his presence.

He was a good man, Edgar knew, but his reluctance, his indifference, made him a terrible ruler.

"It all adds up," King Sovn said, repeating Edgar's earlier words, "but not everything can or should be measured in coin." He squinted at his wife, the Queen Magdalena. "What do you think, my dear?"

Edgar's mother's head turned as the dining room doors opened again. Servants entered with refills and refreshments. "I think Edgar is trying to make the rest of us look bad." She tilted her head at Edgar. "I think I would like to be proven wrong."

"For once," his father chirped.

"That goes without saying." She took her husband's hand. "Think on what you need, and we'll see what can be done." She trained her gaze on one of the servants nearest the twins. "Does that sound fair?" She sounded distant, too absorbed in her own thoughts.

"It does. Thank you." Edgar would have felt triumphant, but his mother's sudden concern soured the moment.

Lena let out a laugh. "Aren't you the savior of the people?"

Vincent nudged his shoulder. "Pay her no mind. Mother and Father both know that if they gave her what she wanted, we'd all be begging at one of your suffer centers."

Edgar nodded at his brother, though he had hardly been listening to him.

The servant which had attracted his mother's interest now had his father's, as well. The man was young, tanned; his hair redder than the soup he carried.

Edgar couldn't place the man. By the confusion that spread like a sickness across Audra's, Auster's, and Horace's faces, he saw that they, too, didn't recognize him.

"My Queen," the servant said, making his way toward her.

By the glint in his mother's eyes, it was clear to Edgar she had seen something they had not. The servant rushed forward, knife in hand. She leaned back in her chair as the man stabbed downward, where her head had been. She stood up, dark tendrils of hair falling from their weaves, and kicked the man's legs out from under him.

With a shout, he fell forward. His chin slammed against the table. Blood blew out of his mouth as he bit through his tongue.

Choking on the fleshy hunk, he hocked the severed muscle across the table, onto a plate.

Magdalena lifted the man up by his collar—her thin arms had never looked stronger—bent him over the table, took the large knife that had been used to cut the mutton, and drove it through his neck.

She released him, but he didn't move. He stayed pinned there, to the wood, like a bug to be dissected.

"As you can see, no matter what you do," the queen said over the assassin's blood-choked cries, "you cannot make everyone happy."

She sighed. Her tongue found a spot of blood on her lips, and she licked it off. "Go to your rooms. Dinner is done."

CHAPTER V

Long were the nights and dark the days, that had followed the Trauma and its malaise.

Under swollen skies, the weary-eyed searched for gods and guidance amidst the lies.

They found a place that scabbed the land with trees like veins torn from man.
In its breast, demons waited, with dark hungers to be sated.

They whispered promises they could not keep.
They desired sacrifices none would reap.

"Royal blood," thus they spake, sick of the poor upon which they'd slaked.
"As you wish," a brave queen said, giving herself to slow the dead.

The demons brought her into that nameless place,
and wept when they gazed upon her face.
Too beautiful to eat, this they knew,
when children she could give to them, strong and true.
Quickly, they learned the folly of their plan;
the queen's blood had been cursed by her own hand.
From seeds on satin, sons did rise,
five in all, with jet black eyes.
They set on fathers when they could,
and with mother took the wood.

Edgar woke in a bed that was not his own, naked and alone. The sheets were sticky with drying blood.

As he sat up, they peeled from him, like butcher's paper. His skin was cold, damp, as though someone had recently tried to wash the gore and smell of metal out of it.

Feet shaking, he stood and started searching the room for a weapon, his weapon, or armor, or anything with which he could protect himself. But there was nothing here. Only darkness, and the chilling light that cut through the doorframe across the way.

"Hold on a minute," a woman said. Her voice was muffled, but he could tell she was close. "You'll break something bumbling around like that."

The door swung back on its whining hinges. An ocean of sunlight flooded the room, which, now that he could see, looked more like a shed than anything else. It was a rickety, rundown hunk of hollowed wood that, for some reason, reminded Edgar of an oversized coffin.

Edgar cupped his hands around his crotch. At the threshold, a woman stood. He could tell by the way she carried herself she wasn't impressed.

"No need, already seen it," she said, coming forward, the long braid of auburn hair the first thing of hers he noticed. "Seen one, seen them all." The words rolled slowly off her lips. "Welcome to Threadbare." She held out her arms, which were taut with muscles. "I think you'll enjoy your stay." She winked, her large, green eyes like those of a reptile's. "I'll make sure of it."

Voice quivering, Edgar asked, "What have you done with my belongings?"

"They... belong to me now." The woman laughed, and shook her head. "I'll give them back once you give me your name and how you got here."

Edgar didn't know what to make of the woman, but he could already tell he would like her. He cupped himself harder to hide this fact. "Edgar is my name. I don't know how I ended up in the Nameless Forest."

"You all still calling it that?" The woman cocked her head, as though she wanted him to drop his hands and grow-up some. "Where do you come from, Edgar? Even us here in nowhere come from somewhere."

Eldrus, he thought, but didn't say. *What would she do if she knew?*

"I'm Lotus, by the way." She closed the gap between them. Near enough now that he could see the faint freckles on her cheeks and neck. "An unbecoming name for an unbecoming woman."

"I think it's lovely," Edgar said, already intoxicated by her mere presence.

"I think if I pissed right here and now, you'd drop to your knees and call it gold."

She was right; he wasn't thinking clearly. "I'm Edgar. Edgar of the royal family of Eldrus."

Lotus didn't seem too surprised. "You don't say?" She bit her lip, one front tooth cracked. She glanced over her shoulder at something outside. "On vacation, then?"

"I was taken."

"Hell of a place to bring a date." Lotus grabbed his hands and pulled him with her out of the room. "Let me give you the tour."

She stopped, looked between his legs, and smiled. "Pants first, actually. Mornings are cold here. They put even the proudest men to shame."

Threadbare was a small, thrown together village that had been built in a clearing surrounded by black barks and red oaks.

What Edgar saw as he came out of the house was all there was to see. According to Lotus, it was all they ever needed. Houses, a lumber yard, farms and barns, and wild animals. There were crops at the back of the village, too. They held crops he couldn't identify and, despite Lotus' insistence, refused to taste.

Given everything he had seen and those that roamed the streets, he assumed the population couldn't be much greater than one hundred. But for a place such as the Nameless Forest, where death bred death, one hundred lives was something of an achievement.

"There was a woman in a white dress. She was covered in blood." Edgar said. He and Lotus stopped in front of a store, every eye of everyone around fixed upon them.

"I know. A bit of her brought you here." Lotus scratched off a chip of blood from his neck. "She could've killed you."

Regardless of what he had seen, it still surprised him when a group of children ran out of the fields and into their homes, where their parents waited with open arms, not butcher knives. *We know nothing about this place.*

"Why didn't she kill me? Who is she?"

Lotus raised her eyebrow, as though she had expected him to have already figured this out. "She has a job for you. Who is she? A mother, a queen, a god." Lotus nodded at someone in the distance. "Stay long, and you'll figure out what to call her."

Edgar's breathing became shallow as the gravity of his situation weighed upon him. "I don't know… what's going on anymore." He rubbed his face. "This is still the Forest, right? Holy Child, what has happened to me?"

Lotus took his hand. "A drink it is, then." She pressed her lips to his ear as he started to sway. "Follow my words, and I'll see you through."

Edgar did what he was told, because he didn't know what else to do.

Lotus brought him to her residence. It was the largest home in Threadbare, and from the greetings and signs of respect she received on their way there, he pegged her as their leader.

She couldn't have been any older than thirty, and yet the way in which she carried herself seemed to suggest otherwise. She had the presence of a commander, and yet emanated an aura by which all who stepped into it were relaxed.

She wasn't beautiful, and yet Edgar found himself more attracted to her than he had ever been to any woman he had known before her. She was a contradiction, and yet he knew he would love her unconditionally by the night's end, whether he wanted to or not.

"In the Old World, when they wanted to remember something, they would take a picture," Lotus said.

Edgar had been staring at her, at this table, saying nothing for a few minutes.

"We've no cameras, but I've several portraits in the back for starry-eyed gentleman such as yourself. If you'd like, I could bring one up, give it a signature. Send you packing with a memento of me."

Caught, Edgar said, "I'm sorry. My mind was elsewhere."

"Oh, that's a shame," Lotus teased. She filled his cup with an unmarked bottle of alcohol. "Who were you in Eldrus?"

"Who was I? No, I'm going back."

Lotus raised an eyebrow. "Wouldn't count on it."

The dark liquid swirled in Edgar's cup. A purple foam gathered on the surface. "If you wanted to kill me, you would have done it already."

"That would've been the logical thing to do, but this place isn't exactly known for that sort of thing, is it?" She snatched the cup and drank half of it. "Matters not to me. Drink's getting drunk, whether you like it or not."

Edgar seized the cup to assert his manliness. "Tell me about the Nameless Forest, about Threadbare. About the woman in the white dress, about how the... how the... I... how I..."

"There, there," Lotus whispered, helping his hands bring the cup to his mouth. "Stop your babbling."

The liquid was thick and burned his throat. All pores and passageways in his body opened wide as the fiery sensation spread throughout his body. The anxiety that had crawled into his speech receded. The alcohol had beaten it back, back into its hidden cove, where it spent most of its time breeding with worry and low self-esteem.

"Thank you."

"Doesn't taste half bad for poison, does it?"

Edgar coughed out a laugh. She was joking, or at least, that's what he told himself.

"It's best not to settle on a definition of the Forest. It changes so much. But some things are constant."

"Like Threadbare?"

Lotus took a drink, her gaze never leaving Edgar's. "Quick as a whip. Yes, like Threadbare. And Anathema, Blackwood, Chapel, and Atlach. All those places, like here, are constant, too."

"What about everything else?"

"If it's been thought or said. Or hell, even if it hasn't, then it's happened here."

Edgar took another drink, his mouth thoroughly numbed by the mixture. "How?"

"Doesn't matter." Lotus scratched the top of her hands. "Figure it out, and the Forest will probably change that part of itself. You're asking the wrong question, Edgar of Eldrus."

I am? He closed his eyes, where he saw Lotus' afterimage on his lids. *A portrait,* he thought drunkenly. *One I'd look at forever.* His eyes snapped open to a sobering realization. *I shouldn't trust her. I shouldn't trust any of this.*

"What question should I be asking, Lotus?"

She grabbed his cup, scowling like Lena would. "Someone's a grumpy drinker. You want to go home, right?"

He nodded, his newfound suspicions robbing him of words.

"Crestfallen. That's what I call her, in case you were wondering. She doesn't let everyone get away. And if she does, she has plans for them, a purpose."

Cringing, he said, "What's that?"

"What makes you think I know?"

"You do. I can tell."

"Ah. Is that why you've been staring me down?" She considered the bottle. "Kill the four, leave the fifth, and she'll send you home, to your black keep and gray skies."

"How do you...?"

She curled the tips of her hair around her fingers. "Not much gets past me. Also, not going to lie to you, Edgar, you're quite a catch."

"The four? The four what?" Edgar backed away from the table. Unsteady, he struggled to his feet. He caught a glimpse of a glint of steel, his sword, behind a curtain across the room.

"Anathema, Blackwood, Chapel, and Atlach. Four men. One in each village. Crestfallen wants them dead. You want to go home? I saw the blood on your blade. I know the sword's not for looks, at least, not all the time."

"I don't believe you." Edgar swallowed hard. His anxiety had returned. It was climbing his ribs as though they were the rungs of a ladder. "You're lying to me."

Lotus coughed out a laugh. "Am I an idiot? Oh sure, I just sat around all these years waiting for some piss-poor warrior to stumble into these woods and do my dirty work. Edgar, I don't give a damn what you do. I'm just telling you what she told me."

"Why do you get to live?"

She shrugged. "There's questions you ask, and questions you don't. Besides, if she asked you to kill me, it would've been your head I took off first. Not your pants."

Edgar knew he shouldn't jump to conclusions, not in a place like this, where things operated on another level entirely.

So, he sighed and said, "Is she a liar?"

"I'm not sure something like her needs to lie." Lotus stood and put her hands on her hips. "I know this isn't the best time, but you'll be leaving soon, and we've our appetites."

Edgar took a step back. "What?"

"Don't make me be vulgar. I know you're not that thick."

"We... barely know each other." He shook his head. "No, I'm sorry. This is too much. I'm so far out of my comfort—"

"Do you get to know your food before you eat it? Your drink before you drink it?" Lotus walked toward him, and put her forehead against his. "I'm not looking for love. Tried it. Didn't like it. Never developed the taste for it."

He chipped away at the red on his fingernails. "What about the... thing that attacked me?" He liked where this was going with her, and didn't; yet another contradiction. "It came out of her dress."

"That's one of her minions. The blood by which we're bound. Hey—" she put her arms on top of his shoulders, "—don't change the subject. It won't be long before we never see each other again. And neither you nor I want to be kept up tomorrow night, wondering what we'd missed."

CHAPTER VI

Forty Days Ago

Audra's fingers moved over the candle, tugging on shadow and light, as though she meant to make of them something more than what the flame had in mind.

Animals and people crawled out of the smoky darkness and onto the wall. Like a puppeteer, she gave them life and purpose. Absorbed in her art, lost in their stories she was now telling, unease quickly fell from her face like a veil.

In this moment, Edgar could tell that she was happy, and beautiful, and all those other things he knew she had convinced herself it was not possible for her to be.

"How did you get so good?" Edgar whispered. He tried to nudge out a similar compliment from her twin, Auster.

"If ever there were a spellweaver in the family, it would be Audra." Auster was as monotone as ever, but sincere.

Audra, sounding angry but looking the opposite, said, "Oh stop! It just takes practice."

She'll be young forever. Edgar watched his sister's hands manifest a tree into the scene on her room's wall. *In every way, and people will make her suffer for it.*

He sighed. "Accept the compliment. You know Auster is rationing them for his future husband. It's a rare treat."

"Fine." Audra waved him off, causing a shadowy wind to ripple across the wall, shaking the figures on it.

Edgar and Auster looked at one another, their faces mirroring one another's surprise.

Audra turned away from her dark world. "What's going to happen?"

The heavy footfalls of the guards outside the door were the answer. She covered her face with shaking hands, and let the terrible thoughts she had been holding at bay finally overcome her.

"We'll get through this," Edgar said. He scooted closer and put his arms around her.

Auster, remaining where he sat, said, "I'm sure this happens a lot."

"That... that is not helpful, Auster," she whimpered, her hot tears soaking Edgar's shirt.

"He's right, though." Edgar shook his head at his sister's twin. "We are who we are, but we're no different than anyone else. Bad things happen, whether you're rich or poor, or—"

"I don't want bad things to happen to anyone." She pushed her head harder into his shoulder. "I know that, Edgar. I'm not a child. But it was an assassination attempt. He was close to us, Edgar. He walked right past me. I could have stopped him if I were only paying more attention for that kind of thing."

"I think Mother did well enough stopping him," Auster droned.

Audra pulled away from Edgar. There was a badge of snot and saliva dripping down the front of him. "I'm sorry." She wiped it off. "I'm tired of being so weak, so... freaking trusting." Biting her nail, she added, "Where do you think he came from?"

Edgar shrugged. "Here, in Eldrus, or I don't know. There's no good reason to try to murder someone, though. I can't believe that."

"I don't know. I think murder is like a potion. Just takes the right amount of ingredients to make it. Two or three things to justify something you would never consider," Audra said. She returned to the candle and, with her hands, raised two shapes from the smoky nether. "Father didn't do anything to help."

"He seldom does." Edgar cocked his head at Auster. "He lacks enthusiasm."

Auster arched his eyebrow. And that was it.

"I feel like..." she searched for her words as she formed a tunnel on the wall for the figures to enter. "I feel like we could be doing more. You've got your programs, your shelters. Lena sits on the council. Horace is practically king from everything he's taken on lately."

"Don't forget Vincent," Auster said. "But no one would fault you if you did."

"Vincent's not so bad." The last of her tears sizzled as it fell into the candle's flame. "He knows a lot about medicine, and myths and things from the Old World. If he wasn't so selfish, he could help a lot of people."

"What about you two?"

Audra's hands took shape into something else, and yet the two figures she had formed stayed on the wall.

Edgar's jaw dropped, but he pressed on. "You, Audra, are the smartest person I know. The most gifted botanist. And how you do what you do with the shadows…" He laughed, pointing at the two, freestanding figures. "I can't even begin to understand."

Auster cleared his throat. "I'm good at a great many things, but I'm not great at anything."

"What's wrong with that?" Edgar said. "I can swing a sword because of you. I can quote stories and poetry because of you. I can name most, if not all, the stuffy dignitaries because of you. You're a teacher, and a great one. No one taught me about the Scavengers or the Sailor's Bane, or the political nonsense over the Divide. No one, except for you."

"I guess," Auster said, smiling. "We should make Eldrus a better place to live, if we're all so damn talented."

"Here, here," Edgar bellowed.

"Shut up," Audra said, giggling. She looked around the room and said, "I want to show you something." She blew out the candle. But for the light of the moon, the room went dark. "You have to keep it a secret. You can't tell anyone."

"That will be easy enough." Edgar nodded toward the door. "We've a whole squadron of guards posted outside the door, though."

"Not a problem." She winked at Auster, who, by his reaction, had already seen what she was about to reveal.

"Should I prepare myself, Auster?"

Audra hopped to her feet and went to the bookshelf.

"One should always be prepared," Auster said, like an asshole.

"We have to be quick." She took out a book and removed an old, rusted key from its hollowed-out pages. "And we have to be very quiet."

Edgar nodded. Audra crossed the room to her writing desk. She went down on her hands and knees and crawled underneath it.

Coughing out the cobwebs that got caught in her mouth, she yanked out the rug there and began to pull and pile up the discolored stones beneath it. She worked quickly. The way in which she stacked the stones suggested she knew their every groove and eccentricity.

Edgar moved towards his sister. Squinting through the darkness, he saw that, as the last stone was removed, there was a metal plate in the floor—a door with a small handle and rusted keyhole.

Audra unlocked the door and pulled it back. A gust of wind blew past her face and filled the room with an old smell, an extinct smell; one that was both instantly recognizable and absolutely foreign.

Softly, Edgar asked, "Where does it go?"

"My hideout," she said with a toothy grin. "There's a ladder. It's slippery, sometimes, so watch your step."

Auster rubbed the back of his head, at the ghost of a past spill. "Yeah, watch your step."

"Audra," Edgar called out, as his sister slipped into the hole and began her descent. "Now doesn't seem the best time. Assassins, re-member? We should be staying with the guards."

Auster crawled past Edgar, under the desk. "All sense and reason leave her when she's like this." He lowered himself into the hole and added, "Let her have her fun."

The ladder was slick, as she had warned. Edgar's vision blurred as he stepped down into the darkness, the small chute awakening dormant claustrophobia. The stone the chute was comprised of told them its story in its colors, like the rings of a tree.

For Edgar, it was as though they were traveling back in time, to the days of Ghostgrave's founding.

When his arms started to ache and his siblings started to pant, their feet found solid footing at the ladder's end. Behind them, bio-luminescent plants lit up the room they stood in, washing the earthen ruin in vibrant, lime green light.

It took Edgar's vision a moment to adjust, but when it did, he couldn't believe what he saw in the room. Old World remnants—boxes, booths, telephones, and turnstiles; boots, books, and coats. All of it was left out in the open, undisturbed. This place wasn't a room at all, but a station; a subway station.

"Audra…" Edgar's words trailed off as he leaned over a phone-book and tried to read its faded text. "What is this?"

She took his hand and guided him to a large fissure in the wall. It was from here that the roots of the bioluminescent plants flowed.

"My happy place," she said, waving Auster over to join them. "See it?"

Edgar nodded. He'd seen the station and, through the fissure, the small makeshift study beyond. It was filled with plants and flowers, and there were tomes and tools atop a workstation which was cov-ered in stolen supplies from their home above.

Edgar nodded again. He saw beyond the study, through a blown-out window, where train tracks laced a chasm, and a subway car sat on its side, like a wounded beast which had long since been left to die, forgotten and alone.

"Holy shit," he said.

"Don't let the Holy Child hear you call him that," Auster joked.

"Audra, when did you find this?" Edgar took a step back, resting against the linoleum wall.

"Two years ago, in a fit of boredom." She moved about the glow-ing garden as she spoke, tending to the needs of her children. "No one looks for me, so no one notices when I'm gone."

Edgar wanted to interrupt her, to tell her she was wrong. But she wasn't; she was right. This was the most he had spoken with his sister in weeks, and it wasn't even until now that he realized it.

Auster leaned into a plant covered in hairs and pods. "You could start a sizeable clinic with all these. Is that your plan?" The pods split open and tendrils shot out, biting at the air, trying to get at his face. He jumped back, and said, "Never mind."

"That's part of the plan, yes." She waved her brothers back to her. "Edgar can secure the places, and we can fill them with food and medicine. Auster, you could educate others, and then they could do the same. We start off small, but if we do it right, others will follow our example."

"I can't believe this is here. How is this here?" Edgar had been lis-tening to her, but only barely.

Auster, keeping a close eye on the plant that had marked him for death, said, "What's the other part of your plan?"

Audra ignored him. "There's so little we know about the Trauma,

Edgar. I think there's a lot of places like this, twisted and displaced. It's like the world was smashed together and pulled apart."

"The other part of your plan?" Auster nagged.

Audra's jaw looked unhinged, like an annoyed snake's. "There, that subway car. Look closer, you'll see it."

Edgar stepped through the fissure, into the study. He went to the blown-out window. Looking closely, he then saw it; a stalk, thick and tough, coming out of the subway car, to taste the new scents that soiled the air.

Audra joined him. With a handful of debris, she reared her arm back and flung the junk across the tracks. Where it landed, hundreds of tiny mushrooms lit up their yellow fear. The light they made crept across the chasm, illuminating the car.

A stalk appeared, and then another, and then several more, followed by roots, engorged and lumbering. They slithered across the subway car, out its windows and doors. Each stalk, each root, seemed to be running from the same place, and when Edgar leaned over the sill, he found it. The appendages were connected to a bulbous base that had grown over half of the seats inside the subway car.

"Audra," Edgar said. Instincts kicking in, he backed away. "What the hell is that?"

"A myth I've been working on. I read about it in a book Amon gave me. I didn't think I'd get this far, but..." Her gaze darted back and forth between her brothers. "It's known as a Crossbreed. After trying forever, this was the perfect place for it to bloom."

For once, Auster's voice shook when he spoke. "What does it do?"

"There's two types," she said, holding up two fingers. "One that kills, a Bloodless, and this one, which soothes. If the people already think we poison their food, then why not introduce something that may calm them down for once? Make them more willing to let us actually help them? We could do a lot if they would just... obey."

CHAPTER VII

The Trauma shattered the world, and from its shards nations rose. In the smoldering folds of the midland, Vold stood unchallenged. It had been the first city to restore order, and so it was to this city people looked for resources and guidance. The accomplishment was not without its shortcomings, however, for it made of Vold's leaders narcissists and egotists with delusions of utopia.

Six sat on the city's council; six sons in each's shadow. Starved for splendor, the six sons turned eastward and saw, in the Nameless Forest, prospects. With forked tongues, they bought favor and labor, and forged their fates in the glories of hell.

The Forest received them on an orange summer day, the cool breeze its cool breath, calling them its way. In the trees they saw towers, and in the vermillion veins gold fortunes. Rivers gave way to crops, and caves to foundations. On the crests and in the crevices, the sons imagined cities, beacons for greatness built on unspoiled plots.

They sent word of their findings to their fathers afar, and went to work on the earth, digging deep, digging hard. The men complained of headaches, hallucinations, and horrors, but the sons paid them no mind.

The excavation took many as they carved out the sweltering depths, and those that persisted did so only by the fortitude found in the vermillion veins above. The six sons did not know why they were digging, for they had all they needed on the surface, but they dug all the same.

In the buzzing night of the third month, the Nameless Forest spoke.

"Drink our blood, and we shall drink yours." The words echoed through the chasm they had created, eroding the will of the workers so that they fled. The six sons shouted commands, threatened violence, but in the end, they ran, too.

The company did not make it very far: The tunnel out had collapsed. The six sons turned on one another, attributing blame and misfortune to everyone but themselves.

"Bring us blood," the Nameless Forest bellowed, as they scuffled and wept in the humid dark, "and we'll bring you home."

The six sons ceased their fighting and did as they were told. The Nameless Forest promised itself to them, and they to it. The six sons fed the remainder of their men to the chasm, to the vermillion veins that waved like reeds in the bloody swamp that their camp had become. They returned to Vold, and to their fathers, with a proposition.

"Let us purify the city, as you've always wanted," they said eagerly. "The un-desirables, the unmentionables, those that do not contribute enough, and those that question too much—give us them all. They will toil in the sun and perish in the night, and the treasures they will find will be yours, and Vold will flourish."

The leaders conceded to their sons' demands after one taste of the vermillion veins. Soon, the damned were packed on the midlands paths, and together marched to persecution songs. The six sons quartered the Nameless Forest in ac-cordance to crime, and over these six wards, they ruled as kings. Those that died were dispersed to the depths and fed to the voice that gave safe passage.

The six sons, with mouths bloodied from vermillion addiction, quickly changed the terms of the agreement. The veins made them feel as gods, and as gods they owed nothing to mortals. The supply lines were broken, and barriers erected, and the six sons took six thousand from the continent and kept them for themselves, so as to appease their subterranean benefactors.

Vold vanished overnight, for reasons lost to history, and the six gods ruled over their tiny kingdom, each indulging in the crime of their governing. And when all that could die had died, they themselves were consumed, and then forgotten.

Many had told Edgar he would be disappointed with his first sex-ual encounter. But as he lay watching Lotus' breasts rise and fall with her breathing, he was glad they had been wrong.

He could recall every detail of the night, and he would remember every detail for all the nights to come. It didn't matter if she loved him, because she had brought him calmness in a place of chaos, and the confidence to keep moving forward.

"I know they're pretty, but there are better things you can do to them than stare," Lotus said, never opening her eyes.

Half-tempted to take her up on the proposition, Edgar resisted and sat up. "Thank you for that."

"No—thank you," she said, still pretending to be asleep. "It's slim pickings around here, let me tell you."

As Edgar freed his feet from the blankets, his thoughts returned to the task at hand. Anathema, Blackwood, Chapel, and Atlach; these were villages of which he knew nothing and yet had been asked to destroy.

With the possible exception of his abductor, he had never killed anyone before. To murder four strangers at the command of some creature clearly capable of doing the job itself seemed ridiculous. No, Edgar wouldn't let the Forest have him so easily. He would appear as though he would do as he was told, but only until the moment presented itself when he could do otherwise.

"What is it?" Lotus asked, finally opening her eyes to find his face wracked with concern.

"I'm so confused."

"Is this not what you expected?" Lotus rose, stretched. "It will be, once you leave Threadbare."

"And if I were to say no?" Edgar had no intention of forsaking his home and family, but Lotus' nakedness made him entertain the notion all the same.

"Then you'd be another drop of blood on Crestfallen's dress."

"How is it you've escaped such a fate? And everyone else here?"

"I'm sure she has her reasons." Lotus got out of bed, her body silencing any arguments. "I don't care to know them."

"What if I stayed?"

Edgar watched with some sadness as the mayor of Threadbare slipped back into her pants. Lotus' room, where they now rested, complimented her well, despite the fact that it was at odds with her tough, assertive personality. The room, much like the entire house, had a softness to it, as though everything were covered in a veil of sleepy haze. The walls were muted shades of gray and blue, and many of the shelves were covered in small, childish trinkets; mementos perhaps, from Lotus' early years.

"And why would you do that?" She looked over her shoulder, green eyes glowing in the candlelight.

"To better understand this place." It was a lie, and yet there was some truth to it. "How you survived, how you've functioned."

Lotus shook her head. Pants still unbuttoned, she walked over to Edgar, pushed him down, and straddled his waist on the bed.

"We survive like everyone else, I imagine. There's no secret to it. You stick with what's constant and make the best of it. When you come back, if you're still dying to know, I'll tell you what I know."

"Come back?" Edgar's hand traveled cautiously to her hips. "Is there a way out through here?"

Lotus shrugged. "Misspoke. Wishful thinking." She shifted her weight down onto his crotch.

"Are you like this with everyone who comes to Threadbare?"

She leaned forward, her lips taunting his as she closed in. "I would be, if more people came to Threadbare."

Edgar tensed, cocked his head. "Crestfallen spared me."

"Guess that makes you special." Lotus pressed her lips hard against his. When she finally pulled away, all the clothes she had put back on were on the floor again.

Lotus was the worst kind of distraction. The kind that would make a man fail to notice the thief in his pocket, or the dagger at his throat—and then not care for either when he did.

The brisk morning air reminded Edgar of this, the cold clearing his thoughts. He followed Lotus through Threadbare. The village glistened in the early light, not one inch of it untouched by dew. They were headed to the gates that surrounded the village, and yet Lotus seemed to be taking the long way, as though she wanted to show off the village. But there wasn't much to see. A few buildings here, empty stretches of grass there. It was a place suspended in time, half-built, wholly forgotten; a place that didn't belong, not here, not anywhere.

Edgar tore his eyes away from the village and looked upward. He shuddered as he stared at the sky, where red clouds lumbered along the flickering firmament. Were they ill omens, he wondered, or an everyday occurrence? Edgar rested his hand on the hilt of his sword, and waited for the dream of Threadbare to come to an end.

"Keep to it," Lotus said. She pointed to the narrow path that wound through the gate and trees ahead. "And you'll get there soon enough."

"Where?" Edgar turned around to have one final look at the village. But he wasn't the only one. The men, women, and children, with their tools, spools, toys, and dolls were standing in the fields and at the stores, watching him as he watched them.

"That's up to you." She spun Edgar around to face her. "You're a pawn. You know that, right?"

He nodded, though he hadn't really considered this obvious fact until now. "Crestfallen could kill me after I'm done."

"Yep." Lotus slapped him gently on the cheek. "But if she doesn't, then something else will. But that something else isn't offering you a way out."

"I'm getting the impression I'm not the first to come through here." Edgar searched Lotus' face for the formation of a lie.

"You're not." She stuck out her tongue to catch the fat drops that had begun to fall around them.

Lotus had given him a cloak. He lifted its hood over his head. "How many quests has she given out?"

"Quests?" She laughed, stepped away, and pushed open the gates. "Are you a hero, now?"

"Feels like it." Edgar cringed as the gate whined open.

"Then get to it, hero. Your princess—" she made a curtsey, "—awaits your return."

Edgar furrowed his brow at the woman, the mayor of Threadbare. In that brief moment, he hated everything about her he had loved, and would love again.

Grumbling, he said, "Just follow the path?"

Lotus smiled and said, "Don't stray. Stay sane."

When Edgar could no longer see Threadbare through the trees, he stopped where he stood and looked over his belongings. Lotus had provided him with the cloak which he wore, a knife, and several curatives; two bags with a week's worth of food and drink, and starters for a fire. The clothes that he wore beneath his armor, which had been thoroughly cleaned, were new as well.

Lotus had groomed him, soothed him, and for what? His being here was too coincidental. He should have died days ago, when the carrion birds came to tear him apart, long before the bell had rung and called them off. Had Crestfallen seen something in him when he sank into the field of satin? Or was the absurdity of her request nothing more than the result of an insane mind too long exposed to an insane world?

"Don't think about it," Edgar told himself, continuing down the path. "Don't stray. Stay sane."

The mantra was easy enough to say, but following it was another matter entirely. Like set pieces from a play, the Nameless Forest shuffled in oddities and impossibilities across the woodland stage for Edgar to behold.

Red suns tempted him to stray from his course, to see better the cracks that marred the orbs. Branches twisted upon themselves, breaking their bark to reveal white bone beneath. Yellow fog poured out of porous rocks, and where it went, plants and weeds burst into flames. Thousands of animal calls, man-made growls, and child-like screams followed Edgar for the better part of an hour.

At times, he even felt the brush of fur, scale, and tooth against his skin, as though these suffering specters walked beside him.

These things he could ignore because, in the end, they were no threat to him. However, what he couldn't ignore was the field of barbed wire that now lay before him, stretching out in all directions, for what seemed like miles.

Crouching, he saw that, where the path went, the metal had formed a series of arches through which one could crawl. To stick to the path, he had to go through here.

So, with a sigh of defeat, he fell forward, face to the dirt, and wondered why his abductor couldn't have taken Lena instead.

"Edgar?" a girl cried out, desperate and pained.

At the mouth of the barbed wire field, Edgar looked up and spotted a rustling coil not too far off. A hand, bloodied and barb-bitten, pushed through the wire.

Again, the girl pleaded, "Edgar?"

This time he recognized, in the slight lisp and soft syllables, a voice he had heard countless times before.

Audra.

It had been Audra's voice.

He plodded forward, because to go backwards would be a betrayal. The field received him without complaint. When he was fully inside, the wire twisted over the portal and sealed it shut, trapping him inside. The metal thorns ran beside him, under and above him.

With every move he made, they tugged and tore at his skin. His palms were pricked, his elbows cut. The field found where his armor wasn't, and left gashes on his side for the oversight.

"Audra!" Edgar winced as the barbed wire contracted. Squinting in pain, he spied a quivering body in the metal bindings and shouted, "Hold on."

His stomach lurched as he saw Audra there, leaking blood to feed the shivering steel. "Don't move anymore. I'll cut you free."

He grabbed the dagger at his side. His sister's eyes widened behind the melting mask of red she wore.

"Don't move."

"I should have died," she said, dropping her head. "It would've been better for everyone."

Edgar started to speak, but before he could, the entire field rushed inward in a silver blur. He cursed and screamed as the barbs sped past him, slicing his skin as they twisted around the place where Audra was held.

With every pass of the barbed wire, a part of her disappeared. She was trying to speak, too, but the shrill cacophony kept serrating her words.

It only took a moment, but when it was over, the field was gone, and Audra was gone, and all that remained was a puddle of blood and a small ball of steel, and the din of a bell ringing out from the church up ahead.

CHAPTER VIII

Thirty-Eight Days Ago

Edgar didn't need to remove the Night Terror's mask to know it wanted to kill him.

The Eel breathed heated, hateful breaths as it knelt before them. Blood dripped from its manacles as it rattled the chains that ran from its wrist to the ceiling. When it came too close, the guard, Brennan, beat it back.

Like all broken creatures, the Night Terror took the beating without complaint, and laughed when it was over.

"Lost its mind," Vincent said. He stared at the Eel's genitals. "Have it all, don't they?"

"Everything but Corruption," Edgar said, rubbing his right arm.

"They've dedicated themselves to murdering humans." Vincent crouched and reached for the Night Terror's mask. "And somehow, we're the villains."

Edgar's stomach tightened into a nauseating knot. "They don't seem much different to us."

"No, they don't." Vincent looked at the guard, and came to his feet. He grinned as Brennan came over and ripped the mask off the creature.

"Huh," he said, surprised. "Well, isn't that disappointing?"

The Night Terror's head didn't come off with the skull, nor did what lay beneath the mask inspire repulsion or awe. It had the face of a man, the flesh of a man, and it bled and sweated like a man. The creature was no less human than those that stood over it, and because of its likeness to humanity, it disarmed Edgar.

He had been expecting it to be what he had been led to believe it was all his life: a half-man, half-animal abomination; a black-eyed, black-souled charlatan. A demon-fanged, specter-held husk; a nightmare torn from Old World slumbers, or a flesh fiend risen from dark world squalors.

Any of those things would have sufficed, and they would have been far less terrifying than what sat fettered before them.

"What do you think?" Vincent asked, apparently sensing his brother's unease.

"There has to be something else," Edgar said. "A deeper difference we can't see."

Vincent nodded. He took the Terror by its hair and inspected its facial features. "We'll find it. The likeness is incredible, isn't it?"

The Night Terror's throat tightened. Its eyes became as an eel's— inky and without conscience.

"I'll cut it open, and we'll see what comes out."

Edgar covered his mouth. He looked to the guard for protest or reassurance even, but received neither. "We're not treading new ground, Vincent."

"Feels like we are."

"No, we're not. It's been too long since the Trauma for this to have been the first time a Night Terror's been captured and studied."

Vincent released the Eel's greasy hair and stepped away. "Sure, but where's the research? Where's the findings? Seem like good questions for the Archivist to answer, don't they? After all, he's the one that got nervous when we first came down here."

Edgar nodded. They were good questions, and Vincent was right; Archivist Amon had acted strangely that day.

"Why don't you go ask him?" Vincent signaled the guard, Brennan, to escort his brother out of the dungeon. "Go on, Ed. You know as well as I do that you don't want to see what I'm going to do next."

Ghostgrave hummed with sounds of suspicion in the midnight haze. Guards and soldiers patrolled the halls with vacant expressions, leaving no shadow or lock untouched. They stopped serving staff and lesser royalty, and searched them for malice and intent.

The queen's decree to increase security had lost her some favor with visiting dignitaries, but for a woman who serves murder at her dinner table, favor, like tradition, meant next to nothing.

Edgar moved about his room, relighting several candles that had been snuffed out by the northern wind. He focused his thoughts on Audra's Crossbreed to avoid the discomfort that came with thinking about Vincent and the Night Terror. He told himself the idea of using the plant was unethical, and the execution of any kind of plan impossible.

While good-willed, tampering with public resources to deliver an inoculation against man's own misguided devices skirted too close to delusions of godhood. Yet, he found himself considering his sister's proposition, working out the details and parties involved, and the lies they would need to tell themselves to see the whole thing through.

Someone knocked on his door.

Edgar straightened up and called out, "Yes? Who is it?"

"My lord," the guard stationed outside his room stated, "Prince Horace is here to see you."

"Please, come in." Edgar wrinkled his brow. What did Horace want with him at this hour?

When Horace entered the room, several candles lost their light. "Just making sure everyone is well tonight," he said.

"That's thoughtful of you, Horace," Edgar said, making no attempt to hide his surprise.

Horace nodded at the guards behind him and slowly closed the door. "I have to act the part I've no choice but to play. Mother practically rules Eldrus herself because of Father's indifference."

"Is everything all right?" Edgar searched his eldest brother for signs of distress. "Don't get me wrong, I appreciate the visit."

"The assassination attempt on our family made me reconsider some things." Horace eyed an empty seat nearby. Had he felt more comfortable with Edgar, he may have even sat in it. "The people are not happy with their rulers."

"Are they ever?" Edgar cringed. He sounded like Vincent. "Who sent the assassin? Are there more?"

Horace shook his head, reached behind him for the doorknob. "I'm sure. We'll find them."

"Horace," Edgar started, stopping his brother to make him roast a little longer in the flames of cordiality. "Would you mind practicing with me in the yard?"

"You're fine with a sword, Edgar."

"I know," he said, rolling his eyes, "but I can be better. Mother won't always be there to protect us."

Horace nodded. "Sure. Tomorrow, then."

For the remainder of the night, Edgar's mind was firmly anchored in a mire of worry. He had only slept for an hour total, so when he finally woke to the early morning light, he did so with the sour taste of sickness on his tongue.

Whispers, that's what had woken him. Bedside whispers, near where his nightstand stood. Edgar got out of bed and lit a few candles. He searched the room for signs of entry or Horace's return, but all he found were a few piles of dust, on the floor and on the nightstand, where before there had been none.

"My lord," his guard called through the door. "My lord, Archivist Amon requests your presence in his chambers."

The Archivist's tower was tall, narrow, and a pain in the ass to climb. If you were visiting Archivist Amon, there would be no surprising him. As soon as one entered the front door, stepped on the first board, the whole place would fill up with decrepit sounds, like a makeshift alarm system. It wasn't so much a place to live in as it was a place to demolish. The only thing that kept the buckled barrel of stone together seemed to be Amon himself. If he left, Edgar often thought, then the tower would go, too.

As for the Archivist's quarters, they were enslaved to cliché, and as far as it seemed Amon was concerned, he would not have it any other way. Books, ancient artifacts, and other oddities of all kinds filled that tower he called home. There was a reverence, too, in the way he handled these items, as though they held for him distant memories or an unresolved longing for their Old World surroundings. Edgar could never make sense of it, and had never tried to.

So when Edgar plodded up that spiraling staircase, the morning sun coming through the cracks in the tower and making his sickness feel sick, the old man already knew he was there.

"It has been too long since you've last visited," Amon cried.

Edgar smiled, caught his breath. He stepped off the staircase and pushed into the Archivist's chambers. Looking back, the tower seemed steeper than he remembered—narrower, too. Looking forward, the quarters seemed larger than he remembered—scarier, too. For a moment, he had a sense of vertigo as he stared into the room, as though he were staring into some great, dark deep into which he was about to fall.

Archivist Amon waved at him. Edgar snapped out of the dizzy spell. The Archivist was sitting behind a desk; the sunlight coming through the window behind him framed him in a heavenly glow. When Edgar had been a child, he had thought heaven might look something like the old man's chambers; cluttered but clean, with a million things to look at, most of which Edgar would never understand. He felt the same way now, except this time, he felt as though they weren't alone. It was hard to tell, because even with the sunlight, the room had its fair share of shadows and hiding places. But there did seem to be something else in there with them.

"I didn't sleep well last night," Edgar finally said, shaking off the feeling and forcing himself to go to Amon. He took a seat on the opposite side of the desk and slouched in the chair. "There's a good chance I'll fall asleep right here if you let me."

Amon shrugged. He had a quill in his hand. Before him, his novel, *The Disciples of the Deep*, lay open. There weren't many blank pages left in it.

"Almost finished?" Edgar looked around the room as he said this. The Archivist's plants had taken over the place. The red rooted things were everywhere, growing into everything.

"Close," Amon said. He set the quill down, shut the book. "Just when I think I'm done, I think of something new to add."

"How long have you been working on that novel?" Edgar tapped his fingers on the desk. He wanted to look through it, but he knew Amon would never allow that. "Ten years?"

"Oh, no, no. Longer than that, Edgar." He smiled, and ran his fingers down the cover. "It's therapeutic, in a way. Truth be told, if I do not give it up, I may never finish it."

"Can you give me a hint of what it's about? I won't tell anyone. I swear it."

Amon laughed and leaned back in his chair. His eyes glinted as he licked his lips. "Ah, I don't know. It's a personal tale. If I tell you what it's about, and you think it's foolish, I'll be crushed."

"So sensitive," Edgar joked. He missed spending time with the

Archivist. Ever since his adolescent years, their time together had been waning. In some ways, Amon had been there for him more than his father.

"I'm old," Amon shouted, going red in the cheeks. "I'm senile. I can't help it!" He snorted. *The Disciples of the Deep.* What's it about? Well, let's see." He leaned forward, elbows to the desk. "You promise you will keep it a secret?"

Edgar sealed his lips.

"Honestly, there's not much to it. It's just a story about a man in a terrible world trying to do the right thing."

Taken aback, Edgar said, "That's all you're going to tell me?"

"Edgar, it's almost finished." Amon took the book and placed it in a drawer. "I'm not going to ruin the surprise."

Edgar groaned. "You're killing me. It needs a better cover, at least."

"It doesn't have a cover," Amon said, dully.

"Exactly."

"Hmm. I think I may need a few more years to figure that detail out."

"If you take too long, you're not going to be able to enjoy all the money it makes from being a bestseller."

Amon nodded and then shook his head. "That's okay. I'm looking to leave a legacy behind. Something that can't be melted down and auctioned off when I'm dead."

Edgar heard something move inside the room. "That's... admirable. Hey, Amon, is someone here?"

"Yes, actually." He gestured behind Edgar. "I would like you to meet someone."

Edgar turned around. Behind him, still as a statue, a man stood, with a smile so wide it couldn't have been anything but insincere. His eyes were penetrating, and his teeth pointed and sharp. He was handsome, though, and well dressed. To Edgar, there was no doubt in his mind this man was a villain. And just where the hell had he come from?

"My lord," Amon said, "this is Alexander Blodworth, understudy of Samuel Turov, the Exemplar of Restraint and a high priest of Penance."

Alexander bowed, and said, "It's an honor to meet you, Lord Edgar."

Is it? Why would it be? "It's an honor to have you in our city. What brings you to Ghostgrave?"

Alexander came around Edgar and stood beside the desk. "Relations. Ours are not great with Eldrus. That is a shame."

"Worse than your relations with Geharra?" Edgar goaded.

Alexander laughed a boisterous laugh. "I don't have the strength to heal those old wounds."

Archivist Amon cleared his throat. "There's more to this world than Eldrus. Your father, and he would agree, has done a poor job keeping you and your brothers and sisters informed."

Edgar, trying to remain as respectful as possible, asked, "Why didn't you call Horace here? I'm last in line. I can't do anything."

Amon folded his hands and rested his chin atop them. "It's always good to be prepared, my lord."

"Penance needs an ear. We've much to offer but none to listen. We're—and I speak for the Mother Abbess—willing to pay more if the Divide would be opened up to us. Between the current tariffs and the Night Terror attacks, shipping on the Divide doesn't show much of a profit. It's not worth the effort."

"Strengthening the bond between cities would give Eldrus more opportunity." Amon reached for one of the red plants growing up his desk, snapped it in half, and ate it.

Edgar didn't trust this Alexander Blodworth, and he was starting to distrust Amon, as well. "This is beyond me, and what I can do. This could be considered treason." His words came out more confidently than he intended. "Penance wouldn't send an exemplar's understudy to discuss these things."

"You're right," Alexander said. He smoothed back his hair. "I've come to spread the word of the Holy Order and trade secrets with your sister, the botanist."

"What? Audra?"

Amon laughed and said, "Certainly not Lena. And Vincent's not a woman. Not yet, at least."

"My lord." Alexander leaned forward, one hand on the desk, the mask of confidence he wore now giving way to cockiness. "We know where the assassin came from."

Edgar made the connection quicker than he could form a sentence, so he blurted, "You? Penance?"

Alexander, impressed, leaned away. Looking at Amon, he said,

"Quick, isn't he?"

CHAPTER IX

The Nameless Forest has always been, and will always be for those who need it. When the Earth turned on itself and all heavenly bodies went to the grave, the Forest stayed. First to leave, and first to return, the women of the Old World rediscovered the Garden and claimed it as their own.

The Trauma had eaten all the children and all their bones, and so the women found themselves elevated, held high by the very hands that had once beat them so low. They repopulated deliberately, mindful of the men they chose and the traits they carried. They studied the past, and by its successes and failures, formed the foundations of the forthcoming future.

Progress, however, was slow, limited by the constraints of the human body and mind. Feeling the burden of their imposed divinity, the women delved deeper into the Nameless Forest for ancient answers. At its center, where reality peeled like paint from a portrait, they found a grandfather clock. It sat atop an island wreathed in red grass, with the clock's hands permanently fixed on the midnight hour.

After some debate, the women decided to swim for the island, but as soon as their feet left the shore, they found the water was not water at all, but worms, hundreds of thick, long, bruise-colored worms. The women turned to flee, but the worms clung tightly to their ankles and wrists, and held them down, so that they could witness the blue light that rose out of the wriggling mass, and hear the words it had to say.

The women returned and shared what they had learned with the women who had stayed behind. By this knowledge, minds were opened and wombs quickened, and soon the Forest was filled with the sounds of children who had only taken a month to gestate. The offspring of the women were considered blessed, and the hundreds that they bore were given as blessings to the villages and towns that had stayed loyal to the women.

The borders of the Nameless Forest were opened shortly thereafter, and the goddesses descended from ascendance to live amongst mortals. They shared their findings with those who could put them into practice, and prayed to the greatness of the Blue Worm in the morning and at night.

The fruits of the women's labors, however, were quick to spoil. The children, who were once so promising, began to turn, on themselves at first, and then others. They tore and ate their own skin, and wore the skin and skulls of those who tried to stop them. Mortified, their revered mothers rallied together to put an end to the slaughter, but the children—the flesh fiends, those terrors—fled into the wilds, leaving behind half-empty towns and half-eaten villages.

Enlightenment soon gave way to idiocy, and the women of the Nameless Forest were rounded up, for the people felt fooled by their promises. The women's methods were questioned and the answers they gave ignored. Upon learning of their encounter at the red island, the women were fixed to a pyre at the Forest's border and burned alive, until nothing remained but their ashes and the worms that had swum in their bellies. Those that attempted to catch the worms failed, and by their failings, their arms were colored crimson, for crimson had been the worms' color before they disappeared into the earth.

Audra was still alive, of that Edgar was certain. He gritted his teeth and forced himself to his feet. Hot, sickening pains from the crooked cuts and gouges left by the barbed wire flared throughout his body. He tried to grab the ball of steel that closed around that imposter Audra. Before his fingers could grasp it, the orb sank into his supposed sister's blood and disappeared. Edgar ignored the urge to dig after it, for the urge was what the Forest surely wanted, and went ahead.

The church sat atop the land, a crumbling mass of spires and glass. The walls that held it together shook and shivered as the bells bellowed a death-knell drone. Had this been the same sound he had heard that killed the carrion birds? He winced, the deep rumblings vibrating his chest and head. Covering his eyes to block out the sun, he saw that above the great, battered doors, the word 'Anathema' had been written in brown and black.

He gripped his sword. "This is a village?" Then he started up the church's front steps.

Like all places haunted and horrible, the doors of Anathema opened on their own. Edgar proceeded cautiously into the church.

As soon as he crossed the threshold, the bells stopped. Sunlight poured through the stained glass windows above, creating pockets of color by which he could navigate this dim place. Pews like mouths full of splinters grinned as he pressed further in. Fallen candles like melted hands reached out of the floor, as though to grab him. A cold wind rolled off the balconies overhead, the stink of rot adhered to it.

He pulled his cloak close, covered his nose, and though every part of him begged him to turn around, he went forward.

When he reached the back of the church, where the wall had sagged and become host to a mess of Stinging Chrism, his nose picked up another scent. He circled the altar here, where it sat swaddled in dusty, dirty sheets, and noticed several cracks at its base. Through them, a warm breeze blew, and rather than rot, it carried the smell of wine and fresh food. He leaned in closer, mouth salivating, stomach growling—too starved to think much of the fact that the sheet that covered the altar had stood up on its own.

But then the spell broke, and he stumbled back, shouting, "Holy Child!" as the dirty sheet fell and revealed a robed man with yellow eyes beneath it.

"Stop, stop," he shouted, as the figure stepped off the altar, his robes streaming like water around him.

"I'll call the others up and tell them you've come," the robed man said. He hurried off, slipped into an alcove, and climbed the ladder there.

Edgar stood by the hollowed-out altar, dumbstruck. The man padded away, deeper into the church.

"Fuck this," he said, stepping away from the altar. "I'm not staying here like an—"

The church trembled as the bells began to rock again high above. It was a signal, he realized; a signal to others unseen that a trespasser had arrived.

Edgar had failed his task, and so, like most failures, he turned on his heels and fled. As he ran down the center aisle, red robed beasts rose out of the pews. He drew his sword, swinging back and forth to keep them at bay. Pale fingers grabbed at his hands and face. He kicked the nearest red hooded horror, and it went whirling into the shadows.

A raspy chant swelled behind Edgar as he hurried toward the front doors. He sheathed his sword and covered his ears to deafen the words, but the words found him all the same. Like hooks, they clung to him, and like hooks they reeled him in.

He was yanked backward, his skull smacking against the floor. His arms shot out and his legs went limp. Like spoiled children, the congregation dragged him across the church, opening old wounds and creating new ones as he bashed and scraped against the deathtrap pews. With one forceful tug, the robed figures chanted him into the air, throwing him against the altar, where he crumpled, powerless to stop them.

"Shouldn't have run," he heard the robed man with the yellow eyes say, somewhere nearby. "Let's have a look at you."

Invisible strings from the strung-together words lifted Edgar and left him to dangle in midair. He held on tightly to his sword. He cursed and screamed, but that was about all he could do. Surrounded, outnumbered, the forlorn lord of Eldrus drifted above a sea of black and red robes and pointed hoods, the waves of their infernal chant keeping him afloat. Fifteen, twenty—Edgar counted the congregation and, out of character, considered how difficult it would be to kill them all.

"Who are you?" a member of the church asked. "What do you want?"

Edgar's mouth started to water again at the smell of the freshly baked bread and picked fruits. He closed his eyes, told himself the sensations were nothing more than conjured temptations.

"Was that you out there?" someone else asked. "Was that you in the fields? I think... I think Crestfallen has spared this man."

A murmur meandered through the cloth. Edgar struggled against his ghostly bindings, and salivated at the hints of cooked meat Beneath his feet, there were small slivers of orange light now coming through the cracks in the church's floor. A force tugged on his wrist, and he dropped his sword to the ground.

"Well, that's different. That's something to consider," a third man said. "A messenger, perhaps? What do you think he has to say?"

The cracks in the floor were starting to spread throughout the church, widening into sizeable fissures. It was as though hell itself were pushing through the holy ground. He heard a ruckus, a clanging of pots and pans. Fork and spoon, too, scraping against a plate, thudding against a bowl.

"Ask him, ask him," a fourth, high-pitched voice shrieked, piercing the ongoing chant. "Just get on with it and ask him!"

Edgar bit his tongue to avoid its loosening, and then he bit into it, drawing blood, as the orange cracks split the floor and pushed pulpits of stone into the air. The congregation stood unyielding as their place of worship was pulled apart like a puzzle; the orange light, now much darker and deeper, spilled over from below, and drowned the church in that hellfire glow.

"Bring him under," a voice commanded from that terrible place. "Bring him to me."

It took everything Edgar had not to beg. He didn't want the congregation to know how cowardly he was.

One by one, the robed figures turned their backs. When they did, the chant ended and Edgar fell. He flailed wildly, hands grasping for purchase on the slick, separated flooring. In seconds, the orange light had enveloped him. Before he could make sense of what was happening, he crashed into the ground, blowing all the air out of his lungs.

"Fuck," Edgar wheezed. He scrambled to his feet, and grabbed his sword off the ground. Batting away the orange smoke of this underground place, he chattered, "Fuck, fuck, fuck."

He was in a kitchen. Blazing ovens lined the room, the smoke they exhaled causing the orange oddity that filled the place. Every type of food that could be cooked was cooking over the roaring flames.

Seeing that, an immense hunger unlike any Edgar had ever known overcame him and, like so many stupid children from so many fairytales, he gravitated towards them, and certain obliteration.

"Leave it," the commanding voice from before boomed. A jagged shadow stood in the swirling smoke at the furthest end of the kitchen.

"That's not for you, not yet."

Edgar cleared the spit, vomit, and fear from his throat, and said, "I seek the ruler of… Anathema."

"Here I stand," the jagged shadow said. "The Woman in White sent you to us. We heard you were coming."

Edgar nodded.

"Is the food not good enough? Is the drink not as she wants it? Who is not satisfied with our offerings? Chapel did not receive the last shipment, this I know and need not be told. The Whore of Threadbare, that's it, isn't it? What did she say?"

In disbelief over the man's trust in him, Edgar just smiled and shook his head. "Blackwood, Atlach." He only mentioned those villages, because the man had not.

The jagged shape came out of the smoke, to show itself to Edgar. He, too, like his brethren, was clad in black and wore a red, pointed hood. But now that he had the light, and a little less fear in his system, Edgar could see that the man, and likely those above, were not beasts at all; this one was an old man with one eye and a cleft lip.

"They have never wanted food before. Is this what she asks of us? It's not, is it? I can tell it isn't. Praise God. You're a wicked man. Tell me, tell me what's brought you here."

Edgar, having suddenly shifted from being a victim to being victorious, was at a loss for words. Finally, he managed to say: "To discuss supply and demand, and dispersion."

The ruler of Anathema nodded with every syllable.

"To discuss this place and your needs."

The last part must have won him over, because he introduced himself. "Father Silas. Welcome to Anathema, Blood of the Cloth."

What that title meant, Edgar couldn't be sure, but it was clear to him that something was wrong with Father Silas. He trusted Edgar as though he had known him for years, and his desperation to be in Crestfallen's good graces blinded him to the fact that she had sent Edgar here to kill him.

The ruler of Anathema led him through the length of the kitchen, and then the larders, garden, winery, and well—all of which was subterranean. The church was not a village, Edgar realized during his tour, but a factory for all things needed to live comfortably in the Nameless Forest. Why would Crestfallen want Father Silas murdered, then? Would it not destroy what little harmony existed between the settlements?

Silas had started bringing Edgar topside, and now they were following a staircase up to the roof.

"Supplies are sent out monthly." He stepped off the final staircase and pushed open the door there.

The sudden blast of light temporarily blinded Edgar.

Going through the door, onto the roof and their loose tiles, Silas said, "Five paths, do you see them?"

Rubbing the sun out of his eyes, Edgar said he did. Five paths, like five splayed fingers. They ran from the palm that was Anathema.

"They are safe roads. Narrow, not well maintained. Easy to stray from, even if you've traveled them all your life." Silas stopped, and when he did, the bells finally stopped booming, too.

Pointing from left to right, Silas said, "To Chapel, to Threadbare." His eyes became as dark as his tone. "That goes to Blackwood, the other, Atlach."

Edgar fingered the hilt of his sword. They were alone on the parapets. If he wanted to kill Silas, he could. "What about the last path?"

"I don't know." Father Silas turned around and headed back toward the stairs. "It's not a safe path. No one goes down there anymore. Wait, over—" he pointed to the church's annex, where several members of the congregation were towing boxes onto a wagon, "—over there. That's the next shipment." He sighed. "It's really been hundreds of years since someone last visited."

Father Silas smiled. He lunged forward and ripped Edgar's sword out of its scabbard. Turning it around, he ran it through his own stomach and pushed the blade into his guts and out his back.

"What are you doing?" Edgar cried. He reached for the sword, but Father Silas twisted away. "Holy Child, let me help you!"

The priest screamed. The flesh on his face started to melt, the glimmer of his appearance running down his robes. Beneath his skin, another face, beaked and scaled, like a lizard's, like a bird's, was there. Great, mottled wings tore outward and stretched through slits in the back of his robe. A second mouth, a chomping umbilical cord of hungry muscle, bit through the front of the garment and snapped at the air.

Carrion bird. Except this one was much larger than the others. Edgar wrestled the sword out of Father Silas's bleeding hole and put several steps between him and the creature.

"You're Blood of the Cloth," Father Silas hissed. Talons burst through his fingernails. "What are you doing?"

"I don't know what that is!" The torso mouth snapped forward, trying to bite Edgar, as though it had a mind of its own. "What is going...? Do they know you're like this?"

Father Silas, despite having lost all his human features, seemed stunned by this. "We're all carrion birds here. It's our curse, our way to redemption." He clicked his talons on the roof tiles. "Is this a test?

Don't you know? Maybe you shouldn't be here."

Edgar leaned over the edge of the roof. Those below were oblivious as to what was happening above, continuing to fill the wagon with the supplies they were hauling out of the church. He returned to Father Silas. If he hesitated, the priest could take flight and flee, or summon his congregation to tear Edgar apart.

Father Silas was already halfway to Death, but if he finished him off, and if he hadn't truly deserved it, then he would have the man's blood on his hands for the rest of his days.

"Why did you stab yourself?"

Father Silas snapped his beak. "You, was it you they saw days ago?" Father Silas cocked his head. He retracted the torso mouth back into his blood-drenched stomach. "You, and the dead man. You, you, you!" His wings started to flap in agitation. "You are disgusted by me? I know why you are here."

Edgar pointed the sword at the massive bird. "No, your people attacked us."

"We are scavengers, bottom-feeders. By our scraps, this forest breathes." Blood poured down the priest's feathered legs and pooled around his feet. "God gives us the living, and we feed the living the dead. That's how it has always been. We do not waste God's gifts. Why do you test me? Have you not come to replace me? Will it be Mother Michelle, instead? I've led Anathema since it was Benediction. I have done my part." He fingered the sword wound. "Do yours!"

Biding his time because he didn't know what the hell was going on, Edgar said, "Would you do anything for your god Crestfallen?"

Father Silas spat. "The Woman in White is not our god. She is nothing more than a vindictive landlord. I have… I have made a mistake." His words started to slur. "I have been too… hasty."

I don't know what to do. I can't do what I'm supposed to do. The Nameless Forest swayed around them, the canopy catching fire in places.

But he hasn't attacked me, yet. Something holds him back.

On the opposite side of the church, great spores were coughed into the air from massive grubs that weighed down the trees.

He would do anything for her. To get away from her. Did she warn him? A raven fell from the sky and exploded when it hit the ground. From its feathery ruin, a person was born.

He brought me up here alone. He wants to die. He stabbed himself. Just do it.

Put him out of his misery. You have to, anyways. Shit. Shit!

"Finish it," Edgar said. He threw the sword at the bird-priest, and Silas caught it. "She wants you to kill yourself. You already know that." Edgar tried to stop his voice from shaking, but he couldn't help it. "Who told you?"

Father Silas reared up, the sword pointing at his neck. "She promised. I always knew." His avian eyes were wet and wide. "I've sinned enough?"

"You have."

"I've converted enough?"

"More than enough." Edgar told himself not to look away.

"Kill myself?"

"As quickly as you… as quickly as…" He nodded. "Yes."

Father Silas nodded and said, "Through hell we find heaven." The intestine-like mouth shot out of his torso. "By our evils we are made good." It snaked around his body and then burrowed into the wound in his chest. At that moment, he pulled the sword back, said to Edgar, "You should run now, Blood of the Cloth," and drove its blade through his neck.

He wandered around for a moment, geysers of blood spewing from his throat. Then, when the torso mouth had grown fat on his innards, he died.

CHAPTER X

Thirty-Four Days Ago

Horace showed no mercy, and Edgar wouldn't have it any other way. Clouds of dirt swirled around them as they blocked, parried, and riposted one another throughout the courtyard.

Edgar's arm ached, threatening to revolt every time his brother's sword crashed against his shield. His legs wobbled as he sidestepped and ducked stabs and swings. He breathed like a dying dog in a deadening heat, three paces from death's door. He was embarrassing himself and losing badly; and Edgar wouldn't have it any other way.

"Tired?" Horace asked.

Edgar nodded. He shook the sweat out of his helmet. "Exhausted."

"You're better than you think." Horace took his brother's sword and shield to put away. "Too cautious, and yet, too imprecise." He stowed both their armaments in the rack at the courtyard's edge.

Edgar doubled over and caught his breath. "I don't want to hurt you." If he didn't get out of the sun soon, there wouldn't be anything left of him but a puddle of sweat and dented armor.

"You won't." Horace nodded at the trainees passing through, and the small crowd that formed in the stands. "Could you kill?"

Edgar shook his head. "I don't want to kill anyone."

Horace approached his brother, straightened him out. "Then what are you doing out here?"

"I don't want anyone killing me." Edgar laughed, coughed, and laughed some more. "What about you? Could you kill someone when the time comes?"

"Yes," Horace said, without hesitation. "I often think of those things which I do not want to do, so that when I must, I am ready for them."

Edgar sighed and stared at his brother. "While you're training to be king, make sure you spend some time learning how to have a bit of fun, too. Because that sounds awful."

Horace nodded with a smile. "Sure, Edgar."

King Sovn and Queen Magdalena were well aware of the assassin's origins, for Alexander Blodworth had told them himself. Afterward, he was apprehended and locked away in a heavily guarded room until it could be decided if he had direct involvement in the orchestration of the royal family's planned demise.

What Edgar couldn't understand was why the understudy from Penance had felt the need to tell him in the first place, and why Archivist Amon had facilitated the meeting to begin with. He had every intention of informing his family of the conspirator's admission, and yet Alexander had beat him to it, by marching straight to the throne room from the Archivist's tower, before Edgar even had the chance to part from Amon's quarters.

"It makes no sense," Edgar said, walking beside Horace as they left the courtyard, far bloodier and bruised than when they had entered. "To begin with, it's not my place to know such things. Why did Blodworth think I could help him?"

"Manipulation, perhaps." Horace stopped where the walkway intersected with another. "I'll speak with Archivist Amon."

"Am I that much of a pushover?" Edgar said, as Horace started down another path. "Never mind. Don't answer that."

Horace didn't.

The Crossbreed had grown larger. It had sprawled itself across the subway station and claimed dominion over the rusty and rotted remains there.

Audra left Auster behind and led Edgar down to the tracks to show him a recent development in the plant's lifecycle. Where the rails had been pulled back off the ground, like beckoning fingers, a cluster of orbs sat glowing in a ditch.

Audra crouched, and said, "This is what we need. These fruits fell from it."

Edgar swallowed his hesitation—the massive plant wasn't far off—and crouched beside her. "What is this?" He leaned in closer. The orbs were covered in a carpet of insects—ants, flies, roaches, beetles, and centipedes—but they weren't moving.

"Not dead, see." Audra gave a few a poke, and they twitched with life.

"Not moving much, either."

"We'll have to find the right amount."

Edgar closed his eyes. He knew he should have put an end to the conversation right then and there, but instead, he simply said, "We have to start small."

"If… if we're going to do this to our people, we ought to do it to ourselves first."

Edgar nodded enthusiastically. "Yes." It was a good idea, one which coaxed his conscience into a calm. "Audra, who else knows about this place?"

His sister stood. She didn't look at him when she said, "No one. Why?"

"Alexander Blodworth. He told me he came to speak with you about botany, among other things."

This time, Audra did face him, and though it was dark in the tunnels, he could see that she was blushing. "Really?"

"We can't tell anyone, Audra." Edgar stood. "If this is what you say it is, and it can do what you say it can do… Don't tell anyone. No one, but especially not Alexander. I know you want to please people."

"No, I don't."

"Yes, you do. You don't have to please anyone, though. You don't have to prove anything. If we're going to do this, it has to be in secret, between me and you and Auster, and for the right reasons."

"Yeah." She waved to Auster, who watched them from the room that overlooked the subway. "You seem… Edgar, I won't be upset if you decide we shouldn't do this. I was expecting you to say no when I told you, anyways."

"So was I."

Audra loosened her hair and let it fall over her shoulders. As she combed it with her fingers, she said, "Why did you say yes? I mean, of all things, Ed, you agree to this?" She laughed, and as she laughed, she smelled the floral fragrances that still lingered in her hair. "I thought you were going to be angry. Or, at least, tell me to destroy it."

"It's just so..." Edgar shrugged, tipped his head back, and groaned. "It's absurd, but there's something about this whole situation. I don't know. It makes sense. It seems right. Maybe it's the assassin, or assassins. I just, I just don't want people to hate us anymore, and they hate us so much. They won't even listen when we're trying to help, and I know that's... you know, you can't make people listen. But, with this, now we can, and if all we need is a month to make things better, and if this works like you say it will, then I guess it's worth it."

Audra nudged him. "I want them to be happier, too, Edgar, but I think your expectations may be too high."

"Theirs are too low, and they shouldn't be. They should expect more, and we should deliver on those expectations."

"It's a myth, not a miracle." Audra went to her knees, and took out a knife. "If it doesn't work, it doesn't work. No sense in talking at length about it until we're sure it does."

Audra was incredibly shy, but also incredibly bold when the situation asked her to be. She started slicing off layers of the orbs, the glowing fruits of the Crossbreed, and somewhere along the way, decided to just take one of the orbs altogether.

Side by side, they marched off the tracks, out of the tunnel, and up to the office, where Auster waited, shaking his head, well aware of what his siblings were about to ask him.

He did what he was told, because he always did what his twin told him to do, and ate a piece of the fruit, which bled a milky white liquid when Audra split it.

"You next," Auster said, cringing as he swallowed the piece.

"No, we have to be thorough about this. One at a time. Don't interrupt, Auster. I'm timing your interaction."

Edgar didn't need to be a scientist to know their experiment was flawed. There were too many variables left unconsidered, and the sample size was too small to do anything but validate their own biases.

He almost expected more from Audra, for it was from her he had learned such terms and considerations, but as he watched her watching Auster hungrily, he knew that, like the rest of the family, she wouldn't be stopped until she got exactly what she wanted.

That's when Edgar realized neither would he.

Ten minutes passed. Auster finally admitted, "I don't feel any different. I wouldn't beat yourself up, Sister. Growing myths is not the easiest of accomplishments."

Audra slipped into her thoughts. Then, she said, "Stand on the top of your chair."

"It's uneven. I will fall and break my neck, and then where will we be?" Auster shook his head, but as he did so, he stood up and stepped onto the chair. "Oh." He looked surprised. "Well, there you go."

As Edgar stared at his brother while he delicately maintained his balance on the unbalanced chair, he said, "What's something Auster would never do, even if you asked him?"

Audra cleared her throat. "Take that knife out of your pocket and cut your hand."

"Hold on. No, wait a minute." Edgar waved his hands, telling Auster to stop, but Auster had already taken out the knife from his pocket.

"What's wrong with you?" he said. He hissed as he sliced his skin with the knife. Stray drops of bright red blood dribbled onto the rickety chair. "I'm done. No more," he insisted, and yet he remained standing, gripping his bloody hand.

"Sit down, Auster," Audra said, giddy. "I'll go next."

Audra ingested half as much of the fruit as her brother had. As expected, she was less open to suggestion; by the time Edgar had her singing a bawdy song about a romance between a well-endowed Night Terror and a buxom human, Auster had recovered.

"I remember everything," he said, out of it. "I hate you. Both of you." He held up his hand. "This is going to get infected." He pointed to the office. "Look at this nasty place. People will not fall for this… this shit!"

"They won't know we're telling them what to do," Audra said, her words slurred, her eyelids fluttering. "Edgar, your turn."

"We have to be able to destroy the Crossbreed as soon as anyone finds out about it." Edgar was beginning to fully comprehend the implications of the plant's qualities; it terrified him. "It works, that's clear to us now, but we don't move forward until we've accounted for everything. Is it addictive? Is it traceable? You said there is a

Crossbreed that kills. The Bloodless. How do you know both creations are not one in the same?"

"Edgar." Audra took a deep breath and exhaled, as though she were physically ridding herself of the plant's influence. "Are you willing to wait the years it will take to find all of that out?"

Edgar shook his head. He wasn't willing to wait years, let alone months, to put their plan into action; Eldrus couldn't afford such a delay. No, he had never truly walked its streets, nor lived a life such as those who called its gutters and sewers home, but he didn't need to; one doesn't need to murder their siblings to know that they shouldn't. He had heard and seen enough from Ghostgrave to silence any doubts that the city should be left to follow its own catastrophic course; a daughter raped by her father, a father raped by his son, children exchanged for coin, coin exchanged for children. Labor that leads to nowhere, and nowhere that leads to labor.

Edgar had heard of roaming gangs leaving blood where they'd roamed, and broken banks leaving behind broken homes. His family could deride him all they liked about his cause. He wouldn't be stopped, and once they saw his good work, neither they, nor anyone else, would ask him to.

"Edgar," Auster said, interrupting his brother's thoughts. "Audra and I have to ask you something."

"What's Vincent doing with the Night Terror in the dungeon?" Audra scooped up the glowing fruit, as though to tell Edgar she would have the truth, whether he wanted to share it or not.

Edgar looked back and forth between the two of them. "How? I wouldn't lie to you, but did Vincent say anything?"

Auster pointed down the tracks, where it was darkest. "These tunnels run deep. They run right beside the dungeons."

"We saw you." Audra wiped the sweat from her brow. "You're right, Auster, you really can feel it leaving your system."

"Wait, can you take me to the dungeon? Can I get in?"

They nodded.

"Show me, please. I need to ask it things, things I can't ask when Vincent or the guards are around. He's not interested in what it has to say, not like I am. Audra, Auster. They look... just like us."

"What about the Crossbreed?" Audra asked, her voice full of pride and the anticipation of it being hurt.

"We start tomorrow." Edgar smiled at his siblings. "We start making everything better tomorrow."

Audra disappeared into the shadows. When she came out, she carried fire. She held the makeshift torch of cloth and wood outward, and led the men that followed behind her down to the subway tracks.

Edgar struggled as they went. He didn't have the foresight to step over every deep puddle and protruding pipe. Under his feet, loose tiles cracked into clouds of dust, while jagged signs and broken bottles threatened to put an end to his walking days altogether.

"Just up here," Audra whispered, pointing to a station outside which a subway car sat. "Have to be quiet. Mean things live down here."

"We aren't prepared for 'mean things,'" Edgar said. "They built Ghostgrave around these ruins on purpose, didn't they?"

Auster made a popping sound with his mouth. "Absolutely. They go on forever, these tracks. It's like the Old World was turned inside out."

Audra lifted herself onto the walkway beside the tracks, went over to the small station, and fixed the torch to a hole in its doorway. She called Edgar over.

As he entered the station, whose ceiling was covered in a thick spider web, she pointed to a place in the back wall where light shone through.

Edgar put his eye to the peephole. On the other side, the Night Terror was still in shackles. Except, this wasn't its cell. It was something else. Something like a torture chamber.

It took Edgar a moment to make sense of everything, but just out of the Eel's reach, Vincent, naked and sweating, was crawling toward an equally naked woman on the floor. She was pregnant, tightly bound, and wore the head of a moon cat.

"How are you so far along?" Vincent asked the female Night Terror. He climbed atop of her before she could answer, and said, "Your belly is so big."

"Edgar," Audra whispered. She grabbed his shoulder.

He swatted her away, unable to pull himself from the revolting scene. His hands became fists, his temples started to throb. He stepped back, turned around to ask his sister how to get into the dungeon from here, to stop Vincent. But he didn't ask. He didn't say anything at all.

Because now there was a knife at Auster's throat, and at his back, a man, bald and grinning, wearing the holy vestments of Penance; the second assassin.

CHAPTER XI

I remember a time when the world was formed and full, and all that could be was, and all that should be wasn't. Songs were sung of such squandered potentials, but when the songs were over, so too were the sentiments. I brought the world to its knees and gave it what it wanted, and it bled all over my feet its willful stupidity.

The Trauma did nothing to humanity that humanity hadn't already done to itself. Some would say the Nameless Forest is rooted in the suffering that followed that conspicuously tenuous event, but they would be wrong. It has always been here, and not in the metaphysical sense. From east to west it has spread, crossing oceans as though they were fields, and now it has arrived here, where I've always wanted it to be, in the graveyard of life and the cradle of death.

When the world writhes, religion reigns. With God gone, the Lillians constructed distractions while waiting for his return. They commanded their congregation to gather the remaining firearms and explosives. With no place to put their deadly haul, they melted it down and built it up, into a great, achromatic tower that signaled to their lord that they were ready.

It wasn't long until the tower became an idol, and like all religions, the Lillians were divided over its meaning. Those that rejected the tower went eastward, filling their ranks with the faiths they had absorbed along the way. Those that held the tower holy stayed behind, christening themselves the Scavengers to make permanent the separation.

Three city-states had been spared the Abyss, and it was to the northernmost territory of Elin, now Eldrus, the Lillians went. Entitlement saw the congregation thinned by blades and imprisonment; the City of Reason had no interest in bending to the commands of the same people thought to have encouraged the Trauma. The Lillians, full of hate and self-inflicted persecution, evacuated the city, their numbers halved to the comforts Elin provided, and continued eastward, where they were certain their lord slumbered.

The Lillians tore across the continent, taking what they willed. It was not until they reached the Nameless Forest, a place towards which they felt a kinship given its infamy, did they rest.

Those too fattened from thieving and fucking ventured into the forest and made it their home. They claimed they saw heaven in its woods, and built the massive church, Benediction, to honor their lord.

Those not taken by the Forest or the strange drink found in the veins that grew there, set their sights on the sea. They claimed they heard God calling them from the foggy isle not far from the shore, and set across the ocean's shallows to answer.

Those beholden to tradition and dogma left the heretical Forlorn behind, and went to where the land was made white and pure. They claimed they felt God in the frozen isolation of the northeastern reaches, and took the forgotten city-state, Six Pillars, now Penance, as their own.

Six Pillars prospered beyond anyone's expectations, for the fanatical have a knack for procreation. Blessed by their God unseen and unheard, the Lillians made of the icy wasteland an escape from mainland chaos. Forgetful pilgrims braved the wild Divide and mountain passes to live with those they had once feared and loathed. The oldest city-state, Geharra, warned of the cruelties that awaited those starry-eyed travelers. They had suffered the Lillians longer than anywhere else, for the city had been the religion's birthplace. Their warnings, however, fell on deaf ears, even as they pointed to the depravities committed by the Scavengers who worshiped the great, gunmetal tower at their territory's edge.

But what could not be ignored were the bodies piling high on the roads to heaven, and the creatures from the Nameless Forest that put them there.

While the sects of Lillian continued to search for God in all the places a god might hide, those that had stayed in the Nameless Forest were convinced they had found him. Believing the vermillion veins brought them closer to God, they drank from them constantly, claiming each inebriation showed them glimpses of God's chambers beneath their feet. The priests of Benediction, determined to find these chambers, then cracked the earth, but they did not find God there; only things that hid in the deep dark that should not have been let loose into the light.

From the Nameless Forest, Nightmares came: Old World terrors that predated the Trauma. Hunters of humanity, dressed in rags and bone, woken and returned to cleanse the world of its Corruption. The Lillians were thought to be responsible for their first Old World appearance, and it only followed that blame would be placed on them for the Night Terrors' return.

Without an army or a god, the Lillians, for the first time in countless years, were quieted. They closed themselves off to the continent and kept to their frozen solitude, hoping that when they finally emerged once more, the Night Terrors would be gone, and their own transgressions forgotten.

Edgar's legs went out from under him as he bolted across Anathema's roof. His palms hit the tiles hard. Scattered pebbles inched their way into the soft, red parts of his palm.

He hurried to his feet, Father Silas' blood licking at his heels, and for some reason, thought of Lotus; beautiful, immaculate Lotus—the woman who had shown him a softer side of sin. He thought of her hair sliding across her chest, her legs entwined with his. He thought of the sensations she had teased out of him, working each one loose with fingers, lips, and tongue. He thought of how short the night had seemed, and how long the next would be.

He then thought of Father Silas, his torso mouth split open at the seams and stuffed with his innards, and told himself the priest wanted this. He wanted this, too, his death, in a way; to get home, but the priest had wanted it first.

"I'm sorry," he said. The torso gave a death spasm and spewed hunks of lung into the air. "I'm so very sorry."

He ran back to the staircase they had ascended to get here. Below, he heard the click of talons on cold stone, and words being murmured in the tongue of suspicion.

"He wanted it, and it was the only way to get home," he told himself.

He was a monster. Edgar ran back across the roof, searching for another way down, other than the stairs. *That's why Crestfallen had me do it. That's why he wanted to die.*

Edgar gripped one of the gargoyles, leaned out, and saw that the supply caravan was readying itself to go down the path that Father Silas said led to Chapel.

I'm doing this to get home, he told himself, Lotus' silhouette in his mind's eye. *I'm doing this because this is what I have to do to get home.* He hadn't killed the man, not really, and yet he still took full responsibility for his death.

Edgar noticed a ladder beneath the gargoyle, one which was bolted to the side of the church and ran the entire length of it. Shaking, he swung his legs over the roof's edge and planted his feet onto the creaking steps of the ladder.

Sharp paint chips along the rungs bit his fingers as he descended. He heard cries coming through a hole in the large, stained glass window beside him. Leaning over, he saw the congregation shedding their robes for feathers, their hoods for beaks. They circled the inside of the church, crying out not in anger, but celebration.

This did wonders for Edgar's nagging conscience.

Edgar's stomach lurched as someone grabbed his ankles and ripped him off the ladder. He cracked against the ground. Two figures shuffled up beside him.

"You killed him," the man with the green hood said. He, like the man beside him, had yet to transform. "You killed Father Silas."

"We saw it," the second man added, the one with the purple hood. "We heard it."

"Please," Edgar pleaded, the sun shining harshly on him, whiting out the scene.

"Come with us." The purple hooded man extended his clawed hand.

"You're not safe here." The green hooded man extended his human hand, which was thick with red Corruption.

Edgar squinted out the light. He sat up and said, "I don't understand."

The purple hooded man looked at Anathema as though he could see through its walls, to his brothers inside. "Father Silas was our leader. They will kill you for killing him."

The green hooded man looked at Edgar as though he could see through his skull to the confused brain within. "Father Silas was wanted dead by all. They will kill you just to pretend they didn't."

Edgar took the green hooded man's human hand and stood. "Why are you helping me, then?"

"The Woman in White wills it." The purple hooded man's eyes went beady and black. His neck opened at the sides and back to let feathers pass through.

Edgar jumped as he heard something snap in half inside the church. It sounded like they were tearing up the already torn-up pews. "If you wanted him dead, why didn't you do it yourself?"

"No blood runs that deep," the purple hooded man said. "My name is Jed."

"No blood runs this deep," the green hooded man corrected.

"And my name is Jes."

Four more robed members of the congregation were stocking the caravan when Edgar snuck up beside it. Jed and Jes introduced him to the workers. They nodded at him with indifference.

Crates of food atop Persist bedding were loaded onto the two horse-drawn wagons. Large, sturdy terracotta vases sat nestled in between them, the liquid inside the vases sloshing as they settled.

When the workers were finished, they turned around and passed through an archway at the back of Anathema, which led down to the depths Father Silas had shown Edgar earlier.

"Those four don't know what you've done," Jed said. He made himself comfortable in the driver's seat of the first wagon.

"They don't, like we don't, feel as the others inside feel," Jes said. He settled into the driver's seat of the second wagon. "We're too young. We don't remember like they do. It's good you killed Father Silas, though. One day, they'll thank you."

"Get in," Jed said to Edgar; then he cracked the reins and the horses started forward. "We've all work to be done in Chapel."

The hooded men, over the clap of hooves and the horses' breathy snorts, continued to speak as they traveled down what they called the Binding Road. Much like the highway, the Spine, which ran the continent from its frosted skull to heated sacrum, the Binding Road connected travelers to the constant places of the Nameless Forest. It ran from the kitchen, Anathema, to the workshop, Chapel, the loom, Atlach, and finally, the mill, Threadbare, with smaller trails here and there that led to the untamed tracts.

Jed was eager to tell Edgar of a few of these untamed tracts. There was the Pit, a hole in the center of a dried basin from which a thousand tortured voices called out unendingly. Also, Agrat's Heath—a fallow plain beneath a blood-red sky, where tens of succubae waited for the wandering unfaithful.

Jes, sensing Edgar's intrigue, then spoke of the Orphanage, a school in a swamp where children worshiped a massive, festering bat. He said it might even be located down the fifth path that ran from Anathema, the one Father Silas couldn't remember the purpose of, but he couldn't be sure.

"There's a small village, no more than a few homes in size really, near a river. It's two days down this way here," Jes said, pointing to a shaded path that peeled away from the Binding Road. "It's said that if you go there, bring a white dress and a jar of graveyard dirt. It's said if you sleep in an empty bed there, with the dress over the headboard and the jar over your heart, you will wake to find a crack in the bed frame. It's said if you widen this crack, you'll find a gray Void beyond. It's said if you look through this crack, you'll find a woman in rags who will take you out of the Nameless Forest."

"That's a lot to say," Edgar teased. He leaned over the edge of the wagon, holding on tightly as it bounced with the bumps in the road. "Take you where?"

"Where you came from."

"Sounds like Crestfallen. I mean, the Woman in White."

Jed cleared his throat. "It's not."

"Sorry, sorry." Edgar didn't want to upset his drivers. He was lucky enough they hadn't butchered him back in the churchyard. "I didn't... Jed watch out!"

From both sides of the Binding Road, an ocean's worth of water was crashing through the trees. Edgar's jaw dropped as waves like sickles rose high into the sky, to reap the world below. Birds were swallowed by the churning flood; clouds were reduced to salt-laden smears.

Edgar did as most do when they don't know what to do: he cursed and shouted and placed blame where it didn't belong.

The waves broke, raining rivers down around them. As the waters reached the road, Edgar knew that the emptiness he felt inside him, the place where his soul had been and had already begun to flee, would soon be filled.

And filled he was; not by the bitter taste of drowning death, but sour relief. As though they were encased in glass, the waters ran against and over the Binding Road. The caravan, its supplies, the passengers—everything that had stayed to the road was untouched.

Like an animal pacing frantically behind its enclosure, Edgar moved about the wagon bed. He gripped the sides of it, a manic smile stretched across his face.

"How is this possible?" The darkened sunlight reflected onto his skin through the waters above, and left his flesh looking scaled.

"Your people would call it the Black Hour," Jes said. He snapped the reins, hurrying the horses.

Edgar watched a shark pass overhead, gear-like legs clicking along its underside. "But it's midday, not midnight." *Holy Child. How long have I been in this place? The sun has been out for as long as I can remember.*

"The Dread Clock cares naught for the hour here." Jed lowered his hood. The feathers poking out of his scalp retreated. "Time is as it wills."

"The Dread Clock?" As Edgar echoed Jed's words, he felt that same emptiness inside him again. "Someone told me a story once about a clock in the Nameless Forest." He closed his eyes. There was a memory in his hazy mind. Something that hadn't been there before; a recollection that had freed itself from his subconscious.

He remembered a room, a heavy cloud of smoke and incense meandering through it. There had been a voice, too, soothing and slow, like a storyteller's.

He fed me until I was full. He kept feeding me, even when I refused to eat. Who... who the hell was it?

Edgar could see a face, but he didn't recognize it. Looking past the face, he saw moonlight.

It was night. It was the night I was taken. The person he couldn't recognize had been telling him about the Nameless Forest.

Was he warning me? Preparing me? Had the Forest really wanted him to forget these moments, or was something else suppressing these memories?

There was something wrong with that person. They, no, he... he asked me to do something.

At that moment, Edgar felt a disgusting weight fill the emptiness inside him.

What terrible thing did he do to me?

"My lord," Jes said. "We're here."

Edgar opened his eyes, and didn't quite catch the fact that Jes had called him lord. In that brief moment of reflection, the ocean had receded. In its place, a massive, toppled skyscraper lay on its side in an overgrown field. He had seen these buildings before, in the books Amon had shared with him from the Old World. The pictures hadn't begun to come close to conveying the skyscraper's size. It was immense, almost too large to take in from just one angle, but there was one detail he didn't understand; a strange, glowing, lattice of lines that covered the building. An architectural quirk of its times, maybe, or...

Edgar's heart stopped. The lines that covered the skyscraper weren't for decoration. They were spider webs. Thick, bloody, quivering, mile-long spider webs.

"Jed, we have to go back," Jes shouted. "Atlach has broken the truce. They must have found out why he was here!"

"What?" Edgar drew his sword. "What's going on?"

Jed, panicked, did everything he could to wheel the wagon around. Something crunched beneath the horses' hooves, and Edgar saw that it was a sign that read "Chapel Industries."

In the distance, figures had begun to emerge from the broken windows and fissured walls that lined the skyscraper. They screamed for help, begged for mercy. Lightning and thunder flashed and boomed throughout Chapel.

A man with a bloody stump for a leg emerged, holding a handgun. He waved to the caravan and fired the weapon into the air—a signal for them to get away as fast as they could.

"That's a pistol," Edgar cried, recognizing the Old World weapon through the confusion. "No one has been able to create—"

Jes wailed in agony. Edgar looked to the second wagon. In the driver's seat, a headless body spewed tongues of steaming blood all over the backside of the horses. His body tensed, his sword tightened. He'd seen something. Something skittered in the second wagon's bed, behind the crates and vases.

"Jed, what is it?" His voice rattled in his throat. "Jed?"

He looked over his shoulder and saw, crouched at the front of the wagon, over Jed's mutilated body, an abomination. It looked like a man, but beneath its arms were another set of arms that had grown out of its side. Longer arms, seemingly boneless, hung down off its back, past its knees; they wept webs from the open veins, and looked like sex organs on their wrists. The abomination's mouth was beset by two fangs that protruded from its gums. The mouth itself was a narrow chamber of swollen flesh that glistened with hissing fluids.

"S-stay back," Edgar warned. He inched forward, sword pointed directly at the beast.

"You're new," the abomination spat. "You're ours."

Edgar's gaze moved past the creature. There were hundreds of the abominations, crawling on all eights out of the skyscrapers, dragging large web sacs that bulged with snared life behind them.

"Wait, wait," Edgar said. "We've the same purpose. I've come to kill the leader of Chapel."

"That's good," the abomination said. It held out one of its hands, put it to its mouth, and blew.

Edgar stumbled backward. Tiny hairs from the creature's hand clung to his eyes and burned away his vision.

"Do struggle," the abomination said.

Edgar, blinded, was lifted off the ground. He tried to swing his sword, but his arm refused to move.

"Struggle fiercely," he heard the abomination say, as it flung Edgar over its shoulder. "You'll taste better that way."

CHAPTER XII

Thirty-Three Days Ago

The first known time that Auster ever shed a tear was now, when Penance's assassin dug his blade into the twin's stretched neck.

"Please. Please," he begged.

"Let him go, god damn it," Edgar shouted. He looked at the assassin's face, which was charming, almost innocent. He imagined ripping that face apart, piece by piece, until nothing was left but the chunks on his fingers.

"What do you want? What is it? What... god, fuck! What do you want?" Audra's voice trembled. She dropped the torch she had ripped from the hole into a pool of water along the tracks. "Please, anything. We'll give you anything." The subway darkened as the dirty water instantly extinguished the torch.

"Oh, god," Auster screamed. Blood bubbled from his mouth between each word. The assassin dug the blade in deeper.

Edgar lunged forward, but Audra grabbed his arm and held him back. In what little light was left, he saw that there was something wrong with the shadows here. They started to thicken, glisten. They became heavy, tangible. They looked like paint splashed against a wall.

Noticing this, all the charm and innocence eroded from the assassin's face. The darkness beside him bubbled and cascaded, like black sand. He gritted his teeth, whispered a prayer. With the look of someone promised the riches of heaven, his arm tightened and started to cut Auster's throat.

Audra screamed. With her screams, the shadows surged forward. They stretched and thinned into spikes. They shot forward, stabbing the assassin through his eyes, mouth, wrists, and heart. Where the wounds should have bled, they decayed instead. It wasn't long until it was the assassin who was screaming, begging for death, as his flesh fell in stinking sheets from his body.

"A-Audra?" Edgar stammered. He stepped away from his sister, fearful of her. "Was that you?"

She shook her head and said plainly, "Mean things live down here."

Edgar didn't believe her. He had almost lost track of where he was, what had happened prior to the shadows, when Auster let out a cough and grabbed his pant leg.

"Auster!"

Edgar dropped to the ground. It was difficult to see; they only had the torture chamber's light to help them. He put his hands to his brother's neck. Expecting to find a gaping wound, he found only an inch-deep gouge that tapered off into a long, superficial cut. Already, there was a dark scab forming across it, as though the shadows had somehow attempted to heal it.

"We've got to get you out of here. Come here. Give me your arm."

"I can do it. I can clean him and stitch him," Audra said.

She crouched down, pulled the torch out of the puddle. Somehow, as though called forth, the flame returned to the torch. With her other hand, she grabbed the assassin's skinless wrist and started to drag him back to her hideout.

"I can do it. We can't let anyone else know what happened or where it happened," Audra said.

"You're right." Edgar looked at Auster. He needed to be disinfected and stitched, but he would be okay. "Audra, what are you doing? Leave the body."

"No," she said.

Auster took up the assassin's other wrist and started to help her haul it down the tracks.

"I can use it." She kicked the assassin's side. "For the Crossbreed."

The hour was late, but Edgar needed to see Alexander Blodworth. He was being held under observation in a small, vacant building directly across the Archivist's tower.

Guards stood posted outside the only entrance at all times. As decreed by King Sovn and Queen Magdalena, they were to forbid passage to anyone who requested it.

Edgar wasn't sure how he intended on breaking into the building, but seeing as his brother had almost died a half an hour earlier, logic was not a luxury he currently possessed.

"My lord," the guard, Brinton, outside the building yelled. He tipped his torch forward to have a better look at Edgar. "My lord, you should not be out this late. Where are your escorts?"

Edgar wrinkled his brow. The man had a point. He turned around, even though he knew his personal guard wouldn't be there. They were supposed to have been outside Audra's room, but they weren't, and he hadn't even realized it until now. Where had they gone? Now that he was thinking about it, Audra's guards had been missing, too.

"I see," Paxton, the second guard, said. "They will be rounded up and left to rot in the dungeons, my lord." He wiggled his moustache, and puffed out his chest proudly. "Allow us to call one from the barracks to see you back to your chambers."

"I need to speak with Blodworth." Edgar felt nauseous and filthy. He was covered in sweat and suspicion. His hands were dirty, remnants of the Crossbreed beneath his nails. He could still smell the assassin's flesh melting from his skull.

Brinton looked at Paxton, his superior, and said, "I'm sorry, my lord, but no one is to see the prisoner."

"Make an exception."

"My lord, you know that we cannot. The king and queen forbid the traitor any visitors. Perhaps if you see your father in the morning...?"

"It cannot wait until the morning."

"If the need is dire, my lord—," Paxton stepped forward, arms outstretched, offering friendship, "—tell us, and we'll aide you."

Edgar rubbed his forehead, and clenched his teeth. A spasm of rage worked its way up his neck. These men meant well, but their well-meaning was getting in his way. He needed to see Alexander Blodworth now, to ask him why he had confided in him that day at the Archivist's tower. Horace had told him that the exemplar's understudy was only trying to manipulate him, but why? Knowing this, why shouldn't he use it to his own advantage? Was that not the spirit of politics? Was that not the future that awaited him when death robbed his older siblings of their duties?

"My lord? Is everything all right, my lord?" Brinton stared at Edgar vacantly, as though when he looked upon him now he no longer saw the man he knew.

"Stand down," a voice said, strained.

Behind Edgar, there was a rustling of cloth and a cracking of bones. He turned around and saw Amon stepping across the moonlit cobblestones, a triumphant smile fixed upon his face. "He only wants a word, nothing more."

Without complaint, Brinton and Paxton tipped their heads at the Archivist and let Edgar pass.

"What is this?" Edgar made his way to the vacant building. "What did you just do?"

Archivist Amon slid his hands into his robes. "I can call them back, if you'd like."

"Why can you call on them at all?"

"Your anger is misplaced." Amon turned around and started up the steps to his tower. "See me when you're finished. We've a lot to discuss."

"Like what?" Edgar's stomach twisted, his heart pounded. He shrank before the Archivist and his glinting eyes. This, this was how it felt to be manipulated.

"Eldrus needs our help." Amon laughed, and disappeared into the night.

By the time Edgar finally entered the building, it was clear to him Alexander had heard everything, for he was waiting there with a smug look upon his face. It had once been a storehouse for excess goods deemed too valuable to divvy up to the poor. Now, it was a holding cell for visiting celebrities deemed too dangerous to be allowed to indulge in their excesses.

The building was decorated and fitted with all the comforts expected by the privileged. However, it also came with an addition befitting the beasts that stayed there. With the pull of three hidden levers, a part of the floor could be made to give way to a five-foot drop and a bed of spikes that always promised the deepest of sleeps.

"My lord," Alexander said, arms folded across his chest, as Edgar

70

entered the building. "It's not much to gander at—" he looked around the room, "—but it sure is homey."

Edgar pointed to the bed. "Sit."

"I'll take the chair, instead." Alexander sat at the desk covered in burning candles. "No offense, but unlike Vincent, I only enjoy women."

Edgar slammed the door shut behind him. "Your second assassin has been found."

Alexander crossed his legs. "Not mine." There were circles underneath his eyes, and the hints of bruising beneath his collar and cuffs. "I'm glad to see you survived him, though."

"Glad?" Edgar wished he had a weapon; and then was grateful he didn't. "Why?"

"Because your father doesn't care, and your mother cares too much. Because Horace has no creativity, nor does he have a heart. Because Lena has no redeeming qualities, other than the amazing feat of having no redeeming qualities. Because Auster could inspire no one, nor have a thought of his own. Because Audra is too precious, too willing; this world would tear her apart."

"So what is it about you, then? That's what you were going to ask next." Alexander grinned. Absently, he picked away at the wax that covered the desk. "Doesn't hurt to ask. Everyone likes to hear good things about themselves. So what is it about Edgar of Eldrus?"

"This is the first time we've met."

"Oh, no. We've met many times before. We've met in rumor and whisper, in letters and deeds. Like the Old World, nothing goes unaccounted for. It's just a bit slower than it used to be."

I've done nothing noteworthy, Edgar thought. *Only a series of failed attempts to make this city a better place to live.*

"You're not particularly special, Edgar," Alexander said. "But you are a summation of all things your family is not. You're adaptable and willing to do what needs to be done for the good of all. Listen, I'm not asking for friendship, because we'll turn on each other eventually. That's just how these things go."

This wasn't the conversation Edgar had expected. "So what are you asking for?"

"Nothing." Alexander stood up and began snuffing out the flames with his fingertips. "I gave you the assassins, whom I was told to let carry out their plot. I gave the Crossbreed, which I was told to forget, to never speak a word of."

"What?" Edgar motioned for Alexander to stop as his finger hovered over the last candle, the last in the place. "What are you talking about?"

"A long time ago, here in Eldrus there lived a researcher, a philosopher and blasphemer, Victor Mors. He discovered that there are many terrible things waiting in the Membrane of the world. Naturally, this didn't sit well with Penance at the time, for he also claimed there was no heaven, only hell. So we killed him and stole his work. In his journals, among other things, were whispers of the Crossbreed. I visited your city two years ago, and I gave your Archivist that coveted page. The Mother Abbess was not… happy about that. Fortunately, she didn't realize it was me, I don't think."

Edgar took a breath, the first one he had taken in over a minute. "Why? Why would you give that to him?"

"Because our cities are run by fools. Because no ruler in his or her right mind would gift such a weapon to their enemy, unless they had good reason to. My reason was good. My city is dying. It's a slow death, but it's dying all the same, and so is yours. And when we've nowhere else to turn, we'll turn on each other. You'll win that war, if the Night Terrors don't stop it, but you'll lose your people, and I'll lose my people. And I think you care too much for people in general to let something like that happen.

"So, again, no, I don't want anything from you, Lord Edgar. But when you're in a position of power, and soon you will be, I will want something. I'll want you to listen and consider what I have to say. The Night Terrors continue to massacre both our people, and Geharra… Geharra sits quietly on the other side of the world, undoubtedly gathering its forces, waiting for us to weaken, so that they can land the killing blow."

Edgar started to back away from Alexander. "Why didn't you use the Crossbreed on your own people?" He reached behind him for the doorknob.

"The climate is wrong." Alexander smiled. He was enjoying this. "We tried for years to grow it, but it wouldn't take. The idea was that if Eldrus was successful, then you would allow us to bring some of it home with us. Introduce some order into the Holy Order, if you know what I mean."

"That's why you wanted to see Audra."

"That's why I wanted to see Audra."

"You're putting a lot of faith in me." Edgar opened the door. The cool night air rushed past his legs and gave him goose bumps.

Alexander laughed and snuffed out the final candle. "I'm not the only one."

Like all things innocuous, the Archivist's tower, rustic and inviting in the daylight, became something more sinister in the dark. It loomed unsteadily over Ghostgrave, as though it were a snake that had been petrified in its attack. The tower's highest window spewed a smoky, crimson light. Rather than dissipate, it wandered across the sky—a sparkling, nebulous cloud like a lonely constellation in search of a lost star.

At night, the tower was known to speak in a sharp, scratchy tongue. The red roots which Amon feasted on were embedded within it.

Even now, as Edgar stood at the tower's steps, he could hear them spreading up the cobblestones, towards the highest point, as though they meant to ensnare the moon itself and bring it closer, to bask in its otherworldly light.

Edgar gathered himself and entered the tower. He climbed it slowly, the spiraling steps there mimicking his spiraling mind. For all his words, Alexander had told him little; however, it had still been enough to take the man's request seriously. But he didn't understand why he had been chosen, when he was the youngest of the royal family and the least likely to be given the responsibility Alexander and, now that he was thinking about him, Amon expected of him. It would have been easy enough with the assassins, putting Edgar into a position of power, and yet Alexander seemed to have gone out of his way to ensure they were caught and killed.

None of it made any god damn sense.

"Please, come in," he heard Amon say.

Edgar stopped and stood at the top of the stairs, which had come much quicker than he realized. He leaned into Amon's room. The Archivist was sitting in a chair beside the fireplace, the flames of which were dangerously close to spilling out.

"I trust our friend has his head on a pillow and not on a spike?"

Edgar took a deep breath and entered the Archivist's chambers. He went to the old man and sat opposite him.

"Amon, what's going on?"

"Many things."

Amon turned in his chair, towards a side table. From it, he took a cup of water that had one of his red roots twisting out of it.

"This will be a long night. Drink. The root will calm your nerves. It's addictive, though. I should know. That's why I allow it to grow here, and why I chew it constantly. You and your siblings always wanted a bite of it—"

"And you always slapped our hands and said no."

"Exactly." He held the cup outward, the red root's crystalline casing glinting in the firelight.

"Thoughtful of you." Edgar accepted the offering and downed it in one swig. He didn't swallow the root, however; he wasn't sure if he was supposed to.

"I like to think so." Amon took the cup from Edgar and filled it with more water from the pitcher on the side table. Beside it was Amon's novel, *The Disciples of the Deep.* "I feel as though I've lost your trust."

Edgar started to fall forward. He caught himself and shook off the tug of sleep. A momentary haze, a surge of adrenaline: he sat back in his chair, now more awake than when he had entered the tower. "You've... whew. You've made me a part of something."

Amon slipped his hand under the cushion of his chair. He rummaged about and then yanked out a foot-long red root that was coiled beneath it. "Yes, I have. I must admit, it all happened more quickly than I expected."

"Amon, they'll kill you if they find out what you've been doing."

"What is it I've been doing?"

Edgar curled his lip. "Conspiring with the enemy, and you've made me a part of it."

Amon coughed, offended. He gripped his side, wincing at a pain there. "I don't recall sending you into the subway tunnels. I don't recall telling you to drug the city."

"Audra told you?"

"Of course. I gave her the ingredients for the Crossbreed. I showed her the tunnels. Have you seen what she can do with the shadows when she gets angry?"

Edgar's eyes widened. "The shadows? What are...?"

"This is about you, though." Amon ignored Edgar's question.

"You're on the right track, Edgar. You always have been, ever since you were a young boy. You always tried so hard to do the right thing, even when it would lead to terrible consequences. I know you better than you think, and that's hard to admit when you realize you don't know me at all. To you, I'm just the old man who played with you when you were young, and kept you out of trouble when you got older. An unremarkable constant in the lives of your brothers and sisters, as well as your own."

Edgar shook his head. "Amon, what are you saying? You're a dear friend of the family. Listen, I'm not saying I don't trust... I just want to know what is going on. I don't mean to offend you, but what you are saying..."

"You're right, though." Again, Amon ignored him. "This city could be so much more than it is. This world could be so much more than it is."

"And what do you think? Some secret alliance with Penance will make a difference? I guess I don't know you very well at all. But don't think you can use my 'bleeding heart' to do yours and Blodworth's dirty work."

Amon took a bite out of the red root. "I know I said this is about you, but if you wouldn't mind, may I tell you a little about myself first?"

Edgar took a drink of the water. This time, he noticed a pungent aftertaste that hadn't been there before. He set down the cup, frustrated, and said, "Go for it."

Archivist Amon's eyes reflected some distant light as he whispered, "I look forward to these rare moments of disclosure. I am very old, you see. Older than I look, which I know must be a horrible thing to imagine."

Edgar shifted impatiently in his chair.

"Stay with me, Edgar. I'm about to tell you a lot of things you will claim are nothing more than ravings of an old man. But where you would be wrong is your calling me an... old man. I'm not an old man. I'm not even a man. This body of mine is nothing more than a costume, and this face, a mask. Don't blame yourself for not realizing this sooner. I wouldn't have gotten as far as I have if I hadn't mastered the art of deception.

"For example, the red root in your drink?" Amon shook the foot-long red root in his hand. "That's not any old plant. It's a vermillion vein, from the Nameless Forest."

Disgusted, Edgar kicked over the cup. He shoved his fingers down his throat, but all he could manage was a dry heave.

"To anyone who knows anything about these insidious growths, they would see through my ruse immediately. But I've been in Eldrus for a very long time, and I have been cultivating my addiction even longer. I know that I am rambling, but do you know what true power is? It's being able to take the truth and pass it off as a lie, or vice versa. Doesn't matter. It's all the same in the end, as long as the end ends the way you want it to."

I need to leave, Edgar thought. *He's lost his fucking mind.* His stomach began to churn. Now that he knew the truth of the red root, he could feel it starting to take hold of him.

"Sorry." Amon took another bite of the vermillion vein. "When you've lived with a secret as long as I have, it's hard to finally let it go. It becomes a part of you. If I give it to you, I give you myself, and I can see by the way you're squirming over there you don't like what you're hearing. But you've been taking a lot of risks lately, so let me do the same.

"I am not a man. I have never been a man. I was not born, and I'm not sure that I can die. At least, in the way that you one day will. I simply was, and what I was, well, was a whisper, a mouth. A smaller part of a greater whole. An organ, if you will, in the body of God. The Vermillion God, and I was content to be that. It was all I knew. Until, one day, someone spoke to the Vermillion God, and It chose me to answer.

"The Ashcroft family, that was the name of those who had spoken to the Deep. They wanted more from life, and with God's grace, I gave them more. At the time, our needs were simple. Sacrifices were all we wanted. It wasn't about the corpses themselves, but the family's dedication and willingness to indulge in desecration."

"Shut up." Edgar held his head. The room began to spin. "Shut the fuck up, Amon. Stop this!"

"We fed them. They fed us. The Ashcroft family, with the Vermillion God's help, grew more powerful, and so did God, though It didn't realize it at the time. Bodies for favors, belief for power. Simple terms, even simpler arrangements. The Ashcroft family had done so well for themselves they started to want for less. But that wouldn't do for me. I had seen them from squalor to supremacy. They wanted less, but I wanted more."

"What are you talking about?" Edgar put his head between his knees and squeezed. He tried to stand, but his legs wouldn't respond to that.

Amon pressed on. "Like everything, the family fell apart, which led to the agreement falling apart. The Vermillion God was content to allow this to happen. It was a simple deity at the time, with simple appetites. But as I said, I wanted more. We had come so far. The simpler parts were becoming more than that. The greater whole had developed a lust, too. The Vermillion God, for the first time in eons, let me do what needed to be done.

"I tortured and taunted one of the last of the Ashcroft line. Until my efforts paid off, and in desperation we were released. Released from the self-imprisonment the Vermillion God had made for Itself so long ago. Deities are simple things, you see, very binary in their understanding of the world and arrangements. But we were out, no longer bound to the Ashcroft line or rudimentary sacrifices or, excuse my language, bullshit like that." Amon rubbed his hands together. "I no longer had to be a whisper or a mouth. A thing without a beginning or an end. Unbound, unshackled from the Vermillion God's breast, I could be something else instead.

"We are creatures of mimicry, you see. Amon Ashcroft was the poor bloke who finally let us out, and when he did, I took his name. I took his form. I took all the whispers with me. I took all the mouths that I could fit inside this skin suit, too. And finally formed, and on two feet, I took to the world I had only seen from shadows and sand. I took a look at it and wanted more. I laid the vermillion vein where I could, our lifeblood, and created children where I went. I was preparing the way, you understand. We all have a master. The Vermillion God is mine. It had freed me, but in return, I had to free It. Free It, the God who could easily do so with a bat of Its innumerable eyes. Imagine the pressure!

"So many rituals, so many deaths. After so many years of stumbles, I thought the world was ready. I sought out a girl. She went by Lillian. She was gifted. She could speak to the Vermillion God. I couldn't do that. I could only listen, carry out Its will. But she could somehow hold a conversation with heaven. So I sought her out and told her the truth of the world, the truth that humanity had masqueraded as a lie.

"That's when it happened, Edgar. It was glorious, at first. Lillian and I, with her gift and my centuries of hard work, we summoned the Vermillion God from its slumber. We woke God, and we gave God to the humans. But this God, the only God, was not what they had in mind, or what they wanted. God sat upon the Earth, and while some worshiped, others bombed It. You see, I had prepared the world, but I hadn't prepared the people. I'm not a man, so it is an easy over-sight. But God hasn't the stomach for such blasphemies. So It left humanity, to return to Its slumber once more.

"I am very old, you see, and though I may or may not be able to die, I am not ready to stop. The world is ready, and the people, though they don't realize it, are willing. I was wrong, and for my mis-calculation, God abandoned us. I see that you don't believe me, but I am telling you the truth of it. Edgar, look at me. Can you not think of a better way to save this world? A God, my lord! Here on Earth. Here to put an end to all your peoples' wants and needs. Humanity has wanted this moment since the dawn of time. I'm offering it to you. Take it. Be what you promised yourself you would be."

With a struggle, Edgar finally pushed himself to his feet. "Go fuck yourself."

Amon sighed. He held out the remainder of the vermillion vein he had been eating. "It doesn't matter what you believe, until you be-lieve as I do. Eat this."

"Fuck you." Edgar started to exit the room. "You're not Amon. I've known him since I was born. We may not see each other more than in passing nowadays, but you're not him."

"You've never known Amon. No one has known Amon Ashcroft for untold years." He shook the vein, encouraging him to take it. "Edgar, I need you to go to the Nameless Forest."

After the pure insanity this man had just vomited onto his lap, Edgar couldn't help but ask, "Why?"

Amon laughed and came to his feet. He lifted his robes over his head and threw them to the ground. Beneath, he was mostly bone and black flesh, and covered in the very same vermillion veins from which he had been eating and claimed to have come from the Name-less Forest. Except these veins were colorless, dried out—a sign, per-haps, of his finite mortality.

"You will eat this," he said, throwing the vermillion vein he held in Edgar's face. "After all, where do you think the Crossbreed gets its qualities of manipulation?" He hobbled toward Edgar, his flesh creaking like charred wood. "Eat it. It's going to help you forget for a while all the terrible things you're about to do for me."

CHAPTER XIII

Edgar woke with a headache, and the feeling that something had been shoved down his throat. Everything around him was gray, sticky. When he tried to reach out, he only did so in thought, because his hands couldn't move. He was cocooned, covered in the same thick webbing he had seen oozing from the abomination's wrists. Where the strands met his flesh, there was a strange, tingling sensation. He might have even enjoyed the sensation, too, if it were not for the fact the strands were slowly eating away at his skin.

Voices. Movement. Edgar leaned forward the best that he could. Mind-numbing claustrophobia washed over him. Through a tear in the sac, he saw on the other side a scene of despair.

More cocoons, dangling as he was, from the branches of trees, and there were more of the abominations—Arachne, he realized—skittering under them, over them, periodically stopping to drip their hissing spit into them. The sacs that had been there longer than the rest were red in color, and when an Arachne crumpled beneath it and punctured a hole in one of the red cocoon's bottoms, he saw why.

Into the abomination's mouth, a thick, sick mixture of hot blood, melted flesh, and bubbling bone sputtered into its waiting mouth. The Arachne drank and drank until the sac was reduced to a drip, and then crawled away, leaving the cocoon to hang there, like a deflated lung.

The strange, tingling sensation from the flesh-eating strands graduated from a hot pain to an unbearable agony. Shifting as much as he could, Edgar realized he still had the dagger from Lotus at his side.

He bent his wrist, and pricked his fingers on the tip of it. His body broke into convulsions as he struggled against his sticky fetters. It made the strands burn quicker, hotter, into his skin, but every time he bucked, they threatened to break.

His arm looser now, he gripped the dagger, but as he did, he watched parts of his hair fell in front of his face, singed by the webs from his scalp.

"Martin, Martin, Martin."

Edgar heard someone shouting a name outside his cocoon. He shifted the dagger towards his wrist and began to saw through the webbing there.

"Martin, this has been a long time coming."

Again, Edgar brought his eye to the rip in the cocoon. Past the swinging, screaming sacs, beyond the constant stream of Arachne running through the trees, he saw a man being dragged across the ground by an Arachne much larger than the others.

"I've often wondered about your taste," the large Arachne said. It stopped and dropped the man he kept calling Martin. Small spiders poured out of the Arachne's reptilian cock hanging between its legs.

"They won't follow you, Anansi," Martin bellowed. He wobbled to his feet in defiance, and then buckled over in defeat.

"They don't have a choice. That's not how it works, and you know it, Martin. If I didn't do this, then that intruder would have. Your death was inevitable. Mine is not." Anansi clicked its fangs. All the Arachne in the forest froze. "Look on, my spawn! We have their ruler, Chapel is ours!"

With all Arachne eyes fixed on their leader and his prey, Edgar cut furiously at his bonds. Anansi, leader of the Arachne, and also the namesake of the growths that had sealed his wounds from the carrion birds. He laughed; he might have even cared if he wasn't about to be eaten.

Edgar freed his hands and arms. He put his hands behind his back, cupped the dagger's handle and tip and sawed upwards, cutting the bindings along his spine. Carefully, so as not to entangle himself further, he cut along his legs and feet. Stabbing and slicing the front of the cocoon, swathes of it fell away, like paper peeling from a wall, and with that, he now had a gap large enough through which he could escape.

"The meat sacs are yours, my spawn," Anansi said. He was still staring Martin down, the man whom Edgar had no doubt now was the man he was supposed to have killed in Chapel. "Let down the others, for we'll need them. They will not refuse us. By law, they are conquered!"

Anansi touched Martin's chin, whispered something to him, and then tore his head off. Blood sprayed and spluttered into the air. Anansi laughed and tipped his head back. He opened his mouth wide, so that the scarlet drops could fall as rain onto his flicking tongue.

Under the cover of the cheering, sneering chorus, Edgar decided to escape. With a loud thump and a wheeze, Edgar fell out of the cocoon, arms bending under himself with the impact. His skin was tender and raw from where the strands had burned it, but the air outside the cocoon was cool and soothed it some. He scurried backward, minding the sacs that swung overhead. Here stood a moment to do something heroic, to save people, like he had always wanted to do. But he had been through enough to know the difference between heroism and stupidity, so he mouthed an apology to the meat sacs and ran into the nearby overgrowth.

"Anathema is next, my spawn!" Anansi released Martin's corpse, letting it crumple to the ground. "But what need have we for old birds in the kitchen?"

The Arachne clicked and hissed and scuttled. The forest floor became a carpet of arms and legs.

"See how fortunate you are, Chapel, that we spared you?"

Anathema, Chapel, Atlach, and Blackwood. Two have died. Two are left. I have to do it. I have to kill him. A cold sweat dripped down Edgar's back as he gazed up at the Arachne's leader. Suddenly, the dagger in his hand didn't seem so useful. Where had his sword gone?

If anything deserves to be killed, it's him. But how?

As Anansi started to spin webs around where Martin had fallen, his Arachne spawn swarmed to release and ravage the cocooned. Those who hadn't already been reduced to thick viscera were released, and those that had were guzzled by the abominations that drank from their red prisons.

Edgar, taking advantage of the commotion, snuck away, back the way they had come, back to the broken skyscraper and the weapons it held.

To Edgar, the silence of Chapel's fields was in some ways more disturbing than the discord he had left behind. He hurried through the tall grass. Mutilated bodies of the first to fight back clogged his path. With every step he took, the toppled skyscraper village rose higher above him, until, when he was close enough to touch it, the skyscraper was the sky itself.

He circled the village until he found a window. Looking in, he wasn't sure where to begin. Though he didn't know what the building originally held in the Old World, he knew that what he saw now wasn't what had been intended at the time.

Edgar climbed into the unconventional village through a broken window and set down on its carpeted roads. Threadbare supplied the lumber, Anathema, the food; this place, he reasoned by the advanced state of things, provided the technology, the tools to make it all possible. But it was so hard to look at it, to make sense of. It was a series of hallways, staircases, and elevator banks, refurbished into something they were never meant to be. There were no clouds in this so-called village's sky; just a white, textured ceiling punctuated by water damage and broken lightbulbs. There was no grass to walk through in Chapel's narrow fields; just carpet and tile with benches here and drinking fountains there. To call this place a village would be like calling Ghostgrave a town. It just didn't make any sense.

In each domicile he passed, which varied in size between closet and conference room, Old World artifacts were on display, in use. A television had become a bowl, a refrigerator, a pantry. Wiring had been reduced to ropes, and computers to science experiments. Each "house" and "storefront" was filled with these dead objects; objects that could live again, if only they had their sparking lifeblood.

Yet, not all was without use. Old World clothing, furniture, books, and magazines were everywhere, offering comforts that rivaled those of royalty, and knowledge that bested any Archivist's.

How quickly the continent would progress, Edgar thought, if this place existed outside the Nameless Forest, for cleverer minds than his own to dissect and disperse their secrets. How quickly the continent would progress, Edgar thought, but would it be towards enlightenment or entropy?

In the end, it didn't matter. He was here, not there, in the outside world, and he had a job to do.

'I don't know. I think murder is like a potion. Just takes the right amount of ingredients to make it.' Audra's words went through his mind. 'Two or three things to justify something you would never consider.'

Edgar had returned to Chapel for one purpose and one purpose only: to find a gun and put a bullet in the spider lord's head.

He had seen the legless man with the pistol, and he had heard the gunshots through the halls of Chapel itself. There had to be more firearms. Although he wasn't sure how to make use of such a weapon, the threat of death often makes of most quick learners.

He was scouring the halls, ducking in and out of what had to be the commercial district, when he heard a pathetic voice whisper, "Please."

Edgar turned and turned, but it wasn't until he had convinced himself it had been his imagination that he saw her: a little girl, hiding underneath a stall in the bathroom beside him. She couldn't have been any older than twelve, and she was dying.

"It hurts so badly," the little girl said. She showed him her blood-stained hands.

Edgar ran into the bathroom—a kind of library—and flung back the stall door. He saw her inside, curled up by the flowerpot toilet, the bloody star of a fatal wound pinned above her heart.

His throat tightened. Something stirred in his chest. "Oh, no."

"I can't. I can't..." Speaking was a struggle, so she gave it up and stared up with her wide, brown eyes into Edgar's.

"Let me help you. I have things." Edgar went to the ground, propped her up against the stall. He searched himself for the curatives he had gathered days ago. "Don't say anything. Please. I can help. Just let me."

The little girl squeezed his hand, and shook her head. Sweat slid in slow beads down her damp hair. She was ready for death; she just needed someone to show her the way.

Edgar nodded, even though he didn't agree with what she was asking. "Can you help me? I'm going to kill Anansi. I'm going to save your people, but I need a weapon. Something to hit him from far away. I saw someone with a gun."

The little girl shook her head. All the color had left her face. "Are you the... the assassin from Anathema?" Her teeth chattered out a desperate code for release. "I... there—" She coughed up blood. "There may be something in the lobby." She coughed, lost consciousness for a moment. "Ahead, and left." The little girl lingered on Edgar's dagger.

"No, no." He brought the girl close to him and held her. "No, go the right way. I'll stay with you."

This is what it means to help people, he thought. *To see and do what no one else wants to see and do. This is how we'll save Eldrus. Not with the Crossbreed, but kindness. Patience.*

"Death won't come," the little girl said. "It's in there." Her hand hovered over her heart. "The spiders put it in me. It…" Her lips trembled, webs of spit between them. "I can't… until it comes out. Please, sir. You're an assassin, right? P-please." She closed her eyes and wept, and as she wept, the bloody star grew larger on her panting chest.

Edgar did it quickly, because if he didn't, he wouldn't have at all. He took the dagger and, holding her as tightly as he could, slit the little girl's throat. In his arms, she went quickly, quietly, but he did not. He sat there awhile, bawling into his blood-drenched fists, wondering what he had done and how it had been so easy to convince him to do it in the first place.

By the time Edgar found the lobby, his dagger was as clean as it was going to get, and even then, it wasn't clean enough. There were no bodies in the lobby, but the place was covered in all the pieces that they were made up of. Swords, daggers, bows and arrows, and pieces of armor were also scattered across the chunky floor and gory barricades.

Edgar wiped the sting from his eyes. He overturned the armaments, the barricades. "It has to be here. It has to be here." A sword required him to get too close, a bow a skill he didn't possess. He kicked a helmet across the lobby and belted, "Where is it? Where the fuck is it?"

He covered his face and broke down.

Why did she call me an assassin? Edgar dropped to his knees. The Nameless Forest had finally worn him down. *How did she know? Word couldn't have spread so fast.*

He put his fists to his eyes, as though to dam the tears. *Is that why I'm here? Does this go beyond Crestfallen?* There had been assassins in Ghostgrave, and now there was an assassin here, in the Nameless Forest, murdering those who ruled it. His forehead throbbed, a tumorous pain behind it.

Why would anyone care what happens here? And why the hell would anyone choose me of all people to do this?

Edgar stood up. "The man had to have died in the field. Hopefully, he still has the pistol." He paused. He caught sight of something—a long, slender container propped up against a pillar in the lobby. "Son of a bitch," he said, heading toward it. "Son of a bitch."

Edgar marched through the fields of Chapel with a bolt-action rifle over his shoulder. The bullets in his pocket clinked against one another. The gun was an older model than the ones he had read about.

Looking at it, he couldn't understand why humanity had failed to recreate the design. It seemed simple enough, and yet, even then, he couldn't fathom its construction; it was as though the concept had been scratched from his mind.

Edgar went to one knee and clumsily loaded a bullet into the rifle's chamber. "I can't miss. What did they call it?" He stood up, and put the rifle into the pocket of his shoulder. That seemed right, after all. "Recoil?"

He turned and aimed at the horse-abandoned wagons of Jed and Jes. Gritting his teeth, he targeted the driver's seat and squeezed the trigger.

A loud crack, and a cloud of smoke. Edgar's heart leapt into his throat as the bullet whizzed across the field and blew through the side of the wagon, not the driver's seat. He kneaded his shoulder from where the rifle had kicked it, and popped the ringing from his ears. He had missed his mark, but not by much.

"Wow," he said, inspecting the rifle. He felt giddy and, for the first time since being in the forest, capable. "I can see the appeal." He loaded another bullet into the heated chamber and hurried back into the forest. If he waited any longer to practice, he might miss his chance to kill Anansi.

The Arachne had done much to the area while Edgar was away. Webs, like walls, had been spun in between the trees, creating a funnel for those entering and exiting the encampment.

Edgar skulked behind the walls, careful to avoid drawing unwanted attention to himself.

Arachne skittered all around him, leaving trails of spit and flesh-eating strands where they went. Through the funnels, the people of Chapel shuffled as their captors taunted them overhead. They begged and balked in their pathetic march, but nevertheless did as they were commanded by the hateful abominations.

"Pay respects to your lord," the creatures growled. "Hurry now, we're hungry."

Edgar followed at a distance, the rifle steadied, ready to fire. The stinging hairs from the Arachne rained down around him, twisting into his skin like needles.

Where did these beasts come from? he wondered, watching these unnatural contortions of the human body. At that moment, stories of the Nameless Forest started to come back to him. Where had he heard them? How did he know them? But none of those surfacing memories told him anything about these spiders.

Was he the first from the outside world to see them? No, probably not. He knew they were called Arachne, and that came from someone else. If he killed Anansi, what would happen to him? The people of Chapel seemed agreeable enough to submit to their new, eight-legged rulers. Would the Arachne do the same for him? For all its complexities, was the Nameless Forest truly that simple in its allegiances? If so, what did that mean for Anathema? Were they now Edgar's to command, too?

Edgar hid himself in the roots of a tree. The funnel opened up to a silken manse that glittered in the sun; it was the plot Anansi had claimed as his own. Inside, the outpost looked like the skeleton of a home, a blueprint writ in web-work. It was all lines and no furnishings.

Looking at it, it seemed as though a weak wind could tear it down, and yet it stood strong, even as hundreds of Arachne crawled over it, expanding its spires into the canopy.

There was Anansi, in the center, in plain sight, basking in the glory of his crystalline creation.

I have to kill now. Edgar wedged the rifle between two roots to soften the recoil. *If I miss, I'm dead. If I hit, I'm probably dead.*

He couldn't believe he was considering this, but he was. It was as though a switch had been flipped in his head. Maybe it had been the little girl, maybe it had been Father Silas; or maybe it was just him, being him, doing what needed to be done for himself at the cost of something else. After all, that was the way of the royal family of Eldrus.

Edgar brought his eye to the iron sights atop the rifle's barrel.

If the Nameless Forest is this simple, the spiders won't attack, because they'll be mine. Or they'll be Crestfallen's, and she'll stop them.

He slowed his breathing and turned the gun until his aim was on Anansi's head.

Or maybe they'll belong to whoever the fuck sent me here.

He hadn't been kidnapped for a ransom. He knew that now.

His finger danced around the trigger. Strange vibrations shook in his chest, but he ignored them.

Don't stray. Stay sane.

A loud crack, and a cloud of smoke: the bullet exploded from the chamber and whizzed across the forest.

Anansi's head snapped back and a chunk of skull and brain sailed across his writhing haven.

Edgar fell back on his elbows, shocked. "Holy fuck," he said, over and over again. "Oh my god. Holy fuck."

The Arachne dropped from the trees. With the smoke still in the air, they knew immediately where to go. They hissed and screamed and pushed past their prisoners, towards the murder tree.

Edgar backed up, and stood. He left the rifle in the roots. Taking out his dagger, he ran along the funnel and cut through its thinner parts, dodging and weaving through web-choked forest. He could feel the Arachne behind him, above him. He could smell the stench of their spit and feel the heat of their hate.

He bounded through the Nameless Forest, crying out as fingers scraped against his ankles, his wrists. They were so close that they could reach out to claim him if they wanted, but they wanted him to be afraid; to get fat with fear. They yelled at him with breathy threats, promising agony, promising despair; promising to tear his flesh, to suck out his bones.

"What gives you the right?" they screamed in a horrifying, dizzying unison. It was something they had practiced time and time again before. "What gives you the right, outsider filth?"

Edgar stopped. Not to respond, not because he had given up, but because something had been shoved down his throat two hours ago, and now it was coming up.

"Oh god!"

Edgar tipped his head back as eight legs pushed through his mouth. They clamped down on the sides of his face, to work its body loose from him.

With a sickening slurp, the creature dropped out of his mouth. With it came hundreds of strings that tore at Edgar's innards, for it had been attached to them, drinking from them. It dangled from his lips, twisting as it tried to tear free of his organs.

Looking at it, barely conscious, with the Arachne inches away, he saw that the creature was a hairy, brown orb. But when it finally wiggled free and hit the ground, the creature cracked open like an egg, and inside the egg, there was an infant. An infant no larger than his palm, with eight stunted legs attached to its gray body.

Edgar's eyes rolled back into his skull. He wavered there, drooling on himself, and fell forward. But he did not fall into green grass.

No, not green grass. His eyes fluttered open.

Not green grass, at all.

But white satin.

"They're all true in their own way," Amon said, forcing a piece of vermillion vein into Edgar's mouth, "but I think you'll find this one most revealing, my lord."

Many years after the Trauma, winter fell upon the continent, and all hearts became as ice in that cruel season. Crops were destroyed by the cold, and towns lost to the snow. People turned to one another for help, and turned on one another when no help could be given. Children were offered up to demons for warmth, and in return the demons gave candles that would not only burn in the coldest of winds, but ensured whoever looked upon them would never be able to look away again.

Those that oversaw the continent found themselves weathered as well. The men and women they had been in the summer were no more: the cold had eaten away their kindness and their morality, and left them nothing but the will to survive and the doubt that they would.

In Geharra, the ruling council disappeared into the dungeons, naked and inebriated, never to be seen again.

In Six Pillars, the Lillian priests tortured themselves, each one-upping the other, like children, to please their absent God.

In Elin, however, the royal family had retained some of its civility, for a visitor in a white satin dress had come to the keep in the final months of Fall. It was this woman who had kept up their spirits in that trying year. Her name was Annaliese, and with the help of her esteemed uncle, the young woman had been sent to Ghostgrave in hopes of finding her lost sister, who was said to have been seen last in Elin. The winter struck before the search could truly begin, and when Annaliese found she could not leave the city, so taken was the royal family by her that they kept her close and as their own.

Queen Vivienne and her five children looked upon Annaliese as a daughter and friend, but King Novn saw something else. He saw a woman more beautiful than he had thought possible, and an equal to him in intelligence and wit. He saw a woman whom he could speak to about his most personal thoughts, a woman whom he could lie down with and wake to every morning of every day of his life, and every life he may live thereafter. In Annaliese, he saw a summer that could melt away the winter that had settled in his heart, long before the one that now ravaged his kingdom.

On a snowless night, Annaliese and King Novn left Ghostgrave, and went to where neither the cold, nor anyone else would follow.

Under many covers and many disguises, and through many bribes and many favors, King Novn had his marriage to Queen Vivienne nullified. He married Annaliese moments later in the presence of a priest suffering from hypothermia. The documents were sealed and placed in an Old World trinket he carried for safekeeping: a ball of hollowed steel.

They arrived at the Nameless Forest months after the escape, their love for one another no less because of this. Just as they had expected, the Forest was untouched by the chill, for the Forest was a world of its own, beholden to neither the rules of man, nor his gods. King Novn had heard many stories in childhood of the place, and had he been thinking clearly, he may have even heeded them.

They built a home on the shore of a river and lake, whose waters were golden, between two trees so tall it seemed as though they touched the stars themselves. They feasted on the animals of the Forest during the day, and on one another at night. They worried little. They were happy.

For a while.

Two months of living in the Nameless Forest had begun to take its toll on the king of Elin. He often woke to find Annaliese staring at him, or kissing him; except that, when she kissed him while he slept, she drew blood and drank it.

When Novn went to the lake to sit by its waters, he found reflected on its surface his guilt. He saw Elin, his wife, and his children, and each in some way were made worse by his leaving. When Novn left to hunt, he found himself stalked by shadows, and when he returned home, he found the shadows in his bed, with Annaliese, asleep beside her. They wore the faces of all the men King Novn hated, including his own.

Three months of living in the Nameless Forest and Annaliese was pregnant. Novn found that he could not sleep beside her, because she would not sleep at all. She never did. One night, after waking from his own hut near the home, he heard Annaliese speaking to someone behind the trees.

"I won't do it," she said into the night. "Let's make it different. We needn't be maidens any longer. You needn't be Pain. I needn't be Joy."

"He's watching you," the night spoke back. "It'll be longer this time if he kills you. Just give yourself to me and we'll live forever. Come down stream. I've a doorway there, my pet. We can have it all. A cult all our own."

King Novn stumbled back to his hut, gathered his belongings, and was gone by the morning. It took him days to work his way out of the Nameless Forest, but when he did, he found the mainland thawed.

He returned to Elin, to his family. They did not ask him where he had gone, for they knew whom he had gone with, and that was enough. King Novn renamed the city Eldrus, for it had endured the cruel winter and thought its name should reflect its endurance. He hoped that this would help the people, himself included, to forget all that had transpired before.

But Annaliese did not forget. Nine months later, four sons ripped their way out of her womb. Annaliese wore the white satin dress while she birthed those boys, and continued to wear the bloodstained garment for the rest of her days. She was not surprised by his betrayal, because, despite her best efforts, she was not human, and who could truly love something so inhuman as she?

Annaliese took on many names over the years, and took over the Nameless Forest, too. To each boy she gave a ward, and they ruled it as kings would rule, for they were of royal blood and would need much practice before they claimed the throne of Eldrus, which, by rights, was theirs to claim.

When their strength was great enough and their subjects many, for Annaliese had begun calling others to the Forest, she promised them the mainland and the city.

But Annaliese became crestfallen and forgot her promise.

The sons grew comfortable in their rulings and forgot their humanity.

Eldrus moved forward and forgot the king's infidelities.

The world was made safer by these forgettings, for what a terrible place it would become if the royal family of Eldrus knew that the true heirs to the throne still lived after all these years. And that, if they were so willing, could give to Eldrus the Nameless Forest and an army of its people and horrors.

CHAPTER XIV

Thirty-Three Days Ago

"You want me to go to the Nameless Forest and kill my oldest living ancestors?"

Amon stared at Edgar. "Yes, you've got it."

"I won't."

"Edgar," Amon said, sitting forward, elbows on his knees, crushing the veins that grew out of them, "by the time you remember this conversation, you'll have already done it."

"No."

"We'll see."

Edgar bit his lip, and then shoved his fingers down his throat, trying, once again, to regurgitate the vermillion veins he had ingested.

"Already in your system." Amon sat back in the chair. "You're already mine."

Edgar vomited onto his fingers, but it was only water and what he'd had for dinner. The vermillion vein was inside him, and it wasn't about to let go. "What... are they?"

"The veins?" Amon ate the last bit of the vermillion vein he had been holding. "You'll see soon enough."

"This is insane." In defiance, Edgar wiped his hands all over the Archivist's chair. "You expect me to kill those four in the Nameless Forest, and then what?"

"Rule."

Edgar laughed out a tear. "You fucking idiot. No one would listen.

There's six before me, my father included. I have no claim, no matter what I do."

Amon nodded. He stood up and circled the chair, so that he came around to the side of his desk. He picked up an object wrapped in dried flesh and tossed it onto Edgar's lap.

"What is this?" Edgar pushed the object onto the floor. The flesh peeled back, revealing a black dagger with red Death engravings.

A figure emerged from the dark and stood beside Edgar.

Amon nodded at it, the eel Night Terror from the dungeon, and said to Edgar, "We'll talk more, when this is finished."

No one stood in the halls of Ghostgrave this night, except for the ghost that haunted it. This ghost, he used to have a name, but now the ghost wasn't so sure of it anymore. In his hand, he held a dagger—so strange was the weight and texture of it—but he couldn't recall who gave it to him. There were voices in his head, too, but he didn't recognize them. They didn't belong there.

The ghost glided soundlessly through the keep, needing no light to find the door that stood so vividly in his mind. He had passed it many times before, but seldom had the opportunity to open it.

When he found the door, its handle felt smooth in his hand. Daily use had worn it down. It was still wet with drunken sweat. The door wasn't locked, and it practically opened on its own. After all, it had suffered much abuse over the years, and no amount of carpentry would see it recovered.

The ghost pushed past the door and into the room on the other side. With the dagger in his hand, he went to the bed and the body tangled in the sheets there.

Lena lifted her head off the pillow. Her cheeks were red, and her eyes dark. Her lips were the color of wine. She moved her mouth, trying to speak, but all she could manage was a series of yawns. She sat up, caught the strap of her gown before it fell too far down her arm.

Lost in the twilight realm of sleep, Lena looked like a child sitting there, and, like a child, she was too trusting to think much of the intruder who stood silently at her bedside.

"What do you want?" She lay back down. "What time is it, anyway?"

The ghost took one last look at what he had done and closed the door behind him. Lena needed the kind of rest that was best left undisturbed.

As he went down the hall, he wiped the dagger against the curtains that lined it. Who would he have to apologize to for the mess in the morning?

He searched the shadows for the staircase he needed to climb—there it was, where it always was—and climbed it to the next floor.

Horace's room was in a transitory state, much like the thing that now inhabited it. He was a heavy sleeper, so when he finally woke, the ghost was almost done with him. Horace's arms shot out to stop the ghost. Any other time, they would have, but not now, not this time.

The ghost worked the dagger like a saw. He looked around the room, taking note of the belongings his brother had packed for his move into the royal quarters. The dead would appreciate him as king more than the living ever would.

The ghost backed out of Horace's room.

Behind him, Auster shouted, "What's happening? What's going on?" He went to the ghost. "I heard screaming." Auster's eyes fell to the dagger. "What did you do?"

The ghost hesitated—*Strange*, he thought—and embraced his brother.

"No, stop!" Auster begged.

The ghost smiled and pulled him closer. He was warm to hold, but after a while, he grew cold. When he did, the ghost opened Auster, to find that warmth again.

When Auster was too heavy to hold, the ghost carried him back into his room and carefully, so as not to wake him, tucked his brother back into bed.

Even when she slept, especially when she slept, actually, Audra looked innocent. She lay in her bed, curled up, clinging to the pillow beside her. There was a softness to her face, a gentleness to her breaths that promised kindness, even in the face of cruelty. Her hair shone silver in the moonlight. When she spoke in her sleep, she did so in childish ramblings. It was as though she were some unfortunate changeling from a far better world.

The ghost never realized how much he cared for his sister, and now that he did, he had to show her.

Vincent wasn't in his room, so the ghost went to the only other place he could possibly be: the dungeon. Stepping into that squalid place, the ghost found locked within each cell many of the guards who were supposed to be guarding Ghostgrave. They stood there with blank expressions on their faces.

The ghost, passing by, noticed all of the guards' jaws were quivering. Going closer to the cells, he saw that their mouths were laced with vermillion veins.

The ghost went to where the dungeon widened and entered the cell where the Night Terror had been. The chamber was empty, the manacles undone.

But he wasn't alone. He heard sounds coming from the back wall. The ghost followed the wall with his hands, until his hands fell away and much to his delight he found a second wall, a cheap trick of perspective, directly behind the first.

He leaned against this second wall, raised the dagger overhead, and snuck down the hidden passage, to the pocket of rotten, orange light at its end.

At the end of the passage, there was a heavy door, and behind it, a torture chamber. He remembered the place. He might have even seen it once, in a past life.

Vincent was at the center of the room, naked. Drenched in sweat and fully erect, he was staring between the legs of the equally naked, table-bound pregnant woman that lay before him. His brother was shaking, breathing heavily. Vincent looked as though he may have done something he finally regretted.

"I didn't think it were possible," he said out of the corner of his mouth. A tongue of blood squirted out of the woman's uterus and onto his feet.

"Oh good," he said, noticing the weapon in the ghost's hand. "Perfect. Let me use it."

Underneath the table to which the woman was strapped, there was the head of a moon cat. Yes, he had seen this place before. He had seen this Night Terror, too. He searched his memories for moments that existed outside these last few dreadful hours, but all he found were vague shapes of things waiting to be defined by even vaguer interpretations.

It hurt the ghost's head trying to figure it all out, so he handed Vincent the dagger, by shoving it through his neck.

"Ed… Ed." Vincent covered the spewing split with his hand. The dagger slid out and clinked on the ground. He stumbled sideways, and fell to the ground.

Whimpering, he said, "Why? I don't deserve…"

To give Vincent time to get comfortable for the long sleep, the ghost turned away and faced the Night Terror. She wasn't moving, he saw that now, but that didn't mean she was dead. With all the blood that had poured out of her, her belly had shrunken some, too.

The ghost stepped closer to the table and rested his hands on it. Beyond the swollen lips of the woman's sex, something was moving, trying to get out.

"Get… away," Vincent warned. "Kill." He spat out a mouthful of blood, and died.

The ghost grabbed the dagger off the ground and leaned in between the Night Terror's legs. Small, clawed fingers pushed through the woman's throbbing folds. Sniffling and low rumbling growls could be heard. A tremor shot through the woman's glistening body.

A bucket's worth of hot, stinking blood oozed out of the Night Terror. The ghost stepped back as a malformed head pushed itself out of the engorged hole and screamed. The baby's lips were thin, its small teeth crooked and pointed. It had large eyes, one red, the other black. Its body was gaunt, severe, as though the act of living would be a great pain to it. Wailing, the infant, tearing at its mother's womb, worked itself free. It smacked against the surface of the table and rolled in the splinters that stuck it.

The ghost considered the fiend. It was too large to be an infant, and too hideous to be human. He thought about putting it to sleep, but he didn't know its name, so he couldn't take it to the place where he took the others. Besides, its mother's body had all the nutrients it needed, and the ghost didn't want any part of her to go to waste.

King Sovn and Queen Magdalena were already dead in their chamber when the ghost arrived. Archivist Amon and the Eel were standing on opposite sides of the bed. Amon held a hammer, the Night Terror a sickle. The ghost's mother and father had been split open, throat to stomach.

Amon smiled, and beckoned him into the room. "No offense, Edgar, but you were taking too long, and, well, you're no match for your mother. Would be a most disappointing end to this complicated plan."

"Edgar?" the ghost repeated the name Amon had called him. "Do I know him?"

"You do." Amon stepped closer to the ghost. "Come to the mirror. I'll show you what he looks like now."

The Archivist took the ghost by the shoulders and led him across the room, past the murder bed, to the large, spotless mirror near the vanity.

"If you're honest with yourself, you'll find nothing about yourself has changed."

Edgar stepped in front of the mirror and saw what he had become. The ghost had gone, and this is what remained. From his shaking head to his shuffling feet, he was coated in wet blood. From it, his skin had a radiant, crimson glow. He was Corrupted through and through, from flesh to bone.

The obvious question was 'Why?', but instead, Edgar asked morbidly, "Why didn't you kill them all yourself?" He clawed at his skin, trying to get the blood off his hands and face. But like the Corruption on his right arm, it stayed.

The Eel laughed and left the room. Before he did, however, Edgar noticed the pained way he walked, and the dark bloodstain on the backside of his trousers.

Amon turned Edgar around to face his parents. Their intestines were intertwined with one another's; a grotesque display of affection.

"To use you, without this—" Amon took out a small piece of a vermillion vein, "—I have to break you. I don't want to use the veins. That's no way to build a following."

Tears streaked down Edgar's bloody face. "I'll just kill myself."

"You might, but I don't think you will. You're too stubborn. You'll want to salvage this, somehow. To spite me."

Edgar thought about slashing the old man's throat, but for some reason, it didn't seem worth it. He stared at his mother and father. A sharp, gnawing pain chewed through his heart. His stomach dropped into the same black pit he was certain his soul now belonged to.

It felt wrong to grieve, because he would have killed his mother and father all the same. But maybe not. Maybe it would have been different. He could have stopped himself, or like Amon said, his mother could have stopped him.

His chest felt as though it were caving in. His legs gave out and he hit the ground. He remembered each one of them—Lena, Horace,

Auster, Audra, and Vincent—and the games they used to play, the conversations they used to have. He remembered how much he loved them, how much he had sometimes hated them. He remembered what they were and would no longer be. He remembered what he had done and would do again.

Edgar tipped his head back and screamed. He screamed until his throat was raw and his lungs were burning, and he didn't stop until he was sure all of Eldrus had heard him.

"Derleth, our Night Terror friend here, will see you to the Divide. After that, another will show you to the Nameless Forest."

Amon bent down, and grabbed Edgar by the chin. Holding his head still, he forced two feet of vermillion vein into his throat. The growth wriggled, and then it adhered to his insides, like a tick.

Edgar didn't put up much of a fight. The concoction he had drunk before, in the Archivist's tower, was still in effect.

"I won't kill anyone else," he finally said.

Amon nodded and patted his back. "It'll be easier next time, because they will deserve it. The Nameless Forest will help you along the way."

"And what you put inside me?" Edgar touched his throat. He was too drugged to do much, other than be detached from it all.

"It will help you forget, and also remember, or maybe nothing at all. Could just be a placebo." Amon shrugged. "You're going to do what you would have done, with or without it. You'll just come to terms with what you are a little more quickly than the rest."

Edgar had a hard time following what the old man was saying, so he mumbled, "Why me?" He fell forward, his lips to the cold tile of what was now his rightful chamber. "Why didn't you do this sooner? Years ago? Why me? Why the fuck did you make me do it?"

"I've waited a long time, Edgar." Amon, apparently not liking his attitude, shoved more of the vermillion veins into his mouth. He laid the last curl atop his tongue, like a holy host. "And my time is limited. I don't know what is going to happen to me. Alexander Blodworth made an interesting proposition, and so did Crestfallen, which is unusual. Worst comes to worst, you die, and the royal family of Eldrus is wiped out. I can work with a clean slate." He sighed, and gently slapped Edgar's cheek. "This hurts me, too. I loved all of you, more than I thought I would. We are family, after all."

"Fuck you. Fuck you! We are not family!" Long strands of saliva ran from Edgar's mouth to the floor.

"Mmm, more on that when you return." Amon patted his back again. "You have enough to think about."

Edgar began to feel the effects of the vermillion veins take hold. His consciousness began to slip farther and farther from his grasp. "Why do you want... the Nameless Forest?" he said, drunkenly.

"I really don't," Amon said. "But you will, eventually. I just want you to bring something back from it."

"Get it yourself." Edgar spat on Amon's robes.

"I would, but I don't think I could survive the trip. That place is beyond our control. But not yours."

Edgar laughed pathetically. "I just have to kill the rest of my family, right? The ones that were abandoned there. Like in your stupid fucking stories."

Amon snapped his fingers. "I'd say you've gotten pretty good at that, so don't complain."

Derleth the Eel heeded the Archivist's call. He returned to the room.

"Get him ready," Amon said.

The Night Terror forced the gore-covered king to his feet. "I hope you cut off your brother's wretched cock."

Again, Edgar looked at the dark bloodstain on the backside of the Night Terror's trousers. To Amon, he said, "Is this how you treat all your allies?"

Several shoots of the fabled veins ran up the Archivist's neck, into his ears. "Strange how everyone acts differently with the vein inside them. You turn into something quite snarky. Allies? Derleth here didn't think much of my offer to join our mission, but your depraved brother quickly changed his mind.

"Enough talking, Edgar. It's a long journey between here and my home, and we haven't the time to waste."

CHAPTER XV

Edgar was alive, but he wished he wasn't, because he remembered everything. It would have been easy enough to blame Amon for what he had done, but the killings hadn't stopped with his family. Under no influence, save for his own need to survive, he had left one crime scene to travel across the continent to create another.

Whether or not the vermillion veins were truly the cause of his actions was irrelevant, because like blaming the Archivist, it didn't bring to life those he'd brought so easily to death.

Edgar had been awake for almost an hour, but he didn't dare show it. He kept his eyes shut, his body still, and his breathing to a minimum. Awful, unspeakable atrocities had ushered him into the Nameless Forest. Why would the end result be any less awful or unspeakable? But this wasn't the end, Edgar realized, because one ruler still remained: the one who claimed dominion over Blackwood.

He opened his eyes, because after all he had done, he knew he had to see this through, to salvage the wreckage of his ruins. He lay in a white field, surrounded by white trees, beneath a maelstrom of white clouds swirling across the sky.

At first, he thought it had snowed, but when he reached out, he found fabric. It wasn't snow, but satin—a single piece of white satin, stretching out in every direction, covering everything.

"How are you feeling?"

Edgar sat up and turned around. Behind him, between the tops of two trees, Crestfallen floated, her dress the source of the fabric that had woven itself around this part of the Forest. At the foot of the trees between which she was suspended, there were innumerable bloodstains, smears, and splatters.

"You've done me a great service," Crestfallen said. Her voice was higher than he expected.

"I killed your children." Edgar came to his feet. The blood on the cloth began to move.

"I would've done it myself, but I loved them too much. It was time, though. They made me something I never wanted to be."

A burning sensation flared within Edgar's throat and chest. He could still feel the open wounds and tears inside him from where the Arachne spawn had dug itself in. Where was it now? And had it left anything behind? He covered his mouth and, to stop himself from vomiting at the thought, said, "What will happen when this is over?"

Crestfallen smiled and leaned forward. The curls of her long, dark hair swept across her face, so that Edgar could see only her hungry eyes. "We'll be free to do as we like, until we can't."

"Did you choose me?" Edgar asked. "Did you choose me to do this?"

Crestfallen shook her head. "Amon did. He chose them all."

The blood on her dress bubbled out of the fabric and popped, spreading the red stains further across the fabric.

"I'm not the only one. How... how long has Amon been sending my ancestors? How many times has that son of a bitch tried this?"

Crestfallen shrugged. "He is a persistent thing. Imagine his surprise when I told him I wouldn't fight him anymore."

An arm shot out of the dress and pushed the rest of its body free. The bloody, glistening thing lay there, adding more color to Crestfallen's fetid canvas.

Edgar, unafraid of nothing but himself, took a few steps forward as the full-grown, newborn creature crawled in circles on the dress. "What are they?"

"The blood in us all," Crestfallen said. With a sigh, she slowly descended from her place between the trees, until she was eye-level with Edgar. "It's everyone that's ever come, every child I've ever had. They're my family, our family. My first true family. Silas, Martin, Anansi." She held out her hands. "They're finally here now, too, with the rest. Where they should have always been."

Shaking his head, Edgar said, "We have no common bond, you and I."

The blood-borne creature melted back into the fabric.

Crestfallen laughed so hard that the dress tightened over the landscape. "I drank so much of Novn's blood that I have more royalty in me than you do in you."

"So you are the ruler of the Nameless Forest?"

"No."

The Woman in White disappeared. The cloth darkened, and more blood rose to the surface. All at once, what had been white was now crimson.

"A mother has to keep her home together. My boys didn't know what they were doing for the longest time. Without me, the villages would have fallen apart, and there were people, and more children to rule. I thought my sons would have a better world in here than out there.

"I wasn't going to let my only chance, the only good thing I've ever done, die. Edgar, we could have done so much more, but we've been in the Nameless Forest a very long time, and it wore us down. I couldn't leave my sons until they were dead, but they wouldn't die. I fought Amon tooth and nail every time he sent someone in, because I knew he would tear our home apart. But after a spell, I knew it had to be done, and no one sews ruin better than Amon Ashcroft."

"You're insane," Edgar said, watching as cracks spread across the sky. "How could anyone live in a place like this? Why would you want to?"

"Watch your world from mine, and you'll say the same thing about it," Crestfallen said. "What happens here has already happened out there untold times over. We accept our places as slaves to chaos. You deny it and then cry, 'Why?' when the blood comes out. But things like this can be hard to see for those who stand so high above the rest."

"So after everything, you're just going to give this to me? That's why I'm here, right? To take the Nameless Forest." Edgar's hand became a fist as he remembered Audra, and how soundly she had been sleeping in her bed.

"I don't care what happens here anymore. I have my boys. I have nothing to prove to myself or my sister anymore."

Sister? Flecks of the sky floated down around him. "No, you don't. Not all of them. There's still the village of Blackwood."

Crestfallen smirked. The dress contracted and lifted her into the air, so that she loomed over him. "The only son in Blackwood is the one you'll call yours. Find him. He's been waiting so long."

Edgar furrowed his eyebrows. He started with a maddened giggle and then broke out into a full-blown bout of guffawing insanity. "My son? What the fuck? What are you...? I don't understand. What the fuck are you two doing to me?" He punched his leg, dug his feet into the bloody satin. "I can't do this anymore. God damn it, I can't!"

"Yes, you can."

Crestfallen tugged on the sides of her dress. All at once, the fabric retreated inwards. As it did, Edgar slipped and fell onto his back.

"You know exactly what is happening. You killed your family, and you killed mine. Eldrus and the Nameless Forest are yours. And now you may go to Blackwood and claim your reward."

"No one is going to follow me." The dress continued to suck inward, causing Edgar to flip and turn over. "Especially not the Nameless Forest." He clawed for purchase on the weave. "It doesn't work that way."

Crestfallen pulled the miles of red satin upward. She spun it around herself, much like the Arachne would their webs.

"The Nameless Forest is a cancer that retained some of the qualities of the thing it grew out of. If it hadn't, the Dread Clock would have torn this place apart the moment it started ticking when the Trauma dropped it here.

"Did Amon tell you of the Vermillion God? If not, you'll see it soon."

"Bullshit," Edgar said.

Crestfallen ignored him. "The Binding Road is stable. The untamed tracts are stable. Each of the villages are stable, too. All of that is because of the Vermillion God's presence and what the Nameless Forest absorbed from exposure to It. A rigid dedication down to the smallest molecule, but only in places, where not even the Black Hour can break through.

"It's not complicated. In the Nameless Forest things are, or they aren't. It just depends what has dominion over that place. You killed the rulers of the villages. Therefore, the villages are yours to rule. Just like your world out there. You conquered them, and your supporters will convince them to follow you. My only stipulation was to keep the land in the family." She winked. "And now that you have it, don't let that pretty little whore snatch it away from you."

Edgar yelled as he tumbled over himself. The bloody, dripping cloth enveloped him, blotting out the sky and any means of escape. Sound dulled and then deadened. He felt the air thicken around him, as though it were coagulating. He punched and scratched the tightening material. It deflected his blows and shot blood black at him for daring to do so.

"I'll try your world again." Crestfallen's words echoed throughout the artery-like tube of satin to which Edgar was confined. "My sister will be happy. I've been ignoring her for so long. We were always stronger when we were together. Her name is Pain. Do you know her? You will."

Bloody arms and fingers shot out of the weave and grabbed at Edgar. They took his ankles, his wrists; they pulled back on his hair, his waist. He held his breath, because the sharp, coppery smell of Crestfallen's children was making him nauseous.

"Please, don't kill me," he begged. The red fingers melted into his mouth. "Please!"

"Kill you?"

A force rushed past Edgar. Looking back, he saw a river of blood flooding through the tube, toward him.

"What do you think I am? A villain? You've confused me with my sister. I'm only trying to help you, my dear nephew. Yes, I made this harder than it needed to be. But I've atoned. Now you must do right by those you've wronged, and make right your wronged world."

Edgar closed his eyes. He gritted his teeth and braced himself for the impact of the crimson deluge. It hit him hard, like a fist, and took him over. It took him where it wanted, further down the narrowing tunnel of satin. A ball of pressure crashed into his gut. His mouth snapped open and hundreds of years of blood poured down his throat.

In a red blur, Edgar was hurled through the satin tube and dumped into the shallows of a mist-covered marsh. Quickly, he surfaced and splashed the gritty water into his eyes to wash the death out of them.

Looking back, he saw that the tube was gone. There was no sign of Crestfallen or her white satin dress. Instead, he found himself checked by a denser part of the Forest that stretched for miles on end. The trees inside it were crooked, bent. Covering each one were layers upon layers of thick, ancient spider webs. Were these the outskirts of Atlach? Edgar wondered. If so, why did they look as though nothing had passed through in hundreds of years?

Edgar preferred to be drenched in water rather than blood, so he soaked himself in the reed-choked marsh until the only red on his skin was the Corruption on his arm.

Don't stray. Stay sane. He missed Lotus, even though he shouldn't. She, like the rest, undoubtedly had her part to play in all of this, yet that didn't seem to matter to him. If he was going to finish what he had started, and live with what he had done, he was going to need her, or someone like her, to keep what little was left of his humanity from slipping away for good.

Enough of the mist had lifted from the marsh to show Edgar what lay further on. Half a mile opposite the tree line, a haggard hill had rolled over the earth. Once, there had been a wood that crowned this hill, but Edgar saw it had since been reduced to a patchy stretch of malnourished oaks. Occasionally, parts of these trees lit up when the sun hit them. It was a reddish light, a winking, refracting signal from a crystalline source. He knew what that was; he should have, at least. He couldn't begin to guess how many pounds of the vermillion veins were inside him at the moment, but what he didn't know about was the thing he saw more clearly when he started trudging forward; the decrepit mansion, further back, at the top of the hill, in the heart of the woods.

"Is that your home, Amon?"

Edgar panted as he crossed the marsh toward the stony path that cut through it. He couldn't remember the last time he had a meal or something to drink. He considered drinking the water here, but figured it would kill him more quickly than drinking nothing at all.

"You said you mimicked someone. Amon... Ashcroft," Edgar rambled, as he shambled on. "The mansion looks old. This must be where it all began." The soil sucked on his feet. "Vermillion God?" He laughed. "No, just you. A manipulator. You're no god, or part of one."

Edgar found the stony path, fell forward, and crawled onto it. A pound of mud slowly sloughed off his ankles. "A son for me?" The rocks that formed the path cut into his skin as he struggled to his feet. "A successor for you. A do-over. Bullshit. All of it."

As he climbed the hill, they came to him in waves. Lena, Horace, Auster, Audra, and Vincent. They begged him to stop with broken lips and bruised eyes. Memories of their murders twisted and coalesced, until he couldn't be sure what was true, and what had been warped by guilt.

Even though he knew they were dead, he still wanted to speak to them, to apologize to them; at the very least, to see them one last time. They were gone, but they weren't really gone, were they?

Tears stung his eyes as shame swelled in his heart. He tried not to think of them, because it hurt to think of them, but he did, anyway. He thought of Lena—oh, how much he would've liked for her to like him—and Horace—oh, how close they could've been. He thought of Auster—so dull, but so damn smart—and Audra—so kind, but so naïve. Even Vincent had his qualities, but of all of them, it was true he deserved to die the most, and if he deserved it, did they, too? Could some justification be made for what he had done, and for what Amon intended?

That's what worried Edgar the most: that if he kept himself alive, and if enough time had passed, he would look back on everything and say it had been worth it.

Coming out of his thoughts, Edgar entered the wood at the top of the hill and confirmed his suspicions about the trees there. They were infested with the vermillion veins. There were hundreds, no, thousands of the veins. He could see the strange liquid inside them, rushing through the crystalline tubes, as though feeding into something yet unseen.

Hand shaking, begging him to touch them, Edgar said, "Drugged me, from Eldrus to here." He could feel the pangs of want, of addiction. He steadied his hand. "What the hell are these things?"

A bell dinned nearby. Then a boy spoke from behind him: "They don't have a name. They don't need one."

Edgar whipped around. He reached for the sword at his waist that was no longer there. Before him, in a decayed grove, a young boy stood, with a small bell dangling from a rope wrapped around his wrist. He had bright green eyes and dark brown hair, and couldn't have been any older than ten or eleven.

"Who are you? What are you doing?" Edgar said.

The boy's bell jingled as he slipped his hands into his pockets. "I wasn't sure you would make it."

Pointing at him, Edgar said, "That was you, with the carrion birds."

"I couldn't have you dying so quickly."

Edgar sized the child up. He looked strange, the proportions and symmetry of his body off ever-so-slightly. It was as though clumsy hands had put him together, from instructions written in a different language.

"Why did you help me?"

"Because we need each other."

The woods rattled as a rotten wind blew through. The mire below belched and gurgled.

The boy continued. "That's why you're here. To take me back to Eldrus."

Edgar looked past the boy, through the break in the trees, where he could see the wreckage of the mansion ahead. "Actually, not quite," he said, drooling on himself. Fading, he said, "I'm just here to kill my oldest living ancestors and take over the place." His face contorted, as though he were about to lose it.

"And who do you think is going to help you with that?" The boy blinked. His pupils dilated, became vermillion in color. "Not Amon. Not after he lets me eat him."

"You're the thing he sent me in after? That makes you my son?" His cheek quivered. "Could have met me halfway."

"No, absolutely not." Edgar's suggestion struck a chord with the boy. "The Nameless Forest grew out of us, but it's not ours anymore. I helped you once, because I couldn't let you die that early. But I have no plan to leave with someone who couldn't have done all that you did to get here."

"So I had to prove myself?" The back of Edgar's throat tickled. It felt as though a finger were wagging back and forth in his esophagus. "Go fuck yourself. You, Amon, Crestfallen. The fucking lot of you."

Ignoring him, the boy said, "Now, the Nameless Forest holds its breath, to see what you're going to do with it. Now, as long as we stay to the Binding Road, I'll go with you, and we can go home."

Edgar gazed at the vermillion veins on the trees. "What are you?" He wanted to suck on the sweet liquid that flowed inside them, to drink himself into catatonia. "Are you a... creature of 'mimicry'?" He mocked Amon's words.

"Amon and I are the same." The boy gestured to the mansion, indicating it was time to go inside. "It took a long time for Amon to become what he has, but he spent too much time outside of heaven, in your hell. He can't hold on much longer. In time, you won't be able to remember the difference between he and I."

"Monsters, then? That's what you are. Just like the Night Terrors. Just like anything else. Except, what? You have some queen or king that's convinced you freaks that it's a god?"

"It is God." The boy beckoned Edgar to follow after him onto the ruined estate. "Why don't I just show you?"

Edgar dug his feet into the earth.

"You killed your family. You just left each of the villages here leaderless. Crestfallen is now free to terrorize the continent again with her sister. Are you really going to let all it be for nothing?"

Edgar stayed silent.

"Besides, wouldn't you like to know where all those veins you've been eating come from?"

Aside from the façade, the mansion was no more than several free-standing walls and battered pillars struggling to keep their place in the overgrowth. The second and third floor of this Old World behemoth had long since collapsed; now, they were no more than dusty piles of rubble that marked the property like forgotten cairns.

Edgar searched for signs of furnishings, indications of the time period which gave birth to this monstrous place. Pacing back and forth, he noted a Victorian style in its construction, but what the word meant or what era such an aesthetic represented he couldn't remember anymore. He just knew he knew it, and knew by looking at it he should fear it.

He became sarcastic when he was afraid, a trait of Vincent's, so he said, "Beautiful place you have here." He paused, and bit his lip. "What's your name?"

"I don't have one. Do you have any suggestions?"

"You're not a child, are you?"

The boy shook his head. "People don't pay children any attention, or they pay them so much attention it borders on worship. Either way is good for our work."

The glowing wood of vermillion veins caused Edgar's throat to prickle again, as though he had swallowed something sour. "What's our work, exactly?" He had seen these things before, when he first came here, so why only now was he tempted to eat them?

"It's better I show you."

Edgar snapped out of it. "I could just kill you." Yes, he liked that, the idea of killing the boy. He imagined strangling him, purple bruising around his neck, red tongue hanging limply from his mouth. He liked that more than he liked to admit.

"If I can stop a flock of Anathema from carrying you off by projecting my powers across the Forest, do you really think you stand a chance?"

Edgar shrugged one shoulder. "Bet you couldn't do much after that."

"Good point. I only just recovered from that this morning." He smiled, shook his head. "Come here, please."

Edgar did as he was told, because at this point, like the boy had said, why not? After everything he had seen and done, despite his defiance, he had to know what it had all been for. He didn't expect anything to justify the murders he was guilty of committing, but he wouldn't be opposed to hearing out a justification if it existed.

Even now, as he followed the boy into the mansion, he found himself making excuses for the deaths of Father Silas and Anansi. The priest had wanted it, had practically killed himself. He had just given him permission, under false pretenses, to carry it out. And the spider lord? Probably not even his mother, Crestfallen, could find something nice to say about him. But how much did they really matter? Actually, about as much as Lena, Horace, Auster, Audra, Vincent, and his mother and father meant to those in slums of Eldrus or penthouses of Penance. It was all a matter of perspective, he thought. Like how the Crossbreed could be good for his city-state.

If God really did exist, was this Its will, like Amon and this boy had been saying, that had led to his family's death? And if It did, could he really say that It, God, was wrong?

The mansion's floor alternated between dirty tile and damp earth. Chandeliers protruded from the mud, while discarded gems and jewelry glinted in the pale sunlight. Half-submerged balconies sat like ship masts in what was some sort of living room. A piano grinned its yellow teeth at the front of a parlor; sticky, decay-stitched bones poured out of its lid. There were dresses here, suits there; ripped portraits and fat safes with faded bills inside, and in the end, from upturned hallways to torn-down staircases, that's all the mansion was: a maze of forgotten memories that had been reduced to scene after scene of indefinable miseries.

The mansion floors sloped as they went past the skeleton of a library. The ground opened up to a second part of the house, a basement that was surprisingly still intact. With its mildewed breath, the basement welcomed them in as they reached the bottom of the slope and slipped past the rubble that blocked the only entrance to the place.

Inside the almost pitch-black basement, a single candle burned at the edge of what appeared to be a circular pool. He followed the boy to the hole in the floor and saw that it wasn't a pool at all, but another doorway of sorts. Attached to it was a spiral staircase that screwed downward into the dark, into the deeper depths that laid beneath this diabolic house.

The boy had a wide smile on his face. Whatever was down there, he was eager to show it to Edgar. But maybe it wasn't even that; human or not, this mimicry of man had probably been left alone in Blackwood for who knows how long. If Edgar had to guess, the boy almost seemed to relish his company.

Candle in hand, the boy went first. Edgar soon followed after. The staircase was narrow, uneven. The steps were short, unstable. Walking down the staircase was like walking across a line of chairs. The whole thing felt as though it were going to give way at any moment. It reminded him of Amon's tower, and if Edgar had arrived here a few hundred years earlier, he figured he may have even spotted some details that were to later inspire the Archivist's current quarters.

After a few minutes, which should have been impossible, the circular chamber became brighter. At the bottom, a few steps further down, a glowing mist rolled across the ground, bubbling and hissing like the spilled contents of a cauldron.

Edgar waited until the boy stepped off the stairs and into it. The boy then turned around and offered his free hand to Edgar, to help him off the spiral and find footing in the deep.

"Almost there," the boy said.

Hesitant, Edgar took his hand and stepped into the glowing mist.

It took Edgar a moment to get his bearings. Because at the bottom of the staircase was a great ballroom that was covered in candles with green and purple flames. Confused, he looked back the way he'd come. The staircase had wound down, through the ceiling of the ballroom, as though it had drilled right through it.

"Almost there," the boy said again, trying to reassure him. He started across the ballroom.

Edgar only made it a few steps before he tripped over his feet. The glowing mist parted around his ankles. There were chains running across the ground, and if he looked hard enough, it seemed the whole floor was covered in them.

"What are these for?" he asked.

"No one, not anymore." The boy ran to the end of the ballroom. Two large double doors stood half-open there. "Fortunately for you, some traditions change over time. Through here." He tapped his fingers on the door. "You have to see for yourself, and then we can go home."

Edgar started to cough. He bent over, growled as he tried to dislodge whatever was holding onto the back of his throat. Hand shaking, he shoved it into his mouth and fished inside it with his disgusting fingers. There was something back there, something thin, waving, like an antenna. He pinched down on it, jerked it forward, and with every inch it gave, he could feel something uncoiling inside his stomach and his skull.

Beside the boy, a vermillion light flared between the cracks in the double-doors. Knuckles grinding into the roof of his mouth, Edgar pulled harder and harder on the object inside his throat. Until, with a tide of vomit and gaseous belch, foot after foot of dried, translucent vermillion veins broke free inside him and spilled with a splat onto the ballroom floor.

Edgar reared back, gulping for air. He stomped his feet on the growths and stormed towards the boy.

Grabbing him by the throat, he screamed at him, "What is this shit? Tell me now! Is this from that fucking spider that was inside me? Is that where this shit comes from?"

The boy's words came out constricted as he said, "No. This is—" he grabbed Edgar's wrists and held on tight until he let him go, "—is from Amon. To help you forget what you did until you were finished here."

"Bullshit!" Edgar slapped the boy's face into the door. "This is what made me kill them."

The vermillion light in the passage beyond the doors flared again.

Baring his teeth, the boy said, "Is it?"

"Don't you dare." Edgar almost hit the boy again, but stopped himself. He took a step back, ran his hands through his hair. Coughing up the last bits of the veins, he said, "You took everything from me. Everything I love. Everything I was."

The boy rubbed his throat. "What if you could have some of it back?"

"Don't you fucking dare." Edgar started forward, kicking the chains on the ground out of his way. "Don't you fucking promise me—"

A red, blinding light broke across the ballroom. Edgar screamed, quickly covering his eyes.

"What the hell is that?" he cried, burying his face in his palms.

"Come and see," the little boy said.

Edgar splayed his fingers, letting in some of the now dimmed light. The little boy slipped in between the double-doors and disappeared.

Edgar looked back at the spiral staircase and then at the chains at his feet. He couldn't have run away, even if he had wanted to. So instead, he followed in the boy's footsteps, through the crack in the doors, and into the vermillion place beyond.

Edgar didn't need the boy to tell him they were no longer in the mansion, and if the boy had told him they were no longer on Earth, he would have believed that, too. The ballroom floor extended a few feet, like the gangplank of a ship, and then dropped off into the gigantic chasm in front of him.

Out of that infinite expanse of impenetrable black ran massive slabs of rock that stretched in every direction, far beyond what Edgar was capable of viewing, let alone comprehending. But he didn't see all of this because of the boy's candle. No, it was the vermillion veins that illuminated the place. The billions of vermillion veins that ran across the walls, pulsating blips of red light, like tiny heartbeats, every time they pushed through a bit of the liquid inside them.

The little boy blew out the candle and set it at his feet. He stood beside Edgar and said to the red darkness, "We're here."

Slowly, the gigantic chasm became illuminated. The vermillion veins were not only on the walls, but inside the chasm as well. The liquid inside them started to move, causing the abyss to be lit up, layer after layer, as though to give Edgar time to comprehend what he was seeing.

First, there were buildings. Skyscrapers, like Chapel, and smaller buildings, businesses, schools, apartments, and homes. There weren't just a few of them, either. There were millions of them. Billions, maybe. Destroyed, obliterated. Packed and piled together with the innumerable amounts of airplanes, automobiles, ships, and tanks that surrounded them. The further down the lights activated, the harder it became to make sense of what he saw, but even from this height, Edgar could tell that there were literally oceans of material goods below this cityscape crust. It was as though a great knife had swept across the Old World and scrapped the scab that was humanity off it.

But it was difficult to see everything. Parts of the chasm had yet to light up. There was a massive patch of darkness in particular, one of which was at the center of the chasm that was making it hard for Edgar to take it all in. Rational thought had abandoned him some time ago, so he proceeded further down the ballroom plank, to try to look around that dark obstacle before him.

But then that dark obstacle lit up, the vermillion veins that laced it finally coming to, and he, both in mind and body, reeled. The darkness hadn't been a wall or more buildings. No, it was something else, something organic, something alive.

At the center of the chasm, an enormous creature sat, rumbling atop a mountain of bones. Miles in width and stature, the winged beast was covered in tendrils and tentacles that were longer than some of the buildings it had undoubtedly devoured and deposited here. Several sets of arms sat at its sides, much like the Arachne, and though its head was down, and a halo of mist surrounded it, Edgar could see that the creature's face had several mouths, and several thousand eyes.

Edgar backed down the plank. He reached for something to brace himself against, but there was only the boy. "What... what..." His eyes darted back and forth between the beast's flesh and the vermillion veins running from it, into the chasm, and up the walls. "What is it?"

"That's God," the boy said. He held Edgar's hand, as a son would to calm a father. "That's God, Edgar."

"N-no." Again, he followed the veins, from the beast, to the chasm and the walls. Again, he looked to the entire continents contained within the chasm. "No, no, no. No. That's not... not God."

"How many gods have you seen lately, Edgar?"

Hyperventilating, Edgar dropped the boy's hand. He ran to the ballroom door, which was now shut and locked. He beat his fists against it, repeating over and over, "That's not God. That's not

God!"

The boy sighed and said, "Don't feel bad, Edgar. You're only mortal. You imagine the unimaginable in a form you can comprehend."

"God doesn't look like that," Edgar shouted.

"God has always looked this way."

He turned around slowly, afraid to look at the beast in full. It seemed to be sleeping, but what would it do to him if it woke?

"This is the Vermillion God, Edgar. The true god. The only god."

"It's... it's feeding off the earth." He pointed his twitching finger at it. "A God doesn't need to do that."

The boy shook his head. "No, those are Its veins. The liquid inside them is its blood. The earth is feeding off God, not the other way around. Part of the reason why the Nameless Forest hasn't fallen into complete chaos. Same for the world, too, I expect."

Edgar touched his lips. "I drank its blood. I ate from... it." He thought back to the feet of vermillion veins he had regurgitated lying in the ballroom. "No, fuck you. I don't believe you."

The boy cocked his head. "Do you know anything else that can do as we have done?"

The Vermillion God stirred, sending a river of skulls down the bone mountain.

"Through hell, we find heaven," the little boy said. He went to the nearest vermillion vein on the wall.

"It had to be you, and it had to happen this way. Your family would never accept the god that sits before you. But ironically enough, it is Eldrus, not Penance, that must accept God, because Eldrus is the only city that can truly save this world."

The boy bit into the vermillion vein. He moaned as he guzzled the liquid inside it. Pulling back, the red drink dousing his face, he plugged the tooth holes with his hand and said, "Amon thought he had to break you to use you. I would have done things differently. But he did break you, and yet, now you stand whole before me."

"Far fucking from it," Edgar said, images of his family flashing through his head. "I am nothing now. There's nothing left of me."

"You are only you, who you were always meant to be."

Edgar threw up his hands. "I was never meant to be a murderer. You and Amon made me one!"

"Maybe." The boy shrugged. "But we also brought you here, to the one place where you can actually make a difference to your city and the world. This is God, Edgar. How many atrocities have been committed in the name of religion? How many could be avoided if you all could just agree on the existence of a god and what god wants? If humans were rid of that problem, they would be rid of others as well. Religion is not the root of all evil, Edgar, but it does have a longer reach than most things."

"Sorry. Humans already have a god." He felt lightheaded, hungry, as he stared at the tempting drink staining the boy's cheeks.

"They like to think they do. The people of the world have lost their way. Now, they worship the little heretic in Penance, along with the great deceiver, the Mother Abbess, both of whom only tell them what they want to hear." He let go of the vermillion vein and sprayed his fingers in its red blood. "Does the world not deserve better than that? Amon tried once, but the world was too big, too complex, too ignorant, and he failed. The world is different now, and God is willing to give it another chance. Give everything another chance. If you're good to God, Edgar—" the boy held out his bloody finger and beckoned Edgar over, "—don't you think It will be good to you?"

Edgar shuffled towards the boy and closed his eyes. Unable to resist the vermillion desire, he lowered his head.

The boy gently touched his lips.

Edgar opened his mouth.

The boy stuck his finger inside his mouth, and from it, Edgar drank the blood of God.

"Let's give them what they've always wanted, Edgar," the boy said, petting him. "After everything, they deserve it."

Threadbare hadn't changed much since he last saw it. The only difference now being that, as he walked through the gates, everyone dropped to their knees, to pay him respect as the new king of the Nameless Forest.

Everyone, except, of course, the woman who probably hadn't ever knelt for anyone. Lotus.

She hurried through the rows of her prostrated people. "Welcome back." She grinned and said, "Edgar, you look terrible."

Lotus opened her arms, and Edgar went into them. He dropped his head against her neck and started crying so hard his body shook.

"Get us out of here," he said between the sobs.

Lotus held the back of his neck. To the boy, she said, "What did you do to him?"

"The Nameless Forest is yours to govern, until we call on you to do otherwise," the boy said.

Lotus nodded.

Edgar straightened up, and said, "What?" Looking at Lotus, after hearing that… being in her arms was no longer a comfort to him.

"I'm your warden," she said. "You can't rule here and Eldrus at the same time."

Spit getting in the way of his words, he said, "But I need you." He knew he looked pathetic, because he felt pathetic, like a filthy rag, something that had been used to clean up shit and left to wither in the sun. "Lotus, I need you. Please." Out of everyone left, she was the only one he still had any connection with.

Lotus took him by the shoulders, looked him dead in the eyes, and whispered, "Not here. You're their king. They can't see you acting like this. Let's go, Edgar. I'll make you feel better."

Lotus led Edgar through Threadbare, encouraging him along the way with nudges and nods to look like the king everyone thought he was. With red eyes, quivering cheeks, and a death-mask smile, he waved to his new subjects—and hated every moment of it. Was this what it meant to rule? Was this why his father had hated it so? Blood Drinker, Heart Eater—that's what they called Sovn, the once-king of Eldrus.

Edgar had thought the titles ridiculous, but now he wasn't so sure. His father had gained a reputation for his indifference towards almost everything, but it hadn't been indifference, he realized that now. It had been numbness, and he felt that same numbness now.

They returned to Lotus' home, where she and Edgar, among other fluids, had shared their first drink. With the boy, they sat down and had one more.

"Here, drink it quick," Lotus said, putting a cup in front of Edgar. "You don't want to taste it."

Edgar poured the alcohol directly down his throat, but he was sure he wouldn't have tasted it either way. He dug his nails into his wrists; didn't feel that, either.

This is what I wanted, Edgar thought, watching Lotus pour him another drink. *At the expense of everything, I can finally make a difference.* He drank that drink and snapped his fingers for another one.

Everyone I love is dead, and I've seen God. There's nothing left for me, and there's nothing I can do.

"What now?" Lotus asked. She took Edgar's hands from across the table and blew on them to warm them.

The boy went to the window and leaned against the wall there. He kept to the sunlight. He seemed to be enjoying it. "We'll go back and pick up where Amon left off. You'll wait here, keep everything together. When we're ready, we'll call you to Eldrus."

Edgar eyed the bottle, hoping for another drink. "The Nameless Forest will listen to her, maybe, but not me."

"They will. We'll start sending aid and support to the Forest, now that there is some stability."

Lotus nodded. "You come from a better off place than we do. We recognize we live in hell. We're not so stubborn to shirk our chances for a moment in heaven."

Edgar poured himself a drink when Lotus wouldn't. "What about the Arachne? Don't think they'll listen to me." He went to pour another cup, but his hand was shaking too much.

"They'll take some persuading, but even they will follow us." Lotus took his cup from him. "Anansi heard you were coming. It scared him enough to mobilize his forces. If it wasn't for you, Edgar, they would be here now, eating us."

"If I had never come here, he wouldn't have mobilized."

"Not true, trust me. I lived with the Arachne when they still held territory in Blackwood. I still have some friends amongst those freaks. I know how to make them listen, to make them fight for you."

Lotus stood up, set the cup down, filled it, and came around the table to stand behind Edgar. She started massaging his shoulders. "You need to rest. It's a long road from here to Eldrus."

The boy leaned away from the window, flecks of vermillion glowing in his pupils. "Can you do this, Edgar?"

Edgar took the cup and slid it closer to him. Monotone, like Auster, he said, "If I don't, it will all have been for nothing. I know that's what you want to hear, that I will try to salvage this, make things right, and that's what I'm going to do. I'm going to use you, like you used me. I'll use you, all of you mother fuckers—" he looked at Lotus, "—until everything is better, and then I'll turn on all of you. And not even God will stop me."

"Sounds fair," the boy said. "I imagine the Vermillion God could make it up to you before then. It could bring them back, if you wanted It to. If you could… live with the questions they would ask you."

Edgar shook his head and leaned over the cup. He paused, confused by what he saw reflected inside it. The ghost; he saw the ghost in the surface of Lotus' black drink. This was the first time he had seen himself since just after the murders of his family. Had he looked this way the entire time, when he had gone to bed with Lotus, or when he had spoken with Father Silas? Or did it go back further than that? If the ghost were sitting here in his place, would he see Edgar reflected instead? Or had there never been an Edgar? Was he just a lie he told himself, about who he was and how he could be different from those monsters that surrounded him?

At first, it made sense to blame the vermillion veins, but now, he wasn't sure. They were rich with the blood of God, and what is God if not a stark reminder of what you are and cannot be?

Edgar raised the cup to his lips and drank the ghost inside. He saw no reason not to let it haunt him just one more time. After all, he had been happy when it did.

PART TWO

THE GRAVEDIGGER'S DILEMMA

CHAPTER I

The Gravedigger had dug too deep, and now there was no way out.

"Will," he shouted, pushing the shovel into the soil until it stood up on its own. "I hear you kicking around out there."

The Gravedigger waited a moment, watching the light waver on the rim of the grave. He could smell the land burning, and the little of his house and barn that loomed over him looked as though it were melting. His house and barn were haggard things; large but run-down, and painted in that faded, murky shade only the poor would know.

"Dad?" His son's voice sounded far away, worlds away, from his place in the ground. A mess of blond hair and a sunburnt face looked down into the hole. "Now how'd you manage that?"

The Gravedigger sighed and rested his arm atop the shovel. "I got a little lost in my thoughts. It don't matter none. Get me the rope, so I can get the hell out of here."

Will grinned, his rosy cheeks cherubic. He was thirteen, almost fourteen, and soon would come the time when he might drift away, from himself and from his family, in search of things he already had and knew, but refused to accept.

The Gravedigger had done it, and so had his wife, when they were younger. It had taken them both a long time to come back round, and the Gravedigger was an impatient man, so he took these moments when he could, so that he could revisit them when he couldn't.

"Hey, Will," he called out, as his son started to walk away. "The rope, not your mother."

A snort, and then: "What's the difference?"

The Gravedigger cocked his jaw as he heard another set of footsteps. "Wife?" he said, shielding his eyes as the sun shifted his way.

"Husband?" she responded, affectionately.

"Our son is trying to get me to dig myself into a deeper hole than I'm already in." He felt a fat bead of sweat slither down his face. Winter had coaxed summer back out of its slumber, and now everyone was going to suffer for it.

"Will, go back inside," the Gravedigger's wife said. She appeared over the plot and waved. "How'd you manage this, Atticus?"

Twenty-five years he'd known Clementine, and for fifteen of them they'd been married. Their hometown of Gallows, which the Gravedigger was currently seven feet below, had seen it coming. Childhood enemies turned adolescent sweethearts, Atticus and Clementine had become something of a symbol of hope for those around them who lacked it. Some would've been honored by this; Atticus and Clementine, however, thought it was the dumbest thing they'd ever heard, and made sure to make fun of those who looked at them all starry-eyed any chance they could.

"Get me some rope, please. Tie it around that stump up there and toss it down," the Gravedigger said.

His wife put a finger to her chin. "Where's that at?"

"Well, there's the house, and then there's the barn."

"Which one do we sleep in again?" Clementine crouched down, her hair—her namesake—catching the sun and coming alive.

"I know which one you'll be sleeping in if you leave me down here."

"If I leave you down there, I don't think you'll be in any position to make me. Now that I've got you where I want you, I think I have some requests."

The Gravedigger pushed his hands against his face, leaving smears of dirt like war paint across his cheeks. He waited a moment, squinting as he stared up at his pale, freckled wife, and shook his head.

"You've got nothing."

"It'll come to me," she said. "What do you need rope for? Just run up the side and jump. I'll pull you up. Why you always have to make things so complicated?"

The Gravedigger grumbled and shrugged. "You going to catch me?"

Clementine rolled up her sleeves and flexed her arm muscles. She was enjoying this far too much for the Gravedigger's liking.

"I'll get you with one hand, just in case anyone's watching. We've got an image to maintain. Oh, I do have one request."

The Gravedigger threw up his arms and said, "What's that, my sweet, precious, milky-white princess?"

To give her a start, he ran up the side of the pit and jumped into the air.

Clementine called him a "son of a bitch," and with one arm, as she'd promised, she caught him.

"God damn, you're heavy, Atticus," she wheezed, lifting him up and back into the world of the living.

Clementine, with the Gravedigger's hand still in hers, fell down to the ground with him and lay there a moment, laughing.

"The rope," she said, smiling too hard to speak right, "it's already under the bed."

For the Gravedigger's family, dinner most often consisted of the "same old, same old,"—a traditional meal prepared by Clementine every evening consisting of the same meats, vegetables, and breads she'd been serving for the past thirteen years. Will used to complain about his mother's lack of creativity in the kitchen. After visiting the homes of his friends, now he was just glad she made the effort.

"Hope you're starving," Clementine said, as she always did, as she came into the dining room, balancing two plates on each arm.

The Gravedigger and his son sat at the table, their stomachs competing against one another's, trying to prove who was the hungriest.

"Instead of the same old, same old," Clementine said, bending down and sliding the plates before her boys, "I thought we could have something a little different."

The Gravedigger and his son went wide-eyed and slack-jawed. Will may have even shed a tear, but they were too caught up in the moment to truly notice.

Something a little different was another meal entirely. It was the holiday that only comes once a year, when no one is expecting it, because they thought they'd already missed it. Something a little different was a dinner cooked in secret, over the course of the week, using the finest meat and most expensive seasonings. Something a little different was a dream made real by Clementine's insistence on finding the finest vegetables, grains, breads, and sauces across Gallows and its borderlands. Ultimately, something a little different was the reminder that they were doing well, and that all good things were well worth the wait.

"You've really outdone yourself this time, Clem," the Gravedigger said. Giddily, he cut through the piece of steak on his plate as though it were butter. He took a bite of the pink square of meat and said, "Mmthasmmmyupgudnkswf," which translated into, "Mm, that's really good. Thank you, my loving wife."

Clementine smiled, took a drink of water, and looked at Will. "How is it?"

Will nodded behind the corncob glued to his mouth and hands. Bits of corn flew onto his shoulders, he went at it so hard.

His father eyed him from across the table, so he quickly said, "Thank you, Mom, it's great."

Clementine took a bite out of a piece of garlic bread. "Digging awfully close to the house."

"Running out of room," the Gravedigger said. He let out a belch even the dead could feel. "Last one this way, I promise. Once the mayor gives me the go ahead, I'll expand southward. I have to get this new body in the ground before it starts to stink up the place."

"Who is it?" Will asked. He leaned back in his chair and undid the top button of his pants. He took a deep breath, and then went at the meal again.

"You remember that uppity boy—Brinton?"

Will shook his head.

Clementine said, "That son of a bitch got himself killed? Did he ever make it to Eldrus?"

"Yup," the Gravedigger said, nodding, "made it all the way into the royal guard."

"Shut up, Atticus. Really? Brinton?" Clementine let out a laugh and hit the table with her fist. "What happened? What the hell is he doing back here? He's got no family."

The Gravedigger shrugged. "He got himself killed guarding the King, I suppose." He took the last steak, cut it into three pieces, and gave the largest two to Clementine and Will. "I don't understand it, them sending his body back here, but they did last night, while you all were sleeping. Two soldiers from Eldrus dropped off the box. I think they're staying at the inn, unless they've already left. Best they do leave soon. Not much love for Eldrus here nowadays."

Will picked at the food in-between his teeth. "Must be a perk to serving royalty. You know, being sent back home."

"It's strange," Clementine said, her mouth full of a little of everything. "King Edgar is a strange one."

"I expect anyone would be after going through what he did." The Gravedigger sighed, slouched in his chair, and allowed the digesting to commence.

"I bet he made it all up," Will suggested, his voice a little too high, a little too unsure to suggest anything other than he was trying to get a rise out of his parents.

"Well, aren't you the rebel?" Clementine said. "He's a king. They all make things up. Surviving the Nameless Forest? Eh, I doubt it." She looked at the Gravedigger, and he nodded in agreement. "But murdering his whole family? Come on, now."

"I'm not saying I love the kid," the Gravedigger said, as though King Edgar were five and not twenty-five, "but he's done more than his father, that's for sure."

"Hell of a lot better than the council did when he was missing," Clementine chirped. "But he hasn't stopped sending soldiers to all the towns, though. They're going to lose support if they keep it up. They ought to send people to Nachtla. Place is a ghost town."

The Gravedigger wiped his mouth. "At least Gallows is far enough out for them to more or less let us be."

Will sat up and drummed the tops of his legs excitedly. "Ronny down the road said that was on purpose, that Archivist Amon screwed things up on purpose so we'd be happy to have King Edgar back. You know, kind of makes sense."

"Ronny down the road is a dumbass," Clementine said bluntly. "He keeps trying to hock Old World artifacts that aren't worth nothing to no one, claiming it's to help pay for his kids, which he don't even take care of to begin with. Ronny's trouble, and if you go around him, you'll get in trouble, too. Just stay the hell away from him, otherwise, the next body your dad will be burying will be his. I'll make sure of it."

Stunned, Will mumbled, "Oh, okay."

"Enough about Ronny," the Gravedigger said. He took his wife's crimson hand and stroked it to calm her. His face had gone hard, and though he didn't show it, he was pissed. "Clementine, thank you for this delicious dinner." He raised her hand and kissed it like a gentle-man. "Let's think good thoughts, before we do bad things."

Clementine smiled, sniffled her nose. "Good thoughts. Only good thoughts."

CHAPTER II

The Gravedigger and his wife weren't the only ones to break a bed that night. Something else had, too.

"Atticus, where are you going?" Clementine said, sitting up, her wrists still bound, her body glistening with sweat. "Let it be until morning. We're not finished here."

The Gravedigger lit a candle and turned around. Many so-called experts on the institution of marriage had warned him he'd tire of his wife and her looks, that he may venture elsewhere to satisfy his needs. He hadn't believed it then, and he sure as hell didn't believe it now. Staring at Clementine there in the candlelight, he felt the same as he had the first time they'd made love. It was as though he had never grown out of being the nervous, overly-excited boy who always finished too soon, and who tried to make up for it too much. If there were other women in the world, then he hadn't seen them; they must've disappeared the day Clementine came into his life.

"You going?" she asked, shaking him from his thoughts. She lay down on the broken bed, her body at odd angles because of the way it fell. "Untie me then, so I can finish what you started."

Thirty minutes later, the Gravedigger emerged from the room, sore but satisfied.

At night, when it thought everyone was asleep or having too much sex to pay it any attention, the house came alive. The floor creaked with phantom footsteps, while the attic howled ghastly gusts of ghostly orders. Things were moved or sometimes broken. If they came down at the right time, when the house was least expecting it, they found rooms shifted slightly, or the staircase somewhat crooked. For the first few months here, they chalked it up to the Black Hour, but now that it was so frequent and it hadn't killed them yet, they figured it was something else entirely; a haunt, maybe, with a soft spot for interior decoration.

So, thirty minutes later, when the Gravedigger emerged from the room, he was understandably confused when he found nothing had changed at all. As he descended the stairs, hot wax from the candle he held dripped onto his hand. Grumbling, the Gravedigger reached the first floor and waved the light about, like a nun at night searching for out-of-bed orphans.

"Will?" the Gravedigger called out, expecting, and getting, no response. His son slept deeper than most of those buried out back, and usually only woke for his girlfriend, Hazel.

The Gravedigger needed some fresh air, so he stepped outside and got some. The night was windy, but humid, and it smelled like wet dog. He took a seat in his father's rocking chair and put it to motion, as his eyes tried to break up the black that blanketed Gallows.

They lived on the outskirts of the town, nearest the Nameless Forest, which, thankfully, was not all that near. It was a good place to be, he often thought, because if something went down in Gallows, they were close enough to see it, but far enough to get away.

He rocked his chair a bit, adding its creaks and cracks to the chorus of bugs and bats that sang around him. Across the yard, where the old chapel sat broken and godless, the graveyard was a mass of severe shapes and mostly bad choices. How he'd gotten into this line of work, the Gravedigger couldn't recall, but he loved it. The money that came with burying the dead was poor—that's what the farm was for—but it also came with a kind of satisfaction he couldn't get elsewhere. Maintaining the graveyard was like maintaining a garden; if only everyone else could appreciate its beauty as much as he did.

A grunt, and then the snapping of wood: He turned his head toward the barn and saw a light through its window; a light that shouldn't be.

The Gravedigger went back inside and grabbed his scythe, because if there ever was a weapon that suited his profession, that was it. He hurried down the porch and sprinted through the grass. Crickets got out of his way as he went.

There were voices in the barn now, hurried but soft. They knew he was coming.

The barn's front door was half-open, so the Gravedigger took it and flung it back the rest of the way.

Two dark shapes froze where they stood. They dropped the lantern they were carrying and slipped through the space between the boards he'd been meaning to fix.

The Gravedigger turned around, and went around the side of the barn. The dark shapes were tearing across the field. Before he gave chase, they'd already disappeared into the woods.

The Gravedigger sighed, and shook his head. He rested the scythe against the side of the barn. He'd been looking forward to a good fight, and they'd robbed him of that. What else had they taken?

The discarded lantern lay face up in a bed of hay, the sharp shadows it produced stabbing the light where it rested. The Gravedigger picked it up quick—the last thing he needed was a fire—and had a look around. No tools had been taken, nor had the few horses been woken. Had he caught them before they could get started?

"Dumbass kids," the Gravedigger mumbled. He'd been one of those dumbass kids once, but he'd long since shed that thick and stupid skin.

After silently vowing to fix the boards in the back wall, the Gravedigger made to leave, but stopped. He heard a whistling—a whining wind through wood—and hinges on rust. Looking over his shoulder, he saw the door to the annex unlatched, with a hole where the handle should've been. The annex was where he kept the dead. What had the little dumbasses wanted with the dead?

Lantern held high, just in case he needed to clobber a straggler on the other side, the Gravedigger crept into the annex. The smell hit him hard, as it always did. No matter how many times he'd worked in here, the pungent preservatives always found a way to make themselves known.

The walls of the annex were not wood, but Rime Rock—stones from the Far North that held a permanent cold. Grave Soil and Devour were applied liberally to the area to prevent decomposition of the corpses inside. These components weren't cheap, nor were they especially common. Dumbass kids always came around trying to get at them.

But not this time.

This time, they'd come for the body.

Brinton's box lay on the long table, front broken and busted, as though the dark shapes had taken hammers to it.

The Gravedigger leaned over the dead man's bed and lit it up. Except for the bone-deep gash running across his neck, Brinton looked like Brinton. He was paler, yes, but the boy never had much color to him. He was thinner as well, but Death will do that to a person.

No, what stood out the most to the Gravedigger were Brinton's eyes. When he lived in Gallows, they'd been an unimpressive brown. But as the Gravedigger pulled back the man's lids, he saw that his eyes had frozen over, and in that icy stillness, there were blotches of red around his pupils.

"What're we going to do with you?"

The Gravedigger knew the body would keep so long as it stayed in this room, but would it stay in this room? Brinton's death looked a violent death. If he'd died with enough hate in his heart, he just might come back to share it with the rest of the class.

The Gravedigger took a jar off the shelf above the table. He shook out a large leaf with sharp edges and crystalline veins, and gave the corpse this Gift of Sleep, which was a little something to help Brinton's spirit sleep better.

"I'll see you in the morning."

He backed out of the room and shut the door to the annex. Whether or not the tiny, faerie-like Inferi would come for the Gift didn't seem to matter; the leaf itself was almost always enough to calm the restless dead.

The Gravedigger emerged from the barn and grabbed the scythe he'd propped up against its side. He felt anxious, on edge. He wouldn't be able to sleep, even if Clementine used every trick in the book on him. He needed something to fix, something to destroy.

Cleaning his teeth with his tongue, he surveyed the graveyard across the dirt path, searching for heads amongst headstones to crack and split. Finding nothing, he returned his attention toward the old chapel. Here, Gallows' outcasts would occasionally have themselves a séance to seduce those grim sweethearts who couldn't be wooed by other means. If he was lucky, he may even catch a few of them in the act tonight. If he was really lucky, he'd even have some new components to show for it, too.

The Gravedigger crossed the path and went quietly through the grass. His ankles itched as the dew-laden blades slid past his skin.

With as much silence as he could muster, he climbed the few stairs outside the chapel, ducked beneath the lopsided archways, and made his way inside.

No longer tightly bound by the words and ways of Penance, the old chapel had learned to relax. Its walls were all but separated from one another. The roof was simply the sky and whatever happened to be in it that day or night. Most of the pews were gone, as well as the candleholders and stained glass windows. The altar was still there—it was too heavy to move, and cursed, or so people said—and that's where the Gravedigger's best friend now sat, snacking on someone's spleen.

"Gary," the Gravedigger said. He dug the scythe into the ground and leaned on it.

The ghoul bit into the bruise-colored organ. "Atticus."

The Gravedigger folded his arms across his chest and sighed. "I expect you heard the commotion?"

Gary kicked his legs into the air as though he were a small child enjoying a sweet. He was the Gravedigger's age, and claimed to have been that way longer than he could remember. The flesh he ate ensured his didn't drop from his bones. His condition itself left his body the color of burlap, and gave it the fabric's texture as well. Supposedly, this made the ghoul's form more agreeable to transforming into whatever it had recently consumed. But Gary had no need for such parlor tricks; the Gravedigger's protection was more than enough to make him feel comfortable in his own skin.

"What was that all about?" Gary chewed on the spleen. "I stuck my head out there to see what I could see. They kept to the shadows, but they knew what they were looking for. They didn't waste no time sniffing about the property." Dried blood mixed with the ghoul's saliva and dripped down his chin. "I can track them if you want. I could smell them from here. Smelled familiar. One was a fatty. I'm sure he didn't get too far."

"I'll think about it," the Gravedigger said. "They went for the body. The new body. Brinton's."

"That son of a bitch got himself killed?" Gary's heels banged against the front of the altar. "How'd that happen?"

The Gravedigger shrugged. Ten pounds of sleep weighed down his eyelids. "Throat was cut to the bone. Who's for dinner tonight, eh?"

Gary set the spleen down on the altar and licked the tips of his fingers. "Judith Myers, row eighteen, plot twenty. She'd been in there a long time." He cringed. "Probably should've just let her be."

The Gravedigger straightened up. "Will you keep watch on the barn tonight?"

"Don't even need to ask." Gary hopped off the altar and shoved the rest of the spleen down his throat. "You know, Mr. Haemo wants his tribute from you."

"Mr. Haemo can kiss my ass." The Gravedigger turned away. "If he wants his tribute, he needs to come get it himself. Otherwise, I'm just going to keep on killing his kids."

CHAPTER III

When the Gravedigger woke the following morning, it was because Will had been shouting for him.

"Dad! Dad!"

The Gravedigger's eyes slowly opened. He'd fallen asleep outside in his father's rocking chair. He leaned forward, his back cracking in a thousand places he couldn't begin to name. His throat was dry and his skin hot. He felt like shit, and probably looked it, too.

"Dad!"

Will's voice flanked him from the left. When the Gravedigger looked over, he saw the shape of his boy running towards him, waving his arms to make sure he had his father's attention.

"Son, son, son," he said. He paused as he rubbed an itching mosquito bite. "Son of a bitch got me."

Will stopped at the front steps and said as he panted, "Didn't... you hear me... calling for you?"

"Thought it was the wind whistling my name."

Will scratched at his poor excuse for a beard. "You've got to see this," he squeaked, his voice snapping, as it always did, at the most inopportune moment.

"Give me a minute." The Gravedigger came to his feet and let his thirst lead him back inside the house.

"Dad, it's the barn."

The Gravedigger stopped. He could see a cup of water sweating in the kitchen from where he stood. "Where's your mother?"

"In the barn. You've got to... there's something wrong with the barn."

The Gravedigger turned and followed his son outside. They went to the front of the barn, where Clementine stood, one eyebrow raised, both hands thrown up in the air.

"We had a break-in," the Gravedigger said. "I scared them off."

"It's not that, Atticus." Clementine pulled the barn door back and pointed to the annex.

The Gravedigger slid past his wife. "What were you in there for?" The broken boards on the back wall taunted him to finally fix them.

"Door was open." Clementine took her husband by his wrist. "How'd Brinton die?"

The Gravedigger considered his wife, but didn't say anything. He reached for the annex door—didn't he shut it last night?—and went inside.

Brinton was where he'd left him—on the table, in his casket—but wasn't as he'd left him. A tangle of bright red, vein-like structures had grown out of his neck. Like ivy, they clung to the places where they touched, and where they touched had been the table, the wall, and half the floor. The annex itself appeared to throb as the veins pumped vermillion liquid through its crystalline casing.

"What is it?" Clementine asked. She whispered something to Will that sounded like "stay back."

The Gravedigger shook his head. A portion of the thick mass slowly spread its way toward the ceiling. What was all this life doing here? The annex had been created and coated in such a way to ensure the only thing that thrived in it was death. Had this been the work of the thieves? The vermillion veins looked similar to Petra's Pest, but the coloration was all wrong. The Gravedigger had heard of something like this before, but what?

On approach, Gallows looked abandoned. It always did. Like the killing thing from which it took its name, the town was wide and made of wood. When the wind hit it, it howled. When the sun touched it, it bled. For those who lived there long enough, they could point to the dark stains on the ground and buildings and say to whom they'd belonged. Gallows was not a nice place, but it was a place made nicer by its lack of pretentions.

Whirlwinds of dirt danced through the center of town, spinning after the children who'd dared to gather there. The sounds of swinging doors and shuffling feet rang out across Gallows, as those that could work went off to ply their trade.

The Gravedigger moved through the rows of sleep-deprived citizens, the hint of their hangovers souring the air, and headed for the place they likely just left not long ago.

The tavern was closed, so the Gravedigger banged on the front door until it wasn't.

"Go away, god damn it," Poe shouted from inside the tavern.

The Gravedigger rattled the doorknob until he heard the barkeep's fat feet bounding across the floor.

"Listen," Poe started, as he ripped the door open and presented himself, shirtless and soiled, to the world. "Atticus," he said, surprised. "Atticus," he went on, stepping outside, crossing his arms to hide his sagging breasts. "I'm sorry. Shit, I didn't know. What... How can I help you?" Poe's body coughed out an odor of oil and sweat.

The Gravedigger gave up breathing for a bit. "Two dumbasses broke into my barn last night. What do you know about that?"

"I don't." Poe took a step back. "I don't know anything about that. Come in, have a seat, have a drink."

"Who you got staying here?" The Gravedigger followed Poe into the building and up to the bar. He dropped onto a stool and stared the man down like he was meat. The bar was sparse but spacious; if one were to take out all the lopsided tables and busted chairs, they could turn it back into the barracks it once served as so many years ago.

Poe stuttered as he puttered about the floor, picking up his garments that lay strewn across it. He dressed himself in the colorful rags.

Once he was satisfied with his squalid appearance, he said, "Just them soldiers that dropped off Brinton."

"Fetch them for me."

"It's best you wait."

"It's best I don't."

Poe made his way behind the bar and had himself a swill of ale. "You think they're the ones who broke in?"

The Gravedigger eyed the drink and then thought better. "Brinton's corpse has something growing all over it. It's spread across my barn. I need to know what it is. I'm not going to bury his body and risk contaminating the property."

Poe's voice grew deep with concern. "You think something hitched a ride on him from Eldrus?"

The Gravedigger shrugged. "I think it's strange they brought Brinton back here to be buried. Never heard of that before." He slid off the stool and onto his feet. "Which room is theirs?"

"Atticus, wait." Poe tripped over his feet as he ran to stop the Gravedigger from marching up the steps. "They had a lot to drink. They got people up there with them. They're not nice men like you or I."

"I don't give a fuck." The Gravedigger shouldered past the barkeep. At the landing, he turned and said, "What'd they do that's got you so scared?"

Poe shook his head. "Nothing. Unlike you, there's just some kinds of people that are best… Just go. Room three, room four." He wandered into his own room underneath the stairs.

The second story floorboards announced the Gravedigger's approach, but no one would hear it. The eight doors that lined the hall ahead were thick slabs of wood that sucked up sound like a rag would water. Because of this, the tavern had developed a reputation. It became a safe haven for those villainous travelers who couldn't distinguish business from pleasure. In the end, not much was done about the matter, because the worst vices tended to bring out the best customers.

The Gravedigger found the third room—after all these years, he knew them by heart—and pushed it open. He didn't have a weapon to defend himself with, but given the soldiers' likely states, he didn't need one.

"No, please," a young man begged as the heavy door swung back.

The Gravedigger's eyes widened as he saw what waited on the other side. In a tangle of bloodstained sheets, James lay naked on the floor. Knees to his chest, chin to his knees. He quivered, the red welts on his backside throbbing, weeping.

"Where'd they go?" The Gravedigger grabbed a pillow from beneath the bed. "Damn it." He dropped it; it was soaked with shit.

James shook his head and held on tighter to himself. The Gravedigger hadn't seen him in three years, not since he'd walked off the farm to chase after a boy he had no reason to be chasing after. He looked at the twenty-two-year-old and wondered what choices he'd made that had led him to this moment. Had it been one "yes" in the place of what should've been a "no"? Or had it been something else, something less obvious? A quiet, seemingly insignificant moment not handled quite as well as it could've been? The Gravedigger thought of Will, got pissed, and then thought of something else.

"Don't tell anyone," James pleaded, sniffling. He wiped his nose on the sheets bunched up in his fists. "I'm sorry."

"No need to apologize." The Gravedigger looked around the room for something to comfort him, but there were only splinters and glass. "Let's get you up and out of here."

When he went in for his arm, James tensed and pushed the Gravedigger away. "Leave me alone, Atticus. I… I can manage."

"Which soldier was it that raped you?"

James swallowed hard. He closed his eyes and whimpered. Clearly, he still saw the night on the back of his lids. "He didn't… I agreed. He just… took it too far." He clenched his legs together.

The Gravedigger could feel the sickly heat of suffering pouring out of James' body. He wished he still possessed some sympathy, some empathy for the boy. But what little he'd managed to muster years ago disappeared the day James skipped town.

James sat up. "That was us last night." He propped himself against the frame of the bed. Embarrassed, he covered his crotch.

"Who's us? Elijah's still with you?" He looked over his shoulder, into the hall, at the door to room four. He imagined finding James' boyfriend dead inside, having finally gotten what he'd so long deserved. It made him smile.

"It was my idea." James tried to look defiant. Now that he wasn't on the floor, the Gravedigger could see the red patches on his neck from where someone had been sucking on it. "We needed money. Figured we could hock some things from the annex."

"You trying to piss me off?" The veins in the Gravedigger's head pulsated with three years of unspoken rage. "I caught you, so you came back here. Ran into them, and they ran you into the ground. You get your money?"

James nodded. "They say jobs are hard to find around these parts. But we've all the parts for at least one job."

"Well isn't that poetic?" The Gravedigger knew there was nothing more to be said. They were both too stubborn to apologize, and too calloused to truly care. "They're gone? Where to?"

James shrugged and said, "Next is Bedlam, but I think they're still around. Said they had another body to deliver. That's where we were going. Back home to Bedlam."

"If you're quick, you just might catch up with them." The Gravedigger turned and left the room. He stood in the hall, staring down room four. "Did you do anything to the body in the annex?" he asked through his teeth.

"No," James said, his voice weak, his resolve gone. "Heard it was Brinton. Thought he might have some badges or something we could sell. Why?"

By the time the Gravedigger got back to the barn, the vermillion veins had completely filled the annex. If he wanted in, he'd have to cut his way through.

Clementine went behind her husband and wrapped her arms around him. "Did you find them?" She rested her head against his shoulder and smelled him. "This scares me, Atticus. Will this cost us a lot?"

The Gravedigger took his wife's hands, and kissed the tops of them. "I'll make the mayor reimburse us, if need be. What is it, though? What's in it? I have an idea, but I don't want to put you and Will in danger if I start tearing it down."

"Got to do something," she said, biting his earlobe. "It'll take over the whole house at this rate."

"I saw James at the tavern."

Clementine gasped and pulled away. "You did?"

"He and that fat fuck Elijah are the ones who tried to break in. After I chased them off, they ran into the soldiers from Eldrus. They did a number on him. Karma, I guess. Whatever that means."

Clementine twisted her mouth. "Were you mean to him?"

The Gravedigger shook his head. "Didn't need to be."

Clementine smiled and, taking her husband by his arm, led him toward the house. "He was a good kid. We did what we could. We didn't have to, but we did. Shouldn't expect anything in return."

The Gravedigger looked across the road to the abandoned chapel, where they'd found James. He then looked at the overpopulated graveyard, where the boy had spent most of his days. He hadn't been a smart kid, nor had he been particularly talented. But with some guidance, their guidance, they had hoped to avoid the very future he had just fucked his way into.

"What's for dinner?" the Gravedigger asked, snapping out of it. Clementine shrugged. "Oh, the same old, same old."

The Gravedigger waited for the evening to go through its motions. He watched the sun crack against the earth, spilling the last of its light like yolk across the land. He listened to the wind as it ripped through the rows of the dead before laying down to die among them. The grass started to tremble, to shake, as things woke to hunt those that now slept. The world dimmed, became intimate, smaller, as though it were closing in to have a look at what deeds were being done in the sweating dark.

The Gravedigger waited for the evening to go through its motions, and then went to work.

Gary sat on a stack of hay. He watched the Gravedigger pace back and forth in front of the annex. "You know what they look like?"

The Gravedigger stopped, entranced by the vibrant liquid coursing through the vermillion veins. "Nameless Forest."

"Never seen it myself, but those things there sure fit the bill."

"It's supposed to be addictive." The Gravedigger ducked into the shadows and returned with a machete. "Any idea what'll happen if I starting hacking at it?"

The ghoul shook his head. "I don't think it's them." He picked at his skin, his doubt leaving a tear on his palm. "You think the soldiers knew? What are their names? What did they—"

The Gravedigger dropped his arms to his sides. "Something's wrong."

"I know. You're not usually this thoughtful."

The Gravedigger sighed and started for the front of the barn. "Let's go... see what Mr. Haemo knows."

It took the Gravedigger and Gary an hour traveling east from the graveyard, but they finally reached Mr. Haemo's haunt. It was a dense, murmuring marsh that had formed at the edge of the fields. Standing on the marsh's sickly shore, the Gravedigger searched for passage.

The waters here were too deep to walk in, and too hungry to swim through. He tapped Gary and pointed to the isle ahead, where the trees, like sickles, curved out of the earth. They skirted the waters, and then came to a stop. At their feet, a path of petrified bodies stretched across the marsh. This bloated bridge of bruised backs was the only way to reach the secluded isle.

The Gravedigger bent down and picked up the candle at the flesh bridge's beginning. "The soldiers aren't gone."

It was always there, and as always, when touched, the candle ignited.

"Soldiers never leave that quickly," the Gravedigger explained to Gary. "They're still around. We need to find them."

An audience with Mr. Haemo came with a strict adherence to ritual. It wasn't a necessity, but it was a good way to get on the good side of the sick son of a bitch.

The Gravedigger went slowly across the slick backs of the bridge of bloated dead. A quarter of the way, he stopped, knelt, and lit the ephemeral candle in the skull floating beside him in the water. Gary, ahead of the Gravedigger, scratched their names into the soggy flesh of the eighth corpse in the chain.

They then moved one after the other, until they were halfway to the isle. There, they each bit their own fingers until a droplet of blood appeared. Holding their hands out, they waited for a mosquito to buzz by and collect their offering. When it did, they proceeded forward, taking off their clothes as they went.

They stepped upon the isle, naked and bleeding, just the way Mr. Haemo preferred all his visitors to be. A wild thicket of black trees greeted them, daring them to enter with sinister sneers and wooden whispers. If they wanted to get to the center, this was the only way through.

A plume of red smoke rose out of the middle of the thicket. "Let's not do this," Gary said.

"Do you know a better way?" The Gravedigger found the entrance. It was a narrow corridor of clawing branches. He placed the candle he held in one of their wooden hands. "What are you afraid of? You're already dead."

"That's cold," Gary said, shaking his head. "You should be nicer to us dead folk. You'll be amongst us one day."

The passage always took more than it deserved, so when they finally slid out of it, they were covered from head to toe in thin, stinging cuts. Crotches still covered, because that was the place the branches liked the best, they walked towards the center of the thicket, where the red plume was finally dispersing.

Mr. Haemo stirred within the crimson cloud and said, "Did you bring me something to drink?"

The Gravedigger cleared his throat. His eyes went to the small, but infinitely deep, pool of blood a few feet away. "I need your help."

Mr. Haemo laughed and stepped out of the smoke. Draped in a cloak of human skin, the six-foot mosquito walked towards them on two legs, its massive, ruby-like eyes staring them down like the pathetic creatures they were to him. His body, black with splotches of pale yellow, moved with an unnatural gait as he strolled over to the blood well.

"Come here," Mr. Haemo said, leaning in to it. He moved his hands over the surface of the pool, divining from the gathering waves its sanguine secrets. He dipped his two-foot proboscis into the swirling cruor and said, "Sit. Now."

The Gravedigger and Gary did as they were told, sitting on their hands to stop the foul-smelling grass from touching their bare flesh.

Mr. Haemo laughed at their obvious discomfort. He suckled stolen blood from the well.

"I need to track two people," the Gravedigger said, too anxious to wait any longer. He'd heard stories of those who spent too much time on the isle; he'd even walked on their backs.

Mr. Haemo's wings started to buzz behind the flesh cloak. "I don't feel compelled to help you, Atticus. You spurn me and mine every chance you get."

"Two soldiers from Eldrus. Blythe… and Bon. You can have every drop."

"In that case, you have a deal." Mr. Haemo snapped his fingers to complete the contract. "But first, a down payment."

The Gravedigger held his arm out over the pool. The blood grew restless. It churned and spilled over itself, like an addict in need of a fix.

"No need," the giant mosquito said. He waved his hand until the Gravedigger withdrew.

Mr. Haemo snapped his fingers. In an instant, the thicket filled with millions of mosquitoes. Sound and space coagulated into a thick tar of buzzing wings.

The Gravedigger tried to move, but the pounding waves of gaunt, gore-filled bodies kept him in place. He could feel their mouthparts probing the cracks in his flesh, searching for blood vessels to pierce and sup. His muscles quivered. He tried to stay upright. The insects were landing on him now, slowly weighing him down by the thousands. The Gravedigger broke out into a cold sweat. When he could literally feel the last of his blood leaving his veins, he knew he had made a—

Mr. Haemo snapped his fingers. With that, his children were gone, spirited away to the secret place from which they'd emerged. "We're good now."

Exhausted, drained, the Gravedigger fell forward, head first toward the pool.

"Atticus, stop!" Gary grabbed his friend and held him there. His ghoul flesh, rigid and harsh, pricked the Gravedigger's back.

Mr. Haemo snickered. "You know, Gary, you don't have to go through all the ceremonies to get here. We're cool."

The ghoul shook his head. "You say that now, but the day I don't, you'll have changed your mind." He scoured the Gravedigger's body for the bites that should've been there but weren't.

Mr. Haemo shrugged. Again, he put his hands over the blood well, but this time, a light came through the waters and shone into his thousand emotionless eyes.

"Khr'ka elhx uhri. Tch'xa slvf uhri, Mhr'la roij uhri. In blood we're born and by blood we're bound. Through this, their blood, the hidden will be found!"

Mr. Haemo submerged his entire head into the pool and sat there a moment, the crimson waters bubbling around the base of his neck. The skin cloak slid off his body, giving his wings free rein to beat violently in the air.

"Is he... is he doing it?" The Gravedigger lifted his head weakly and stared into his friend's dead eyes.

"He's doing something."

Mr. Haemo threw his head back, slinging a rope of blood across the panting ground. "They're in here, I found them," the mosquito said, blood pouring down his face.

Barely conscious, the Gravedigger whispered, "W-where are they?"

"Are you trying to waste my time?" Mr. Haemo rubbed his proboscis. He looked like he was seriously considering plunging it into the Gravedigger's chest.

"What? No? Where are they?"

Mr. Haemo glanced at Gary.

Gary shrugged. "I'm just tagging along."

"They're in the house, Atticus," Mr. Haemo said. "They're in your house."

CHAPTER IV

Head throbbing, heart pounding, the Gravedigger bounded towards his house. No soldiers, no screams. With Gary following close behind, he staggered across the yard, crawled up the porch, and burst through the front door.

"Clementine," he shouted. "Will!"

The Gravedigger dragged himself through the house, knocking over a vase here, a shelf there. Dizzied and dead-eyed, he went in circles around the first floor, calling their names while he beat his fists and feet against the walls and floors. He darted through the living room, the dining room, and the kitchen. He checked every closet, but found nothing.

He made his way to the front of the house and headed up the stairs. The Gravedigger sniffed the air for the smells of men and metal, leather and liquor. He blinked, widened his eyes; he saw everything through a fog of exhaustion. With every step he took, the fog thickened.

He stumbled off the stairs and ran through doorways, shouting their names in his head rather than saying them aloud. Where were they? He checked the spare rooms; they hadn't seen visitors in several years. Tears fell from his eyes as he grew frantic and faint. Where were they? And in his state, could he even do anything to save them?

"Atticus, god damn. What are you hollering about?" Clementine barked from outside.

Like teeth, the stairs bit the Gravedigger's ass as he tripped and slid down them. Clementine stood on the porch, looking in the house, her hands gloved, her face masked, and a machete—his machete—in her freckly grip. Her head nodded, nodded, nodded, as he went down, down, down each step.

He smacked against the landing, legs spread, as though he were giving birth to the pain he'd just made.

Clementine smiled and laughed. When she saw her husband wasn't doing either, she turned grim. "Atticus, what? What's wrong? What happened to you? Shit," she said, going to him and taking both of his outstretched hands. "Come here."

The Gravedigger held onto his wife as though she'd already died. She smelled like a bonfire. He buried his face in her neck and left some tears there for her to wonder about later. "Where's Will? Is he okay? Did the soldiers come?"

Clementine let out a kind laugh as she patted his back. She kissed his head through her mask. "Honey, what the hell you been up to? I'm fine. Will's fine."

When his senses settled and the feel of his wife balanced him, the Gravedigger stepped back and said, "Why you dressed like that?"

With her husband in tow, Clementine brought them out back, behind the barn, where Will, equally masked and machete equipped, stood over a burning pit. It was the grave his father had been digging a day ago, for Brinton.

Will nodded at the Gravedigger and slid through broken barn boards that still needed fixing.

With enough blood built up to be more or less himself, the Gravedigger scowled at his wife and moseyed over to the fire. "Clementine, you shouldn't—"

Clementine's mouth dropped open and she put her hand to her ear. "What's that? I didn't quite... What you say?" She smiled and stuck out her tongue.

Ever since she'd been little, Clementine had a severe allergy to being told what to do. It made her heated and gave her the shakes. If it was a man who'd done it, she came down with a full-blown case of go-fuck-yourselfitus.

"It had to happen, Atticus. It was spreading to the barn. Once it got out of the annex, you know we wouldn't be able to stop it."

The Gravedigger looked into the pit. Six feet further down, writhing together like a ball of snakes, the vermillion veins hissed and popped, staining the sides of the grave with their bright blood.

"Coming through," Will said.

With an armful of veins, he brushed past his father and dumped the quivering things into the pit. He stood there a moment, admiring what he surely considered manly work, and lumbered back into the barn.

"I went and saw Mr. Haemo." The Gravedigger closed his eyes and screwed up his face.

Clementine slapped the back of his head. "Atticus, what the hell is wrong with you? Why? To find out what these were? It don't matter. You always make things so damn complicated." She took a deep breath. "I'm sorry. I am, really." The machete fell from her grip and stuck in the ground. She kissed the Gravedigger's cheek and said, "You know we know how much you do for us, right?"

"I know it. I'm keeping tabs." The Gravedigger brushed his nose against his wife's. "Mr. Haemo said soldiers had come. You didn't see any?"

"Been out here ever since you left with Gary. There's a couple of critters in the graveyard causing a ruckus, but other than that, it's been quiet."

Will carried out another few pounds of veins.

"It's coming out of Brinton. I can't bury him like that," the Gravedigger said.

"Atticus, no one's going to miss him. He's got no family left here. Unless you think Gary would want a bite out of him, it's probably just best to burn him."

The Gravedigger shook his head. "Gary thinks it's those things from the Nameless Forest that have come out of Brinton. You know, those plants. The ones that make everyone crazy. I don't expect he'd touch them, even if we paid him to."

"All right then," Clementine said, pulling the machete out of the earth. "Let's get to work."

It was half past the Black Hour when the Gravedigger and his clan of vein-cutters finally called it quits. They'd cleared the barn and the annex of the overgrowth, and now sat on a pile of hay in aching bliss. The horses there, apathetic as usual, neighed every few minutes, trying their best to guilt the humans into a late night snack.

The Gravedigger, rubbing his utterly useless arms, analyzed the annex from where he'd collapsed. As difficult as they were to remove, the vermillion veins hadn't actually damaged anything in the room. Sure, Brinton's body had literally burst open, like a sack full of sharp objects, but Brinton was dead and, well, it was Brinton.

"This is something we don't tell anyone else about, isn't it?" Will said, sniffling his nose. The dark circles under his eyes were getting darker with every passing second. He needed his precious beauty sleep.

"Mmm," the Gravedigger mumbled.

"Can I marry Hazel?" Will blurted out.

The Gravedigger looked at his wife. "If you got to ask, then you got your answer."

"You only been seeing her a year, Will." Clementine lay back in the hay and neighed at the neighing horse looming over her head. "Tell me five things about her you like. And me and your father, we'll consider."

Some color came back to the boy's cheeks while he fidgeted and fretted over what to say. "You guys don't know her like I do. Okay, listen." He smiled, giggled, which made his parents do the same. "Listen, okay. Listen. Number one, okay, she's beautiful."

"Beautiful?" Clementine repeated. "Well, I'll be."

"Two," Will waved his hands. "Two, okay, she's like the smartest girl in town."

"She don't exactly have much competition," the Gravedigger remarked.

"Three." Will had gone red in the face. If he weren't so tired, he would've had something smart to say to his doubters. "Three, she's… she's…"

"Uh oh," Clementine said, snickering. "Beautiful and smart? That's great and all—"

"Funny!" Will interrupted. "She's funny, you jerks."

The Gravedigger shook his head and made a face. "If you say so, Son."

"Forget it. Forget it." Will stood up, and on shaking legs dragged himself to the front of the barn. "You hate her. I get it. It's fine."

"Holy Child, you're dramatic." Clementine covered her eyes with her arm. "We're just kidding you, kid. You know we love Hazel."

The Gravedigger nodded and gave his son the thumbs-up. "She's a catch. But you're thirteen. You can't even clean up after yourself. Gary's got better breath than you. Take it slow. The world won't, so make sure you do."

"You and Mom got married at seventeen," Will said. His voice rose an octave. A sound outside startled him.

The Gravedigger lay beside his wife, cheek to her chest. "Yeah, but we didn't want you coming out a bastard. That's a heavy title to be holding—"

"What?"

"Goodnight, Will," the Gravedigger said, not facing him. "Thank you for all your help tonight. Help me finish up Brinton tomorrow?"

"Dad?"

"Hmm?"

The Gravedigger waited a moment. Very slowly, he sat up. Every part of him hurt. He wondered if that's what it was like for the dead; an absolute state of absolute agony.

"Hmm?" He turned to face the front of the barn, and then he felt a hurt unlike any he'd ever felt before.

Because there was Will, holding his stomach, desperately trying to stop all the blood from coming out of it.

CHAPTER V

The Gravedigger and Clementine caught Will before he hit the ground. Pulling up his shirt, they saw his stomach had been stabbed.

"Stop, stop," Will said, pushing his parents' hands away while they tried to apply pressure to the wound. Blood streamed down his pants and dribbled onto his feet.

Clementine grabbed her son's wrists and held them away. The Gravedigger ran into the annex and returned with a bandage coated in Null and disinfectant. He fastened it to Will's stomach, and pressed down hard. He took the boy's kicks as he lashed out in pain.

"It's okay, it's okay," Clementine said, brushing his hair and holding him back. "It's not deep, is it, Atticus?"

"It's not." The Gravedigger wasn't a squeamish man, but having his son's blood on his hands made him one. "Who did this? Will? Will?" The Gravedigger took his chin. "Will, you'll be okay. I swear it. But who did this?"

Clementine nodded at her husband. When his hand left Will's stomach, hers replaced it. With enough hate in his heart to fill the graveyard again, he grabbed a machete and scythe, and went like Death into the dark.

Where had Gary gone? For a brief and betraying moment, the Gravedigger thought the ghoul may be responsible for this. But he knew that wasn't true. His eyes darted back and forth between the church, the graveyard, and the house. Night was more than a period of time. It had a texture to it, as though all it touched were covered in grain. He didn't have much light, but the Gravedigger knew someone was out there. He could feel them moving through the night, breaking it up, leaving gaps in the grain from where they'd been.

Blythe and Bon, the soldiers from Eldrus; they were responsible for this. Mr. Haemo had been right, but somehow, the Gravedigger had overlooked them. It had to do with the vermillion veins, he was sure of it. Too many strange coincidences had come together too quickly to suggest otherwise.

The grass crunched beneath the Gravedigger's feet as he ran towards the house. His brain felt too large for his skull. Ruminations filled it on how he could kill the men. Because they were soldiers of Eldrus, they were granted some unspoken protections in the Heartland. But that didn't matter much to the Gravedigger. It's not as though anyone would be able to prove he'd done anything, anyway. When he'd finished with them, there'd be nothing left but what could be wrung out of their shredded clothes.

By the time his foot found the porch, he knew he'd made a mistake. He heard a rustling first. Then, when he turned around, he saw Blythe and Bon rush out of the graveyard, their drawn swords grinning in the moonlight. A third figure followed—Gary. But when the ghoul passed the last headstone, he hit the ground and fell into the fog there.

"Atticus!" Clementine screamed.

The Gravedigger tore through the dark. Another scream, a howl, broke across the dead land. But it hadn't been a woman's, and it hadn't been Will's.

The Gravedigger crashed into the barn, rounded the corner, and went, weapons readied, into it. Bon was bent over, holding onto the stump where his right hand should've been. He gagged as the fountain of arterial spray doused his lips.

"Atticus, don't move," Clementine said, still standing beside Will, the machete she gripped slick with the soldier's blood.

The Gravedigger said, "Where's—?"

Clementine shook her head as Blythe stood up and stepped out from behind her. A blood-soaked rope dangled past his legs. It was attached to the pointed blade, a kunai, he held.

Blythe bared his teeth as he pushed the tip into Clementine's side, stopping only when he broke the skin.

"Get in there and fix yourself up," Blythe said to Bon, nodding at the annex. "Gravedigger, drop your weapons. Gravedigger's wife, you ought to do the same."

Will moaned on the floor. The bandage on his belly was holding tight. The Gravedigger did as he was told, his wife the same. If not for their son, they may have done differently, but there he was, bleeding on the ground, reminding them of the value of restraint.

"This thing?" Blythe said, admiring the kunai. "Got it from some asshole named Ronny down the road. Never seen one before. He said it was from the Old World. Didn't think it would work, but…" Blythe focused on Will's stomach. "Cuts right through the air. Guess I have a better aim than I give myself credit for. Bon, you all right in there?"

Bon stumbled out of the annex, stump wrapped tight, mouth stained with whatever painkillers and mind-breakers he'd gotten into. "What… what are…?" He doubled over and fell on his ass. "This isn't supposed to hurt. He promised."

Blythe kicked the back of Clementine's legs. Crying out, she dropped to her knees.

"It'll hurt, but you'll get it back." Blythe sighed and took Clementine's hair in his hand. "It's Atticus, right? Atticus, listen, I know this isn't your fault. Get your boy, your wife, and let's go inside and talk this out. We could kill you. We could have killed you. I didn't cut young Will here and run for no reason. I'm sorry it happened like this. It's not your fault, but nevertheless, let's try to salvage this situation, okay?"

The Gravedigger had never been so powerless in his entire life. He felt as though he were standing beside himself, above himself—a ghost haunting his own useless body. Seeing his son lying there, whimpering, shivering, and his wife kneeling there, Blythe tugging on her hair, it made him so sick with rage he would gladly follow the men into death just to have the chance kill them again.

But truth be told, all that was pride and posturing. He would be as clay in their hands, to be molded and degraded, if only for no more than the promise no harm would come to his family.

With Blythe and Bon at the rear, the Gravedigger, Clementine, and Will were forced out of the barn and into the house. They were forced to sit around the kitchen table, dirty and disabled, like a trio of convicts having dinner with their jailers. Muddy elbow marks marred the tabletop from where Clementine had leant in, concerned. Will slouched in his chair, struggling to find the right position to keep from stretching the stomach hole.

The Gravedigger, however, remained unmoved. His back stiff, his mouth watering, he waited for orders to be given and chances to be taken.

"Here it is," Blythe said, sitting at the table, too. He swung the kunai by its rope. "Here's what's going to happen."

Bon groaned and clenched his bloody stump between his legs. With his other hand, his only hand, he gripped the pommel of his sword and eyed the Gravedigger's family. "Don't bother."

Blythe ignored his companion and said, "What you saw in Brinton is something new. All across the Heartland, the soil is turning sour. If nothing's done about it, the crops won't grow, the animals won't eat, and you sure as hell won't want to keep living on it. You'll suffer, and Eldrus will suffer, too. What you saw in Brinton is an attempt to avoid all that. It makes the soil fertile, fruitful."

Clementine cleared her throat, and took Will's hand. She lingered on the blood spot on his belly. "Then why're you hiding it in dead bodies?"

"Let's face it: if we came into the Heartland towns and started planting the stuff, you all would have turned it up by lunchtime."

Blythe released the kunai, and with a clink it hit the floor. He held onto the top of the rope as the rest of it spooled over the blade.

"We need the Heartland. We need it more than you all need us. It doesn't make much sense for us to poison it. Otherwise, we'd be poisoning ourselves, right?"

"You hid them in dead bodies," Clementine persisted. "You could have paid someone off, did it in the dead of night." She squeezed Will's hand, closed her eyes to cut off the tears welling there. "You almost killed my son, you fucking piece of shit."

The Gravedigger noticed a stirring within Bon, as though his insides were clockwork that had finally started to turn. The soldier gritted his gritty teeth. Pieces of Null were still in the gaps. He tightened his legs against his arm.

Blythe smiled at Will, in the same way one smiles for telling a bad joke. "You two," he started, looking at the Gravedigger and his wife, "have a reputation in these parts. Your boy will be all right. We just had to split you up. Blame it on that ghoul of yours. Didn't see that coming."

"Eat shit, you fucking cocksucker," Will mumbled.

The Gravedigger heard a buzzing in his ear. Was Mr. Haemo still watching? He offered silent prayers and promises of servitude, but it seemed the blood lord wasn't listening. Did he need his help, though? Bon was crippled, hardly conscious, and Blythe was so full of himself he put most cannibals to shame.

"Clementine," he started, tonguing his gums and blinking twice to signal his wife to attack. "What say you—?"

Bon slid back in his chair, cracking it against the wall. "Blythe, quit fucking with them."

Will gasped and got up, crying, "What the fuck, what the fuck, what the fuck?" as Bon showed off what he'd been doing between his legs.

On the arm that should've ended at the wrist, there was a hand, yet it wasn't made of flesh and blood but the red veins that had grown all over the barn. The soldier flexed the monstrous appendage, balling his hand into a fist.

"Don't move, Atticus," Blythe said, coming to his feet.

The Gravedigger turned to Blythe, confused. He jumped as something silver flashed before his eyes. Screams like waves broke over him. When he looked down, he saw why. A wet piece of rope dangled out of his chest and ran opposite him, across the table and into Blythe's hands.

The Gravedigger coughed. The kunai twisted like a key in his ribs and unlocked unknown agonies.

"Don't... don't... please... my family," the Gravedigger pleaded.

Bon pushed Will to the ground, and took Clementine by the neck.

Blythe tugged on the rope until it went taut and said, "You won't be around to know."

The Gravedigger looked at Clementine, then looked at Will. He said everything he could without words.

As Blythe jerked the rope, he flew forward, the kunai wrenching out of his chest. His head bashed against the table. A red tide washed over his face.

He tried to tell his wife and son that he was sorry, that he loved them, but there was too much blood in his mouth, so he died instead.

CHAPTER VI

Atticus woke in darkness to the feeling he was falling. He couldn't see his body, nor move it. After a while, he doubted he actually had one. The only true kindness of life had been that it always ended in death. And he was dead, wasn't he? He distinctively remembered dying. So what was he doing with these memories? And why was he doing anything at all?

After a short spell, the black appeared to thicken, harden, until it became brittle. Up ahead, pinpricks of light pushed through, causing the darkness they touched to curl back. Streaks of sinewy color shot past Atticus and attached themselves to the flaking hollow. Like the rope that pulled his life out, the pink, pulpy streaks went taught and snapped back. From where they'd been attached, large chunks were torn from the darkness, letting in just enough light to scorch the rest away.

Atticus gasped, screamed, and flailed. He had a body, and he was falling, falling through a tunnel of flesh. He flung his hands forward, reaching for the ribbed walls upon which cities of refuse had been built. He looked down at his naked body, at his chest and the gash gasping with his breaths, his feet and the Abyss below them. The gravity of Death pulled him toward it. Now that he knew there was an end, and a chance to avoid it, he had to fight back.

Where the flesh tunnel had scabbed over, Atticus dug his fingers in deep. He slid down the wall, until his hands and feet found purchase in a patch of carbuncles. The abscesses ballooned in his grip. With every second that passed, they threatened to rupture. Despite there being no air to breathe here, he took a deep breath and set his sights on the scabby shelf below.

I should let go, he told himself, moving off the spitting pustules and onto a sheet of teeth. He could feel oblivion tugging on his bones. It was tempting, the Abyss below at the bottom of the flesh tunnel. Though he'd never seen it before, he knew its meaning, its purpose. Nothingness had a kind of comfort to it he didn't expect to find anywhere else. But what if he wasn't dead? What if he gave up when Clementine and Will hadn't? He wouldn't know, but he would: it was the kind of thing that would always be, even if he were not.

Atticus climbed across the wall. Once he was over the shelf beneath it, he let go. Distance didn't mean much in these parts, because what should've been a fall ended up being a plummet. He crashed onto the shelf, which was wide enough for his body and then some, and lay there a moment. He expected pain, but got none. The only thing he felt was the Abyss, shifting him with its undertow.

Atticus came to his feet and didn't move further. A thin curtain billowed before him. Somehow it reminded him of a dress his wife might've worn. He took it in his hands, and with the utmost care, pushed it aside.

Behind the curtain, the tunnel turned inward, slanted downward, until it disappeared past the small outcrop that stood above him. From its stony lip to his cut-up feet, a blanket of Death's Dilemma stood in between them, their bone-white pedals tucked beneath their ice-blue stalks. He didn't want to trample them; it was bad luck to step on the flowers of Death's beloveds. But he heard a noise ahead, atop the outcrop, and had to see what it was.

Where does all this come from? Atticus wondered, half-turned, looking at the towers of trash across the flesh tunnel. He faced the high outcrop and went forward on the tips of his toes. Death's Dilemma was a species of flower whose soil was suffering, and whose individual lives were as long as the sorrow that spawned them. Each one, it was said, represented a love of Death's, who had dared to love and let It love them in return. The dilemma, then, was in the kiss, the confirmation, the moment of knowing and then not.

Atticus cleared the field and started up the outcrop. He stretched his limbs to their limits in search of holds. At the top, he dragged himself over, grinding his stomach and crotch against the edge. Scratches and scrapes broke like lightning across his skin. It was good he couldn't feel their thunderous pain.

He meant to stand, but what he saw up here required him to sit instead. Across the way, where the tunnel broadened, a grotesque village festered atop a dried-out lake. Despite its appearance, the village had a sensuality to its symmetry, as though put together by a poet from whatever he'd had on hand. Bound by rope and stuffed with waste, the sprawl of rubble laid out like a body on its side, rising and falling where shoulders and hips would've been. It reminded Atticus of the women from Gallows' tavern, and the way they looked on the beds before the lights went out.

"It's always good to see a new face," an old man said.

Atticus crouched low, furrowed his brow. "Who said that?" He scanned the village outskirts, and looked backward over the outcrop to the field of Death's Dilemmas. "Show yourself, you son of a bitch."

"I'm right here," the old man said. He waved. The old man was only a few feet away, leaning against the tunnel wall before it opened up to the lakebed. "You really ought to pay attention in these parts. One false step and that's it, you're done."

The old man came forward, his hand outstretched. Like Atticus, he was naked. And like Atticus, he bore the mark of his undoing. From jaw to clavicle, the old man's neck had been ripped open, as though something had dug its way out.

"Atticus," he said, shaking the old man's hand. Unlike him, this guy had no Corruption on his right arm.

"Herbert North." The old man smiled, let his gaze wander down Atticus' body. "Did it hurt?"

Atticus felt his chest, fingered the wound. "Not as much as everything else."

"Too true." Herbert clapped his hands together, and dropped them to his sides, where they swung excitedly. "You're a fighter. Wouldn't be here if you weren't."

Atticus laughed and nodded. "Aren't you perceptive? I suppose you know my next question?"

"Where is here?" Herbert's gaze ran along the cracks in the flesh sky over the village. "The Membrane. That's what we all seem to call it, even though no one told us to."

Atticus hesitated, then just said it: "Are we dead?"

"Yes," Herbert whispered. "It's good you asked. I wasted too much time working up the nerve to."

Atticus didn't feel much here in the Membrane, but that didn't stop Herbert's words from hitting him like a punch in his gut. His feet shuffled some to break up the Abyss' pull. He remembered everything. Now that he knew he was dead, he wasn't sure he wanted to remember anything anymore.

"What is this, then?" Atticus tried not to think of Clementine and Will, but did anyway. "These things, the village. Where did it all come from?"

"I took me a while to figure it out," Hebert said. He offered for Atticus to follow him to the lakebed, which he did. "There weren't too many around when I arrived. I don't know why, but when we die, we take what we see with us. A copy of it, at least."

"I was in my kitchen when it happened," Atticus admitted, stepping with the old man onto the shore. There, toys and tiny shoes poked out of the dirt.

"Then somewhere in here, there's your table and whatever else. Without those things, we wouldn't have been able to build this place."

"You got a name for it, Herb?"

The old man laughed. "Pulsa diNura."

"That got a meaning?" Atticus twitched as he heard waves breaking on the shore; phantom waves of a phantom lake.

"I'm sure it did to someone at some point, but I don't remember now. I've been down here awhile."

"How long?" Now, there was a breeze—constant and cool. It kicked up the water that wasn't around his feet.

Herbert shrugged. "There's no time here. You can't measure it. No point. Maybe it's been a few minutes or a couple hundred years." He paused, scratched at his neck. "I don't know how much longer I can do it." He laughed. "Then again, I don't know how long I've been saying that for. Pain in the ass, you know?"

Atticus wrinkled his face. "This place doesn't scare me. Actually, I don't feel much at all here. That normal?"

The ropes holding Pulsa diNura started to shake, sending out thick throbs of noise. The junkyard village rattled with each vibration, causing portions of it to fall apart.

Herbert smiled at Atticus. "We're dead. Not supposed to feel much, in general. There isn't much to torment us here other than ourselves."

The old man quickened his pace across the lakebed. Finally, they reached the rickety supports and platforms upon which Pulsa diNura had been built.

"No one will bother you. In fact, you may not see anyone else besides myself for a while."

"How many live here?" Atticus gasped. There was someone watching him through the breaks in the platform.

Herbert gave a rigid shrug. The neck wound wouldn't let him do much else. "Never did a headcount."

"Why call it the Membrane?"

Herbert went around the supports. He led Atticus to a ramp that ran up into the village.

"Because it acts like one. It runs between our world and the others, overlapping it. Keeps things out, and sometimes lets things in. Come on, Atticus, I know a place you can call yours."

"Hold it. I'm not staying, Herbert," he said, digging his feet into the ground, like Will used to when Clementine asked him to clean his room.

"You need a routine. Come here. Please." He went up the ramp and waited until Atticus joined him at the top. "See them?"

Atticus did, but he didn't want to. The old man was offering him something he had no intention of accepting. He saw them all right, the bodies in their beds of rope. Sleeping like the dead they were, in their homes made out of copied memories. A routine? No, either he was getting out, or he was going out. Nothing could change his mind on that.

"They lie like that, under all the ropes, so the Abyss won't take them while they sleep. It's an easy thing to forget about, Atticus."

Again, the sinewy streaks of color slithered across the fleshy sky, leaving gossamer patches in their wake. A soft light shone through the thinnest parts of the firmament. In it, Atticus saw another place, a desert, empty and vast. The white dunes there started to shiver, shedding the sands they were comprised of. It was as though something were waking within them.

"Where is…?" But before he could finish, the plane pulled back, the sky scaled over, and the scene was finished.

Herbert nodded at Atticus' feet.

Atticus had slid a few inches across the platform, toward the direction of the Abyss.

"Distractions are the danger here."

"If the Abyss gets me, that's it, right? I'm done?" Atticus echoed the old man's earlier warning.

"I mean, can't really confirm anything, but I think it's like a switch, like turning something off. For a long time, my business was the supernatural."

Herbert nodded at a nude woman with wild hair as she rolled out of bed and disappeared into the thick of the village.

"Seen a lot of things that were supposed to be dead come back and go on living. The Abyss is the end, but only until it isn't, you know? In it, you cease to be, until something pulls you back out."

"A ritual, a spell," Atticus guessed.

"Exactly. I assume the same works for us, heh, rebels. Unfortunately, I didn't leave too many friends behind. No one's going to bail me out of here." He sighed. "I lived a long time. Got so used to it... not quite ready to stop, not just yet, even if no one is coming to get me."

Pulsa diNura rocked with the phantom waves that still possessed the lakebed. If things were different, Atticus may have been moved by the Old World artifacts that surrounded him. But the cars, the computers, the crooked streetlights, and storefront signs didn't much muster more than an "eh."

So he looked past it all, to the furthest point in front of him, beyond the village, where the Membrane stretched on, and searched for something that suggested there was more to all this than what he'd already seen.

But there wasn't. Not really.

"Have you ever been to the other side of the Membrane? Or farther up?" Atticus mumbled. He hated that he kept asking questions about the place he desperately needed to leave.

"Occasionally." Herbert moved as though to put his hands in his pockets. "Death made me a kinder man, but a more cautious one, too. Also, a lot more talkative. It's the only pastime we have down here, other than building shit out of shit." He grinned. "You can't climb too high past here. Nothing to hold on to. I bet there's thousands in these walls, just waiting for the day they can finally claw their way out." Herbert stopped speaking, turned his head. "Did you... Do you hear that?"

Atticus got the impression the old man had finally lost it. "No?"

Heavy footsteps pounded against the platform, with the sound of something being dragged following close behind.

Herbert threw his arms around Atticus and pulled him into the nearest house. They found the darkest place to hide and hid, using a pile of wiring and mason jars as a barrier between them and the thing lurking outside. Bunched up there, the way he used to be when his dad went on a bender, it dawned on Atticus just how little it upset him to think of Clementine and Will. Recollections should've ripped him apart, but they hardly even registered.

Through the glass jars, Pulsa diNura looked warped, like something out of the sideshows that sometimes came through Gallows.

Sitting up, Atticus whispered, "I don't see anything."

Herbert's calm demeanor was gone. With the thing's arrival, he'd grown frantic and scared—feelings Atticus figured the Membrane wouldn't allow.

It gives just enough of yourself to keep you out of the Abyss, Atticus realized. *The kind of torture you don't realize is torture; the kind that almost seems charitable.*

"I haven't seen them enough to figure out what they are," Herbert said, lowering his voice. The footsteps grew louder. "They only seem to—"

A figure lumbered into view and dropped the body of the boy it'd been dragging. Dark blond hair spilled out from under the ragged hat it wore, obscuring the figure's face. A leather coat covered in stains and cracks ran down to its knees, stopping at its boots, which were all buckles and straps. Its right hand had disappeared somewhere up its sleeve, while its left held a shepherd's crook.

Atticus gritted his teeth and gripped his chest. It burned, like he'd swallowed a piece of the sun.

Herbert mouthed, "Are you okay?" and Atticus gave a weak nod when the heat died down.

The shepherd took a step, draping the ends of its coat over the boy. Thump, thump, thump. It banged the crook on the platform, but the boy didn't stir. Out of curiosity or impatience, it leaned forward and continued to crack the crook against the ground.

"What's it doing?" Atticus whispered.

Herbert shook his head. "I think, maybe, this is how we got here."

Atticus raised an eyebrow. "No, I don't think that's right. I remember—"

The shepherd reared up. Its right hand, wrapped tightly with pink bandages, lowered out of its sleeve. One by one, the strips of gauze unraveled. Together, they fell into a pile on the platform. The shepherd stretched its hand, picked at the green paint splattered across its nails.

"Oh, fuck!" Atticus fell back and gripped his chest. Between his ribs, metal ground, scraped his bones. He put his arm to his mouth and screamed into it.

"Atticus. Atticus, stop."

Herbert took him in his arms and held him there, deafening his cries and putting an end to his rocking.

"We can't interrupt it." He patted Atticus' back as he came to again. "You okay? You're okay. Let's go, let's get out of here."

"I'm sorry, Herb. I'm not sure what's happening to me." He straightened up and then, looking over the pile of wire and glass, said, "What the fuck?"

The pink bandages shot into the air. With a will of their own, they twisted and extended, until they made themselves into a rudimentary human form. The shepherd dug into the jacket's linings and came back with a vial of orange liquid. It threw the vial hard at the ground.

When it shattered, a cloud of sparking smoke engulfed the bandages. Scratches like suicide attempts rose out of the gauze, forming runes.

Atticus fell forward, crashing into the wires and glass, giving them away for good.

"I'm sorry," he started. "Oh fuck!"

The Echoes of his death pummeled him to the platform. He felt the kunai in his chest, the hairs of its rope sticking in his skin.

"Make it stop!"

The shepherd stared at Atticus with indifference and went back to the bandages. With both hands, it clutched the crook and held it over its head. The sparking strips shuddered, retracted, and exploded, full and whole, into the form of an ephemeral corpse. Colored like bloody milk, the soul, the boy's spitting image, immediately went to the ground, crawled atop the child, and sank into him.

When the boy's eyes opened, the shepherd suddenly took interest in Atticus' presence. Like a dog protecting its property, it went down on its haunches and bayed behind its blond hair.

"Scoot back. It'll tear you apart," he heard Herbert say. "The things it can do to you… On your ass, god damn it!"

Out of nowhere, a sinewy streak of light bore down on Atticus and broke through the top of his skull. Scolding tendrils of suffering spread like roots through his body.

Herbert North was saying something now, but there were too many voices in his head for him to hear.

Atticus' throat closed shut as the shepherd's crook looped around his neck. But before it could jerk him back, the sinewy streak threw him into the air, toward the clouds like tumors in the flesh sky.

The voices multiplied in his head as he hurtled toward the vortex of skin. They were hurried, desperate. He recognized Gary's and Mr. Haemo's among them. But the one that stood out the most was the one that wasn't in his head at all.

Clementine's.

Fighting against the streak, which he moved along like a bead upon a chain, Atticus turned his gaze toward the ground. He had to squint to see her, but in the shrinking outskirts of Pulsa diNura, Clementine stood. She was naked, and she was alone, and once again, no matter how hard he fought, no matter how hard he screamed, he was leaving her behind.

CHAPTER VII

It happened fast, but not fast enough for Atticus to forget what he'd seen. There was a place beyond the flesh sky, where the Membrane ended in a colossal knot of open arteries. The streak shoved him into one near the heart of the nest. The blood there did the rest.

Inside the artery, he was surprised to find its sides covered in pale green tiles. Back in Gallows, some fifteen odd years ago, there had been an Old World swimming pool colored and checkered the same; it had sat in the marsh Mr. Haemo now inhabited. Until he moved in, all the kids had flocked there. The pool had been a good place to catch a date or a bad case of diarrhea—which one you ended up with just depended on how much you opened your mouth.

"Who's that?" Atticus remembered asking his friend one lonely day. In the deep end, a girl sat at the bottom of the pool, her hair like a halo of fire around her head.

The blood was pushing him harder now. The farther he went up the artery, the more tiled it became. He tried to grab onto the walls, like he had in the Membrane, but he was moving too fast. There was no stopping the momentum.

"Nmw'gla fhtha xu… ek'mwn uh'fh'xu ma'ta."

The words rippled through the blood, each syllable a blinding smack across his brow. Going upward, he went backward through time.

He saw Will in waves, birth to last night's late-night beating. He felt the weight of his boy, and then on his neck, like a sigh from spring, Will's warm breath. He traveled back some years, to when

Will had come home crying. He hugged Atticus, and told him how much he hated the first girl he had ever loved.

"Nmw'gla fhta xu … ek'mwn uh'fh'xu ma'ta."

Now, Atticus' father rose out of the blood, eyes shining something fierce. He got the closest he'd ever been to his father. In the man's reptilian eyes, he saw his mother. Her knuckles were chewed up from all the teeth they'd cracked, because she gave what she got twice over. The fear between them was palpable, a force of its own. It pulled them together, and kept them apart.

"Nmw'gla fhta xu … ek'mwn uh'fh'xu ma'ta."

Atticus bucked in the blood, tried to get himself caught in a bend. One of the sanitarium-green tiles was missing. Through the small square, he saw Clementine standing in the dark, her hair the only light there.

No, no, no! I can't do this anymore.

Clementine's fashion changed with her furor. Her scowl evened out into a smile, while her dirty pants loosened into a skirt. Her stomach swelled and flattened and swelled again.

Please, stop, he begged, but no one was listening. *I can't see that again.*

But again he saw it, Ronny down the road coming up it, mighty and triumphant.

"Nmw'gla fhta xu… ek'mwn uh'fh'xu ma'ta."

Ahead, oily shadows danced on rims of light. Atticus pulled back and made for them. Whether it brought him to the Membrane or the Abyss, he didn't care. Either he had his wife and son, or nothing at all. The torture he deserved, yes, but fuck it, he didn't want it, couldn't handle it.

"Nmw'gla fhta xu… ek'mwn uh'fh'xu ma'ta."

Atticus gasped and touched the darkness. Fresh air, wet grass; the sour smell of rot. He shot out of the artery and collapsed. Pale and ephemeral, every part of him in pain, he looked like the soul that had settled into the boy moments ago.

"Nmw'gla fhta—"

It was after the chanting stopped that Atticus realized where he'd emerged. The sky curved over him, the stars like white eyes looking down from black heavens. Beneath him, the ground thrummed, spitting out red smoke and shrouding him in it. He could taste the air, that swirling mire of iron and ichor, and listening closely, heard whispers.

I can't be here. This can't be right. He sat up, cried out. At the edge of the artery, he found his nude corpse lying in the grass. Like the cruelest truth, the sight tore through his mind and left it naked and raw. With its rigid limbs and sickly sheen, Atticus' body looked like an insect that'd crawled out to die in the light. All that he was and all that he'd done, that body didn't hold. To know him would be to know those he knew, and they were most likely no better off.

"Atticus?"

The question was a confirmation, the voice, a trigger. A ravenous urge overcame him, but this ghostly form of his had no interest in earthly pleasures. He wanted life, wanted to swallow it whole. He needed to push it down his gullet, feel it thrashing in his stomach. Atticus looked at his corpse and, like an animal turned on its master, went for it.

He scurried across the grass and mounted his body. He had to be in it, inside it. He had to have what it did and he didn't. The carcass pulled him closer, its skin like hooks piercing his translucent tissue. He relented, the envy too heavy to hold, and sank into his rotten shell.

"Hey... hey, is he okay?"

Atticus shot up, digging his heels into the dirt, his fingers into his palms. As the last of his soul went back where it belonged, strands of excruciating pain threaded throughout his body. Like needlework, they pierced his bones and his organs, creating a patchwork of anguish. The sensation was suffocating, but it was real; by it, kicking and screaming, he was made new.

"W-where... where are they... t-they..." Atticus addressed Gary, who was standing in the grainy dark. "What... what happened? Why am I... Why are we at Haemo's?"

The ghoul gestured for him to calm down. With a bum leg and bad cough, he closed the gap and helped Atticus up.

Gary's rugged flesh scraped against Atticus' hand, but he didn't mind much. What gave him pause, however, was the way he wavered, the way the dead thing looked deader. He remembered Gary falling that night. That night Clementine and Will...

"Where are they?" In his lust for life, he'd forgotten their deaths. The memories boiled in his brain and spilt out as tears down his face. "Gary, tell me!"

"They're gone, Atticus. Killed," he whispered, mouth quivering.

He cupped Atticus' head with his half-bone hand and held him. "I tried to stop those sons of bitches, I did. I promise you."

"I know you did," Atticus whimpered.

"They had a weapon. Caught me catching them. A Death weapon. One nick was enough to send me down. I'm so sorry. Look at me." The ghoul wrapped both hands around Atticus' head and managed a glint of sympathy in his glassy eyes. "We brought you back. We can make this better." He paused, trembled. Ants fell out of his mouth. "We can make this better."

"Brought me back?" Again, a surge of images overtook him. The kitchen, his dying; the Membrane, his afterlife; the artery, his rebirth. "What did you do to me?"

"He didn't do much but provide some of the ingredients," Mr. Haemo buzzed behind Atticus, his jagged shadow growing across the grass. "Give credit where credit is due. You don't know how much work I've put into you."

Atticus turned, his nudity once again giving him some qualms in the presence of the blood lord. Behind him, the mosquito stood, wrapped tightly in his cloak of flesh, the hood of it resting atop his proboscis. In one claw, he gripped a ball of Atticus' bloodstained clothes. In the other, a rolled portrait of him and his family.

"You were dead. This one here begged me to bring you back."

Red smoke coughed out of the well. A fine mist of blood washed across the isle, speckling what it touched.

Atticus glanced down at himself. He looked like a harlequin with all that splotchy, stiff skin of his. "How did—?"

"Blood, of course," the mosquito continued, voice shrill with glee, "and bits of you, for the delving."

Atticus shook his head. He didn't know what he was; dead, un-dead, on borrowed time. But he did know this: he'd seen Clementine in the Membrane.

"We have to get her back! I saw her there, before you pulled me out. Gary," he said, turning to appeal to his friend, "we're going to, right?"

"Atticus," Gary said, cringing as something inside him tore through his composure, "we already tried."

"What?"

Atticus went back and forth between the ghoul and the mosquito. He could feel Mr. Haemo's children sucking on him, to replenish lost stock.

"What the fuck are you saying? You choose them over me, every time! That's what we say, what you promised, god damn it! You promised me."

Mr. Haemo plodded forward, hints of his wings emerging from his cloak. "Don't give him a hard time, you ungrateful prick." He shoved the ball of clothes and portrait into Atticus' chest. "You need something dead to get in, and blood to track the soul. Memories to coax it out, and a body to hold it. And words, hungry ones, to keep it all together."

"It took us days to bring you out of the Membrane," Gary said. "And we had more than enough blood to do it. Mr. Haemo's children have been feeding on you for decades. And the well is the other half of the old swimming pool... for the memory."

Atticus raised an eyebrow, his once-dead muscles struggling with the gesture. "What went—?"

"A soul without a body is a cruel thing. For you, it was only a moment, but you remember the feeling, don't you?" Mr. Haemo sounded as though he were enjoying himself.

Atticus understood what he meant. In that brief, bodiless moment, he had wanted nothing more than to consume life, to hoard and covet it, if only so that nothing else could have it.

"Give him a moment," Gary pleaded with the monstrosity. "Let him catch his breath."

Mr. Haemo threw back his hood and trained his bulbous eyes on the ghoul. Mosquitoes phased in and out around them. A low rumbling bounded across the island.

"What went wrong?" Atticus started to unravel the portrait and then stopped. Dead, undead, or on borrowed time, he still felt a dreadful loss.

"You and yours are a stubborn kind."

Mr. Haemo shouldered past Atticus and dipped his hands in the well. Blood pooled in his yellow-streaked palms. He carried the offering to the ghoul, who lapped it up.

"I've always liked your family. You treat us creeps with kindness. And I didn't much care for what the soldiers did to you all. Gary said you would never accept the Abyss. After we did some delving, we saw that to be true."

"Clementine was in the Membrane."

Gary's eyes rolled back in his head. It made Atticus' stomach turn. *What the hell is wrong with him?* He said, "Is Will down there, too?"

Mr. Haemo nodded. "Stubborn sons of bitches. Always putting up a fight, even when it's Death you're fighting. We tried for—" he and the ghoul exchanged nods, "—awhile to bring them back, but the ritual wouldn't take. We could get their souls right now, but that wouldn't do. You wouldn't want them like that."

Eyes readjusting in his mossy skull, Gary said, "Wouldn't do."

Atticus cocked his head. "You have the blood… the memories… everything. What else do you need? I'll get it, just tell me." Atticus stopped speaking, finally catching the mosquito's meaning. "Their bodies." He spun in place. "Where are their bodies? They're not here?"

"No, they're not," Gary said, finally coming to. "Because the soldiers took them."

CHAPTER VIII

Atticus tore westward through marshland, Gary behind him and Mr. Haemo above. They warned him as he left the isle that something had gone wrong with the summoning, that the wrong words had been spoken, that too much ghoul flesh had been used. They told him to take it slow, because if he went any faster, he'd be right back where he started.

So he told them to get the fuck out of his way and headed home.

He didn't recognize the farmhouse when he found it. Trauma will do that to a thing. He started up the porch, stopped to catch his breath. Not that he needed to. Was the haunt still here? In its late-night tinkering, had it seen something that could be of some use?

By the time his friend and enemy had caught up with him, he pushed through the front door and was heading toward the kitchen.

They'd made an effort—that much was true. Pieces of the floor, wall, and table had been torn up, ripped away, to get at the blood that stained them. Atticus grabbed the chair he'd sat in when it happened, and took a seat. He put his elbows to the table, hands to his temples, and lost it.

"We have to get them back," he said, spit and tears running off his face. Atticus pushed his hands through his hair. He dug into his scalp and thought about ripping it out. He needed something to fix, something to destroy.

"Bedlam."

No one was listening, but he kept talking all the same.

"Bedlam," he repeated, plunging the word like a shovel into his mind. He dug at it until he recollected what'd been buried, and who'd been buried long before it.

"James."

Atticus let go and looked up. He had said the soldiers were going to Bedlam, to deliver another corpse, and that he was going to the town, too. It'd been a week, but Blythe and Bon had left the boy in a bad way. He might still be there, at the tavern, collecting coin and pity. He'd used Atticus for years; it seemed only fitting Atticus should finally do the same in return.

Poe stood on the tavern's porch, puffing out a cloud of smoke from his pipe. His face glistened in the torchlight as his thick fingers tucked in the places where his fat had pushed out his shirt. One of his girls screamed upstairs, making him jump. After all these years, it still got to him. The gesture wasn't much, but it was better than nothing, even if in the end that's exactly what it amounted to.

Atticus crept in the dark toward the tavern. "James here?"

"Holy Child in hell!" Poe coughed and beat his chest. "Who's that? Atticus?" He leaned forward, squinted, his small, rodent eyes disappearing in the folds of his face. "Come out here. Where you been?"

Atticus was careful not to show too much of himself. He hadn't had a good look at his body since he'd climbed back in it. The clothes he'd thrown on when he left the house were in a terrible condition, too. But at this point, what did it matter?

"What's happening?" Poe chewed on the pipe stem. "Why you acting all timid?"

Atticus took that as a taunt, so he came out of the shadows and stopped at the front steps. The pipe dropped out of Poe's mouth and fell between the crooked planks. He put his hands out, like he wanted to help.

"James?" Atticus insisted.

Over Poe's shoulder, through the tavern's open doorway, two drunk women danced near the bar. They were kissing each other's foreheads, and singing a tuneless song.

"He – he's inside, same place as before. He's fixing to leave in the morning." Poe cringed. "Elijah went ahead without him. Didn't want to wait around until James was right enough to ride again." He puffed out his cheeks and exhaled. "Who did this to you? Do you know even what…? Come here, come here."

Atticus let Poe lead him inside, to the barkeep's retreat beneath the stairs. He could count on one hand the number of occasions he'd gone in the room. The first time, he'd been twelve, when he had no place to go, because no one wanted him. The second and third had been because of a bloody blur of bad jobs. The fourth time he found his way in was by way of Will's birth and its celebration. And the fifth had come shortly thereafter, when Atticus had to beat his retirement out of the fat man's grip.

"You hungry? Thirsty?" Poe ducked under the stairs and pushed open his door. "I could have something fixed up for you."

Atticus shook his head. A fog of incense rolled lazily out of the room, too long left inside to know what to do with itself. It smelled hot, felt hot; the aroma it carried was of sweet perfume and chopped wood. His senses were intact, but hunger and thirst were conveniently absent. He shook his head again and wandered in, over to the mirror Poe now stood beside.

Anyone with a pair of eyes and half a brain could see Atticus had died. His skin was pale, splotchy—shaded darkly where bone bulged against it. The hair on his head went wildly in different directions, held in place by whatever foul stuff greased it. His body as a whole, not to mention the actual hole in his chest, appeared both stiff and stretched, as though Death hadn't been able to decide what to do with him. In that revealing moment, he felt embarrassed, ashamed, not fit to be amongst the living or in the flesh that had once served him so well.

While he was dazed, Poe fingered the collar of Atticus' shirt and pulled it down. "Who did this to you?"

The wound was a hard gem of gore buried in his chest. When did Poe discover kindness? Atticus searched the room, its Old World artifacts—the microwave, the air conditioner, and sculptures made of out of circuitry. Perhaps he'd found it with these dead things that outlived those like him.

"You don't know?" Atticus said at last.

"Hell, you made it very clear to us simple folk of Gallows you want your privacy. When's the last time you had visitors?"

Atticus gritted his teeth.

"My point exactly."

"The soldiers from Eldrus came." He paused, eviscerated the tale until it sounded generic. "We were attacked. They took Clementine and Will to Bedlam. I'm going to get them back."

Poe's lip quivered. He took a seat at his desk and ran his fingers over a keyboard. The sensation was one he often used to calm his nerves. "But why would they do that?"

More corpses to deliver, Atticus remembered. *More corpses to bury, to spread the growth.* He glanced at Poe, snarling as he thought: *they put those veins inside them.* If he took too long, would their bodies be ravaged beyond resurrection?

Atticus hurried out of the room, up the stairs, and burst through James' door. The twenty-two-year-old prostitute was in bed, blanket up to his chin, a small candle burning on the table beside him. Even now, three years later, he couldn't fall asleep without some light to keep him safe.

"Get up," Atticus said.

Immediately, James woke and screamed. In sweaty convulsions, he kicked his way across the bed until he hit the wall. He reached under his pillow and pulled out a knife.

"It's me," Atticus continued.

"Atticus?" James kept the knife pointed at him, not entirely convinced. He called him forward with his free hand. "What's wrong with your face?"

"Clementine and Will are dead. Those soldiers you fucked killed them and took them. I need their bodies back. And I need you to help me draw them out."

"Clementine and Will are—"

Atticus found James' clothes in a pile on floor and threw them at the boy. "I need your help, not your sympathy."

James caught the clothes and immediately started getting dressed. "Okay," he said, his tears soaking his shirt as he pulled it over his head. "Okay, okay. Okay, okay, okay," he repeated, the words becoming more and more incoherent, until he was shaking too hard to button his pants. "God, oh god, Atticus, I'm sorry. I'm so, so sorry."

"There's an Eldrus outpost there." Atticus kept his composure, because if he didn't, he'd lose it for good.

"There is, that's where they're going. That's what they said. Will you tell me what happened?" He stared at Atticus, who stared back, grimly. "If they know you're coming, then they'll know why. They'll lie to you. I can figure out what they've done with... with... I can call in favors. Hex, maybe. When do you want to leave?"

Two hours later, Atticus and James were back at the farmhouse, saddling the horses and stocking weapons and supplies. Dawn glowed at the corners of the sky, finally letting him know just how long he'd been awake. Hunger and thirst had yet to find him. Fatigue, if it was there, had long since been suppressed by the focus he needed to see this all through.

Something had gone wrong with the ritual, Gary and Mr. Haemo had warned. If these were the symptoms of their mistake, he was glad for them.

He didn't need James, he thought, as he watched the boy mount the horse. Not to track down Blythe and Bon. His reasons for dragging him across the countryside were selfish, ones he wouldn't admit come hell or high water. No, bringing James was an apology, an unspoken acceptance and forgiveness. Atticus needed someone at his side for this, someone who knew Clementine and Will and would keep him going when late-night doubt set in. Above all else, and god damn if it didn't hurt to admit it, he needed someone to love.

"What's this?"

Atticus snapped out of it. He looked at the graveyard. Gary was shambling between the plots, his body covered completely in ratty clothes and scarves—the ghoul's idea of a disguise.

"Where y'all going?" he asked in a mocking drawl.

James stopped what he was doing and stared down the creature. His face twitched out a smile. Bedlam was home for him, but his true homecoming was now, as the two dead things welcomed him back into their stunted lives. He went to Gary, threw his arms around him, and let his tears soften up the ghoul's dried flesh.

"Does he know?" Gary asked, pulling away from James.

"Knows enough," Atticus said. "You better get back to the chapel. Sun will be up soon."

"I'm coming with." The ghoul hurried back to the graveyard and pulled a cowboy hat out from behind a grave. "I'll sleep until we get to where we're going." He lowered it on his head and kicked up some dirt. "No one will know."

There was a third horse in the barn, a small brown Quarter he'd found in the wilds a year back. The thought of leaving it behind hadn't sat well with him, anyway.

"If someone finds out what you are…" Atticus said.

"I'm on borrowed time, buddy." Gary passed between Atticus and James to reach his mount in the stalls. "If you leave, I'm done for. Simple as that. I need you. And I want to help you. No one and nothing has ever been as good to me as you and yours were to our kind."

"Fair enough," Atticus rumbled, putting his foot in the stirrups and mounting the horse. "Don't suppose Mr. Haemo would care to join our motley crew?"

"You can't be serious," James said, doe-eyed. "That thing's still here?"

"No, he's a bit of a homebody," Gary said, leading his horse out of the barn.

"We ought to pay him a visit," Atticus said, watching horror spread across James' face, "and see if he can't track Clementine's and Will's… b-bodies. Find out where they're at exactly in Bedlam."

Gary shook his head and got on the horse bareback. "Tried. Can't track something if there's no blood left in it."

"They bled them dry?"

Gary closed his eyes, shook his head, and said, "Yeah."

Atticus closed his hands around the reins and held them tightly. The hate and hurt he felt was unbearable. There was no doubt in his mind he would've long since killed himself if he didn't already know what awaited him in the Membrane. Not the Abyss or the Membrane, but Clementine, and her bitter disappointment.

"Let's go," he said, kicking the horse into a gallop. He looked back, at the farmhouse, at the land, and hoped never to see them again, not until he saw them again.

CHAPTER IX

The massive snake and its slithering brood had come out of nowhere. In one scaled second, it sprung from the woods and struck Atticus' horse in the neck. The beast whined as the serpent tore a chunk out of its throat. As it fell sideways, legs kicking wildly at its attacker, Atticus jumped from the saddle and hit the road hard.

"Get away from him," James screamed, his own horse on its hind legs, terrified. He drew his beat-up sword and held it limply.

Atticus reached into his pack and pulled out his machete. He scurried backward, heels leaving grooves in the dirt. The snake's brood shimmered like silk as they slid in unison towards him. He hacked at the air to hold them at bay, but they kept coming all the same.

"No, James," he heard Gary shout. "Stay the hell back."

The Hissing Monarch hurried ahead of her children and threw the bulk of her weight over the horse. The beast cried out, slammed its hooves into her side. Little by little, the venom in its neck sapped its strength.

The Hissing Monarch took the hits excitedly, its forked tongue tasting the beast's fear-drenched coat. Slowly, carefully, patiently, it wrapped itself around the animal. When all that could be seen of the horse was its head, it squeezed.

The horse's scream was cut short as the broken bones inside it stabbed every which way into its organs. Its wide and wet eyes blew out of its skull and into the Hissing Monarch's waiting mouth. She gulped them down too quickly to taste them, and turned her sights on Atticus.

"Get back! Get back, god damn you," Atticus hollered.

His heart pounded in his chest. He hacked head after head off the smaller snakes. But the brood continued unabated, breaking like a wave around him and then reforming behind, so that he was surrounded. He looked at them, the Monarch's gawping children, and hoped that his scraps would give them the shits.

"Xu'chil utuk ah g'hu'uhl," Gary belted, as he dropped from his horse and hurried, bow drawn, arrow readied, to his friend. Though it was no spell, the words drew the Monarch's ire.

Atticus threw caution to the wind and jumped to his feet. With the Hissing Monarch distracted, he turned and ran through the field of bared teeth. The brood sprung through the air, clamped down on his ankles, calves, and thighs. He felt their fangs in his flesh, their venom in his blood, surging throughout his body.

He only got a few feet before his legs were too heavy to lift. He stopped, turned around, stumbled as he lost circulation in his legs completely. Back where he'd started, the Hissing Monarch thrashed, one of Gary's arrows jutting out of her head.

Atticus glanced at James, who sat upon his horse, just as stunned as his animal. He'd made a mistake bringing the living to do the work of the damned.

"Atticus!" Gary screamed.

He didn't have any time to react. The Hissing Monarch swung herself into him, flattening him against the ground. Fang after fang after fang ripped out his flesh. The brood that had surrounded him retreated, to give their mother space, and to give Gary chase.

"Bring me back," Atticus wheezed, as the massive snake coiled around him.

He was speaking to Gary, who'd fled. But if the Monarch was willing, that'd work, too. One day into his mission, three hours from Bedlam, and this was how it was to end.

"Bring me back," he cried. The Monarch's crucifix-shaped pupils widened. Her weight now became the weight of his failure.

The Hissing Monarch opened her mouth, revealing two fangs as long Atticus' forearms. Her gigantic head moved closer, blocking out his field of vision. He heard more words, more commotion. But what could they do? The brood had already killed him. The Monarch was just coming to get the credit.

The snake flicked her black tongue, reared back. Pop. Snap. A geyser of blood blew out of her throat, onto his face. The Hissing Monarch unraveled from him.

He wiped the blood from his eyes, the Monarch's own flashing all the shades of hate. She twisted around. Having given up glory, Atticus saw what had wounded her.

Three female Night Terrors stood behind the Monarch. An unmasked one was closest to the snake, her jet black spear goring the Monarch's side. The other two, the Bison and the Horse, were further down the creature, their swords pinning parts of her body to the road.

"Atticus, get up," James shouted, turning his horse and galloping towards him.

The Unmasked shoved the spear in deeper, grinding it through muscle. The Monarch whipped around. Her tail tore from the swords, and split down the middle.

James came around behind Atticus. He reached for his hand. His legs were swelling in his pants, pushing against the fabric, ready to explode.

The Hissing Monarch lunged forward, venom like spit spewing from her mouth. The Unmasked ripped the spear out, bore down on the beast again. The Monarch went sideways, jerked back, and clamped her mouth over the Unmasked's head.

"Drag me, god damn it," Atticus said through his teeth.

James, halfway out of his saddle, held his hand tight and towed him off the road. Gary was circling the perimeter, the words he kept repeating distracting the snapping horde.

The Horse and the Bison rushed to their companion. The Monarch choked down the Unmasked, her last line of defense against their steel. The Night Terrors raised their swords over the snake. The Unmasked's shoulder, arms, and hips disappeared down the Monarch's gullet.

"She's dead," Atticus heard the Horse say. If she wasn't, to kill the Monarch would be to kill their companion; he'd never known the Night Terrors to show sympathy.

But that's just what they did. One after the other, they stabbed and chopped through the Monarch, through their friend, until the snake's head was separated from her body, and the Unmasked's body from her head.

"We weren't here," the Horse said, her grotesque face, half-flesh, half-skull, beaming down on Atticus.

"Watch out," Gary shouted, the brood having changed their course back toward the Monarch.

The Bison grabbed the snake's still sputtering head, lifted it up, and shook it until the Unmasked's decapitated corpse slid free. The Horse rooted through the Hissing Matron's gory remains and pulled out her companion's head. Holding it by its long hair, the Horse knelt down and scooped the Unmasked up into her arms.

"You should be dead by now," the Bison said to Atticus. The Night Terror turned away and walked with the Horse into the woods, leaving a thick trail of blood in their wake.

Fixing his disguise, Gary said, "Up, up." He ran over to Atticus, slung his friend's arm around his shoulder, and lifted him.

Beside them, the brood slithered over Atticus' dead horse. They shoved themselves inside the Matron's wound. Her body swelled and bulged, while her children consumed her from the inside out.

"Something went wrong with the ritual," Atticus whispered into Gary's ear. The ghoul and James worked together to lift him onto James' horse. "I can't be alive like this." He threw up on himself and the world went dark.

"We keep going," he heard Gary say, his voice faint, distant. "I'll explain the mistake…"

CHAPTER X

Atticus woke up, naked and alone, on a bed that may as well have been a boulder. Lacerations ran up and down his legs from where he'd been bled. From his stomach to his toes, the skin was tender, inflamed—one unending landscape of raised, red flesh. It bubbled when he moved, so he stayed put instead, and wondered where he was.

The room was small, windowless. It smelled like feet and dust. *Bedlam?* He could hear people outside, a horse trotting down the street. Across the room, his bag, and James' and Gary's sat. *I hope they didn't make a big fuss dragging me in.* He tried to move his leg, but the dried blood kept it in place. *Otherwise, Blythe and Bon will know we're here.* He thought of water, and though the thought appealed to him, the need wasn't there.

"They were hunting it," Atticus mumbled, counting the bite marks on his body. "I shouldn't be here." He touched two large holes. The skin around them felt soft, sticky, like the inside of an old apple. "One of those little snakes should've been enough to put me down."

The door to the room opened. Atticus shot up. His hands pawed around for weapons, but there were none. "Who's that?" he snarled.

"Shush," Gary said, coming in crouched, like he had a cramp. "How are you feeling?"

"I'm not." Atticus moved his legs. They shed dried blood in their bending. "Where are we? Bedlam?"

"Rode in at sunset. It's night now. Looks like they're gearing up for their regular bacchanal. James is out doing reconnaissance. Got a contact from way back." Gary shut the door, went to the bed, and started prodding Atticus' legs. "You should be dead."

"Technically, I am."

"No, you're not. Or you shouldn't be." The ghoul stuck his finger into one of the deeper holes, but Atticus kept quiet. "When we brought you back, we brought you back alive. That's the way it works."

"What went wrong?"

"Mr. Haemo had a hard time tracking you down in the Membrane. We used more ingredients than necessary. He added a few of his own. We were, well, I was desperate."

"I haven't had a need to eat or drink or sleep. Only reason I passed out was because of all that venom in me."

Gary pulled out his finger and tasted it.

Atticus cringed but held his tongue.

"Everyone comes back different," Gary went on. "They act like something's gone or something's suddenly so damn important. Apathetic, you know, or obsessive. They come back with a goal, usually."

"I'm feeling a bit of both." Atticus swung his legs over the side of the bed and contemplated standing.

"You should be dead," Gary said, moving to stop Atticus, but stopping himself instead.

"And if I am?" His legs went rubbery and wide, yet they held. He sighed and took a step forward. A fire erupted across his muscles. Sheer stubbornness saw the flames doused. Again, he said, "And if I am?"

Gary rubbed at his side, hand disappearing entirely into his ribcage. "Even the dead can die, Atticus."

He took another step forward, towards the bags. "And if I can't?"

"You don't want that."

Atticus glanced down at the hole in his chest and wondered, if he looked hard enough, could he see his soul on the other side? Was it comfortable there in this reclaimed husk? Atticus rubbed his Corrupted arm. Death had made him thoughtful, philosophical. He hated it.

"You're something in between." Gary sounded despaired, as though he blamed himself for his friend's condition. "I'd go through the motions, though. Eating, drinking, sleeping. You might be dying and not even know it. Or die out of nowhere."

"Whatever it is, it'll do." Atticus' face hardened, and he let hate have its way with him. "You keep bringing me back until it's done. Clementine and Will won't go to the Abyss. They're stubborn, like me. They got to die right, Gary."

"We could send you back. You all could walk off the edge together. Be done with it."

Atticus didn't much care for his rationality. He wanted revenge, and he wanted certainty. But most of all, he wanted purpose.

"We weren't ready to die. I'll not give in if there's means to do otherwise. We slaughter the soldiers, and then we save my family. Where's James? We're finishing this tonight. I'll not have this drawn out."

Gary went ahead and started rummaging through their bags for weapons. "Your horse died."

Atticus furrowed his brow. "I know," he said. "What're you getting at?"

"Remember its name?"

Atticus stared at the ghoul for a moment. He didn't.

Bedlam was divided in two by the river that ran through it, and because of this division, those who lived there deemed it necessary to divide themselves as well. To the east of the river went the poor, and to the west of the river the less poor. When the people of Bedlam weren't working in the woods or fishing in the streams—both of which were threatening to take the place over in the next ten years— they had turf wars. In the end, neither side really wanted to claim the other, but down home rivalry was as good a way as any to pass the time in a place where the hours moved like years.

Atticus and Gary leaned against the last standing Old World house in town. Above them, the moon hung large in the sky, leaving the dark silvery and gray. Midnight neared and still Bedlam bustled, its narrow streets filled with obnoxious youth and the generation that loathed them. The town records laid claim to three hundred and forty residents, but by the swell on the riverbank alone, it seemed double that.

The revelry wouldn't last forever, Atticus knew. But until that sobering moment came, when all coin was wasted and all debts were renewed, Bedlam's bedlam would provide the perfect cover for his kill.

"There's James," Atticus said, pointing at the figure crossing the bridge. The house howled behind him, still feeling the phantom pain from the shotgun blasts that had riddled its second floor ages ago.

Gary tightened the scarves across his face. "You did a shit job preparing for this."

"If you want your bow, go get your bow," Atticus said, who'd made him leave it behind to appear less obvious.

"I could be perched up on these rooftops, raining arrows on the wicked."

"Our undead lord and savior."

Gary smirked. "Don't talk about the Hydra of Penance like that. Hey, did he always walk with a limp?"

"James?" Atticus squinted to have a better look at their spy, who was halfway across the bridge.

"Something..." Gary sniffed the air, turned in place to face the house, and then came back round. "What's he looking at? Where's that sword he's so proud of?"

Again, Atticus squinted. It was true, the boy was unarmed. He slowly brought the machete out from behind him. "You told him we'd meet him here?"

"Yeah." The ghoul took a deep breath, tongued it. "They're close, or were here. One of them is, at least. The soldiers. I can smell them."

"That's a black eye." James' face looked swollen. His shirt was covered in blood. He walked stiffly, as though on a leash or by command. "Fistful of coins says they're behind—"

An arrow tore through the air, goring Atticus' shoulder and pinning him to the house. He gripped the shaft, blood spurting over his knuckles.

"Move your hands!" Gary broke the arrow in half. Taking Atticus' arms, he pulled him off what remained of the shaft.

"Holy Child," Atticus gasped. Pain curled inside him, like a palm closing shut.

James screamed and hobbled towards the end of the bridge, but the gawking crowd slowed him to a crawl.

A second arrow caught Atticus in his leg, slinging blood and leftover venom across the grass.

"Mother fucker!" He reached for the shaft. A third arrow sent him reeling as it hit him in the neck.

"Stop, stop," Gary said. "The soldier doesn't know. He thinks this will kill you."

Atticus covered the bubbling wound and fell to the ground. He felt faint, sick. The archer had struck an artery. If ever there was a moment to die, then this was it.

"You're fine," Gary said, cheering him on. He knelt down, had a glance at the inquiring crowd. "See him?" He pointed across the river, where a dark shape jumped off a roof. "Let him in close. Play dead."

Atticus' teeth were bright red as he said, "I have to... know where the bodies are."

"Can you fight?" Gary jumped to his feet. "It doesn't hurt. You just know that it should." He brought his knives out and shouldered his way to the bridge, to James.

Atticus had to look defeated, so like the defeated, he retreated, up the yard and through the Old World house's front door. It wouldn't take much for the archer to find him. He'd left about a half a gallon of himself on the way inside.

Don't die, don't die, don't die. Atticus stumbled into the foyer. He considered the stairs and turned left into the living room that had long since been stripped. There, he collapsed beside the bay windows, and, with the machete across his lap, waited.

"Should've had a plan." He stared at an outlet across the room, and wondered if the world would ever have the chance to use it again. Beside it, the words "Kelly Zdanowicz was here!" had been shakily carved.

"I'm sorry, Clem," he said, his voice laced with lunacy. "Sorry, Will. Nothing's ever simple with this simpleton."

Outside, the crowd grew restless. He could hear someone pushing through the onlookers, drawing curses and gasps. It had to be one of the soldiers. They'd beaten James into bait and betrayal. He almost asked himself why they attacked him in broad moonlight, but, again, they were soldiers. His living was an affront to the absolute authority given to them by King Edgar in the Heartland. How dare he refuse their demands and then not die when told to.

"Is that you, Gravedigger?" Bon's, not Blythe's, voice echoed from the front of the house. "Did you come to your senses and have a nip of the veins? We stuck Brinton in the ground after we did you. Kept some for yourself, eh?"

The floorboards creaked as the soldier moved towards the living room. "Hope you brought some for tonight. Hope you brought a lot."

A flash of purple flooded the blown-out bay windows. On the east side of Bedlam, fireworks exploded across the sky, raining diamonds of light onto the squalid houses below. In that brief moment, Bedlam was beautiful, and as rich as the people told themselves it could be.

"Can't say they don't put on a good party," Bon's voice boomed as he strolled into the living room. "About time we dispelled the distraction."

The soldier from Eldrus stood in plainclothes, bow and quiver on his back. He wore a black leather glove on his right hand—the hand Clementine had cut off and he'd regrown. He walked right up to Atticus and crouched down, so that the two were inches away from one another. Bon glanced at the machete, smiled, and turned his attention to the windows. Tens of townsfolk had gathered outside to watch.

"You're a tough son of a bitch," Bon said. "Your... friend? Lover? That James boy. He is not." He touched the tip of the machete and pointed it directly at his crotch. "Come for your revenge? I can appreciate that. You've earned it, but that don't mean you'll have it."

"You're from here, aren't you?" Atticus coughed out bloody phlegm onto Bon's doublet.

Bon smiled. When he smiled, he looked feral. His features stretched back, fitting to the shape of the monster he was underneath.

"You'll bleed out soon, so we'll talk." He eyed the arrow in Atticus' neck. "What gave me away?"

"Was just a guess." Atticus closed his eyes, saw Clementine and Will there. "Did you have yourself stationed here on purpose?" He opened his eyes, saw Gary and James on the edge of the crowd.

In a flash, Bon grabbed Atticus' wrist and wrenched the machete from his hand. "Bedlam can be better," he said, throwing the blade across the room. He came to his feet and kicked Atticus hard. "They appreciate me. Admire what I am. Get, Gravedigger."

Atticus struggled to stand, so Bon heaved him up and held him close. "How'd you do that with your hand?" He sniffed the soldier: he smelled too clean, as though he'd spent the better part of his life trying to scrub off the filth that formed it.

"You had your chance to learn, Gravedigger." He pushed him back and turned him towards the foyer. "But we can still teach these idiots here in Bedlam something. And you're going to help me do it."

With an arrow aimed at his spine, Atticus let Bon lead him out of the Old World house and into the streets. A mob stood there in festival drab, shifting back and forth and murmuring amongst themselves. Twenty or thirty blocked the bridge, while even more stood in scattered pockets by homes and storefronts.

"What's going on?"

"How is he alive?"

"That looks bad. What'd he do?"

Atticus tilted his head to squeeze out one more spurt of blood.

"Holy Child, that's disgusting."

"Don't look at him. You know what he'll do if he sees you looking at him."

"James, get back."

Atticus followed James and Gary as they melted into the crowd. *Stay back*, he thought. *They can't hurt me like they can hurt you.*

More fireworks took to the sky, sending off a chain reaction of urchin-shaped lights. A few soldiers waited in the wings, swords drawn, watching as the local bully had his run of the schoolyard.

"Gather round, people, gather round," Bon said. "Hold this, would you, Mary Lee?" He lowered his bow and handed it to a skinny woman on the street. "I know you've had your doubts, but let me show you what happens when you defy the king's command." He kicked Atticus onto the bridge. "Let's make it crystal for you all."

Torches blazed on both sides of the bridge, tiny cinder sprites circling the cracking flames. People parted as they approached. If Atticus listened hard enough, he swore he could hear Bon's grin tearing across his face.

"Where's their bodies?" Atticus asked softly.

Bon ignored him and continued to address the crowd. "Your King Edgar has promised all those who have enlisted a proper burial. Most of us are from the Heartland, people, you know that. Is it so wrong to want to be buried back where you came from? With your family or friends? No one wants to die hundreds of miles from home."

Atticus couldn't help but laugh as Bon spoke. Now that everyone was looking at him, he lost the delinquent, shit-kicker accent and replaced it with something more preacher-like. He was holding a sermon, holding himself up to be a shining example of what they could be. But Atticus had a look at his congregation, and he saw only blank faces and balled fists.

From somewhere amongst the masses: "Did the king promise you soldiers our livelihood, eh?"

And another, closer to the front: "We don't need you here!"

Bon grabbed Atticus' hands and held them tightly. "Yes, you do need us here. The Heartland is out of control. If it falls, we all fall. We are here to maintain order. God damn morons, don't you see?" He snarled and whipped Atticus around to face the Old World house, where at least seventy stood. "This man is from Gallows. We brought him a body and he almost killed us when we asked him to bury it. You fight to fight, just to say you did."

A woman shouted from the heart of the revelers, "What's he doing here, then?"

"We are everywhere, and we are not going anywhere. He is an example of our reach." Bon nodded at two soldiers. They pushed their way through the crowd to the woman who had challenged him. "Do as your king wills and we will be as good as invisible."

"Good speech," Atticus said, tipping his head back. "Where's my family?"

Bon dropped Atticus' hands. He slipped his right arm around Atticus' throat. He took out a dagger hidden in the glove and pressed it to Atticus' neck, into the arrow hole.

"Where are they?" he persisted.

"Where Blythe should've sent you." He cleared his throat. "Resistance will not be granted the glory of a trial and the trappings of an execution." He stuck the tip of the dagger into Atticus' neck, drawing blood. "You will be gutted and left to rot in the street. Remember this, my people."

"Couldn't have just killed me quietly?" Atticus winced as the dagger went in deeper, pushing out a hot squirt of blood.

"Two birds, one stone," Bon whispered. "I'm impressed you're still standing." He kissed the side of Atticus' head. "Couldn't have just let bygones be bygones?"

"Two birds," Atticus said, turning his head towards the dagger, causing the blade to slip into his neck with ease.

Bon mumbled "What the fuck?" He ripped the dagger outward. Arterial spray sputtered out of the wound, like crimson sparks from one of Bedlam's many fireworks. Atticus' neck opened like a book and revealed its glistening pages.

A tremor of disbelief rocked the crowd. Atticus stood there a moment, bleeding all over himself, to watch them. Some covered their mouths and shielded their children. Others looked to Bon and his brothers in arms, perhaps hoping for a fight or permission to start one. They were terrified, that much Atticus could tell, but it was more than that: they were curious; one hundred or so now stood before him.

Glancing back, he saw even more across the river. Bedlam was holding its breath, and had been ever since Eldrus arrived, and they were about to get the wrong impression they could breathe again.

Atticus spun around and grabbed Bon's face. He twisted his neck and shot blood into his eye, blinding him. "Where's my family? Where did you take their bodies?"

He kneed Bon. While he was doubled over, he brought him to one of the torches. "Where are they?" He held his head against the fire. "Tell me!"

"Stop, stop," Bon screamed, swinging his arms and trying to make his body dead weight. "Help me, god damn it. Someone!" A flame licked his skin and singed his eyebrows. "Ah, god, please!"

Atticus glanced over his shoulder, where several soldiers stood, swords out, more concerned about the crowd around them than their comrade. They looked at Atticus, damning him and Bon for putting them in this position, and walked away.

"Just us," Atticus said. His ears caught the sound of something. Footsteps; James was behind him. "And that boy, James. Now, quit your squirming."

"Let's see how you like it," James said, grabbing Bon's dagger off the ground. He came behind the soldier, took him by the loose of his shirt. He paused, smiled, and drove the dagger into his ass.

"Blythe!" Bon screamed, eyes wide, mouth agape. His legs gave out and he went forward, busting his lip against the torch's center. He wailed and reeled, balked and begged as blood poured down his legs. He pawed at the dagger hilt-deep inside him, but every touch of the thing sent him into pained convulsions.

"Where's Blythe?" Atticus ripped the torch from the bridge's wall. Pushing Bon down until he was flat on the ground, he held the fire to his face and asked again. "Where is my family?"

"I don't know!" Bon covered his face with his hands, but the flames burned too hot to keep them there. "Blythe had the corpse cart. We went, oh god, please!" With wide, wet eyes, he looked back at Bedlam for help, but the crowd's attention was fixed on Atticus.

"Where'd he go?" Atticus stepped on Bon's chest, brought the torch in closer. His neck no longer hurt, he realized, but he felt sick, as though his soul had rotted inside him. "Where's Blythe?" He pulled the torch away as the smell of burnt hair reached his nose.

"I can't tell…" He closed his eyes and cried out. Inside his mouth, Atticus saw vermillion veins weaving through the gaps in his teeth, heading toward his lips, to repair him. "The plantation, the plantation outside Cathedra," he admitted.

Seeing the veins, Atticus knelt down and stripped the glove off Bon's right hand. Bedlam gasped as he gasped. The soldier's entire hand was infested with the growths. They seemed to be pumping something into his bulging skin.

Do it, Clementine and Will whispered inside him, and so he did. He took the glove and put it on. Believing Bon had told him all he could, he stepped down on his ribcage, pushed the torch into his face, and held it there, until there was nothing left but charred bone.

CHAPTER XI

The woman he heard called Hex was the first to Atticus' side. As he stood there, staring at what he'd done to Bon, Hex grabbed his hand and ran off while pulling him behind her. Gary and James covered him as the crowd converged, eager to touch their new undead lord and savior.

"What's going on?" Atticus cringed as Hex, who was no more than a blur to him, ripped out the remaining arrows from him. His surroundings slowed, smeared. He'd done what needed to be done, and now his body was going to get what was coming to it. "Who are you?"

"A friend, I'm thinking." Hex led him off the bridge. "There," she said, pointing to the nearest alley on the east side. "Down there."

"Your information was good," James, no Gary... no, James, said. "Bon just found me first."

"I'm sorry," Hex said.

The alley widened as they went in. Its tops stretched skyward, into a space of sand and bone.

"If I had known—"

Human shadows peered over the precipice of the alley. He could feel their judgment, their hate, spilling over from above.

"How is he still standing?" A grotesque shape that must've been James stirred beside him. "He doesn't look good."

"I think he's dying." Atticus followed Gary's voice. Where the ghoul should have been, he found a patch of Death's Dilemma.

"You said that wasn't possible—"

The buildings dissolved. In their place, the walls of the Membrane grew. Thick curtains of flesh cordoned off the alley, preventing him from going any further. He stumbled, fell to his hands as the ground gave way to gray matter.

"No, no!" He pulled back, ripping his fingers out of the tough folds. "Herbert, help," he cried. Maybe the old man was somewhere nearby. *I can't go back.*

Thump, thump, thump. Atticus' eyes darted back and forth as he turned and searched for the source of the sound. White sand cascaded in front of him from the vermillion heaven above.

Thump, thump, thump. Atticus knew the noise but couldn't place it. The Membrane grew over where the shadows had been. But he could still see them there, behind the translucent film, clawing at it.

Thump, thump, thump. Atticus closed his hand. Hex's hand still held it, even though she was gone. He went backward, back the way they'd come, hoping to stumble into Bedlam. As the gray matter sucked on his ankles with every plodding step, he sensed the pull of the Abyss on his very bones.

Thump, thump, thump. *It's behind me*, he thought, turning around. Out of the darkness, a shepherd came, cracking its crook against the ground. It walked with its head down, hair and hat hiding its face. From the pockets of its coat, pink bandages hung, swaying back and forth.

"Hold it," Atticus said. "Stop."

The shepherd outstretched its arm and pointed at him. Holding that position, it ran. Before Atticus could do anything, the shepherd was already there, choking him—it's long, painted fingernails gouging his throat.

"Get off me, god damn it," Atticus rasped. The creature lifted him by his neck. The veins in his forehead bulged. Legs flailing, he punched its arm and spat in its face, but the shepherd would not be moved. It was going to do what it had to—

Atticus shot out of bed and crashed onto the floor. The pus sacs on his legs burst. He willed his eyes to sight, to see where he'd ended up now. Another room, not much different from the last. It may have been the same from before, Atticus couldn't be sure; but instead of it just being Gary visiting him, he now had James and the stranger, Hex, as well.

"You can stay," he grumbled, speaking to the woman. "Don't

smell so bad with you here, perfuming up the place."

"Appreciate that," Hex said. She crossed her arms, both of which were Corrupted, and smiled.

The woman was young, pretty, but appeared as though she didn't want to be. She wore a plain green dress that kept her modesty intact and her figure featureless. Her hair was a mess of dyed blue braids and strands going every which way. What she had, regardless of how it looked on her, wasn't cheap, but unlike those as well off as she probably was, she didn't wear make-up to make up for her flaws. It was the kind of confidence that men wouldn't understand, because what she did, she didn't do for them. Atticus knew this, but only because Clementine had taught him how to see it.

"Do you know who I am?" she asked.

"No." Atticus gently ran his finger along his neck. Someone had stitched it back up.

"I told them," Gary said, coming forward like a witness to give testimony. "They needed to know."

"He did." Atticus gave a weak nod to James. "She didn't." He touched the arrow holes, felt their fatality with the tips of his fingers.

"Explains a lot," James said. He crossed the room and dropped to his knees. "What the hell?" Carefully, as though trying to comfort a cactus, he put his arm around Atticus. "You don't want to talk about it, do you?"

"Don't know if I should." Atticus' eyes went back and forth between Hex's arms. "You must be real popular with the Night Terrors."

"Popular with most," she said. "I can get you to Blythe."

Atticus scowled at the woman. Sighing, he said, "You don't know me. Don't worry on my wants."

"They killed you and your family. Took their bodies but left yours. Your friend here brought you back. Said he can bring them back, too. You just need them bodies."

Gary coughed and bit the inside of his mouth. Atticus had known the ghoul long enough to know he was hiding something.

"I can get you to Blythe," Hex carried on.

"You trust her?" Atticus slowly stood. Using James for support, he made it to the bed.

Back when he worked for Poe, he would've kept clammed up, wouldn't have said a damn thing around that damn woman. But to make sense of this secret, he had to share it. Dead or alive, it wasn't a burden he could bear alone.

"It's been awhile." James sat beside him, close enough that their shoulders touched, like the old days. "I know a lot of people I didn't before. I trust her, though. She's—"

"I can speak for myself," Hex interrupted. She pulled open the door, left, and came back with a rickety chair. "Let's hope it holds," she said, as she took a seat, weight giving it the shakes. "Name's Hex, which I'm guessing you gathered. Kind of name you only need to hear once to remember. I own a few businesses. A jewelry shop, a tavern, and the inn next to it."

"That where we are?"

"The inn?" Hex shook her head. "No, this is my home."

"Look about the same."

"Part of the attic. It's unfinished," she said, offended.

Is this what'll be for me from now on? Blackouts and backroom gatherings? He squinted at Hex, and tried to look past her, through the doorway. *How many more rooms like this will there be until it's all over?*

"James and I met each other a few years ago, back when my husband was living," she continued. "Dead now, though. Obviously."

"You don't sound broken up over it," Atticus remarked. He closed his eyes and saw Bon's face, sizzling flesh oozing off it.

"I'm from the coast, down south a ways. He found me there and never brought me back. He mined those parts, mined the people that took interest in the trade, too. He was a kind man, taught me a lot. But there wasn't much love between us."

"He died and left everything to her," James said. "She opened up shop here in Bedlam. Took me and Elijah in after… everything that happened. Hex has no love for Eldrus. Atticus, she knows how to get back at them, and has the money to do it. We'll need more preparation if we're going to get to Blythe. Hell, or even get out of Bedlam."

"All right," Atticus said. "But I'm not leading some rebellion. I saw the way the crowd was looking at me. I'm not doing that." He furrowed his brow and, to Gary, said, "You're awfully quiet."

The ghoul cleared his throat, tainting the air with his cough. "I thought you were dead for good."

"No, but I saw something this time. It was more than passing out." He ran his hands through his oily hair and realized how badly he must smell. "You sure you told them everything?"

"More or less."

"I imagine if someone told me all that, I'd have a hard time believing it."

"I watched you die twice, Atticus," James said.

"Once was enough for me," Hex quipped. "Gary's a ghoul. Not all that hard to believe someone can come back."

"I never died," Gary corrected. "Ghoulism is different."

"The Membrane? The Abyss? Mr. Haemo?" Atticus expected outrage. These were matters of the afterlife, after all, but they couldn't have appeared any more unimpressed. Were they planning a conspiracy? Mutiny? He looked at his friends and, for another paranoid moment, saw enemies.

Gary nodded. "All of it."

"I'm a selfish woman," Hex said, shifting on the chair. "I'm helping you because if you can't die, then you're my best bet at getting my brother back."

Atticus raised an eyebrow. "We're not in the resurrection business, ma'am."

"He's not dead, I don't think. Ichor, my brother... the last letter he sent me was about the plantation. Carpenter Plantation. The one outside Cathedra where Blythe's at. Got it out, somehow, the letter. Said they were holding him prisoner there with others. Protestors."

"That's where Clementine and Will are."

"Lots of bodies go through there. Ichor said the land around it is sick. Cathedra is a proud place. Eldrus or not, they don't take what the soldiers are doing there lightly."

Gary, twitching, said anxiously, "Hence the protests."

"I want to see the letter," Atticus said. The warmth coming off James comforted him. "A lot has happened a lot faster than I can handle."

Hex nodded, saying, "I understand." She stood, headed for the door. "Think of it as a contract. I'll pay you in weapons and supplies. We'll both get what we want."

"I'm not interested in turning the murder of family into a partnership," Atticus spat angrily.

"We're down a horse," James said. "We didn't bring much with us. I trust Hex, Atticus. You brought me here for my connections. She's one of them, and I trust her. Things have gone... unexpectedly... but I don't know if we'll get this opportunity again."

"Mmm." Atticus swallowed hard. A few stitches snapped; his neck opened up where they broke.

"What did you see?" Gary followed Hex with his glassy gaze until she left the room. "When you died, what did you see?"

"You holding something back?" Atticus gripped the bedsheets as he spoke. "Can't get you to shut up half the time. I'm not right, I know that, but neither are you. Not since Mr. Haemo. Are you sick from the ritual? What?" Atticus exhaled and got to his feet. "Close that door and say what's on your mind, god damn it."

Gary did as he was told and slammed the door shut. Pulling up his pants, which were halfway down his bony ass, he said, "The ritual took a lot of me, boss." He lifted his shirt. His chest was flayed, and half his ribcage was exposed. "A lot of ghoul flesh went into finding you. But I'll be fine. Did you see the Membrane when you slept?"

Atticus lowered his head. He felt like an asshole; so, like an asshole, he just nodded weakly.

"Until you woke up on that bed, you were gone. Body went stiff and cold. The Abyss is trying to get you back, but somehow, you're fighting it off."

"Like a cat. Nine lives," James added innocently.

"Nine or nine thousand, I don't know. But you're not dying right away. It's like you're getting used to it. Next time, it'll take longer, I think." The ghoul grabbed his head and groaned. "Did you see it? The shepherd?"

"Yes," Atticus blurted out, nodding as he spoke. "Yes, yeah, I did. The first time I was down there, and then just now. What are they?"

"They are their name. I'd heard of them, but Mr. Haemo... we... he explained... explained it to me." Gary stopped speaking and, when he'd stopped stuttering, started again. "Fuck, sorry. Don't mind..."

Atticus cocked his head. "What's wrong?"

Gary ignored him and said, "When something escapes the Membrane or the Abyss, the shepherds follow. They give you some time to die again, but if you don't, then they come for you. They won't kill you, Mr. Haemo said. They'll just take you, all of you, body and soul, back to the Membrane. If that happens, that's it. No ritual can pull you out again."

"Are you still alive when a shepherd sends you back to the Membrane?" James asked, his voice quivering.

Gary covered his face as though he were about to cry. "I don't know," he whimpered. "Atticus, if you saw one, that means it'll be coming for you soon, too."

"If I bring Clementine and Will back, they'll have shepherds of their own, right?"

Gary stared at him blankly.

"Right?" he snarled.

"Yeah." The ghoul picked a tooth out of its gum and flung it at the floor.

For the first time since he woke, he thought of Bon's glove, which no one had bothered to strip off him. The murder was no more than a memory that, like a knife, would dull after daily use. But this trophy, on the other hand, would outlast all recollections. For as long as he controlled it, the glove's texture would hold its history. He touched it, tightened it, and as he went back once again to the bridge, found himself imagining what else he may add to his new collection.

"Can the shepherds be killed?" Atticus said at last. He splayed his fingers to stretch the glove's leather.

"Everything can die. It's just a matter of finding their weakness," Gary said.

"We better hurry then," Atticus said, hand balling into a fist. "Before they find mine."

CHAPTER XII

Getting out of Bedlam was going to be more difficult than it should've been. Atticus had been dead through most of it, but during the night and the dawning hours, his resistance had inspired a revolt. Those who'd watched him kill Bon without recourse from the other soldiers took this as permission to be shitheads. They marched through the streets, stirring up the anger the festivities had settled.

According to Hex, who'd ducked out to have a look shortly after she found the letter from her brother, "Gravedigger" had been written in several places across the town.

"Someone probably heard Bon call me that," Atticus mumbled, when Hex had told him what she'd seen.

"You're their hero," she joked, as she hauled crates full of random pieces of armor out of the basement.

"Not my intention." He moved to take the crate, but she, like Clementine, hadn't the stomach for unnecessary gentlemanly gestures. So he scratched his crotch instead and said, "His 'brothers' should've stopped me."

"Well, you see a good thing and you take it." She dropped the crate and disappeared down the stairs for another one. Shouting, she said, "He had it coming. Just no one knew when it was going to get here."

When the morning fog had finally rolled in, blanketing Bedlam in otherworldly breaths, they mounted their horses and made their move. Soldiers patrolled the streets, drawn swords sneering silver in the pale light.

Hex, who'd cloaked her new companions from head to toe, kept them to the denser parts of town. She made sure to point out the graffiti across the buildings and ground, which read "Gravedigger," just as she'd claimed.

"How are we going to get out of here?" Gary asked, from the middle of their procession.

Atticus' heart dropped. The last time the ghoul had left Gallows' graveyard had been over thirty years ago. He kept expecting Gary to abandon ship and swim for safer shores, but still he stayed.

"Very carefully," Hex said. She led them off the main road and down to the riverbank. "We're a ragtag-looking group, what with all these cloaks and this secrecy."

"Have any friends in Cathedra?" Atticus asked, grateful that the surging river masked the sounds of their horses.

Hex shook her head. "None worth more than how far I can throw them. I can sweet-talk us out of a bind. Maybe. But once we reach the woods, we're on our own."

Near the edge of Bedlam, where the river widened under a collapsing archway, the fog sat thick and unmoving. It was as though some ancient spider had passed through, leaving its web atop the waters, to catch insects who'd thought they'd slipped their captors.

Hex and James rode side-by-side, buddy-like, and steered them in the right direction. When they told Atticus and Gary to go left, they went left. And when they told them to go straight, they went straight. And then when they told them to quit their jabbering, they did that, too.

The leather armor irritated Atticus' wounds. He tried to explain to them he didn't much see the point in armor, but then Gary made a point himself that, even if Atticus couldn't die, he wouldn't be much use to anyone if he lost an arm or a leg. They still hurt, though, the wounds—still throbbed with gut-wrenching pain, but he was getting used to it. His father once told him a man could get used to anything given enough time. He'd always admired how philosophical his daddy got before the belt came out.

"Eat," he heard Gary whisper behind him.

The fog was too dense to see him, but nevertheless, Atticus knew the ghoul was staring him down. He fumbled for the satchel at his side and slipped some bread into his mouth. If he was constantly coming back from the dead—a concept he wasn't willing to even begin to process—then he needed to keep his body in working condition.

"When Clementine and Will come back," Gary had said before they left, his voice shaking, his eyes elsewhere, "what do you want them to see? Take it from me, love isn't that blinding."

A shush shook Atticus from his thoughts. He leaned forward, hand tightening around the machete's handle. Hex only had three swords, and Atticus passed his to James on account of being dead and all.

Another shush. A new set of hooves were clapping ahead. Neighing. Atticus strained his ears to overhear what was happening behind the river's noises. Slowly, he cantered forward, machete out, hoping Gary behind him had the same idea.

The wind kicked up, caught his cloak and made it snap. Curtains of mist wavered back and forth across his path, wetting his face with its delicate fabric. He could make out two shapes now—Hex and James—and then two more ahead of them, tall and imposing.

"Stop," one of the shapes boomed, the clink of steel the punctuation to his sentence.

Atticus took a few steps forward and stopped. Close enough to make out their armor and adornments, he saw that the shapes were soldiers of Eldrus.

Gary trotted up beside him and planted his horse in front of Atticus, as though to hide him.

"What is this?" the soldier with the loud voice asked. His face looked as though it'd been carved out of rock, or dipped in acid.

"Why can't you all just listen?" the second soldier added. He held his sword like it were his dick—proud but without a clue as to how to use it. "Turn back—"

The ugly soldier raised his hand to interrupt. "Who's this you have with you, Hex?" He squinted his bloodshot eyes. "That you, James? You've got sand, I'll give you that. There's a warrant out for your arrest, you know that, right? Plenty saw you there on the bridge." The soldier paused, stretched his neck, and got pissed. "Who's that behind you?"

A mosquito landed on Atticus' wrist and had a nip. The machete felt light in his hand, but he put it away. It was too easy to become the thing he hunted. The last thing he needed or wanted was a trail of bodies by which those seeking revenge could find him.

"Just friends passing through," Gary said.

I can't keep having these delays. Ignoring the soldiers' shouts to do otherwise, Atticus rode forward, between Hex and James, until he was within killing distance of the men.

He dropped his hood and said, "I expect you're looking for me."

The ugly soldier pulled his sword back. One swing and he'd hack Atticus' head clean off. "Might be." He took in for a moment the ruin that was Atticus' neck. "Drop the weapon. Get off your horse. Jonathan," he said to the other soldier, "grab that one back there."

"No, you stay put." Jonathan stopped Gary, who'd gone sideways, to hide his ghoulish face.

Atticus slid off his horse, machete back in hand.

"Drop it," the ugly soldier barked. He put himself into a stance the royal must've found fancy. The fog rolled past, unimpressed.

"Bruce, what's the word around the campfire?" Hex turned, and crossed her legs. All that black armor on her made her look like a bug.

"Don't you start," the ugly soldier, Bruce, said.

"That he's dead, right? Killed Bon and died elsewhere."

Bruce's mouth hung open; a mosquito buzzed by it. "Someone helped him off that bridge. A woman. Too dark to tell who."

"I'm guessing I don't need to spell it out for you." She dropped off the horse. Her feet hit the ground hard, mud exploding out from under them. "I've done a lot for you. Hey, Jonathan," she said, noticing he'd been shuffling closer to Atticus. "This man burned Bon's face to the bone. You think he gives two shits about you? Let's re-think this, boys."

Bruce furrowed his eyebrows. His face stayed like that a bit, as though it were putty. "Not going to happen. I can't do that."

"You saying him killing Bon wasn't, in some way, a favor to you?" Hex fiddled with the sheathed sword at her side. "Favor to your wife, I imagine. Didn't he beat her bad? Didn't I patch her up?"

Bruce growled, raised his hand as though to hit her.

"Jonathan, you know James here," Hex carried on.

James smirked. "Boohooed in my arms one night after Bon went to work on him. What'd you do with that dress Hex made you? What'd you do with all that time I bought you?" He sounded tough, sounded the way Atticus had always intended for him to be.

Hex sighed. Before anyone could react, she drew her sword and stuck it to Bruce's gut.

"'Gravedigger' is dead, or just about, to most. Bon was a matter of revenge. Bedlam just took it the wrong way. You bring him in, you're just going to make everything worse. Let this go."

Bruce bit his lip. Hex put some pressure on the sword, working the tip of it into his armor. "Dead or alive, it doesn't matter which. We just need a body to show. I'll forget this happened, Hex. I'm willing to."

"No one knows we're here." James kept his eyes locked on Jonathan as he spoke. "We're just passing through. We won't be back. Let us leave before the next patrol comes. The fog's going to clear soon."

Jonathan's lip trembled. With fire in his eyes, he stomped forward and ripped James off his horse. "Asshole!"

Mud splattered over James' armor. The ground sucked him into place. He moaned and rubbed at his spine.

Jonathan stood over him. He raised his sword up, ready to drive it through James' heart. "What'd you do to Elijah—"

Atticus barreled into Jonathan. The sword flew out of his hands and crashed into a pile of rocks.

Bruce tried to make a move, but Hex drew back and busted him in the mouth with her sword's pommel.

Atticus punched Jonathan in the stomach. Lifting him a few inches off the ground, he threw him into the river. His screams came out garbled as the currents crashed into him, taking him further downstream.

"Stop, stop," Bruce begged.

Atticus glanced over at Hex, who was straddling the soldier. Her hand's Corruption glowed like an ember as she pressed it against his face.

"What's it going to be, eh?" She leaned forward, blue braids like blue ropes touching his cheek. Her throat quivered, bulged slightly. "Take my house. I've others. You see that one there?" She nodded at Gary, who'd finally come to join in the fun.

Gary peeled back his hood, his ghastly visage made all the worse by the fog that passed in and out of it.

"He's a ghoul," she said. "And Gravedigger, there? Well, I don't rightly know what he is, but he's still kicking when anything else would be gathering flies. James' exploits aren't any mystery to you, and my stirrings, well, you know all about them. This is the company I keep. Does yours measure up?"

Bruce shook his head.

Contented, Hex leaned back. Her throat returned to normal as she let out a cough. "Then you better get on your feet, soldier, and fetch a towel for your friend. I don't want him to catch a cold."

An hour south of Bedlam, in the oldest part of the surrounding woods, Annaliese's Deceit cuts through. Seldom traveled, the forgotten trail stretches from the church of Cathedra to the roaring cataracts near the Nameless Forest. Smugglers once used the path as a means by which they could trade their goods to the towns and villages along the way. But when the trail started eating the smugglers, the criminals of the Heartland turned to more obvious but less murderous routes to pitch their pilfered wares.

After Atticus and his companions cleared Bedlam, that's where they found themselves, each in quiet awe of one another's capabilities.

"This is the quickest route to Cathedra?" Atticus asked. He still had his machete, and now Jonathan's sword as well.

They'd been on the trail for fifteen minutes. Already, he felt cut off from the world. It seemed segregated from the rest of the woods, as though it'd been pushed out, like a splinter from a cut.

"Don't know much about it," he added.

"No," Hex grunted. Her horse struggled with the uneven terrain. "But no one'll see us coming. And it runs right behind Carpenter Plantation."

Gary coughed until he had everyone's attention. He said quietly, "Know anywhere a guy can get a bite to eat?"

Atticus noticed how disgusted James looked when the ghoul had said that; cannibalism had never sat well with the boy.

"There's an old graveyard a few hours in. Bet we can find something there for you to munch on," Hex offered, not missing a beat.

"How long's it been?" Atticus fell back and rode beside Gary.

"Since Bedlam. I think that's part of the reason I haven't been right."

"Where's Elijah?" Atticus threw the question out, to see how much James would fumble for an answer.

"Never... never... never came back to Bedlam," he said, going red in the face. He took a drink of water. "Gave him up."

"What'd you do to him?" Atticus saw the ever-steadfast Hex glance back. He didn't like being out of the loop. When they made camp, he'd be sure to right that wrong. "That soldier, Jonathan, said you did something to him."

With a burst of anger, James shouted, "I hit him." He stopped his horse. He squeezed the reins until his knuckles went white. "I got tired of it. You were right. Been waiting for you to ask. I broke his nose. His hand and foot. Couldn't take it. Sleeping around and… and the manipulation." He rubbed his face. He'd have a few hives soon, be out for the whole night when he finally turned in. "I don't want to talk about this right now, Atticus. I don't want to get into this with you."

"That's fine," he conceded. *You don't need to prove anything to me anymore*, he thought, but didn't say.

"I don't mean to interrupt," Hex said, "but these trees—" she pointed to a cluster of engorged oaks that had grown into one another, their bases twisted into petrified sneers, "—stay clear of them."

Atticus smashed a mosquito sucking on his neck. "Why's that?"

"They'll eat you," she said, her grin almost as large the one on the grotesque growth. "As old as they are, these Adelaide, they're surprisingly spry."

A few hours in, just as Hex had promised, they came upon a graveyard that had been built twenty or so feet off of Annaliese's Deceit. Only a few headstones remained there. Ten to fifteen carnivorous Adelaides sat around the perimeter as well, doing their best to look as maniacal as possible as the group settled in.

"He's different," Atticus said to Gary. He watched Hex and James from the far end of the graveyard. "She is, too, in her own way."

The ghoul grunted. He paced back and forth, stopping sometimes to sniff the air and sample the soil.

"How long have you had the hunger?"

Gary shrugged and settled on an unmarked mound. "Since the snake, actually." He looked at the sun, and sighed; deeds such as these were often done in the dark.

"You put us at risk."

"No, I would never. I wouldn't do that." Gary's glassy eyes went wide. He couldn't cry anymore, but that didn't mean he wouldn't. "I didn't want to take away from what you had to do."

Gary clawed through the topsoil. Dirt and grass flew every-which-way. His tough ghoul flesh flexed and tightened, taking on the earth's various tones. How many graves had he gone through over the years? Atticus wondered. And would he ever stop to lie down in one of his own? He himself could stop, Atticus thought, but what would happen if he did? Once he found Clementine and Will, would he even have the chance to speak to them? Hold them? Or would that be when Death finally arrived, to collect what was owed? Atticus considered what would happen to him if he were to leave them to the Membrane, to spare them their painful rebirth. He considered this, and then scratched his head until it bled.

"Shallow, and fresh," Gary said. He was four feet into the ground when his nails caught on a coffin. "Someone's still kicking around in these woods." He cracked the front of the coffin and said, "Oh, shit."

Atticus furrowed his brow at the ghoul. He leaned over the grave. The coffin inside was already covered in the Adelaide's roots. "What?"

Gary pulled back on the cracked wood until it snapped off. Inside the coffin, a little girl lay, her hair turned gray from the cobwebs spun across it. She wore a woman's dress, her mother's maybe, and held a bundle of rosy Peace against her chest. She couldn't have been dead more than a week.

Gary turned her over, where he found the little girl's broken spine jutting out against her dress. "I don't want to do this," he said. "It's disrespectful."

"There has to be someone else." Atticus eyed the graveyard and knew by the state of things there probably wasn't.

"Nothing I can get anything out of." Gary touched her cheek. "Every meal is a murder, you know."

Atticus wiped his eyes. The little girl reminded him of Clementine and the time they spent together the first summer after they met, rough-housing.

"You know, I know, that she could come back. Everyone I eat I take that away from." He shooed away the spider who'd webbed up her hair. "Her dad might be out there now, gathering up ingredients."

"I don't think so, Gary. Bringing someone back is a selfish thing. You see to it they're laid to rest for good. I need you with me. And I imagine her dad, whatever his plans may be, only wants the best for her. I don't think having another go at this world is that."

Gary fell back on his heels and placed his trembling hands atop his thighs. "That makes you a hypocrite."

"I know."

"What if… what if Clem-Clementine and Will… what if you find them but it's too late? And we can't… do another ritual?"

Was it sadness that caused his friend to stutter when mentioning his family? It seemed closer to guilt than grief, but now wasn't the time to ask, so Atticus said, "I have to try. No one's going to do it for me."

Gary nodded and leaned into the grave. He put both hands on the little girl and lifted her out of the coffin. Like a doll, he laid her on the ground carefully.

"When's the last time you ate a child?" Atticus asked, gripping Gary's shoulder.

"Long before I met you." Gary slid off her dress and placed it back in the coffin. "I don't want to stain it. Meant something to someone."

"I know." He squeezed his shoulder, patted his back. "I imagine you've seen all manner of awful things."

Gary wiped his salivating mouth. He picked up the little girl's pale arm. The faint hairs that ran along it glowed golden in the afternoon light. "Everything ends for a reason. Things aren't meant to go past their expiration." He pressed her flesh to his lips. "I'd turn away."

Atticus shook his head as the ghoul's teeth came out. "I don't think I will."

It took about twenty minutes until the little girl was gone. Gary placed her bones back in the grave, buried the coffin, and used what little dirt was left over to cover up the mess he'd made. The ghoul looked better than before, more like his usual self. But now that Atticus thought about it, there appeared to be more to his starvation than a lack of opportunity to feast. It almost seemed like penance.

Two mosquitoes buzzed past Atticus and Gary as they walked to the center of the graveyard. Hex and James were small figures in the distance, coming off the Deceit.

"How you like being dead?" Gary asked, throwing his hood over his head.

"Haven't had time to think about it. Not sure I want to."

They reached the horses, which were tethered to the only tree that appeared as though it wouldn't gobble them up. Atticus gave the horses some of their own food; otherwise, they weren't likely to eat.

"It's like I'm getting chance after chance after chance. Like I'm rebounding from the Membrane." He showed his neck and the three arrow-holes. "They're healing. Slowly, but still. I got to thinking on the way here. Do I need all this? If someone cuts my heart out, will I keep coming back. What's the thing that truly fuels this mess of flesh, you know what I mean?" He paused a moment. "No, I don't want to think about it, being dead. Or not dead. That's when complications will set in. When I'll inherit my legacy of decrepitude."

"I can respect that." Gary took out his sword, gave it a slow swing. "Haven't had to use one of these in a while."

"You never died, that right?"

Gary aimed the sword at the nearest Adelaide, as though he meant to spar with it. "Like I said a million times before, ghoulism is different. It's a disease."

"Came from… what'd you say his name was? David? Dandy Dumbass? No, what? Deacon, right?"

Gary laughed and sheathed the sword. "Yeah, Deacon Wake. Dandy Dumbass was his brother." He snorted. "I'm thinking about him, too. He went to the Membrane. But he didn't die. Somehow, he found a way in. That's how he contracted the disease."

"The shepherds get out somehow. Makes sense." Atticus swallowed hard. For a moment, he'd forgotten he was hunted.

"That thing is out there, Atticus. We're not going to let it get to you."

"Appreciate it." Atticus nodded at Hex, who, with James, was almost close enough to hear their conversation. "This has gotten bigger than I like."

"She's a good woman. James looks up to her, like a sister. We need her, and I can tell you like her, so you're just distrusting her for the hell of it."

"We're not tracking Gallows' most wanted. These are soldiers of Eldrus. It has to be bigger if we're going to finish… How do you think Deacon ended up in the Membrane?" Atticus changed the subject, as Hex and James were in earshot of them.

Gary shrugged. "That was a long time ago. Story changes depending upon which ghoul you ask." His speech became rapid, excited, as though he were sharing something important. "He was killed somewhere up north, I know. I heard he used a black chalice to open the gateway to the 'margins and the folds,' but who the hell knows where that chalice is, if it even exists? Eldrus, maybe, what with that old coot Amon collecting up relics and all. Would make sense. Few said they'd seen something of the like in Ghostgrave."

"That's okay, Gary, I'm not planning on going into the Membrane again," Atticus said, screwing up his face. "What you and Mr. Haemo did should still work, right? You're talking like it won't. That's the second time today you said something."

Gary nodded, looked away; nodded and smiled some more. "Yeah, yes, of course. Sorry. Ghouls get anxious after eating. It's… no, no. It'll still work, Atticus. Nothing's changed."

"Howdy," Hex said, stomping across the graveyard. She rubbed her stomach. "Better?"

"Yeah," Gary said. "Thanks, Hex."

"No problem."

Staring at James, Atticus said, "How's the trail looking?"

"Fine," James said, still sore about when he'd ambushed him on Elijah. "Gets rough, but we'll manage."

"All right boys," Hex said, crossing her arms across the black breastplate. She blew one of her blue braids out of her face. "We've got about a day until we hit Carpenter Plantation." She went around them to the horses. "There's a good place to camp about thirteen hours from here."

"You been here a lot?" Atticus stole a glance at one of the Adelaides, which had opened its mouth slightly, to suck in a snake.

"Off and on." She smiled. "It's good to know your getaways. My husband understood that. Anyways, let's get to it." She slapped one of the horses on its rear. "We need to catch up with the rest."

Atticus' hands were fists before he had a reason to use them. "What?" His neck tightened until some of the stitching snapped again. "The rest? Hex, I like you, but if you're holding something back… I won't."

She waved him off and started rummaging through the saddlebags. "You're my best bet at getting my brother back, like I said in Bedlam. But I financed a team before I met you. I was on my way out when James came storming in, asking after Bon. After you agreed, I told them to hold their position a little longer until we arrived."

"Didn't think to mention that earlier?" *This woman*, he thought, *is using me. If I have to kill her, I might lose James for good.*

"I… thought I did?" She smiled and mouthed an apology. "There's at least fifty soldiers stationed there. Probably more, now. Carpenter Plantation is a corpse factory. Bodies are coming in daily from Holy Child knows where. But that's all we got so far. It's a big secret they're doing a shit job of hiding. I like to think we're a capable bunch, but we aren't breaking in just the four of us. You'd do anything to get your wife and son back, yeah?"

"Yeah."

"Then do this, with me, with us. I could be asking you to do a whole lot worse."

"Hex," Atticus said. "I saw what they put in one of the bodies. Looked like something straight out of the Nameless Forest."

"It is," she said in a cheerily, sardonic way. "They're trying to grow another one."

CHAPTER XIII

They built a fire in a fallen Adelaide and huddled closely around it. Its nearby brethren wailed over the desecration, but Hex assured the men this was the only way the trees would learn to respect them. Atticus didn't put much stock in the statement, so he offered to keep watch while they slept.

"Mighty big of you," Hex said, face sweating from the fire. "But this is fool-proof, I promise."

"Eh." Atticus leaned in a little. "This Adelaide isn't dead yet. I can hear it whimpering. The only message you're sending them out there in the dark is that we deserve to be eaten."

"It's fine." She smiled, dug her heels into the leafy dirt. "We'll douse it in the morning. Takes more than a fire to do these things in. This is just to tell them we mean business."

Atticus gave up. "Whatever you say." He touched the hole in his chest from Blythe's kunai. The wound he'd had the longest seemed to be healing the slowest. "The Nameless Forest. I don't see the point."

"Can't go wrong with a plan that doesn't make sense," James piped up. He'd settled down some since they made camp. They'd called it quits for the night outside a dilapidated cabin and woodshed. Both were too far gone to lie down in, but James took to them all the same.

"Blythe said they were transporting the roots in the bodies to avoid anyone catching on." Atticus remembered Brinton, the no-good nobody who'd spun this all into motion. "So either the bodies are part of the process, or there's something else to it."

Gary cleared his throat as he inched closer to the flames. Ghoul flesh was thick and didn't hold much heat, so he took advantage of the chance to cop some anytime he could.

"Still doesn't make sense. Let's say they are the vermillion veins. As soon as people see them start growing, they'll tear them out, most likely," Atticus said.

"Sounds like they're sending them all over as well," Hex said. "That's too wide a net to manage. But in Ichor's letter, he was convinced they were from the Nameless Forest."

Gary raised his hand and said, "Think about it. When's the last time anyone's seen the veins? The Nameless Forest has about a million stories to its name. Nobody's gotten much further than the outskirts in who knows how long. We're going off myths here."

"Ah," Hex interrupted, smiling. "Not true. King Edgar had himself a sojourn in that fanciful place."

"So they say." Atticus thought on this for a moment. "Does add up with what his soldiers are doing. But how'd he haul all that out of there? And what for? Clementine hacked off Bon's arm and he used the stuff to grow it back."

"New resource, maybe. New drug, like you said, to heal." Hex leaned back, gazed upward into the star-pricked sky. "A new distraction to draw us away from what's really important."

"They killed us for it. It's important."

Hex's face went limp. She dropped her head, and the tough woman act went along with it. "Sorry," she mumbled. And then, standing up: "I have to piss." She looked at Atticus, took her sword, and then disappeared into the mourning night.

"I miss them," James said. "I didn't want to say anything. Figured you didn't need that. But I miss them, Atticus. I do. You were… are my family. Clementine and Will… when I sleep, they're all I see. It makes me sick." James covered his mouth. Tears streaked down his knuckles. "I know you don't want to hear it. That's fine. But I'm not just here to help you. I'm here for them, too. To get them b-back." He shut his eyes tight and started to cry. "I'm sorry. I'm s-s-sorry I left you. All of you."

James wiped his nose on his arm. Holding his forehead, he whispered, "That night, when we broke into the barn. It was Elijah's idea. Not mine. I lied to you about that. I was just protecting him. Again, like always. I was going to... to see you that day. But he said we should rob Brinton, first." He cleared his throat, took a deep breath. "If we hadn't broken in, none of this would've happened."

He went still, letting his words wash over Atticus, and then, all at once, began to bawl. "I'm sorry. I'm so sorry. I'm so, so, so... so, so... so."

Gary moved closer to James, and put his arm around him. James buried his face in the ghoul's rotted chest and soaked his innards with a flood of tears.

Patting his back, Gary said, "When I went into that kitchen and found all three of you, I thought that, maybe, that was it. I thought it was the end. You, your family, gave me something to live for. And seeing you there, all of you, dead... Almost nothing has hurt as much as that. Thought about killing myself. I did. I wanted to. Holy Child, did I want to.

"This, this is your journey, Atticus, we know that. But know that you're not doing it alone, whether you like it or not." Gary paused and closed his eyes. "However it ends, you'll have us. Right, James?"

James nodded as he pulled away from the ghoul. "Sorry," he said, smiling. "Needed a good cry." He pointed to Gary's ribcage. "I think I got some snot your heart."

Gary waved him off. "Don't worry about it. Hasn't worked in ages."

Atticus sat there in silence, the flames of the fire licking his feet. His friends were waiting for him to say something, but what could he tell them? It hadn't even crossed his mind the effect the deaths of Clementine and Will would've had on them. He'd brought them for their company and for their skills, not for the investment; for the connection to his wife and son.

He shouldered the hurt like he would've a corpse—on his own and with every intention of burying it himself. But he wasn't the Gravedigger anymore. He'd outgrown that role, just as he had the role of Hangman for Poe in the days best left forgotten. He was Atticus now, a mere human without a local legend behind which he could hide. Immortal, maybe, sure, but what did that matter if he lost his humanity along the way?

Atticus sat there in silence. Shedding the last of his old, thick skin he said, "Thank you. This is about all of us doing what's right. You didn't do nothing wrong, James. You never did. And I'm sorry I made you feel like that. And Gary... you son of a bitch." He smiled at the ghoul. "I can't repay you enough. I wouldn't be here if not for you, both of you. I don't know what's going to happen when this is over. I don't know if that's when my time will run out. But I know that, when we bring them back, they'll be okay, because they have you two to keep them out of trou—"

Gary's grin became a grimace as he said, "Atticus? What?"

Behind James, about four feet away, a shepherd stood, the Adelaide around it gone quiet. It tipped its crook forward, pointing its bloody top Atticus' way.

"Oh shit," Gary and James said in unison, looking back.

"You can see it?" Atticus wondered where Hex had wandered off to. He grabbed his sword and machete. "You can see it?"

Paralyzed, James and Gary sat there, mouths agape, as though in the presence of a deity.

"You can see it?" Atticus shouted, snapping his head to the left as Hex came out of the bushes.

Buttons unbuttoned, she shouted, "What in the fuck is that?" She grabbed her sword and held it in both hands.

"That's it, that's the shepherd."

A clammy gale blew through the Deceit. The trees flattened as it rushed toward the shepherd. When the wind hit it, the creature's hair parted and, in one slowed second, Atticus saw, for the first time, its face.

The shepherd's eyes and mouth were sewn shut. Its forehead had been split down the middle. Inside the gash, there were trinkets, mementos. A lock of red hair, an old toy. A piece of parchment, and part of a painting, too. The painting he recognized—it'd be the same Mr. Haemo had used to track him in the Membrane—and then he remembered the other items as well. Clementine's hair, and a toy of Will's Atticus had made himself. There was something else in the gulf, something oval-shaped, like an egg or an organ, or a curled-up infant.

But before he could make sense of it, sinewy streaks of color shot from the ground and wrung the shepherd out of existence.

"Are you okay?" Hex asked no one in particular.

What was that in its head? "When it had me alone, it was ruthless. Maybe it was a warning just now. Or maybe it knew it couldn't kill us all."

"Maybe it can only hurt you," Gary whispered.

"We'll stay up." James nodded.

"Won't sleep none anyways," Hex said.

Gary crossed his arms and put his back to the fire, going sentry-like for the night ahead. "You'd do the same for us. Get some rest, Atticus."

Their intentions, good as they may have been, were no match against the fatigue. Half past the Black Hour, they began to drop like flies. James first, then Hex. Gary held out the longest, but mid-sentence, mid-joke, the ghoul's resolve gave and forty winks turned into forty thousand.

Atticus was sitting with both hands on both of his weapons when he heard Hex mumble, "You don't smell so good."

He looked over at the woman, who was face-first in the bags they'd brought, which she now used as pillows. A blanket was in a tangle around her ankles. She'd been slowly kicking it off over the course of the night.

"I think you caught a whiff of yourself is all," Atticus said.

"Mmm." Hex licked her lips and forced one eye open. "Could be that." She stretched out her arms. "You're rotting somewhere. Let me see you."

It was his legs. The long ride through the Deceit had left them swollen and raw. Pulling his pus-soaked pant leg back, he spotted a patchwork of splotches across his skin. The smell of piss and rotten meat sent his stomach reeling.

"I didn't have much to treat you with back in Bedlam. Supplies were getting scarce. Honestly, didn't even know if I should. You looked dangerous." She sat up, tied her hair back, and got serious. "Got to cut out the necrosis. The way James described them, the snakes sounded like Malingas. It's a strange venom, theirs. Kills flesh quick, but lingers after treatment. We might have to do this again. You ready?"

"Here?" Atticus wondered how many more times he'd have to die until infection and pain were no longer a part of the equation. "I suppose."

Hex yawned and gave herself a few slaps to the face. She tore into the bags she'd slept on and pulled out a black case. "Old World doctors used these. Handy to have around." She undid its clasps and pulled it open. "This is what I was before I left the south. A healer. It's what they told me to be."

"Your family did?" Atticus sprawled his legs out, while Hex did a quick inventory of what she'd packed. "Where's home?"

"Angheuawl. Say that five times fast. It's a little place in the swamps before Kistvaen's foothills. Not much to it. You keep moving through or you're there in it forever. One of those places." She closed the case, came over, opened the case, knelt beside him, and took out a thin scalpel. "Nothing like a little flaying to bring friends together."

"How old are you?"

She pulled out a vial, doused the scalpel in what Atticus identified as a sanitizing solution. "Twenty-seven. You?"

"Thirty-five and some change."

"Strip," Hex said, waving the scalpel. "Don't worry." She nodded at James and Gary. "They'll be out till morning."

Atticus undid his pants and, carefully, so as to not irritate his legs further, slipped out of them. "Not much gets to you, huh?"

"Not much, no."

"On account of your upbringing?"

"That, and what was passed down to me." She licked her teeth. "Ichor's the same. We weren't really all that close until I was married. Then I couldn't shake him. Guess he felt he had to protect me."

Atticus twitched as she touched his legs. They looked like pincushions. Any other time, he'd be counting bite marks, tallying up the fangs for future boastings. But with Clementine gone, he didn't much see a reason to.

Hex lingered on a black patch of skin near Atticus' knee. "Nicholas Harrington was my husband."

"Sounds familiar. Can't say from where."

"That was the case with most. Drove him mad. Never got to be the big-shot he'd hoped to be."

She continued to chart his flesh, testing each stretch with the tips of her fingers. The smell was getting to her. She kept holding her breath, until she couldn't.

"Your other wounds look good, on your neck and shoulder. Just the legs have gone bad."

"Do what you have to. It's a mystery to me what I'm capable of healing anymore."

His heart skipped as she started to quietly count the places she needed to remove.

"Giant snake was one thing. The Night Terrors chasing after it… Never known one to let a human go."

"Seen plenty back home." She mouthed the word twelve. She prodded the last of Atticus' necrotic flesh, making him cringe. "Seen plenty kill us 'Corrupted.'" She laughed and held out her crimson arms. "I guess they didn't know what to do with me."

"I appreciate what you've done for us, Hex." Atticus took a deep breath, filling his lungs with the thick, burning bark taste of the campfire. "We'll get Ichor back. I apologize for mistrusting you."

"Getting a man to take his pants off is one thing, but getting a man to let you cut into him… I figured I had your trust, Atticus."

She put the scalpel to his skin and scraped away some dark crust. With her other hand, she pulled out a thick rag and threw it at his chest.

"Bite down and don't pass out. I need you keeping an eye on things in case that shepherd friend of yours decides to show up again."

"I'll trade you this rag for some anesthetic."

"That's for all of us after the plantation. This won't kill you, so I can't bring myself to waste it. You understand?" She shrugged. "Most likely, this won't hurt. It's dead tissue. No feeling. Problem with Malingas venom is that it heightens the sensations around the decayed site, to avoid its removal."

Atticus balled up the rag. "Then be precise, or I'm going to start singing." He wedged it in his mouth.

Hex laughed and leaned in. "I bet you have the voice of an angel. Bite down, big guy."

She brought the scalpel in sideways, catching it on a hunk of dry, dead flesh. It passed through painlessly, slicing off the foul gristle and exposing more beneath it. He didn't feel much at first, only the dull tug every time she tore a piece off him. But as she went deeper, the scabby chunks held on tighter, as though they'd grafted themselves to the tender flesh they hoped one day to spoil.

Hex stopped and chewed on her lip. "This is strange."

Atticus spat out the rag. "What?"

"Your body." She squinted, and got closer to the putrid patch. "It's… it's trying to absorb the dead parts."

"What?"

"Here, scoot closer to the fire."

Atticus did as he was told. Leaning forward, his untrained eyes only saw a glistening gash that hurt like a son of a bitch.

"Here, and here." She pointed the scalpel at the last bits of dead tissue. Fresh flesh had begun to grow over it. "Humans can't break down necrosis like this. It's too much. That's what this is for." She wiggled the scalpel. "Your body is attacking it, absorbing it."

Atticus remembered what Gary had told him his first night in Bedlam, after the snake attack. *"I'd go through the motions,"* the ghoul said. *"You might be dying and not even know it."*

"If you leave it, necrosis can spread. Poison you. Kill you."

Atticus reached for the rag. "Keep going then."

Hex looked almost disappointed. "You sure? In your case, I think you'll be fine."

"I can't be relying on this. I may recover, but every time I die I'm putting myself at risk." He scanned the dark for signs of the shepherd. "I have to go through the motions. It's going to heal me, but if I'm spiriting off to the Membrane every five minutes until it does because of infections or bleeding… then that's when they'll have me."

"You're a brave man," Hex said, nodding. "You'll get them back. We'll make you a hero yet."

Atticus laughed and told her to get on with it.

She slid the scalpel back into his leg. "What's it like? Death and the Membrane?" She continued to saw slowly. Fresh blood bubbled out and dripped over his thigh.

Fuck you, god damn bitch, Atticus screamed in his head, as she peeled back the last of the dead tissue.

"One down, eleven to go," she said, giddily.

"They're lonely." He threw the rag into the fire. She poured a foamy concoction over his leg. "Both of them. God damn, woman!"

"Hush child, you're going to wake the neighborhood." She tilted her head at a stirring Adelaide. Its roots curled and uncurled, like fingers flexing before a kill. "What's it look like?"

"Funnily enough, you're the first to ask."

"Not surprised." She reached into the case and pulled out a thick roll of bandages. "James doesn't have the stomach for it. And for Gary, this is his afterlife. Don't think he's ready for another."

"But you want to know?"

"I want to know everything about everything." She lifted his leg, brushed off the mosquitoes that had landed on it. "I come from a curious family."

Do I want to tell you? His was a secret only the dead truly know. Perhaps it was privilege that gave him pause, but how could she appreciate what he told her? *Hell, how many more are out there that are like me?* Realizing that secrecy was, in part, what had resulted in his family's demise, he described what he'd seen.

While he walked her through Pulsa diNura, Hex finished tightening the bandage on his leg. She smiled as he spoke, her tongue slightly out, like a child enraptured by a fairy tale. At times, her eyes would flash blue, like jewels catching wintry light, but Atticus was too invested in his story to stop and ask what that was all about.

"Did you happen to see god while you were there?" She put the roll of bandages down and picked up the scalpel again.

He followed her hand as she deliberated back and forth between her next necrotic victim. "No."

Choosing his knee, she dug the scalpel in and said, "That's a shame. If we could haul its corpse up out of there, people might get the point."

"Penance, you mean?"

James mumbled something in his sleep. The only time he did that was when he was dreaming about his father.

"Nah. They stopped worshiping god years ago. It's all the Holy Child and the Hydra, sorry, 'Mother Abbess Justine' now. The people of Penance just haven't realized it yet."

"Wonder what that must feel like? To be worshiped?"

Hex took off a large chunk of skin. He punched the ground and growled.

"Probably a little bit like what you're going through right now. Being taken apart and put back together until all the flaws are the ones you can't see." She poured liquid on his leg and broke out the bandages. "Better watch yourself, Atticus. The Gravedigger's graves might just become gateways to heaven."

"Nobody's deifying me," he said, helping her tie off the cloth.

"Nobody's going to ask if you want to be. Two down, ten to go."

CHAPTER XIV

Cathedra crowned the hill ahead. With the help of the rising sun, the town blinded Atticus and the others who looked at it. Cathedra's stark white walls and towers were modeled after Penance's own, because many years ago, according to Hex, this was supposed to have been the new home of the city-state. At the time, the Holy Order of Penance had fallen ill, sickened by the beliefs and practices of the old priests and exemplars who refused to give up their positions. Their decisions led to the destruction of the city's economy, as well as most of its food supply. The relentless blizzards that barraged the city-state thereafter for months at a time only added insult to injury.

"God is in the hearts of all who follow him, but not in the heart of the land itself," Hex said, quoting something as they stood staring at the distant town. "That's where the name came from, you know? Heartland."

When it became clear to the rest of the world that Penance, for the first time in a long time, was actually going to go through with something they said, Hex told them the Night Terrors responded. They left Cathedra alone, but struck at any organizer for the mainland movement. The Divide became hotly contested, resulting in the demolition of several bridges that spanned the river, as well as the deaths of hundreds of Corrupted and Terrors alike. Old World fears resurfaced concerning the creatures. Afraid they would become targets themselves, Hex explained that many supporters turned on Penance. Desperation led to a restructuring of the Holy Order. Like all religious blowhards, they took no responsibility for their actions by decreeing that what had transpired had been, in the end, the will of god.

"The Heartland would be a very different place if it had all worked out," James said.

They continued down the Deceit.

Gary nodded, scratching his horse behind the ear. "Wouldn't be much room for people like us, Atticus."

"Not sure there is now." Looking at the town, Atticus wondered how something so beautiful could remain beautiful so many years later. "Where's Carpenter Plantation?"

"Annaliese's Deceit winds around back of Cathedra," Hex said. "The plantation sits about two miles outside of town. It'll get dense again and then marshy. That's where my team is. From there, we go half a mile south and we're at their front door."

"This team made up of people you know?"

Atticus had one last look at Cathedra and the tiny figures on the road, before the Deceit closed around him, swallowing the view.

"Some. They're led by a man named Warren. Real big fella. Met him near Hrothas a few years back. Team's mostly his. Warren's a good guy. He'll do just about anything for a bit of coin."

"How much did this search and rescue run you?" Gary asked, ducking before his head collided with a low-hanging bough.

"A bit," Hex said, grinning. "But I'll make sure to get my money's worth."

Atticus searched the trail for signs of the Adelaides, but the last one he'd seen had been a few hours ago.

"If Cathedra catches wind of what we're doing, they going to stop us?"

"They're protesting, remember? Nah, they'll join. Banking on it, actually." Hex paused, said something under her breath about Ichor. "For Cathedra, it's not about what Eldrus is doing at the plantation. They don't give a damn about that. They're still preparing for the day Penance comes. So anything that gets in the way of that is a problem. Real shallow folks that only care about appearance. I kind of think it's them that's given Penance a bad name, and not Penance itself. I mean, how often do you really run into someone from that place?"

"Faith's a hell of a thing," Gary said.

Hex hummed and, clicking her tongue, hurried her horse. "Ought to find a way to bottle it. I've yet to find a better anesthetic."

"Aren't you a little heretic?" Atticus said, teasing her.

Even now, he found himself surprised by the woman's openness. He expected she was the kind of person that, when she spoke her mind, everyone listened; not because they agreed, but because it would be better than the beating they'd get if they didn't. It was the kind of confidence that attracted people and alienated friends.

Maybe Ichor's all she's got, he thought, watching her braids sway with every gallop. *Or maybe he's all she deserves.*

Hex giggled and put her hands together as though to say a prayer. "Aren't we all heretics in our own ways?"

"I'm not," James said proudly, though his nervous tone suggested otherwise. "I still have faith."

"Good, James," Atticus said, smiling at the boy. *I hope you're never given cause to lose it.*

Annaliese's Deceit didn't know what color it wanted to be, so it tried them all on at once. As the trail went wide outside of Cathedra, the leaves alternated between dark oranges and vibrant greens, subdued yellows and yearning reds. The soil, too, ran the spectrums of brown and gray, creating a path that it almost seemed a shame to trample.

When things had quieted down, Atticus asked Hex who Annaliese was and what her deceit had been, but she only shook her head and said, "At this point, that story is as good as gone. Sure left some nice things behind to look at, though, didn't she?"

Fifteen minutes from their rendezvous, Atticus got to thinking about Clementine and Will. He'd been avoiding it and most things associated with their memory. Talking seemed to help some. He'd said more words in the last few weeks than he had in the last few months. But at best, disclosure was a dam built to hold back an ocean Yet he couldn't always think of Blythe, either. He could only mutilate the soldier so many times in his mind before he started to repeat himself. So fifteen minutes from their rendezvous, Atticus got to thinking about Clementine and Will, and wished he hadn't.

He'd never even seen Will down there. As far as he knew, Clementine could've taken the plunge into the Abyss moments after he abandoned her. There was no telling they even wanted to come back. All he had was what he knew, and how much of that remained true in a place like the Membrane? The longer they stayed, the longer Death would erode them, break them down, until, one day, they became something he would be better off leaving behind.

Death had made him doubtful, pitiful. He abhorred it.

"No, no," he said under his breath. *I just need to find them. Once I see their bodies, I'll know.*

There was a rustling somewhere off the path. Atticus straightened up. Slowing his horse, he searched the area. He sought out the sounds, his gaze moving between the skinny trees and the razor thin grass that grew wildly amongst them. Probing the gaps in the Deceit, he caught glimpses of the landscape beyond, sun-shocked and shimmering. It was a sight for his sore eyes that he hadn't seen since Will's birth, when he put behind him Poe's bounties and shakedowns.

A branch snapped, and ripped him from his reverie. He shifted his attention to the source—a few trees bound at their canopies by black ivy. He'd touched the stuff once. It took two months and a whole lot of prayers and promises before the itching stopped. No, there wasn't anything there. A soldier, he thought, spying, maybe, or an animal stalking, more likely, but no, there wasn't anything.

But it was when he'd made up his mind and went to turn away that it was there. The shepherd stood between the trees, covered in fungus from the brim of its hat to the heel of its boot. It was the same he'd seen last night, but it seemed like it had been here for years. It was watching him, following him with eyes it didn't have.

The horse kept going until he couldn't see the shepherd anymore. He glanced back the way they'd come, but it wasn't giving chase, and he knew that was the point. Every second he spent looking over his shoulder was a second lost to seeing the thing that was in front of him all along.

A few miles and many memories later, the land grew soft and the air turned damp. Before them, a stream babbled in protest at the branches and rocks that sat in its way. A turtle roamed the banks, its parasitic shell greedily gobbling up what had been washed onto the shore.

"There," Hex said, at the head of the line, wheeling around. "Past here." She pointed at the tops of two tents hidden amongst the foliage. "They've probably seen us already, but even so, don't do anything stupid. I'll take the lead."

They steered their horses northward, until they found a place where the stream was shallow and not coated in leeches. Atticus followed behind Hex, reins in one hand, machete in the other. He could hear Gary and James whispering amongst themselves, one telling the other—he wasn't sure which—everything was going to be okay.

Somewhere in his soul, Atticus heard a whispering, felt a hungering. He reached into his pocket, pulled out Bon's glove, and slipped it on. If he tried hard enough, he could still conjure up the smell of the soldier's burning flesh.

Past the stream and berry-choked bushes, they found several men, surrounded by sagging tents, sitting in a circle, warming their hands by a pile of heat rocks. Some had been cracked open to get at the last of the warmth inside. Each man was armed and armored; a few even had shields. They didn't so much as budge when Atticus and company came bumbling in.

"Good afternoon to you," Hex said to the men. She hopped off her horse and let it graze about the camp. "They're with me."

The men nodded, and grunted. They made room for her to sit, but she thanked them and stood instead. Three more, archers, emerged from the woods, one carrying a fawn, while the others each held a dead Eldrus soldier over their shoulders. Long lines of blood ran down those archers' backs, from their victims' mangled mouths.

Atticus got down with Gary and James, and kept close to Hex. The archers dropped the bodies near one of the tents and stripped them. They piled the soldiers' clothes and weapons separately and kept any valuables for themselves. Afterwards, they spat in their lifeless faces, dragged them back into the woods, and rolled them into a large pit.

"How do you like our grave, Gravedigger?"

Atticus turned to a tent and found there was now a massive mountain of a man standing outside it. The shit-eating grin on his face told Atticus this was their leader, Warren. His arms probably weighed more than James and Gary combined. Hundreds of scars ran across his bulging muscles, as though he'd been put together from the parts of others. His hair was long, pulled back tight into a greasy bun, and his beard hung like moss off his chin. He looked like what most men of Gallows had hoped one day to be, before the drink had drowned their dreams.

"Kind of you," he finally responded. "Seems a bit cramped."

"Oh yes, there are a few down there already. Stragglers. These soldiers are due back this evening, so it's best you arrived when you did. We have to get moving." Warren grinned. Half his teeth had been busted. "I've got to see it, Gravedigger. Won't you show me?"

Atticus, looking at Hex, said, "What's that?"

Warren rubbed his hands together, almost did a jig he was so excited. "You know, the whole not dying business."

Atticus' face turned red, as though he'd swallowed some horrible swill. He was about to make a big deal out of what was, admittedly, a big deal, but instead pointed to his neck. "This?"

"Oh my, that looks troublesome."

Warren laughed as Atticus pulled up his pant leg.

"We're getting a peep show here, boys."

Warren cringed when he saw the skin underneath.

"How are you still standing, my man? You don't look like the toughest cat in town."

"Hold on," Atticus said. "How the hell do you know who I am?"

"Look," Hex said, interrupting, "we're here for Ichor, not to measure our dicks."

Warren, staring at his crotch, mumbled, "Thank god for that. I've had enough embarrassment this week."

"Show us the plans," Hex commanded.

"Who are these others with you first?" Warren made a motion for his men to stand, and they stood. "Why are they with you to begin with?"

"James," she said, pointing to James, "and Gary." She nodded at the ghoul. "Gravedigger was coming this way, anyways. Blythe stole something of his. He means to get it back. A man who can't die is a man I want at my side."

"Can't argue with that." Warren bit his lip, picked at a callus on his meaty hands. "You got a ghoul with you?"

"You getting squeamish, Warren?"

"I just like to know what I'm getting into. You a ghoul?"

Gary nodded, sending a part of his spine through his flesh. "You going to do something about it?"

Warren shrugged and shook his head. "Not unless I have to. This is a merry band of murderers and monsters we have here. Follow." He pointed to the tent he'd come out of. "Step into my humble abode."

There was a woman in the tent, Warren's second in command, Francis. She sat at a small table, pouring over the blueprints of Carpenter Plantation. She, plus the men outside and the three women he saw coming in from the field, put the team at twenty. Hex had told them to expect at least fifty soldiers at the plantation. The odds didn't sit right with Atticus.

"Gravedigger?" Francis was about the size of Warren, except she was more fat than muscle. She looked like a toad sitting on that stool of hers, and when she spoke, she croaked like one, too.

"Starting to feel popular around these parts." Atticus did a double-take of the tent as Warren drew back the flap. "Big place you got here."

"Better than the one I've got back home," Warren said. He went to the table and waved them over. "They're fine, Francis. What Hex wants, Hex gets. For a little more coin, I offered to give her a strip-tease, but she didn't bite."

Francis rolled her bulged-out eyes. "Keep saying stupid shit like that and she just might."

Warren went solemn. "Don't mind her. She's grumpy. Come here, come here. Have a gander at the grinder we're about to throw ourselves in."

"He's a ghoul." Francis repositioned herself on the stool, perturbed. Pointing at James, she added, "He's too young."

"And he can't die," Hex said mockingly. She looked at Atticus. "What're you getting at?"

"I like to know who's tagging along and why. If Hex wants you, fine. That's fine. But I heard you say something out there about how Blythe stole something. What did he steal?"

Atticus gave no response.

"I'm not trying to get in your personal business. I'm forming squads, so I need to know where to put you."

"Blythe killed all of us, my family." He pulled down his armor and shirt, revealing the crater in his chest. "He left me and took their bodies. I've come to get them back. To see they're laid to rest right."

Francis opened her mouth and then shut it. It was probably the first time in a long time something had left her at a loss for words.

"You really did die?"

"I did."

"Hey now, how'd you come back?" Warren asked.

Atticus shrugged. "Unfinished business, I suppose. I don't care to know until what I need to do is done."

"I know where to put you," Francis said, softening up some. "Commit this to memory, everyone who is coming. Eldrus couldn't have picked a better place to do terrible things. You see it? The architecture? The insanity of it? Look, look at it."

It was true, every word of what the woman said. Carpenter Plantation was madness made manifest. The blueprints stated there were three floors and a basement, but all Atticus saw was a cramped labyrinth of walls and half-rooms, with hallways that ran in circles and staircases that led nowhere. There were pits that plummeted into the basement, and areas on the third floor that were inaccessible altogether. In places, doors lined the floor, leading to crawlspaces where one could scurry like a rat the length of the place. And elsewhere, there were rumblings of a second basement—the scrawl beside the plans demanding it be placed on the third floor... upside down.

"Guess they never heard of the word 'attic,'" Atticus said. "Where'd you dig this up?"

"We got it from an old man we interrogated," Warren said. His face went dark. "Nice guy. He had quite the collection of Old World memorabilia. He said he kept the blueprints updated. It was a project of his. Damndest thing, though. We went easy on him, didn't we, Francis?"

She nodded.

"We went easy on him, but the excitement was too much. His heart gave right out. He just keeled over his coffee. Scared the hell out of me."

Francis sighed and said, "We did right by him, though."

"We did do that, we did. He was a sweet old man. Didn't have anyone, and we didn't want Eldrus grabbing up his corpse, so we gave him a proper send-off. Francisco, that was his name."

"Well, aren't you sweethearts?" Hex said.

"Honey, not all monsters are monsters." Warren bit his lip and then continued. "It's not just the plantation's construction that's got us worried. You can hear things coming from it."

Francis nodded. "Screaming. Wailing. For most of the night, that's all there is. No animals come near the area anymore because of it."

"And they're taking corpses?" Gary asked. He sounded worried, as though Eldrus would eye his husk and get the need to have it.

"Mostly," Francis answered. "Dead body is a dead body. You put it in the ground and you forget about it, like a seed that's never going to grow into anything. But some of the protestors have gone missing after a rally. So they're not above taking the living, either."

"It's because they have an excuse with the protestors," James said, biting his thumb. "They're interfering, trespassing. Whatever they're up to in the plantation… with those plants… they're terrified of it getting out."

"Something about it has them spooked," Atticus said. "This is a delicate thing they must be doing."

"Ichor," Hex whispered. "Have you heard any more about him?"

Warren shook his head. "Nothing. We know they still have prisoners." He looked at Atticus. "We know Blythe brought in the last shipment. There's still hope for the both of you."

"Better be." Hex rubbed her fingers together. "I'm getting what's mine, whether it's my brother or the coin I put in your pocket. We're not leaving here empty-handed."

"Yes, ma'am," Warren said.

"So you know about the plants? The vermillion veins?" Francis was slow on the draw, but she caught up all the same. "James, is it?"

Atticus raised his hand and responded instead. "I saw them, in the dead body they brought back home for me to bury. Blythe and Bon, I mean. My… wife cut off Bon's arm and I saw them grow it right back, the veins did."

"I think they're from the Nameless Forest," Gary threw in.

"Yeah," Hex said dryly.

"Well, I could see that." Francis tapped on the table with her thumb. "We've heard about the growths. Sometimes, they come through the yards in Cathedra, like roots trying to spread. When the soldiers find out, they dig them up and more or less quarantine the spot."

"And we've been thinking," Warren said, "that, sure, Carpenter Plantation does have that kind of cozy, crazy charm to it that makes it perfect for bad business, but there's got to be more. Nameless Forest or not, whatever they're doing to the bodies, it must come from there. They set up in that place not by choice but by necessity. Eldrus knows better than to trifle with Cathedra."

"Eldrus has been sending soldiers into the Heartland for a while now," Atticus said. "Blythe told me that what they were doing, putting the veins in the corpses, was to stop the land from dying."

Hex added, "Ichor said they're trying to throw together another

Nameless Forest."

"Well, I could see that," Francis said again, "but I don't see why they would. You said they healed a man, didn't you?"

Atticus nodded. "I did."

"It could be they're putting this crap in the ground to call on later. Has some sort of will, don't it? Or can be controlled, at least. Eldrus has been wanting the Heartland awhile now. If the towns don't give and keep trying to push them out, they could just call on these ver-million veins and that'd be that. Can't rebel if your town is over-grown. Can't fight back if the soldier you're cutting at can't be killed."

"You're so smart, Francis," Warren said, leaning and planting a wet one on her forehead. "Hex, I love working for you. Makes me feel less like a mercenary and more like a do-gooder."

Hex laughed and shook her head.

"Are you okay?" Atticus whispered to her. She didn't look it.

"Yeah," Hex said back, without opening her mouth or speaking at all.

Atticus raised an eyebrow "How the hell did you just—?"

"Sir." One of Warren's men hurried into the tent. "Sir, we saw a woman outside the camp."

Warren perked up. "What's that? Eldrus?"

The man shook his head. "Might be a villager. Long coat, big hat. Shepherd, maybe. Want me to follow her?"

Warren nodded. "Just to be sure."

Atticus swallowed hard and said nothing.

"All right, enough chit-chat," Warren said, returning to the table. "Francis, tell us our teams and how we're going to help these fine people."

"Okay, listen closely, because the rest of us aren't as patient as Warren and I. Hex, the prisoners are being kept on the third floor. Gravedigger, the shipments come out of the back of the house, but there's some strange tunnel connected to the basement, so that's where we're thinking everything is being loaded.

"I'm going to split you all up, because while these aren't Eldrus' finest, they are better than most. Hex, you'll go with Gary, James, Marco, and myself. Gravedigger, what you want is heavily guarded, so you'll need a tougher crew. Take Jessie, Miranda, Elizabeth, and War-ren."

Warren nudged Atticus. "Looking forward to watching you

work."

"We are the Cabal," Francis said. "For as long as you're with us, you're one of us. Don't make it personal. We shoulder each other's burdens. So yours are now ours. We're expecting about thirty-five soldiers. Most likely we're going to have to kill them all.

"Two of ours will go in disguise, thanks to those our archers caught. There'll be five teams altogether." She pointed to the blueprint. "Hex, you'll come in from the east, through the kitchen. Gravedigger, you'll circle around back and wait until the grounds are clear, then you'll work your way through the study." She dabbed her finger on the small compartments shaped like stars on what was now their map.

"We've been hearing a lot of construction, or deconstruction. It's hard to say. They're either building the place up or tearing some of it down. It probably won't look like what you've imagined. So don't lose your head and stay close to your team. I'll explain the rest at sundown." Francis looked over at Atticus and his companions. "Gravedigger, I hope you don't mind dying, because you might be doing a lot of it tonight."

"I don't," Atticus said.

"Good, that's good." Francis finally got up from the table. "Because I'd rather it be you than any of mine. You can appreciate that, can't you?"

"Just get me to my wife and son and I'll fall on every sword that's put in front of me."

CHAPTER XV

In the cold dusk and descending gloom, Carpenter Plantation waited. Its shiny eyes cast their burning gaze over the property, to singe the shadows until they showed the secrets they kept. Screams, desperate and disbelieving, bellowed out of its locked-up mouths, to be heard by those chanting outside the gates, fevered and frothing.

Atticus and his team lay on a hill, surveying the eastern side of the estate. Somewhere, an order cracked across the grounds. Ten men poured out of the slave shacks at the end of the house. They hopped on their horses and rode down the quarter mile stretch to the gates. The protestors hooped and hollered as they neared.

Several soldiers emerged from various doors, the sounds of their chainmail preceding them. They started patrolling the length of house, up and down the wraparound porch. Occasionally, they would survey the hills around the place, where sentries should've been posted and were not; because the Cabal had cut their throats.

The other teams moved through the outskirts, bunching up against the wall that blocked off parts of the estate. Atticus blinked, and then they were gone, into the tunnels they'd dug under the weakest, most overgrown points. It was a short crawl, he was told, but for the sake of cover, they suffered the thorns on the other side of the wall until the coast was clear.

Voices rolled off the second floor balcony as three soldiers stepped onto it. A painted-over door opened on the side of the third. Someone with a bucket slung a gallon of red water over the edge.

At the back of the house, where four carriages were parked, massive steel doors in the earth flung back. A group of three Eldrus soldiers sprinted out, horsed-up a carriage, and drove it through the doorway, down a ramp and into the basement. Ropes attached to the doors pulled them back, to seal off the loading area.

"It's like they want people to see how it works," Atticus whispered. "Couldn't be any more inconspicuous if they tried."

Jessie, Miranda, and Elizabeth—Warren's so-called Deadly Beauties—simultaneously looked at Atticus and told him to shut the fuck up. He didn't have a lot of time to get a feel for the women, but by the way they carried themselves, he was sure he was in good hands.

"Don't be rude," Warren said, not bothering to lower his voice. "You know why that is, Gravedigger? Why they're running around, showing everything off?"

He didn't.

"Because nobody knows anything," Jessie answered instead. She looked younger than James, even with the armor on, but Atticus was pretty confidant she could give the boy a run for his money.

"No plans, no one really in charge." Miranda slid back, holding tightly to her bow. She was the oldest of the group, at a whopping thirty.

"It's all word of mouth. No records, yeah? And the assumption it'll get done." If Hex had a sister, it was probably Elizabeth. Her ears, lips, and nose were heavily pierced. He'd only spied a few, but her arms were covered in enough tattoos to hide her Corruption. "No one knows anything, yeah? That's why. There's nothing to know."

"Can't get blood from a stone," Atticus said.

"Everything bleeds," Miranda said, rearing up. "And there's always something you can do with what comes out."

Warren tapped Miranda's head. "Should've named you all the Chatty Cathies. Wait for the signal before you sing."

"Gary and James better be all right," Atticus said, to no one in particular.

"If they have a lick of sense," Jessie said, mocking Atticus' accent, "they'll come out just fine."

"I wouldn't worry, Gravedigger." Warren nodded toward the front gates. "Hex alone is a one-woman army. I just sent Francis with her so she wouldn't pitch a fit. See the new shift there?"

At the gates, the protestors had been flanked by fifteen of Eldrus' soldiers who had come from Cathedra. The demonstration was on the edge of dispersing, what with all the dirt kicking and hand wringing.

"Hex said fifty soldiers. You said thirty-five," Atticus said through his teeth.

"Never was good with math. Watch closely," Warren said, grinning, "and you'll see a firework show that puts Bedlam's to shame."

When the reinforcements had the protestors shaken from their perches outside the gates, the soldiers took up their spots and formed a barricade between them and the bars. There was shouting and there were blows. One wise soldier went to his knees and touched the ground. He seemed surprised by what he found there, so he showed it off to the rest. His brothers looked at his hands—they were covered in something—and started to panic.

"See that fella right there?" Warren said, pointing to a male protestor in bright red. "That's one of ours."

The protestor pulled back his arm and threw something, a pouch perhaps, at the gates. In one hellish second, green flames shot out of the ground and immolated the soldiers. Helmets and breastplates fell to the ground as their bodies were melted instantaneously.

"Brimstone and Rapture," Atticus said, in awe. "How did you even find those powders?"

The protestors had coated the grounds in Brimstone, and the cabalist in disguise had ignited it with a pouch full of Rapture. The fire only burned where the accelerant had been poured, and like all things heated and hateful, it burned out quick.

In fifteen seconds, the fifteen soldiers were no more than one puddle of flesh and fat, sticking to the soles of the townspeople that now trampled through them.

"Miranda, sing us a song," Warren said.

As the protestors rocked the gates and worked the locks, the mounted guards on the other side were shouting something to those patrolling the house. Miranda stood up, nocked an arrow, and shot it at a guard on the grounds. Before it met its mark, the soldiers on the second floor and those circling the first hit the ground, too, each with an arrow through an eye or throat. The Cabal archers elsewhere had a song to sing, too.

"Let's go, Gravedigger, yeah?" Elizabeth said, kicking his ankle.

Warren urged them up, so they got up. Under the cover of Miranda's volleys, they rushed down the hill, surprising the few soldiers that hadn't yet been skewered. Atticus' legs were tight as he bounded towards Carpenter Plantation. Each step was like another snakebite. If he closed his eyes, he saw them there, the Hissing Monarch and her brood.

I've come so far, he thought. Two teams emerged from their tunnels beside the walls. *It's almost over, Clementine. We'll be going home soon, Will.*

When the front gate burst open, Atticus drew his sword. Protestors rushed the estate. The mounted soldiers hesitated for a moment, waiting for orders they knew would never come, and went at them. Eldrus rode the townspeople down, hacking off heads and arms, showering themselves in Cathedra's blood. The fallen begged for mercy, but the best they got was a hoof to the mouth and a throat full of teeth.

By the time the soldiers on horseback realized what was happening behind them, the Cabal were already at the house. Atticus and his team clambered over the railing of the wraparound porch. To their left, more of the Cabal intervened in the front yard slaughter, ripping the men off their horses. To their right, the teams from the walls converged at the back of the house.

"Through there," Warren said, shouting over the screaming and the sounds of footsteps in and outside of the house. He ran to the end of the porch, where it stopped at a discolored wall. "Paint's still fresh." He kicked the wall with his massive legs, flinging back what was now clearly a door. The chain locks lolled off it like tongues. "Skedaddle, god damn it!"

Atticus and the Deadly Beauties bounded through the doorway, leaving the cacophony outside for the chaos within. The study they entered was egg-shaped. The room held one desk with a chair, all iron-maiden-like. There were bookshelves bolted into the ceiling, far out of reach and long since emptied. Glancing down, Atticus spotted a window in the distressed floor. Behind it, a precious specimen lay crumpled and stiff: a pair of women's underwear dyed in menstrual red.

Warren shouldered past his people, slammed the door shut, and threw the desk in front of it. "No one's stabbing me in the back."

Something hit the ground hard on the floor above and rained dust down on their heads. Elizabeth said, "Let's get going, yeah?" and then shut up quick as the door they needed to go through slammed back.

Three soldiers ran into the room and stopped, surprised to find the Cabal there.

They drew their swords at about the same time they drew their last breaths, give or take a few seconds. Elizabeth punched one in the face and pulled him down on her sword, sending it out his back. Atticus vaulted across the room and, with the machete he'd brought, split open a soldier's gut and spilt his innards. The last man tried to escape, but he slipped on the steaming intestines. Atticus crawled over his body, grunting as the soldier tried to kick him off, and broke his face open.

"Hell, I like your spirit," Warren said.

"Thanks," he said, tightening Bon's glove on his right hand.

He stopped feeling so sore about being separated from Gary and James. It was better this way. He felt less responsible for their wellbeing, and they probably felt the same about his.

"If we're quiet, we should miss most of the action," Jessie said. She slipped past Atticus and leaned out the doorway. "It's clear."

"There's more going on here," Atticus remarked, machete in one hand, sword in the other. "This is an assault, not just a rescue."

"Well, we've been gathering information and planning for about two months now." Warren looked at Miranda and Elizabeth; they went to the doorway and joined Jessie there. "Now's not the time, Gravedigger."

"Hex waited two months to get her brother back?" Atticus persisted. "Does she even got a brother?"

"Three months, really," Warren said, holding up three fingers. "She delayed some to bring you along. But brother? I've met a man named Ichor who said he was her brother. They were at each other's necks. Literally. Teeth and knives and all that jazz."

"You reckon she's here for other reasons?"

"I reckon she is. Hex is a person of ulterior motives. We all are, in our own ways."

Soldiers ran through the hall outside the study.

"Does it matter, Gravedigger? You're using her, after all, to find your family. Just like she's using you to sweeten the pot, to make sure the mission is completed."

It doesn't matter, Atticus heard Clementine whisper in his ear. *You're so close. You've come so far. Nothing stands between us now, other than the re-*

mains of those that would try.

"Hey, dead man," Elizabeth said, "you first."

Miranda nodded and, with her, the Deadly Beauties parted. "Earn your place," she said, as though she resented his presence here. "Earn your myth."

Though he thought myth was a stretch, Atticus let it go and took the lead. The hallway outside the room was narrow and split into three different directions. The walls themselves were the color of rust. They stretched into the attic, so that the ceiling here was the roof itself. Prison bars had been installed into the walls on the second floor. More soldiers, apparently not looking down, hurried past them.

Atticus put his finger to his lips. Some of the blood from the soldier he had crushed had stuck there. The taste of him made his tongue curl. He waved Warren and the Deadly Beauties forward, shrinking into himself as they passed. Even now, after everything, it didn't sit right with Atticus to be taking orders. He'd sworn off letting others run his life long ago. It was too easy a role for him to slip into, the simple servant, dutiful and dangerous; Poe had known that, and had milked it for all it was worth.

Warren went to where the hallway branched, closed his eyes, and chose the leftmost path. "This should cut through the center of the house, to the sleeping quarters. If we're quick, we'll cross paths with Francis and Hex."

"Could be a lot of soldiers still there," Atticus said.

He heard a tapping. The shepherd was on the second floor, staring at him through the prison bars. *Shit, shit, shit.* The team was too focused on the hallways in front of them to notice it.

"Front of the line, Gravedigger," Miranda said, not letting him off the hook. She smiled when she said it; probably could tell she was pissing him off.

Atticus looked back at the second floor, but the shepherd was gone. *It won't try nothing here,* he thought. *It can't with them around. If it comes down here, I'll have them kill it.*

"You got a name, Gravedigger?" Miranda asked.

"Gravedigger is fine," he said, going down the hallway.

He expected Warren to put a stop to the Beauties' behavior, but he didn't seem to care, and, really, Atticus couldn't blame him. If he met someone claiming immortality, he'd put them to the test, too.

"Got a good ring to it, yeah?" Elizabeth said, taking out the piercing in her lip and slipping it into a pocket. "Real broody. People will like that."

The team worked their way through the winding hallway. They couldn't take more than a few steps before it would abruptly change directions. Screams and clashing steel pierced Atticus' ears, the sounds being more amplified here. He had a sour taste in his mouth, and his stomach felt sick. But it would be over soon, and he hoped it wouldn't take long to put this—Eldrus, the Membrane, the vermillion veins—all behind him. He could do that if he needed to, suppress and deny. He'd gotten good at it. He would have died a long time ago if he hadn't.

The hallway split into three more corridors. They took the one that went past a small chapel. Peeking inside, Atticus found an altar bathed in candlelight, with a skull on a bundle of vermillion veins atop it. Cracked stained-glass windows hovered over the cramped spot, imposing their forgotten deities onto this offering.

"What... please... don't."

Atticus stopped, doubled back. At the end of the chapel, in the last pew, a young soldier sat, bawling.

"Please," he blathered on, coming shakily to his feet. He dropped the sword he held. "Please, I'm sorry. We... we stayed in this house too long. It changed us. I don't know anything."

Miranda sighed, handed Warren her sword. She raised her bow, nocked an arrow, and shot the soldier in the neck. Blood spurted out across the altar, across the face of the crucifix behind it. The young soldier fell to the ground, disappearing into the dark there. They didn't bother to check his pulse.

The sleeping quarters made about as much sense as their plan to slip through them. Chain-bound beds, twenty in all, dangled from the ceiling. There were doors, too, in the floor and the walls, some of which were ajar, most of which went nowhere. Garish stone slabs shot out of the ground, the blood on their edges a testament to their sharpness.

"I don't see any signs anyone slept here," Atticus whispered.

"Can you blame them?" Warren and the Deadly Beauties parted and scoured the quarters. "We didn't tell you the story of this place."

"Didn't care enough to ask." Atticus opened a door in the floor, but there was only dirt behind it.

"Not much for details, are you, yeah?" Elizabeth tapped one of the beds. "They're upside down. Bedposts, see, flipped around."

"Gravedigger strikes me as a thoughtful man," Warren said, as though Atticus weren't there. "Single-minded, but thoughtful."

Atticus' arms went taut. "Do you have a problem with my being here?" He imagined what damage he could do with them, the sword, and the machete.

Warren smiled. "The old man, Francisco, said it happened long before the Trauma, back in the days when they kept slaves."

Miranda interrupted. "We don't have time for this."

Warren nodded, shrugged. "Might be relevant. Why don't you scout ahead, sourpuss?"

Miranda gave him the middle finger and marched to the end of the room.

Warren laughed. "I should be harder on the Cabal, but I'm just too damn nice."

"You're buying time," Atticus said, realizing how much the man had been stalling lately.

"Hush now," he said, giggling like a schoolgirl. "But, yes, yes I am. I don't have to pay if the person's dead. The more we stall, the more that fall. The Cabal isn't the securest of jobs, right, Jessie?"

Jessie clicked her tongue and pretended to hang herself with a noose. "Right, boss."

"Most of the men you saw were hired-on. We four and Francis are the backbone of this operation. Maybe you'd like to join us?" He waved off the offer. "Anyways, the story, Gravedigger. The Carpenters went into business with a family from a distant country. Can't remember why. Can't make heads or tails of that nonsense. The Ashcroft family, that was their name.

"So the old man I told you about, Francisco, he said the Ashcrofts sent two people to the plantation. Ruth and her uncle, Amon. He showed me the records. It's kind of amazing what's survived over the years."

"We're good to move," Miranda said.

Warren winked and sent Elizabeth and Jessie to her. He shouldered up next to Atticus and walked with him to the end of the sleeping quarters.

"The Carpenters did well, but somewhere along the line, the father of the family, Abel, lost his mind. He became obsessed with Ruth Ashcroft, and then, and Francisco couldn't ever figure out why, he turned on her. Amon left at some point, but it seems like Ruth may have stayed.

"Abel became convinced there was something wrong with the house, and that the girl had put it there. But he didn't leave, man. No, sir. He stayed and remodeled everything. Francisco said Abel was at it for years, tearing the place apart."

"A man needs a hobby," Atticus said. His eyes darted back and forth, following a sound somewhere ahead.

"He stayed with the house, because he was trying to stop whatever was inside from getting out. Clearly, the poor soul was insane. You and I both know there's better ways to handle things like that. But not Abel, no sir. He lived here until he died, constantly building and repairing, turning this plantation into an unsolvable maze, to keep the thing from leaving."

"You thinking Eldrus found what Abel was trying to hide?" Atticus didn't need to ask. He knew this was exactly what Warren was getting at.

"I'm thinking that, if he wasn't as crazy as a shithouse rat, then, yeah. Whatever he was hiding, it was either too cruel to just kill him, or too simple to just leave. Yeah, I'm thinking Eldrus found something and they've conscripted it to their cause."

"The vermillion veins," Elizabeth said, raising an eyebrow.

"My Deadly Smarties." Warren shook his head, too pleased with himself to stop smiling. "All right, people. Break's done. Let's get to kill—"

An Eldrus soldier ran screaming into the room and cut Jessie's head in half. The top of her skull spun off, slinging a spiral of blood over her wide-eyed sisters. As her body hit the ground, they could hear, and then see more soldiers—*five, no. Ten… twelve. Fuck!*—burst into the sleeping quarters.

"Jessie!" Elizabeth lunged for her corpse.

Miranda grabbed her and dragged her back to Atticus and Warren.

"You mother fuckers," Warren bellowed.

Atticus' neck twitched with every squirt of blood that spurted out of the girl's bisected head. Her severed brain slid out. A soldier crushed it under his heel and smeared everything she had ever been across the floor.

The soldiers didn't speak, just swarmed. Atticus and the others broke apart, forcing the wave of men to do the same. Three soldiers converged, each taking a turn slashing at him. The sword shook in his hand as he deflected their blows. He couldn't hold it much longer, not without his other hand. So he swung his machete and let it loose mid-swing, catching the red-headed soldier in the thick of his thigh.

The man stumbled back, went to one knee. Atticus hoped for a break in their attacks, but the other soldiers continued unabated. Their swords sang and shivered. Atticus ducked, gasped as he felt the wall at his back, the wall they'd been pressing him toward.

"Fuck!" he said, all teeth and spit.

Elbows bent, he didn't have enough room to do much with his sword. He shimmied down the wall, bounced off it, and crashed into one of the suspended beds. A hot, wet pain slithered through his gut. Looking down, he saw a sword there, bleeding him like a stuck pig. The soldier holding it grinned, his eyes lost in the dark that circled them.

Somewhere, someone shouted Atticus' name. He stumbled, the tug of a current at his ankles, at his knees. The sleeping quarters flickered and pounded. Something swelled and popped like a balloon. Another sword, the other soldier's, the bearded one, in Atticus' side, through his lung. He wheezed, fell forward, sending the blades in deeper, severing tendons, splitting muscle. He heard a throbbing, a thumping. A cracking like a crook beating at the door of his soul.

Atticus died for a moment, and lived again. He reared up, ripped himself free. Like a man possessed, he shrieked and flailed, drenching the redhead he'd thrown the machete at in hot cruor. He ripped the machete out of the soldier's thigh, whipped around, and chopped off the dark-eyed soldier's hand at the wrist.

The bearded soldier stabbed Atticus again, through his stomach. As he twisted the sword in deeper, Atticus hacked at his bearded face, cutting off his nose and lips, until the soldier finally stopped and fell to the floor to die, disfigured.

"You piece of shit," the dark-eyed soldier cried.

Stump in his arm pit, he slashed with his bad hand at Atticus' chest. The sword grazed his breastplate, but got his attention. When the man came back for a second strike, Atticus knocked his sword aside and rammed both his weapons into the dark-eyed soldier's gut. He stood there for a moment, churning the soldier's stomach with steel, and breathed in the coppery smell of death. It was his now, the life in the man's chest, and he'd keep it forever.

Atticus kicked the man into the corner and turned around. Warren, Miranda, and Elizabeth grunted and yelled as they traded blows with the six soldiers still standing.

"Gravedigger," Warren called, taking a soldier's arm and breaking it. He moaned as another soldier snuck up and cracked his head with the hilt of his sword.

Miranda backpedaled, went to her knees, and fired at Warren's bludgeoner. The arrow ripped through his eye socket and killed him quick.

Elizabeth shouted, "Watch out," but Miranda was too slow. A stocky soldier from behind ran his sword into her shoulder. She shrieked, her neck stretched to the point of snapping. Tears in her eyes, she feebly pawed at the blade, unable to reach it.

A feral beast, Atticus bounded to them. Elizabeth saw him coming and fought her way toward him. She repelled one soldier, riposted the other. Grabbing one of the suspended beds, she pulled it back and let it rip, causing it to smack into the stocky soldier that had Miranda impaled.

"Get up," Elizabeth said, air catching in her throat as she sidestepped a soldier's thrust. "Get up," she begged Miranda, who stood there unmoving, alive, but paralyzed with pain.

Atticus stumbled. His ankle bent until it sprained. His eyes fluttered. The Membrane kept getting in them, like stinging drops of rain. He saw it on the wall, in the ceiling, its fleshy pillars and piles of trash. He slashed at a soldier and fell short, his torn lung doing him no favors.

Atticus crashed to his knees and died again. He saw Pulsa diNura on the dried lakebed, same as it was and would probably ever be.

"Clementine," he shouted, but before his words could be heard, he was in the sleeping quarters again. He was coming back quicker now. His resistance to death growing stronger every time his heart stopped.

A soldier fell in front of him. She writhed on the ground. Looking up from the blood-soaked, corpse-clogged floor, Atticus watched Elizabeth and Warren close in on the last three soldiers.

A greedy thought clotted up his mind: *I need more.*

Atticus started to crawl over the corpses, towards the three, no, two soldiers still standing. One, a captain by the bulkiness of her armor, caught him out the corner of her eye. She turned.

Before she could make her move, Atticus stabbed the machete through her shoe. He then pulled it out and pushed her down and, grabbing onto her leg, heaved himself onto her.

She went for a dagger, but he grabbed her wrist and used that to propel himself forward. Her face, so panicked and red, and cheeks, tear-streaked and quivering… He had to have it. He had to eat it.

CHAPTER XVI

"That'll do for now," Clementine said, caressing his face.

She smelled so good, but where was she? Not here, not beneath him; that was the captain, still struggling so sweetly. In her eyes, maybe.

Atticus put his forearm to her throat and pulled back her lids. In the pupils, perhaps, mingling with her soul, coming through from the Membrane. She wasn't there, but she was near. Somewhere below, in the basement, with Will. But no, not here, not in this distraction.

"I'm sorry," he said, ashamed of what he'd become. He took the dagger she'd been reaching for and slit her throat. "I'm sorry."

Warren's trembling arms wrapped around Atticus and pulled him to his feet. Though he couldn't see them, he could hear what sounded like hundreds of mosquitoes congregating over the corpses, laying claim to what was now their new, bloody mecca. It made him think of Mr. Haemo and all the favors he'd have to do to get the giant insect to perform the ritual one last time.

"Jessie," Atticus said, the girl's body bringing him out of his thoughts.

He looked at Warren, who held him from behind, and Elizabeth, who had just put down the last soldier. He lingered on Miranda. She was moving now, but not much, and she kept touching her left arm, which had gone limp and rubbery.

Warren let him go and walked away. "Miranda, what's wrong?" The big man had big tears leaving bloody smears down his face.

"They killed Jessie," she said. She unlaced her bracers and pinched the skin on her left forearm. "They killed her."

Elizabeth was shivering. She stepped over the bodies towards their fallen friend. She started stripping off pieces of armor as well. They fell with a splash into the pools of gore.

"Don't do that," Warren said to her. "You'll need it."

Elizabeth shook her head. She ripped off her breastplate. The blood that had collected behind it spilled out and soaked her feet.

Atticus wheezed when he breathed, on account of only having one functioning lung. Most of his armor, that patchwork of colors and craft, was damaged, so he removed those pieces. He left his legs protected, as well as one of his arms. Bending down, he took the captain's helmet and slipped it over his head. At this point, he need only worry about the essentials.

"I can't feel it," Miranda admitted when Warren went to touch her left arm. "I can't move it."

He sighed and spun her around to look at the hole the soldier had put through her back. He pulled out a pouch and poured some powder from it into her wound.

"Nerve damage. Leave the bow. Your sword arm is still good?"

She nodded.

Elizabeth knelt beside Jessie's body. She rooted around her neck and inside her breastplate. Something clinked. She pulled out a necklace made of shells.

"Can I wear it for a while?" Miranda asked.

"Of course. Seventy-five percent yours, anyways."

"You were there, too." Miranda hobbled forward. Elizabeth met her halfway and fastened the trinket around her neck. "Can't believe she kept it."

She smiled, put her forehead to Miranda's. "We all kept something from back then."

"She died the way she would've wanted to: spectacularly," Warren said, his lip quivering. He was trying to make the others feel better, but as for himself, he was on his own. "Through hell, we find heaven."

"Through hell, we find heaven," Elizabeth and Miranda repeated as one.

"I didn't know her," Atticus said, breaking his silence, "but I wish I had. I know that hurt too well."

"You really can't die, can you?" Elizabeth said. She pulled Miranda in close and patted her back, shushing her cries.

"Couldn't even if I wanted to."

"Lift up your shirt," Warren said. He wiped his eyes, snapped his head to the doorway as though he'd heard someone. "Lift it up. Quick."

Atticus did as he was told. The shirt was sticky, ruined, so when he was able to peel it off, he dropped it to the floor. Warren covered his mouth, while Elizabeth and Miranda gawked at the blasphemy of flesh that was his body. Two wicked slits, one in his chest, the other in his stomach, pumped out blood like a spigot. Large gouges and deep lacerations ran across his purpling flesh. The injuries from Bedlam had opened up as well, the arrow holes now glistening and smelling sour. His neck had more or less healed, but still the wound from Blythe's kunai remained untouched. It seemed he could fix what needed fixing now, but the past was beyond him, forever damaged.

"You keep nodding off, Gravedigger. Are you okay?" Warren said. He seemed as though he wanted to touch Atticus, to marvel at what, surely, this man of muscle and brute strength could only dream of.

"Yeah, just dying is all." He looked at his stomach wound and noticed it had already started to shut. "It's getting easier. Maybe I'll explain it better when we're done."

Warren nodded and looked back at Jessie's corpse. Voice quivering, he said, "I'd like that. I think we all would."

After ten minutes of pitch-black hallways and above ground sewage tunnels, Atticus and the others finally reached the swimming room. Surprisingly, the pool was still filled, but the water looked more like ink than anything else. The numbers on the side of the pool varied between two and fifty-five feet, sometimes directly after one another, as though the owner hadn't been entirely sure himself of its depths.

There were a few bodies bobbing in the kiddy-pool, blood from their backs streaking across the black water.

"Couple of our own," Warren said, recognizing the cabalists. "Third team. They cleared the place." He craned his neck. "Whatever killed them left."

Noticing there was no obvious way out of the room, Atticus said, "Where to?"

Miranda started to cry again. Like a reflex honed from years of looking out for one another, Elizabeth immediately went to her.

"I'm fine," she said, flicking Elizabeth's nose ring. "Just need to think of something else."

"There's one way into the basement. Francisco said it was the most fortified. So, he had another suggestion." Warren rubbed the back of his head. He hissed as he touched the tender skin there. "A secret passage, in this room. It wasn't on any of the maps, he said. Something he found a long time ago and kept quiet about."

"You sure it exists?" Atticus said.

He followed Warren and the others to a second, smaller pool. It was empty, a few people in width, about three feet deep, and held a garden of Haruspex drops.

"Saw a man take a bet and bite into one of these," Atticus told them. "Lost his mind before the bulb left his mouth. Lost the bet, too."

"Great story," Miranda said snidely.

Elizabeth nudged her and told her to stop.

"Gravedigger, find the deepest marker and stand on it." Warren crouched down, his hands hovering over the Haruspex. "Elizabeth, Miranda, go to the east and west walls. There should be pentagrams on them."

Ten, thirty-three. In the dim light here, Atticus had to squint to see the markers on the pool's edge. *Five, eleven, five.* The black liquid smelled like run-off, he thought, or some by-product. *Eighty-eight, seventy-two.* He straightened up as a ripple broke across the surface. *Ninety-nine.* He backed away, just in case something got grabby in the grubby muck. *Zero, negative four, negative thirteen.* He rounded the corner, sprinted, rounded the other. *One, two hundred.*

Elizabeth shouted she'd found something.

Six hundred and sixty-six.

And then Miranda did as well.

Atticus covered the last stretch of the pool and returned to that telling number: Six hundred and sixty-six.

Elizabeth stood on the tips of her toes. Arm outstretched, she pressed her hand against a patch of cracks high on the wall. "This is it, yeah?"

Warren nodded and said to Miranda, "And you have yours?"

"It's here." She was standing near the doorway, looking at something beside a light switch.

"Gravedigger." Warren reached into the Haruspexes and something clicked. "Put your weight on the numbers."

Atticus did that.

"Miranda, go for it."

And so she did.

"Elizabeth... Wait." Warren tilted his head.

Thump, thump, thump—the sound rang out through the halls they'd left behind.

"Soldiers," he said.

But Atticus knew better.

"All right, press it," Warren said, sounding rushed. "No one moves until I say."

Elizabeth, grunting, rammed her palm into the pentagram. Without missing a beat, the room went to work. Grinding gears inside the floor gave the pool the shakes. Behind the walls, ropes tightened, stretched. A death-rattle gasp, a snake-rattle shake. The Haruspex pool's bottom dropped back like a plate and plummeted the plants into the dark below it.

It was said that, by the plants, one would see their death. Atticus kept that detail to himself.

Warren told them that was enough so, equally intrigued, they hurried over to him. Taking a stone out of his pocket, he crushed it, blew on it until it glowed, and dropped it through the opening. A sharp din sounded as it hit the wrought iron staircase hidden a few feet further down.

Thump, thump, thump. The shepherd was getting closer.

"I'll go first," Atticus volunteered.

Holding her arm, Miranda's eyes lingered on the entrance to the poolroom. "What is that sound?"

"Rather not know." Warren nodded at Atticus. "Hop to it, then."

Thump, thump, thump. It was right outside the door, just out of sight, grinding the end of its crook into the ground.

Atticus stepped into the pool, sat down, and threw his legs over the edge of the opening. He gripped the sides, turned around. Lowering himself into the dark below the pool, he watched the door, his heartbeat now matching the cadence of the creature that had come to collect him. Quiet as he could be, he let go and fell onto the rickety staircase.

The air in the dark below, in the secret hell of the house, was clinging and cold, like something that'd been left alone for far too long. Dead as he might be, Atticus had to cover his nose to get away from the smell here. The thick musk of mucus and milk was just a little too much for him to take.

"It'll do," he whispered, looking up into the swimming room. "One at a time, though." He grabbed the glowing stone and held it outward, seeing where the stairs led to. "Don't know how much it'll hold."

To avoid putting too much weight in one place, Atticus started down the staircase. Miranda dropped, and then Elizabeth and Warren. Atticus couldn't hear the shepherd anymore, and no one said nothing about it, so he put it out of his mind.

Warren nudged the Beauties until they gave him the thumbs-up. "Okay, if we follow this and hit the switch at the bottom, we should come out into a storeroom, right next to where we need to be."

"Most of the soldiers will be there," Atticus said. He took a step; he heard what sounded like breathing.

"Probably twenty-five or so, yeah?" Elizabeth blew on her hands, to burn the chill of battle. "A few stragglers, maybe."

Warren nodded. "All the teams were told to converge on the basement after taking their points. Hex and your friends may or may not be there. Depends on Ichor's health."

"Hey, Gravedigger," Miranda said, "how'd your family die?"

"Two soldiers from Eldrus put us in a predicament." Atticus was surprised Warren hadn't already told them his story. "And then they put us in the ground."

"You crawled out, though." Miranda sniffed her nose, calmed a tremor in her cheek. "How?"

"I don't know," he lied.

And she knew it. "What makes you different from your ghoul friend?"

Atticus sighed. "If I knew how to bring Jessie back—"

Miranda shook her head, looked away.

"I'll take vanguard," Warren said.

Atticus went sideways and let him pass.

"I want to show you guys something."

The wrought iron staircase slumped and swayed as they plodded down its steps. Atticus had heard breathing before. He continued to hear it now, coming from inside the crumbling walls. Someone was sniffling as well. Thinking it was Miranda, he thought nothing of it, until he glanced back and saw that it wasn't.

"I'll be," Warren said, stopping where the staircase went wide. He pressed his face to the wall, picked away at the bricks. Looking through the hole, he said, "The old man Francisco was right."

Elizabeth stopped and said, "Not a good time to be withholding information, boss."

Smiling, Warren stepped back and waved Atticus over. "Cathedra thought this place was haunted. The noises they heard coming out of the plantation didn't start when Eldrus showed up. They'd—come here, Gravedigger—they'd always been here."

Atticus went over to him. Before he looked in the hole, he said quietly, "You all right?"

Warren kept on smiling, but the smile seemed sadder now, forced. "Oh yeah. Thought you might appreciate this."

Atticus put his eye to the peephole, to see what haunted this forgotten hollow. The space beyond was larger than he expected. With the support beams and scaffolding that ran along the untouched earth, he had a feeling this was meant to be another room for the house.

"What am I looking—"

And then Atticus got his answer. A glistening sack of a man sat up out of the shadows and turned. The man's face was no more than ears, jaws, mouth, and nose. His brain was there, though the top of it was pulled back by wires that were fixed to the gray flaps and tips of his skull. His arms weren't arms, not anymore, but shredded pieces of skin, like ground beef, stretched to impossible lengths. They ran like straightjacket sleeves across the floor, feeding directly into the foundations of Carpenter Plantation. As for legs, he had none. The man had nothing below the torso, except for a steady spurt of black fluid that squirted out the bottom of his spinal cord.

"What is this?"

Atticus' shoulders dipped as Elizabeth and Miranda leaned over him. He gave up his position to the Beauties and joined Warren, who was further back on the staircase.

"Abel, the master of the estate." He put his hands on his hips. "He became the thing he hated. The old man said he's been haunting this house for hundreds of years. Hell, he might've been the only evil thing left in this place until Eldrus arrived. I guess he got comfortable."

"You trying to learn me something?"

Warren shrugged and said, "I saw what you're capable of. You have your purpose. When you've done what needs to be done, you should be done."

"Kind of you. But you're singing to the choir. That's the plan."

"That stuff in the pool, that's from him, yeah?" Elizabeth said, peeking back.

"Yeah," Warren said. "I guess Mr. Abel used to be a force to be reckoned with. But time got him, like it gets us all."

"He did this to himself, then?"

Atticus was getting impatient. Warren's delays, however strategic they may have been, were starting to piss him off.

"Well, no, not entirely. There was a letter Francisco recovered. Abel threw a few parties before he boarded the place up for good. Letter talked about a woman in black that showed up, a local Witch of some sort. Guessing she offered him power and turned him into that Horror. He's been stuck here ever since."

Atticus started descending the stairs. "We should put him out of his misery."

Warren laughed and followed after him. "Misery is all he has. It's better he's forgotten. People can do a whole lot with a little bit of misery."

The stairwell ended at a brick wall flanked on all sides by engraved plates. Warren put his ear to the wall, said he heard nothing, and pressed the plate that was more faded than the rest. The wall shook. The outline of an archway formed at the center of it as bricks pulled away from one another. Without warning, the entire wall collapsed, spilling the ancient bricks into the room beyond.

"Fucking shit," Warren said, coughing as a cloud of dust blew into the hidden stairwell. He kicked at the bricks until there was enough room to cross the wreckage. "So much for subtlety."

Atticus was the first to go through. He was too close to Clementine and Will to hang back. The longer he waited, the less there'd be of them, and himself.

There was a storeroom on the other side, like Warren said, but instead of supplies it held rows of cots. But how anyone could sleep here, Atticus couldn't figure, because the air was like molasses. Thick, clammy, the soupy atmosphere had given rise to the hundreds of mushrooms and fungi that sprouted from the floors and walls.

From where he stood, he spied a large room through the doorway yonder. It was the basement, lantern-lit. This was where the carriages had gone into at the back of the plantation earlier. Muffled shouts and buckling wood told him there was a barricade somewhere, most likely between the soldiers and the cabalists ordered to get in.

"We still have the element of surprise, yeah?" Elizabeth said.

"Might not hear us," Atticus said.

He marched between the beds. Belongings were stacked under most; the soldiers to whom they belonged unlikely to ever claim them again.

"Got to be quick."

"Blythe's yours," Warren said. He and Miranda caught up with Atticus. "But don't leave us hanging, Gravedigger. If we call, you come."

Atticus nodded, said "Of course," but didn't really mean it. He pushed through the shower of spores that the mushrooms kept coughing up and went to the doorway. The basement was huge, triple the size of the house and only half furnished, as though necessity had forced it beyond what had originally been intended. Long, tall curtains sectioned off portions of the basement, like sheets left out in the sun to dry.

But what he initially mistook as a poor excuse for privacy, he quickly realized was something else entirely. Stepping out of the storeroom, he saw that the curtains weren't curtains at all, but massive sheets of fungal growth. And all of them were exhaling in unison towards the back of the house, feeding something yet unseen with their toxic breath.

"Hold them back! Hold them!"

Atticus followed the shouting, the strained groans. To his right, through the gaps in the fungal walls, he saw a barricade. Ten or more soldiers manned the mess of desks and chairs that stood in front of the chained double-doors.

Now that he had his bearings, Atticus looked to his left, where the sheets were blowing toward, and knew, further back, he'd find the carriages and, inevitably, the corpses.

"Leave them," Warren said, surprising him. "They didn't hear us, which means neither did Blythe."

"Let the men break through and chop them down," Miranda said, her arm limp at her side. "Or vice versa."

"Whatever pays the bills better, yeah?" Elizabeth chimed.

Miranda shook her head. "Yeah."

"We'll watch your back, Gravedigger," Warren said. "Press on and get what's yours."

Atticus avoided touching the sheets as he steered himself towards the back of the basement. Even being near the fungal walls made him feel faint, sick in the head. *How many are there?* he thought anxiously, passing between one after the other. More spores rained down on him from mushrooms above. With every layer he passed, the fungal walls grew darker in coloration, their exhalations weaker. Were Warren and the Beauties still behind him? He couldn't tell and didn't care enough to turn around to check. His wife and son were up ahead, and the shepherd. The shepherd.

Thump, thump, thump, he thought, thinking he heard that familiar call not far off. *It's down here with me. It's going to try to take me as soon as I have them. I know it.*

Wood buckled behind him. One wave of screams crashed over the other. The barricade had broken, and soon, so too would the loyalty of those who had manned it.

A terrible thing was easy to shoulder, as long you didn't shoulder it alone. With every crack of the shepherd's crook—*Fuck, it's close,* Atticus thought—he, now sole proprietor of certain miseries, suffered an onslaught of old agonies.

Thump: There, in his hand, his father's knife, and in the other, Poe's.

Thump: There, in his ear, Will's voice, and the sound of toys overcome by work that didn't need to be done.

Thump: And there, in every piece of him he had left, his daughter crying, her life as long as her fit.

The fungal walls continued to transition in color, until they were ashen and riddled with black, gawping growths. Atticus stopped, thought he caught a glimpse of the shepherd between the rows. New voices now, he heard, not far from where he stood. He followed the fungal wall as it ran unyielding alongside him, searching for a breach to breach.

"There," Warren said, apparently still behind him. "Right before it dead-ends."

The boss man was right. There was a desk. Beside it, an opening that had been cut into the fungal wall.

Atticus hoofed it, his helmet sitting loosely on his head. The voices were getting louder—was that Blythe on the other side?—and he heard horses snorting amongst a general commotion.

We're here, Clementine told him. *Take us home, my love.* He started crying for the hell of it, taking pride in the fact he still could, and walked, weapons at the ready, into the loading area.

It took Atticus a moment to register what he was looking at, because it wasn't something he'd ever seen before. It was a tree, or maybe it was a hand, twisting out of the ground. From its branches— or were they fingers?—thirty corpses hung, their naked bodies like fruit still waiting to ripen. There were no ropes around their necks, though. What kept them in place were the thick bundles of vermillion veins running from the tips of the branches, feeding into and latching onto their gaping mouths.

Where are you? Atticus felt cold, weak, as though all he'd been through was finally catching up with him. There were soldiers further back, in the loading area, by the metal doors, stocking the three carriages there with coffin after coffin. But they hadn't seen him, and, really, he didn't give two shits if they had.

He wandered over to the tree. It had no base, he realized, coming to the place it had ruptured out of. How large was it? How far down did it go? Was it some alien appendage? He gazed upon it's rotten canopy, that arthritic nest of knuckles and human-shaped nails. *Where are you?*

"Gravedigger," Miranda whispered. She sounded scared that they would be spotted.

Atticus ignored her. A hush fell on the soldiers ahead, so he was sure they'd already been seen. It didn't matter. It was going to be over soon, anyway. He searched the corpses like they were cattle, weeding out those that had the defect of not being Clementine or Will.

"What the hell is this?" a soldier belted.

"Shit, hurry it up! Hurry it up!"

And then Blythe: "What's wrong? Oh, who's that over there?"

Where were they? He wheeled around the gateway, not afraid or reluctant to skirt the edge of it. He couldn't begin to guess how far down the tree went. Miles, maybe. Eternities, even. He couldn't die, but he wasn't impervious to imprisonment by way of a bad fall, so he stepped back.

Thump, thump, thump.

And then the pounding of boots.

Where were they? Plenty of kids, with their distended bellies, apple colored and shaped. And teenagers, too—cut and stabbed and bludgeoned. Atticus could feel a finger being pointed at him, words being spoken of him. Where were they? He stepped over a root, an arterial thing. Older folks, hanging better off the boughs than the skin from their bones. Youth, he needed youth. The machete started swinging of its own accord, a response to the guard he saw in his periphery. Where were they? A woman, Clementine's age and build, but, no, wrong color, wrong hair. A birthmark behind the knee. That tell-tale sign. Just had to find it. Unique to her. Unique and perfect. Will? A young man, throat bulging, vermillion liquid leaking from his ass. No, not him. Where were they? Where were they? Thirty, forty, no thirty here. Was he too late?

He wheeled and wheeled, a sky of heels. Where were they? Red hair, there, red hair. It sparked his heart. He stumbled over a root to reach it, but that's all it was. A severed head, a mess of hair, with a neck that'd gone soft and separated from its body long before he'd gotten there. It was a woman, but it wasn't his woman. Where were they? Where—

"Gravedigger?" Blythe cried out to him. "As I live and breathe. What are you doing here?"

Atticus spun around, every muscle in his back trembling. Blythe. The son of a bitch stood there, arms out and exhilarated, as though he'd run into a friend he hadn't seen in years. The man was unchanged. It seemed no amount of depravity could messy that freshface he had.

Atticus started to wheeze when he breathed. Still bare-chested, he glanced at his side and saw the slit that led to his lungs had reopened again. He decided to let it bleed, to give the bastard a good show before this grueling play came to its much needed end.

Blythe set the lantern he was carrying at his feet. It lit up the cloak he wore, shone some light into the hood over his head.

"I apologize for not giving credit where credit is due."

A few soldiers sauntered over to him, but he told them to get back to the carriages.

"Hi, there," Blythe said, suddenly addressing Warren, Elizabeth, and Miranda. "Like I was saying—" he turned back to Atticus, "—I apologize for not giving credit where credit is due. We received a warning yesterday morning about a riot in Bedlam. Said some suspicious figure named 'Gravedigger' might be headed this way. That was you, wasn't it?" He laughed, and as he laughed, Atticus realized the man was completely unarmed. "I didn't even make the connection. What's your name...? Doesn't matter. Man, oh man, how... how are you here?"

Atticus dropped the sword, the one he'd stolen from the poor sap of a soldier by Bedlam's river. If he was going to kill Blythe, it was going to be with something that was his from home.

"Where... are... they?" He could barely speak. His soul burned so hot that it charred his speech.

A horse neighed. A carriage door slammed shut. There was a banging, too, on the huge, metal doors that led outside, to Carpenter Plantation's backyard. The piles of unused coffins, dark, like they'd been left out in the rain, shook beside them.

"Go ahead," Atticus said to Warren and the Beauties. His eyes never left Blythe's. "I'll... I'll be fine."

Warren nodded. With Elizabeth and Miranda, he went not to the carriages, but back the way they'd come, to assist the other cabalists, who, after Jessie, maybe didn't seem too expendable to the big brute.

"Interesting choice." Blythe leaned back, watching them navigate the fungal walls. "And here I was thinking we were under attack because of what we were doing here." He batted away a mosquito. "Where the hell are all these things coming... I'm sorry. Where are they? Gravedigger, what do you mean?"

He held the machete out, walked towards Blythe until the soldier took a step back. "My wife and son."

Blythe furrowed his brows. He stepped forward, so that the tip of the machete was touching his chest. "You're not here for revenge?"

"Oh, I am," Atticus said, licking his lips. Blythe's life was making him hungry. "But I can wait on that. Give them to me. Give me my god damn wife and son."

"What did Bon tell you? You're the Gravedigger, right? You killed him and he told you...? Huh." Blythe's eyes darted back and forth in his skull. "Your wife and son are where we left them. At the kitchen table. In the chair and on the floor. Where you ought to be."

"Don't lie to me," Atticus snarled. He pulled the machete back and socked Blythe in the jaw.

Blythe reeled. He knocked over the lantern and stumbled toward the tree. "Not bad for a dead man. Sheesh." He stretched his mouth out. "You are dead. I killed you. Looks like a few others have, too. What are you? A ghoul? Like that friend of yours?"

"Where are they?" Atticus repeated.

The soldiers had finished loading the coffins into the carriages. For some reason, they had stood up another six of the coffins in front of the metal doors.

"No small talk. No more delays. Tell me!"

"You boys done back there?" Blythe yelled, ignoring him.

The soldiers in the loading area gave him the thumbs up and dispersed into the carriages. One hung back, to open the massive metal doors.

"Hold it," he said, pointing up. There was movement in the tree limbs above. "One more for the road."

A corpse, a teenage girl, plummeted from her branch and crashed between Atticus and Blythe. She crumpled like a doll, her broken legs going every which way legs shouldn't. The vermillion veins that had held her up were still dangling out of her mouth, like parasitic anemones. The growths sat there a moment, stilled, and shivered to life. With a slurp, they retracted into her mouth and down her throat. Her legs quivered, corrected themselves; bones snapped into place, and the skin they'd punctured repaired itself. She didn't live afterward, but she looked better than before.

Blythe waved. "Come get—"

Atticus stepped in front of the girl, blocking her from the soldier who'd started over.

"—Never mind."

The soldier stopped, shrugged.

"Have a safe journey, Johnny."

Johnny smiled, nodded, and turned with a skip back towards the doors.

"Your wife and son aren't here. We killed them, yes, but we didn't take them. I don't know what to tell you, Gravedigger. I don't know who told you that we did."

Grinding his teeth, Atticus twisted his arm back and forth; the machete blade caught the lamplight and blinded Blythe.

Clementine? He bit at the inside of his mouth and drew blood. *Will,*

I'm here. He searched the tree again, Blythe staying where he stood, but his family wasn't there. Maybe the fucker had told the truth. Maybe they had never been. *Answer me,* he begged. *Please.* But they'd gone quiet. Because he'd failed them.

The soldier, Johnny, flung back a lever. Slowly, the loading area doors pulled back. The sleepy light of dusk wandered into the basement and stopped at the standing caskets. Outside, on the threshold, a handful of cabalists waited.

"Let me... have at the coffins," Atticus said, desperate.

"They're not here. I'd tell you." Blythe began to back away. "You want to bring them back. Like how you came back." He laughed, took a few more steps away from Atticus. "I'd like to see that. I'd help you for that reason alone. But you've gone quiet, Gravedigger, so I'm thinking you've realized you've been misled." He slipped a hand into his cloak. It closed around something. "That's Bon's glove, isn't it?"

Gary. Atticus remembered how jumpy the ghoul had been every time he brought up Clementine and Will. How unlike himself he'd been ever since he came out of the Membrane. *He lied to me. Him and Mr. Haemo both. Why? What did they do to them?*

The cabalists from outside marched down the slope, shouting at the soldiers in the carriages not to move.

"The Rapture and Brimstone at the front gates was impressive," Blythe said. He went to pull his arm out of the cloak and—

Atticus ran forward and stabbed Blythe. He rammed the machete upward, into his ribcage. The soldier gasped, the hood falling from his head. With his last bit of strength, he revealed what he'd reached for inside his cloak—a syringe—and stuck it in the slit of Atticus' throat. He pushed down on the plunger and smiled a bloody smile.

"What did you..."

The liquid inside the instrument drained into his skin. Immediately, his neck went numb. He ripped the machete out of Blythe and cleaved his skull.

After his neck, his face froze, too. Playing out before him was a scene he'd seen before. The cabalists were mumbling to themselves, inspecting the freestanding coffins while ordering Eldrus' carriage not to move. His eyes became as rocks, his tongue a slab of stone. The numbness worked him over like a bad drink. He heard what sounded like wood splitting and fell to his knees.

"Get back, get back!"

Atticus couldn't turn his neck anymore, so he turned what he could of his body instead. Each of the six coffins exploded open. Hundreds of vermillion veins blew out of them. They gored the cabalists, running through them as though they were paper thin. The veins shot every which way, the force of their stretching ripping apart the men's bodies. Arms and legs and entrails spilled across the basement, while impaled torsos, stuck on the net, wept blood onto the quivering strands.

Atticus would've dropped his jaw if he could have. He heard Warren coming—that booming voice of his preceding him—but when he raised up to find him, he found the numbness had overtaken him completely.

"Burn it," a carriage driver shouted.

As the vermillion veins lost their grip on the basement's walls and fell to the ground, lanterns and burning rags were hurled from the carriages. End over end, they flew through the air, crashing into the stacks of unused coffins. The coffins erupted into massive flames.

Thump, thump, thump.

Atticus cried out pathetically. He could feel the shepherd's crook pounding the floor, but couldn't move at all to find it.

Thump, thump, thump.

The fire slithered out of the loading area, towards the claw-like tree. And like a claw, it splayed its branches, shook, and retracted into its ancient gateway, taking all the bodies still attached with it.

Thump, thump, thump.

Atticus screamed. The fire crept toward him, ready to overrun him. *Warren! Warren!* He thought and wanted to say. *This can't happen. Clementine. Will.*

Thump, thump, thump.

A shadow grew over Atticus. Out the corner of his eye, he saw the crook and felt its crack. *I… I'm sorry.*

From behind, the shepherd laid its hand over his face, took off his helmet. It pushed its finger into his mouth and gums. With its other hand, the shepherd pushed through the wound in his side, dug into his lung, and started scrambling his insides.

CHAPTER XVII

The inferno spread fast. It shot across the basement and over the fungal walls, creating a deadly display of colors that almost made Atticus forget how much he'd fucked things up. When the fire started towards them, he prayed, begging for the ashy release of immolation. But the shepherd saw it coming. With a jerk of its head, it willed the fire away from them.

There was no pain as the creature lifted Atticus by his gum and lung. He should have felt something. The serum Blythe pumped into him was used to enhance sensation during vivisections. Yet, he didn't.

As the basement burned around him, the Membrane began to materialize in billowing clouds of smoke.

"Why you always have to make things so complicated?" Clementine had asked him, that day he'd gotten stuck in Brinton's grave. He never gave her an answer, because he never really had one. For as long as he could remember, that's how he always did things. It worked for him. But as he swayed there in the shepherd's hold, too feeble to fight back, he decided to try the simpler alternative.

He was going to give up.

The serum was already starting to wear off, but at that point, it didn't matter much. The Membrane had begun imposing itself upon his reality. The fungal walls lost their mushrooms and became fleshy instead. The ground sucked inward, becoming like a narrow throat, resembling the tunnel he'd fallen through when he'd first died. Another town of trash materialized in the dark distance, where the metal doors to the outside should have been and were no more.

Atticus didn't need to make this journey, make himself some sort of rumored hero, just to find them. He just thought they deserved better. Was the Membrane really all that different than life? It was same the shit-show, but without the dressings. Clementine and Will could make him forget that, though. Forget everything. Everything he'd done to find them, everything he'd become to save them.

"A shepherd watches over her flock," the creature whispered into his ear. It sounded like his wife and son, and its breath smelled like theirs, too.

Atticus could turn his head, so he did. "You come to put me back with the rest of the sheep?"

The shepherd said, "No," and lifted him higher. "You are a wolf. A shepherd watches over her world, to protect it from things like you."

In the gash that ran down the shepherd's head, he saw distilled memories gathered inside, like rivulets of water, beaded on grass.

"Take me to them," he said. "I won't fight you no more." The fire closed in, the basement almost completely engulfed. "I just want to be with them again."

The shepherd shook its head. It's sewn-shut eyes and mouth fluttered as it said, "Too bad."

A mosquito buzzed past Atticus' face and landed on his shoulder. The Membrane heaved forward, became more defined, more distinct, as it grafted itself into his mind. Wind rushed past him, into him. The shepherd hummed a spell to take them back to that terrible place.

Fire snapped at his feet, rushed up his legs. Sacs of pus popped on his thighs as his hard skin cracked in the heat. Any other time, he'd have fought the shepherd tooth and nail. But he'd been fighting long enough. And maybe he didn't deserve them after all.

The mosquito lifted off Atticus' shoulder. A pillar of smoke shot upwards, enveloping them. The shepherd shrieked. It tore its fingers out of his gum, pulled its fist from his lung.

Atticus fell. When he hit the ground, the image of the Membrane was dispelled. Arms his again, he pulled himself across the scorching earth, until he backed against something hard and boney. Ignoring it, he fumbled at the ground, for his machete.

"He's mine," the shepherd roared from somewhere in the gritty smoke.

A clicking laugh cut through the smoldering air. All at once, the smoke parted around Atticus and the shepherd stood aside. And there, framed by fire, Mr. Haemo stood, the six-foot mosquito's frantic wings beating back the hungry blaze.

He lowered his skin hood, offered a claw to Atticus, and said, "Deus ex mosquito."

"You can't," the shepherd shouted, breaking the stitching across its lips.

Mr. Haemo pulled back his claw and stepped over Atticus. He stood up to the shepherd and then knocked the hat off its head.

"You sure about that?" The giant mosquito bent down, so that his proboscis touched the shepherd's chest. "Your kind are worse than my kids."

The shepherd reached for its crook. Before it could grasp it, Mr. Haemo grabbed the shepherd by the crack in its head, where the memories and trinkets of Atticus' clan were wedged. With a roar, the mosquito ripped open the shepherd's head, sending its blond hair every-which-way. A deluge of imitations poured down its face. A lock of Clementine's hair, a piece of Will's jeans; an apron, wedding ring, and a flower; Will's first lost tooth, fairy coin and all, and Clementine's last letter, addressed to Vale. Where did it get these? Why did it have them?

The creature went limp and slumped to the ground. As the fire climbed over the shepherd's corpse, it dissolved into orange dust.

Atticus was right enough to walk again, so he got up and grabbed his machete. He could hardly open his eyes, so bright was the blaze. He went the opposite way of Mr. Haemo, to where Blythe lay, burning like Bon had. He tore off the soldier's cloak, beat the fire out of it, and threw it over his head and shoulders. *Two trophies. One for each of you*, he thought, appealing to his family, his brain bubbling like the fungal walls around him.

"Come to me," Mr. Haemo shouted through the blackening smoke.

There was fire everywhere, enough to reduce the plantation to cinders, which was most likely Eldrus' intent the entire time. Because he hadn't had a shirt on, Atticus' skin had been cooked to varying degrees. The heat was too hot to think straight. He found himself wandering, searching out spots where he wouldn't roast completely if he stood there. Hopefully, Warren and the Beauties got out. They were good people. Or good bad people, at least.

Mr. Haemo buzzed through the choking, swirling death and grabbed Atticus by his arms. "Surprised to see me?"

"A bit."

Mr. Haemo pulled Atticus close to his disgusting insect body. "Figured you would have gotten my not-so-subtle hints. Hold on tight."

"Let me be, god damn it," he said, unable to break free. He screamed as the fire climbed up his leg.

"There's hope for you and yours yet." Mr. Haemo's wings became a buzzing blur. They started to lift him and Atticus off the ground. "Hear us out first, before you pitch a fit?"

"Us?"

Atticus' feet left the floor. They rose to the ceiling. He looked over his shoulder, to the hole the vermillion hand had grown out of.

"You and Gary. You lied to me, you fuckers."

Mr. Haemo dove through the flames, towards the metal door that led outside. Atticus dangled from the creature's claws, which were a few inches deep into his skin. A searing itch of pain shot through his body as small fires started on his feet and thighs. He beat himself against himself, against the fungal walls. All this skin was getting in his way, he thought, the basement rushing past him, a blinding orange blur of spores and secrets. If only he could do without it, this skin.

Atticus gasped as they flew past the metal doors, into the backyard. The air froze his bones. Mr. Haemo brought them to the slave quarters and landed. He pulled his claws out of Atticus. With a quick whisper, the blood slithered up his claws and into his proboscis.

Taking a deep breath, Atticus fell to his knees and screamed. Every inch of him hurt so bad he couldn't help but cry. When he had hope, when he had purpose, he'd been able to suffer through the suffering. But not now, not anymore.

Carpenter Plantation moaned as its roof buckled and caved in upon itself. Waves of fire shot out of the house's crackling corpse. The second floor sagged, slouched. The third split, slid forward, crushing the porch and the bodies on the front yard. Smoke exploded upward and joined its thick, entwined brethren blackening the night sky.

"Falling apart so fast... you'd think the house wanted this," Mr. Haemo said. He threw the flesh hood over his head and added,

"Here come your cronies."

Out of the smoke, several people ran. Cabalists, he realized, as he tried to rub the sting out of his eyes. Mr. Haemo made a sound behind him. When he looked back, he found the mosquito had vanished into one of the rickety, run-down cabins behind them.

"Can't be seen, not yet," Mr. Haemo said from the shadows of the slave quarter. "Might want to cover up yourself."

Atticus fell back on his heels. He unfastened Blythe's cloak and dropped it beside him. He took off Bon's glove and rested it in the grass. By the hellish light, he read himself as he would a map, touching every bleeding landmark that gave definition to his body. Gallows: A rotting crater in his chest, surrounded by faint scars from days past only he could see. Bedlam: A stretch of necrosis from foot to thigh, with a slit-neck crowning his arrow riddled torso. Cathedra: A bruised wasteland of skin, charred and tendon-tight, cut to the quick, down to the deflated lung sacs like smashed mushroom caps. He would heal, but he wouldn't forget, just as a land doesn't forget the wars waged upon it. Will wouldn't have seen the scars, Atticus figured, but a woman's eyes, Clementine's eyes, peered much deeper. She would've seen them and thought differently of him. The notion alone hurt more than the violence chronicled in his skin.

The cabalists were coming. Gary was among them. He'd grab the ghoul by his neck when he was close enough and choke the truth from him. But maybe Blythe had lied. Maybe they were still down there, in ashes, or bound up, boxed up, bobbing along whatever road the carriages took. It had all happened so god damn fast. And then there was the shepherd, who died by diabolical intervention. What for? How come?

Atticus gripped the grass and howled. *This isn't over*, he thought, face quivering between a sneer and a smile. Though he had nothing but the word of the monster who'd murdered his family, he decided that they hadn't been there; couldn't have been there. They would live again, where the living belonged. Not where the dead were digested and shat out into the infinite unknown.

Atticus smiled and sneered, sneered and smiled. He wiped his nose and told his soul to stop its ramblings. Hungry as it was—he laughed and stood, drenched in sweat, and grabbed his trophies—it would have to wait.

"At-Atticus?"

That had been James' voice. Atticus hunched forward and squinted. He didn't know most of the faces of the approaching cabalists, and the dark sure wasn't helping any. But, wait, there he was. James. And Hex. But she looked different. Not so cock-sure. She hadn't found her brother, he reckoned. If she had, she'd left what remained of him inside the house to burn.

James went ahead of the cabalists, shouldering past a large shape that must've been Warren.

"Are you okay?" At arm's length, James stopped and gasped. "Atticus, what the hell happened to you?"

Atticus ignored him, focusing instead on James' arm and hand. His Corruption was patchy, marred by defensive wounds. His hand looked like a fist, but that was only because he was missing most of the fingers on it.

"I guess I'll have to get good with my other hand." He forced out a laugh. Eyes widening, he said, "Did you find them?"

Atticus stared at James, teared-up, and said, "No. No, I didn't."

Gasps, whispers. Those cabalists who didn't know him were close enough to see the extent of Atticus' wounds. Not including Warren, Elizabeth, and Miranda, who were at the rear of the group, only four cabalists remained of the twenty-five brought here, and there wasn't much left of them, either.

"Gary," Atticus said, calling him out.

The ghoul didn't respond, nor did he move. He just stood there, slack-jawed, mouth still blood-wetted from a mid-battle snack. With a dead gaze, he appealed to Hex beside him. She shook her head, turned to Warren, and whispered something that made the others, Warren and the Beauties included, disperse.

"You all have been treating me like a god damn fool." It took everything Atticus had to hold back from going off. "Gary." He sighed. "Gary, you haven't been right since the ritual."

Hex stirred. Her eyes turned a darker shade of blue; her braids tightened.

James went sideways, looking back and forth between the ghoul and Atticus. Then he stopped and craned his neck toward the cabin where Mr. Haemo hid; strange noises were coming out of it.

If he waited for Gary to say it, they'd be there all night, so Atticus said it. "They're not here. They never were. Where are they?" He walked past James, and got in Gary's face. "You said you couldn't bring them back because the soldiers took their bodies."

He prodded his finger against the ghoul's ribcage. "They're not here. And you knew it this whole god damn fucking time."

Atticus slammed his palms into Gary, pushing him to the ground. "What did you and that fucking mosquito do to my family?" He stood over his friend like an executioner would a prisoner on the chopping block. "You lied to me. You've never lied to me before. What the fuck did you do, then? Answer me!"

"I'm… I'm sorry." Gary crawled backwards. Carefully, hands out in case Atticus came after him, he got back on his feet. "I don't know why I did what I did. I didn't know what to do, and I didn't want to hurt you. Man, I swear it, I didn't. We did, we did bring them back." The ghoul nodded; a centipede crawled out of his nose and into his mouth.

"Gary," James said, breathily.

A crash came out of Carpenter Plantation. The house coughed a fireball at the smug moon on high.

"You did?" Atticus' heart started to beat fast. "Were they not like me? What happened?" And as he finished asking the question, his mind went ahead and gave him the answer. "Shepherds."

Gary nodded and said, "The shepherds, yeah. It worked, they were fine. I did what you asked. I helped them first. They were fine. Out of it, but they were okay. We dusted them off and put them to bed and went to work on you. The shepherds came and grabbed them in the night. Only caught a glimpse of them and then they were gone.

"Atticus, listen, I didn't know about them, the shepherds. And Mr. Haemo, he said he forgot, wasn't even sure if they were still around. He's a son of a bitch, but he loves that blood well. And resurrection rituals drain it quicker than anything else."

"I don't care about that," Atticus hollered. "That's why there were no corpses. You left Clementine and Will alone and the shepherds took them, body and soul, back to the Membrane." He raised his hand to strike Gary, but stopped himself, knowing it would do him no good, at least for right now. "Why didn't you tell me? You wasted my time!"

"You weren't supposed to come back," Gary shouted. He panted as his words rung out across the yard and surrounding forest. "We tried for days to reach you. Nothing. No signs. Nothing. The blood well was breaking down. We had to stop." Gary started to smell the air, to smell, undoubtedly, the presence of Mr. Haemo. "But the words finally took, delayed as they were, and you came crawling out.

"I wanted you back. You're my best friend, Atticus. But when we couldn't reach you, I thought, well, maybe that was best. You'd be with them. But then there you were. I had to say something."

"The truth. I would've appreciated the truth," Atticus growled. "What did you think was going to happen when we got here? Did you think I'd die before I found out? Is that what you thought? You selfish shit. Were you going to eat me when this curse of mine gave out? Prolong your living some?"

Where was his machete? He looked around for a weapon. His soul was hungry, and though Gary had no life to take, he could make do with the scraps left in that corpse of his.

"Atticus, wait," James started.

"Shut the fuck up, James," Atticus snapped back.

"I thought I could buy some time." Gary took a few steps backward. "I thought Mr. Haemo could find another solution. I don't have a good answer. I thought if I told you, you'd kill yourself."

"You didn't tell me about the shepherd until it came for me." Atticus grabbed the ghoul by his throat. He pushed his thumb through the open airway and hooked it on a tendon. "Until I fought it off. And you knew it would come."

Voice choked, Gary muttered, "I am selfish. I wanted you with me. And then, sometimes, I thought it would be better to let you get your revenge on Blythe and Bon and have the shepherd take you. I didn't know you'd be fucking un-killable." He took Atticus by the back of his hair. "So many things are happening that could lead us to them. Kill me if you want. I would. I'm not going to lie. If I knew it'd bring back my wife… my daughters… I would. I'd kill all of you. I know how you feel. God, how I miss them. But I have you, and having you helps getting me through.

"Listen, these things… I can—"

Atticus squeezed harder on his throat.

"–There may be another way. Hear Hex out. Please."

Atticus let go of Gary and gave him one final push, like the dumbass kid he was supposed to have outgrown. He lumbered towards Hex, and she met him halfway, her pupils bluer than ever.

"I knew there was something about you I didn't like."

Hex's cheek quivered. An ash landed on her lip and melted there like snow. Close enough to bite his nose off, she said, "Don't start with me, Gravedigger. Your friend didn't tell me or James his little secret. My loved one wasn't there, either. You aren't the only one suffering."

Hear her out, Clementine whispered in Atticus' ear. He stopped breathing and shed a tear. The mood swings were coming too quickly to predict, and the madness propelling them too strong to stifle. *Get ahold of yourself, Dad,* Will scolded.

"We've been talking behind your back. That is true." Hex's eyes dimmed. "But Gary didn't tell me or James what had happened to your family. I was rooting for you the whole way."

"Appreciate it," Atticus said. He gave Hex some space.

"I don't know where Ichor is. If I hadn't waited for you, he might still be here. I'm trying not to blame you and your friends for that, but it's hard." For the first time, she showed James an unkind look. "But this wasn't always about a break-out.

"Eldrus has gotten too big for its britches." Hex spat out some blood. She had lost a tooth during the battle. "And King Edgar has lost his mind. He's brought more than just that boy back from the Nameless Forest. Warren told me what you saw in the basement. Vermillion veins. Nameless Forest. Like I said."

Atticus shook his head.

Again, a noise came out of the cabin, as though Mr. Haemo was getting impatient.

"Carpenter Plantation is the beginning. The first meaningful punch from the Heartland since Eldrus started this fight. You know they're doing this in other places. It isn't that much of a stretch of the imagination.

"But this isn't my gig, Gravedigger. I'm a hired hand, like you were to me. My benefactors' reach far extends my own. It's pure coincidence things have gone the way they have. I was going to ask you this, what I'm about to say, regardless. So don't go thinking I'm trying to exploit your family. I don't want to have to kick your ass in front of everyone."

"I don't want your lip right now. What do you need?" Atticus threw his arms into the air. His side wounds stretched and shot out blood. "Are you saying you can get me into the Membrane?" He looked at Gary and James. "Is that what she's saying? That's all I care about."

A murmur broke out between the cabalists, Warren, and the Beauties. They were listening, overhearing everything. Atticus finally noticed that Francis wasn't among them.

"You have a gift. Curse, gift, whatever. A man who can't die, who can take the worst beating and shrug it off, is a man to get behind. It was going to be Warren, but he and I don't think that's right. From what I heard, you have a following in Gallows. And you were on every lip in Bedlam. And you can be sure you'll be the talk of the town in Cathedra tomorrow."

Hex sighed and came out with it. "We're going to Eldrus. We're going straight to Ghostgrave. I'm not asking you to lead but to lend your image to us. You're an inspiration. I can't think of a stronger symbol than one that cannot be killed.

"Gary told me about all the occult crap they've got stored up there in Ghostgrave, and now that I know he's been scamming you, I know why. And I've heard the stories, too. Come with us. Do some fighting, some inspiring, and you can have it all."

Atticus couldn't help it: he started to laugh and shake his head, causing Hex to shrink before him. "I'm not... I ain't leading some fucking rebellion. I don't have the constitution or care to do it. And I sure as hell don't have the time it would take." He stopped for a moment and saw that she was sincere. "Why you going to Ghostgrave?"

"To kill King Edgar," she said plainly. "I reckon you're not the only one who has qualms with him and his men. Listen, I also know you're not the charitable type, but revenge gets you hard like the rest of us maniacs. I guarantee you, you're not the only one missing your family right now. But I'm pretty sure you might be the only one among them who can do a damned thing about it."

From behind, an insect's clicking: "My cue!"

Mr. Haemo emerged from the cabin, in all his grotesque glory.

Hex recoiled, screaming "What the fuck is that?" as the cabalists further back shouted and drew their swords.

The mosquito took great strides as he moved towards them, his million unblinking eyes boring through those blood bags called humans.

"That's—" Hex's eyes glowed again, "—that's the thing that brought you back?"

One for dramatics, Mr. Haemo raised his claw up, as though he were commanding the minions of hell to rise, and said, "One and the same."

"Hex," Warren belted, sword drawn. "What the fuck is that shit, god damn it?"

"Hold," she said, eyes wide in awe.

Mr. Haemo cocked his head, twitched his wings. "Interesting," he said, staring at Hex intensely. "You're gifted, too, aren't you?" He laughed and turned to Atticus. "I do like meeting new people, but hell, let's give them a break some."

The giant mosquito took the edge of his hood and lowered it over his face. He grabbed the cloak and pulled it tight, until it seemed as though it were going to rip.

Chanting, "Bl'xhzhka ukul'qntk," the cloak stretched beyond what seemed possible, down his arms and his legs, until the mosquito's entire carapace was covered in old, stitched skin. Then, the flesh began to mold itself, give detail to itself. It pushed in on the mosquito's head, and the mosquito's head deflated until it was more skull-like. It grew heavy on the mosquito's shoulders, and the mosquito's body shrank, losing a foot every few seconds, until he was the same height as Atticus. His arms retracted, his claws became fingers; his feet and legs became meaty and human. His stomach sucked inward, while his chest rippled to give the appearance of ribs. A penis far larger than normal dropped from his still-forming pelvis, and he laughed when he looked at it, pleased. Two eyes with every possible color grew in his shallow sockets, until they were lidded and lighted. When he opened his mouth, teeth pushed through his gums. And the proboscis inside his maw retracted, flattened, until it was close enough to be mistaken for a tongue.

"Better? Or did I make it worse?" Mr. Haemo chuckled, his ashy, scarred skin a patchwork of the long-dead. "Woman's got a point, At—" he smirked, "—woman's got a point, Gravedigger."

Carpenter Plantation drew its final breath, and went on to die a smoldering death, collapsing completely upon itself. A wave of heat exploded across the property, leaving those that stood before it drenched in sweat. Screams rode in on the searing wind. The smoke rising out of the rubble turned to fog and, for a moment, looked like a face.

Abel, Atticus thought. *Now that there's nothing he can do, I wonder if he's relieved?*

"I'll come with you," Mr. Haemo offered, his human suit in some ways more disturbing than his insect form. "Been with you this whole way already."

Atticus took Blythe's cloak and wiped himself down. The Membrane flashed before him. *Huh. Died again.* He rubbed his temples as a sudden headache cracked his forehead open. *I'm losing my fucking mind.*

Finally, voice hoarse, he said, "Why?"

"Blood well's busted. They're delicate things. We overdid it." Mr. Haemo's voice still buzzed when he spoke, as though he had a throat full of bugs. "A mosquito needs its blood well. I'm not much without it. I've been watching you since you left. You've been tearing across the country, leaving behind so much blood it makes me want to cry." Mr. Haemo covered his crotch and winked at Hex. "Apologies, but not really. Got a dress I can borrow?"

"Don't talk to her like that," Atticus threatened. "So, what? You trail along and drain those we drop? Why? You can't get me into the Membrane. You'd have done it already."

"Gary's got it right," Mr. Haemo said. He snapped his fingers at the ghoul and gave him the thumbs up. "I've been around a long, long time. I remember when Archivist Amon was pillaging the continent for artifacts. He's got plenty of things we could use to tear a way into the Membrane, or at least power a blood well to make it large enough to pass through. Hell, I know for a fact that the first ghoul, Deacon Wake, had a black chalice which is up there."

Atticus shook his head. "How?"

"Seen it. Been to Ghostgrave a few times. Before I retired to the marsh."

Mr. Haemo strolled over to James and extended his hand. "Howdy, buddy. Long time, no taste."

James stepped away and went shoulder to shoulder with Hex. "Fuck off, freak."

"I need to sit down, lie down." Atticus stared at the ground and disappeared into a reverie for a moment.

"Atticus," Gary started. "I don't like this son of a bitch, either, but I think this is the answer we were all looking for. I wish it hadn't taken so long to get here."

"I'm tired of waiting," Atticus said, his voice cracking. "I'm tired of it! I just want them back. I've died so many god damn times that life is this fucking close to losing all meaning to me." He curled his fists, told Clementine to shut up, even though she wasn't talking. "I've endured all manner of mutilations. I've traveled I don't even know how fucking far. And I can't die. I can't even give up. I'm too fucking stupid to do that, too unlucky." He put his hands to his head. "I feel my mind tearing in two. And I guarantee you that I'll take the worst of the parts when the time comes, because the worst is what'll serve me best. Always have. I cannot let that happen. If I'm going to save them, I need to be what I always was to them."

He covered his mouth, gave everything he had to hold back the tears. "You all are using me, and I don't rightly believe you'll come through with what you promise. But what else am I going to do?"

Atticus went quiet for a moment. He closed his eyes and saw his wife and son, sitting down at the table, eating the same old, same old and telling stories to pass the time. God, he wanted that back so bad. He'd never been happier than in those "insignificant" moments. He'd collected them, he had; like pretty, polished rocks too often over-looked in a creek bed. He'd get them out from time to time, to re-member why they'd caught his eye. Dinner, farming, small picnics in fields. Bad jokes, stupid arguments. Will trying to ride a pig. Clemen-tine trying to write a book.

He remembered when Clementine taught Will how to fight, and when Will went to practice on him after. Boy got lucky, and then knocked his daddy out cold. What was the name of the ship Will meant to build? So he could sail the Widening Gyre and see what sat at the center? They were supposed to do that one day. And Clemen-tine was going to fight off the sea hags, because just between the two of them, Atticus had confessed to his son, Mom was the far better beater.

They were talking to him—Hex, James, Gary, Mr. Haemo—but he wasn't listening. He was trying to remember what Clementine had told him the first time they had met, back at the abandoned swim-ming pool, a million years ago. She'd been so nervous, he knew that much, and he could never figure out why. She was popular enough. She'd even been the one to approach him. What had she said?

I knew before, but not anymore. Atticus looked at the people who claimed to be his friends and whom he'd once claimed as such.

I knew before, but not anymore. Atticus looked down at himself, at the body that was his but at this point could've been anyone's.

I knew before, but not anymore. Atticus looked inward, at the things he'd done or sworn off, and was willing to do again.

I knew before, but not anymore. This, he realized, was what terrified him the most. That his mind would rot before his flesh would, and he would do everything he could, only to forget why he'd done it at all.

"Who's your benefactor?" Atticus said, breaking his silence.

"I can't say. But there's a meeting," Hex replied quickly.

"Where?"

"Cathedra. Two days."

Atticus repeated again: "With who?"

Hex shook her head. "Gravedigger, I can't."

"You can, and you will."

Hex sighed and stomped her feet, like a child who wasn't about to get her way.

Finally, she said, "Geharra."

CHAPTER XVIII

Beauty had been sorely lacking from Atticus' life of late. He'd seen it here and there, on the road, in Hex, but it'd been brief, and quick to ugly. Now, as he sat on a bench on Cathedra's streets, marveling at the buildings in the midnight moonlight, he knew he'd found it again. And for the next twelve hours, it was his to have.

Hex had patched him up as best she could, which was a thing of beauty in and of itself. But he'd tired of flesh and blood, of death and destruction, so when he was good to go, he had to go. Anywhere would do, he said, hurrying from the hideout they'd bought in Cathedra. Gary and James had tried to follow him, but when he started rolling up his sleeves, they went back to bed.

The burning of Carpenter Plantation had brought a lot of the town running, which was how they'd slipped into Cathedra unnoticed. At this moment, many of the townspeople were still at the property, dousing the fires to prevent them from spreading further. While others were rummaging through the wreckage for the bodies of those unfortunate protestors who'd gotten, in some ways, just what they'd wanted.

So Cathedra was quiet, almost silent, and for mostly terrible reasons. Atticus didn't pay that much mind, though. Instead, he sat with his legs crossed, his hands folded over his knees, while the cool air gave to him a much needed baptism.

This was as close as he was going to get to Penance, Atticus figured. The white buildings, somehow grand in their minimalism, were not cold but comforting. They had a sophistication to their architecture, a happy marriage of aesthetic and function. Atticus always imagined himself being a builder. He'd even tried his hand at it for a while, after Will's birth. It never went anywhere, all that practice and studying, but he did end up learning a few fancy words to impress the easily impressed at Gallows' tavern.

Atticus uncrossed his legs and took a deep breath. Things were better when they didn't smell like blood. He stood up, stretched, and crossed the road. First time he saw the road, he thought it was covered in snow, but the road was just white rocks cobbled together and cleaned on a constant basis. Did they still think they had a chance of Penance moving here? Cathedra struck him like the room an innkeeper keeps ready at all times, for that special guest who will almost certainly never arrive. The people of Cathedra probably knew this, too, but there was a discipline to be had in blind obedience. And that wasn't bad at all, Atticus thought, leaning out of the shadows to touch the sculpture of the Holy Child on the corner. Not bad at all.

Since the plantation and the offers of Hex and Mr. Haemo, he'd slowed his mind to a crawl. He had to; otherwise, he would've gotten belligerent and said to hell with the lot of them.

Atticus moved past the sculpture, ducked past candlelit windows. Cathedra was a wide town, spacious, like heavenly places.

How do I get up there? he wondered, gazing at cathedral upon the hill. It was magnificent. The way the world seemed to bend around it made it look alive. The stained glass windows were huge, bright; they cast their multicolored stories across the town. He couldn't make much sense of them, but he kind of wanted to.

"Go to Eldrus and kill the king?" he whispered to himself. "I could do that."

Somehow, after all that fire at the plantation, he was cold. He pulled Blythe's cloak tight and studied the cathedral some more.

"You'd like this place, Will," he said. "Sure beats all that wood of Gallows." He smiled, almost went to put his arm around his kid.

Is that her? He squinted at the cathedral and the tall, wrought iron fences that surrounded it. *I'll be damned.* There was a statue where the street started up the hill. He couldn't get too close. There were too many open windows nearby and not enough cover. But as he crept forward, hugging the edge of a seamstress' building, his suspicions were confirmed.

The statue was of Justine, the Hydra of Penance, Mother Abbess, and High Priestess of the Holy Order; or at least that's what the stat-ue claimed on its weatherworn placard. The Hydra had developed a reputation over the years, where it was said that her appearance was always changing. Though it wasn't illegal to reproduce her likeness, many superstitious subordinates assumed it should've been. That, in combination with the rumor she rarely looked the same, made images of her hard to find and even harder to trust. But this was Cathedra, Atticus figured, the would-be capitol of the Holy Order. If any place got it right, they probably did.

Justine. He'd only heard her called by her name once or twice in his life. It was pretty, like she was, or had been at the time of the statue's carving. She was slender, elegant, with large eyes and a smile that was just as endearing as it was devious. He was certain the sculp-tor had taken some liberties, but even so, she didn't strike him as the leader type. And how did she even get to be the head of the Order? It was strange standing there, in the dead of night, alone with the rare likeness of one of the most powerful people in the world. This was who he needed to see, he thought, because if anyone knew anything about otherworldly matters, it would be her.

"One at a time," he said, slinking back into the shadows. "King Edgar first, and then you, Justine, if need be." He collected the memory of Justine and put it somewhere safe in his mind.

"I wonder if they'll carve a statue of me, Clementine," he mum-bled, heading back towards the hideout. "I bet Hex has her people working on it right now. We'll be famous when you get back. Our friends back in Gallows will shit themselves."

The hideout was a literal hole in the wall of a hole in the wall tav-ern that the good people of Cathedra surprisingly never remodeled. There was a side entrance near the stables that didn't see use any-more, and Atticus went through there. Where the stable checked the tavern, a few boards were loose. He pulled those up, knocked on the door behind them, and went through when Hex opened it.

"Feel better now?" Hex asked, sounding slightly annoyed. She shut and locked the door behind him and said, "Anyone see you?"

Atticus shook his head. The room in front of him was all they had. It was small, cramped; the three beds inside it took up most of the floor space. Elizabeth and Miranda were asleep together, while Warren was sitting at the edge of his bed, which he shared with Hex.

James was high on painkillers for his hand. When Atticus eventually settled in beside him, the boy was probably going to try to snuggle up close. Gary and Mr. Haemo, being the creatures they were, slept under the beds, though Atticus was pretty sure the human-shaped mosquito was faking it.

He searched the room and said, "Where's the rest of the Cabal?"

"Paid them and sent them on their way." Warren swallowed hard. There was a glint in his eyes.

"Won't they rat us out?"

"No, they're too shaken to squeal. Plus, I don't recruit squealers."

The big man lay back down, his massive body causing the bed's center to sink. His head disappeared behind his wide shoulder, into the pillow.

Hex shook her head and said, "Eat something, and then get some rest."

Atticus lingered on Warren, noticing how he shook there, sorrow freezing him to the bone. "When you've done what needs to be done, be done," he said, reciting what he'd told Atticus in the hidden stairwell.

Warren snickered, and said, "There's always something that needs doing. Always some wrong that needs righted." He wiped something off his face. "People like us, we'll be done when we're dead."

"And what about the dead? When will we be done?"

Warren shrugged. "When god gets around to it."

Like any self-respecting secret meeting, this one was held at the Black Hour. They'd spent the whole of that next day in the hideout, so when it was twenty minutes 'til, Atticus and Hex almost blew the doors off the place trying to get out. To no one's surprise, three grieving mercenaries, one pain-wracked prostitute, a festering ghoul, and a blood obsessed mosquito didn't exactly make for good company in close quarters.

With Carpenter Plantation's fire extinguished and everyone on alert, Cathedra was a much different town this night than it had been before. Candles burned on every sill and fires blazed in every shop. There were voices all around, at Atticus's and Hex's backs and to their sides. It was a neighborhood watch done right, the kind that could be felt but not seen, yet respected all the same.

Atticus and Hex leaned out of the stable, searching for a good street to start down. "No soldiers or patrol?"

Hex shook her head. "The tavern owner has had a few of his bar flies spread rumors about you, Gravedigger. We gave them our old camp in the woods to find as a distraction."

Footsteps cut her short. A couple wandered past, hands all over each other. They disappeared into the dark.

"Everyone's spooked, but curious, too. Cathedra has no love for Eldrus, either. If we mind our business tonight, most'll turn a blind eye."

"What's the tavern owner been saying about me?"

Atticus threw the hood of Blythe's cloak over his head. He followed Hex out of the stables and down the street that ran along the back of the businesses.

Hex tugged her braids apart. Quickly, she put them into a blue bun. "That you led the attack on Carpenter Plantation. That you can't be killed. That you wait in the graveyards at night, looking for new recruits for your cause."

Atticus grabbed her shoulders. "Did you leave my family out of it?"

"No."

A few more buildings and they'd be in the open again.

"No names, of course, but a monster needs a heart if people are going to follow it."

Atticus twitched. "That's what I am to you now?"

"You saying you're not a monster?" She smiled, took his hand off her. "Don't worry. We'll figure this human business out together when it's all over."

If it were up to Atticus, he wouldn't have held the secret meeting at the center of town, but as he'd come to realize over the last few months, not much was up to him anymore. Revenge had gotten him a little further than his front step, but everything after that was because of someone else. This was a personal matter, and yet it didn't feel personal anymore. The fact that his loss had become entwined with fanciful thoughts of revolt made him want to spit.

Time was different in the Membrane, he knew that. The days he'd spent down there were no more than hours to him. But going to Eldrus and holding up his end of whatever deal they struck tonight was going to take time. If this was the course he was going to follow, it would be many more months, a year, even, before he had the chance to see them again.

Just how long in hell could one wait until they started to call it home?

"All right," Hex said, nudging him.

They slipped into an alley between two bone-white buildings.

"We're getting—"

Atticus held up his hand. He heard voices, chanting; feet shuffling and stomping out a beat. "What's that noise?"

"Ah, yeah." Hex beckoned him to follow her to the end of the alley, where an intense light was coming through. "Have a look."

Atticus curled his lip and slipped past her. At the edge of the alley, he leaned out and had a look.

In front of a lighted gazebo, thirty or so figures swayed, humming and holding their hands high. In the gazebo itself, a man sat in snowy robes, reading from a heavy book that had to have been the Holy Order's holy text *Helminth's Way*. Beside him, a portly woman stood and sang in tongues. Even though it was gibberish, it didn't sound half bad.

"Midnight mass," Hex whispered. "If you're going to get right with the lord, may as well get a head-start, you know what I mean?"

Atticus wouldn't admit it to the woman, but the hymns, the movements—it was starting to get to him. It centered him, made him feel right on the inside. He didn't expect that. Wasn't sure if he liked that he liked that.

"Take it you're not the church-going type?" he finally said.

"No, afraid not." She pressed her body against his, as she peeked out of the alley to look at the mass. "Saw god when I was a little girl." She glanced at Atticus from the corner of her eye. "Didn't much care for it."

"That so?" Wedged between her and the alley, his Corruption against hers, Atticus realized how much he missed a woman's touch. "How come?"

Hex worked herself loose, tightened up her bun. She retreated and leaned against that building's side door.

"Didn't see the big deal. God seemed like an asshole, like the rest of us." She raised her eyebrows, and smiled.

Atticus didn't believe her, and he didn't care if she knew it. "What's god look like, then?"

"Has some blue to it," she said, blowing a loose strand of hair out of her face.

"You saying you're god?"

Hex shrugged, and said, "We're all gods of something," and then threw her weight into the side door, flinging it open.

Atticus took a few steps forward as Hex disappeared past it. "What're you doing?"

Poking her head out, she said, "What? Oh." She held out her hand, shook it until he took it. "We're here. Come on, Gravedigger."

Atticus dropped Hex's hand and followed her. On the other side of the door, they entered a small workshop that time had gutted. All that remained now were a few tables, some tools, and about a fourth of the wooden floor. The rest of the workshop was cut-off by rubble and the building beside it, which it appeared to have been attached to at some point. Faint moonlight poured in from the gaps in the roof.

"Won't they hear us?" Atticus asked, searching for Hex's so-called benefactors.

"Not with all that praising going on out there." She swung back around and shut the side door. "They'll be at it for another hour."

"They late?"

There wasn't a lot to look at in the workshop. It was empty, flat; no corners or crevices to check.

"We're early." Hex found a few chairs folded up against the wall. Bringing them over to a table, she said, "Here, cop a squat."

Atticus eyed Hex.

"What?" she said. She set up six chairs and sat in one.

He buried his paranoia and sat opposite her.

She sighed, put her hands behind her head, getting real comfortable. Smiling, she finally said, "How are you?"

"Eh?"

"How are you?"

"I'm... fine."

Hex waited a moment, tonguing her teeth, and said, "I'm fine, too, Gravedigger. Thanks for asking."

Atticus laughed. "What is this?"

"I'd really like to get to know you." She leaned forward, elbows to the table, and looked him in the eyes. "Tell me about your family."

"Heh, uh, thought I did."

Hex shook her head.

"Well, I mean, what do you want to know?"

Hex undid her hair and started to braid it in the way she always wore it. "It's not a test, man."

Atticus took a deep breath and exhaled slowly. "It's not easy. I avoid it, if I can, because it makes me feel like they're already lost. Gary and James, they're invested, too, but, I don't know. Pretending I'm alone in this makes it easier to focus on what has to be done."

"I understand."

"I, uh, well, Clementine was, is, my wife. I'd always seen her around, but we didn't really meet until we were ten." He smiled. "There was this Old World swimming pool outside of town, in the mire. Water was cleaner than you'd think, but we mostly went there to get away from our parents.

"One day, Clementine was at the pool. I mean, she was always there, but for some reason, that day, I don't know. Guess I noticed her, finally."

"The stars aligned," Hex said.

"Hormones more like it, but yeah, something like that. I thought she was real pretty. In Gallows, everyone kind of knows everyone. Kids don't really grow up scared to talk to the opposite sex. At that point, I'd probably seen half the town naked."

Hex laughed. "Very open community."

"Yeah, sure," he said, shaking his head. "So, you know, I wasn't scared to talk to her. But she always had her friends around. They didn't much care for me." Atticus paused, considered putting an end to this confession, and then went on ahead. "But I got her alone one day. Struck up a conversation."

"You strike out?" Hex asked.

Atticus chuckled. "Big time. I'm sorry to say it, but Clementine was a bit of a bitch back then. I'm sure I did something wrong, don't get me wrong, but I think that girl was born with a stick up her ass."

Hex leaned in closer, chin on hand. "So, of course you fell in love."

"That's how it goes." Atticus looked around the workshop, for uninvited guests, but they were still alone. "She didn't really come from a good family. I didn't, either. It was bad, but it was good we found each other. My parents died early."

Atticus closed his eyes, saw his father dead on the floor, his mother standing over his body, in celebration.

"My parents died early, and a family friend took me in."

He opened his eyes, but the workshop was gone. He was at Poe's again, his father's knife in hand, his mother's blood all over his face.

"Clementine wasn't so lucky. Her dad lived a lot longer than he deserved."

"I'm sorry to hear that about your parents," Hex said softly.

"Don't be. I'm not." He flexed his killing hand. "Poe, the family friend, raised me. Or whatever you want to call it. He's a piece of shit. Not much better than my dad, except he never laid a hand on me. When I was old enough to do something other than chase down debts, I became the Hangman. Fancy name for a killer. Scarier, I guess. Money was good, so I got Clementine away from her dad. I did a lot of bad things for Poe."

"Did Clementine mind? Them bad things?"

Atticus shook his head. "No, she understood. She wasn't no saint, neither. She's got a few bodies notched into her belt, too. Don't get any romantic inclinations about us. We cleaned up okay, but we weren't much more than scum."

Hex bit her lip. "Will's your only kid?"

"No, I mean, yes." Atticus' mouth hung open as he tried to come up with an excuse.

"He's got a sibling? Listen, I was just curious about you. If this is something you haven't told Gary or James, maybe it's best you don't—"

"Vale," Atticus said, forcing the name past his lips. "Vale." Saying it felt strange, like remembering a word from a different language; something you'd always known but at some point forgot. "Vale was our daughter. A few years before Will." Atticus covered his mouth. "You got me on the right night to have me talking about her. You spell-weaving this out of me or something?"

Hex shook her head. "No, don't got that power."

"She... died." He exhaled. His saliva was thick, tasted like sadness must taste. "Clementine fought and fought to give birth. But my little girl, my little Vale..." He tapped the table, fidgeted with his fingers. "Too small, too eager to see us. That's what we used to say. She couldn't wait to come out. We—" he took a deep breath, "—we got a few minutes with her." He started to rock in the chair. "At least we got that. It wasn't her fault, though. She didn't know better.

"Someone was supposed to fetch the doctor, this man named Ronny, but he didn't. Said he would, and we waited, but he didn't. He had always wanted Clementine, always hated me for having her. I don't know if Vale would've made it if the doctor had come. I wanted to kill Ronny, because I knew he'd done that on purpose, but I couldn't. In those... in those few minutes with Vale... I knew her. And I knew she wouldn't want that."

Hex sat there in silence. When he stopped breathing so heavily, she reached across the table and took his hand. This time, he didn't pull away.

"Will's a good kid." Atticus nodded. He liked the way Hex's fingers rubbed his knuckles. "Clementine didn't want to have another child, but it happened anyways. I quit being Hangman when he was born. Poe sent a few men to my house that night to help me reconsider."

"Did you?" Hex asked, hanging on his every word.

"Reconsider? No, no, I didn't. But I did such a good job on those men's bodies when I was done that the mayor made me gravedigger." He took his hand away from Hex's. "Poe and I were all right after that."

Hex groaned and said, "Men are stupid."

Atticus shrugged. "Will grew up quick. For the life of me, I don't know how it happened so fast. Doesn't have a mean bone in his body. I was afraid, think Clementine was, too, he'd turn out like us. But he didn't. He got the best of us. Which was good. Made us better ourselves.

"We definitely sheltered the boy. He kept hearing things about us, what we'd done in the past, and thought it was a big joke. We were just a bunch of boring farmers who wouldn't let him have no fun."

"No swampy pools to play in?"

"Nope. At that point, Mr. Haemo had made himself comfy in the area, so Will didn't get to meet the love of his life there, like I did."

"Does that giant mosquito have to come with us?" Hex asked, cringing.

"I need to have a sit down with him. I've got no qualms killing him at the end of this. Kind of hope I get to.

"I don't talk about Will much, not like I do Clementine, because it hurts too much. He's too good to be down there in a place like that. I know he isn't prepared for something like that. We didn't let him see the world the way it really is."

"You can't blame yourself," Hex said. "If he's your son, I'm sure—"

Atticus' lip started to quiver. He'd cried enough, so he looked away until the urge passed.

"I don't know if he's down there. I know Clementine is. I saw her. She saw me. But Will? The Abyss might've got him. I could see him giving in. If he was lost… alone."

"I bet he's still down there," Hex said, eyes going kind. "What's he going to be when he grows up?"

"Everything. He could be, too, if he wanted. But if he had to settle on something, I think he'd be a farmer, like his old man." Atticus bit his nail. It fell off into his mouth and made him wretch. "You want to tell me about Ichor?"

Hex leaned back in her chair. "Guess that'd be fair, on account of having you spill your guts and all."

Atticus shook his head. "Please, don't joke about that," he said, grabbing his stomach. "It'll probably happen at some point."

"Ichor's different." Hex bit her lip, chewed on her words. "When we were little, in Angheuawl, he wasn't really ever around. He was a loner. Kids used to make fun of him, beat him up. He's very smart, but has a temper like you wouldn't believe. I think if he had grown up somewhere else, he might've turned out different. All that bad business made him a bleeding heart. And all the world's going to do to people like that is bleed them dry."

Remembering what Hex told him awhile back, Atticus said, "You mentioned you weren't all that close 'til you got hitched."

"Yeah. I got it. Made sense. Parents marrying me off to some stranger like I was some fucking set-aside bride. I'd get all brotherly, too, if I were him. But I think he did it for the wrong reasons. He was trying to prove something or something."

Atticus thought back to Ichor's supposed imprisonment. "Bleeding heart? Take it he's an investigator type?"

Hex threw her hands up into the air. The chair tilted back. "Shit," she yelled, balancing it.

"You don't have much love for him, do you?"

Hex mouthed "No," and snapped her head to the side door they'd come through.

"You trying to prove something, too? By rescuing him, I mean."

"Hmm?"

Hex got to her feet, so Atticus did, too.

"Oh, no. No."

The side door creaked open. Figures stood behind it. Atticus went for a weapon, then remembered Hex hadn't let him bring one.

"No, I came to get Ichor to kill him," Hex said, plain as day. "Ah, come on in, everyone."

Atticus' eyes went wide. "Kill him? What the hell you talking about?"

But before Hex could answer him, three Night Terrors were in the doorway. One wore the skull of a fox, the other a mask of centipede carapaces. The last one, the one who kept closest to the Fox, had pale scars running across his body. At first, Atticus couldn't make sense of his skull, but if he had to guess, he would have said it looked kind of like a bat's.

CHAPTER XIX

The midnight mass hit a howling crescendo as the creatures came into the room. A small woman trailed behind them, her half-lit face about as worn down as the workshop itself. She was dressed in men's clothes, and the spectacles she wore were large enough to give Mr. Haemo's eyes a run for their money. She, along with the Night Terrors, took a seat at the table, while Atticus and Hex just stood there, one far more shocked than the other.

"Timely, as always," the woman said to Hex.

Atticus' gaze moved back and forth, between the woman planning fratricide and the creatures known to kill humans. When he'd been attacked by the snake, there was too much going on to consider the Night Terrors. But now that they were in the same room as him, he felt the chill of myth and superstition; even had the goosebumps to show for it.

"Gravedigger." Hex nodded at the chair he'd been sitting in. "I'll introduce you to everyone."

This feels like a god damn set-up. He didn't have a weapon, but when it was harder to shake off a cold than it was Death, that didn't seem to matter much. The Night Terrors followed him as he pulled out the chair and took a seat.

Pointing to the Fox, Hex said, "This is Johannes."

The Night Terror, Johannes, was the thinnest of the murderous bunch. He wore little in the way of armor, but had a handful of daggers, knives, and unmarked pouches lining his waist and legs. There were several patches of fur still attached to Johannes' mask. By the jagged bands of black and red that ran across them, Atticus would have guessed the skull came from a lord of the Blasted Woodland. Looking into its weathered sockets, he noticed the Night Terror had black paint around his eyes, to give a more fearsome impression.

"You've been through a lot," Johannes said, offering his hand. "This must be like icing on the cake."

"Yeah," Atticus grunted.

He took and shook the Terror's hand. Johannes cocked his head, as though he hadn't heard him, and then pulled away.

"This one—" Hex smiled at the Centipede, "—this one gracing us with her appearance tonight, her name is Mara."

Mara's mask was a mean mound of centipede carapaces that had fused together. They were fashioned in a such way that it gave the Night Terror the appearance of having horns. Unlike Johannes and the Bat beside her, she didn't wear armor at all. Her clothes looked like something that would've washed up on Bedlam's banks, and by the way she carried herself—so cocky you would've thought she'd sprouted one between her legs—this was probably on purpose.

"Hex has high hopes for you," Mara said, her voice sounding much older than her body looked. "This is Deimos." She nodded her head at the Night Terror beside her. "He's a real chatterbox."

"Atticus, is it?" Deimos asked, standing up. He held out his hand.

This isn't right. I can't be sitting here, alive, conversing with these things. "Gravedigger will do."

Atticus paused before shaking the Bat's hand. From the tips of his fingers to the bones in his wrist, Deimos' skin was covered in pale, shiny scars. He accepted the gesture, went in closer. Deimos' skull was not one bat skull but many smaller ones, that had been fused together to give him this unnerving visage. The mask had a strange hue to it, too, like the color of disease.

"Sit, then, Gravedigger," Deimos said, following his own advice. Beside the mask, he wasn't all that imposing. And his kind voice wasn't doing him any favors, either. "I do not know how much Hex has shared with you, so I'll leave the rest to her."

Atticus sat again and looked at the woman, the Corrupted (he had to make sure), who'd come in behind them.

"My name is Kevin," she said, taking off her spectacles. Her eyes lost half their size when the lenses left them. She rubbed the bridge of her nose. "I sit on the council of Geharra. I've called this meeting here tonight. I understand that you cannot die." She put her spectacles back on. "Show me."

Atticus tilted his head to show where Bon had opened his neck. He pulled up his shirt, to show where Blythe had gored him.

Kevin snapped her fingers at Johannes. He handed her one of his knives. She tossed it on the table in front of Atticus.

"I'd rather not," he said, pushing the knife back towards her. "I've done it enough already."

Kevin flicked the knife, sent it spinning back at him. "I try something before I buy it, Gravedigger."

Hex said to him, "You'd do the same."

Lip curled, Atticus leaned forward and grabbed the knife. He searched its blade for evidence of runes, of powders—things that may reverse his life-sustaining curse. Did they trust him by giving him this? Or did they trust in their numbers to overwhelm him if need be?

"We're on a time crunch," Mara said. Her mask quivered with life. "Hurry it up, please."

Deimos shook his head. "Give him a moment. It's good this isn't something he takes lightly."

Suddenly agreeable, Atticus pressed the knife into his wrist. "This will take a minute."

"What?" Johannes turned his head. "Oh, no. It's tainted with Thanatos."

Atticus gritted his teeth. With the knife only touching his skin, he could feel a lightning storm blowing across the muscles below. "How long 'till this shit is out of my system?"

"It's quick." Johannes sounded excited, like the herbalist he probably was. "Like blowing out a candle."

"Hex, I don't know if another one is coming—" Atticus closed his eyes and exhaled, "—but if a shepherd shows up, you take it down. You hear me?"

Hex nodded. "Of course."

Kevin went wide-eyed and said, "Shepherd? What is he—?"

Atticus slipped the knife's tip into his wrist. Blood welled around the puncture, thick and dark. He gripped the knife and ripped downward. His forearm split open, the seams of skin giving way to the blade. Hot, red blood poured over his flesh, like water over the edge of a tub. He dropped the knife and grabbed the wound, his hand adhering to the sticky slit. Sight and sound ceased to be, and like a breath to a flame, Thanatos snuffed his life out.

When his senses returned, Atticus found himself sitting in the same seat, at the same table, on a scabby cliff overlooking a white desert. A thin film, veined and rough, hung from an unseen place high in the sunless sky. It ran before him for as far as he could see, blocking off the desert entirely.

"Is this the Membrane?"

He stood up, noticed his forearm had already begun to heal itself. Craning his neck, he found that familiar tunnel he'd fallen through before, streaks of sinewy light inching across it.

"Guess so."

Atticus walked over to the film. He touched it. Like the insect wing it resembled, it buzzed. *Why am I still here?* he wondered. The Thanatos. Looking at his slit wrist, he figured it hadn't left his system yet. Atticus put his nose to the film. The pale desert on the other side sat quietly, a wild wind slowly undoing its many dunes. Where had he seen this place before? The first time he died, he realized, and in Bedlam, the first time the shepherd showed.

I should try to look for Clementine and Will. Atticus stepped back. *If I keep using the Thanatos, maybe I can find them. Maybe I can tell them what I'm doing for them.* But before he could turn away, the desert drew him back in. Small figures started to emerge from the sands. They were human, but their bodies were hazy and black, like literal shadows of their former selves. He didn't turn away, but he did back away, because something about the sight of the shadows made him uneasy.

"Will! Clementine!" Atticus shouted. He noticed he'd drifted a few feet from the film, the Abyss' pull ever-present.

The shadows were coming out in droves now, by the hundreds, by the thousands. They were coming for him.

"Fuck, fuck!"

He panicked as the shadowy swarm disappeared under the lip of the cliff, out of sight.

Am I stuck down here? What the fuck did I do? Atticus went past the table and chair, to where the cliff ended and the Membrane's tunnel began. He peered into the dim depths, searching the fleshy walls for hints of Pulsa diNura.

Take care of them, Herbert, he thought. *Or whatever the hell your name was.*

"Son of a bitch!" Atticus turned around and jumped as he saw the shadows there pressed against the other side of the film. There were hundreds of them, each one fighting their way to the front. Thick, glistening saliva poured out of their chomping mouths. The sight of Atticus had driven them into a frenzy. They clawed at the film in desperation, and from their desperation, Atticus could tell they were suffering.

"Are you in hell?" he asked, in awe, like a child.

Some were praying, others looked like they were trying to make the signs of Penance, but it kept coming out wrong.

Someone snapped their finger in Atticus' ear.

"Are you there?" Hex asked.

Atticus screamed. He kicked his feet and fell out of the chair. The workshop's floor met his face like a fist and chipped his tooth. He lay there a moment, breathing in the puddle of blood his suicide had formed.

"I'm very sorry," he heard Kevin say. "We will never ask you to do that again. You... are amazing."

Atticus grunted. He stood up and threw himself in the chair. He was covered in blood, and his arm had torn back open.

"Someone going to stitch me up?" He bit the inside of his mouth as the cool air got inside the wound and worked over his nerves. "I'd like to be conscious for whatever other bullshit gets asked of me."

Hex, as always, had a small amount of medical supplies on her. It probably wasn't a coincidence, but Atticus had, in part, done this to himself, so he wasn't about to bitch about it.

"Hex already told you our goal: to force Eldrus out of the Heartland and kill King Edgar," Kevin said as Hex fixed Atticus up. "We have dissidents across the Heartland, but they're timid. The Heartland hates Eldrus' involvement, but for most, it was an inevitability. So they're used to it."

Atticus looked at the Night Terrors. Every time he was reborn, he felt renewed, so with renewed confidence, he muttered, "Why are they here?"

"To keep the balance," Deimos answered.

Mara yawned and nodded. "Don't mistake us for our bloodthirsty brethren in the south."

"You saying you don't kill 'Corrupted'?"

"We do," Johannes added cheerfully, his fox skull bobbing up and down. "But we try to be a little more meaningful about it."

"You're not what I had in mind," Atticus admitted.

Mara fiddled with her thumbs, bored. "That's generally the goal."

"When you sneak around killing in the dark, that'll happen."

Atticus thought back to Gallows, where at least twice a year, a neighbor was found slaughtered, Corruption stripped from their arms. It scared him at first, the Night Terror attacks, and then it just became business.

Mara crossed her arms. "When you're done sneaking around, killing in the dark, you think you'll be the same in the light?"

The Bat cleared his throat. "Our people keep the balance through whatever means necessary. All populations, be it natural or supernatural, must be maintained. The city-states and the Heartland have their place on this traumatized continent. Eldrus has forgotten its place."

Atticus tilted his head at Hex. Rolling his eyes, he said, "Dress it up how you like, Terror, but murder is murder."

"Are your hands clean, Gravedigger?" Johannes asked, jumping to Deimos' defense.

"No," Atticus said. "Haven't been most of my life. But I know what kind of monster I am. Not sure you all do." He looked at his arm as Hex tightened the last stitch. "I can wash this blood off all I want, but I know it's always going to be there." He paused. The gears in his mind cranked out a notion. "Letting Geharra go to war with Eldrus doesn't sound like the best way to keep your balance."

"Not war," Kevin said. She reached into her pocket and popped a piece of candy into her mouth. "We're forcing them out, nothing more."

"Killing the king isn't an act of war?"

"They won't know it was us."

Atticus bit his lip. "Sure they won't."

"The Nameless Forest changed King Edgar," Johannes said. He touched a dagger on his belt. "It rotted him from the inside out."

"He needs to be replaced," Mara said. "He can't be reasoned with. And since he brought that child back from the Forest, he can't be reached, either. It's going to require brute force."

Hex took out a vial of Numb and doused his arm. "To make a difference, he has to die. The body farms and the vermillion veins, they're only the beginning."

Atticus tried to flex his arm, but it wasn't there yet. "Beginning of what?"

"You're going to help us," Kevin demanded. "There is no turning back. If you betray us, we will chain you to a rock and leave you to burn on the sands of the Ossuary."

"Funny you should mention a desert. No, I want my wife and son back more than…" He sighed. "I'll do anything, even if it means I'll regret it later."

"That's good to know," Mara said. She crossed her legs, leaned out of her chair, and said, "Mass is almost over."

"King Edgar," Kevin began, "is trying to mobilize the Nameless Forest. We don't know what he found when he went in there, but we do know he's trying to bring it out."

"Our people occasionally measure the borders of the Nameless Forest," Johannes said. "It hasn't moved, not even an inch, in the last hundred years. But in the last six months, it's moved forward one mile. In every direction."

"It's spreading," Mara said. "Testing the waters. What you saw in those bodies are the very same vermillion veins found in the Forest. King Edgar is preparing the land, making it agreeable."

Johannes nodded. "They're also weapons themselves. The soldiers are burying them deep in the earth. But you saw what happens when they are triggered."

"It was a massacre," Atticus said. He remembered Carpenter Plantation's basement, the web of mutilated bodies from the coffin bombs.

"During King Edgar's disappearance, he discovered new allies," Deimos said, joining the conversation. "We've noticed an increase in activity around the Nameless Forest, too. Messenger birds and men made of veins. He's communicating with what's inside of the Forest. We've seen the rare supply line here and there as well."

"What's inside the Forest?" Atticus asked. "Does anyone really know?"

"Old World monsters, maybe," Hex said. "People said a lot of them fled there after the Trauma. But they got caught in the chaos of the place and couldn't get back out."

"Some believe the Dread Clock sits at the Nameless Forest's center," Deimos said. "Some believe that's what perpetuates the Black Hour. It's creations, in combination with the insane things that normally live there, would make a wave of death not even the greatest of alliances could break."

"An army." Atticus picked at his stitches. "Except, it can't move unless the conditions are right."

"Immortal and intelligent," Mara said sarcastically. "A man after my own heart."

Kevin shook her head and said, "Tracking the corpses is difficult. Their operation is not well organized, and it doesn't matter if they meet their exact destination as long they're buried. So anywhere, in the end, is good. But we're doing our best to rout the convoys, and Carpenter Plantation was a blow to their operations, you can be sure."

"So he brings the Nameless Forest to the Heartland. Then what?" Atticus asked.

"Then whatever he wants," Hex said. "If it works, if it's like what we're thinking it's like, he'll be able to take over anything. And if it doesn't, then the Nameless Forest will probably choke the life out of what's left of this shitty continent. I don't think it matters what happens. The man is insane. He's going to go along with whatever outcome he gets."

Atticus raised an eyebrow. "Let's say it happens like you all think it will happen. But it's not hell on Earth. Don't think there's any good that can come out of this?"

The Night Terrors shook their heads in unison.

"Balance is everything," Deimos said. "Diversity is everything in this dying world."

"Your movement is just, I agree," Atticus said. He lowered his voice as he heard the midnight parishioners shuffle past the workshop. When they'd gone, he whispered, "What happens next?"

Mara straightened up in her seat, exhaled as though to say "finally."

Kevin reached back into her pocket and laid a large, blue, slimy snail shell on the table. "You, Hex, and your men will leave tomorrow morning and go west to Islaos. You'll make yourself known, bolster morale, give a speech, kill if you can, and be on your way. After that, you'll double back east to Hrothas, then north to Nyxis. After every town, leave a rebellion in your wake. Eldrus will have to stretch itself thin suppressing each uprising. Like I said, our people are timid, because they do not fight for war, but equilibrium. Humans don't stand particularly well on the middle ground. It is on extreme soil that they find their footing. So give them your image, your story, your ability, and help them understand the importance of standing up for themselves, without having to tear everything down in the process."

"And after Nyxis?" Atticus asked. *I can do this*, he said to his wife and son. *I can do this quickly, I promise.*

"Geharra has been smuggling weapons into the Heartland for a while now. Mercenaries, too, like Hex's friend, Warren. After Nyxis, if you've done what you're supposed to do, and we'll know, you'll go with a smaller, more covert operation into Eldrus. As the city-state tries to quell the fighting at its gates, you move into Ghostgrave and kill Edgar. We have people inside the keep. We'll be tracking his movements, or supposed movements, the best that we can. We will be providing that information."

"Geharra stands to benefit a lot from this," Atticus said, addressing the Night Terrors. "You guys not as cozy with Penance, I take it?"

"Geharra knows it place," Mara said. "And they know what will happen if they forget it."

"You know why I trust you?" Kevin said, interrupting the Mara.

Atticus shook his head.

"Because of your cause. It's good for all of us, yourself included, that you can't die, but that alone isn't enough for me to trust you. There's plenty of things out there that can do a good imitation of you, Gravedigger. It's your cause. It's simple, to the point. Heartfelt. When I look at you, I don't see a man with grand aspirations for profits or politics. You're going to do what you have to do until there's nothing left of you, and then you're going to take what's yours and put this all behind you."

"Yeah, that's the plan."

"Archivist Amon keeps his artifacts in his tower," Mara said. "You take what you need and leave the rest."

Atticus' heart started to beat hard. "Is what I need in there?"

"Yes," Deimos said. "Archivist Amon has led an unnaturally long life. And there are rumors King Edgar has tried to bring back his dead family members. But he doesn't have your gift, so he can't make the journey into the Membrane just by killing himself."

Mara laughed. "If nothing else, I'm sure your mosquito friend can figure something out, what with all that fresh blood to weave with."

Atticus shot a damning glance Hex's way. "How have you been in contact with them? I've kept a close eye on you since Bedlam."

Johannes made a clicking noise with his mouth. "Oh, Hex. You spilled the beans about our plan, but you didn't tell him about that? You've got your priorities backwards, girl."

Slamming his fist into the table, Atticus shot up and said, "What the hell is he talking about?"

"Sit down, Gravedigger," Kevin said. "This—" she picked up the large, blue, slimy snail shell, "—we call it an heir. It lets us communicate over vast distances."

"Where'd it come from?"

Kevin looked at Mara.

Mara shook her head.

The councilwoman of Geharra said, "Hex has been keeping in contact with us through the heir."

"You have one of those? In that bag you carry around?" Atticus got calm, got seated.

Hex shook her head and said, "Don't have one. Don't need one."

"It really only works one-way," Kevin said, slipping the device back into her pocket. "We mostly just listen and hope Hex gets the fragments of our answers."

Atticus grinned. "I don't understand. You don't have one?"

"Don't need one. I know you've seen it, when my eyes turn blue like they do. I can cast my thoughts." She struggled to find her words and then finally said it: "I'm a telepath, Gravedigger."

CHAPTER XX

The midnight meeting came to an end shortly thereafter. The Night Terrors scattered to the wind, Mara going one way, Deimos and Johannes, hand-in-hand, the other. Kevin of Geharra went to the local inn, because she was supposed to be in Cathedra, anyways, for a symposium. Atticus and Hex stayed in the workshop awhile longer, staring each other down.

"A telepath." Atticus ground his heel into the ground. "I poured my god damn heart out to you."

"I can't always control it."

"Sure seems to come on at the most opportune of times."

"It really doesn't. I said I came to find Ichor to kill him, and that was true. You know why he hates me? Because he's a telepath, too. Except, he's better at receiving than sending. Every time he fucked up, every time I made fun of him, hated him, he knew. And I didn't. Had no idea he could read my thoughts. Didn't know until the day he tried to kill himself. Then he told me."

"But you still want to kill him? I'm sorry but that doesn't make a lick of god damn sense."

"It's… it's m-mutual."

Hex was giving him everything, and in return, Atticus knew she was hoping to buy back no more than his favor.

"We've been hunting each other since my wedding night."

"How come?"

"Ichor is generally a receiver, not a sender, like I said, but during the wedding dinner, I caught his thoughts. What he thought about me, what he wanted to… do to me." Hex swallowed hard. She mouthed the words, "Spread you open." Her face darkened several shades of Death. "I leapt across the table and put every fork and knife I could get ahold of in his chest. He got away, though. Ichor always gets away.

"He came back a few weeks later, in the night. Husband was gone. Fought then, too. He'd show up every month or so after that and we'd beat each other to a pulp. He'd get away, or I'd let him get away. I don't even know anymore. The only connection we have to each other is how much we hate one another."

Atticus considered her and said, "Did you get involved with Geharra to find him? Or because you actually believe in them?"

Hex shrugged. "Both. I can't explain it, Gravedigger. It's… sick. But I have to find him again."

"To kill him?"

"To try." Her eyes went bright blue. "But maybe this time will be different."

"All that about Ichor, what you said earlier. Him protecting you. That was a lie, wasn't it?"

"It was. I don't tell the truth when it comes to Ichor."

Atticus loosened up. "Guess I wouldn't either. You enjoy this, don't you? This cat-and-mouse game."

"Yes," Hex admitted. "The more complex, the better. I'm glad he wasn't at Carpenter Plantation. But I do worry about him."

"Is there another person inside of you? I don't know who you are right now."

Embarrassed, she looked at her feet. "We all have our flaws. You're covered in them. You enjoy killing. Don't you say you don't, I know you do. And, yes, I enjoy every awful thing my brother and I have done to each other."

Atticus shrugged and then whispered, "Why?"

"The thrill of it. What do you call it? A fetish? Some degrading thing no one would admit to? I don't know, Gravedigger. I just want us to be on the same level. That's why I'm telling you. We're partners, you and I."

"You want to come over for dinner when this is done?" Atticus laughed. "I'm glad you told me. I feel like I can trust you better knowing how fucked up you are."

Hex did a curtsey in her seat.

"Telepath, huh? How'd that happen?"

"Born that way, I guess," Hex said.

"Can you read my mind?"

"No, not unless you can send your thoughts, too. The way it works: I transmit my thoughts, and whoever can receive usually does. More of a burden than a gift."

"And the heir?"

"Night Terrors came up with that," Hex said, sounding guilty of something. "Never told me where they got it."

"Uh, huh." Atticus scrutinized her. "You're awfully chummy with them. Why's that?"

"Husband was in the mining business. Had to get on their good side a few times to work some areas. Seen Mara in passing here and there. She's not the killing type. More diplomatic." She came to her feet. "Any more questions?"

"One," Atticus said, doing the same. "Why'd Ichor try to kill himself?"

Hex chewed on her lip. He could tell she despised him right now, because he knew that look better than anyone else; he saw it every time the Hangman came.

Balling her fists, she said, "Because I wanted him to. I was fucking tired of his whining, the sick shit he used to pull. I was embarrassed by him, playing the victim all the time. I thought to myself, you should kill yourself, Ichor.' And he heard that, and because I wanted it so bad, he thought he did, too. He thought it was a genuine, bona fide thought of his own.

"I'm not a good person, Gravedigger, so it's a good thing Ichor and I hate each other. Who knows what damage I could do if I didn't have him to hurt?"

ISLAOS

It took them three weeks before Atticus and his followers crossed into the Blasted Woodland, a blown-out mess of trees, valleys, and crags that sat on the edge of the much larger, much drier Dires. At the middle of the Woodland, a steep, Y-shaped valley stretched for miles across the emerald expanse. In it, Islaos waited at the bottom, the sounds of axes and pickaxes constantly coming up from the valley's floor.

Geharra had been good to them thus far, that much was true.

They'd come to Cathedra in hand-me-downs, and left the town looking smart. They were given, by unnamed confederates, full sets of armor, weapons, new horses, supplies, and enough money to bribe their way out of any situation from here to Nyxis.

Atticus had been given a special blade, a sword with a skull at its hilt. But it looked hokey, and he'd grown partial to his machete. He kept the special sword stowed, until someone with lower standards than himself came along to wield it.

"We need a name," Hex said, trotting on her horse beside Elizabeth's and Miranda's. "The rebellion doesn't have one yet."

Gary raised his hand.

Hex cut him off: "And anyone who suggests calling it the Resistance is going to have my boot in their ass."

Gary lowered his hand.

"The Cabal isn't a household name, but some know it," Warren said, gripping the reins tightly. His horse hadn't taken kindly to the big man's weight; ever since they'd left, it'd been trying to shake him off.

"We're different now, though, yeah?" Elizabeth added.

Miranda massaged her shoulder. She hadn't given up trying to bring life back to the dead nerves there. "Gravedigger is leading now. Let's let him decide."

Atticus looked at James, who rode beside him. "What you think?"

James shrugged and laughed. "I'm not the Gravedigger. That's up to you."

Atticus grunted. He looked at the trees, the ground; marveled at the way everything seemed to be frozen in the moment right after an explosion. The Blasted Woodland. Name made sense now. But how it happened, he couldn't figure.

"I like the Cabal," James said. He winced, his right hand, or what was left of it, giving him some issues. It was a good thing he was ambidextrous, or so he claimed. "But I agree with Miranda."

"Thank you," Miranda chirped from the back.

"It's got to be something people can get behind. Something that'll inspire them." James ballooned out his cheeks and then exhaled. "How about the Marrow Cabal?"

"Why?" Atticus liked it, but he wanted James to defend it, the way he used to make him defend things back on the farm, to build confidence.

"Well, I mean, we have the Spine running through the Heartland, so there's that. But Eldrus is making the land sick. We're going to heal it, bring some strength back to everything."

"I like it," Warren bellowed. His horse neighed as he gave it an excited slap.

"All right." Atticus smiled and nodded at James. "What do you think, Gary?"

"Hmm?" The ghoul swallowed something—an eyeball by what Atticus could see through the holes in his throat. He gave the thumbs up. "Sounds perfect."

"I like it, too," a human-shaped Mr. Haemo buzzed, flanking them from the side. He and his horse were so covered in blood, it was hard to tell where one stopped and the other began. "Found a lumber mill."

"We said scout ahead, not slaughter ahead," Hex growled.

"They might have seen us."

Mr. Haemo balled his fist. In an instant, he absorbed the blood off himself and the horse.

"Besides, we're going to need a lot of the sticky stuff to get Clementine and Will back."

Ahead, the land began to pull apart, the background separating from the foreground. By this, Atticus knew they'd found the valley.

"What's the plan, Hex?" he asked, as they brought their horses to the edge. The valley was large enough that it was almost a stretch to consider it part of the Blasted Woodland. With its rivers and lakes, fields and forests, it was a place all its own. It had a paradise quality to it, all sun and shine, which made him second guess for a moment the extent of Eldrus' rumored atrocities here.

"We can't even be sure how many vermillion corpses have been buried in Islaos," she said. "This is where Eldrus started doing it first."

"Hex, how long has this been going on for?" Gary asked.

"Maybe two or three months after Edgar got back from the Nameless Forest. Two years, then?"

"Holy Child," James whispered.

"Rebellions take time to build," Warren reminded them, before the accusations started.

"So no grave digging for infected bodies?" Mr. Haemo sounded sad. "What a shame."

"Seven hundred people live in Islaos," Hex said. "More above the valley. We have about one hundred to one hundred and fifty committed to our cause, which doesn't mean a whole lot, other than they showed up for refreshments."

Miranda cleared her throat. "How many soldiers?"

Hex shrugged and said, "Hard to say. It's a wide area to police. We don't know exactly what's going on in these woods, either. Islaos is a frontier town, though. We won't have a lot of pushback. People move out here because they value privacy."

"No more killing, mosquito," Atticus said. He noticed a trail not far from where they stood that led into the valley. "You got that?"

"I have to kill to keep this appearance, boss," Mr. Haemo said, riding up beside him. "Taking out that shepherd for you—you're welcome, by the way—took a lot out of me."

Atticus cringed at Mr. Haemo's ashy, patchy, sagging face. "I know. Thank you. You only helped to save yourself. I know that."

Mr. Haemo tried to smile, but his cheeks wouldn't cooperate. "Save? No. I just don't like being weak. I can do this on my own, but it'll go faster with you." He paused and then said, "There's another shepherd coming, I'm sure. Grab them by the cracks in their head, like I did. It's the only way."

Hex coughed, drawing attention to herself. A wave of leaves blew past, sticking a few twigs in her hair. "King Edgar has one of his famous suffer centers in Islaos. We'll meet our contact there."

Atticus could feel all eyes on him. He glanced back and saw Warren nodding in his direction. *Son of a bitch*, he thought. *This was supposed to be your gig.*

"Let's go, then," he said finally, kicking his horse toward the trail. "Before someone sees us."

The trail was one of many that had been carved into the valley's steep slopes. Each went to different locations above Islaos, with the trail to the distant Spine being the busiest. Where the valley was highest, elevators had been installed. In constant use, they transported workers and gathered resources back and forth between the town and the various encampments around the Blasted Woodland.

Elizabeth rode to the front of the party. "You should get some ink, Gravedigger."

Atticus raised an eyebrow. The new armor had more or less covered most of her tattoos, but even now there were a few thick lines creeping up her neck.

"Afraid it might hurt?"

Atticus unbuckled his bracer and showed the Deadly Beauty where he'd killed himself. "Not particularly."

She curled her nose. "You smell awful."

"Consequence of dying all the time."

"You're too skinny, too."

Atticus tugged his horse as they went around the last bend to Islaos. "You come up here to give me a hard time?"

"Just saying you look a little rough."

Elizabeth waved at a group of women in robes coming toward them. They waved, went another way, and started whispering amongst themselves.

"Might want something to cover up all that damage you've done to yourself, yeah?"

"Don't see the point. Whatever tattoo I got, it would probably just be torn off." The hot sun was starting to get in his eyes. He lowered his head until it stopped pissing him off. "Besides, I wouldn't know what tattoo to get."

"Something meaningful is a good start." She grumbled as she tried to lift the armor on her side. "See it?"

He did notice the scarred slits on each of her hands, but she was getting at something else. On her lower back, there was a tattoo of a nun with the face of a demon. In her right hand, she held Penance's holy text, *Helminth's Way*, and in her left, a rosary made out of teeth and eyeballs. At her feet, four stones—red, white, pink, and purple—were placed.

"The Bad Woman from the Our Ladies of Sorrow academy." She covered herself, deflected the glare Miranda was giving her from the back of the line. "I'm the red stone, Miranda's the purple. Jessie... was the pink."

"Who was the white?"

"Emily... our friend who didn't make it out of that place. This, and what we—" she pointed to Miranda, "—remember is all that's left of her."

"What'd you do with the Bad Woman?"

The trail evened out into the grassy floor of the valley.

"Put her in my skin. She's still alive. A spellweaver wove her in, body and soul. The Bad Woman always kept a close eye on us at the academy. Always kept in range of the cane." Elizabeth smiled victoriously. "Now she doesn't have to worry, because we're always together." She took out a knife and stuck it to her side. "We don't have a cane, yeah? But this works well, too. I make sure she gets her daily stabbing."

"Take it you can't feel it?"

"Couldn't even if I could."

Atticus was their leader, but Hex was in charge, so when she vetoed subtlety and told them to ride through the front gates of Islaos, they did just that.

"There's no point in hiding anymore," she told them as they navigated the throngs of people on the main thoroughfare. "We want them to know we're here. It'll give them a chance to change their tune."

Islaos had a rustic charm to it that Atticus found endearing. Laid out like a star, the town was all dark wood and black knots, with each radial street filled to the brim with houses, businesses, and stalls. Eldrus' presence was undeniable, because a few seconds couldn't pass without Atticus seeing some armed soldier moving through the crowd or going into a shop. Nobody looked uncomfortable with them being there, but even the sick sometimes forget the disease that's killing them.

The suffer center stood out like a sore thumb. As the first part of what people now realized to be Eldrus' encroachment, the city-state had constructed these pantries and shelters years ago to serve the poor and misfortunate. Eldrus kept the places well-stocked and well-manned by community members, but under one condition: They did not alter in any way, shape, or form the look of the suffer center. They were not meant to fit into the surrounding environment. They were meant to stand out, black and angular, like the city-state itself, as a constant reminder of Eldrus' charity. Most of the Heartland found King Edgar's demands reasonable and worth the eye-sore.

Except Gallows, of course. They tore the suffer center down the first day it went it up, claiming they were suffering just fine without it.

Their contact's name was Benjamin. By the looks of it, he was the poor bastard in the front of the suffer center swamped by the lunchtime regulars. When Atticus turned to ask Hex if there was a back entrance, the crowd of thirty went quiet and took notice of them. Whispers, murmurs. People parted, pointed. Some tried to look at Atticus, but when he caught their gaze, they quickly looked away, shaken and scared. He didn't like this, having a reputation. He used to, back when it kept him out of fights he couldn't win. But not anymore, especially when he didn't even know what it was for.

"Let them through," Benjamin shouted. He handed off some food to a few workers nearby and let them take over. Staring at Atticus, grizzled and grinning, he said, "Come down. We'll take care of the horses."

"It's okay," Hex said to everyone.

"Doesn't look like it." Gary made a circle with his finger. All around them, small pockets of Eldrus' soldiers had formed. They were too far away to attack, but they were close enough to see and hear everything.

"We've got tens of human shields between us and them," Mr. Haemo buzzed, several of his children humming around his head. "Let them try."

Atticus grunted and dismounted from his horse. He took out his machete and started through the crowd. He eyed the people like grass that needed to be cut back. And like grass they shivered, and like grass they parted.

What role do they expect me to play? He heard the others drop from their horses. *Undead maniac? Reborn savior?*

"They're here."

"—Gravedigger?"

An old woman whipped around to the younger woman behind her. "Look at his neck."

Some men, too muscular to be begging, said loudly, "About time. I'm ready to do this."

Atticus tried to read the faces of the people outside the suffer center, but he couldn't make sense of them. Had they never expected him to arrive? Had they even believed that he existed at all? Maybe he'd died too much to understand those unspoken subtleties anymore. Or maybe their faces reflected his own; that is, the sudden, pants-shitting realization that now they had to make good on their not so good word.

"Please," Benjamin said, waving them on. "Please, people, let them pass."

"Is that the Gravedigger?"

"Is that him?"

Benjamin heard the questions and nodded to no one in particular.

"Can't say I like being out in the open like this," Warren rumbled.

Benjamin walked towards Atticus, hand outstretched. "You're safe, I give you my word."

Atticus took his hand and shook it.

"Let's go inside, sir."

"Gravedigger's fine," Atticus said. He flinched as he heard the crowd clamor at the confirmation. In his periphery, he saw more joining in. "Let's go inside, Benjamin."

Benjamin shuffled the Marrow Cabal through the front of the suffer center, locked the doors behind them, and led them through the building, until they emerged into a small gathering place. Several long benches stretched across the room. There wasn't enough space to hold Hex's supposed one hundred to one hundred and fifty loyalists. But there were enough nooks to cram together those that counted most.

"I'm so glad you're here." Benjamin was a young man, but to Atticus, it seemed following Geharra's goals had aged him. The twenty-something enthusiasm was there, but so, too, were the dark circles of thirty and the creeping wrinkles of forty.

"We are the Marrow Cabal," Hex said. She nodded at Warren, and he bolted the door. "And now you are, too."

Benjamin smiled so hard his teeth looked as though they'd blow out his skull.

"This is James, Warren, Elizabeth, and Miranda," Hex said, gesturing to each. "That's Gary. He's a ghoul. He has his shit together, though, so don't worry."

Gary nodded innocently and said, "I ate on my way here."

Benjamin, star-struck, waved him off and said, "No, no. No, you're fine. Hi."

"This…" Hex scowled at Mr. Haemo, but he was too busy fighting with his skin suit to pay her much mind. "Just come to us if he gives you any problems."

"Yeah, yeah." Again, Benjamin was shaking Atticus' hand. "Gravedigger."

"Yeah, we met about ten seconds ago."

"I hadn't heard anything. I thought maybe Geharra gave up."

"You didn't receive any correspondence?" Hex asked.

Benjamin shook his head. "No, but Eldrus might've got to them first. We've been preparing, though. Everyone knows what's coming. We've just been waiting for the orders. You saw the soldiers out front? They've been here for a while. I'm friends with a lot of them. Most of us are. There's some jackasses, sure, but a lot of them are decent people."

"Sounds like you're having a change of heart," Atticus said.

"No, not at all." Benjamin sounded scared, as though he feared the Gravedigger was questioning his loyalty. "What I'm saying… what I'm saying is that it doesn't need to be a bloodbath."

"Whoa, hold on. Pump the brakes," Mr. Haemo said.

Atticus held up his hand.

"The soldiers don't want to be here, either," Benjamin continued. "But it's their job. But… they don't want to die for it, you know? I think most will leave without a fight, but we have to fight. Otherwise, they won't leave. Does that make sense?"

Atticus and Hex nodded.

"People in Islaos are worried that we'll push these soldiers out and then worse ones will replace them. I don't blame them. Eldrus definitely has to go, don't get me wrong. We've dug up a lot of the bodies they've buried and I don't even know what they're doing."

Hex lied and said, "We're not sure, either."

"Exactly. They've got to go. We realize this. But the people need to feel confident that this is worth fighting for. There's been a malaise of apathy lately in Islaos. I'm sorry if I sound scattered. We've worked and worked to get people this far. But they need a shove in the right direction. If they fall back to their old ways, then at that point, I don't think there's anything anyone can do to convince them."

"You can say it." Atticus cleared his throat. He didn't want his next sentence to sound as nervous as he now felt. "You want me to give them a speech."

Benjamin nodded, put his hands together. "Please. That's all they need. I figured you would, but I wasn't certain. If you tell them what you've been through, what you've done."

Atticus glanced back at Hex. "What's that exactly?"

"The plantation in Cathedra," Benjamin said. "The riots in Bedlam. You broke the supply lines in the lowlands. Raided the ports along the Divide. You've been digging up all the tainted corpses and putting them to rest in consecrated ground."

Still looking at Hex, he said, "Yeah, seems I've been busy."

"And… and–" Benjamin swallowed hard, "–and you can't die. At least, not until you've avenged your wife and son."

"Yeah, one day that day will come." He shook his head at Hex, and then at Warren, whom he was sure was also propagating these rumors.

"You… you really can't die?"

Atticus unfastened the straps of his armor. His chest piece cracked against the ground. He lifted his shirt.

Benjamin gasped. The neck slit, the kunai gouge, the red ravines of rot leading to his lungs—they were all there. He loosened his tassets and his greaves, and then, with his pants, let them drop around his ankles. The skin on his legs was pale and stiff, like petrified wood. Across them, the hundreds of tiny fang holes left him looking porous, spongey. The necrosis had returned, but as Hex had predicted, his body had absorbed it. What other pieces of filth were floating around inside him? he wondered. If someone cut him open, really cut him open deep, would they find a dam of decay built up inside? And what would be held back? A great deluge of insanity? Or just the dredges of his poor excuse for humanity?

Atticus came to his senses. "I really can't die? No." Taking a page from Elizabeth's book, he said, "Couldn't even if I could."

If Atticus was going to give a speech to inspire people to get off their asses and attempt something other than look for an excuse to sit back down on them, then he was going to do it right. He had the benches hauled out of the gathering place, to the front of the suffer center. He was only going to say what he had to say once, and he wasn't about to say it only to the so-called leaders who wouldn't do much fighting to begin with. People would stand, and people would sit, and everyone would know what they were getting into.

"I don't think this is a good idea," Benjamin said as he, Atticus, Miranda, and Gary worked the last bench through the suffer center's hall. "If we're out in the open, then they will have to respond."

"Let them," Atticus said. For a moment, he worried about pulling a muscle, and then he realized it didn't matter. "Hopefully, they'll try to assassinate me."

"Wouldn't that be nice," Miranda said snidely.

"Hey, you looking for a boyfriend?" Gary asked. "You and Mr. Haemo both have the same shitty attitude. I can put in a good word for you, if you'd like."

Miranda smiled her first smile since meeting Atticus, and put her guard back up.

Atticus returned to the gathering place a few hours later and started to pace the length of the room.

"Feeling about as far from my comfort zone as I can get," he said to James, who stood in the doorway. "Feels like we rode out of Gallows yesterday."

"I don't know a man better than you." James came into the room, hands in his pockets. "You've put yourself through almost everything to get them back. No hesitation, no complaints."

"None that I voiced." He sighed. "Please tell me I didn't get myself elected to be leader of some half-assed rebellion."

"No," James said, laughing. "You're a convenient figure is all. I'm sure they have several 'Gravediggers' lined up if things go south at some point. As soon as Hex brought you back to her place in Bedlam, she went to work on your story. She has a good eye for people. I think she was going to offer you a lot of money to work for them, before she found out what happened to Clementine and Will."

"Yeah, I guess money don't mean much to me anymore."

"What are you going to say tonight?"

Atticus' mouth hung open. "Still working on that. Waiting for divine inspiration, I suppose."

"You're a holy man now, Atticus?" He winced as his butchered hand begged to be amputated.

"Comes and goes. All this dying I've done, can't say I've seen god in any of it."

"Well, I don't know if you're looking in the right place. The Membrane sounds like an in-between."

Atticus stroked his chin. "Guess I got to find the correct keyhole to look through. Might be god's not what we expected."

James shrugged and said, "Might be that, for heretics like yourself, you can't recognize god, even if god kicked you square in the ass. God will never live up to your expectations."

"I suppose, little priest."

"Hey, uh," James rubbed the back of his head, "You know, I tried to find my family after I left the farm a few years back."

"I figured that was part of it." *It's time*, Atticus thought. "How'd Elijah fit into all that?"

"He told me where they were. He told me a lot of things. I guess I just… I couldn't help myself. That's why I ran."

It took everything Atticus had from going off. He saw Elijah in his mind's eye and regretted every day he hadn't dismembered him. "Did you see your family?"

"Oh, yeah." James took out his mangled hand. With the other, he took out a vial and poured something into the bandages. "It didn't go well. Not at all."

"Well, having sex with your brother will do that. Hard thing to forgive." Atticus cringed and said, "I know you didn't know."

James looked surprised, as though he hadn't expected him to be so blunt about the issue. "I didn't know. Not when we were little. But, Atticus, I have no excuse for after that, when we were caught. When Mom and Dad told us."

"Elijah manipulated you for years."

James' cheek quivered. He looked away, eyes gone red. "I hate talking about it. There's no good way to put it. I feel so fucking disgusting having done it. When were kids, okay, fine. Kids play games. They don't know any better. I looked… up to him."

Atticus said, "You do something long enough, and if no one says otherwise, it's going to seem normal."

"But how do you explain after my parents found us? They beat the hell out of me. Not him. Me. And then we kept doing it, anyways. We were teenagers. We knew better, but we did it, anyways. How can you possibly explain that?"

Atticus couldn't, so he didn't say anything.

"I wish someone else got it. What it's like. I knew all this time he was using me. But I didn't look at him like he was my brother. Dad wouldn't talk to me. Mom wouldn't look at me. This was before they even found out. There was only Elijah. And I knew it was sick, our secret, but he listened, he looked at me. The trade-off seemed all right."

James sighed, pulled down on his cheeks. "I know you and Clementine and Will poured a lot into me. All your love and compassion. I can't believe after all that running away I ran into people like you."

"So why'd you answer when Elijah came calling?" Atticus asked. "You knew all these things, how wrong and sick it was."

"It was like someone flipped a switch in my head. All you guys did for me... it was like none of it happened. Seeing him took me back. Caught me off-guard. And he made promises. Said we could be a family again. I did miss it, us together."

"Do you still miss it?"

James hesitated and said, "Yeah, sometimes. It's like it's tainted. Sex, that is. I've been with other men, but even then I found myself missing him. I'm sorry, I know it's disgusting to say that. Years of it. God. Fucked me in the head so bad."

"Was it his idea to sell yourself for money?"

"It was both our idea. After a year of it, we weren't intimate with each other anymore. Didn't want nothing to do with me."

Atticus took a deep breath. He didn't want to hear these things, but for James' sake, he had to.

"I did want to leave him, Atticus, about six months ago. But I couldn't. What if I couldn't do any better? What if someone found out? I mean, some people knew, but it was mostly a joke they really didn't think was all that true. Him, the whoring—it became routine. My family disowned me. I disowned you. He was all I had. My body was all I had. All it seemed I was good for."

"You turned on him, though," Atticus said, stepping closer to James. "Why'd you do that?"

"After we broke into Brinton's casket, it hit me. That feeling you get when you know you've done something just... wrong. We were breaking into your place. Your place. Being back there, brought it all back. You, Clementine. Will. Dinners and going to school and working in the fields. Everything caught up with me. And looking at Brinton, I think I saw myself in him. That's what I had in store for me. Some asshole in a casket who no one really liked and never did much for himself. I didn't want to die like that, be remembered like that. The whore who fucks his b-brother and robs his friends. No, I'm not that. Never was supposed to be that. I know that now.

"I struggle with it, though. I do. Did I make a mistake? Was I wrong? Maybe he'll... forgive me for leaving him? I try to ignore my doubts." He sighed. "Thank you for listening to me."

Atticus nodded, pulled James into a hug.

"Thank you," he said, holding him there. "Thank you for not giving up on us. Holy Child knows I deserve it. We've both been through enough."

James smiled and said with tears in his eyes, "Isn't that the god damn truth. I think they're ready for you."

"I doubt it," Atticus said, smoothing out his shirt. "But we'll see."

Outside the suffer center, Islaos waited. The benches were packed, with everyone sitting so close they were almost in each other's laps. Looking through the front doorway, Atticus saw even more behind the fifty or sixty that were seated. They shuffled back and forth, murmuring to themselves and pointing when they probably thought they caught a glimpse of the infamous Gravedigger.

Behind them, stationed along the street and atop the nearby roofs, were Eldrus' soldiers, each armed to the gums. Out in the open as they were, it was clear they weren't trying to hide themselves for the demonstration. Like the suffer center itself, they wanted people to know they were there, and to remember what they were capable of.

"Everyone is in place," Hex said, coming up behind Atticus. She put her hand on his shoulder. "They'll fall for it. Remember, don't mention the Nameless Forest."

"Yeah, don't want to overdo it," Warren said, coming from the gathering place. He stood at the threshold with Atticus and added, "Glad it's you going out there and getting them all rowdy. Public speaking makes me want to puke."

Atticus cocked his head and glared at the big man. "Why'd you agree to help with the rebellion in the first place? Don't seem all that passionate about it."

Warren shrugged. "Sounded good at the time. But then you showed up and did your undead thing. I know when I've been upstaged, and when I need to follow rather than lead."

"Did you pay him off, to let me take over instead?" Atticus asked Hex.

She nodded. "Of course. He's a greedy son of a bitch."

Warren smiled and bobbed his eyebrows up and down.

"Put a lot of faith in me, Hex," Atticus said.

"You haven't let me down yet." She paused as the crowd started to grow louder outside the suffer center. "We can make a hero out of anyone."

Atticus put his finger to her chest. "What's that mean?"

"Means you're not the only one we're hedging our bets on. Means when you get your wife and son back, I'll do everything I can to get you out of this."

Atticus looked back outside. People had begun chanting "Grave-digger," each syllable slow and deep, like a hand thudding against the skin of a drum.

Hex punched his chest and said, "You're on."

Atticus nodded and, without hesitation, walked outside to greet those who knew him better than he did them. The crowd stopped it's chanting. Again, there were whispers, but they were quickly snuffed out by harsh shushes. Benjamin had built a small platform in front of the suffer center, so he stepped onto that. Standing there, exposed and more or less unprepared, Atticus felt like the fool he surely seemed.

What do I say? He looked to those sitting, to those standing, and those farther off, disinterested. *What have I done?* He looked up, to the top of the valley, where torches burned brightly against the darkening sky.

Clementine, this isn't me. He looked inward, to the memory of the Membrane. *I can feel you laughing at me, Will. Your father's an idiot.*

"Do... you... know who I am?" Atticus mumbled, each word louder than the last. It was a start, even if it was a shitty one.

The crowd gave the only response he deserved: silence.

He swallowed hard. With a shaking hand—*This is worse than dying*—he pointed to the soldiers of Eldrus. "They know who I am. They know better. That is why they keep their distance and hide in the shadows."

Those sitting whispered to themselves. Some glanced over their shoulders at the soldiers, to see how they were taking it.

When he was eight or nine, a man by the name of Anthony Proust came to Gallows once. He claimed to be the descendant of Marcus Proust, a religious zealot who tried to wipe out the Night Terrors in the south. Before reaching Gallows, Anthony had marched across the Heartland, giving speeches and gaining followers to help him take up his family's genocidal dreams.

Atticus could still remember when Anthony came to town and gave the speech he gave. He sounded confident to the point of delu-sional, and though he spoke clearly, he spoke like a madman. Others would've been booed off stage, but when he came to Gallows that day, people listened, because Anthony himself believed he was worth listening to.

Atticus took a deep breath. He worked his words over in his head, until they lost most of his accent and took on another tone entirely. "I know that you all did not come out here to seek an easier life. These lands are hard lands, like the palms of your hands and the soles of your feet. You came out here to get away, like the rest of us across the Heartland. If Penance came into your valley, would you put up with their being here?"

Numerous heads shook throughout the crowd.

"You would think you were being overthrown. You would think you were under attack. How come..." Atticus cleared his throat. "What makes Eldrus different? We may trade and offer services, but for as long as I can remember, that has been the extent of our relationship. They've gone too far, have they not?"

Numerous heads nodded throughout the crowd.

"You've seen what they've put in the soil. Turning our loved ones into weapons. That's right, weapons. I have seen what happens to those bodies when Eldrus activates them. They explode, ripping apart everything in the area. Do you want that? Do you want to have to worry about your child stepping outside and being torn to pieces because he put his foot on the wrong patch of grass? Do you want to take the risk that, when you die, you'll be dug up and desecrated and used to kill others? They say the tainted corpses will heal the land, but all I see is an attempt to control it without us knowing."

The soldiers started to get antsy. Slowly, they inched forward, their weapons sheathed, but not for much longer.

"I am not asking you or anyone else to go to war." Atticus closed his eyes and apologized to his family. "They killed my family. They killed me."

He stripped off his shirt and showed the extent of his scars. The crowd leaned in, gasped in disbelief. Those standing, and those even further back, pushed in with the soldiers, to have a better look at this monologuing monstrosity.

"I have died more than anyone ought to. I have lived many lives from Gallows to here, and all of them were cut short by Eldrus' swords. And do you know why? Do you... do you know why they killed me and my... Do you know why they murdered my family? Because we discovered what they were putting in the ground and refused to take part in it. What do you think they will do to you when you say no? Do you think they will care if they kill you? At this point, you're useful to them, whether you are dead or alive."

The crowd grew louder, more animated. People started to stand up, while others slinked off, afraid of what may come. Atticus heard doubters amongst the commotion, but even they didn't sound convinced of themselves.

"I am not asking you to go to war," Atticus repeated. He was starting to get the hang of this. He kind of liked how powerful it made him feel. "I know that you have friends amongst these soldiers. They are human beings, like the rest of us. But like the rest of us, most of them will do what they are told, because they have to protect themselves as well. I do not want any killing here tonight. But they cannot stay. If they do, the wounds they have made will worsen, and they will fester, until one day, our Heartland dries up and dies out."

Atticus forced himself to stop talking. The words were coming too quickly, too easily, and Islaos had gotten so loud, he wasn't sure they were hearing him anymore. People were shouting and throwing their hands into the air. Debates had broken out in the back rows.

One down, Atticus thought. *Two more to go.*

Atticus returned to the crowd. "You would not be sitting here—"

His throat closed shut. In the wings of the audience, a woman sat. She was leaning forward, but the long, blonde hair spilling out from under her large hat made it impossible to see her face. Loose bandages hung from both her hands, and across her lap, a shepherd's crook lay.

"You would not—"

Immediately, his eyes went to the opposite side of the gathering. On the edge of it, another woman stood—another blonde with long hair hanging messily in front of her face. In her left hand, a bundle of bandages, and in her right, a twisted shepherd's crook.

Hex came up behind him. "Is everything okay?"

"There's two of them," he said, his voice gone hoarse. "There's two shepherds now. Keep Mr. Haemo close."

She nodded and said, "You're doing great. Just a little more."

Eyes fixed on the shepherds, Atticus continued. "You would not be here if you did not, in some ways, agree with what is being said here tonight. People are fighting across the Heartland, but we must fight together. I would and will die a thousand times over to see Eldrus thrown from—"

A voice shouted, "And you will!"

Something whistled through the air. Atticus felt a pressure in his chest, like a palm pushing him back. He looked down and found a massive bolt from a crossbow there, inches deep into his heart. The crowd gasped, stunned. Soldiers pushed themselves towards the front, to detain the people there.

Atticus dropped to his knees, ripped the bolt out, and died. Like a curtain falling, the Membrane closed in around him.

"Clementine! Will," he shouted. He had to take advantage of these moments. They had to know what he was doing for them. "Clementine! Will!"

He blinked his eyes. He was back in Islaos, now standing, but still shouting for his wife and son. The hole in his chest gave a glimpse of his wounded heart. Though it had been torn open, it still beat, and it still bled.

"He... he... he's alive!"

"Look at his heart. Look at it!"

"That bolt would've killed a bear!"

Atticus touched his chest, seeped the blood into his hand, and held it high. "Eldrus bleeds us dry. Have my blood, until the Heartland's flows again."

In an instant, Hex's one hundred loyalists emerged. They filtered through the crowd and seized the soldiers who hadn't seen them coming. Those seated in the front hadn't been devoted to Geharra's cause, like the soldiers might've thought. They were just people passing by who needed to rest their feet and wanted to see a good show.

"Take them," Atticus said.

With their swords, knives, and spears, the loyalists forced the soldiers into a surrender.

"But do not harm them!"

The soldiers on the roofs shouted to one another. As they loaded their bows to loose arrows on the people below, loyalists came up behind them and killed them dead.

Frantic, Atticus searched for the shepherds. *Where are they? Where did they go?*

"You fucking morons! I am captain Kellin," a soldier shouted. By the medals fixed to his breastplate, he appeared to be in charge of this suppression. "There are hundreds of us higher in the valley. You think Eldrus will let this happen?" The loyalists holding him kicked out his legs and sent him to the ground. "Let us go, and we'll only make an example of these… deceivers who organized this mockery!"

To his left, Gary, James, and Mr. Haemo stood. And to his right, now there was Hex, Warren, Elizabeth, and Miranda.

"Go," Atticus shouted. He waved goodbye to captain Kellin as the loyalists dragged him away into the maddening swell of people.

"Beat them back!"

The crowd, likely half of Islaos at this point, began to disperse. They tore through the streets, tackling the soldiers who were trying to flee.

"Retake what's yours!"

Screams fell around him. At the top of the valley, in the light of the torches there, soldiers were being thrown off the cliffs, their bodies breaking on the boulders at the valley's bottom.

"Kill them all," he shouted, spitting the words. "Kill them!" His soul salivated inside him, its black, barbed tongue becoming his own. He smelled blood in the air, and it excited him. "Kill them, and then bring their bodies to me!"

Smiling at Mr. Haemo, he screamed, "My friends and I will see they do not go to waste!"

CHAPTER XXI

HROTHAS

Islaos had gone well.

Hrothas did not.

Atticus and the Marrow Cabal rode into the town two months later and found another Gravedigger had beaten them there. The pale skinned impersonator with bad prosthetics stood on the steps of the town hall, shovel in hand. When he spoke to his crowd, he shouted. And when the people of Hrothas shouted back, he recoiled. Eldrus' soldiers were in attendance as well, but they almost looked disinterested in the display.

"What is this?" Atticus asked.

He and the Marrow Cabal hitched their horses to a few nearby houses. They moved down the winding avenue, towards the town hall.

Hex's braids started to unravel and twist, unravel and twist. Her eyes went wide and, for a moment, became so blue it was almost blinding. A vein bulged on the side of her head and inched across her skull, like a worm looking for a hole to hide in.

James went to touch her arm. "Are you okay?"

Warren grabbed his hand. "She's trying to receive. Trying to see what thoughts are out there. Maybe from the heir."

Mr. Haemo licked his lips.

"Can she do that?" Gary leaned away from the group. "Things are getting worse up there, guys."

"Sometimes." Warren nodded and turned to Elizabeth and Miranda. "Right?"

"Yeah, I've heard her say she can do it," Miranda said. She took out her sword, having seen what Gary had seen.

"Can you hear what that son of a bitch is saying?" Atticus said.

The crowd had morphed into a mob. If he had to guess, he'd say they were about sixty strong.

Hex moaned and blew the air out of her lungs. Her legs quivered. She braced herself against James. "He's not one of us." The vein in her head stopped throbbing. "I... heard something about Eldrus hiring... impostors."

Atticus said, "I'm not the only Gravedigger, right?"

Hex shook her head. "None of them are nearby, though. They're in the field, fighting. He's not one of us."

"I can make out some of what he's saying," Mr. Haemo said. He pulled his waxy ear further back until it started to tear away from his head. "Don't you see they're here to help?" the mosquito repeated, his words matching with the impostor's lips. "We don't need to fight back. We don't need to... Ah, ah, oh my god—"

A wave of people crashed into the impostor Gravedigger.

"—Please, no, please. I'm not him. I'm not him. I'm not." Mr. Haemo cleared his throat. "The rest is gurgles. And... wait for it."

A severed arm was flung high above the mob.

"Wait for it."

And then a handful of intestines.

"There we go. Now he's dead."

Turning to Hex, Atticus said, "To Nyxis, then?"

"No." She mouthed she was okay as Elizabeth patted her back. "No, this is perfect. Just need to give them something to do with their anger."

The mob begun to tear through the town. Doors were kicked open and windows shattered. Small fires erupted where torches were torn down. People ran into shops and came out with armfuls of stolen goods. Proprietors tried to chase the thieves, but they were beaten down by others nearby, others who had probably once bought from them before. One would've expected Eldrus to intervene, but instead the soldiers stood there and let Hrothas have its temper tantrum, because after all, it was their toys they were breaking.

"Idiots," Warren shouted.

"We can't do nothing now," Atticus said. Somewhere in the uproar, he heard the thump of a shepherd's crook. "Let's go before they string us up."

Mr. Haemo held out his hands. The skin sagged off his arms, like an old woman's in a wind tunnel. "I got this," he said cheerfully. The mosquito had gotten blood-drunk in Islaos. Ever since, he'd had a skip in his step.

"No," Hex and Elizabeth said simultaneously.

But it was too late. The mosquito had shed his skin and taken to the sky. Mr. Haemo buzzed high above the black-eyed looters, his gangling magnificence going unseen. Thick swathes of his children phased into being from their unseen lairs. They formed clouds with their fragile bodies. In a matter of seconds, dark, whining nimbuses were roaming the sky, droning threats of an impending downpour.

"Don't do it," Hex said. She shook Atticus. "Call him off!"

"What do you want me to do? Swat him down?"

"You employed this thing!"

"We're almost to Eldrus. If this is what it takes, then let it happen."

"Wind smells like metal," Elizabeth said, covering her nose.

"Geharra isn't going to back us if we end up doing more damage than King Edgar!" She tilted her head back. "Feels like it's going to… Oh, son of a bitch."

From every pulsing proboscis, blood poured in choking sheets. The red rain washed back and forth, dousing the mob in the very thing they were eager to spill. Dumbstruck, the dumbasses stood there, eyes open, mouths agape, gawping and gulping down the gory shower.

"Your Gravedigger is here," Mr. Haemo shouted.

Not one for waste of the sticky stuff, he shut down the show seconds later. But it'd been enough; he had everyone's attention, and everyone's horror.

The giant mosquito outstretched his gaunt, burn-black arm. "Eldrus wants you to think we've given up." His million eyes got a glint to them—a sheen of triumph from their terror. "The Gravedigger reminds you the Marrow Cabal has not!"

The mob turned slowly. Mr. Haemo's children fell around them and sucked up what they could of the blood they'd spent.

"I am the Gravedigger," Atticus shouted to them. He was off-guard, put on the spot. He looked past the dripping mob, to the soldiers shuffling forward, swords drawn. "I am—"

Thump, thump, thump, from somewhere nearby.

"—I am here to fight alongside you."

"What's… what's going on?" a man asked. The jewelry he'd stolen hung limply from his pocket.

The mob ducked as Mr. Haemo flew past them and landed beside the Marrow Cabal.

Another man shrieked, "What is that thing?" And then he slipped on the slick stones and fell on his ass.

"Is this another one of Eldrus' tricks?"

"Holy Child, go, go! Run!"

"This isn't worth it. What's going on?"

"Move, damn it! Run!"

People fled in every direction, leaving a trail of red footsteps by which one could follow, if one were so inclined. Mr. Haemo's demonstration had impressed, but it had also doused the fires they needed to keep the rebellion burning here.

Horse hooves. The clinking of chainmail. These sounds and distant orders rose unexpectedly around the mob. And then, as they grew louder and closer, a voice, raw with authority, belted, "Round them up!"

Mounted guards mowed down the milling mob. One after the other, until there was too much chaos to count, Eldrus' finest in shining mail split the ranks. Those too slow to flee were knocked down, and quickly picked up by the soldiers on foot. Those too fast to catch caught an arrow in the calf, and quickly learned the virtues of obedience.

"We have to go," Hex said. She looked about as pissed as she sounded.

Atticus threw out his arms. "We wasted months getting here!"

"Are you kidding me? You're the one who just said we should leave."

The rest of the Marrow Cabal, Mr. Haemo included, didn't need much convincing. They were already hopping on their horses.

"You can't die, Atticus," Hex snarled. "But we can. Get on your horse and get."

"This rebellion is a fucking joke."

Thump, thump, thump.

Atticus spun around, trying to locate the shepherd. "Eldrus is just going to kill them." Why was he fighting her on this? He didn't give a shit.

"They were going to do that, anyways." She mounted her horse. "Go, save them. Better yet, why not beat the shit out of your mosquito friend for getting up there and showing his ass?" She sighed. "Geharra will send more groups in to destabilize the town. It'll help pull more reinforcements away from Eldrus."

She went to his horse and untethered it from the support beam he'd wrapped it around. Throwing the reins at Atticus, she said, "Get, Gravedigger."

NYXIS

After spending twenty minutes in a town that took two months to get to, the last thing the Marrow Cabal wanted was to ride for another twenty days into a town under martial law; which was exactly what had happened in Nyxis, thanks to the events that had occurred in Hrothas.

So a mile outside of Nyxis, in the folds of the farmland there, they abandoned their horses and made for a barn with a busted-up car sitting outside it. Slipping inside the barn, Atticus and the others found three old women, robed in red, sitting at a small table, reading one another's palms. They were Hex's contacts in Nyxis, ones which she had apparently been conversing with mentally since Islaos.

"Hex, lend me your hand," the smallest woman said. She looked over her shoulder coyly. "You won't worm your way out of it this time."

Hex shook her head. "Tell you what. Get us in to Nyxis and I'll even let you read my feet."

The largest woman chuckled as she said, "Can't do nothing with them monkey toes."

"This him?" The skinniest of the three closed her hands into fists. "This our Gravedigger?"

Atticus stepped forward. Tapping his machete against his leg, he said, "The one and only."

The skinniest shook her head. Pointing to herself, she said, "Name's Helena. Don't worry about the others." She waved off the two women, who were now trying to get her attention. "Those old crones couldn't tell you what they're called if their lives depended on it."

"You look like witches," Atticus said.

"We are witches," the smallest one chirped. "You and your dead friend over there—" she pointed one crooked finger at Gary, "— smell like borrowed time."

Helena gasped, finally taking notice of Mr. Haemo. "We want nothing to do with him!"

The mosquito, back in his man suit, acted shocked. "You wound me, Dark Sister."

"Interesting, yeah?" Elizabeth nudged Miranda.

"Can you get us into Nyxis?" Warren sounded impatient; looked it, too. "There were soldiers posted at every entrance. Liable to be more the longer we wait."

"Yeah, yeah, yeah," the largest witch said. She stood with the smallest witch. "Don't move."

Helena took a curved dagger out of her robes and said to Hex, "How badly you need that creature?"

"Mr. Haemo?" She glanced at Atticus, and said begrudgingly, "Pretty badly."

Helena's eyes went shark-black. She put the dagger away. "Next time, bug."

Mr. Haemo smiled until the sides of his mouth split. "I'm sure."

"Look up," the largest witch said.

And they did.

Above them, a pentagram had been seared into the barn's ceiling. The intricate details inside it writhed, as though each line and cut had been packed with maggots.

"Don't take your eyes off it," the smallest witch added.

"We need to have a talk, Hex," Helena said. "About the company you keep."

"That means we'd have to talk about you three," Hex snapped back.

"You ladies going to weave us away?" Gary asked.

"Hold on," James said. "What's going on here?"

"Don't take your eyes off it," the smallest witch repeated. "Or they'll be picking up pieces of you from here to the Divide."

The witches closed in on the Marrow Cabal. They wrangled them into a small a circle and stood at their sides, forming a triangle around them.

"Don't see how you're going to get much done in Nyxis nowadays," the largest witch said. She put her hands together as though she were praying.

"Soldiers have a stranglehold on the people. Can't imagine many will fight," the smallest witch said. She went to her knees and put her palms to the ground.

"Might be some merit in letting Eldrus do what they're trying to do," Helena chimed in finally. She grabbed her breasts and tipped back her head. "Already the world feels different, more alive. Your kind may not like it, but ours are flourishing. But no matter." She sighed and made a clicking noise. "Even to monsters, money is money."

James' hand closed around Atticus', then trembled beside him. They'd seen so many strange and terrible things of late and this was what made him sweat? At this point, Atticus himself would walk through a den of werewolves just to be through with this cursed campaign. Maybe that was selfish of him—he didn't think of life like they thought of life—but all the traveling and the speaking and lonely nights spent thinking of his loved ones was getting mighty old.

"Keep your eyes on the sign," Helena reminded. "It has a sister in one of Nyxis' row houses." She smiled. "Quite the dedicated bunch you've got there, Hex. You've even managed to make Warren fall in line."

Warren cleared his throat. "Don't think I'm not still a little bit sore about you dumping me."

"You were beautiful, for a time," Helena said, voice gone dreamy. "You've all been good sports, but the Disciples of the Deep have been better. Bye now."

From the lines of the pentagram, pale, writhing maggots fell and landed on each of their faces. Insects touching his skin, Atticus' face went completely numb. The maggots crawled over his lips, into his ears, over his eyes. He tried to stop them from getting inside him, but they got in all the same. When they touched his tongue, they turned to garbage-flavored water. When they hit his nose, they smelled of flowers and the grave. And when they wriggled into his ears, they sounded of distant horns droning in the deep of a storm.

"Ah'ka'bukal. Ah'ba'kubal. Ei'ha. Ei'ha."

Mr. Haemo leaned into Atticus and said, "Sound familiar? I'm not the only thing that sucks life out of the world."

Atticus could only manage a confused hum.

"G'ba. N'ta. Agulafpa."

The mosquito spat out something. "See how long it takes to wake when we've landed. You think this trip is free?"

Atticus' chest tightened. His eyes glazed over, leaving the world blurry and smeared. His heart beat slowed down, stopped altogether.

"N'ta. A'ta."

The barn dimmed to an apocalyptic dark.

"Ah'ka'bukal."

His feet left the ground.

"Ei'ha navul!"

And then there was a line of light dividing the dark. When it opened, it took them all.

Atticus lay in bed hours later, staring up at the sister pentagram that had brought them to this row house in Nyxis. Outside, soldiers marched past, but they never stopped to enter. Hex had told him the houses were abandoned, boarded up. And since they hadn't entered the row house through any window or door, those passing by would be none-the-wiser to their presence here.

Atticus had been the second to wake from the witches' spell, with Mr. Haemo being the first.

"Took a little life from us," the mosquito had said, in his original form, as he stared out a window. "From Hex and them, mostly. Shaved off a few minutes to get us here. They won't notice. Won't never know unless you tell them."

"Guess that's fair." Atticus went to the window. "How do you know the witches?"

"They've always wanted to kill me. Get at my power. We've all been around awhile."

"How long?"

"Too long to be sure anymore."

"Since the Old World?"

Mr. Haemo hummed. "They all get old after a while."

"You still think you can get me into the Membrane?"

"Going to try."

Atticus tilted his head. "How much blood you need?"

Mr. Haemo deliberated for a moment. "Hard to say. That blood well wasn't of the finest stock, but I'd been cultivating it for years. The fresher, the better." He pointed to his chest. "I keep it here." It started to glow, become translucent. A liquid coursed behind the insect's carapace. "I keep it close and listen to what it has to say."

Atticus nodded. He didn't want to know any more about that. "How do you think Hex knows them? The Witches?"

Through the window, he noted several skulls painted across the street on a nearby wall. Beneath them, it read "Gravedigger."

The giant mosquito shrugged its slender shoulders. Lumbering over Atticus, he said, "Woman like that... she gets around. And I don't mean no disrespect when I say that."

Behind them, he heard Hex start to wake.

"You trust her?" Atticus asked.

"Doesn't matter." Mr. Haemo backed away from the window and headed for one of the doors that led out of the room. "I can kill you all whenever I feel like it. Don't need to trust no one."

"Kill me? Wouldn't be so sure about that."

The mosquito ducked through the doorway. "You hear the witches mention the Disciples of the Deep?"

"Yeah, what's that?"

"A new religious movement in Eldrus. Wouldn't be surprised if the witches fell in with them."

"What do you think that means?"

Mr. Haemo shrugged. "Witches are already untrustworthy, so could be nothing. Or could be a good idea not to sleep tonight. We'll see, won't we?"

Atticus was still in bed, except now he was staring up at the sister pentagram that had brought them to this row house in Nyxis. His recollection of the conversation with Mr. Haemo began to fade as his eyelids started to flutter. Maybe it was the residual effects of the witches' transportation spell, but god damn did he feel, for the first time since Gallows, absolutely exhausted.

The row house was large enough that each of them had a room to themselves, so they took advantage of their lodgings and split up. *Maybe not the smartest thing to do*, he thought, feeling fuzzy. *But it's nice to have a breather from them mouth-breathers.*

"Hey, you awake?"

Atticus' body gave a jerk. He tilted his head. Gary stood at the end of the room.

The ghoul came in, went to his bedside. "Sorry man."

"It's fine. It's not like I haven't had a good sleep in half a year." He folded his hands across his chest but didn't sit up. "Do you want me to read you a bedtime story?"

The ghoul's ghastly face lit up the best it could. His skull shone with the dusk coming through the window. "Yeah, I want to hear the one about the asshole farmer who united the continent and, in the end, got the glory and the babe."

"You find someone's stash in this dump?" Atticus snorted. "Your breath's getting me buzzed."

With little grace, Gary sat on the edge of the bed.

Atticus scooted his head back. Wrinkling his nose, he said, "When's the last time you took a bath?"

Gary touched his chest. "You're going to make me blush." He laughed, looked out the window. "The day I died, believe it or not."

Atticus coughed and covered his face. "I believe it."

"I ever tell you how it happened?"

Still he stared out the window, but Atticus knew what he was looking at no one else could see.

"I was naked as the day I was born. Kids were out back on the swing sets. Wife was in the garage, tinkering with something or other."

Now, Atticus did sit up. "You were alive in the Old World? Didn't think to mention that in all the years I've known you?"

"It's not a memory I like to come back to."

The ghoul finally pulled away from the window. He lifted up his shirt. There was almost no flesh left on his ribcage.

"You'll be a skeleton soon," Atticus said.

"Already am. We both are, in a way." Gary groaned. "The Trauma is what did my family in."

"Do you remember what it was?"

"Kind of. Not really. I don't know. It's a blank. Like, when you go to write a sentence, except half the words are missing. They're in your head, but you can't remember what they were?

"It was Sunday; I do remember that. Church day. The girls were playing outside. Wife was fixing up the car. I was getting all pruney in the tub, trying to shake off a hangover. Now it's coming back to me.

"I remember hearing someone knocking on the door. Odd, but

not that odd. We lived in a big neighborhood with a lot of nosey no-bodies. I didn't think much of it. Then the house started shaking. Felt like an earthquake.

"I burst out of the bath and ran butt naked outside to my kids. There was a cloud over the city, like a demolition crew had taken down a building. I guess seeing their dad naked was worse than that, because my kids forgot about the shaking right away and ran inside. Embarrassed them pretty good." Gary stopped for a moment, closed his eyes, and held that memory a little longer.

"I forgot about the knock on the door. That was my mistake. If I hadn't, who knows. Might not be here talking to you."

Atticus whispered, "What happened, Gary?"

"She screamed. I had never heard my wife scream like that before. It was the scariest thing I've ever... I ran inside. My wife had beaten me to the front door. She was there, on the floor. Half her head was gone. Gone. Just, there was nothing left. And there were these people standing over her, with guns. They'd come in from outside. Thing is, I recognized them. They were our neighbors. And they were in their church clothes. Like, they were going to do this and then go to mass, like it was nothing.

"I thought about my kids. And the neighbors must have read my thoughts, because when I did, they shot me in the stomach. My kids were crying, then. Could hear them running down the hall. They wanted to know what was going on." Gary dug the heels of his palms into his eye sockets. "I tried to tell them to go away. Not to come in.

"They shot my little girls, too. I crawled to them, to see if they were okay. At first, I was happy. Their faces, it didn't look like them. The... I wasn't thinking right. I thought, maybe, they were someone else's kids. That mine were okay. That they had got away. But it was them. They hadn't gotten away. There was just nothing left of their beautiful f-faces. N-nothing to touch or kiss. Everything just fell apart when I tried to hold them. Right in my hands. My little girls. Delicate as we always said they were."

Atticus put his arm around Gary and brought him close.

"I couldn't figure out what the fuck they were babbling about, my neighbors. Now, I know, of course, a million years later. They were Lillians. They were part of the fucking Holy Order of Penance before Penance even existed. I went to church with these people. These... god-fearing Christians. And here they were, door-to-door death dealers, going on and on about some cult and God."

Gary sighed. Atticus rubbed his back the way he used to rub Will's when he had a bad day. As he did that, he noticed the ghoul's flesh had begun to change, taking on the tone of someone he'd eaten earlier.

"They said some words. One of them cut his hand and bled it in my mouth. Then they shot me again on their way out. I didn't die. I should have. But I didn't. The blood was infected with ghoulism. I don't know if that person did it on purpose, but it kept me hanging on. Hey, maybe that mother fucker was the first ghoul, Deacon Wake. I don't… I don't know.

"For a while, it was like I was hibernating. I knew things were going on around me. I was aware, but I couldn't see anything. I felt people around me. Police officers, paramedics. I could tell when they moved me. Buried me. Or maybe it was rubble that fell on me. It was dark, like I said. And in that dark, all I could do was think about my wife and little girls, and what I was going to do to the people who had killed them.

"Then, there were these awful sounds. After weeks of it, I could finally move, see again. And things were all wrong. There was smoke everywhere. Barely any sun. People were screaming, killing each other. There were explosions, and, again, that awful noise, all the time. Never stopped. It was like everything in the world was falling apart, all at once. It's hard to describe. Hurts to think about. Like my brain doesn't want to. I missed what started the Trauma, but what came afterwards was hell. No doubt in my mind. Can't relive that for you, not now, I'm sorry."

Atticus didn't know what to say, so he played it safe and just said nothing.

Gary continued. "I was 'hibernating' for years. It's part of the process, I guess. That's why you don't run into many ghouls." Gary exhaled and got up. "I couldn't save my family, even if I wanted to. But you can. And… if you can, then I think I'll feel like I've finally saved mine, too. Atticus." He laughed. "Atticus, oh Atticus. That's why I put you through this, instead of putting you out of your misery. Selfish, I know. My wife always said I was, too."

"I'm glad that you are," Atticus said. "Though it may not always seem like it, I'm grateful."

Gary nodded. "I hope so. Who would have thought we'd have

gotten this far?"

"I'd go further, still," Atticus said.

"I know." Gary started to shamble out of the room. "I think Hex really lucked out when she hired you to speak for the Marrow Cabal. When you love something, you'll give everything for it. You're the only person I've met who I believe would actually do that."

"I'm not sure I love this rebellion of theirs. Just using it like they've used me." Atticus thought of something and then said it: "When I go into the Membrane, you think I could find them? Your wife and kids?"

Gary stopped in the doorway, his hand already pulling the door shut. "I hope not. And don't tell me if you do. Get some rest, my man. Hex's contact will be here in the morning."

Atticus didn't even realize he'd fallen asleep until someone stabbed a sword through his stomach. With a choking gasp, his eyes snapped open to the soldier of Eldrus who stood over him, impaling him.

"Atticus! Atticus," Hex screamed from outside his room. "Get, god damn it! They've found us!"

Atticus grabbed the soldier's arms and pulled him downward, onto him. The blade ran through Atticus' body, out his back and through the bed. With the soldier up close and personal, Atticus plunged his thumbs into his eyes, and worked them over until they were white jelly. He spat blood in the soldier's eyes, for good measure, and died.

Then, rebounding from the Membrane in record time, he ripped the sword out of himself and plummeted onto the floor.

"Take this," Hex shouted.

Atticus turned his head. Hex and the rest of the Marrow Cabal were in the other room. There were more dead soldiers in there, too, and a few others in the grasps of Warren and the Deadly Beauties that were about to be added to the pile.

Hex threw something at him. He barely snatched it out of the air. It was a large, blue, slimy snail shell. The heir.

"Hide it! In case we get split up. I'll take care of the others." She went sideways and showed that everyone was okay. "They only want—"

The pounding of boots cut her off. Vibrations rocked the row house, from the other soldiers inside it. He could hear them, the reinforcements, heading their way. He took the heir, looked at his stomach wound. Holding his breath, he rammed it through the slit and lodged it inside himself.

"There's too many. Fifty, at least," James said, shouldering past Hex. "But we'll stay if you want."

Atticus shook his head, coughed up more blood. "Can you get away if they take me?"

Hex nodded. "Probably."

He heard voices outside the other door to his room. "Where's Mr. Haemo?"

"Gone," Gary said, voice shaking. "There's a secret passage out of here. Guessing he went out of it."

"Don't let them get the heir," Hex said. She slammed the door on him and, behind it, shouted, "Listen for me. I'll find a way to get you out of this! I promise."

The other door cracked open. Tens of Eldrus' soldiers flooded the room. Atticus reached for his machete, but he was quickly pinned down.

"Fuck you," he screamed, grabbing at their ankles, clawing at their legs. He bit the hands that held him down. The bigger the scene, the better the chance he'd have for the others to get away. "You fucking bitches. You fucking Eldrusian whores!"

Someone punched the back of his head into the ground. His nose broke on the floor. Glancing up, the room was packed to the brim with soldiers. Each one seemed to be waiting for him to do something.

"Shackle him!"

Chains were passed around the room, as though someone had brought them out for show-and-tell. Atticus' arms and legs were yanked back. With the bindings, he was shackled at the ankles, wrists, and neck. They finished it off by hog-tying him with the chains and kicked him on his side.

"You think this will stop me?" Atticus yelled, struggling to turn himself over. "We are everywhere!"

A woman emerged from the crowd. "Cut open his neck." She wore a cloak that was almost as dark as her skin. "I don't want another fake Gravedigger."

The soldiers grabbed his head and jerked it back. Several men, eager to please the woman, went in and hacked at his neck until he died.

"Is he breathing?"

"I'm not sure, Captain Yelena."

Atticus snapped back from the Membrane. He held his breath, stayed still. Someone kicked him in his stomach, burying the heir deeper inside him. He cried out and curled into a ball. The soldier continued to drive their boot into his organs, as though they were trying to pop them.

"Amazing," the woman, Captain Yelena, said. She crouched down in front of Atticus and picked his head up by his chin. "Sorry for the rude awakening, but we're on a bit of a time crunch."

She smiled, and looked deeply into his eyes, trying to find something there. "I heard you were headed to Eldrus. Don't worry, though."

She came to her feet, took one of Atticus' chains, and started dragging him across the room. "Your friends left you behind. Sometimes, it takes something like this to really see just how much someone cares about you. But hey—" she stopped; her forearms bulged as she held the chain up, like he was her marionette, "—good news, you're still going to get to meet King Edgar. Because we're going to take you to him."

CHAPTER XXII

After a while, Atticus lost count of how many times they'd killed him on the road to Eldrus. The soldiers, Captain Yelena included, were transporting him in a large, covered wagon with two compartments for prisoners like himself. By the third or fourth week, the compartment they kept him in smelled so bad they had to take a break from the torture for a few days to clean it. Afterwards, they stopped trying to bleed him dry and started hacking off pieces of him altogether. With a quick tourniquet and a damp cloth of Clot, much to his surprise, this turned out to be far less messy than repeatedly cutting open his neck, wrist, and thighs.

As it turned out, Atticus wasn't completely out of luck when it came to losing a limb. He couldn't grow another one—even immortality had its limits—but as long as they fastened it to the place where it fell off, his body would repair the damaged site and make everything, more or less, good as new. So far, he had reattached both his hands and his feet.

If there was a benefit to be had from this mutilation-by-the-minute madness, it was that it left Atticus weak enough to explore the Membrane for longer periods of time. He was dying so quickly, so often, that it was taking longer and longer for his soul to return to his body. With every mortal wound they inflicted on him, he bought himself a few more steps toward Pulsa diNura and, hopefully, his wife and son.

Any other day, he would have fought these fucks off for the hell of it, but in a way, they were doing him a favor. If they kept him dead long enough, he could see Clementine and Will, know that they were okay, and tell them it would all be over soon.

Captain Yelena tightened up the chains that bound Atticus to the compartment. "What do you think would happen if we cut off his head?"

Her two lackeys, George and Robert, shrugged.

"Might be too much, sir," Robert said.

George ducked out of the compartment for some fresh air. Outside, he said, "Sir, don't you think we've put him through enough?"

Captain Yelena grabbed the bucket they'd been bleeding Atticus into and threw it at George. "King Edgar said to put him to the test."

"It's just... it's getting old, sir." George brushed the blood off his armor. "If we break him…"

"Then he's not the Gravedigger, is he?"

Robert cleared his throat and crossed the compartment, minding the strips of flesh that slickened its floor. "George has a point, sir. Immortal or not, he might have his limits, too. Sir, say we have the genuine Gravedigger here and we find his weakness and kill him? King Edgar wouldn't be too happy about that."

Captain Yelena groaned. She grabbed a knife and ran it into Atticus' neck. Blood spluttered out, but he didn't flinch. Didn't even feel it. Not anymore.

"King Edgar would be happy. Because King Edgar doesn't want anything to do with something that has a weakness," Captain Yelena said. "You two shut your mouths and go do something else. I will not have you ruin my one chance."

Captain Yelena went to work on Atticus after that. But as the day grew darker and the road more run down, even she began to lose interest in testing him. Her cuts became less precise, more superficial. She resorted to weak punches rather than forceful stabbings.

Now, with the sun dipping behind the horizon, she was trying to remove his head from his body. By the time she hit bone, she was too tired and too worn down by the routine of it all. Captain Yelena's saw ground to a halt in his spine. Before he did the dying thing, he saw a softness in her face, a disgust in her eyes—a realization of what she'd done, what she'd become. In those not-so-final moments, he crossed his fingers and hoped she'd kill herself soon. After all, he was about to die, and if she did commit suicide, he might be able to find her in the Membrane and teach her a thing or two about suffering.

Atticus fell forward. Before he hit the compartment's floor, he was already plummeting through the Membrane on a sinewy streak of light. The fleshy walls of the place shot up around him. He willed his body towards them, hand reaching out for an outcrop. Looking down the vertical drop, he wondered how much further he could fall before he hit the Abyss and it swallowed him up.

Maybe I'll always stop myself. His fingers skidded across the walls, over hair and cloth. *Maybe, for me, all these ledges lead to the same place.* Atticus turned himself and brought his other hand to the wall. *Maybe this place can't take me. Maybe I have to give myself willingly.* His hands closed shut on a stony ledge. With everything he had, he locked his arms and stopped his falling momentum.

Come back, keep going, Yelena. He clenched his teeth and hoisted himself onto the ledge.

Atticus didn't know why he did it—time was not something he had to waste; he'd be alive any moment now—but he looked back, over the edge. In the past, he'd never seen anything but darkness at the bottom of the tunnel. But as he leaned forward, feet kicking off the Abyss' pull, he saw, in the darkness, lights and clouds of color. It was as though a piece of the night sky had been cut away and woven across the tunnel's end. It was an unexpected beauty in a place that had about as much beauty as the bottom of a boot. The star-like light, the astral swathes of purple and pink—was that the Abyss, or those within it?

Atticus turned around and headed down the path there. It wound through the walls of the Membrane, past groves of Death's Delirium.

Please, take me to Pulsa diNura, he thought. *All roads lead to the same place.* The floor slanted upward, and he climbed a rocky hill. *This is my damnation, and I'll be damned if it doesn't do as I say.* At the top of the passage, he saw light creeping across the walls; around the bend, the path seemed to open up to something wide and—

"Atticus?"

He stopped dead in his tracks. The voice. Her voice. Clementine's. Had it been hers? He squinted. Ahead, someone was leaning out from the bend in the passage. A woman. Red hair. It was her, but was it her? The thought, the possibility—it left his mind paralyzed to the point that nothing made sense. A woman. Red hair. Was it—?

"There you are!"

Clementine came out from behind the wall. She ran and threw

herself into him, knocking him off his feet. They smacked into the ground, her arms and legs wrapped around him.

"Where were you?" she cried, kissing his face and neck. "Oh my god, what happened to you?"

"Clementine." About all Atticus could muster was her name. She was here. She hadn't given up. There was a stab wound in her side, from where Blythe and Bon had killed her, but that didn't matter now. She was here. With him. And she hadn't given up.

"What did they do to you?" she begged, unwrapping from him.

She smelled good. Or maybe she didn't, and he thought she did. He touched her hair, touched her skin. He looked into her eyes, ran his thumb across her lips. He'd lost so much of himself, and yet all it took was a moment with her to feel whole again.

"I'm okay," he said, coming out of the shock of seeing her. He caught his breath. "I know I look like hell. Are you okay?"

"I am now. Yes." She smiled and held his face. "You're mangled, Atticus. What did Blythe and Bon do to you?"

"Not them. Listen. Where's Will?"

Clementine bit her lip. "He's here. He's here. It took a long time to find him. He's with that man, Herbert North. He said he knew you?"

"Good, okay, good." Atticus took her by her shoulders. "I'm going to be gone in a second."

She pushed him back, screaming, "What? No!"

"I don't have a choice!"

As she curled into a ball, he grabbed her and held her close.

"I can't die. Which means I can't stay in this place for long. I don't know what happened, but I can't die. It doesn't make sense, I know, but Clementine, listen to me." He lowered his head, to her ear. "I'm going to get us out. I've been working at this for months, you hear? I'm going to get us out. There's a way. I need you and Will to hold on until then, okay?"

Clementine shook her head. "I don't know what the hell you're saying. You can't, anyways. The shepherds brought us here. Herbert said we're stuck, like him."

"He was taken too?" Atticus moved past the question, because it didn't matter right now. "I can. I will get you out. I love you, and I'm not leaving you, not ever. I'll be back." He buried his face into her hair and kissed her everywhere he could. "I'm going to open this place up and take you and Will out."

"Okay," Clementine said. "I trust you, Atticus. I believe you. I know you will, baby."

He moaned. "I don't want to leave you again."

She shook her head. "Please, don't."

The sight of Clementine alone was enough to make him forsake everything he had planned. For months, he'd been starved of her, and now he was so absolutely ravenous for her affection, he'd sacrifice just about anything to have a morsel of it.

"I won't," he said, having decided to stay in this place, having instantly forgotten that he could not. "You're right. I'm here with you. I'm not going anywhere. We'll make this work, you and I and Will. It's not so bad. It's worse up there. We can make this—"

Atticus sputtered to life in the cramped compartment and sat there awhile, drinking his own blood in bitter disappointment. He could still feel her body pressed against his, the warmth of it radiating through his skin. For now, that would be enough to get him through the cold nights to come.

By the time Atticus realized they were in Eldrus, they were already pulling up to the gates of Ghostgrave. Five soldiers in slim, obsidian armor were waiting for him as Captain Yelena and her two lackeys hauled him out of the wagon.

"Looks like you had your fun with him," one of the soldiers in obsidian boomed.

"I didn't want to embarrass myself again," Captain Yelena said. She kicked Atticus to his knees. "He is as they say, Roderick." She handed the chains to the soldier in obsidian. "Keep him on a tight leash. He'll fight like a rabid dog."

Roderick yanked on the chains until they were choking Atticus. "I doubt it." He loosened his grip and then said, "Ever been to Eldrus, Gravedigger?"

Atticus decided to stop breathing, because it was making his neck hurt too much.

Eldrus. It finally dawned on him that he was here, where he needed to be to put an end to all of this. His eyes were dirty, encrusted with blood and sweat and whatever else they'd manage squeeze out of him. But he could see the city-state well enough.

Similar to the armor the soldiers wore, Eldrus was all right angles

324

and black stone, like ancient obelisks unearthed and commercialized for use. The sky overhead seemed to be constantly overcast, as though it reflected the grim living of those who lived beneath it. Of course, Ghostgrave didn't look much better. The keep sat on the hill, a bloated mess of uneven walls and crooked towers, with sagging balconies from which the privileged could observe the city and only see its pretty superficialities. But, hey, unlike Eldrus, at least the keep had character.

"Real nice place you've got here," Atticus said at last. He hadn't eaten or drunk anything in a month and a half, so when he vomited all over Roderick's feet, he vomited blood and bile. He grinned and said, "My bad, sir."

Roderick smiled. "Think nothing of it. Captain Yelena, where's his confederates?"

"The Marrow Cabal?"

Atticus shut his eyes tight, as though that would somehow dampen the news.

"Gravedigger was the highest priority. The Marrow Cabal took down a few of our men and escaped." She shrugged. "This movement is pathetic. Once they realize we have their one trump card, they'll break."

Roderick pulled on Atticus' chain. "So you let them get away? Word is he was traveling with a few creatures similar to himself. You may have just elected a new problem for us to deal with in the future."

Captain Yelena exhaled slowly. She turned her back, saying, "Then you go get them. Oh wait." She looked over her shoulder. "You don't give a shit, either. No one does." She started walking away, beckoning her lackeys to follow after. "Have fun with the Gravedigger. I'll be expecting payment soon."

Roderick snapped his fingers. One of his men came forward and threw a hood over Atticus' head. He tightened it in place with a belt—it wasn't as though he didn't already have enough bindings— and helped Atticus to his feet.

With the assistance of this soldier and another, Roderick forced him forward, through the gates, up a set of stairs, past a door, and another door, around a corner, up a flight of steps, down a flight of steps, through a heavy door, and then a small door, around another corner, into a long hall, down a winding staircase, through a triple-locked door, and into a moist room that smelled of mildew and shit.

Roderick ripped the hood from Atticus' head. He gave him a moment to take in his surroundings, as though he would be surprised by where they'd brought him. Atticus had seen his fair share of dungeons in his lifetime. Being Poe's Hangman would do that to a person. But this was easily the worst of the lot. The prison cells were festering pockets of filth, fleas, and flies. The ceiling and the floor were crooked and crumbling. Rats ran freely in the rotund area at the dungeon's end, chittering and clicking, probably boasting about all the diseases they were going to spread.

"Did you bring me some company?" a woman called out from one of the cells.

Atticus cocked his head. It was then that he noticed that, besides this woman, there were no other prisoners here.

"I don't know what Yelena did to you exactly," Roderick said. He started forward, tugging on Atticus' chain for him to follow. "But I want to apologize for her treatment of you. I can see that she took things too far." He stopped at the center of the dungeon and turned Atticus to face the cell where the woman sat. "King Edgar asked that you be isolated. I think you've been isolated long enough. I'm not saying she's good company."

Atticus squinted and tried to pierce the shadows the woman waited in. She looked small, fragile, like she'd been down here a long time.

"But she's better than nothing," Roderick said. He ordered the jailer, who Atticus hadn't even noticed until now, to open the cell beside the woman's.

"Why the kindness?" Atticus asked. Roderick had his men unshackle him and, for a moment, he considered running.

Holding out his hand for him to enter the cell, Roderick said, "Because I am a kind man, like most here in Eldrus. Don't let people like Yelena convince you otherwise."

Atticus nodded and walked into the cell. His neck, wrists, and ankles felt strange out of their fetters. The skin where they'd been fastened was pale and raw.

The jailer closed the cell door and locked it.

Roderick leaned into the bars. "I don't have any advice to give you, Gravedigger, other than you better figure out how to die, and you better do it fast."

"Your momma give you that name?" the woman in the next cell over asked.

Atticus ignored her, gripped the bars, and pressed his face against them. He watched Roderick and his soldiers leave the dungeon, along with the jailer, who was probably too repulsed by the place to stay in it any longer than he had to.

"I got a weird name, too, so I guess I shouldn't talk," the woman went on. She stood up and went to the bars that divided her cell from his. "Name's Lotus." She extended her hand for him to shake.

"Atticus." He took her hand and gave her the once-over. She wasn't much to look at, and the two shiners and busted lip weren't doing her any favors. Yet he found himself attracted to her. Maybe it was the blood loss talking, or maybe there was something about her, something unseen, in the air, that gave her that alluring quality.

She nodded. "Atticus, again, I have no room to talk, but have you seen yourself lately?"

He hadn't. But when he turned his neck, he felt it gape open, which meant Captain Yelena's sawing attempt hadn't healed yet. Holding his hand there, he noticed the gouges and patches of stripped flesh along his forearm. At some point during his ride from Nyxis to Eldrus, he'd gotten in the habit of not looking at himself. He doubted now that he was missing anything.

"Do you know who I am?" Atticus took his hand back and moved away from the bars.

"I'm guessing I should, but since I've been locked up in here for a few months now, I can't say that I do." She raised her eyebrows, twisted her mouth. She went back to her place on the floor. "Have a seat. It's about all you can do in here."

Atticus chose to remain standing. *I'm here, in Ghostgrave,* he thought. *If I can get out, I can get to the Archivist's tower and get what I need.*

"Not much of a talker?"

"Hmm?" Atticus snapped out of it. "No, not particularly." *Can I use her?* he wondered. "How, uh, did you end up here?"

"It's better you not know." Lotus pointed to her swollen face. "Looks like you've been through enough already."

Atticus shrugged. *It was convenient to run into Clementine when I did,* he thought. *Why was she out there? Was she looking for the Abyss? To end everything? Was that even really her?*

"What's that about you not being able to die?" Lotus laughed, wincing as she did so. "Does it help with the pain? Because if so, I'll have some myself."

Maybe she was just passing time. Atticus could see Lotus was waiting for a response, so he quickly said, "No, doesn't help with the pain. But yes, I can't die."

"Guess I know why you're here, then. Seems like something the king would want to have a hand in."

"That's half of it." Now, Atticus did sit. A rat scurried past him, into Lotus' cell. "What's King Edgar want with you?"

"Not really sure." Lotus caught the rat, broke its neck, and flung it across the dungeon. "My chances aren't good, Atticus. I'm not sure if talking to you will make them worse."

"Kind of seems like you're going to tell me anyways," he said.

"You're the first person I've had a conversation with. Tried talking to the rats, but it's the same old shit with them. Yeah, ha, I'll tell you. Why not?" She slicked her short hair back, took out a clump of it when she pulled her hand away. "I'm from the Nameless Forest. Most people don't believe me when I tell them that, but since you can't die, I'm sure that's not all that surprising to hear."

Nameless Forest. Now there were two words that knew how to get Atticus' attention.

"No." Lotus' voice hardened and she scooted a little further away. "This is a test, isn't it? To get me to talk? I don't know who you are."

After that, Lotus shut down.

Atticus learned to count the days by the faint dinning of a bell somewhere above the dungeon. It rang twice in the morning, and four times in the afternoon. In the evening, the bell thudded out six dark notes and went dead until the midnight hour, when it rang once, sharply. Atticus was down there for a week and a half before Lotus started talking again.

"Aren't you hungry?" she asked after finishing her meal. It was breakfast for dinner. A way to throw them off, he figured. "They've barely fed you."

"Can't die. Should be skinnier, but I guess my body has me covered."

Lotus pulled a piece of biscuit from her teeth. "Why can't you die?"

"Don't know." If she was going to keep him at a distance, maybe it was best he did the same. No one else had been placed in the dungeon since he arrived. Either there was a dearth of prisoners of late, or it was on purpose.

Lotus got the sniffles and said, "I miss my home. Never thought I would, but I do."

"The Nameless Forest?"

"Yeah, but my village, Threadbare."

"Didn't know there were towns in there."

Lotus held out her hands. "Yeah. I mean, how much do you know about the place?"

"I'm from Gallows," Atticus offered.

"Hey!" Lotus shouted. "Guess that makes us neighbors."

Atticus smiled. "Yeah, in a way. What's Threadbare like?"

"Small. Everyone in everyone's business. But they are good people. It's batshit madness outside the village, like you'd expect, but nothing's perfect." Lotus paused and then added, "I am, well, was the mayor."

"You must have really pissed King Edgar off."

"I guess." Lotus started to rock back and forth, the only form of stimulation she probably had in this place. "What about you?"

"Got wrapped up in a rebellion against Eldrus." *How much do I tell her?* "Can't die, like I said, so I'm sure that's ruffling his feathers, too."

Lotus came to her feet, went to the corner, and took a piss. "Damn," she said, going back to where she was sitting. "Why'd you do that?"

It was getting easier to talk to her. "You first."

"I don't know, Atticus."

"All right."

Lotus groaned. "King Edgar wants to take over the Nameless Forest. He wants to turn it into a state. He wants its people to fight for him."

"Figured as much," Atticus said, trying to assuage her worries of confession.

"Is that what the rebellion is all about?" Lotus scooted closer.

"Yeah, stopping that from happening. Stopping the Forest from spreading."

"Spreading?" Lotus cocked her head. "With the vermillion veins?"

Atticus nodded. "What are they?"

"Oh, I don't know. No one knows. You stop asking questions

when you live in the Nameless Forest. You said spreading? It can, I guess, but... that's no good unless he gets the people to spread outward, too."

"Why not?"

"Eh." Lotus covered her mouth and shook her head.

"That's why you're here, then."

"This is making me nervous," Lotus said. "Not a big fan of the feeling."

"Doesn't make no difference to me," Atticus said. He stood up and went to the opposite side of his cell.

Lotus pounded her fists against the dungeon's floor. The words were coming out, regardless of if she wanted them to or not. And here they were: "The Dread Clock."

"I don't know what that is."

"Everyone in the Nameless Forest does, though. And that's what pisses me off. He could have taken anyone, but he took me."

"What is it?"

"The source of the chaos in the Nameless Forest. The Black Hour? That's where most of us think it comes from. And because the Forest is so close to it, that's why it is the way it is. Black Hour all the time in there."

Atticus faced Lotus and went to the bars she sat beside. "King Edgar wants it?"

"Yeah."

"Why?"

"It's chaos. It's everything. The Black Hour is capable of showing and creating anything. If you can control that, you can do whatever you want. If he—you better not be a fucking spy, I swear to god—if he gets a hold of it, then he can make the Forest grow beyond its borders, and make the people leave them. Or maybe just use the Black Hour to destroy his enemies. All sounds terrible to me."

"Huh." The gears in Atticus' head started churning out thoughts, but he tried not to show it. *If it were mine, if it works the way she says it does, I wouldn't need Mr. Haemo or anything else to bring them back.* "And he thinks you know how to reach it?"

Lotus nodded. "He does."

"Do you?"

"I do."

"Don't want to tell him?"

"I did. It's not a secret." Lotus straightened up. She looked towards the front of the dungeon. "But nothing living—" her words faded as she turned her head back towards him, "—nothing living can get close to it."

"That's why I'm here?" Atticus could see the panic in Lotus' eyes.

"You tell me." She jumped as the dungeon doors were unlocked and flung back. "You son of a bitch. I'm so stupid." She punched the side of her head and leaned into the bars. "What do you know? Here comes the king."

CHAPTER XXIII

The only thing King Edgar looked like he could rule was a kindergarteners' playset on recess. With five guards surrounding him, the red-cheeked royal had about as much presence as the ground Lotus kept pissing on. Beneath the fancy garments that swaddled him like a blanket, it appeared Edgar had the body of a brawler. But whether or not the baby-faced boy was willing to make use of his training remained to be seen.

"I've been looking forward to meeting you," King Edgar said. He pointed at Lotus' cell and, again, from out of nowhere, the jailer appeared and unlocked it. "Please, accept my apologies, Lotus. This has to be a private conversation."

The king's guard moved into her cell, rounded her up before she could make a fuss, and hauled her out of the dungeon. They returned, two fewer, and, with the jailer, went to and unlocked Atticus' cell.

"Put this on," one of the guards said, tossing Atticus a hood to wear.

"We're going somewhere else," King Edgar said. "Lotus doesn't need to know that. I prefer to keep her in the dark at all times."

Atticus stretched the hood between his hands. "What do you want from me?"

A guard shouted, "He is your king—"

King Edgar held up his hand. "A king earns his people's respect. I have not earned this one's yet. Gravedigger, if you wouldn't mind."

Atticus stared down King Edgar. He'd die a few times, but he could probably tear out the man's throat in the process. *Do I even need to, though?* That part of the plan was finished. He was already here, without the help of Geharra and their "team." He slid the hood on and put his hands behind his back. Everything went dark. *I'll play nice and see where it gets me.*

The guards entered his cell. He heard the familiar clink of the jailer's keyring. His wrists were shackled, and a gag was stuffed into his mouth. Swords were unsheathed, and their tips went into his side, neck, and at the back of his head. With the speed of molasses, they transported him out of the cell, turned him right, facing the back of the dungeon, and pushed him towards that rotund area, where, with the help of their swords, the guards forced him into another cell, against a wall, and then flattened him and slid him across it, until the wall gave out and he stumbled into a passage, past a heavy door, and then, finally, another open place altogether.

Atticus tried to shake off the hood. Before he could, a guard punched him in the face and shoved him backward. He smacked against a cold, stone wall. As he shook there, stunned, they ungagged and unshackled him. The guards grabbed his arms and legs and stretched them outward, so he stood splayed. They moved his arms and legs into iron cuffs that protruded from the wall and clamped them shut. The guards tightened the cuffs to the point where he lost circulation in those areas. In a frenzy, they cut off his clothes, tearing them from his body, until he was completely nude.

"Leave his neck unsecured," he heard King Edgar say. "Otherwise, it'll be too difficult for him to speak."

Taking a bit of his hair with it, a guard ripped the hood off Atticus' head. His eyes burned as they adjusted to the rotten, orange light that burned brightly in this room. It was a torture chamber if he ever saw one. The amount of blood and mangled skin here put his compartment back on Captain Yelena's wagon to shame. There was a table beside where he stood, and it, too, was drenched through with gore. Further back, behind King Edgar, a wall divided the room, running across it and from floor to ceiling. It looked new. The only way past the wall was a small gate large enough for a dog to pass through. Something was back there—he could hear noises coming through the gate—but what it was, he couldn't be sure.

"Leave us," King Edgar demanded.

Without hesitation, his guard nodded and left the way they'd come.

"Captain Yelena and Captain Roderick tell me you're the real Gravedigger." King Edgar grabbed a stool and planted it right in front of Atticus. He unfastened his cloak and excessive adornments and dropped them onto the disgusting floor. "Do you know how many 'Gravediggers' we've gone through in the last month?"

Atticus didn't respond.

"Five." King Edgar held up five fingers. "They weren't innocent. They deserved to die for their treason against Eldrus. But they didn't deserve to be tortured like they were, like you have been.

"I know Geharra is funding this little rebellion." King Edgar crossed his legs and sighed. "I've known about it for a while. Eldrus, Penance, Geharra. We all play these games with one another. But sometimes, someone takes it too far, and Geharra's done just that."

"Why'd you wait to stop it?"

"You're not a military-minded kind of man, I take it? I'm not, either, to be honest. This is not where I saw myself a few years back."

King Edgar's pretty face didn't look so pretty this close. It was covered in make-up, to hide the scars that uglied it.

"A problem isn't a problem until you make it one. I was willing to let this fire burn a while, and then burn out. The Heartland has nothing that can stop Eldrus, not even with Geharra's help. Except for you. Or rather, the idea of you. You're a powerful symbol, but in the hands of a bunch of bumbling idiots. They know nothing of patience. Instead of letting you increase your influence naturally, they sculpted imitations and planted them where they would take."

"Speaking of planting things," Atticus started.

"Why are you fighting for Geharra? A man who can't die has better things to do than take orders from someone who can."

"Don't you know the stories?" Atticus tested the iron cuffs, but they wouldn't give.

"Of course. My men killed your wife and son, and now you want revenge for their deaths. And that revenge has become something political and galvanizing."

Atticus shrugged. "There you go."

"But you didn't turn yourself into a symbol to save the Heartland from Eldrus." King Edgar stood up, shaking his head. "For everyone who believes your story and is touched by it, that's one more death on your shoulders. You know this, don't you? Your inspiration is their damnation. I'm not saying you're some messiah sweeping across the continent, but everyone you inspire is your responsibility. Can you live with that?"

"I care about what I'm doing." Atticus tried to sound sincere, and failed.

"Do you think the Heartland's hate for Eldrus only has to do with my soldiers occupying their towns? Or planting... crops... in their soil?"

Atticus could a sense a monologue coming on.

"I think you do believe this. My reports tell me you've been to Bedlam, Cathedra, Islaos, Hrothas, and, for a moment, Nyxis. You never stayed long. You never took the time to get to know the people and their problems. You just gave a speech, acted like you cared, and carried on."

"That's my job," Atticus said.

"No, it's not." King Edgar's neck tightened, and his make-up started to run. "No, it's not. In Bedlam, there're more jobs in the underground markets peddling stolen goods, prostitutes, and mind-killer substances than anything else. They've already divided the town between the east and west side, and now they've started harassing people whose Corruption is lighter than most. Criminal organizations, like your former Marrow Cabal, go there and find cheap workers to carry out their jobs. There are good people in Bedlam, but they are forced to do bad things. And I will hold them accountable for their actions, but I will not judge them for it, because I would do the same.

"In Cathedra, we have rape cases every day, from men and women in town and the surrounding woodlands. There's not a lot of murder in that beautiful place, because most families just beat each other into submission at home, in private, under the guise of holy discipline. The cathedral knows about this but does nothing, because nothing fills pews faster than self-loathing.

"In Islaos, people work themselves to the bone. The unsafe conditions of the lumberyards, mining tunnels, and, in general, the Blasted Woodland, lead to more deaths than anything else. Families are large there, because life is short and unpredictable. Mind-killers are popular, and alcohol even more so. Children are raised to be complacent in Islaos, and to be responsible for its well-being. Those who leave the town for personal reasons are considered outcasts, because they refuse to contribute to the place that gave them the life they live.

"In Hrothas, murder runs rampant. The law enforcement agencies are corrupt and paid to look away from illicit activities. The misogynistic mayor of Hrothas has tried several times to enact a bill that would allow women to be rounded up and processed like cattle, to identify undesirable defects and personalities. The people fight this, because the people in Hrothas are strong of will, and brave. They may be the strongest in all the Heartland, and most loyal. And what did you do there? You made it rain blood, and then, when things weren't going your way, when my men outnumbered yours, instead of staying and supporting your people, you ran.

"And Nyxis? I can forgive for you not knowing Nyxis well, as your stay there was brief. But in Nyxis, the land is dying. Those fields outside the town are fallow. Inside the town, wombs are barren. Disease spreads through the streets from the same mosquitoes you probably employ. Birth rates have plummeted. Violence has increased. Sex is a distraction, and sexually transmitted diseases are considered an inconsequential consequence. My soldiers have to break up community meetings. Somewhere along the line, excommunicated members of Cathedra's cathedral and followers of the witches who betrayed you have formed a coven. And they're wreaking havoc, using Geharra's rebellion as a cover for their activities. Using my Disciples of the Deep as weapons.

"I didn't mention Gallows. I know you're from there. I know you know it's hardly a happy place to live. It's an unregulated, backwoods bum fuck of a town, isn't it? Everyone taking what they want, when they want, and just barely hanging onto what they've got. But it's home, isn't it? All these places are homes. All these places are great, in their own ways. Bedlam's culture, creativity, and once liberal ideology. Cathedra's tradition, architecture, and devotion to spirituality. Islaos' work ethic, production, and sense of community. Hrothas' bravery, intelligence, and political savvy. Nyxis' love for the land, for the things that grow out of it, and their need to do right by others. I don't know Gallows as well as you do, Gravedigger. Tell me its positive qualities."

Atticus' lip quivered. He felt the weight of King Edgar's words on his shoulders, in his heart. "Gallows' no-nonsense living, and being like a world all its own. Simple folk, simple needs. Privacy. A touch of the supernatural you can't get nowhere else."

King Edgar nodded. "Sounds lovely."

Shaking his head, Atticus said, "How... how do you know these things?"

"The pantries, the shelters. My 'suffer centers' as they are called. I have workers in the community gathering data. They report it back to me. Moving my soldiers into the Heartland and planting those crops, they are calculated moves to correct the wrongs done unto the people of the Heartland, by themselves and others.

"I must admit, then, Gravedigger, that when I think of you, I grow jealous. I have been forced to do many things I otherwise wouldn't—" King Edgar's face went dark, and tears welled on the rims of his eyes, "—for the betterment of this world. I am jealous, because I care, because I sacrifice and suffer, and yet people like you are the ones to whom the world looks."

"If you want the publicity, go ahead and take it," Atticus said.

"I don't want publicity. I want change. I want to give the people what they want. And I want meddlers like you and Geharra to stay out of it, to stop trying to exploit the exploited."

Atticus bucked against the iron cuffs, but they did not move. "You going to keep me locked up in here forever, then?"

"No, I'd rather not." King Edgar let out a heavy sigh and took a seat on the stool again. "I'd rather employ you, like Geharra employed you, but this time, to use you to do the right thing."

"Why should the dead take orders from the living? Isn't that what you said?"

King Edgar nodded. "I did. But you want something. You took on this monumental task for a reason. Was it just revenge? I heard whispers you were coming here, anyways, to kill me. Revenge really brought you this far?"

"No," Atticus said. He lowered his voice, lowered his head. "I'm trying to get them back."

"Your wife and son?"

"Yeah."

"How would killing me bring them back?"

"I don't give two shits about killing you."

King Edgar scooted closer to Atticus. "Then why were you coming to Ghostgrave? If I have something to help you, I'll give it to you. But only if you'll help me."

"I'm not leading anything anymore," Atticus said.

King Edgar slipped something from his pocket into his mouth. It looked like a vermillion vein. "That's okay. I just want to be like you. I, too, have people I want to save."

"The Heartland? Or your family you slaughtered?"

King Edgar swallowed down the vein. With his hands balled, he said, "A vicious rumor from Geharra. What do you need, Grave-digger? To get them back?"

I can't help him be like me, Atticus thought. Spit bubbled on his lips. *But I can string him along.*

"Gravedigger, what do you need?"

"An Old World relic." He looked up. "From Archivist Amon's collection. To open a way to… reach them."

King Edgar's eyes went soft, sympathetic. "I'm sorry, but the Anointed One had those relics destroyed months ago. They were a liability to our Disciples of the Deep. I cannot help you with that."

"You're a fucking liar," Atticus snarled.

"I'm trying to get you to help me. Why would I lie to you about the very thing that would do that? I respect you too much to play you like Geharra has played you." King Edgar sighed and came to his feet. "I want you to meet someone." He snapped his fingers and shouted, "Alexander, please, enter."

Atticus turned his head towards the torture chamber's door. A man in fitted robes came into the room. With a wide smile, Alexander joined King Edgar's side and stood there like a statue, his features chiseled, his emotions fixed. Close enough for Atticus' bleary eyes to see, he noticed Penance's holy symbols running up and down the man's dark robes.

"This is Alexander Blodworth, understudy of Exemplar Samuel Turov, and envoy of Penance."

Alexander bowed. "It's a pleasure to meet you," he said, his eyes never leaving Atticus' crotch.

"Gravedigger is guilty of treason," King Edgar said.

"Undoubtedly," Alexander agreed.

"But I hope to win his loyalty back."

Alexander's grin grew wider, his focus more intense on Atticus' nudity. "An immortal seems like a powerful ally."

"Your favorite city, Geharra, has been funding the rebellion."

Alexander gave a slight shrug. "Not surprised."

"I know I've rejected your offers before, but I would like to send

Geharra a message."

Now, Alexander did look away from Atticus. "Don't tease, Edgar."

"How is the Crossbreed?" King Edgar asked, as he stared at Atticus, making sure he knew whatever decision he was about to make would be his fault.

A bead of sweat started down Blodworth's forehead. "Very healthy, and very ready to stretch its limbs."

"Can you convince Penance to let you go to Geharra?"

"It may take some time, but I'm sure we can... come up with something to get Mother Abbess Justine's permission."

"Good." King Edgar patted Blodworth's back. "When you do, you may take the Crossbreed with you. Use it to change their minds about a few things." King Edgar paused and then added, "Oh, the Night Terrors have given Geharra their blessing to carry out this rebellion. Isn't there a village of theirs along the way to Geharra?"

"There is. Alluvia, I believe."

"Make sure you change their minds as well. We'll have that Eel, Derleth, assist you. He's from there."

Again, Alexander bowed. Backing away, giddy and bothered, he said, "Thank you, my lord."

King Edgar waited until Alexander Blodworth was out of the room before saying, "All actions have consequences. They may not be immediate, but they are there, echoing through time. You may not see or hear or feel them now, but you will, when you're ready to take responsibility.

"I can see that this is a lot to consider." King Edgar started for the torture chamber's door. "I will convince you to cooperate, but before I do, I need to be absolutely sure you are what you say you are. I do not trust Captain Yelena that much."

Atticus smirked. Tears poured down his puffy face. "Then where are you going? You want to hurt me some more? I can't think of a better place. You too much of a little bitch to do it yourself?"

"No," King Edgar said, smiling a sad smile. "I've done my share of despicable atrocities. But my... nephew... has a stronger stomach for this sort of thing. His father was my brother, Vincent. He may mention his name as he puts you to the test."

King Edgar slammed the torture chamber's door shut and locked it more times than Atticus could count. After a moment, he heard mechanisms working inside the walls, and the stretching of ropes. Something creaked, groaned across the chamber. He looked to the newer wall that divided it. The small gate slowly lifted upward, and the thing he heard before now sat behind it, waiting to be freed.

CHAPTER XXIV

The flesh fiend crawled forward on all fours, its sticky, stolen skin stretching to accommodate its wild movements.

"Shit, shit," Atticus screamed, rocking violently. He tried to break his wrists, to be free of the iron cuffs, but couldn't. "Edgar!"

The creature's claws clicked and scratched against the floor. As it bounded towards him, it scooped up chunky handfuls of gore and shoved them down it's throat.

Atticus strained himself against his fetters. "I'll help you! I'll help, god damn it!"

As though it'd been struck, the flesh fiend stopped a few feet in front of Atticus. Slowly, like a child learning to walk for the first time, it stood. The flesh fiend's red eyes widened, its bisected pupils pulled further apart. Its jaw sat slightly unhinged, while its tongue ran frantically back and forth across its chapped lips, tasting their sores. Thick flaps of skin hung off its wiry frame, and they quivered while it shook, overwhelmed with deviant delight.

The flesh fiend started forward, flexing its claws.

"Get the fuck away," Atticus cried.

Like abhorrent adornments, bands of veins were wrapped around the creature's arms and torso. And by the way the fiend stroked and caressed them, it seemed these pieces of profane jewelry meant much to it.

"Edgar!"

The flesh fiend rushed forward. It grabbed Atticus and pushed itself against him, grinding its bare, swollen pelvis into his leg. With both hands, the creature pried open Atticus' screaming mouth and locked its nails behind his teeth. It pressed its infected lips to his and tongued his gums. Before he even tasted the creature's sour spit, Atticus was dry heaving, coughing bits of stomach acid into the fiend's mouth, which it gobbled up with glee.

The flesh fiend worked its hands down Atticus' arms. It bared its crooked, sharp teeth and ran them across his chest, snagging them on his nipple. By now, the fiend's hands were at his hips, and they were going still further down.

"Stop, stop," Atticus begged.

But the flesh fiend did not. Its hand found Atticus' testicles and closed tightly around them. The creature continued to bend its knees. As it did so, it dragged its trembling mouth down his stomach. In an orgasmic spasm, the flesh fiend regurgitated hot blood onto Atticus' navel, watching in fascination as it dripped onto Atticus' spread legs.

"Please," Atticus rasped. He started to cry, to shake uncontrollably. He wanted to die. He needed to die. "Please, don't."

The flesh fiend went to its knees. It let go of Atticus' testicles. He exhaled in a cold sweat.

"Vincent," the flesh fiend said. It's hot, stinking breath rolled under Atticus' frenulum. "I'm so hungry, Vincent."

The flesh fiend went forwards, unhinged its jaw, and closed its mouth around Atticus' penis and testicles. It looked up at Atticus, dug its claws into his thighs, and then started to chew.

CHAPTER XXV

When Atticus came back to life, all he saw was bone. No skin, no hair, only bone. His muscles were gone, and his fat chewed away. His veins had been stripped, his arteries torn out. He looked at his hand and its skeletal digits. He looked at his chest and its rungs of ribs. He looked inside himself, to where organs should've been, and to the floor, where they should've fallen.

He turned his head to the table beside him and found, at some point, a mirror had been placed there. Before he could shy away, he saw himself as he was now, completely incomplete. His face was gone. No nose, no lips, no ears, no flesh. The flesh fiend had left nothing but his teeth, tongue, and those bloodshot eyeballs of his that gazed back madly.

Elsewhere was the same. The flesh fiend had eaten everything. He wasn't Atticus, not anymore. He was just the Skeleton of that man, the thing he should've always been the very first time he died. It was incomprehensible. Was it even him? There were no defining features, no hints of his personality. His living defied all logic, all reason. Was it even him? Or perhaps he just seeing himself as he ought to be, as he deserved to be.

His arms, so thin now, slid out of the iron cuffs and landed at his side. He fell onto the ground. He felt the impact, but without any nerves to call his own, knew that the sensation was only a memory in his mind.

"It'll all grow back," he said, on his hands and knees, staring at the ground. His voice sounded higher, as though all the screaming he'd done stretched it too far. But how could he speak at all? He had a tongue, but no vocal cords.

"It'll all grow back," he repeated. He took a deep breath, even though he had no lungs. "It just needs time to take." Sanity was a slippery thing, and now more than ever, he could feel it slipping through his boney fingers.

The Skeleton raised up and sat on his heels. His head went back and forth, in search of the flesh fiend. But before he could find it, something else in that rotten, orange light caught his attention instead. In a steaming pile of himself, a large, blue snail shell sat, unharmed.

"The heir."

The Skeleton scrambled forward and snatched the glowing object. He'd forgotten about it, and hadn't had a chance to use it while imprisoned by Captain Yelena. How did it work? He pressed it to his skull, and then felt like an idiot, because he had no ears.

"But I can still hear," he said, his own voice and the sounds of the torture chamber coming clearly to him.

Without realizing it, he was moving his fingers in a spiraling motion along the shell. It started to glow vibrantly. Each individual ridge pulled away from one another, expanding the shell in his hand.

"Atticus," Hex whispered.

The Skeleton held the heir outward. He scanned the room, but no, he'd heard it right: Hex's voice had come from inside the shell.

"Atticus. There… no team. Get out… your own. I'm sorry."

He pressed the snail shell to his skull again. Hex's words were drenched in noise. He could hear layers of her voice behind each utterance, as though she'd sent the same thought over and over again.

"I am taking Marrow Cabal… east. Taking them to… home. An island. In… Gyre. I am… them to Lacuna. I think… can get in again. There is something there… help us all. I will do right by you. Get yourself out. Get to… Nachtla. We'll wait… as long… takes."

Footsteps outside the torture chamber. People coming down the passage.

"Put… heir on… tongue. Will your thoughts. It'll hurt."

Hurt? The Skeleton laughed. As the locks unlocked on the torture chamber door, he put the heir onto his tongue and willed this: *The artifacts are gone. King Edgar told me so. He might be lying, but what can I do? I have another lead. The Dread Clock in the Nameless Forest. I can get out of here. Eldrus can't hurt me anymore. I just need an opening. I'll see you in Nacht-la.*

The torture chamber door swung back. Behind it, King Edgar and his guard of five stood, swords drawn. Dark material flowed from the king's hands to the floor.

The Skeleton closed his mouth to hide the heir.

"Gravedigger?" King Edgar's voice was beyond surprised.

His guards tried to remain stoic, but even their stone-hard faces were starting to crack.

King Edgar went forward. "Gravedigger, can you hear me?"

The Skeleton nodded. He locked his jaw and imagined how terrifying he must look. It was a nice notion.

"You are remarkable." King Edgar bent down and laid the dark material on the ground. "Captain Yelena gave us a few of your belongings."

Bon's glove, he realized. *And Blythe's cloak. My trophies.* The Skeleton nodded and, to feign subservience, crawled forward to collect them.

The guards got uppity, but King Edgar took a step back and said, "He who has nothing stands to gain everything. You won't hurt me, will you, Gravedigger?"

The Skeleton shook his head. He outstretched his pale arm—*Heh, no Corruption anymore*, he thought—and took the trophies. He slipped his bones into the glove, put on the cloak. He threw the hood over his head and crawled backward, like the loyal mutt King Edgar clearly wanted him to be.

"Take him to his cell," King Edgar said. "He who has lost everything will do anything to get it back."

The Skeleton didn't put up a fight. He wasn't even sure if he could. As the guards dragged him back to his cell, he tried to familiarize himself with his limbs. Everything worked right, but it all felt so effortless. There was no weight to his movements, no resistance. He could throw a punch, but if it hit as hard as a feather, then what did it matter?

The guards pulled him into the rotund area of the dungeon, across the floor, and threw him back into his cell. The jailer did his reappearing act and locked it up tight. Not a moment later, Lotus was led in by a chain leash from the front of the dungeon.

"This is getting old," she screamed, spitting in the face of the guard who held her leash.

The Skeleton bunched himself up in his cloak, so that Lotus couldn't see what he'd become. He spat the heir into a pocket inside it.

The guard busted her lip. With the other guards, he gathered her up, undid her leash, threw her into the cell, and locked the door behind her.

"Oh, hey, you're back," Lotus said, going immediately to the bars that barred them from one another. "Where'd you get that cloak, buddy? Looks good. Whose dick did you have to suck for that?"

"Actually," the Skeleton said, cringing, "it was the opposite."

Lotus let out a laugh. "What'd they do to you? Let me see you."

"Tell me about the Dread Clock."

"What? What? No. Are you kidding me?"

"I want it," The Skeleton said. "Not for him. For me."

"Bullshit." Lotus kicked the bars; they rang out an unnerving tone. "He broke you, and now he's using you. I'm not that stupid."

The Skeleton threw back his hood and stared directly into her widening eyes. "If I don't answer to Death, why would I answer to him? The Dread Clock, the Nameless Forest. Tell me everything."

"Holy shit," she said. She wiped her bloody lip on her arm. "Holy shit." She did a double-take, looked around the room as though to confirm with someone else what she was seeing. "Atticus, what the hell? How are you…?" She swallowed the blood in her mouth. "Oh god, what did they do to you?"

"What it looks like." The Skeleton went to the bars, wrapped his fingers around them. "I can't die, like I said. This is bad, but it'll heal."

"Are you… are you sure?"

He stared at her for a moment, doubt destroying his certainty. "Yeah. I am. Always does."

Lotus looked about as convinced as a convict in a convent. "What do you want with the Dread Clock?"

There was no holding back now. He had to tell her. "My family and I were killed by Eldrus' soldiers. My wife and son stayed dead. I didn't. I came back. There's a place between life and death, between this world and others. The Membrane. I got out, but they didn't."

"I've heard of the Membrane," Lotus said. Her breathing was shallow and rapid. "And things coming out of it. Creatures. Shadows.

Could be the Dread Clock is part of it?"

"That's why I need it. How do I get to it?"

"But, Atticus, the rebellion. Why… why are you here, then?"

"Artifacts from the Old World," he said. "There were supposed to be some here I could use to open the way into the Membrane. King Edgar said he had them destroyed."

"Oh shit, oh shit." Lotus covered her mouth. "Yeah, I guess that was it."

"What?"

"When they brought me in, I wasn't a prisoner. They were civil. We went up top, passed the Archivist's tower. Have you seen the thing? It's covered in vermillion veins, and no one says anything!"

The Skeleton shook his head.

"Anyways, they took me past it. There were all these things laid out in the courtyard. Shrines, urns, goblets, jewelry, gems. And they were melting it down. The metal, Atticus, it begged when they burned it. Like it was alive."

"Even if I get out and what I need's left, I can't get up there, get it, and get home. So, the clock. Tell me about it."

Why you always have to make things complicated? he heard Clementine whisper in his skull. *What the hell are you doing? Do you even want to save us? Or do you just want to prolong this?*

"I know you can't die, but you know what the Black Hour is, right? If you're going toe-to-toe with the source of it, the source of the Nameless Forest's madness, you're not going to come out the way you were before."

"I'm resilient," the Skeleton said, undeterred. "I don't care. I am tired. I want this to be over. I want them back."

Lotus nodded and, with a pathetic look on her face, began: "The Nameless Forest is easy to get into. There's nothing to it. The Forest wants visitors. It thrives on them. It will do and show you anything. But you must stay to the path. There is a road, the Binding Road, that runs, much like the Spine, through it."

"Where does it begin?" the Skeleton asked.

"Wherever you do. It doesn't matter where you enter. It'll be there. But you have to stay on it. If you do, it'll lead past my village, Threadbare, to a church, Anathema. There, the road splits in five different directions. Each one goes further into the Forest, to different villages. The one you want is furthest from Anathema, where the trees are darker.

"After a while, you won't think you're in the Nameless Forest anymore. The trees will disappear. The land will become swamp. And the fog will be so thick, you'll lose track of the road. But if you don't, you'll find the Orphanage."

"The Orphanage?" The Skeleton twitched. Something thumped outside the dungeon.

"Yeah. I've only been there once. Wouldn't be bummed out if I never went back. It's run by children, and the massive bat they worship. They guard the lake the Dread Clock sits in. If you want the clock, you'll have to get right with them."

Thump, thump, thump.

Lotus turned her head. "What was that?"

"Nothing," the Skeleton said quickly.

"That's all I know, Atticus. I swear."

Thump, thump, thump.

Lotus went to the front of her cell. "What the hell…?"

Oh no, the Skeleton thought. *Oh god damn it.* He tried to close his eyes, but he had no lids to hide them behind. "Lotus, what's going to happen if I tamper with the clock?"

"I don't know. I figured King Edgar wanted it to control the people of the Forest and force them out. But if he's not there when you do it, the people can maybe decide for themselves if they really want to follow him."

Thump, thump, thump.

"Okay what the hell is that?"

The Skeleton threw the hood over his head. He tightened his glove and said, "Start screaming, Lotus."

"What? Why?"

"Something's coming. Might be our way out. Need to get the jailer in here."

"Atticus?" she whimpered.

The Skeleton felt his non-existent heart stop. "What?"

"What the hell are those things standing behind you?"

The Skeleton turned around and, there, at his back, two shepherds stood. The creatures weren't trying to hide their faces anymore. Their sewn-up eyes and sewn-up mouths were swollen lumps of ashy flesh. Their foreheads were glossy gulfs of gore and trinkets, like the nest of some mad magpie. In appearance, the shepherds were identical, from the cracks in their hats to the buckles on their boots. The only difference was the nail polish. One wore green, the other, yellow.

Lotus started screaming.

"The wolf has lost its fur," the shepherds spoke in unison. "It can hide among the sheep no longer."

The green-nailed shepherd swung its crook and cracked the Skeleton's skull. He went sideways, crashing into the bars.

"Guards! Guards!" Lotus screamed.

The Skeleton didn't feel the impact or the pain that should've come with it. He reared up and launched himself at the shepherds.

"Stop it, Atticus," the shepherds said. They beat him back, their crooks breaking his bones. "Because we won't."

The Skeleton ignored them. Hairline cracks ran along his bones, but they healed almost as quickly as they formed. He threw himself into the green-nailed shepherd, knocking it to the ground.

"Guards, get in here! Someone is trying to break him out," Lotus belted.

The yellow-nailed shepherd slammed its crook into the back of the Skeleton's head. He took the blows like he took a breeze. Remembering Mr. Haemo's words, he grabbed the green-nailed shepherd by the fissure in its head and dug his fingers in deep.

The dungeon doors unlocked and flung back.

"What the hell is going on in here?" he heard the jailer shout.

The Skeleton head-butted the green-nailed shepherd. "I'm not going anywhere." He bit down onto its face and held on tight. Screaming, he strengthened his grip on the shepherd's forehead. Like tearing bark from a tree, he split it open with ease. Hundreds of tiny objects—toys, corks, fingernails, eyelashes—poured out and turned to dust.

The yellow-nailed shepherd's crook caught the side of his skull and sent him flying across the cell.

"Get in there!" Lotus yelled.

The Skeleton looked up and saw the jailer and several guards standing outside his cell. They didn't know what to do.

But the Skeleton did. He let the shepherd pull him into its arms.

"Stop it," he said, to the guards. "Stop it. It's trying to take me out of here."

The shepherd shot the humans a damning glance, and like the damned, they wilted within it.

"The king wants him," Lotus said. She was rattling the bars, looking far more panicked than the Skeleton would've expected. "You have to do something!"

The jailer was the first to snap out of it. He unlocked the cell. With the sound of its unlocking, the guards remembered their responsibilities and headed in.

"Get away," the shepherd said, dragging the Skeleton towards the back of the cell. "He's mine."

The guards drew their swords and pressed forward. Five of them in all, it seemed they hoped to overwhelm the creature with their number. But the shepherd wasn't impressed. It dropped one hand from the crook, reached into its coat, and threw a bundle of pink bandages onto the floor.

"Get back," the Skeleton warned, knowing damn well they would do the opposite.

The closest guard did just that: He raised his sword and slashed at the shepherd's head. As the blade touched the brim of its hat, the pink bandages exploded. Pale, ephemeral tentacles shot out of the fabric and punctured the guard's throat. Like ghostly tapeworms, the tentacles fed on the man, slowly sucking the soul out of his body.

"Anointed One, Anointed One," the guards murmured, instead of saying "Holy Child."

The Skeleton elbowed the shepherd in the stomach and slid under the crook. He stumbled forward, past the bandage, dodging the tentacles that whipped out of it.

"Stop," the guards cried.

The Skeleton took up the soulless man's sword and ran it through the nearest guard. The others swung at him, but their swings were cut short. The shepherd bore down on them, breaking, in one swipe, their heads and necks with its crook.

"What is going on?" Lotus cried out.

The Skeleton grabbed the jailer before he could flee. He stabbed him through the heart, took his keys, and lobbed them into Lotus' cell.

The Skeleton bolted across the dungeon, the shepherd in pursuit. He tore through the doors, up the winding staircase beyond, and stumbled into the long hallway it led to.

"Oh my god, what is that?"

The Skeleton's eyes darted back and forth between the royalty gathered in Ghostgrave's hall. Their dresses glinted in the evening light, their lips blood red from the wine in their hands.

"Guards! Guards!"

Where am I? What do I do? There were doors and more hallways everywhere around him.

Thump, thump, thump.

The shepherd was following after, making its way up the stairs.

"Guards!"

The Skeleton spotted more of Eldrus' men moving through the crowds of people. *I can't go back down there. I can't.* He took off, following the wall and going wide around the room.

"Stop him!"

He pushed through the people that stood in his way, throwing them to the ground. Their jewelry broke under his skeletal feet. *I can't die*, he told himself, bloodshot eyes fixed on the massive, low-sitting, stained-glass window ahead. *I won't die.*

Guards flanked him from the right, pinning him against the wall beside the window. Without thinking, because if he had, he may have done otherwise, the Skeleton threw himself through the window and over the edge of Ghostgrave.

CHAPTER XXVI

The Skeleton fell fifty feet through the air and broke into a million pieces on the boulders below. His brain blew out of his skull and left a sickening smear across the earth. In a matter of minutes, his body began to reform. The scattered remnants took on a life of their own, gravitating towards one another to form a pile of bones and bone fragments. One after the other, the pieces of the Skeleton were put into place, until his completed frame stood where the pile had been.

Alive again, the Skeleton found his cloak and glove and got dressed. Even this far down from Ghostgrave, he could hear from the keep the ruckus his escape had caused. They'd be here soon, to investigate what surely seemed like a suicide. So he turned on his heels and, with Eldrus and his mind behind him, headed eastward, to begin his long journey to the Nameless Forest.

With no need to eat or sleep, the Skeleton was relentless. He traveled day and night, pausing for neither pain nor threat of death. He stole horses when he could, and went by foot when he couldn't. There was purity in bone, he realized. A raw power that could be expressed without fear of damage to the flesh. In the light, he looked human, but truth be told, he was anything but. The thing that had been Atticus was no more. His skin hadn't regrown, and his organs hadn't returned. All that he was and all that he'd done, these bones didn't hold. To know him would be to know those he knew, but he doubted even they would recognize him.

The Skeleton was immune to most things, except his emotions. After several weeks of solitude, he began to hold conversations with

Clementine and Will. And because they weren't there, he had to speak for them on their behalf.

"Why don't you think of me much?" Will asked as the Skeleton skirted some rocky foothills.

"I do."

"Not like you do Mom."

"I love your mother." And then: "I love you, too, Will. Where's this coming from?"

"You always think of her. Talk about her. You don't remember me like you remember her."

The Skeleton stopped. He thought he'd heard something in the wilderness, but chances were he scared it off with his ramblings.

"Clementine this, Clementine that," Will went on.

"Stop it," the Skeleton shouted. He threw his hood over his head and said, "I'll have no more of this."

"You say you love me but you never show—"

"Stop!" He scratched at his skull. "What do you want me to say?"

Clementine joined the conversation, so the Skeleton's voice rose a few octaves. "Tell him the truth, Atticus. Tell him why you act funny around him. Tell him about Vale."

"He knows about our daughter, god damn it," he growled.

"Do you know that's why your father tries not to get attached to you?" Clementine asked Will.

"Is he afraid I'll die like she did?"

"He is."

"Please, I don't want to talk about this anymore," the Skeleton said.

"When he comes back here, will he take me with you?" Will asked.

"God damn it, Will, of course," the Skeleton said to his son, to himself.

"You going to give the boy the love he deserves?" Clementine sighed. "You have to love him like you love me."

The Skeleton sighed and whispered, "We've been through so much, me and you. It's different."

"No," Clementine said. "It's not."

When the Skeleton wasn't talking to himself or talking to himself about talking to himself, he was checking the heir for new transmissions from Hex. About the time he reached the Divide, the massive river which separated a portion of the Heartland from Penance's peninsula, the snail shell began to glow again.

The Divide was busy this day, as it probably was most days. Ships small and large sailed its turbulent waters, as others unloaded their goods at the wharfs than ran up and down both sides of the shore. Most of the ships flew the sails of Penance, as trade on the Divide was their frozen wasteland's lifeblood.

It was hard to tell how many people were in the area. The dock-yard workers moved in swarms, and the roads saw light, but constant traffic. But all it would take was one blabbermouth to flap his jaws about a living skeleton to put this Skeleton's months of careful travel to waste. So he hit the ground hard, hid in some grass, and reconsidered his options.

"Any news?" he asked the shell, as he let his fingers work its grooves.

The Dread Clock? Atticus, no, don't be an idiot. Did you escape? Hex's voice was clearer than before. He swore he could hear James in the background. *Mr. Haemo is here. He says the clock could work. He says he's seen it. Mara, too. You seem to trust this bug more than I'm willing to. Mara wouldn't lie, not to me. Think she... wants to see if... you can pull it off. Just hope you know how to get to the damn thing. Don't bother going... Nachtla, then. It's better... split up. Are you...? You sound different. We're okay. We... spreading word... Gravedigger. Never know when... need allies.*

The Skeleton was about fifty feet from the nearest wharf. As far he could tell, no one had seen or heard him. He lay back down, put the heir on top of his tongue, and willed this: *I got out. I'm at the Divide. I'll catch a ship and keep going. I know where the Clock is. Mr. Haemo wants to use me to return to his former glory. So, yeah, I trust him. What is Lacuna? What's there? Hex, if you're using me, too, then tell me. Is Lacuna your actual home? You trying to prove something?*

He covered himself up the best that he could and made for a small dock beside the wharf. There, a few boats were grounded, and a few men were dicking around. The Skeleton came in quiet. But when he'd been spotted, he threw back his hood and revealed himself.

"Holy Child, Holy Child," the men shouted, tripping over their feet.

"I am Death," the Skeleton said. He walked towards the men, cornering them like mice. "I have come to judge you all."

"No, please, I swear I've given up that life," one man cried.

"One more chance, I beg of you," another pleaded.

"I have a family. I haven't.... it was one time! They need me," a third blubbered.

"Let us strike a deal, then," the Skeleton boomed.

"Anything."

"A boat for your lives."

The men glanced at one another, dumbfounded, and said, "Uh, yeah, sure!" and high-tailed it into the river.

After crossing the Divide, the Skeleton began to lose track of things. Suddenly, his mind, or what little of it hadn't been dashed on the rocks outside Ghostgrave, didn't seem so sharp. He found himself wandering the Heartland, haunting the small settlements along the way for days at a time. He would tell people he was the Gravedigger, what he'd done, and where he was going. They would listen, as most would to a talking skeleton, and give him gifts to save their own skin, just in case he a the hankering to wear it.

"What are you doing?" he asked himself one night in Clementine's voice. He was standing in the fields outside some family's farm house. He'd knocked down the scarecrow there and taken its place.

"What?"

"Get your shit together, Atticus."

The Skeleton pulled himself off the scarecrow's post. "I'm doing the best I can."

"You're dragging your feet. Why?"

"I'm not."

"You are. We need you. Every day gets harder down here and you're up here screwing around with the locals."

"Maybe I should've made sure all the artifacts were destroyed. Should I go back to Ghostgrave?"

The Skeleton's skull went sideways as he pretended that Clementine had slapped it.

"You afraid you'll get to the Nameless Forest and find something that'll really put you to the test?"

"No," he said.

A little girl passed in front of one of the farm house's windows. She waved at him. He waved back.

"You don't want this to end, do you? Been at it so long it's become routine."

He started marching through the fields, back towards the road.

"No, that's not it."

And then Will asked, "What is it, Dad?"

"Maybe you all would be better off without me." He stumbled on-to the road, the moonlit ribbon of white. "I'm not anything like what I was. Look at me."

"You think any of us are what we used to be?" Clementine pushed him. "You think I'm that shallow? You weren't exactly the cream of the crop way back when."

"You can't give up on us," Will begged. "What is wrong with you?"

"Keep going, love," Clementine whispered. "Bring us back."

Having grown up in Gallows, it surprised the Skeleton to think he'd never visited the Nameless Forest. But as he approached it, he was glad he hadn't. He wouldn't have been able to appreciate it then. In fact, he wasn't sure most could. It was a place of myth and mad-ness that, for many, had become nothing more than a campfire tale. People feared it, yes, but only because they filled it with their fears. They knew it only by nouns and the tenuous terrors that strung them together. He was like them once, but not anymore. When he looked at the Nameless Forest now, he didn't see its massive size, didn't no-tice the way it moved when there was no wind to move it. He didn't see abstract horrors or folklore freak shows. Instead, he saw King Edgar moving through the trees, a cape of vermillion veins trailing behind him. Instead, he saw the Dread Clock chiming out wrath and ruin, and hordes of creatures clamoring at the borders to be set free. Instead of a forest, he saw a weapon, one which could cleave humans like scabs off the continent.

The Nameless Forest loomed over the Skeleton as he made his careful approach. Abandoned wagons and pilfered crates were scat-tered across the outskirts of the Forest. Small piles of rotten food had been left in the fresh footprints in the mud. There were a few tents, too; torn open, they'd been stripped of whatever was inside.

"Eldrus' supply lines," he mumbled. He tried to find signs of any soldiers, but there was no life here, himself included.

Bending wood begged for his attention. Before him, the Nameless Forest's trees had parted. A warm gust that smelled faintly of flowers blew through the new passage. The Skeleton took the hint like a shot of whiskey. Cringing, he went reluctantly into the place where he should've always been.

The Binding Road was where Lotus had promised: right in front of him. It started at his feet and stretched indefinitely to infinite green ahead. He did a quick search for the vermillion veins, but they were nowhere to be found. He did spot a gathering of dandelions with lightning storms instead of flower heads, but they were off the beaten path, so he ignored them and let common sense take the wheel.

It didn't take long for the Skeleton to lose track of time in the Nameless Forest. He'd entered in the afternoon. Hours later, the sun still hadn't moved. Granted, it had developed a growth that protruded from its side, like an orbiting moon, but he didn't really know what to make of that.

He'd seen several people as well, in his periphery, or he'd heard them, at his back. The Skeleton ignored them the best he could, but the longer he did so, the more of them there seemed to be, until they were everywhere, except right in front of him. They started to whisper his name, touch his neck. He could hear them run past, even though no one did. He twitched as he heard blades sharpening against stone, teeth grinding on bone. Hands touched the back of his skull. He felt fluid filling it up from the inside, the pressure of it pressing on his eyes.

Finally, he spun around, crying, "What do you want?"

They gave no answer, because they'd vanished. In their place, they'd left headstones. More than he could count. He found himself drifting from the Binding Road to read their inscriptions.

The Skeleton went to the closest headstone. It read in bloody scrawl: Jessie Miller, death by Gravedigger. He stumbled, falling back on his hands. On the opposite side of the road, another headstone read: Blythe Keller, death by Gravedigger. He ran up and down the road. On each headstone the death of someone he'd known had been written onto it. And he was always to blame.

"That's not right," he said. Deeper into the Forest, many more headstones sat in cold, silent judgment. "I didn't kill that many people."

"But you did," a voice whispered.

The Skeleton spun in place. Great hills of headstones had formed behind him. The rotted corpses of children protruded from the pregnant mounds. All their eyes, bulging and maggoty, were on him.

"I didn't kill no kids!"

Again, the voice whispered, "But you have. But you will."

The Skeleton covered his face, but because he had no flesh to hide behind, he saw everything.

"You have thinned the flock," the voice said. "And now you have come home, where all wolves belong."

The Skeleton dropped to his knees and buried his skull in the dirt. "No," he said, thinking of every person he'd murdered for Poe, for Clementine and Will.

"No!" he said, thinking of the rebellion members who'd died for Geharra's cause and his need.

He reared back, muddy tears in his eyes. The headstones were gone. The body hills, too.

He stumbled upon Threadbare a few hours—or weeks, he couldn't tell—later. Lotus' village was too busy working the lumber to take notice of him. Besides, chances were a walking, talking skeleton didn't exactly incite surprise here like it would back home. But what did surprise him was the presence of Eldrus' soldiers. They were there, they'd made it to the place, but they weren't occupying the village. They were working the fields, the lumberyard, and helping the villagers construct new homes. There wasn't any animosity between them. A part of him wondered if this had been what King Edgar wanted for the Heartland all along. And if so, why had he been successful here when, at the same time, he'd failed so miserably in Bedlam and Hrothas?

Anathema rose out of the land a few weeks—or years, he couldn't tell—later. The crumbling spires and crooked walls that comprised the church were covered in thick spider webs. Large carrion birds circled the sky, while robed figures worked in their shadows below, hauling crates from Anathema's cellar. As the Skeleton drew closer, the belfry bellowed out a low, droning tone. The front of the church opened. A congregation came pouring out.

"Halt," a hooded woman shouted at the front of the line. She held up her hand. The congregation behind her stopped. "Who are you?"

The Skeleton pointed to himself and played stupid. "Me?"

"Wait here," he heard the hooded woman whisper.

She crossed the churchyard, avoiding the spider webs slung across it. When she was up close to the Skeleton, she said, "Oh," and got all soft on him. "Sorry about that."

He flinched as something wet splatted on his head. He glanced up and saw the carrion birds were now only ten or so feet above them. Their stomach mouths were fully extended and drooling everywhere.

"You don't need to worry about them. We like our food to have a little more meat on the bone." The woman lowered her hood and a mess of mousy hair spilled out. She was young, heavyset. Cannibalism, it seemed, was a good way to pack on pounds. "I'm Mother Michelle, leader of Anathema. Is there anything I can do for you?"

The Skeleton stared at Mother Michelle's congregation on Anathema's threshold. "You all expecting me?"

She shrugged. "Where are you trying to go?"

He nodded at the webs that seemed to be holding the church together. "Guys got a bug problem?"

Mother Michelle laughed. "New neighbors."

"You with Eldrus?"

"Of course," she said. She looked sick when she mumbled, "Edgar is our king."

The carrion birds quieted as they lifted higher into the sky.

"You don't seem too happy about that."

Mother Michelle forced a smile.

"I'm going to the Orphanage," the Skeleton admitted. His eyes followed the Binding Road, to where it split into five different directions past the church. "That going to be a problem?"

"No." A tear ran down her cheek. "Not at all." She turned and pointed to the farthest road, where the shadows were thick and the Forest dense. "That's the road you want. It's a good thing you don't have any blood left in your body."

"Yeah? Why's that?"

"Because they might actually listen to what you have to say, rather than fight to be the first one to suck you dry." Mother Michelle put on her hood and headed back towards Anathema.

A few minutes out of Anathema, like Lotus had promised, it seemed as though the Skeleton was somewhere else entirely. The sky had thickened and turned black, as though tar had been smeared across it. What little light there was came from the red stars trapped in the churning firmament. By their crimson courtesy, he found he stood at the edge of a wide and seamless swamp. The Nameless Forest, if he was even in it anymore, was nowhere to be found.

"Don't go anywhere." The Skeleton was talking to the Binding Road. It was still there, at his feet, but the roaming fog made it hard to keep track of its course.

"Do you see it?" he asked himself, pretending to be Will.

"See what? Can't see much in this fog."

"The house."

The Skeleton imagined Clementine and Will standing at his side. They were pointing at something in the distance.

"Atticus," Clementine said. "Wait until you get out of the Nameless Forest before you use the Dread Clock."

"I'll take it to Nachtla," he said. He kissed the air where he told himself his wife's cheek would be. "I'll make that mosquito help me make it work."

Will smiled. "I love you, Dad."

The Skeleton smiled back, or at least tried to. "I love you, too, Will."

The further the Skeleton plunged into the swamp, the clearer it became "house" wasn't a strong enough word to describe the Orphanage. It was a three-story mansion, all red-brick and black mortar. The windows were barred, and the property itself protected by the ten-foot, wrought iron fence that surrounded it.

"You don't want to go in there."

The Skeleton stumbled off the Binding Road and quickly stepped back onto it. He swiped at the fog and said, "Who's there?"

A little girl, doing it's damndest to sound seductive, whispered, "Whoever you want."

A wave of rapturous moans broke over the Skeleton. The sweaty exhalations seeped into his bones. Warmth radiated through his ribcage, swelling in his loins. Again, he stumbled from the Binding Road. But this time, when he'd gathered himself, it was nowhere to be found.

"Atticus. Gravedigger. Skeleton."

Panicked, he went down and crawled on the ground. *Where's the road, god damn it?*

"So many names, so many roles."

Holy fucking Child, he thought. The fog swooped in and blinded him in its embrace. *This isn't happening.*

"You need only one name. One role."

The Skeleton lost control of his arms as the fog rolled under them and lifted him to and off his feet. He clawed at it, bit at it, but like him, the fog felt no pain and gave no mercy.

"You've forgotten happiness. Be a lover again, Skeleton of the Gravedigger, Atticus, and let us love you in return."

The fog lifted him high into the red-starred sky. A mildewed wind rushed in and swept the rest of it away, to show him what he'd been missing. All across the swamp, bodies writhed in the inky waters, displaying in bloody, orgiastic bliss the sexual limits their flesh could endure. There were hundreds of them, thousands of them. They were all, in some way, connected to one another. By hand and foot, mouth and tongue, and every form of possible penetration, the men and women formed a chain of lust around the swamp that refused to be broken.

"Clementine's in there. Will, too, if you fancy that sort of thing," the voice continued. "Come into our waters."

The Skeleton shouted, "Get off!" and flung himself in the fog until it finally let him go. He plummeted onto the Binding Road. His feet hit the ground sideways, shattering immediately.

"You're not stopping me," he said, crawling forward, the fog having dropped him at the Orphanage's gate.

A soft laughter rang out across the swamp. The little girl said, "Wouldn't dream of it."

All of a sudden, the Orphanage's wrought iron fences started to rattle. The front gates shook and, with a whine, slowly crept open, leaving just enough space for the Skeleton to squeeze through.

"Come in," the little girl said. "We're all so excited to meet you."

CHAPTER XXVII

Crawling towards the Orphanage, the Skeleton's fingers closed around the edge of a sign that had sunk into the mud. The front of it was heavily faded, but after a moment, he could make out what it said.

"Our Ladies of Sorrow Academy," he read, tracing the silver lettering. He remembered Elizabeth's story about the Bad Mother at this same school who had treated her and the other Deadly Beauties so poorly; the Bad Mother she'd had tattooed into her skin. He sighed and kept crawling, repeating "son of a bitch" over and over again under his breath.

By the time he reached the Orphanage, his feet had healed and he was able to walk again. The moans from the swamp grew louder, but he knew a trap when he heard one. Under different circumstances, when he wasn't a walking pile of bones, he probably would've fallen for it. But the flaying had taken more than his skin. It'd left him with purpose, and that was about it.

"Knock, knock," the little girl said. Her voice was leathery, chirpy, like a bat and its wings.

The Skeleton ignored her and pulled on the gigantic wooden doors. They refused to give. It was only until he gave up on going in this way that they started to creak open on their own.

"Knock, knock," the little girl persisted. Her voice came through the widening doorway. She was somewhere inside.

The Skeleton grumbled. "Who's there?"

The little girl giggled and said, "You're stupid."

Fog poured like an avalanche over the front of the Orphanage and filled the swamp until it was completely covered. The moans continued to rise higher and higher in pitch until they twisted into screams.

"Are you coming in or what?" the little girl asked snidely.

The Skeleton nodded and entered the Orphanage. Immediately, the front doors slammed shut behind him and locked. He didn't go much further because, inside, the mansion was pitch-black.

Thinking the little girl enjoyed bantering, he said, "Spare some light?"

The little girl laughed. "For you, anything."

One by one, small flames came to life above him. At first, he thought the candles on which they burned were floating in the air. But as more light filled the room, he saw that wasn't the case at all. There were bodies, hundreds of them, bound and hanging together from the ceiling like a grotesque chandelier. And it was in each of their hands, atop untold years of hardened wax, that these candles burned.

"What do you think?"

The Skeleton jumped backward as he noticed the little girl at his side. She was small, pale, with white hair done up in thick braids. She wore a long, dark blue dress with a red collar. Dirty rags were tightly wrapped around her hands. The little girl looked like a student of the place, and couldn't have been any older than twelve or thirteen.

With her smiling eyes fixed on the dead above, she said, "My name is Gemma. What's yours?"

"Atticus."

"It's nice to meet you, Atticus."

The Skeleton continued to take in his surroundings. Inside the building, it was all doom and gloom. The walls were dark green; golden words in the deader-than-dead language of Latin were written across them. Sharp, wooden adornments and busts jutted out from every possible perch, making the mansion itself look more like a weapon of torture than anything else. A few feet from where he stood, the central staircase ran upward to the second floor, and doubled back to the third. What waited on the upper levels was difficult tell, because of the large, violet curtains draped over the balconies and catwalks there.

"It's nice to meet you, Atticus," the little girl persisted, sounding overly polite.

"It's nice to meet you, too, Gemma."

She smiled. "You've had better days, I take it?"

"Something like that." He pointed to the corpses. "Who're they?"

"Those are our moms and dads," Gemma said, joy in her voice where hurt should've been.

"What'd they do?"

"They gave up on us. Mine are up there, too." Finally, she looked over at the Skeleton. "After everything I did for them, they still didn't learn their lesson. Can I call you Skeleton? I know what it's like to be reminded of something you only want to forget, so Skeleton?"

"That's fine," he said. *She's enjoying this*, he thought.

Gemma took his hand. She fingered his bones, giggled at their texture. "The Dread Clock means a lot to me."

"So you know why I'm here?"

"Lotus sent you to get it."

The Skeleton dropped her hand. Something sharp had pricked his own. "Lotus is locked up in Ghostgrave. How the hell you know that?"

Gemma laughed and rubbed her hands together. "Because that was the plan? Atticus, I mean, Skeleton, listen: When a monster starts leading rebellions and winning the respect of humans, other monsters, monsters like ourselves, take notice."

He ground his teeth. "Figured I was being used."

Gemma wrinkled her nose. "I doubt it, but, yeah, you are. Sort of."

"King Edgar put Lotus up to this, then? Telling me about the Dread Clock and sending me in after it?"

Gemma nodded.

"How the hell do you know that?"

"We're in the Nameless Forest, dude. Is it all that hard to believe Lotus can communicate with us?"

"Sounds like a bullshit answer."

"Sounds like the only one you're getting." She nudged him. "Skeleton, it's not all bad."

"Lotus was beaten to a pulp—" Something glided through the air above, landed on one of the balconies, out of sight. "—I had to beg her to tell me about the clock."

"Lotus… is a freak." Gemma made a popping sound with her mouth. "That was her idea. She'll be and do anything it takes to get what she wants. And King Edgar thinks she wants what he wants. That's why he put her up to it. But we have more planned."

Whispers wound down from the ceiling. Slick-skinned creatures hopped back and forth between the hanging bodies.

"King Edgar came in here and took everything over. Fine. No big deal. We needed a change, anyways. He went to work on the villages and united them. Good. About time, I say. But there was one condition."

"Fight for him," the Skeleton said.

"Well, he said 'support,' but even the dumbest that live here can read between the lines. All right. Fair enough, we agreed. One problem, though. The Dread Clock. It won't let us leave."

"Why?"

Gemma started forward and swung her arm for him to follow. "I know you're on a tight schedule. Walk with me."

"Why can't you leave?" the Skeleton asked as they crossed the main hall. The ratty, wine-colored carpet soaked up their sounds.

"The Nameless Forest is complex, but also really simple. After the Trauma, people went insane. They were hunting down anything that wasn't human, because they thought us creatures had caused the Trauma. You'd think being a monster during the apocalypse would be paradise, right?"

The Skeleton shrugged.

"Nope. We were almost wiped out. And then there was this forest, one the humans over the years became afraid of. It didn't have a name at the time—hence the name, ha, ha—but it sounded safe, especially since they were steering clear of it. We thought we'd hide out here for a while until the humans forgot about us. And they did forget, but when we tried to leave, the Nameless Forest wouldn't let us.

"Parents ever tell you a fairy tale? Such and such can only be killed by water on the fifth day and all that crap? Don't feed after midnight? Sometimes, that's what the Forest is like. Somehow, something decided all us creatures couldn't leave, so we couldn't leave.

"It's the Dread Clock."

She went up the stairs, flung her hands back, causing the first door on the second floor to open.

"It's what keeps it together. It's what ticks out the rules. It soaks up everything that's ever happened, could happen, like a sponge. Every thought, every action. Have you figured out what caused the

Trauma yet?"

The Skeleton said, "No," as they went through the door and entered another hall. Here, the bones of children were on display. Except there were strange, dried-up, tube-like organs running up and down their arms. "Do I want to?"

Gemma nodded. They rounded a corner into another hall.

"The humans did. They caused it. They woke up God and then tried to kill It when It turned out to be something other than what they had in mind."

She knocked on a door covered in spikes and it swung back. Stopping at the threshold, she said, "This forest is a small part of Its domain. Where It really comes from… I don't know… somewhere deep down, maybe in the Membrane. Somehow, the Dread Clock ended up here, though. Maybe someone put it here to make sure God didn't wake up again."

"Is that what King Edgar wants? To wake it up?" The cause of the Trauma? A god? He should've been hysterical, but his broken mind couldn't manage it.

A pale hand emerged from the dark of the doorway and beckoned them in.

"I think he does." Gemma went through the doorway.

The Skeleton followed her into the next room and stopped, surprised. There were more children like herself inside. They were sitting on the floor, unraveling the rags around their hands as they stared at the gigantic, metal door on the opposite side of the room.

"I'm no chemist, Skeleton, but when you combine an object of pure madness with a place of otherworldly power, well, you're probably not going to get the best results."

One of the children looked up at the Skeleton and moaned hungrily. Gemma shushed him and shook her head.

"King Edgar has sent so many men through to take down the Dread Clock. We're grateful," she pointed to a toddler in the corner, who was ravaging a soldier's corpse, "but we're not stupid. And we know you're not working for him. So if you pull this off, why should we follow him?"

The Skeleton realized they were moving towards the massive, metal doors. Behind it, he could hear raspy, hard, and heavy breathing.

"You're not following me," he said. The empty gaze of the children here was getting to him. "I'm not leading no one no more."

"We'll see. Lotus is doing her best, though. She's human, so she can get out of this place. She fights for us. Hey, you two would make a cute couple." Gemma grabbed the handles to the heaving doors. "You do know that, if you take the Dread Clock, we'll be set free right?"

"If it'll do what I need it to, I don't care."

Gemma smiled. "We'll see." She pulled back on the doors.

The first thing the Skeleton saw was the bat. The massive, twenty-foot long, semi-decayed bat that hung from hooks fixed into the ceiling of the church-like room. Though it looked dead, the creature seemed anything but, for it was from its gaping mouth the heavy, rank breaths poured. The bat's wing span was beyond impressive. In the room, it looked stunted, but the Skeleton was sure that, if stretched, they could envelope the Orphanage entirely.

"We are vampyres," Gemma said. "This is our master, Camazotz." She drew his attention to the pews that ran under the bat and across the room. "They are waiting for her blessing."

In the pews, innumerable children sat, their hands held high, their tongues flicking out bestial praises. They kept their palms toward Camazotz as they worshiped. When the Skeleton stepped closer to the children, he saw why; each of their palms were slit, and in each slit were mouths.

Gemma unraveled the rags around her hands. "Biting necks is all well and good." She pressed her hand to the Skeleton's arm. The slit in her hand sucked on his bones like a leech. "But who notices a small touch? A quick graze? Ah!"

She outstretched her hand and caught a drop of blood that fell from Camazotz's body. She closed her eyes and licked her lips as the beast's blood coursed through her.

"Delicious," she said, finally coming out of it and looking more alive than before. "Now that you've seen us, you sure you want to let us out?"

The Skeleton nodded and ignored Clementine's and Will's pleas for him to reconsider.

"Probably didn't get to see the spider people, did you? Oh well. If we don't make you turn on your heels, bunch of bugs won't, either." She pressed her head against the Skeleton's shoulder. "Hundreds of years ago, I might've stopped you from taking the Dread Clock. I know what it's capable of. But I like to think I grew out of that selfish girl I used to be, so it's yours. You, you seem selfish, though. You're doing this to get your family back, right?"

"Right," he said. *Why is she trying to stop me?*

"They must mean a lot to you to put the whole world in danger."

The Skeleton said, "Maybe the world needs monsters like you. Otherwise, we just end up with monsters like us."

Gemma grinned. She flicked her finger and two blue flames came to life at the far end of the room, directly under the bat. Between the flames, there was an opening, and it led outside, to a tranquil lake with a small island wreathed in red grass. And at the center of the island, alone and unguarded, the Dread Clock waited.

"Go for it," Gemma said, nudging the Skeleton along. "Let's see how immortal you really are."

CHAPTER XXVIII

It wasn't water that filled the lake, but hundreds of long, thick, bruise-colored worms. As though fused to one another, the slimy, hissing creatures circled the island together in a slow, hypnotic rotation. The Skeleton stood at the end of the passage, the Orphanage behind him, watching their movements. What were these sluggish sentries capable of? he wondered. What was it that did the King's men in? The worms? The vampyres? Or the Dread Clock itself?

The Skeleton stepped out of the passage. He heard a click, like a latch, and when he turned around, he found that the passage was gone. Being outside, he expected to see the Orphanage, but the mansion had vanished. Whatever portal he'd entered, it'd taken him further into the Nameless Forest, further than most had ever gone.

But, really, it didn't matter where the vampyres had led him. What mattered was the Dread Clock was here, fifty feet in front of him, and for the first time since he'd started this goddamn, mother fucking, piece of shit journey, it felt like there was actually an end to it in sight.

For an instrument of insanity, the Dread Clock sure fit the part. It was tall, ten feet or so, with two wicked horns curving outward from its notched pediment. Its body was narrow, impossibly black. The moon dial glowed hellfire red, the celestial bodies it depicted surely the homes of chaos, madness, and despair. Below it, the hour and minute hands spun psychotically around the clock face, refusing to land on the numbers scratched into the metalwork. And further down still, at the Dread Clock's center, a tumorous pendulum swung back and forth, ringing out a song only those at midnight might hear.

"I guess I expected more of a fight," the Skeleton said.

He put one foot into the lake. The worms tightened to support his weight. But as he brought his other foot in, a thought crept into his mind and paralyzed him, from his bones to his soul.

How did I get here?

He had been a simple man, reformed to an extent, with a little bit of land and a family to call his own. He hadn't any grand aspirations, or wild notions about the world and the worlds within it. Satisfaction came in the form of a good farm and a job well done. Happiness was Clementine's smile and Will's laugh, and some of that same old, same old to fill an empty stomach. When his time came, he had figured history would go hard on him, but he always kept his fingers crossed there'd be a footnote with a little fancy asterisk that said, "Atticus wasn't a great man, but he sure tried."

But all it took was one night and three murders to take that all away from him. Over the last year, that simple man had died more times than he had ever lived. He learned there was more to death than death. He realized that it had a structure, a system, like a country all its own. Over the last year, he'd became a symbol for a rebellion he couldn't give two shits about. He'd taken part in a secret alliance between humans and Night Terrors. He'd discovered what Eldrus was putting into the earth, and what King Edgar was trying to dig out of it. Over the last year, he'd been hunted by shepherds, lied to by friends. He'd killed more people than he ever thought he could stomach, and god damn if each killing didn't make his stomach growl. Over the last year, he'd become nothing more than a proper noun running across the continent, like a mad dog with too long a leash, feebly trying to claw out treasures that were probably better off being left buried.

And here he was. Here he was. He'd come from Ghostgrave, his initial destination, to the Nameless Forest on the word of a stranger alone. He'd seen and heard more profane and sacred secrets here than most, and yet they did little to move him. Maybe it was a fact that he'd been eaten alive dick first, but clearly, after all he'd gone through, something wasn't right with him. Not anymore.

Finally, he started forward. The waves of worms quickly took over, however, and guided him to the red-grassed island. As they did, he remembered the flowers he'd seen in the Membrane; Death's Dilemma they were called. Each one represented a love of Death's who dared to love Death in return. It made him laugh to think it, but he felt a kind of kinship with Death now, for the Gravedigger had a dilemma of his own. In place of flowers, he imagined headstones, each one representing someone he'd tried to save, and someone who'd tried to save him in return.

Like a pit of snakes, the worms writhed and undulated until they practically heaved the Skeleton onto the island. He caught his balance, told himself this was it, that if this didn't work, nothing would, and went to the Dread Clock.

His dead eyes couldn't help but be fixed on the swollen, cancerous mass that was the clock's pendulum. At the height of every swing, a sinking feeling came over him, as though he were swallowing himself up. But it wasn't the pendulum he needed. That was only one part of the machine. What he required was its infernal engine. He reached for the handle of the glass door the pendulum sat behind and pulled it—

Yellow flames flaring under a wilting sky. Hundreds of horses pounding across a flooded desert. Caskets like chrysalises glowing in a new dawn light, the world below them empty and unformed.

—The Skeleton ripped his hand away and screamed. The images had torn through his skull like a knife. Shaking it off, he went in again and—

Metal stars in a blood-drenched night. Babies in a barn, chains at their feet. Skyscrapers on fire. Cars dead and rusted in a lake. Men in suits with body-shaped briefcases. Mountains of eyes blinking from the folds of space. Guns. Flesh fiends. Women holding hands as they cut each other's wrists. Tornados of the dead. Entire cities reduced to rubble. A small girl frothing at the mouth. Fissures in the earth. House catching the sunlight on a hill. White grass. Red Death.

—Again, he pulled back and then fell to the ground. What little was left of his mind had been stretched to its limit, and it was starting to tear. The power in the clock was overwhelming. Each image was a lifetime. He felt them completely with every sense he possessed, and every sense he didn't even know existed.

"I… have to focus," he said, slurring his words. He got up and grabbed the clock.

Nursing home nurses stalk the halls, crawling on the ceiling, like bugs on a wall. Tired-eyed students reach into their laptop screens. Pestilence in a synagogue. Ancient flowers subjugating human pulp. Organs in revolt. Torn-open books. Backyard spacecraft. Nightmares from a canvas.

The Skeleton gritted his teeth. The images clawed at his sanity, leaving most of it shredded. He gripped the glass door's handle. Struggling, shaking from a seizure, he pulled it open.

Dance hall devastation. Prom queen cannibal. Crime in a classroom. The dead marching down an upside down street. Hollowed-out children. A cackling coven. Wars raging across a vomiting cityscape.

He gritted his teeth and grinned through the onslaught. His arm slipped past the pendulum. He worked his fingers between the arterial pulleys.

Pink rivers clogged with human glaciers. Suburban violence in gangland haunts. Infected satellites falling to earth. Wedding vows made in flesh.

Focus, the Skeleton told himself, drowning in the deluge of past and possibilities.

Children killing children. Snuff films taped over birthday parties.

He needed the heart, and a heart it had. He could hear it beating behind the complications, somewhere further back.

Poisoned water. Forgetful kings. God on Its throne, vermillion and vengeful.

Pressing his face to the clock, letting the hour and minute hands grind at his skull, he dug deeper.

Clementine and Will in heated debate, as she tries to fit him back inside her.

The Skeleton shook off the scene. The Dread Clock was reacting, which meant he was getting closer.

Carnage at the zoo. Ligaments for hair. Bursts of color in gawping throats. A masked orgy in an abandoned warehouse. Cold skin. Milky blood. Airplanes bombing countries into dust. Diamonds on drying brains. Politicians with nails through their teeth.

Shoulder inside the Dread Clock, he reached past the weights. There, through a layer of mush, a cradle.

Blythe and Bon, raping Clementine and Will, making new orifices when theirs wouldn't suffice.

The Skeleton could smell their sweat. He could hear their cries. He could taste what they tasted, could feel what they felt inside. He hesitated, and then kept clawing at the cradle.

Tanks roll over an open field, as artillery pummels the writhing gates of heaven.

His fingers broke through the hard barrier. Freezing liquid poured out, shattering his bones.

Earthquakes cough out hailstorms. Dark tabernacle in a forbidden grotto.

His bones reformed in an instant, his cursed soul empowered here, and he kept at it.

A mass of humans a million strong, their creations in upheaval, filling up the sky.

The Dread Clock's body split apart. Fleshy, gear-covered sacs ballooned from it. Astral tendrils shot out and pierced the Skeleton. They bore into his eyes, into his tongue. They split open his bones and drilled through their centers, carving him out and filling him with fathomless pain.

Frozen oceans. Consuming shadows. Spinal cord currency.

Screaming, the Skeleton grabbed the tendrils and shoved himself inside the Dread Clock. He broke his face through its mechanical innards, gears like crumbs spilling from his chattering mouth. With both hands, he clutched the Dread Clock's heart—

Howls from the underworld. A great, grinding machine, making meat to feed the slugs lying bloated in space.

—and, with all his strength and the strength Clementine and Will leant him, he—

Candlelit homes. Empty wells. Gurgling stomachs spitting out wine and host. Animal skulls on sunburnt shoulders, moving from palms to heels.

—ripped the heart out of the Dread Clock and fell backward, collapsing into the red grass. He grasped the clicking, bleeding trophy and held it high. Dark oil dripped from the throbbing heart-work onto his tongue and stained it black.

"That's it," the Skeleton said. He opened a pocket in his cloak and dropped the heart inside. As soon as it left his hands, the images began to fade. "It's done."

Without it's heart, the Black Hour's vessel could not keep. It collapsed in upon itself. The glass doors blew outward. Wood splintered, metal rusted. The tumorous pendulum had one last swing and then was flung from its confines, out of the clock and into the lake of worms.

The Skeleton got up, laughing. "Show me what I want." He dug into the cloak's pockets. He couldn't wait. "I need to know you work." Gasping, he grasped the Black Hour's heart and said, "Show me Hex. Show me Lacuna. And take me there."

Islands in the ocean. Waves over beaches. Nimbuses crowding the firmament. Hex in Bedlam, in Hrothas. Hex in a forest. Hex digging in the dirt. Cold water, thick spray. Night Terrors carrying a tribute, Corrupted in tow.

The Skeleton sifted through the images. "Show me the Widening Gyre," he demanded. He would treat the heart like the heir, willing it to do his bidding. "Lacuna, an island off the coast of Nachtla." He felt like throwing up, but he didn't have a stomach, so he was solid on that front. "Hex, age twenty-seven, maybe twenty-eight."

Hex standing over her husband, cracking a whip across his face. The Widening Gyre spiraling inward, ship masts disappearing beneath its surface. Mara in Corrupted garb. A centipede mask sitting in the shadows. A pile of children's bones. A wriggling, blue mass, nesting like a spider in all the minds it could.

He had to refine the visions. The Black Hour absorbed time itself and forged its own hellscapes from it. He had to cut away those dark simulacrums; otherwise, he couldn't be sure what would happen if he mistook them for being real.

"Show Hex, in Nachtla, with James, Gary, Warren, Elizabeth, Miranda, and Mr. Haemo." The Black Hour's heart pulsated a blisteringly hot heat. "Show me Hex sending her thoughts in Nachtla." If he had flesh, he wouldn't anymore. He could see why others had failed here. They had the disadvantage of being human. "Show me their boats in the Widening Gyre."

The gears in the Black Hour's heart ground into one another. Its dark, fleshy surface tightened. Center glowing a wintry white, it assaulted the Skeleton's mind with tens of timelines of Hex, Nacthla, the Widening Gyre, and an island that had to have been Lacuna.

To go where he needed to go, he had to stick with what he knew.

Like pieces to a puzzle, he arranged every scenario until it reflected his own experience. Starting in Nyxis, he moved with the Marrow Cabal into the barn where the witch Helena and her sisters had weaved them into the town. He found the fragments of his conversations with Mr. Haemo and James, relived the attack on his friends and his inevitable capture. There, the timeline split, and rather than follow himself into weeks of torture with Captain Yelena, he trailed after Hex and the others as they escaped the town and headed eastward.

He didn't know if he was doing it right—who could claim to be an expert on the Black Hour?—but it felt like he was getting somewhere. He watched as the Marrow Cabal navigated the land, stopping in town after town, village after village. He spotted anomalies that couldn't have been—James with the wrong hair color, the Marrow Cabal in the Old World, Mr. Haemo not being a freak. He disregarded them, and went back to the source at Nyxis again, to scour other annals.

If he let the scenarios play out as they occurred, he'd be here for months. There was too much information to process, too many details to take note of. He could, assuming the heart wasn't lying to him, spy on each member of the Marrow Cabal, overhear their every conversation, oversee their every private action. But now wasn't the time for that. It was interesting to see, though, that as the Marrow Cabal traveled toward Nachtla, their ranks continued to grow. Hex had told him true; she wasn't going to let his name go to waste.

There, there it is. He stopped the Black Hour's heart on a scene in Nachtla. Hex was transmitting something to him. He pulled away from the village, but before he did, he heard someone mention something about a Red Worm. He scanned the horizon, to ensure the season was right. And then, holding that timeline in his mind's periphery, he tracked down his own journey, from Ghostgrave to the Nameless Forest, and overlaid them.

As he trucked toward the present, his present, the anomalies became fewer and the branches in time shorter. The Dread Clock hadn't had a chance yet to forge new midnight nightmares from the events of the last few weeks. He replayed his struggles of tearing out the heart, and while he did, Hex's timeline showed them departing Nachtla, twelve strong, for the coast.

"Shit."

The images were coming to an end. Everything was playing out in real-time. From the heart, he watched himself on the island, watching himself from the heart on the island. And as this was happening, the Marrow Cabal were marching through a cove, to a small dock with three boats tethered to it.

"This has to be it." The Skeleton sounded convinced, but only because he had to be to keep going. How he'd managed in the last few minutes to have done what he did, he couldn't even begin to understand. It was like the heart was guiding his every move, teaching him how to make the most of it. For any well-adjusted individual, that should've thrown up enough red flags that even the blind would do a double-take. But the Skeleton had never been one of those people. If he had been, he would've said "no" twenty-five years ago, when Poe put a knife in his hand and left it up to him as to what to do with it.

The Skeleton put the Black Hour's heart to his teeth. "Take me there," he spoke into it. He held the moments in his mind, him on the Dread Clock's island, the Marrow Cabal setting sail for the sea, and willed that past into the present once again. "Take me, god damn it."

The heart throbbed in his hands, his demands clearly heard. The gears fixed to it started to grind and turn. With every pulsation, the fabric of reality before him became twisted and torn. Against his view of the lake and the Nameless Forest further back, small slits were cut into air in the form of an upside-cross. From them, salty spray and the sounds of the sea blew through.

This has to be it, the Skeleton thought as he pocketed the heart and gripped the tears in reality. Laughing maniacally at what was happening, he pulled the slits further apart and realized the portal sat high in the sky. Looking through, he could see the shore behind an evening haze, while below, the ocean spiraled inwards, throwing massive waves in a childish tantrum.

That's the Widening Gyre. He pushed further into the slit, until half of him was in the sky, and the other half still in the Nameless Forest. *Where are...* On the edge of his field of vision, three boats were struggling against the current. Beside them, Mr. Haemo hovered in the air, hauling someone out of the water who'd gone overboard.

The Skeleton felt a phantom smile form across his face. "This is it, guys," he said, talking to Clementine and Will.

For a moment, he thought about the fact he had never seen the

Membrane in the Black Hour's recordings, but ignored it.

He pushed the rest of his body through the portal, said "We'll be home soon enough," and fell like a heretic out of heaven from the sky.

CHAPTER XXIX

The Skeleton must've fallen off-course, because when he woke up, he woke up in half, in the dark, on a beach. Had he even died? He didn't remember going to the Membrane, even for an instant. Apparently, having his spine snapped off from his pelvis wasn't good enough for Death anymore.

The Skeleton sat up and started blindly rooting around in the sand. "Son of a bitch," he said. A few crabs snapped at his digits. He gave them a good smash.

He grunted as his hands closed around the rest of himself. "God damn son of a bitch." He lined his upper and lower spine up to one another and let his body do the rest. "Where the hell am I?"

Light would've been nice, but all he had was the moon, and the clouds were doing their damndest to hide it. The ocean sounded fairly calm, so either the Widening Gyre was winding down for the night, or he'd come out of the portal much further up the mainland's coast. There were trees, however, higher up the hill he lay at the bottom of. Palm trees and sprawling mangroves, and massive, mutant succulents large enough to get lost in. He'd been to Nachtla once or twice in his lifetime, and didn't remember any plants like that there.

The Skeleton froze. The Black Hour's heart. He patted himself down and, lo and behold, it was in the pocket where he left it.

"Tough son of a bitch," he said, touching it through the fabric, trying and finding no damage done to it.

He dug into the opposite pocket and found the heir there. It hadn't weathered the journey well. The object was in pieces, looking like the innocuous snail shell it resembled. "Not good," he said, hanging onto the fragments. "God damn it."

He started moving his legs well before he realized his spine had reconnected. *I did it*, he thought. He let out a wild laugh and beat the sand with his fists.

"Ha, ha! I did it Clementine!" He jumped to his feet. His cheeks went red, even though they were technically lying in a pile of the flesh fiend's shit in Ghostgrave.

"So bring us back," Will said through the Skeleton's mouth.

He shook his head and said, "Soon. I don't know where I am. I don't know how much more I can get out of this heart." But what the Skeleton was really thinking was this: *I have to do this right, and I'm afraid to do it alone. I don't have a life to risk. You do.*

"Now to get my bearings—" a strong gale blew across the beach and flattened him into the sand, "—what the hell?"

In a matter of seconds, a windstorm had settled over the area. The sound of the bending trees and the wind ripping through their canopies was deafening. Buffeted to the point of bruising, the Skeleton got up and went on all fours up the hill, to have a better look at his surroundings. He found a dented breastplate along the way and put it on, for old time's sake.

As he crawled over the hill's crest, the clouds above started to part and let a little light in. Using a tree for support, he stood and surveyed the sights. He was on the edge of a dense jungle, a jungle that, judging by the violent tempest charging across it, was on the edge of extinction.

"This has to be Lacuna," he mumbled. Sharp, stinging rain ran sideways like razors across the area. "Or an island close by."

The Skeleton grabbed his hood and cloak and held them shut. He needed to start somewhere, so he checked the sky for the North Star and headed its way. The circumstances weren't great—he was walking more crookedly than a drunk on payday—but it didn't matter. It was done. He had the heart. He knew how to use it. It was done.

Maybe I could go back, back before all this happened. He noticed, far off, what looked like a house. *Go back in time and make this all... No,* he decided, heading for the building. *No. We live with what we've done. That shit's more trouble than it's worth.*

Small streams poured past the Skeleton, tripping him up with the debris that floated down them. It wasn't a house, he realized, the wind throwing him against the building, but a storage shed. House or no house, it was a sign of habitation. And, better yet, it was a place he could hold out until the storm had its fair share of being a full-blown asshole.

But as he rounded the shed, the slick door handle slipping out his grasp, he noticed something else further off. Torches, twelve of them, and the cloaked figures holding them. They were winding through the jungle, hacking at it with moonlit weapons. He could hear them shouting to one another, but what they were saying was lost in the cacophony of the storm.

The Skeleton chose to follow, because although he couldn't see their faces, there was a good chance it was the Marrow Cabal. Their numbers checked out. They sounded about as pissed off as he imagined they would be in this situation.

The Skeleton went low to the ground. His bones were covered in mud and it was getting hard to walk with the wind and that extra weight. He missed his eyelids, because the rain was doing its best to stab his eyes out of his skull. The cloaked twelve hadn't spotted him yet, but he did see, as the wind shoved a portion of the jungle aside, where they were going.

It was a village. An arboreal, half-in-shambles village.

"What's that?"

The Skeleton stopped. While he'd been watching the village, he hadn't been watching those he was stalking. They'd seen him. Him, the hooded skeleton, with bloodshot eyes and a Black Hour-blackened tongue. All twelve had turned, their torches in front of them, making of their faces smoldering vagaries.

Not needing the element of surprise to win a fight anymore, he just came right out and shouted it: "Are you the Marrow Cabal?"

A few torches went down; a few glances were exchanged. A hooded figure came forward, their torch their shield, their sword their only hope.

"Are you the Marrow Cabal?" the Skeleton repeated. He pulled his cloak closer. Regardless of who they were, he didn't want them to see all of him, not yet.

The one who came forward said, "Who—?"

A woman's voice. Hex's voice. Quickly, the Skeleton cut her off and said, "It's me. It's me. It's Atticus."

"Drop your hood!" She shoved the torch at him, so he couldn't see her at all. She swung back her killing arm. "Drop it!"

The wind did the work for him. A blast of wet air blew across the jungle and flung the hood back.

"Fuck you," Hex said. She drove the sword at the Skeleton, but he caught it with his bare hand and held on tightly. "Help," she cried, the others coming to assist her.

The Skeleton knocked the torch from Hex. It hit the ground and sputtered in a puddle. With his free hand, he grabbed her cloak, pulling her face inches away from his and said, "It's me. It's Atticus. I'm here. It's me."

"Bullshit!" She shook and tried to break free. "Get this fucker off of me!"

The Skeleton's teeth chattered, probably because he remembered they were supposed to in a storm as cold as this. "It's me," he repeated. He brought her in closer, her nose in his nose cavity. "You're a telepath. Ichor, your brother, he can only receive. All your life you hated him—" He pulled her back as the rest of the Marrow Cabal tried to overtake him. "—You hated him and now you two hunt each other, beat the living shit out of each other." He looked into her pale blue eyes and saw the faintest glimmer of recognition. "I had a daughter," he said, his voice as pained as he now felt. "I had a daughter named Vale."

Hex's lips started to quiver. Her blue braids unwound and brushed against them. "Atticus?" She threw up her hand and the Marrow Cabal came to a halt.

"You patched me up," he said, continuing to appeal to her. "That night in Bedlam. There was a riot. And again, on the way to Carpenter Plantation, on Adelaide's Deceit." Her eyes went bright blue. She was transmitting everything now. "You told me you were from Angheuawl, but you told me through the heir you're from another place. An island. Lacuna."

Hex got all soft on him and started crying tears fatter than the rain drops dotting her face. "Atticus? Oh my god, Atticus?" She let go of her sword, but he kept holding its blade. She touched his skull, her hands shaking. "Atticus… how are you… what the hell…?"

At this point, the rest of the Marrow Cabal had put two and two together. Gathered around, the Skeleton saw James, Gary, Warren, Elizabeth, Miranda, and Mr. Haemo in man-mode. There were five additional members now, too. Three more women, and two men.

"At-Atticus?" James stammered.

Gary, beautifully decayed as ever, dropped his hood and torch and managed only a pathetic, whispered, "Oh no."

The Skeleton nodded and released Hex. She backed away from him. He couldn't blame her for that.

"You look like you've been through the wringer," Warren said behind his bulky hands.

"That, and then some." The Skeleton felt an immediate wholeness now that he was in their presence again. He hadn't realized how much he missed it, missed them. In the months away from his friends, and friends they were—there was no denying it now—he'd lost more than his flesh and blood. He'd lost himself to his cursed crusade.

"What happened to you?" Hex was speaking for everyone, though that wasn't anything new.

The Skeleton went sideways as the tempest blasted them from the west. "King Edgar and his flesh fiend pet did this to me. Too much damage. Couldn't fix it." He grabbed the guttering torch that Hex had dropped and handed it to her. "It's a much longer story than the time we have to spare right now."

"You're creeping me out, bag of bones," Mr. Haemo buzzed, his skin suit not doing a good job of adhering to his insect form.

"Compliment as far I'm concerned." He even missed Mr. Haemo, but mostly because he still planned to use him for everything he was worth.

"I got it, Hex," he said, tapping his cloak where the heart sat somewhat safely.

"What?" she said, confused.

"The Black Hour's heart. And I used it. That's how I got here."

The new recruits into the Marrow Cabal looked at one another, baffled.

"Atticus... you can't... I don't believe... Wait, where's your family?"

"Did you find them?" James stepped beside Hex.

Gary hung back, looking less excited than the Skeleton would've imagined.

"No," the Skeleton said. "Haven't tried yet. Got to do it right. With you all. Back in Gallows. Is this Lacuna?"

All of a sudden, Hex snapped out of the trance the Skeleton's arrival had put her in. "Yes!" She grabbed the sword in his hand and said, "Shit, yes. This is… there's too much… just follow. I'll try to—" She gave him a pathetic look.

He missed them, but he didn't miss their pity. He'd spent months traveling the continent, and not once did he look at his reflection. People were a confirmation of his condition he could've done without.

"—I'll try to fill you in on the way," Hex finished. She nodded at the others.

Together, they darted through the sheets of rain that stood between them and Lacuna.

The Skeleton had to pace himself as they ran, because the purity of bone made him faster than them all. He kept deflecting the glances the others were giving him. They dug too deep, those wide and sympathetic eyes. He didn't need that right now; couldn't handle that right now.

"This is my home," Hex said. "I'm a child of Lacuna. This island belongs to the Night Terrors."

The Marrow Cabal grunted and groaned as branches and bushes tore at their cloaks and gouged their flesh.

"It'll be easier to explain later, but I was born here." She worked her way to the front of the group and veered them past a gurgling ravine. "The Night Terrors have been running experiments. They're not a fertile people anymore. They've been trying to fix that for Holy Child knows how long." She slipped on a patch of wet leaves but quickly caught herself.

Hex was talking so freely, the Skeleton assumed she'd filled the others in on her history. "You're one of the experiments?"

"Yeah," she huffed.

Lacuna wasn't far now. Another thirty seconds, at best.

"They mate humans with their kind. Those that come out like them, they take to their villages. Those that come out Corrupted like me, they convert to their cause."

"You're a Night Terror?" The Skeleton didn't want to sound judgmental—after all, who was he to judge anyone?—but he did.

"In a way," she said. They stopped at the outskirts of Lacuna. Hex made a motion. The Marrow Cabal fanned out, flanking the center from all sides.

Catching her breath, she added, "Don't have a mask. At least, not one you can see."

"It don't matter," the Skeleton said. He touched his cloak to make sure the Black Hour's heart hadn't fallen out. "Why'd you come back here? You said in your message you finally figured out how to get back? Did you forget or something?"

"Sort of."

She reared up and took off. The Marrow Cabal had searched enough of Lacuna and were moving towards a large tree that sat off to the side of the village. Its front had been carved out, and a tunnel ran through it, and then down into the island itself.

"It took me a long time to tell them, Atticus. But you... you've seen some shit, so I'm not going to sugarcoat it. There was something living here. I don't know how they made me forget about it, but all of us, all the children born here, we are telepaths in some way. We share thoughts, and that's how we stay connected to the Night Terrors, to receive orders."

They ran across the village center and regrouped with the Marrow Cabal at the passage that ran underneath the tree.

"The thing living here, they call it the Blue Worm. I remembered seeing it when I was a little girl, and then here and there, off and on. I put it together over the last year, from fragments of my family. And Mara dropped a few hints, too. She runs this place, you know?"

"They went down here," Warren interrupted. "We'll go on ahead." He led the charge down the passage, into the bowels of Lacuna, leaving the Skeleton and Hex topside.

"The Night Terrors can't reproduce right," she said.

She was shivering so hard she looked like she was going to pull a muscle. The Skeleton thought about comforting her, but couldn't see how something that looked like him could be of much comfort to anyone.

"They woke up this creature, this Blue Worm, years and years ago. It taught them how to have children. I think it put a little bit of itself in each of us, the offspring. That's why we're telepaths, why we're all connected.

"I thought I'd come here and get its help. Get its help to save your family and save the Heartland. Took forever, Atticus, to get in. The Widening Gyre is a real son of a bitch. Then we saw Mara and two other Night Terrors, a woman and a girl, while we were out to sea. And after they got on the island, everything went to shit. The Gyre calmed its ass down, but the Blue Worm was gone. We went into its chamber and it wasn't there. Whatever they did, it's gone. Have you heard of the Red Worm?"

The Skeleton shook his head, even though it did sound familiar.

Hex said she wasn't surprised and headed into the tunnel, down the ramp that followed after. It was almost impossible to see where they were going or who was waiting at the bottom besides the Marrow Cabal. But it was nice to get out of the rain.

"Geharra's dead," Hex said. "We think Penance killed everyone there. I heard talk of a Crossbreed."

The Skeleton stopped and fell against the side of the passage. "What is it?"

He shook his head. "Go on."

Eying him curiously, she continued. "Penance went into the city, took it over. They used a Crossbreed, an ancient plant, to brainwash them, and then they killed them. All of them. Thousands." She caught her breath. The sounds of the storm outside thudded down the passage. "It was a sacrifice. They summoned something called the Red Worm with all the dead."

"Any relation to the Blue Worm?" the Skeleton asked. He was trying to focus on what Hex was saying, but all he could think of were King Edgar's threats in Ghostgrave's torture chamber.

"Hex," he said, before she could answer. "When I was being tortured, King Edgar brought someone in named Alexander Blodworth from Penance. He promised... he said... because he knew Geharra was running the rebellion, he promised Blodworth could take a Crossbreed to Geharra to... to 'change their minds.'"

"Atticus," Hex said breathily. "Holy shit, Atticus. That's... that's huge."

"Wait, no, wait. Can't be right, though. Blodworth said it would take years to pull it off. It's not possible. It took me awhile to get to the Nameless Forest, but not long enough for them to pull something like that off."

Hex cleared her throat and mumbled, "Atticus. Atticus, you were gone a long time."

"No." He crossed his arms, shook his head. "What do you mean?"

"The last message you sent me, outside the Nameless Forest, that was a year and a half ago." Softly, Hex took his hand and rubbed it, the way she did in Cathedra, that night when he bared his soul to her. "You were gone so long, we thought you'd finally died. We came here to get your family out of the Membrane, anyways. It seemed the right thing to do."

The Skeleton couldn't stop shaking his head. "A year and a half? I was only in the Forest for a few days at—"

"The Night Terrors who did this to the Blue Worm are getting away," Hex said. "They're down there, in the dockyard. The others already sailed out of here. We need to stop them, Atticus."

Hand in hand, the Skeleton and Hex hurried down the rest of the ramp, until it went wide and curved around and into the dockyard she'd mentioned moments before. The dockyard wrapped around the cove, and had been built into the exposed rock. The storm hadn't been kind to it, though. Most of the boards and walkways were torn off and were now resigned to the piles of driftwood congesting the ocean below. The Marrow Cabal were meandering around the edge of the area, rifling through some of the supplies that had been left behind.

A year and a half? The Skeleton let Hex lead him to the others. A fucking year and a half? How long had he been staring into that god damn heart? A year and a half? Were Clementine and Will even still…? No, they were. They were. They understood these things took time.

"Oh fuck," he said, dropping Hex's hand. He dug his fingers into his skull. "I don't even know what the fuck these Worm things are, but are they my fault? Did I make those happen by helping you?"

Hex shook her head. "No, Atticus."

Gary noticed his breakdown and came over to comfort him. "Hey, man," he said. He pulled the Skeleton's hands away and looked him in his glassy, bloodshot eyes. "We're going to get them back. As soon as we get off this island. If anyone knows about guilt, it's me. It's not worth it. Don't worry about that, right—"

"A year and a half!" the Skeleton screamed. "Look at me!" He showed off his bones the best he could. "This happened to me up here! What do you think they've had to go through down there?"

James chimed in, saying, "Gary's right."

Elizabeth and even Miranda nodded in agreement.

"My eyes aren't what they used to be," Mr. Haemo said, ignoring the Skeleton's outburst. "But our ladies haven't gotten far." He pointed to where the dockyard opened to the vast ocean beyond. And he was right: On the edge of darkness, a small boat floated, an emerald orb of light at its bow.

The Marrow Cabal converged at the furthest point of the dock they could. The Skeleton hung back, alone, the Black Hour's heart beating as fast as his would've been if he still had one.

A year and a half? I led a rebellion and... how could they kill a whole city? The tempest up top blew the last of its rain into the cove. *Red Worm? Blue Worm? What the fuck happened to the world? Oh god, did I take too long?*

"Want me to chase after them?" Mr. Haemo asked from the back of the Cabal. He started shaking his shoulders, as though to let loose his wings. "As long as the storm steers clear—"

"You can still save us," the Skeleton said, speaking on Clementine's behalf.

The rest of the Marrow Cabal were watching him now, watching him speak to himself, like the schizophrenic skeleton he'd slowly become.

"We're okay, for now, but you have to hurry, Dad," Will pleaded.

"I will," the Skeleton said. His hand drifted towards the Black Hour's heart. "I swear to god I will save you. Just give me a few more..."

The emerald orb from the bow of the Night Terrors' ship arced through the sky. At its highest point, it exploded like a firework, bathing the dockyard in nightmarish green light.

As the Marrow Cabal lowered their hoods, probably to let their escapees see who exactly they were fucking with, the Skeleton pushed his way to the front of the group.

"You want them?" the Skeleton practically spat the words into Hex's face. He needed something to fix, something to destroy.

He limped gracelessly to the edge of the dock, his legs suddenly remembering the snake bites they once bore, and threw back his hood. As the emerald gems of light cascaded across the cove, he raised his hand high and started to wave.

"I'll get them for you." His other hand went to the Black Hour's heart inside the cloak. "I'll get them for you good."

Black ice. Darkness. Dunes of death in a desert dream. Chitin taste. Old World sewers coughing up infants, rats in their eyes. Crystal shards. Crystal spires. Crucified orphans. Clementine in bed. James in the graveyard. Carpenter Plantation. Sky-

scrapers looming high. **Winter in Gallows.**

They were trying to get his attention, but they weren't going to have it. His mind was swamped with images, from the past and never. Like an architect, he built his tribute to insanity, cobbling the disparate objects together in his mind. Skyscrapers here, snow there. He imagined the ocean a sheet of frozen ice to grind their boat to a halt. Shadowy figures kept cropping up in the corners of his creation, so he let them flock beneath the ice, for good measure. They wouldn't get away from this, he thought. *Blue Worm? No, Hex, the heart is enough. Let's just kill these Terrors and be done with it.*

"Atticus?"

"Is he okay?"

"Mr. Haemo's headed back. He doesn't have them."

"Is he okay? It's been like an hour."

The Skeleton pulled his hand away from the Black Hour's heart and, with it, willed what he'd conjured into reality. The Marrow Cabal gasped as the ocean froze over in front of them, long fields of snow-dusted ice growing across the water at an impossible rate. Further in the distance, red lights began to wink below the frigid landscape.

The Skeleton started to laugh, started to laugh until he cried. With every passing second, the laughter rose in pitch, until it warped into something like an infant's wail. It was high, piercing, loud enough to be heard clear across the sea. He laughed endlessly, because he had no lungs to stop him. When the skyscrapers started winding through the ice, blowing massive chunks of it across the sky, he stopped. He stopped and looked out upon the sea, upon the great, frozen, dead city of his imaginings. He looked upon it, proud as any father would be, and said that it was good.

CHAPTER XXX

Warren's hands wrapped around the Skeleton's neck and flung him into the dock. "Atticus, stop!"

He tried to get up, but Miranda and Elizabeth were quick to hold him down. The heart had come over him. He expected the temptation, but hadn't expected to fold to it so quickly. After he opened the portal to the Membrane and brought Clementine and Will through, maybe he'd toss it to the Abyss. Let nothingness have its way with it.

"Cut it out, yeah?" Elizabeth said, giving him a slap across the skull.

Miranda shook her head at him and mumbled something under her breath.

"I'm sorry," the Skeleton said. With his hand off the heart and his mind no longer holding the images, his temporary Black Hour was over. Nothing broke, nothing collapsed. It all just ceased to be.

Hex leaned over him, planting her foot on his ribcage. "Appreciate the help, Atticus."

"I'm sorry," he said. He felt like laughing again, but thought better of it.

"It's great to see your new fancy tool works and all." She outstretched her hand, and he took it. "But we're leaving the old fashioned way. By boat."

He nodded and set aside ravenous considerations. The new recruits were terrified, but Hex did a good job calming them down.

Mr. Haemo flew in from the ocean and landed on a pole, pleased as punch with the Skeleton's work.

Warren, Elizabeth, and Miranda joined together and moved in a pack, as they always did, towards the back of the dockyard, to talk badly about him.

But James and Gary, they didn't budge. They didn't speak. They hardly even blinked. Instead, all they did was stand there at the edge of the dock and stare absently into the distant dark. The Skeleton felt bad about what he'd done, but he felt even worse about it when he saw their faces. They had a look about them, a look he'd known and mastered. It was an absent gaze, an absolute indifference to the events around them. They looked empty, because they were empty. Their thoughts, their feelings, they were many miles away, back in Gallows, both the place and its memory, with the Atticus they remembered and loved. This flayed thing that stood before them, it wasn't Atticus, not to them, at least. Not anymore.

They left Lacuna not long after by way of the three boats they'd brought there. The storm had beat them up bad, but they were sailable. It was always a risk going out into the Widening Gyre, especially at night, but Hex had been able to convince the others that, because of its unusual, prolonged calmness, it was a now or never sort of situation.

Like the loser picked last at recess, the Skeleton had found himself sitting in his boat alone, on the beach, while the others drew mental straws to decide who would be stuck with him. Unsurprisingly, he ended up with Hex, Gary, James, and Mr. Haemo. But now, as they rowed through the dead of night, he found the other boats crowding his, Warren, the Deadly Beauties, and the new recruits eager to hear what he had to say. They were like his farm outside Gallows: close enough to see if something went down, but far enough to get away, if need be.

He'd spent awhile listening to the waves lap against the boat. The rock of the boat and the sounds of the water calmed him considerably. He could still feel the Black Hour's heart calling to him, but the weight of his guilt over what he'd done kept his hands firmly planted on the seat.

"After Nyxis," he volunteered, "I was captured and tortured for weeks."

With everyone's attention on him, he told his story, starting from the back of Captain Yelena's wagon to the Dread Clock's island in the Nameless Forest, although he left out the bit about possibly free-ing the creatures who live there. No one interrupted. No one ques-tioned him. They just sat there silently, rowing mindlessly, all eyes focused on the spot in his cloak, waiting for the Black Hour's heart to make its big reveal.

"There's a cost to using it," he said. With the hand that wore Bon's glove, he reached into his pocket, and closed it around the heart. He waited for the images, but none came. It needed direct con-tact.

James twisted his mouth. "Atticus, I don't know if you should take it out."

"That's what she said," Gary said, grinning. He looked around, but no one was laughing. "Sorry. Old World joke."

The Skeleton ignored James and brought out the heart for all to see. Everyone leaned forward, transfixed. The boat tipped, their curi-osity almost capsizing them.

"I didn't realize how much time it took to use it. You said I was on the docks for almost an hour? Was only seconds for me."

He paused, noticing that the heart looked different than before. It appeared harder. Parts of it were crystallized. The gears weren't the same, either. They had undergone a metamorphosis of their own; the metal pieces appeared as though were decaying into some kind of bone-like material.

He quickly put it away and started to row quicker. Without a ves-sel, maybe its life was limited.

Mr. Haemo adjusted his human suit. "We got to find a way to get rid of it when you're done, you know that, don't you?"

"Plan to." The Skeleton cocked his head. "Surprised to hear you say that."

The mosquito in disguise shrugged. A bit of his wing broke through his flesh. "Don't feel comfortable around it. That thing is a myth for monsters, too. If you're using it, it's because it's letting you. That thing has history hidden inside it. Better off letting it terrorize people than letting people use it. It's a problem for everyone. Get rid of it."

Warren said from the boat beside them, "If the bug doesn't like it, then it's got to go."

James went forward. "Atticus, you've been through hell. Literally. Are you... how are you...?"

"How are you not absolutely insane?" Hex asked, matter-of-factly. "You know you're not right, right? In the jungle, you were like yourself. On the docks, you were something else."

"I know that," the Skeleton said. "I recognize that. But that's something, right?"

"You do know you're only bones, yeah?" Elizabeth asked.

The Skeleton snapped his skull to the Deadly Beauty. An irrational anger told him to drown her in the sea. "I know," he said, focusing on the waves to cool off. "But I'm still me." Changing the subject, he said, "Hex, you going to introduce me to the new recruits?"

"Hmm?" Hex's sleepy eyes shot open. "Yeah, sorry." She pointed to the boat that held the newcomers, the three women and two men. "You all have tongues. Use them."

The skinniest man cleared his throat and said, "Sean. My name's Sean, sir."

The Skeleton waved off the formality like a gnat.

"Allister," the second man said. He was bald, badly sunburned, and piggish. "It's an honor."

"Likewise."

"Maya," one of the women offered. She looked to be in her fifties, and had about as many scars on her face as Elizabeth did tattoos on her body.

The woman beside her, a mousey brunette with shark eyes, said quietly, "Kristin. We won't tell anyone about any of this."

The Skeleton shrugged. They were addressing him like a leader, a role he'd tried and failed miserably at. "If Hex thought you would, you'd be in the ocean talking to the fish, not me."

Hex nodded and snapped her fingers. "That one," she said, pointing to the last woman, a leaner version of Warren. "That one is Bruna. Say hi, Bruna."

Bruna, whose cloak was now obviously too small for her frame, waved at the Skeleton.

"Bruna is a holy roller," Hex said. "Thinks you're a demon. I know you don't need to sleep, but in case you do, watch out for her. She's got daggers in her eyes for you. Mr. Haemo was one thing, but you're just too much."

Bruna's mouth dropped open, her face going bright red. "You don't—"

"Shut up, Bruna," Miranda interrupted, rubbing her nerve-dead arm. "You're in the middle of the ocean with a living skeleton, a giant mosquito, and a handful of murderers. Just what do you expect to accomplish?"

Hex laughed and winked at Miranda. "These five were all we had on hand when we left Nachtla. Didn't think the six of us would be enough for Lacuna. Took a chance. Guess it paid off."

A large wave rolled past, tossing a bit of itself into the Skeleton's boat. He turned. They were getting close to the mainland, though it seemed they'd sailed far off-course from the dock in the cove outside Nachtla. Turning back around, he asked, "What's happened to the world, Hex?"

She laughed, her eyes flashing blue. "Where to start? Geharra's rebellion died out. People just stopped fighting."

"Do they know I was captured?"

"Not widely. King Edgar didn't even announce it. People just didn't care anymore. Geharra stopped supporting the rebellion once he removed a good seventy-five percent of his soldiers from the Heartland. The Night Terrors, my people—it's a relief to be able to admit it—were fine with that. It's all they wanted."

"What about the bodies? The vermillion veins?"

"Still out there. Still being planted, but not as many, or at least, not as out in the open. I kept the Marrow Cabal going after the rebellion died out because I actually give a damn about doing the right thing. There were still some who wanted to fight. So we moved out to Nachtla, far away from Eldrus, and started building up again. We did that awhile. Numbers fluctuated. I'd say we have about one hundred who're loyal. They think you're out there, fighting, so don't ruin it if you meet them."

The Skeleton's eyes drifted to the sky, to greet the moon, which, in some ways, reflected himself better than any mirror could. It was worn-down, roughed-up, pale and cold; too distant to reach, but impossible to ignore.

"There's more like you. Children of Lacuna. And Worms? How did they kill a whole city?"

"I don't know what the fuck the Worms are." Hex's eyes flashed blue again and, for a moment, she disappeared inside herself. Then, she said, "From what you told me, it sounds like Eldrus put Penance up to invading Geharra. I don't know if King Edgar wanted them to kill everyone, but they did. And one of our villages, Alluvia, too.

Whatever they did, it summoned that thing, that Red Worm. Last I heard, it was moving across the continent, but that's it. I've been cut off from news awhile now. Stopped getting so many transmissions, too. And ever since Mara and the others did what they did to the Blue Worm, I haven't heard anything. Not sure I can even send or receive anymore.

"Used to be I'd hear things all the time. Thought I was crazy. I'd get glimpses when I was a little girl. Even saw the Blue Worm a few times. Didn't know what it was then. Just figured maybe it was god. But not anymore. Around the time Penance did what they did in Geharra, all the other Children of Lacuna went dark. Like we were cut off from each other."

"Sounds suspicious," the Skeleton said.

"Yeah." Hex's voice sounded hoarse. Not one for talking, all this talking was taking its toll. "Thing is, it's not something you're aware of, being a telepath. They have to teach you, unlock it. People send and receive without really realizing it until someone like Mara helps them hone the ability. Like I said, I'd hear or see things all the time. I've met a few—Ichor's one of them—and they did, too. Guessing some Children of Lacuna still don't know what they're capable of all these years later, because no one told them. Didn't stop them though from using it all the same. With all them pieces, that's how I remembered Lacuna and the Blue Worm. Now we just have to figure out what the hell it was, what the hell this Red Worm is, and if there's more coming our way."

The Skeleton noticed his hand drifting to the Black Hour's heart. He stopped it and played it off, although everyone noticed, anyway. "You think King Edgar wanted this to happen? For these creatures to wake up?"

"They sure sound like something the Nameless Forest could spit out." She sighed and shook her head. "Hell, but if Mara and two scrawny girls can take one down, maybe we don't have so much to worry about."

After many starts and stops and somehow going in circles, the Marrow Cabal finally made landfall. Physically and mentally exhausted—the latter more so than the former for the Skeleton—they dragged themselves up the coast and found shelter in a shallow cave. The Skeleton offered to keep watch. Because only Mr. Haemo could match his stamina at this moment, they let him do just that.

He spent most of the night patrolling outside the cave, talking to himself in his head. He told Clementine and Will how much he loved them, and they talked about what they wanted to do when he finally brought them out of the Membrane. At some point, far down the coast from where they camped, he noticed a small spot in the dark, a fire on the beach. It was back the way Nachtla would've been. If he had to guess, it was probably the same Night Terrors who had put an end to the Blue Worm. He considered waking Hex, but with the Black Hour's heart in its seemingly decayed state, he decided against any further delays.

They worked their way towards Gallows in the weeks that followed. The Skeleton, Gary, and Mr. Haemo had spoken at length about the best way to use the heart, open a portal to the Membrane, and get his family out.

"We'll treat it like a blood well," the mosquito said, agitatedly.

The Skeleton was making everyone repeat the plan on an hourly basis.

"You didn't see the Membrane when you were tinkering with it? Might be because time runs different down there. I don't know. We'll go back to your house, gather up anything personal, if the locals haven't already hocked your stuff. We'll treat it like a blood well. Do everything we can to make your visions as pointed as possible." Mr. Haemo turned and tore off his skin suit, growing several inches and several times more sinister. "And then you get rid of it."

The Skeleton started pushing them hard on the last day as they entered the swampy outskirts of the town. They were about eight hours out from Mr. Haemo's haunt, though the bug didn't sound too homesick when Gary brought that fact up.

"We need to rest," Hex said, forcing them to stop on the only dry patch of land for the last few miles. "You've waited this long, Atticus. We've stuck by you this whole time. You telling me you can't let us get some sleep before your big day?"

The Skeleton roamed around the dry thicket, like a feral beast looking for something to maim. "We're so close," he shouted, his words echoing through the swamp, waking up half the place.

"Then go!" She threw her hands up. "Take bug boy here. You don't need us to do what you have to do. We're just people. We'll get in your way."

As the rest of the Marrow Cabal settled in for the night, the Skeleton decided to stay. Hex wasn't usually like this, but he understood why she was, because she was trying to prove a point. She recognized his impatience, probably remembered his bloodlusts. Calling him out, seeing how he responded, it was all a litmus test, to see how much human was left in that scourged soul of his.

At daybreak, before the others had woken, Hex started screaming in her sleep. Thinking a snake or a gator had got to her, the Skeleton rushed over to save her.

"What's wrong?" he asked. Her eyes were still shut, but she was screaming. A nightmare? He touched her face as he searched what he could of her for wounds. "Hex, what's wrong?"

Slowly, her eyes opened. The Skeleton gasped as he saw them. They were a radiant blue, surely bright enough to blind her. But as the rest of the Marrow Cabal crowded in to see what had gone wrong, her eyes started to dim. She stopped screaming and started breathing again.

James knelt down beside her, one of Mr. Haemo's children sucking on his forehead. "Are you okay? What happened?"

Hex took a moment to respond. She slapped her lips, curled her hands until Miranda filled them with a flagon of water. After she gulped down most of it, she poured the rest over her face, took a deep breath, and said, "Sorry. I don't know what happened."

"Your eyes," the Skeleton said.

She nodded. She wiped the sweat off her chest and started nervously twisting her hair. "I saw something. But I think it was just a nightmare. Holy Child, it felt awful."

"What'd you see?" Mr. Haemo asked, not one to miss out on a juicy bit of despair.

Using James' shoulder for support, she came to her feet. Squinting, the morning sun in her glazed-over eyes, she said, "A gray place. Mountains and pits. And then there was this... these things. One was this pale woman barely wearing anything at all. And the other was some kind of... horror. It was at the woman's side. It looked half-human, half-bird, like a raven. The woman was petting it." She took another deep breath, exhaled hard. "And there was this necklace around the raven's neck. Blue gem. Kept shining in my eyes. Couldn't stand to look at it."

"Was it a vision?" the Skeleton asked.

Hex shook her head. "I don't know what to make of it."

CHAPTER XXXI

By the time they got to Gallows, the Red Worm was already there. Like a covetous centipede, it had curled itself around the town. From the ten thousand faces that covered its bulbous head, blood poured out in thick, unending streams, reducing most of Gallows to a muddy pit of deepening gore. As people tried to escape, the creature drummed the ground with its thousands of severed human legs. The vibrations knocked people off their feet, sending them face-first into the mire of filth that had become their home. And while they lay there, struggling to be free of the blood-soaked and sucking earth, the Red Worm would close in with its thousands of writhing, severed arms and bring them into its crimson embrace.

Standing on the sun-soaked outskirts, the sick run-off pouring past their feet, the Marrow Cabal couldn't help but simply watch the scene in awe.

"Mother Abbess," Bruna whispered. She made the sign of Penance and started to pray.

"Back into the swamp," Hex said. "It hasn't seen us."

James rubbed the nubs on his hand where his fingers had been. "Is that it?"

Already retreating, Gary said, "Has to be. Come on, let's go."

The Skeleton shook his head. "No."

"What?" Elizabeth punched his arm. "You're kidding, yeah?"

"He's insane, don't bother," Miranda said.

"What are you thinking, Atticus?" Mr. Haemo muscled his way in between the Skeleton and Hex. Being back home, he had neglected to put on his skin suit. After all, he had appearances to maintain.

"He's not thinking a god damn thing." Hex nodded at Warren. "We're leaving. If we're quick, we can get Clementine and Will out at the farm."

The Skeleton interrupted, saying, "What would be the point? Bring them back with that thing tearing through the town? Through the world? I will not bring them back to have them die again!"

"We can hide until it passes," Maya said. Her and Allister were already a few feet from the group, taking the initiative.

"No," the Skeleton repeated. "Hex, how much do you care about your cause?"

She puffed out her chest. "What you say?"

For a moment, he found himself channeling King Edgar as he proposed, "You want to make a difference? You want the Marrow Cabal to mean something? You want people to—"

The Red Worm let out a hiss. Lightning quick, it whipped its gore-encrusted trunk. Houses exploded across Gallows, sending massive amounts of debris and corpses into the air.

"You want people to follow you?" the Skeleton shouted over the destruction.

"What're you saying? Kill it?" Hex laughed. She looked at Sean and Kristin, who'd gone pale at the suggestion. "You're insane. I see what you're saying, but we have nothing."

"We have the heart." The Skeleton took out the Black Hour's throbbing heart and held it in his gloved hand. "We have everything."

Screams. Loud, strained, almost-familiar screams lurched into the outskirts. They weren't screams of terror, of horror. They were primal pleas, deep, hard, and grating. The Red Worm was reducing the Skeleton's town to ruin, and his neighbors' minds to nothing.

It was hard to hold court so close to a massacre, so the Skeleton put away the heart and simply said, "I'm going."

Warren grabbed his cloak. "Gravedigger, what's wrong with you, man? Do you even want your family back?"

At this, he spun around. He planted his fingers in the big man's chest and dug till they started to get wet. "I can't bring them back to die again. I can't sit here and watch these people, even I didn't much care for them, be killed. I've known most of them all my life." He let go and pushed Warren back.

Looking at Hex, he then said, "Who's to say Eldrus or Penance or whoever is controlling this thing isn't trying to destroy Gallows to make another one? Hell of a way to take over a continent. You think anyone's going to fight back with two or three of these things running around?"

The Red Worm grabbed a handful of children from the streets and shoved them into itself. At first, they didn't fit, so the gore-beast crushed them until they would.

"But they will fight back, with us, if we've shown we can stop the Worms."

"We?" Hex snarled. "You actually give a damn now? Last time I checked, this has only been about your family."

"I'm not bringing them from one hell just to throw them into another," he said. "I'm sure there's something in the Black Hour to kill it."

James pleaded, "Atticus, you can't. That takes too much time."

"No, not if I'm not searching for something. I'll just grab what it shows me."

"What do you want us for, then?" Miranda, gripping her bad arm, asked. "Bait?"

"To get people out. To do what the Marrow Cabal is supposed to do."

Elizabeth shook her head. "You were gone for a year and a half, yeah? And deader than dead. You don't get to lead anyone anymore."

Hex grumbled. She fingered the hilt of her sword. "The heart won't show you the Membrane, will it? I heard you say that to Mr. Haemo."

The Skeleton went stiff. He exchanged glances with the giant mosquito, who realized, along with Hex, his intentions all along.

Mr. Haemo snapped his fingers. A million of his mosquito minions shivered into existence and sat like a suffocating cloud above them. "You want to turn Gallows into a blood well."

"I want to save it—"

"With this much of the sweet stuff, I can drop you at your family's feet."

"We kill it, I get Clementine and Will back, and you get your following," the Skeleton said.

"It's the right thing to do," Mr. Haemo appealed to Hex.

"Shut the fuck up, bug," she said.

Mr. Haemo stepped up to her, loomed over her, the top of his proboscis touching her scalp. "Using the Black Hour seemed like a good idea at first, but not anymore. He uses that heart to tear into a place like the Membrane... a lot of bad things could come spilling out. Last thing we need is another me."

Gary was grinding his teeth so hard one shattered in his mouth. "You don't give a shit. You just want the blood."

Mr. Haemo laughed. "We all just want something, ghoul. Let's just be honest with ourselves and go ahead and get it."

There wasn't much to the plan, but they tried to carry it out all the same. Miranda and James, on account of being paralyzed and maimed, took off for the Skeleton's farm, to gather up any personal belongings.

Warren and the new recruits went southward, where most of the damage was done, to rescue anyone still trapped in the wreckage.

Mr. Haemo, with his children in tow, plunged into the thick of the slaughter, to begin the ritual.

Those that were left—Gary, Hex, and Elizabeth—were those that stood beside the Skeleton now, beside Poe's bar, staring up at the grandeur of the walking grave that overshadowed them.

"We shouldn't be this close," Elizabeth said. She held onto Hex as waves of blood crashed against their knees.

"I have to see it to know it," the Skeleton said. And see it, he did.

The Red Worm towered over them, its upper half reared up, stretching a good sixty feet into the air. With its head still turned towards the center of town, where it continued to vomit torrents of gore, the Skeleton had a chance to glimpse its underbelly. Like the centipede it resembled, the Red Worm's body was divided into seams and segments. Each segment, fifteen, maybe twenty feet in width, was a hard shell of human sediment. In each division, reams of skin, piles of bones, and swathes of muscle formed the beast's crimson carapace. The paste that held it all together was a mix of pulverized entrails, coagulated blood, and a kind of eldritch glaze. In between each segment were the seams that connected them. They consisted of thousands of animal carcasses and their innards. But what somehow caught the Skeleton's eyes were the wet patches within the seams, where a second body, perhaps the Red Worm's true body, worked tirelessly to accommodate the monster's spastic movements. Everything had a weakness, and the Red Worm's was the body beyond the bodies.

Screams stole the Skeleton's attention away from the horror's anatomy. To his left, past Poe's bar, where Gallows opened to the town's center, people were wading through their new lake of blood; some to rescue stragglers, others to escape. They carried weapons, but only because it seemed the right thing to do, not because they thought they might get the chance to use them. The Red Worm could've killed those trudging beneath it, but the thing seemed to be enjoying itself. Instead, it stirred the steaming pool with the hundreds of arms that hung off it. By doing so, the Worm began to create a tidal pool that even the strongest struggled to escape.

Quickly, the Skeleton moved onto Poe's porch. He looked through the doors for the fat man, didn't find him, and then said to Hex and Elizabeth, "I know what to do."

Hex and Elizabeth moved onto the porch, to temporarily get out of the blood pool's pull.

"We don't have hours to wait for you," Hex said. Her eyes hadn't stopped glowing bright blue since this all began. Whatever had halted her telepathy before, it was gone now. "We have minutes, at best."

"That's all I need." The Skeleton reached into his cloak, closed his hand around the Black Hour's heart. "Stay here, by me. If the Red Worm sees us, hit me as hard as you can."

Elizabeth gave a weak nod. She was listening, but only barely. The Skeleton was one thing, but the Red Worm was another matter entirely. For once, since Ghostgrave, he'd be one-upped by something worse looking than him.

"Do it," Hex said. She took out her sword. "If we can't snap you out of it, you're on your own."

He took out the heart with his gloved hand and said, "That's fine. Worm can't do no worse to me than what I've been through already."

As he transferred the Black Hour's heart to his bare hand, he noticed a young girl creeping alongside the edge of Poe's bar. He knew everyone in Gallows, but he didn't know her. She was a teenager by his guess, dark skin, with a mess of hair that was having a hard time hiding the scar that ran from neck to ear. Strange, talon-like daggers were fastened to her side, and in her hand, she carried an ax that looked better suited for battle than chopping wood. After a moment, she took her eyes off the Worm and noticed him, too. She went pale.

Her mouth dropped open, as though she recognized him. Carefully, with her Corruption running like mascara down her arm, she backed away, and took off.

The Skeleton didn't have time to make sense of the situation, so he let the Black Hour's heart touch his bones and went to work.

Blood moon rising over a howling fjord. Horned doctors dissecting a stillborn. Canopies billowing. Sewer pipes clogged with wiring. Family of five having a dinner that could only feed two. The poor standing outside a bank, checks in hand, waiting for the guard to let them in. Rain clouds.

"Atticus, hurry it up," Hex said, smacking his skull.

"How long?" he blabbered.

"Forty seconds."

He had to focus. He needed something large. The Black Hour wouldn't give him what he wanted, he realized that now. He'd lost a year and a half because he thought it would. He had to make do with the sights it showed him, and go where they would let him.

"I need the skyscrapers again," he said. He clutched the heart. "I need what's inside them. Can't destroy Gallows."

Kids in a coffee shop. Snakes in tangled sheets on a motel room floor. Strobe lights blinking across bleeding tattoos. Sanitarium blues. City on the horizon, brake lights in its smog.

That's what I need. The Skeleton focused harder on the recollection, pushing further into it.

Pedestrians on the crosswalk. Children skipping intestinal rope. Summer camp social by the waterfront. Yellow-hatted workers digging up the road.

Hex shook him again, but he ignored her. The ground rumbled—the Red Worm had to be moving—but he ignored that, too. He focused on the worker in the image, the truck they kept going back to.

Construction yard. Barbed wire fences. Junkies hocking copper for coin. Black dogs having the run of the place. Tools. Windstorm. Tools.

"Atticus," Elizabeth shouted.

Trucks idling in a garage. Foreman screwing around with his secretary. Supply depot. Protests in the streets. Supply depot. A Molotov celebration at a daycare. Supply depot.

Hex shook him by his shoulders. "Atticus, it's looking right at us!"

Supply depot. Construction workers. Yellow hats, blood in-

side. Wrenches. Nails. A sign that says rebar. Steel bars, as long as a building—a whole mess of them.

Hex gouged out his eye with her thumb.

The Skeleton broke out of the trance. His eye reformed in a matter of seconds, to confirm what the other saw: the Red Worm looking down on them, drooling its fetid body water on the roof of Poe's Bar.

"Oh god," Elizabeth said, repeating herself over and over.

"Atticus." Hex held onto him from behind, as though he were a shield. "You have to do—"

The Skeleton closed his eyes, grasped the image of the piles of rebar he held there, and willed them into being.

Like javelins from hell, thirty-five, sixty-foot steel bars shot out of the earth. One-by-one, they tore through the Red Worm's body, puncturing each segment and seam. Gallons of gore and disease-infested filth fell from its ruptured carapace, raising the blood level of Gallows' lake. Once the steel bars broke through the creature's back, rather than blow through completely, they stopped instead. By staying fixed inside the earth, they kept the Red Worm impaled there, to bleed it out and kill it for good.

"Holy shit," Hex said.

The Red Worm's patchwork of appendages worked at the rebar, but they wouldn't budge. Its ten thousand faces wailed in agony. It writhed in deafening desperation.

Elizabeth started to cry. "You did it."

Blood rained down upon Gallows in choking sheets. The Red Worm gripped each bar, tried to hoist itself off them, but couldn't. Great, steaming mounds of meat clumped together in the center of Gallows, sucking in those people who were caught in their wake.

"You think that's enough?" The Skeleton held onto the heart, to keep the rebar in place.

Hex nodded and came out from behind him. A geyser of blood squirted out of the Red Worm's side and blasted the front of Poe's bar. The Skeleton, Hex, and Elizabeth flew backward, crashing into the building.

"It's dying," Hex said, spitting up the blood that had gotten in her mouth. "Just give it a minute."

So they did. They sat where they were, crumpled on Poe's porch, watching as the Red Worm made matters worse for itself. Like an animal caught in a trap, it twisted and turned, doing more harm than good. Whole bodies began to fall from its segments now. With them, a dam of soggy, pale corpses formed in the lake of blood, stemming the rising tide.

From where the Skeleton had spotted the strange, young girl, he heard James say, "Was that you?"

He turned. James and Miranda were standing beside the porch, arms full of things from his farmhouse. The blood was up to their waists now, and was lapping at the edge of the porch itself. Holding their findings to their chests, they had brought pictures, letters, toys, clothes, blankets, and surely other things crammed in between the aforementioned.

"I can't believe…." Miranda smiled and dumped her haul onto the porch of Poe's. "You did it."

The Skeleton wished he could smile back at her, but instead he gave her that skeletal grin and went to help her and James onto the porch.

James dropped what he carried as well. And as the Skeleton offered him a hand, he said, "Wait," and told him there was something else.

"This is enough," the Skeleton said, the Red Worm in his periphery, slowing down.

James shook his head. He crouched, chin to the blood, and reared up, producing the Skeleton's scythe from out of the crimson water. Handing the weapon to him, James said, "Saw it. Thought you should have it."

The Skeleton took the scythe, and then he took James up onto the porch. They stared at each other a moment, each seeing past what the other had become. He had wanted to kill the Red Worm, in part, to prove he still had some humanity inside him. And as James' gaze went soft and looked at the Skeleton the way he used to years ago, when he was young and proud to be a part of his family, he knew he had succeeded.

"Thanks, James," the Skeleton said. He rested the scythe against the front of Poe's bar. "But I think we all need a break from killing."

At that moment, the Red Worm bore down on the steel bars and ripped itself apart. Massive chunks of the gore-beast flew through the air in opposite directions, spinning wildly. They crashed into buildings, landed like boulders in the lake. Huge waves of red built across

Gallows, before breaking on the homes in their way, or the outskirts further off.

The Skeleton finally put the Black Hour's heart back into his cloak. As he did so, the thirty-five pieces of rebar returned to the nightmare they'd been called from. Pieces of the Red Worm still attached to them fell as the steel bars disappeared, because it seemed not even the Black Hour wanted anything to do with the creature.

Hex stumbled across the porch. She started to say something like, "It's dead," but stopped herself, because the Red Worm wasn't.

It wasn't dead at all.

About a stone's throw away, six large, bear-sized pieces of the Red Worm rose out of the blood, until they were floating in it. Rows of teeth, human and animal alike, comprised the entirety of the vestiges' fronts, making most of the gory, gem-hard hunks of meat nothing more than mouths. With their tens of arms and dangling legs, they lifted themselves up, until they were standing on the blood itself. All six of them, fixed on the Skeleton and his friends beside him, swarmed.

"Find Mr. Haemo!" the Skeleton shouted. He grabbed the scythe and started down the porch steps to greet the abominations. "All of you."

Hex and Elizabeth didn't need to be told twice. With James and Miranda, they gathered up all the personal belongings and dropped off the side of Poe's, disappearing around the back.

The Skeleton dropped into the lake, the blood going up to his waist. The abominations were bolting towards him, killing any survivors that weren't quick enough to get out of their way. He wanted to use the heart, but he didn't have time. They'd be tearing him apart before he could even process the first image.

"Atticus! What the hell you doing?"

The Skeleton's gaze shot across Gallows, where he spotted Gary, Warren, and the new recruits emerging from in between several destroyed houses. Bruna was limping, and Allister had a little girl on his shoulders whose hair was half torn out. Maya, Kristin, and Sean were lagging behind. They looked so absolutely worn-down by their surroundings it seemed they were trying to go slow enough to be forgotten by the Cabal.

He waved them off, said "Gary, turn around," and then knew he'd fucked up. Immediately, the closest rotted vestige of the Red Worm identified them as his friends and changed its course. It barreled towards them, mouths within mouths chomping in anticipation.

"Nmw'gla fhtha xu… ufv'la ufv'la axtu."

The Skeleton spun around, looked clear across town where, atop the general store, Mr. Haemo stood, cloaked in human skin. His thousands of tiny children were going back and forth, between him and the lake, feeding him the blood they carried. He spotted James, Hex, Elizabeth, and Miranda, working their way up to the general store's roof, with the last of Atticus' family's most cherished items.

"Oh god!"

The Red Worm's vestige slammed into Gary and Warren's group. With a ceaseless hunger, it grabbed the little girl Allister was shouldering and crammed her down its toothy gullet. Bruna screamed, ran her sword through the vestige's side. It batted her back, breaking her nose as it did. Gary got brave and drove his sword in deep—

The Skeleton sank beneath the blood as the first of the five vestiges bashed into him. In his concern, he'd lost track of their whereabouts. Tens of hands held him down in the muck, to drown him. Because the beast didn't know better, he stopped flailing after a while to make it think it had.

The Skeleton, scythe in the hand, broke free and rose up out of the blood. He swung the scythe and slashed through the vestige's mouth. Its flabby, quivering jaw split apart and handfuls of teeth rolled out into the lake.

"Nmw'gla fhtha xu… ufv'la ufv'la axtu."

He drove the scythe's blade through the top of the vestige, until it went all the way in. He ripped outward, sloppily bisecting the lump of a monster. As death deflated it, the four other vestiges trampled over it and piled onto the Skeleton.

"Nmw'gla fhtha xu … ufv'la ufv'la axtu."

The Skeleton struggled to stay above the blood as the vestiges weighed him down. Several fleshy and boney hands clamped onto his face and pulled his head back until his neck broke. Momentarily paralyzed, he watched as the other two vestiges started disassembling him. With their rubbery appendages, the solidified pieces of gore tore out his bones and tossed them to the last vestige, who scarfed them down greedily.

"Nmw'gla fhtha xu… ufv'la ufv'la axtu."

The Skeleton died and descended into the Membrane. He fell, as he always fell, through the organic tunnel that, now that he was look-ing at it, bore some resemblance to the Red Worm itself. But as he realized this, he realized another thing as well: he could still hear Mr. Haemo chanting out the ritual.

It's working, he thought. His soul rebounded, started hauling him out of that limbo. *The ritual is taking hold.*

It wasn't a good thing for the Red Worm's vestige to have eaten him, because when he reformed, he reformed inside the creature. Like an oversized infant cramped in its womb, the Skeleton started kicking and clawing at the vestige's interior. He ripped through layers of fat and cartilage, stomped on the organs and bones it had no use for, but had assimilated all the same.

The vestige must've felt the attack. All of sudden, the Skeleton flew forward as the creature dunked itself into the lake and guzzled it. Heavy, coppery mouthfuls of blood flooded the vestige's chambers, but it wouldn't be enough to stop him. Laughing wildly, the Skeleton started biting and ripping at the creature's side. The vestige's flesh tore, its meaty exterior pulling apart, one sinewy stitch at a time. With not a hint of white left on his bones, the crimson Skeleton burst through the vestige's torso, killing it immediately.

"Nmw'gla fhtha xu… ufv'la ufv'la axtu."

Standing there in the vestige's carcass, he saw its three other brethren had fled. Two were gallivanting across the lake, dead-set to knock dead Mr. Haemo mid-ritual.

"Help them," James cried out from the roof where the rites were being completed.

The Skeleton looked back towards Warren, Gary, and the others. They weren't in the lake, but scrambling across the piles of pale car-casses that had dropped out of the Red Worm. The first vestige was wounded, yet still it limped speedily across the bulwark of bodies. The third of the four that had swarmed the Skeleton was in the lake, swiping at their legs, biting at their toes.

He grabbed his scythe out of the blood and ran as fast he could across the lake. His strides were huge, his hypothetical heart beating fast. People he'd known all his life floated past him on their broken backs, their faces fixed in disbelief. He saw Mary Beth here, Johnny and his boy Jimmy there; Katie, whom he'd crushed hard on before Clementine, and old man Carruthers, somehow looking younger than before. He even caught a glimpse of Poe, the fat pimp popped open like a pimple. It was good he died, the Skeleton thought, because he could only imagine what business opportunities the man would pursue in the wake of this hell.

"Fuck," Gary cried out, the vestige in the lake sinking a few claws into his thigh.

The Skeleton hurried faster. "Hold on," he said. "I'm almost there."

Gary yanked himself free of the vestige. Stumbling backward across the slippery corpses, he knocked Maya into the water.

"Maya!" Kristin went down on her knee, but as she extended her hand, the vestige took Maya by the arms and bit her in half.

The lake of blood started to churn. Smoke began to rise off the surface. Below the waters, a light grew from some otherworldly place.

"Nmw'gla fhtha xu... ufv'la ufv'la axtu."

The Skeleton looked over his shoulder and saw the other two vestiges climbing the general store.

"Holy Child," Gary screamed again.

The Skeleton snapped back to the scene atop the corpses. The vestige had Gary pinned, but the ghoul had plunged his sword through the beast's gut.

"Get off him," Warren bellowed. He, Allister, Sean, and Kristin attacked the vestige from all angles. They stabbed at it repeatedly, turning its skin into pulpy, paper Mache, but the beast would not relent. Every time Warren went in to drag Gary out from under it, it would snap forward, nearly taking off his arms.

Gary screamed, driving his legs into the vestige's stomach. He fixed his hands under the beast's mouth, to hold it back. But his arms were weak, rotted, so when the vestige threw its weight forward, the ghoul's arms gave.

After that, there was a moment where time seemed to slow, where it seemed as though the Skeleton could do something other than watch what was about to happen. It was a moment of hope, where the anti-villain had one last chance at heroism. Time was slowing, but the Skeleton wasn't; maybe it was the Black Hour doing its one good deed for the millennium.

I can save him, he thought, his best friend just a few feet away. Warren and the others continued to chop and mutilate the beast, but the Skeleton knew it wouldn't be enough.

Has to be me, he thought. *Us dead things have to stick together.*

He plodded forward. If not for the blood, he'd already be there, helping him up, laughing off the close encounter.

I just need more time. His best friend turned to look at him, the teeth of his undoing right above his head. *I just need—*

But time was not that kind, and would never be. In the next second that followed, the vestige bit down on Gary's head and tore it off, spine and all, from the ghoul's quivering body.

"No!" The Skeleton took two lunges, closed in on the corpse pile, and drove the scythe into the haunch of the vestige in the lake. The beast bucked and flung him backward. The scythe, lodged in its back, stayed there.

"Nmw'gla fhtha xu… ufv'la ufv'la axtu."

He's okay, he's okay. The Skeleton struggled to his feet. More smoke rolled in over the now bubbling lake of blood. *Gary will come back.*

He ran forward, the vestige distracted by Warren and the remaining recruits, grabbed the scythe again. Gritting his teeth, he drove it in deeper. The vestige wheeled, trying to grab the Skeleton as he corralled him away from the others.

Meanwhile, with blood-colored tears in his eyes, Warren ran his sword into Gary's killer's mouth, hilt-deep, until he was up to his shoulder in the vestige's maw. He pulled out, went again, pulled out, went again, until the thing reared back, a torrent of red spewing from its throat. As it toppled over, the vestige's arms shot out and ripped off Kristin's face. She screamed, and died about the same time it did.

He's coming back, the Skeleton told himself, feeling the recruit's gaze pierce him as Kristin lay there, the folds of her facial muscles glistening in the lake's new light.

"I'm not like you," the Skeleton said to himself, speaking on Gary's behalf. The vestige in the lake galloped across the blood in circles.

A crimson wave washed over the Skeleton. Warren dropped into the lake. He walked over to him, looking deader than the Skeleton himself. Two hands on the hilt of his sword, he raised it up. With all the hate and hurt wreaking havoc inside him, he rammed the sword through the vestige's head, killing it instantly.

The Skeleton worked the scythe out of the Red Worm's vestige, to take back what was his. He said to himself in Gary's ghoulish droll, "How many times do I have to tell you?"

"Atticus," Warren said, breathless, nearly lifeless.

"I'm not dead." The Skeleton made eye contact with the big man, but he wasn't really seeing him. "I'm just a ghoul. It's different."

Warren sighed. He threw his arms around the Skeleton. His bloody bones stuck to his sweating flesh. "I'm so sorry."

"I can't come back like you," the Skeleton rambled on. "I'm with my wife and daughters now. I'm doing just fine."

Warren, bawling into the Skeleton's cloak, said, "He was a great guy. I don't know... what to say. I've lost too many... people doing this."

The Skeleton snapped out of it. Holding the back of Warren's head, he said, "I could get them back."

"No. Let's leave them be. I failed them once. Don't want to fail them again."

Waves of smoke rolled over them. Atticus and Warren pulled away from one another and found most of Gallows gone, hidden behind charcoal-colored clouds. Above them, blood-swollen mosquitoes buzzed in the sky, muddying the rays of the midday sun.

"Go get Clementine and Will." Warren looked at Sean and Allister. "Go get them, or we'll annihilate you for putting us through all of this."

The Skeleton glanced at Gary's headless body. He started to shake, to feel sick. He remembered the first time they'd met, so many years back, in the graveyard, at midnight. They'd both been drunk as hell, which was why they probably hadn't torn each other's throats out at first blush. After a lot snarling and shit-talking, they roamed the graves side-by-side and made fun of the names written on them, like the sophisticated country boys they were.

"We'll get him out of here. Go, Atticus."

The Skeleton nodded at Allister and Sean. "Where's Bruna?"

Warren shrugged. "She ran. Who gives a fuck? Get out of here."

The Skeleton left the scythe with Warren, made sure he still had the Black Hour's heart, and headed through the roiling lake. The lights beneath the blood were bright, beaming, and the smoke dirty, sulfurous.

"Nmw'gla fhtha xu... ufv'la ufv'la axtu."

Mr. Haemo's voice boomed through the clouds. Looking down at the surface of the lake, the Skeleton noticed the blood was headed in one direction, as though it were draining into something. He picked up the pace, letting the current tugging at his legs do most of the work.

"Nmw'gla fhtha xu… ufv'la ufv'la axtu."

The Skeleton pushed through a thick layer of smoke and found himself at the foot of the general store, where Mr. Haemo, James, Hex, Elizabeth, and Miranda waited. At the bottom of the building, the last two vestiges were lodged into crimson whirlpools, slowly being taken apart by the pressure inside each.

"It's ready!" Mr. Haemo pointed to the place in front of the Skeleton. "Are you?"

Gary should be here, he thought. *He started this. He should be here with me, god damn it.*

"Atticus, what is it?" James hollered.

The Skeleton shook his head and said to the mosquito, "I'm ready."

Giddy from all the gore about him, Mr. Haemo spread his wings and floated down to the lake. He flew forward, until he was face-to-face with the Skeleton.

"Do it."

Mr. Haemo raised his claw. "This place is mine."

"What?"

"This place is a blood well, and it is mine."

The Skeleton lowered his voice. "People live here."

"No one's moving back after this. I want the blood. You promised me."

"Gary's dead."

Mr. Haemo gave a slight sigh and shrug. "Sorry to hear that."

"Fuck you." Reluctantly, the Skeleton nodded. "Gallows is yours. But you have to share it with the Marrow Cabal if they want it, too."

"Fat chance they do." Mr. Haemo laughed, put his hands together. "Nmw'gla fhtha xu… iha'iha' mjuv iha'xuvul!" He nodded at something behind the Skeleton. "There you are. Go get them, tiger."

When the mosquito said that, he didn't move. Not because he didn't want to, but because he didn't believe this moment was finally happening. He could feel it alright, the blood well opening behind him, just as he had felt it the first time they brought him out of the Membrane. But he couldn't believe it. Saving them had guided his every decision, had been the purpose of his every waking moment. Could he just stop? There was no going back to the way things were before, not with how he looked, what he'd done and become. Did he want to stop?

Death had given him guidance, purpose. He missed it already.

"Is this really the end?" he blurted out, sounding naïve.

The mosquito shook his massive head. "Doubt it."

"Will they be okay leaving the Membrane?"

"Should be exactly the same as when they went in."

"Shepherds going to come for them?"

Mr. Haemo started to rise into the air. "Why wouldn't they?" He paused and then: "Get rid of the heart, Atticus. Toss it into the Abyss."

The Skeleton's hand touched the heart through his cloak. "Thank you, Mr. Haemo."

"I should be thanking you, but I won't. Don't want to give you the wrong impression." He took off, back to his perch on top of the building. "Hurry," he shouted. "It won't stay open forever." Then, darkly: "Toss the heart in."

Finally, the Skeleton turned around. A few inches from where he stood, the blood well swirled, a sanguine portal to the secret places of the universe.

"I'm sorry I made you wait so long." The Skeleton exhaled the air he hadn't breathed in over a year and a half.

He walked forward, one foot over the blood well. "I'm sorry this is all that's left of me."

And then, as he went forward and stepped into the churning gateway, thought: *I hope I'm still enough.*

CHAPTER XXXII

There was no tunnel to fall through in the Membrane this time. With all the fresh blood Mr. Haemo had amassed, he'd been able to create a portal that opened directly outside the deranged Pulsa diNura. Maybe it was because he was only bones now, but as the Skeleton stood there, in the dry lakebed, looking out over the village, he realized he no longer felt the Abyss' pull. It was a good thing, until he started thinking about why it wasn't.

He started forward, going slower than one would've expected of a man who was about to be reunited with his family. The citizens of Pulsa diNura crowded around the platform the village was built upon, watching his approach. They whispered to one another. Some took off to tell others. If Clementine and Will were still here, it wouldn't be long 'til they got the message.

The Membrane hadn't changed much since his last visit. It never did. The Skeleton couldn't really consider himself a tourist or guest in these parts, anymore. How many times had he died? How many times had he seen these same scabby walls, the same endless Abyss? In the fleshy tapestry of the Membrane's sky, sinewy streaks of light continued to dart across them. How many of those had he ridden now, out of here and back there? As many times as they had penetrated him, he would've thought the damn things could've at least given him their name.

Several people were coming down the ramps that ran from the village to the lakebed. In their dirty, death-marred nudity, everyone looked about the same. It was like a uniform for those trapped here.

The only hint of personality, however, wasn't in the persons themselves. That was impossible. Emotions were too suppressed, and memories ever-fleeting. No, the hint of personality was in the way that they had died. A slit neck, gouged eyes. A nasty stab wound, or an overdose. That was the future Clementine and Will, or even himself, had coming to them; an eternity of sitting around on the edge of death, staring at the walls, and talking about how they died. Maybe the Skeleton wasn't himself anymore. And maybe they weren't either. And maybe the world had gone to shit while they were gone, but anything was better than this. It had to be.

Several had started down the ramp, but only two actually stepped off it and onto the lakebed. Clementine. Will. The both of them, dirty, naked, and death-marred, but still them, his wife, his son. Ten-feet between them, and what could he say? Should he shout? Run to them? No, that didn't seem right. So instead he stopped, studied their every detail, to make sure he hadn't forgotten anything, to make sure nothing had been lost.

Every perfection and imperfection was present. Clementine's hair, and the small curl near her ear that would never straighten, even if she threatened to cut it off. Will's face, and the small gap between his front teeth where a bit of his dinner always ended up. Mr. Haemo was right. They were as they had been. Their skin looked good, their bodies healthy. And this was them he was looking at, he realized. Not their souls or some sad imitation by the Membrane. It was them, their flesh and bone. The shepherds had taken them away from him, but in doing so, they had preserved them, kept them just the way he remembered them, wanted them. It was a shame someone hadn't been able to do the same for him.

The Skeleton started forward. When he was only a few feet away, Clementine held up her hand. Immediately, he stopped in his tracks. Murmurs like clouds passed overhead, from the rope-bound rape victim that was Pulsa diNura.

She said it first, because nothing ever got past her. "Atticus?"

Will covered his crotch. "What?" His son's stomach was split, like it had been when Blythe first attacked him. There were several holes in his back, too, as though he'd been stabbed to death trying to protect his mother. "No, no. No, you're wrong. How can you…?"

Ignoring him, she said dreamily, "It was… so long ago. But I think it could be him." She reached out to touch him. Her face flashed red and she shouted, "Speak, damn you!"

Leave it to Clementine to get angry in a place where anger and indifference mimicked one another. The Skeleton fumbled for his words. What he said and how he said it would determine if they'd go willingly through the portal behind him, or kicking and screaming.

Will's throat tightened, as though looking at the Skeleton made him sick. "Prove you're him," he said, wanting and not wanting to hear what he was about to say.

The Skeleton racked his mind for memories only he and his wife and son would know. But there wasn't much left in that skull of his to probe and prop-up as proof. He could remember back as far as he needed to, but his uncertainty made him mute; because here he stood before the only two gods he'd ever worshiped. He had to get this right.

Clementine made fists. "Look in his eyes, Will. It's him, can't you see?"

Will, shaking his head, backed up towards the ramp. "No, I can't." And he didn't. "You're just seeing what you want to see." He tripped on a soda can filled with quarters. "I know you said you spoke to him, but that's not Dad!"

"It is me," the Skeleton said, at last. The Black Hour's heart beat against his chest, and he mistook it for his own. "Clem. Will. It's me. I swear it."

Will, eyes large and wet as saucers, quivered out a pathetic, "What?"

"It's me."

The Skeleton wanted so badly to embrace them, but if they ran or rejected him, or showed the slightest discomfort, he was certain he would die for good.

"I'm here now. Like I said I would be." He nodded towards the portal behind him and added, "We're going home."

A non-existent wind swept through Pulsa diNura. The ropes that held it together hummed like guitar strings. Bored already, most of the people on the platform started to disperse. Except for one. An old man, eagerly watching the scene from the top of the ramp.

"Prove it," Clementine demanded. "Prove you're you."

"I saw you here once. I told you I couldn't die, that I'd be back." The Skeleton didn't want to remind them of their deaths, but he had to. "That night when Blythe and Bon killed us, we were lying in the barn. Will was trying to prove how much of a catch Hazel was."

"Hazel," Will whispered. The name meant something to him, but he clearly couldn't place it anymore.

"More," Clementine commanded, her words heavy, desperate.

The Skeleton had to stop himself from throwing the hood over his head. He wanted to hide, but these weren't the people to hide from.

"We had a daughter—Vale," he said. "She didn't live long, but we loved her like she had been with us from the beginning."

Clementine went stiff. She pawed for Will's hand. He came to her side and took it.

"You wrote letters to Vale, one every day. Like she was still with us. You didn't stop until you found out you were pregnant with Will." The Skeleton dared a step forward. "She's buried behind the abandoned church." He swallowed hard. "Gary keeps watch over her. That's why he stays there."

Clementine's face twitched. Spasms throbbed through her neck. The Membrane had hardened her, but its grip on her wouldn't hold much longer.

Will caved in first. "What happened to you?"

The Skeleton reached out. His fingers brushed against Clementine's.

Will left his mother's side. He went to his father, kicking off the pull of the Abyss as he went. "Will you always be like this?"

The Skeleton put his hand on Will's shoulder. "I don't know." Seeing his boney fingers on his son's pink flesh, it didn't look right. "I'll explain everything, I promise. But not here."

Clementine threw her arms around the Skeleton. She dug her face into his bones. "I love you," she said, her fingers inside his ribcage. "I know it's you." She nodded at her son. "It's him, Will."

"Get us out of here." Will nudged his cheek against the Skeleton's fingers. "I don't care if you're not him. Not no more. Just get us out of here."

The Skeleton took both Clementine's and Will's hands. With them, he turned around and started toward the blood well's portal. Through its bubbling, foaming surface, faint traces of Gallows could be seen.

"Home is going to look different," the Skeleton warned. "It's safe for now, but it's never going to be the same."

"Don't matter," Clementine said.

"Wait!" Will broke free of his father's grasp. Facing Pulsa diNura, he shouted, "Herbert! Herbert!"

Herbert? The Skeleton grabbed Will's arm. But he shrugged him off and said, "He watched over me and Mom. Shepherds took him, same as us. We have to bring him back, too."

Clementine nodded, said, "It's the right thing to do, Atticus. Didn't he help you once?"

"There he is!" Will pointed to the old man who had stopped on the ramp. "Herbert, come on! You're coming with us."

"They're good friends," Clementine whispered. "Will about walked straight into the Abyss after I saw you here. Herbert saved him."

Herbert North raised his arms high and waved. "Good man," he shouted. He hobbled down the ramp, across the lakebed, his sun-spotted legs going this way and that.

Will met him halfway. He threw his arm around Herbert's shoulder and led him back to his mother and father.

Sinewy streaks of light shot across the area. Thunder rumbled behind the cancerous nimbuses that congested the flesh sky. The Membrane had always looked and felt the same, every time he came, but now, something was different. The air, or rather the idea of air, started to make the Skeleton's black tongue prickle, and he could see that the Abyss' pull on his wife, son, and Herbert had grown stronger. The Membrane was reacting. The Membrane was coming for them.

"Thank you, Herbert," the Skeleton said, "for taking care of them." He ushered them towards the portal. "We have to hurry."

Herbert North, close enough to get a good look at the Skeleton, mouthed "Holy shit."

The Skeleton extended his hand.

Herbert North took it and said, "They took care of me, too."

"Appreciate it." Pointing to the blood well, he said, "What do you think?"

"Most beautiful, awful fucking thing I've seen all my life. Love it." Still bone-struck by the Skeleton's appearance, Herbert said, "You got room for me? That's one more shepherd to add to the mix."

"Funny you seem to know what they're about now."

"Didn't want to scare you."

Clementine nudged the Skeleton. "Let's go, men."

The Skeleton took up his wife's and son's hands again. With Herbert, they both bowed to Pulsa diNura, the home they never wanted, and yet always had.

"Do you know what they are? The shepherds?" Will asked. "Do you—"

Thump, thump, thump.

The Skeleton didn't need to turn around. He already knew what was behind him, in between him and the blood well's portal. It was perfect fucking timing on the Membrane's part. And if he hadn't been so short-sighted his entire life, he may have even seen it coming. But did the shepherd that stood behind him—or shepherds, now that they were all getting out—know that he knew how to destroy them? Did they know he held all the power of the Black Hour's heart in his cursed hand? They sure as hell were about to find out.

So the Skeleton turned around, ready to go toe-to-toe with the only creatures that could kill him. Except there wasn't one shepherd standing with them on that dried out lakebed. Not even three or four. No, standing there on that dried out lakebed, in between him and their sanguine salvation, there were hundreds upon hundreds of the shepherds, each of which were dressed in their identical, iconic garb. With their crooks, they pounded the scabby ground. Each thump they released was a violent tremor that rocked the Membrane like a demonic pulse. Portions of Pulsa diNura collapsed completely to those rapturous repetitions.

Despite each shepherd looking no different from those that surrounded it, there was one the Skeleton recognized. It stood in front of the others, its fingernails painted yellow. It was the shepherd from Ghostgrave's dungeon.

The yellow-nailed shepherd raised its hand. Immediately, the others went silent.

The Skeleton took the Black Hour's heart out of his cloak, to show off to these show-offs. To his satisfaction, the shepherds recoiled. They pulled the brims of their hats further down their faces, to block out their view of the unholy organ.

"We don't want you," the yellow-nailed shepherd purred.

The Skeleton didn't believe the shepherd, so he took a step forward, forcing the creature one step backward. "Come on."

"Orders have changed."

Clementine, confused, said to the Skeleton, "What is that thing,

Atticus?"

The Skeleton held the heart high above his head. It started to throb in his gloved hand. Black, chunky secretions oozed out of its porous ventricles.

"We're leaving," he said, heading for the portal.

The yellow-nailed shepherd stepped aside. When it did, its brethren did as well.

"Orders have changed," it repeated, twisting its crook into the ground. "But we will not stop."

The Skeleton shrugged, said, "Doesn't seem that way right now."

At this, the shepherd smiled. It smiled so hard the stitching in its lip split and a chain of tongues spilled out. "You haven't suffered enough. We'll get you. When you're good and fat with the stuff."

"I'll be waiting," the Skeleton said.

"No, orders have changed from our Lepidoptera," the shepherd said. It started cracking the crook against the ground again. One by one, the others followed its example. "You won't, Atticus. And that's what we are looking forward to the most. When you've bared your teeth and ravaged everything, and moved past that point of wanting to die because of it. When you've grown complacent with your sick soul, when you've convinced yourself all the terrible things you've done were justified—that's when we will come for you, and remind you that it was not."

"Stay the fuck out of our way," the Skeleton said. He pocketed the Black Hour's heart and grabbed onto Clementine and Will. With Herbert North creeping behind him, all four passed through the ranks of shepherds, and walked into the blood well's portal.

The world twisted itself around, turned itself upside down. They walked out of the Membrane on two feet, and fell face-first into Gallows' lake of blood.

"Atticus! Atticus," Clementine screamed, spitting up and sneezing out the red water.

Will struggled to find his footing. Gallows' own lakebed had become a slippery stretch of bloody mud. "Dad," he cried, grabbing for Herbert North, instead.

"It's okay," the Skeleton said, wading through the blood. He packed them together, Clementine and Will, and held them there until they were right again. "It's okay. We're out."

Herbert North let out a laugh. He plodded away from the Skeleton's family, dropped to his knees, so that the blood was covering his mouth. He wasn't afraid, wasn't horrified. The old man was happy, damn near ecstatic. It was a sad state of affairs when the scenery here somehow surmounted that of the Membrane's.

"What is this?" Clementine clung to the Skeleton, like Vale in her weakest moments. "Atticus?"

Will kept coughing. The plumes of smoke from Mr. Haemo's ritual, though weaker than before, were still roaming the lake.

"We're out." The Skeleton tried to kiss Clementine's head, but he had no lips. "We're out. This is Gallows. I know it doesn't look it, but it's home. A lot has happened, but we're safe. I swear it."

From behind the sooty clouds, Mr. Haemo called out: "Is that you, Atticus?"

Slowly, the smoke started to part, as though the mosquito were doing its best holy prophet act. A hazy outline of the general store began to form, and there, at the bottom, the Marrow Cabal waited, bloodied and beaten, but more or less, minus James' few fingers, in one piece.

Clementine, pointing at the boy, shouted, "James!"

He waved his mangled hand. "Oh, heavens, is it good to see you again."

It was odd to think it, but there was a kind of serenity in Gallows. With the Red Worm and most of its population dead, the place had an aura of finality to it that was not only morbid, but calming.

"This is the Marrow Cabal," the Skeleton said. "They've been with me the whole way. I would've never done this without them."

"That's Warren."

The big man nodded, but just barely. He was covered in so many slashes that half the blood in the lake was probably his.

"And Elizabeth and Miranda, part of his Deadly Beauty squad."

Elizabeth made a curtsey. Miranda gave a half-grin, gave more of a shit than usual.

"And that's Hex."

Hex smiled a half-smile. Eyes glowing brightly, she said, "It's a pleasure to meet you."

The Skeleton rolled his eyes. "You know Mr. Haemo."

The mosquito came forward, bowed, but Clementine and Will didn't pay him any mind.

Pointing to the recruits, he said, "That's Sean and Allister. They're new. They could've run, but they stayed to fight."

Neither of the men really knew what the hell was going on, so, blood-shocked, they just smiled back and went back to minding their own business.

"This is Clementine, my wife," the Skeleton said, holding onto his wife tightly. "And my son, Will." He threw his other arm around Will. He wondered how long he could keep them this close. He had all eternity, after all, but them, not so much.

"And this is Herbert North," the Skeleton added, nodding to the old man. "Don't know much about him. But word through the grapevine is he kept them safe for me. So if we have any spoils from our efforts, this man deserves them."

Herbert didn't seem to hear the compliment. Instead, he kept staring at Mr. Haemo. Finally, he asked him, "Do I know you?"

The giant mosquito threw the skin hood over his head. Blinking his million ruby-like eyes, he said, "We'll, I'll be. Herbert fucking North. How you been, brother?"

As those too reunited with one another, Clementine leaned into the Skeleton, pointed at Hex, and said, "Hey, who's that?"

"Hex," he said. "Weird name, but yeah."

"No, the little girl."

"What?"

Clementine pointed harder. "There, right behind her."

The Skeleton cocked his head. She was right. There was someone standing behind Hex. Someone smaller. A child. "Hey, Hex, who's that behind you?"

Hex took a deep breath and stepped aside. "I'll let her tell you."

It was the young girl he'd seen earlier, the one with the scar on her head. She still had the ax from before, but in her other hand, she was carrying what looked like the hollowed-out body of an octopus. The smeared Corruption he'd noticing running down her arm earlier was gone, too.

"Who are you?" the Skeleton said.

"R'lyeh." The young girl came forward. "R'lyeh, of Alluvia."

Alluvia. The Skeleton glanced around the lake of blood, the remnants of the Red Worm lying foul and festering in the red water. "You're a Night Terror?"

She nodded. "My mother and father are here, in all this."

"I'm sorry. I heard what happened."

Will and Clementine came at him from both sides with, "What happened? What happened?"

R'lyeh sounded stone cold as she said, "I was there, in Geharra, when Penance did this." She took the octopus and slid it over her head, donning it like the mask it was. "You brought them back from the dead?"

The Skeleton looked at his wife and son. "In a way." He let go of Clementine and met the girl where she stood. "Hey, are you okay?"

"No." Taking the ax with both hands, she said, "I was there, in Lacuna, when the Blue Worm was destroyed, too. I know a lot. More than you."

"I'm sure you—"

"You brought them back from the dead."

"Uh, yeah." Did he need to protect them from this girl? What was she getting at?

"If I help you, tell you everything I know, will you help me?"

"R'lyeh." The Skeleton butchered her name. "I'm not who—"

"A Witch named the Maiden of Pain took my friend. My friend, Vrana. I'm going to get her back. I'll kill anyone you want. I'll do anything. She was... is all I have. If you and the Marrow Cabal can do this, I know you can find her. Help me save her."

Before the Skeleton could reject her offer, Hex said, "Remember why we killed the Red Worm?"

He looked at his wife and son. He remembered. They killed it to turn this place into a massive blood well, only to save two people. The others that were saved as a result were a nice consequence he never cared to consider. But by the look in Hex's eyes, he knew this wasn't what she was getting at.

"Because we are the Marrow Cabal," she continued. "Because we are going to put a stop to things like this from ever happening again." Now she was talking to Clementine and Will: "Your husband, your father, risked everything not only to bring you back, but to fight against Eldrus."

Clementine's jaw had dropped. She had already seemed impressed with the Marrow Cabal, but now this? "Atticus, is that true?"

Will didn't need to hear his confirmation. He was already looking at the Skeleton as though he were some seasoned, celebrated war hero. When he finally spoke next, it would probably be to sign up for the Marrow Cabal.

"It's true," Hex carried on. She was smiling at the Skeleton, making sure he knew that he was hers now. "Now's not the best place to tell it, but we've been everywhere. Your husband is famous. We were stumped as to how to proceed, but R'lyeh here has given us all the fire we need to burn our overlords to the ground."

Clementine came up behind the Skeleton and took his arm. "You really did all that?"

He knew she wasn't herself, yet. She sounded tired, looked tired. The fight that had been thirty-one years strong in her, since the day she was born, was still trying to find its footing in her resurrected body. Hex was taking advantage of her and their son's state. The same way the Skeleton had taken advantage of the situation here. Son of a bitch.

"I did," the Skeleton said. "A lot has changed. I've… changed."

Clementine touched his bones, her eyes struggling to stay open. "But you're still you. That's all I want. You're still you?" She stared at R'lyeh. "You still do the right thing?"

The Skeleton looked at R'lyeh and, for a moment, was reminded of his daughter, Vale. Here stood another test of his humanity. Clementine and Will had more or less completely accepted him for who and what he was back in the Membrane. The ordeal that would've been convincing them should've taken months, and yet he'd managed it in five minutes flat. Maybe the Membrane hadn't worn off. Or maybe this is what the Membrane had made of them, and that dull gullibility of theirs was about all he could expect from here on out.

He just wanted to tell Hex to fuck off, to go home, back to the farm, and live out, with his family, however many days he had left with them. But how could he do that now? Now that Hex had him cornered and this little girl was begging him for help? If he said no to either of them, then Hex would tell Clementine and Will about his insanity, his bloodlusts; everyone he'd killed and the Black Hour heart which, in a way, had become his own. His wife and son had wrapped him in love, and so perhaps all they saw was what they remembered and expected of him. With a few sharp words, Hex and the others would have him unraveled, stripped to the bone and put on display as the monster he truly was. And if that happened, if those who had stood behind him suddenly turned against him, and took from him the only two things that mattered to him in the world, then he knew, without a shadow of a doubt, his hungering soul would eat them whole. And it wouldn't stop there. If he lost Clementine and Will again, he would be lost for good.

So the Skeleton stepped forward, outstretched his hand, and said, "Welcome to the Marrow Cabal, R'lyeh. Help us make the world a better place, and we'll save your Vrana." He touched his chest, where the Black Hour's heart stirred. "I am who they say I am."

The Gravedigger had dug too deep, and now there was no way out.

PART THREE

THE SINNER AND THE SHADOWS

CHAPTER I

Heaven had to be empty, because the Holy Child hadn't heard anything from it in a very long time. God was still around, no doubt about that, but he was pretty sure he and everyone else were sending their prayers to the wrong place. The exemplars liked to call him gullible, but since he didn't really want to know what that word meant, he just assumed they were jealous he had figured everything out before them.

The Holy Child sat on his bed, a faint light coming through the frosted windows beside it. "Gullible," he said with a snicker. Shaking his head, he slipped on his quietest shoes and laced them as tightly as he could. "If you pray for good things," he said, as though the exemplars were standing in front of him. "Then god will make good things happen!" He hopped to his feet and, with his secret journal and pen, went to the door. "Gullible." He rolled his eyes and opened it. "Idiots."

No matter how hard he tried, he never could manage to wake up before everyone else. As he stepped out of his room, he saw, even now, in the gray hours of dawn, Pyra was packed. Yes, the sprawling abbey was the headquarters for the Holy Order of Penance, but didn't these people ever sleep? The guards had an excuse—they were guards—but what was theirs? With so many people running around Pyra all the time, he still couldn't figure out how Exemplar Samuel Turov had managed to smuggle him into the South last year. Heck, he still couldn't figure out why he had even done it in the first place. But he would soon enough, he thought, closing the door behind him, and suddenly feeling like he needed a bath. Eventually, Mother Abbess Justine would cave in and tell him the truth. She always did.

His quarters sat at the highest point of Pyra, the Ascent. It was here where he, the six exemplars, Mother Abbess, and the dedicated guards who protected them resided. For the longest time, he'd had the same two men watching over him, ever since he had been chosen as god's speaker when he was a year old. But not anymore. He got new guards after Penance's soldiers finally found him in the South. Justine told him his old guards had been fired, because they hadn't kept him safe like they were supposed to. That made sense, but why he had butterflies in his stomach when he thought about them didn't.

"Where you off to this morning?" Avery, one of his two guards, asked. He was standing where the circular Ascent jutted outward, to the hall and cloister that connected it to the rest of Pyra.

Quickly, the Holy Child put his journal and pen behind his back. "Nowhere. You didn't see me."

Avery hummed. He tapped on his scabbard a catchy hymn from mass. "Who are we spying on today?"

The Holy Child bit his lip as a few people passed in the hall ahead. The cloister had the most traffic, and everyone there seemed to be in a hurry or shouting about something. What was going on?

"Where's Mackenzie?" She was the Holy Child's other guard. It was weird not seeing her and Avery together.

"She's around, but sick." Avery shrugged. "I wouldn't worry. So you didn't answer me. Who are you spying on?"

"Isla Taggart."

Avery laughed. Glancing around the Ascent, he said, "Really?"

The Holy Child took out his journal, tapped the front of it. "She has a page now."

"If you say so." Smiling, he shook his head. "Have fun with that."

"You didn't see me, right?"

"I don't even know who I'm talking to right now." Avery went cross-eyed and looked crazy. "Hey," he added, as the Holy Child started for his hidden place.

"What?"

"Don't let anyone see you."

"I know."

"Don't listen to anything anyone is saying."

The Holy Child looked at Avery, and then at the instruments in his hand, which he used to keep track of every nitty gritty detail about those living in Pyra.

"Get out of here," Avery said, his smile slowly becoming a frown. "Be back before breakfast, or I'll have the Night Terrors come for you."

The Holy Child didn't get adults. They didn't make any sense. After they brought him back to Penance, they wouldn't let him out of his guards' sights. But now, a few months later, Justine often had him running off on his own, completing her "special missions." Maybe he didn't know what gullible meant, but he was smart enough to realize "special missions" meant keeping tabs on people the Mother Abbess didn't really like. As the Holy Child, he could go almost anywhere, and everyone would be nice to him, whether they wanted to or not. It wasn't a good thing, he eventually realized, but it was a handy thing to have when it came to what Avery called "holy espionage."

Isla Taggart. Halfway to his hidden place, the Holy Child opened his journal to her aforementioned page. There wasn't much written there, and none of it was anything of particular use. She was a girl, obviously, and twenty years old. She was the niece of the Exemplar of Innocence, Augustus Enfield, and a hermit. She spent most of her time going back and forth between the library and refectory, and getting, according to Justine, very bad advice from the Demagogue on religion and politics.

The Holy Child went to where the Ascent ran widest, where there were several portraits of previous exemplars, as well as the Mother Abbesses from the past. Justine had been Mother Abbess for the last thirty years, but the thing was, all the other abbesses kind of looked like her, too. The Holy Child was pretty sure it had always been her all along. She worked for god, after all, and everyone loved her, so why find someone different? He didn't see why she had to hide the fact she could live longer than anyone else, but that was her business. The important thing was that she was his best friend, and he hers. And it made him happy to know she'd be with him forever.

His hidden place was in this gallery. Behind the several bookshelves that lined it, there was a small passage that ran from the Ascent to a small closet on the upper level of the cloister. Inside the place, he kept his disguise—a boring, hooded, servant's robe, a wig, and some of Mackenzie's makeup—so that he could put it on, pretend to be a girl, and get around Pyra more or less unnoticed when he needed to, like today. He also had a set of skeleton keys in there, to get into almost any room. That was nice. Cheating, probably, in the grand scheme of holy espionage, but definitely nice.

The Holy Child did his usual rounds to make sure the coast was clear. Like a cat after a rat, he crammed himself behind the bookcases and into the hidden place. There, he put on his robe and wig, and, with a heavy hand, his makeup. He looked like a half-mad doll with all that blush and eyeliner, but most importantly, he didn't look like himself.

Isla Taggart. Why did Justine want to know more about her? The Holy Child crawled on all fours through his hidden place, turning as it turned through the walls of Pyra. She didn't seem dangerous like the other people he had investigated. Annoying, yes, but not dangerous. Isla Taggart was the kind of person who had only one hobby in life: outrage. And if you weren't like her, you were her enemy.

The Holy Child dropped out of the hiding place, from the ceiling and into the abandoned closet. Fresh spider webs and not-so-fresh bugs tried to break his fall, but they ended up grossing him out instead. It was pitch-black, but he had been here so many times before he could find the door easily enough. The closet sat alone in an unfinished, unvisited part of the cloister, so when he unlocked it and stepped out, no one was there to bust him.

The Holy Child locked the closet and headed out of this forgotten place. Sunlight shone through the passage ahead, where tens of people were moving in groups, whispering and shouting. He went to the beginning of the passage, peeked through the few boards that were supposed to block it off from the rest of the cloister. There were other doors here, the steel one was especially intriguing, but the skeleton key didn't work on it or the others, so this was the only way out.

While he waited for a chance to slip through, he tried to figure out what everyone was saying.

"What does this mean for us?"

"It means everyone will…"

"You know who did it? I know who did it."

"That's a sin to suggest so."

"There's no proof, though."

"She's been lying to us."

"No, he has."

"How could god let this happen?"

Are they talking about the monster in the West? The Holy Child slipped through the boards. A light snow blew through, dusting the exterior arcades that ran along the cloister's winter garden. He pulled his cloak tight. It was always cold in Penance, always snowing, and he always forgot to pack something warmer for his missions. If he missed anything about his time in the South, it was the warmth. To see trees and grass that were every color but white was something he hadn't even considered until Samuel Turov took him there.

The Holy Child hurried past the gossiping busybodies and took the stairs to the first floor. *Justine said not to worry about the monster*, he thought, going through the door that would eventually take him to the infirmary. *I didn't tell anyone.*

He looked back into the cloister, at the frenzy of robed figures pacing in the snow. *The Demagogue was the only other person who knew. Did he tell someone?*

Avery said not to listen, so the Holy Child wasn't going to. His old guards always said he knew too much for a child his age. Maybe that was why he always felt so nervous all the time. Because he knew things he wasn't supposed to. Even worse were the things he had done. He couldn't talk of them, either.

There were two infirmaries in Pyra. The first was in the central terminal, the main, open to the public area of the abbey, and the second near the private quarters, on the third floor. Isla Taggart lived alone, in an unfurnished room—unfurnished because she rejected all materialistic things. The room sat beside the third floor infirmary that was for, as the Demagogue had put it, the "important people." Supposedly, Isla was training to be a doctor, but she actually spent most of her time trying to convert patients to her beliefs.

The Holy Child grinned as he put the people's gossip out of his mind. He stopped, cracked open his journal, and made a correction to Isla's page. After "Taggart" he wrote "the Torturer," because that was what her patients called her after being forced to listen to her for hours on end.

He shut the journal and hurried to the infirmary. It was open, but the staff inside were asleep at their desks. Under the cover of their snores, he slipped in, crouched low, and scampered past. There were only a few patients resting in the infirmary today, but they were out cold.

Mother Abbess Justine had told him there was another hiding

place he could use. It sat at the back of the infirmary, in the corner, behind a grate everyone seemed to have forgotten was there. It used to be a vent from the Old World, she told him. Most of the remodeling to Pyra had cut it off from where it used to go, but if he crawled inside it and went right, left, and right again, he would end up in Isla Taggart's room, under her bed.

Justine had been very specific about when he should carry out his special mission. He had to be in the vent, under her bed, by sunrise. So he padded across the infirmary's frigid floor, found the grate. Carefully, he gripped the heavy, metal covering and pulled it away. It shrieked shrilly as he worked it out of the wall. Heart pounding, he was almost certain the sound would give him away. But he remembered his page on the doctors of Pyra and their fondness for sedatives.

"Too easy," he mumbled, sliding into the vent backward. He grabbed the grate and lodged it into place. "All too easy."

The vent was cramped, uneven. He curled into a ball and turned himself around. Right, left, right. Easy enough. It didn't look like he could go anywhere else, anyway. Every other direction was caved in or cut off somehow. Right, left, right, he went. He saw light, and also, shadows.

The Holy Child found the grate Justine had told him about and camped out in front of it. He opened his journal to Isla Taggart the Torturer's page and pressed his pen to the paper. He saw her shadow on the opposite wall. Her legs dropped over the side of the bed. She was awake, but she wasn't doing anything. Reading, maybe? One of her favorite hobbies was to read about issues from the Old World and use them to invent new problems for this world.

Did she find out about the monster? Did she tell everyone? The Holy Child started writing down a description of Isla's room. It was a stark, stone, square of a room. There were a lot of dirty clothes everywhere, and a lot of books, too. *I bet she did. That's why Justine wanted me to spy on her.* She had several mirrors in her room as well, but they were so caked with dried makeup they reflected very little.

Why before sunrise, though? He noted the single portrait on the wall, sitting higher on it than the icon of Penance. It was of her, and only her, and though he thought she was pretty in person, in the portrait, she had been made ugly.

As the Holy Child lifted his eyes from the journal, he noticed a second shadow beside Isla's on the wall. It was coming out of hers. He heard the bed creak, saw it sag a little, as though someone had just sat on it. But no one had entered the room since he got here.

"I have to be quick," a woman who wasn't Isla said. She sounded scared, thirsty.

And then Isla did speak, but in a whisper. "How did you...?"

"Will you help me now?"

"Yes, of course. Have you told anyone else? If you have, I won't."

The woman sighed. Whoever she was, she sounded fed-up with Isla's selfishness. "What does it matter?"

"Because we have to do this right, or no one will believe you."

The bed shifted again. Two legs dropped over the edge, beside Isla's. They were bare; dark green bruises ran up the backs of them.

Isla continued. "You have to show me how you do it."

"It doesn't work like that."

"Part of the deal, Audra."

Audra? The Holy Child started writing frantically on the page, the sound of his pen's scratching growing louder and louder.

"This was a mistake." The women pulled up her legs. Her shadow started to draw closer to Isla's.

"No! Where are you going?" Isla dropped from the bed, her feet falling into a pile of expensive, crumpled undergarments. "We have to do this right. I can't just come out and say it."

"I'm Audra of Eldrus!" Audra shouted. "Your city has been keeping me prisoner for years! You don't think that won't get anyone's attention?"

The Holy Child's eyes went wide as Audra's shadow disappeared into Isla's. *Audra? From Eldrus?* He started backing away, down the vent. *That doesn't make sense. The royal family of Eldrus... they're all supposed to be dead.*

CHAPTER II

The Holy Child had to run as fast as he could to get back into bed before it was time to do his daily duties. As he tore through Pyra, ditched his disguise in the hiding place, and snuck through the Ascent, he found himself slowing down as he thought about this woman who claimed to be Audra. Obviously, that was what Justine had wanted him to record. So did she know a surviving member of the royal family of Eldrus was staying here? Or was it just a lucky guess?

The Holy Child turned the corner, clipped Avery as he did so, burst into his room, and threw the covers over his head. Ten seconds later, Avery and a sniffling Mackenzie came to collect him.

"Still have a little blush on your cheeks," Mackenzie said. She took out her handkerchief and cleaned him up. "Learn anything juicy today?"

The Holy Child got out of bed and let Avery dress him in his sacred robe. He nodded and, barely paying attention to them, said, "Oh, yeah. Definitely."

The Holy Child had several tasks he had to complete every single day. They began with breakfast, where he, Justine, the six exemplars, and almost everyone else in Pyra sat down and ate together in the gathering hall. But before they could eat, they had to listen to him share any news he had received from god during the night. Most of the time, he just made something up on the spot—god wasn't exactly a chatterbox—but here and there, Justine would pull him aside and tell him what to talk about.

Given the chaos in the cloister today, it was no surprise to the Holy Child that, after his guards left the room, Mother Abbess Justine entered, a look of concern etched upon her usually warm and inviting face. She wore a long, hooded, light blue dress that shimmered when she walked, and white gloves that looked as pure as the snow outside. He didn't know as much about Justine as he would have liked, but he did know that she often dressed opposite to how she felt that day. According to her, it reminded her to "try harder."

"I want to hear about Isla Taggart, I do," she said, noticing how antsy he looked on his bed. "But god has spoken, and had a lot to say." Her pale skin became flushed. She started to pace back and forth. "It's about the monster in the West."

The Holy Child nodded. "Someone spilled the beans?"

"It takes a long time for news to reach Penance when it's not coming from god directly." She stopped, combed her fingers through her long, brown hair. "That's a good thing. We don't need gossip and lies out here, in our cold wilderness. The monster was in the West, but not anymore."

The Holy Child stood up. He felt his heart quicken. "Where is it?" His shoulders tightened, in preparation for the bad things about to come.

She waved her hand for him to sit, and he sat. She took a seat beside him. "In Gallows."

Up close, she always looked sickly to him, her skin moist and almost translucent. Up close, she smelled strange, too. She did smell good, most of the time, but behind the perfume, there was always a pungent odor, like burning wood.

"Gallows? That's all the way across the continent."

"The monster made it there is no time." She took his hand and squeezed it. She did this a lot, to borrow his courage. "It's dead now."

His eyes went wide and he exclaimed, "That's great!"

Justine shook her head, a bit of her hair brushing his arm. "No, because now people think the monster is our fault."

The Holy Child raised an eyebrow. "Why?"

She closed her eyes and nodded. "Because they think we made it."

"What?" His hand started to shake. She squeezed it harder, giving him some of her strength. "What? Did we?"

"No," she said. "No, Eldrus did. That's what we're going to tell everyone today."

"But did they?" He searched her face for signs of a lie, but as always, she was unreadable.

Sounding sterner, she said, "That's what we're going to tell everyone today."

Breakfast always began with a prayer, but the Holy Child was afraid to give it today, because he knew he would sound afraid. He sat at the front of the gathering hall, at the small table he shared with Mother Abbess Justine. To their left and right, two longer tables ran, where three of the six exemplars occupied each. He didn't mind talking to them. It was the rest of Pyra—the priests, nuns, staff, students, and various visitors—now seated before him that made him scared. There had to be at least one hundred people here today. How could he say something that would make all of them feel at ease?

"You'll do fine," Justine whispered, leaning into him. "You always do."

The Holy Child nodded, swallowed hard, and came to his feet. As soon as he did, the rest of Pyra went silent and fixed their eyes on him. After all, he was as close as they could get to god. The respect they had for him wasn't necessarily earned, but understood.

"To the almighty lord who watches over us, we give our thanks and praise. For this day and those days to come, lend us your guidance and your love, so that we may serve you faithfully and honor through action your teachings. To those who do not yet know of your love or have refused it, be merciful, for in time, they shall know it and accept it wholly. We are your servants, and by the bones of your blessings, we shall bring to life the parts of the Earth that have withered without your grace. Through hell, we find heaven. And through heaven, we find you. So let us suffer and make better those who have suffered, so that we may be strong enough to sit at your side. To the almighty lord who watches over us, we give our thanks and praise. We shall honor you at every moment of every hour of this joyous day. Amen."

As those gathered said "Amen," the Holy Child took a drink of water. Prayer always managed to parch his throat. Looking out across the gathering hall, he saw everyone was on the edge of their seats, waiting for him to address what Justine had called the 'Red Worm." He started guzzling the water, his thoughts turning to escape. Between the age of five and his current age of eleven, he had spoken to most of these same people every day during this time. He wasn't good at math, but he didn't need to be to know that should've been enough time to be prepared for this moment when he, not Justine, finally gave the people his first bit of bad news.

Will they hate me? He looked at the exemplars, both tables, and set down his cup. *Will they turn on me?* A monster had killed all of Geharra, some Night Terror village of Alluvia, and ravaged most of Gallows, on behalf of King Edgar of Eldrus, yet here he was, worrying about himself. He felt like Isla Taggart; that is, selfish and sick.

"Forgive me," he began. His leg started to shake. Justine touched his knee and it calmed. "God has spoken to me. It is dark news I bring to you today. But by the light of the lord's words, we will lift this darkness and see the truth for what it is."

The Holy Child's confidence began to return. Like always, once he started speaking, he became eloquent and fearless. People would often compliment him on his speeches, but he couldn't accept their praises. When he spoke as well as he did, it was because god was inside him, guiding him. Benefit, he assumed, of being the lord's chosen speaker.

"Many months ago, a terrible thing happened in Geharra." The Holy Child closed his eyes and, as he replayed what Justine had told him, began again. "As we revealed a few weeks ago, Alexander Blodworth, understudy of the traitor, Samuel Turov, went with a group of priests and soldiers to Geharra. He believed I had been taken there, and with the blessing of our benevolent Mother Abbess Justine, went to rescue me. But when Alexander Blodworth arrived, he found the entire city had been murdered by Eldrus' soldiers."

A hush fell over the room. People began to lean so far forward they slipped off their benches. Small whispers erupted like fires amongst the congregation, but the piercing eyes of Justine quickly snuffed them out.

"Our relationship with Geharra is a strained one, but ten thousand deaths transcend all past and present transgressions. Let us pray that, in their final moments, they accepted our lord's love."

In glorious synchronicity, the congregation bowed their head and said their silent prayers, and secret good riddances.

"Eldrus desecrated the bodies of Geharra, and in a terrible ritual, used them to summon a creature they have named the 'Red Worm.' They thought by creating it across the continent, it would go unnoticed. They intended to send this bloody weapon here, to Penance, to destroy us. And as many of you know as of today, they tried. But by the time it reached Gallows, our god intervened and smote it from the earth."

The Holy Child took another drink of water. Everyone else did as well. While he must have sounded tough to those before him, inside, he was as weak as could be. Just looking at his food made his stomach do a backflip. But he had to see this announcement through. He could, and would, cry about it later.

"There is a rebel group trying to take credit for stopping the Red Worm. I assure you, no man could harm such a foul beast. Do not believe the lies of vultures, for they speak with the stink of carrion on their breaths.

"It is with a heavy heart that I report to you that Alexander Blodworth has perished. He sits with god now." The Holy Child looked over to one the exemplars' table, at a young, brown-skinned woman seated there. "But it is with much happiness that I elect Alexander Blodworth's assistant, Karyl Elesh, to join the exemplars. Behold and give praise to your new Exemplar of Restraint."

Slowly, the rest of the room rose to their feet. In sporadic, forced bursts, they clapped for their new beaming exemplar.

What do they care? the Holy Child thought as he watched Karyl soak up the applause. *It's too soon... unless Justine wanted people to think of Karyl when they thought of this tragedy.*

When the weak show of support died down, which didn't take long, the Holy Child continued. "I am very sorry to share such grave news at such an early hour, but our lord wishes to keep nothing from us. God does have a plan, and when it is time—" the Holy Child looked at Justine, "—it will be shared with us. Fear not, for we are his sheep, and a shepherd will always protect their flock."

After that, breakfast moved at the pace of a funeral dirge. Most of the food remained untouched, because baseless speculation was far more savory. To avoid a panic, which was only permitted when the Demagogue had manufactured it, Mother Abbess Justine dismissed everyone from the gathering hall earlier than usual and sent the Holy Child on his way to finish the rest of his duties.

After morning prayer, announcements, and breakfast, the Holy Child was confined to a classroom with one of the exemplars until lunch. Today, oddly enough, he was with Isla Taggart's uncle, Augustus Enfield, Exemplar of Innocence. They were supposed to be studying the treaty of non-violence that existed between the quarters of Penance when it was known as Six Pillars. But the only thing the Holy Child heard during these lessons were his own thoughts.

Ten thousand dead? Eldrus is responsible? And we might have the only surviving member of the royal family locked up here? He gazed outside the classroom window. He had to squint to see Penance through the falling snow. *Justine is planning something. Is she testing me? Don't feel bad about the ten thousand, don't feel bad. They're with god now.*

Augustus Enfield cleared his throat to get the Holy Child's attention. And the Holy Child gave him no more than a tenth of it.

I need to tell her about the nightmares. He started taking notes, but all he wrote was gibberish. For the last month, almost every night, he had been having the same dream. In it, he was in a gray place, a kind of Void. But he wasn't alone. The Night Terror who had saved him from Samuel Turov, the one who had the raven head, she was there, too. But she looked different. She had feathers instead of skin, and wings. Around her neck, she wore a pretty necklace that always shone bright blue. He'd even tried to talk to her once in his dream, but when she tried to talk back, she could only make choking sounds. The strange thing was, every time he woke up, this morning included, the scar on his thigh hurt. He had a few scars there. Most of them he was trying to forget how he got them. But that one, the one that hurt, that was the one from the lake monster the Night Terror had killed.

After lessons came lunch. With a company of guards, he ate his food in the small chapel that crowned the main terminal. During this hour, people lined up outside the chapel to speak, one at a time, to him.

"A lot of people here to see you today," Avery said. He and Mackenzie stood behind him, while the other, less familiar guards, manned the entrance. "Think you could take a break from that peanut butter sandwich to talk to a few of them?"

The Holy Child shook his head as he took a big drink of milk. The only person he wanted to talk to was Justine. He wouldn't see her again until their private evening dinner. Besides, peanut butter sandwiches were his favorite. At the moment, it was the only thing stopping his anxious heart from bursting out of his chest.

"Bring someone in," Mackenzie said to the guards at the front. "We're ready."

Ten thousand dead, a monster made from their remains. The Holy Child gulped down some more milk. He hollowed out his sandwich until the crust was left, and left them there, for the birds. *God, did you not help them because they were sinners? I know they were our enemy, but I feel bad for them.*

The first to enter the chapel was a bearded old man with a bad knee. He went to the Holy Child's table.

With ten feet and Avery and Mackenzie between them, the old man bowed the best that he could and said, "It is an honor to stand in your presence. I mean no disrespect to the others, but you are the greatest of the Holy Children to come before you."

Nodding, quickly dodging that sore subject, he asked, "What is your name?"

"Bart, your holiness."

"It is an honor to meet you as well."

"I know that a lot of people want to talk to you today, so I'll be quick."

The Holy Child nodded. "Many need guidance in these dark times."

"Will there be war?" Bart's eyes bulged as he asked the question.

"I don't know yet," the Holy Child said. "I hope not."

"We were blamed for the Trauma. I don't want Penance to be blamed for tearing the continent apart."

"Nor do I."

Bart scratched his bristly beard. "Did the lord tell you a long time ago about the Red Worm? It sounds like it's been a long time since what happened in Geharra. I'm sure you were waiting until the right moment to tell us."

The Holy Child felt as though he were being tested, so he said, "Thank you, Bart, for talking to me," and sent the old man limping on his way.

The more people that came into the chapel to see him, the shorter he found himself becoming with each of them. Unsurprisingly, they wanted to know about the Red Worm and how Penance would respond. But the same question they kept asking him was the one that hit him the hardest: Why hadn't god told him sooner? He didn't have an answer, because aside from knowing the monster was out there, he had never been told where it came from or why it existed at all. He hadn't heard anything from god. In fact, god hadn't even been the one to tell him at all. It was Justine who broke the news. Most of the time, it always was.

The Holy Child sighed as he watched another man being ushered into the chapel. For a moment, he doubted himself and who he was supposed to be. *Maybe Justine should be the speaker. She sure seems better at it than—*

The man cleared his throat. His arm wasn't Corrupted like most. Instead, the Corruption was freckled, splotchy, and it ran from his fingers all the way up to his neck. The Holy Child had seen this man before. He was in charge of the main terminal and its upkeep.

"Your holiness," he began, bowing. His eyes darted back and forth between Avery and Mackenzie. "I know your lunch is almost over. Thank you for taking the time to speak to me."

"If only I had more time… Grant," he said, remembering the man's name at the last minute.

A big smile spread across Grant's face. He hadn't expected that.

"What can I do for you?"

"You can…" Grant's voice deepened. He bared his teeth, clamped them together. Small pricks of blue light started to shine across his irises. "Tell them the truth."

Avery and Mackenzie reached for their swords, but the Holy Child told them to stop.

"Tell them about the cult." Grant's lips quivered. Drool seeped out the corner of his mouth. "The cult of your nightmares." The blue light in his eyes grew brighter. "The Cult of the Worm!"

At this, Avery and Mackenzie grabbed Grant by his arms and hauled him out of the chapel, through the back entrance. He didn't resist, he just kept staring at the Holy Child, his eyes glowing, mumbling, "Maiden… Maiden…" over and over again.

After morning prayer, announcements, breakfast, lessons, lunch, and afternoon guidance, the only thing the Holy Child wanted to do was go back to his room and disappear for the next century into his journal.

This is too much, he thought, trudging through Pyra, to his next duty. *Please, god, let me get through this day. Please, I need you more than ever.*

After afternoon guidance, the Holy Child met with the governing bodies of Penance, to receive updates on the city. These sessions often ran long, and were mostly for the exemplars, who also attended them. He was supposed to use what he learned during these sessions to guide his addresses to the public, so the Holy Order would always appear current. But with everything on his mind, even after a particularly delicious peanut butter sandwich, all he could do was watch Penance through the window and wonder how life would be different if he hadn't been chosen to be god's speaker.

I can't be the only one, he thought, staring at Penance. The large, fluffy white clouds over the city were always there. He was pretty sure they hadn't moved in years. *I mean, there's always another Holy Child after the last one turns eighteen.* The clouds seemed to have an endless supply of snow. Lately, though, there hadn't been any blizzards.

Except for Cadence, he didn't really get to see much of the buildings of the South. But as he stared at the tall, sleek, white, and somewhat sparkling buildings of Penance, he doubted there was anything down there that could best them. *Heaven must be cold*, he thought, the buildings like giant icicles. *It's cold here, and when you do speak to me, lord, your words chill my mind.*

Sighing, he set his eyes on the streets of Penance, where people went about their business wrapped in scarves and thick, billowing cloaks.

How many people live here now? I guess I could ask. He looked to the front of the room, where the minister of agriculture and the Exemplar of Knowledge were arguing about crops.

But then they might remember I'm here.

The Holy Child turned away from the city. He folded his arms over his desk, rested his head against his arms, and went to sleep. Nobody noticed until it was time for supper.

"You've had a long day, haven't you?" Justine asked as the Holy Child shuffled into her chambers, hours later, for dinner. She was bathed in candle light, and enveloped in the smoke of incense. She pulled out the chair of the table she sat at and said, "Sit, and tell me why you hate me."

"I don't hate you," the Holy Child mumbled as he did what he was told. Tonight, everything about him hurt. His legs, his head, his throat, his brain. He felt sick from the stress of it all.

Justine smiled. Maybe it was because of the dim lighting, but she always looked better in her chambers. Less sickly, less translucent. And he couldn't blame her. Justine's chambers were one of his favorite places in Pyra. The massive bed, the thick curtains. The bookshelves and their odd trinkets. She even had a small jungle towards the back, with various plants and beautiful flowers. It was a place he could fill several journals on.

"I feel like..." The Holy Child bit the inside of his lip. He looked down at the table, where she had fixed him a plate of steak, greens, and potatoes, and filled him a cup full of wine. "I feel like... you're testing me."

Justine nodded, her pale, grayish eyes glinting. "I am," she said.

"Why?"

"The world is changing." She nodded at him to eat.

The Holy Child picked up his fork and knife and started cutting the steak into smaller pieces.

"We need to change, too. After the Trauma, our people were scared of change. They clung closely to their beliefs and their place in the world."

"Why did we get the blame?" The Holy Child took a bite of the steak. His tongue prickled, a warm sensation spread throughout his body. Instantly, he felt better. "I don't get it. Somewhere, shouldn't it be written down what we did?"

"It's been a long time," Justine said. "So long, and there have been so many stories. It would be hard to say anymore which of them were true." She paused, nodded to herself. "If I had to say so, we were blamed for the Trauma because god didn't save them."

"Kind of getting that feeling today." He took a drink of wine. She'd given him a lot more than usual. "Do you... want me to do something? Is it because of the Red Worm?"

"I want you to be with us until you're old and wrinkly." She smiled and nudged his leg with her toe. Becoming serious, she added, "You will not be replaced when you turn eighteen."

The Holy Child dropped his silverware. "What?"

"I'm asking you to continue to be at my side. Every time we elect a new Holy Child, we have to start over. We have to teach them, train them. We have to introduce them to the people and hope the people take to them like their predecessor. In the past, it was necessary. People didn't trust the Holy Order like they do now. Back then, many years ago, the Holy Order didn't even trust itself. To invest so much in one child for a lifetime was dangerous. But we are an institution now, with a direct line to god, and you, my dear, are a genuine and wonderful individual, and the people, they love you. I've wanted to do away with this tradition for a while, but I couldn't until I found the right person. It wouldn't work unless it was the right person."

"Does... does god want this, too?" He wouldn't be replaced at eighteen? It wasn't something he often thought about—eighteen seemed so far away—but when he did, it made him shiver with fear. The Holy Children who had aged out of their position as speakers were given a final ceremony, and then never heard from again.

"God and I want the same. Do you want this as well?"

"Yes," he said, in a whisper. "I don't want to die at eighteen."

"Die?" Justine laughed and held his hand. "They don't die. That's a nasty rumor. They live long lives, serving the Holy Order. God gives them new identities when they are finished. That's why you don't hear or see them anymore. You, though, won't get that. Serving the Holy Order will be your life. It will be difficult, but it is also god's will that you do this."

"I knew you were testing me," he said.

"We just had to start somewhere. This business with the Red Worm made me move a little faster. Penance, the world, needs us more than ever. There's a new heresy in the West, and to respond, we must change."

What does she want me to do? The Holy Child kept waiting for her to come out and say it, but what was it she was trying to say?

Justine, as usual, hadn't touched her food. She never did. "Do you remember the rumors that King Edgar returned from the Nameless Forest with a child?"

He nodded.

"Those rumors are true. Up until now, very few had seen him, let alone remembered the rumor at all. But the child is real. They are calling him the Anointed One. King Edgar and this child are accusing Penance of not only creating the Red Worm, but of worshiping a false idol. You see, they have started a new religion in Eldrus, a religion they claim follows the true God. It is called the Disciples of the Deep. It started in Eldrus, and has taken over in Nyxis."

"True God?" The Holy Child wrinkled his forehead. His neck got hot and sweaty. "No, they're wrong."

"They are. You and I both know better than anyone else that they are." Justine's hands became fists. "But Eldrus and the Heartland are convinced we are responsible for the Red Worm. And we've lost many of our footholds in the Heartland, as well. People don't believe like they used to. King Edgar foretold the death of the Red Worm, so when it happened, he found himself with new followers from this 'miracle.'" She shook her head, looked as though she were about to spit. "Do you see now why we must be consistent, as well as adaptable?"

The Holy Child nodded. As the blood boiled in his veins, his heart began to beat hard to the thudding rhythm of newfound purpose.

"I will have new missions for you. Some of them may be dangerous, and it hurts me to put you in danger, but we must learn how to weather adversity if we are going survive."

"You're talking about Audra of Eldrus?" The Holy Child wished he had his journal. He wanted badly to show her all he'd observed this morning in Isla Taggart's room.

"Yes. Alexander Blodworth smuggled her out of Ghostgrave after the rest of her family had been murdered. We've kept her here, out of sight and out of the loop, because having her was a liability. Geharra had always been our rival, but it is clear to us now that Eldrus is our true enemy. If we are to learn anything about our enemy, it would be from someone who lived amongst them.

"She is a gifted botanist, but she has other gifts as well. I believe she may be a spellweaver of some sort. I want you to befriend her, get to know her, and if you can, convert her. Find out how and why she's been talking to Isla Taggart, and if others know about her."

"People will find out if I start seeing her," the Holy Child said.

"We'll create the necessary story." Justine paused and studied him. "I know you're thinking I should just do it myself, right?"

He nodded.

"People don't trust me the way that they trust you. They call me the Hydra, because they think that I am two-faced and have my hands in everything. No, it has to be you. If you can do this, then you can do anything. The Anointed One will claim he is the true Holy Child. We have to show the people he is nothing more than a fake. Our god is the true god, but that won't matter if we've lost the faith of the flock."

The Holy Child closed his eyes. He had been looking forward to supper as a means to clear his mind. And in a way, somehow, it had. He felt trusted, more informed. He didn't grasp the exact implications of working more closely with Justine, but now, for the first time in a very long time, he actually felt important again. Sure, he knew he was important—he was the speaker of god—but even that had become routine. The same thing, day in and day out. Now, he could make a difference. He wouldn't be waiting for orders but giving them.

"There's one more thing," Justine said, a wave of smoke from the incense washing over her. "I heard you had an incident in the chapel today with Grant. He mentioned nightmares and a cult."

"I don't know what that was about." The Holy Child responded so quickly, so thoughtlessly, that even he believed the lie he told. And it seemed Justine did, too.

She nodded and stood up from the table. "Get some rest. You've had a long day. Tomorrow will be very different. Think about what I've said, and tell me your decision when you're ready." She went over to him and kissed his forehead gently. "You and I will make the world a better place. The way god has always wanted it to be. Never forget how fortunate we are to have you. Goodnight, Felix."

CHAPTER III

When Felix woke the following morning, he had already missed prayer, announcements, and breakfast. If he'd had a nightmare last night, well, he'd missed that, too. Fully rested, but in an absolute panic, he crawled out of bed and started dressing himself.

Why didn't anyone wake me up? His arms and legs were still asleep. They fought him every chance they could to stop him from getting ready. *Not good, not good. People are going to freak out.* Finally slipping into his sacred garments, he went at the speed of a sloth to the mirror and gave himself the once-over. *Justine did this*, he thought, spitting in his palm to flatten the explosion of hair on the top of his head. *She really is testing me.*

Without knocking, Avery and Mackenzie entered his room and shut the door behind them.

"What's going on?" he asked, a fresh glob of saliva sitting in his hand.

Mackenzie shook her head in amusement. "All the spit in the world won't be enough to tame that travesty of a hair-do." She went to him, took his hand, and wiped it on her armor. "You look like you slept well."

"Too well," Felix said. "Why didn't anyone wake me?"

Avery went to one knee, his armor rustling as he rummaged about on the ground. He stood up, brush in hand, and said, "Mother Abbess Justine ordered us to let you get some rest."

"Why?" He tilted his head downward. Mackenzie grabbed the brush and went to work on him.

"Because you'll be too busy talking to god today," Avery said.

"I will?" He hissed. "Ouch, Mackenzie!" If she brushed him any harder, he'd have a concussion.

She stopped, said, "Don't be a baby," and tossed the brush onto his bed. She slipped her hand into a pocket and took out a thin, white key.

"What's that?"

Mackenzie pressed the key into his hand and closed his fingers around it. Taking him by the shoulders, she turned him to the door and said, "Everyone's still eating. Go do what you do best."

Felix raised an eyebrow at Avery.

The guard raised his even higher. "I heard there's a room in the unfinished part of the cloister. Behind a steel door. Seems as good a place as any to listen to god."

Felix ran his finger along the teeth of the key. "I've always wondered what was behind there."

"Be back here fifteen minutes before afternoon guidance," Mackenzie said. She and Avery started out of the room. "Or we'll send a Night Terror in to—"

Before Avery could finish his sentence, Felix grabbed his journal, pen, and keyring and bolted out of the room.

He hurried to the hiding place and slipped inside. His disguise was there where he left it, but he didn't need it. Justine had told him Audra would trust him because of who he was. If he went to her as someone else, she'd never open up to him.

I can't believe she's letting me do this on my own, he thought, backing out of the hiding place and down into the abandoned closet at its end. *Can't be that dangerous. She wants to keep me around. She wouldn't take that big a risk.* He unlocked the door and, crouching low, entered the unfinished part of the cloister.

Felix jumped as the wind howled through the boards at the passage's beginning. He could hear it rattling the pathetic barricade, like the undead returning home. As he turned to lock the closet behind him, he noticed wet patches like footprints along the semi-tiled ground. They started at the front of the passage and went past the closet, father back into this forgotten place.

But where the footprints led to, Felix couldn't be sure. By the time he reached the first junction, he was too far from the front to see anything. He had to go left, that's where the steel door was, but what if whoever had come through here went left, too? Suddenly, the cold and muted darkness that surrounded him didn't feel empty like it should have. Standing there, teeth chattering, he swore he could see something in that frigid black, something darker than the dark it hid in. It was large, jagged, with a point like a beak jutting from the top of it.

"It's just my imagination," he said aloud. His voice echoed down the left passage. "It's just my imagination."

And maybe it had been, because after he said this again, the figure vanished.

Felix puffed out his chest, said a prayer to god, and plunged into the darkness. He started at a snail's pace. When the wind rose to a wail, he booked it down the passage, stubbing his toes and nicking his legs on the rubble in the way.

When he came here before, he'd had a candle, so he knew that if he ran his fingers along the wall, they should catch on three doors—wood, rock, and glass—before they hit the steel door. And one after the other, they came, until his nails ground to a halt on the thick, heavy door he often daydreamed of.

Quickly, he took out the key. After a good ten seconds of struggle, he unlocked the door. Something buzzed inside the metal. A pinching shock ran up his arm. He quickly let go of the key. But the key didn't need him. Slowly, it continued to turn on its own, until after two thuds and a click, the key stopped and the door popped open.

Felix, cringing, reached for the key and tore it out before it shocked him again. As he pulled the door back, a sliver of dirty, white light flickered on behind it. He let go of the door and crept through the crack. On the other side, a single fluorescent bulb sat fixed to the ceiling, blinking out a spastic distress signal.

"What is this?"

In awe, Felix closed the door behind him. Before he had the chance, it locked itself. But he didn't care, because here he was, in one of the most rundown parts of Pyra, and there was electricity coursing through it. He'd challenged Justine and his teachers every chance he could about the Old World technologies, and every time, they swore they were an impossibility.

He squinted, the harsh light starting to agitate his eyes. "I knew it."

Felix continued forward, to a second, circular, metal door at the end of this small passage. It was locked, so he took out the white key again and changed that. The door shook and opened inward. Light poured out from behind it, like water breaching a dam. With it came a gust of warm air, moist and earthy. Covering his face, he crossed the threshold and pushed the circular door shut.

Felix rubbed his eyes until they were right again. Then, blinking hard, shouted, "Holy crap!"

Statues, tens of them, covered almost completely in long, waxen sheets stood before him. They were tall, double his height, with humpbacks and star-shaped heads. Their feet were exposed—the statues looked to be made out of marble—but when he went to pull the sheets up, he found he couldn't. They were stuck to the statues, as though a part of them. What were they doing down here? Was there something wrong with them? Felix's imagination began to run wild, which meant it was time to move on.

But after he cleared the statues, he found there wasn't much further to go, because past them, there was only a small greenhouse. Most of the glass was covered in flowers and vines. As Felix drew nearer, he saw through the openings a woman inside. She was sitting on a bed in a dirty slip, her back to him, facing the wall of the hollow this place had been built against. And, though he couldn't hear her, he could tell by the way she moved her hands that she was talking to someone.

Felix bent down and laid his journal on the ground. *Should I play stupid?* He heard rocks crumbling behind him. He spun around, faced the hallway where the statues stood. There was no one there, but a few of the sheets that covered the statues were swaying slightly, as if someone had walked by.

Or should I pretend to be her friend? He turned back, towards the greenhouse, and froze. The woman was gone.

"What do you want?" the woman called out.

It was Audra, Felix was sure of it. She sounded the same as she had in Isla Taggart's room. Not responding, he went to the front of the greenhouse, where an ugly jail cell gate acted as a door. It had no keyhole, no way to unlock or open it. The frame of the door was fused to glass surrounding it with nether oil, which meant nothing short of another Trauma would be able to knock it down.

"What are you doing here?"

Felix looked through the bars of the gate, into the greenhouse.

Eggs of light hung down from the ceiling; from front to back, they covered the plants growing there in artificial light. In random places, sprinklers would sputter to life and spray the greenery they cowered behind. At the farthest end of the greenhouse, there was a long work bench covered in pots, bags, potions, and tools.

If someone told him all the plants of the world were growing here, he'd probably believe them. Felix didn't know much about that kind of thing, but some of the flowers were colors he hadn't even seen before. And there was a small stalk at the back, red markings like teeth running up it, that, when he looked at it, made his veins bulge.

Audra stepped out of the overgrowth running along the side of the greenhouse. "Holy Child or not, you shouldn't be here."

Audra of Eldrus. Here she was, not just as a name in a conversation or a shadow on the wall. And she wasn't what he expected at all. Her hair was long, but greasy, thick with knots that would have to be cut out. She was gaunt, her legs and armpits unshaven. Dry skin fell from her lips as she chewed on them. Her nails had so much dirt under them, they probably had a garden of their own. Felix remembered Justine had said she'd been here since the royal family of Eldrus had been murdered, but why were they treating her like a prisoner?

"Did you come to stare?" He could see through her slip, but he knew he wasn't supposed to, so he kept looking at her feet, instead. "Did they decide to turn me into a zoo attraction?"

"Isla…" Felix had said something just to say something, but when he said that, he noticed Audra's eyes widen. "Isla Taggart told me about you."

"How did you get in here?"

Felix took out his keyring.

"Let me out."

"I don't know how." He heard more rocks crumbling back the way he'd come. He looked at the statues. Again, some of the cloth that covered them was moving.

"You're lying to me," Audra said. She padded across the greenhouse, her feet making sucking sounds in the soil.

"You met with Isla Taggart yesterday morning in her bedroom."

Audra stopped and shot him a nasty look.

"You asked her to help. She wanted to wait until the right moment." Felix took a deep breath. He had to be careful. "She said you weren't happy."

"So she went and told the Holy Child of Penance?" Audra laughed. Her bones pressed against her thin skin as she did so. "I'm not stupid. The Hydra sent you."

Don't call her that, Felix thought. He grimaced.

She started to pace. "What do you want?"

Audra had been down here a long time, and short of death, there wasn't much worse that could happen to her. She would pretend not to trust him, he realized, but she would try to, every chance she could get. He knew what that was like. It was the only way he could get through those days in the South with Samuel Turov.

She growled, "Don't stare at me."

Felix's eyes went to his journal on the ground. "I'm sorry," he whispered.

"Do you know how to get me out of here?" She sat down on her bed. It sagged with her weight.

"I don't see a way to unlock the door."

"You can't." She threw up her arms. "I've had a long time to search this place. I can't find the way out. The glass isn't glass. I don't know what it is, but I can't break it." She bared her knuckles, which were scabby and uneven. "I tried. A lot. But they come in here some-times, to fix this Old World stuff or to leave food or supplies."

Felix's eyes found hers again. "How do they get in?"

Audra shrugged. "They fill the greenhouse up with gas. I don't wake up for a long time until after they leave."

"I'm sorry you're here," Felix admitted. He wanted to cry, he felt so bad for her. She didn't deserve this. No one did. God wouldn't want this.

Audra grunted. She picked her nose and ate what came out of it. "The Hydra would know how to get me out."

"The... I got this key from Mother Abbess Justine's room. There might be something... or I could talk to her for you."

Audra scoffed. "After what your city is saying that my brother did? I don't think so."

"Did Isla tell you?"

"No, my real friends did." She looked at the wall behind the glass beside her bed.

"Who?"

"She didn't send you." Audra stood up and walked over to the cell gate. "She wouldn't forget that detail."

"Shadows," Felix blurted out. He remembered how she seemed to come out of Isla's shadow.

Audra furrowed her brows. "Alexander Blodworth told me about the Worms of the Earth."

Felix's voice broke as he asked, "The what?"

"Ask the Hydra," she said with a smile.

"Like the Red Worm?" Felix was starting to sound like the child he was. He straightened up and took a step back, trying not to look at Audra's chest.

She grabbed the bars of the gate. "The Hydra knows more than she lets on. Did she tell you why she let Exemplar Samuel Turov kidnap you and take you into Night Terror country?"

"What?" Felix's manliness deflated. "What are you...? She wouldn't."

"I could kill you where you stand," Audra said. "She probably knows that. But she let you come and see me, anyways."

"She didn't send me..."

"You're a pawn. She moves you to her advantage." Audra let go of the bars and started to walk away. "Even if you wanted to help me, you couldn't. You'd turn against me. I know enough about your 'Holy Child' kind. I don't blame you, but I don't need you." She disappeared back into the overgrowth and said, "Hear anything from god lately? I prayed a lot that first year. Guess god can't hear me all the way down here."

Felix had lost her, but he had to leave anyway, because it was almost time for afternoon guidance. After Audra, all he wanted to do was sit down with Justine and ask her questions. He knew the woman was probably lying, but what were these Worms of the Earth? And why did she say Samuel Turov had taken him on purpose? And Audra could have killed him if she wanted to? He doubted that, but if there was a chance, why did Justine even take the risk?

At nightfall, Felix made his way to Mother Abbess Justine's quarters, only to find she was gone. Her personal guards told him she had been called away on important business. She would dine with him tomorrow.

"Are you sure?" he asked, sulking. "I need to talk to her."

"I'm sorry, your holiness," one of the guards said. "She thought you would appreciate the time to yourself, to reflect on god's word.

God's word? He almost laughed. *God hasn't told me anything.*

"Dinner was delivered to your room, your holiness," the other guard added. As though he were speaking to a lost dog, he said, "Mother Abbess Justine is not here."

Felix returned to his quarters and stayed there the rest of the night. He ate half his dinner and gave the rest to Avery and Mackenzie, who finished it off before he could hand them the silverware. Not wanting to think any more about Audra or what she had said, because he knew his mind would make those things worse than they probably were, he drank a bit of Respite and went to sleep.

After a month of nightmares, he wasn't surprised to have another. But this time, he wasn't in the gray place, or with the Night Terror who saved him. This time, he was in the South, back in the house Samuel Turov had kept him in. The old man was in his underwear. He had a switch in his hand.

"Recite," he screamed at Felix, who was cowering in the pile of blankets on the floor. He was in his underwear, too, and he had almost soiled himself.

"Thou shalt not…"

Samuel Turov clenched his teeth and grabbed Felix by his ankle. He dragged him out of the pile and whipped the switch against Felix's bare thighs.

"Stop me! Stop me!" Samuel Turov cried, eyes heavenward, as he branded the Holy Child with his cruelty.

Felix squirmed free of the exemplar's grip. He got up and went for the sword against the wall, but Samuel Turov wrapped his arm around his neck and flung him down to the ground. "Thou shalt not worship false idols!"

Felix bit into the old man's sunburnt arm, but it only made him choke him harder.

"Stop me!" Samuel Turov screamed.

Felix's eyes rolled back in his skull.

And as his consciousness faded, he woke, drenched in sweat, tangled in his blankets. He threw his legs over the side of the bed and bawled into his hands.

"Don't think about it, don't think about it," he repeated over and over, fingers sticky with snot and saliva. "She wouldn't leave you with him. She wouldn't do that to you."

Felix wiped his hands on the covers and rose shakily to his feet. He sighed, his breath hot and potion-soured, and went the window, to stand in the moonlight coming through it.

"God give me strength," he said. He put his elbows on the sill, his nose to the iced glass. "God give us all strength."

Felix took a deep breath and blew on the window. The glass fogged. As he put his finger to it, someone croaked behind him, "Help me."

Mackenzie? Felix looked over his shoulder, but it wasn't Mackenzie he found there. It was the Night Terror who'd saved him, the woman with the raven's head. She was in his room. He wasn't dreaming.

CHAPTER IV

The Winged Horror ran forward and tackled Felix to the ground. The feathers that covered her pricked his skin, leaving numb bumps where they touched him. She wrapped her human-like claws around his face and tilted it back. The Night Terror leaned forward, into the shaft of moonlight coming through the window above. Her head was literally a massive raven's skull. With it illuminated, Felix could see two sad, black eyes sunken deep inside it.

"Help me." Her voice was high, but hoarse. The words came out muffled from that scarred beak of hers.

Felix shook his head. "I don't... I don't..."

The Winged Horror squeezed his head in anger, and let go. She reared up, her mottled wings splayed outward. He had been wrong. She did have skin, but it looked bleached, and there wasn't much of it. It had been a long time since he'd seen her, but she looked wrong, starved. Her arms, which were attached to the inside of the wings, were sinewy, stretched. But she clearly remembered him. And if he looked at her hard enough, he could see what he remembered of her.

Felix scooted back, against the wall. "Who did this... to you? What can I...?"

She lowered her wings and rose to her feet. The talons that had burst from her boots clicked on the ground. "The cult... the cult."

She gripped her head and bent over. The feathers on her back stood upright. Her spine pressed hard against her back.

"They're coming," she said, clawing her skull. "Find them. Tell them." She looked up at the ceiling. "Two men." She glanced back at him, shivering with fear. "I am... V-Vrana. Tell them!"

Felix cried, "I don't know who you're talking about." He slid up the wall. "I want to help you, Vrana, but I don't know—"

Gray fog formed above her. From it, a long, pale arm fell down in front of Vrana and grabbed her by the beak. The Night Terror screamed, sunk her talons deep into the arm. A second arm, longer than the first, slipped through the fog and, with its boney hand, choked her throat.

"Naughty, naughty," a woman's voice whispered. There were voices behind the voice, words within the words.

"Vrana," Felix whispered.

Long, wet, black hair fell from the fog, draping across Vrana's skull. Then, along with the arms, like a spider crawling down its web, a head and two shoulders appeared. It was a woman, the woman who had spoken.

The Witch twisted her neck, the veins and muscles in it bulging, and said, "Go back to sleep, little boy. This is only a bad, bad dream."

Felix jerked awake. He was on the floor, curled up in a ball. The morning sun was coming through the window, slowly creeping towards him.

Avery and Mackenzie opened the door. Their eyes went wide. They ran to him.

"What happened? Are you okay?"

Felix tried to get up, but he was so covered in sweat he kept slipping.

Avery and Mackenzie went to his side and gently put him back in his bed.

"Bad dream," he said, now shivering. He grabbed his pillow and held it tightly.

Mackenzie shoved Avery toward the door. "Get a doctor."

"Not necessary," Justine said.

The Mother Abbess was standing in the hall. As though nothing were wrong, she strolled in. Flicking her wrist, she sent the guards out of the room.

When the door slammed shut behind her, Justine said, "We can't miss morning prayer again." Her morning gown, a pinkish white, pooled around her feet.

Felix peeled himself from the pillow. "Where were you?"

"A few months ago, we sent another party to Geharra, at Blodworth's request. They made it back last night, with two survivors from Blodworth's group." Justine's lip quivered. "You have to learn how to live without me sometimes."

Felix's cheeks went red. He could tell he had let her down. Yeah, he was only eleven, but he was the Holy Child, god's speaker, and one of the highest ranking members of the Holy Order of Penance. He couldn't crumble every time she wasn't there to support him.

"I don't know who the two survivors are. I've never met them before. They were too traumatized to talk. Maybe you can talk to them." She fingered a chain around her neck, mumbled "Ouch," when it moved. "Are you sick?"

Felix shook his head. He was perfect. There was absolutely nothing wrong with him. He might have just seen his nightmares come to life, but how did that make him different from anybody else?

Justine wrinkled her nose. Her pale eyes darted back and forth as she stared him down. She could tell he was lying this time. But apparently, she didn't care, because she ignored it and said, "Did you speak to Audra?"

"Yes." He tossed the pillow onto his bed, got up, and started getting dressed. He had to keep busy, to keep the images of Vrana and the Witch off his mind. "She said—" he searched the ground for feathers, scratches—anything that would prove it had really happened, "—something about the Worms of the Earth?" He threw on a tunic, slipped into some pants. He touched the back of his head and felt a stinging cut. "And something about—" he still had a few of the numb bumps on his arm, "—Samuel Turov. But I know it's not true."

Justine touched Felix's shoulder, to slow him down. "I wouldn't sleep well, either, with all that on my mind."

He closed his eyes and took a deep breath. Her hand on his shoulder, its cold warmth comforting him. This was what he needed last night. She wasn't his mother, but to him, she was. Without her, he only had god, and sometimes, god wasn't enough.

"Did she say that I let Samuel Turov take you on purpose?"

He nodded.

"That is a vicious lie that Isla Taggart and the Winnowers' Chapter have been trying to pass off recently. If Isla wasn't the Exemplar of Innocence's niece, I'd cast her out to the tundra."

"I know." He smiled, fought back a tear. "Doesn't make sense, anyways."

"What doesn't?"

"Letting Samuel Turov steal me."

"Exactly." She patted his head. "A lot of people lost a lot of trust in the church when that happened. And I… lost a lot of faith in myself."

She apologized a million times that day the soldiers brought him home from Cadence. He had never seen her look so scared in his entire life. She had never said she loved him before, but in that moment, he knew. Nothing made Justine cry. But that did.

"Samuel Turov… Worms of the Earth. She's already trying to turn you against me." The smell of burnt wood rolled off Justine and made Felix's nose curl.

"What are they?"

"Ancient, mythological creatures. But apparently, not that mythological." She smiled, ran her fingers through his hair. "Eldrus' Red Worm seems to be one of them. Get through the day, Felix, and I'll give you the writings on the creatures tonight at dinner to read. I'm not worried, though. It's nothing god can't handle."

As she finally took her hands off him, he felt his stomach sink, the burden of his lie about the nightmare weighing it down. But that wasn't the only thing making him sick. Samuel Turov. Something didn't add up about him, about how he'd taken Felix. He acted like he believed her, only because he hoped to fall for the act himself. She loved him, but that didn't mean she wouldn't hurt him.

Felix shook the stupid idea out of his head.

"After the usual morning business, I want you to go to Penance. Meet these survivors. The people of Penance need to see you, too."

"What about Audra?"

Justine laughed, her face flashing all the colors of cruelty. "She can wait. She's not going anywhere."

The road to Penance proper from Pyra was a short one—the monastery sat high on a hill at the edge of the city—but the weather had been poor the night before. Helminth's Pass, the road on which Felix's carriage traveled, was covered in a few feet of snow. The weather workers were out in full force, as they often were, maintaining the roadways. For some reason, though, they hadn't made it to Pyra yet—a place that was supposed to be taken care of before anywhere else.

Felix rode alone, but outside the carriage, he was at the center of everyone's attention. Avery, Mackenzie, and several additional guards rode alongside him. But with all the armor and furs they wore, even he had a hard time recognizing them. They looked like a bunch of wild animals on horseback, pretending to be human. It made him smile, and made him think of Vrana.

There was a ragged copy of *Helminth's Way* on the seat beside him. He grabbed it and opened to a random page, to forget about the Night Terror. The sacred text of the Holy Order was everywhere in the city. There were definitely more of them out there than any other book. And he was pretty sure it was the only book most people ever read.

"The Five Commandments of Helminth," Felix started, focusing as hard as he could on the prophet's words. "The First Commandment: There are no other gods but god. The Second Commandment: Lillian was the first mother of the Holy Order, and the first speaker of god; her words are divine truths. The Third Commandment: God's followers are missionaries; it is their duty to save those who have strayed from god's grace."

Felix bobbed in his seat as the carriage cleared a mountainous drift. The driver shouted something at the horses. With a snap of his reins, the carriage bucked again and landed, at last, onto cleared road.

Felix lost his page, but quickly flipped back to it. Of course, he didn't have to. He'd had the Five Commandments memorized long before he could speak them.

"The Fourth Commandment: Do not do harm to god's people, lest harm is done unto the people of god. The Fifth Commandment: The Holy Order is the embodiment of god and, therefore, infallible."

He hated to admit it, even in his head, but thinking about the Commandments, it made him realize how people like Isla Taggart and the Winnowers' Chapter were right about the way they were written. Helminth was a Trauma survivor, a prophet who created the sacred text and many of the Holy Order's rules, but why was his name on everything? Shouldn't he have given god credit? The same went for Lillian, about whom even less was known.

Justine had made him attend a Winnowers' conference in secret once, to see how extreme some individuals' views were when it came to their religion. They had claimed that people didn't worship god anymore, but the Holy Order itself; the "institution" as they put it. It had made him so mad that he begged Justine to break up the Chapter, but she told him it wasn't worth it.

"There's always someone who thinks they're smarter than the rest," Justine had said, ushering Felix's red-faced self out of the meeting. "It's not about worshiping, but being the one who is worshiped."

"Isn't that blasphemy?" he had said, cursing them in his head.

"Everything is a blasphemy. The Night Terrors are right, in a way."

Felix remembered he had stopped and looked at her like she was crazy.

"It's all about balance. But not an equal balance, as they know it. The scales must always favor evil. Otherwise, there will be no motivation to do good."

"No," he had said, shaking his head. "I don't think that's true."

"Would you rather it be the opposite? Good outbalancing evil? That's how we end up with groups like the Winnowers' Chapter. Good is never good enough. Honestly, it's not even about balance, Felix, but maintenance. Life is best enjoyed with the faint taste of rot in one's mouth."

"God doesn't think so," Felix had boasted boldly.

Justine had smiled at this and said quietly, "Is that what god said?"

Outside the carriage, Avery shouted, "We're almost there!"

Felix closed the sacred text and tossed it across the compartment. Realizing what he'd done, he said, "Sorry, god," and prayed a quick prayer of penitence.

The carriage picked up the pace once Helminth's Pass wrapped around and joined with Lillian Avenue. Penance's main road, it ran from north to south across the snow-sieged city. When Penance had been known as Six Pillars, Lillian Avenue was the way in which the religions housed here could come out of their quarters and interact and build good relationships with one another. When Six Pillars became known as Penance, Lillian Avenue was the way in which the newly formed Holy Order had been able to take over the city and absorb the faiths that were too weak to fight them off.

The two surviving soldiers of Geharra and the group who had found them were waiting for Felix at Saint Priscilla's Hospital for Maladies. Saint Priscilla had been the first Mother Abbess, after Lillian; her namesake hospital was mostly used for quarantining patients.

According to Justine, the survivors may have come into contact with a plant Eldrus had used to take Geharra over. They had since been tested and cleared, but to avoid a panic and mob, were yet to be released.

Two knocks sounded on Felix's door. Then Avery's voice shouted through it: "There's a few people here to see you. Do you want to address them?"

You do, god said to him, so Felix nodded and said, "Yes."

Avery shouted something to the other guards. He heard them dismount. The horses all snorted in appreciation. Felix opened his door slightly. A few people? Even through the crack, he could tell the area was packed.

Mackenzie pulled the door open all the way. A cold wind funneled through and blasted Felix with a face-full of ice.

"Tell Avery his math skills suck," he said, as Mackenzie wiped him down.

"Your math skills suck," Mackenzie shouted at Avery, who was securing a perimeter outside the hospital.

Avery looked back angrily, and shrugged.

Felix strained his ears to make sense of the crowd, but too many people were saying too many things all at once. "What are they saying?"

"The usual. They know you're here for the survivors." Mackenzie pulled back, gave him the thumbs up. "Say something sassy about Eldrus. The Demagogue has been whipping them up all morning. They'll love it."

"The Demagogue?"

Felix dropped out of the carriage into two feet of snow. Despite his layers, the cold found him at once. The frozen needles of this forever winter stabbed at his feet, worked their way up his legs, and prodded him for warmth to take.

"He's here?"

"Unfortunately."

Felix wasn't very tall, but the crowd stretched so far and was so loud, that he didn't need to be to know there were more behind those bunched up outside Saint Priscilla's Hospital for Maladies. They had to have been standing there for a while, all the men and women, and the children like glue that wriggled between them. Their faces were bright red, their whole bodies solid, stiff. An inch or so of snow sat on top of their shoulders. Altogether, they looked and moved like hunks of ice. But that didn't stop them from crying out to him, reaching out to him, begging him for blessings and god's guidance.

With Avery and Mackenzie to his left and right, he trudged toward Saint Priscilla's. The hospital had been a shell of itself after the Trauma. Mother Abbess Priscilla took that wreckage, gutted the Old World machines and objects, and rebuilt it. Now, it stood two stories high, pillars running up and down its length, with more stained glass windows than most of the churches nearby.

The Demagogue was standing, arms crossed, at the foot of the steps that led up to the hospital. Dressed in a long, tapered, black robe, with a red clerical collar like a fetter around his neck, the man, with his craggy face and crooked nose, still looked like an absolute tool.

"Your holiness," the Demagogue said, kneeling. His greasy, shoulder length hair slid across his face like an oil spill.

Cringing, Felix held out his hand; he yanked it back as soon as the Demagogue kissed it. This was a formality he kept trying to forget. But he did it today, because he knew the Demagogue wouldn't forget. He didn't forget anything.

The Demagogue rose to his feet. "Are they supporters or traitors?"

"Who?" He had to shout it, because the crowd around them was getting restless.

"The survivors." The Demagogue's hand dipped into his pocket and took out a rosary. He started rubbing each of the wooden beads.

Supporters, god said, so Felix said, "Supporters."

"That's a shame." The Demagogue bowed and stepped aside. "Nothing like a little gossip to warm up a city."

Felix smiled the fakest smile he could manage and started up the steps. The Demagogue; his real name was Joseph Cleon, but if you called him that, he'd throw a temper tantrum. What a freak. Why Justine continued to use him, he didn't understand. And she seemed to like him, too. He caught them flirting every once in a while. It made him jealous.

Felix and his guards stopped at the top of the stairs, where several nurses stood, eyes shining and happy to see him. He nodded at them and turned around to greet those who now stood below him, two hundred strong.

"It's freezing out here," Felix started, a big grin on his face.

Penance, below him, laughed. They nodded and nudged one another, but never broke their gaze from his.

"Thank you for coming here to show your support for our soldiers. These brave men have endured unspeakable horrors, but their faith remains unshaken. God has a plan, but expectations, as well. I know that you want to know what we are going to do about Eldrus, but before we make a decision, we need all the information we can get. God expects us to learn, to make use of these minds given to us. God has all the answers, but sometimes, we have to find them for ourselves. We must be patient. We must be diligent. We mustn't become what we once were, what led us out here to the edge of everything."

Applause broke out through the crowd. In the snow-covered city of Penance, all sound was dampened, so each clapping hand was like the crack of a snare, the thump of a drum.

But Felix could see that some of the people weren't pleased with his speech. Winnowers, probably, or people with close ties to the blabbermouths of Pyra.

So he added: "There are whispers that Eldrus has abandoned god for a false idol. There are whispers that King Edgar has formed a new religion, the Disciples of the Deep, with an imposter holy child. God has spoken to me, and god has said that anyone who pledges allegiance to this new heresy will be cast out from the flock, from god's light. Remember—"

The Demagogue nodded at Felix. He was practically rubbing his hands in excitement. In that moment, he knew he had screwed up.

"Remember this," Felix said, voice cracking. He turned on Penance and headed inside.

I'm in trouble, he thought, as he, Avery, and Mackenzie followed the nurses from outside through Saint Priscilla's. *I shouldn't have said that. They might not even know about that new religion. Crap.* They turned down several corners, the doctors that lined the halls forcing patients back into their rooms. *Crap, crap, crap.*

"They are through here, your holiness," one of the nurses said.

She and her sisters took the lead and pushed open the double doors at the end of the hall. Prayers from the patients they had left behind echoed around them.

"Mother Abbess requested that you meet with them alone," Avery said as they filed into the infectious disease ward of the hospital.

"They are still somewhat sedated," another nurse said. She led them past the front desk, down a hall, to a large metal door, with a peephole at the top of it. "And restrained."

"Restrained?" Felix looked at Avery and Mackenzie. "Why?"

"The Mother Abbess said that if you were going to meet with them alone, they should be restrained. For your safety."

"Do they know I'm here to see them?"

The nurse shook her head. "They went mute after the Mother Abbess visited yesterday."

"We're out here, okay?" Avery drew his sword.

Mackenzie did the same. "Leave the door unlocked," she said to the nurse. "Your holiness, if you feel threatened, don't hesitate to run."

"I'll be fine." Felix turned to the nurse. "I have god on my side."

The nurse nodded. She took out a keyring that was positively overflowing with keys and, somehow, immediately picked out the right one. She unlocked the door, smiled, and mouthed something that looked like "Be careful."

Felix opened the door and went through. The room on the other side didn't have much going on. Just two beds and the two men on them, haggard as heck and not having much fun with the chains around their wrists and ankles.

The man on the left looked almost feral. His hair and beard had, more or less, taken over his face. But what scared Felix the most about him was his eyes. They had a strange, green sheen to them, like the back of a bug.

The man on the right, however, was different. Felix felt bad for that man. He looked hurt. Not a recent kind of hurt, but the kind of hurt someone carries with them a long, long time. This man didn't have much of a beard, and no hair. One of his eyes was bright blue, while the other was clouded over, as if he were blind in it. He was covered in scars, too, all over his face and body.

"Nobody said the Holy Child was coming to see us," the man on the left said. He sounded like a jerk.

"It is an honor, your holiness," the man on the right said, lowering his head.

"I'm sorry about the restraints." Felix closed the door behind him, stepped further into the room. "I didn't know."

"We understand, your holiness," the hurt man said.

The jerk nodded. "It's kind of you to grace us with your presence, my... your holiness." He smirked at the hurt man and rolled his eyes.

"Please, forgive him, your holiness," the hurt man said. "He is without his medicine. And we have seen many things to trouble our minds."

"I've come today to help you unburden yourselves." Felix started counting the scars on the hurt man. When the hurt man noticed this, he stopped... stopped at fifty-three. "I'm sorry to ask you to relive what happened in Geharra, but it may save even more lives if you..."

Felix stopped speaking, the word of god lifting from his tongue. His eyes darted back and forth between the two men. Something clicked in his mind. Words he'd heard hours before now made sense. *Two men are coming*, Vrana had told him. So he stared at these two men, who had come from so far, and wondered: *Are these them? Would it hurt to ask?*

If they did know who Vrana was, then they would know she was a Night Terror. That would make Felix look bad, but it would make them look suspicious, too. He was the Holy Child, though. If he had to play that card to get himself out of a bad situation, he would.

Maybe they know her. Maybe they met her on their way back. Justine did say Night Terrors were killed along with Geharra, too.

"Is everything okay, your holiness?" the hurt man asked.

"Do you know..." He hesitated, looked at the Corruption on these men's arms. It was faded, pinkish, like most children's looked; like his did.

The jerk cleared his throat. "We told the Mother Abbess everything, your holiness."

Felix shook his head and forced himself to say it. "Do you know someone named Vrana?"

The hurt man's mouth dropped open slightly.

The jerk started to laugh. He cocked his head and said, "Uh, what?"

"Vrana," Felix repeated. "Do you know her?" But he already knew they did. He had caught them off-guard.

The jerk said, "No, sorry, we—"

"Yes," the hurt man interrupted. "She saved your life."

Felix checked the door, to make sure it was shut. His face got hot and his heart started to pound. *This was a mistake. Crap, crap, crap—*

"She saved your life," the hurt man continued. He leaned forward. "The Exemplar of Restraint had taken you. She found you accidentally and killed him. She took you to Cadence, where Penance finally found you. We know her, because we are looking for her."

"She came to me... she came to me." Felix pulled down on his face and fell against the wall. "She visits me—" He lowered his voice to a whisper. "—Visits me in my dreams."

The jerk gasped. "Deimos, she is dead."

"No," Deimos said. "That doesn't mean anything." He turned to Felix. "Your holiness, we must find a way to help her. She has something, and someone terrible is using her for it."

"I saw that someone," Felix said. "She was... awful. Who is she? No, no, who are you?"

"Night Terrors," Deimos said. "This is—"

The jerk shouted, "No, stop, idiot!"

"—Is Lucan. We know that you are kind, your holiness, and that you are wise beyond your years. We did not come here to cause trouble, but to stop another Worm from laying ruin to the Earth."

"You went to the wrong city," Felix said, praying to god no one could hear them. "Eldrus started this!"

"Vrana is a dear friend. We received correspondence that something may have happened to her. There are people here in Penance, in Pyra, that are changing because of her."

"Changing how? The cult?"

"Cult? I don't know. But if you are in contact with her—"

Someone knocked on the door.

Felix jumped so high, he almost went through the roof.

"Your holiness, it's time to return," Mackenzie said.

"You're Night Terrors?" Felix didn't know how the prophets of old did it. All these revelations would be the death of him. "No, you're sick. That's why you're in here. It's a sin to lie to the Holy Child."

Lucan sneezed onto his bedsheets. "If we were lying, we'd lie about something that wouldn't get us killed immediately."

"We can help you, help you help her," Deimos said. "But you have to get us out of here. She's coming to you in your dreams? Your holiness, you are not safe. Have you told anyone else?"

"No, I haven't, I—"

Another knock. This time, Avery: "Is everything okay in there, your holiness? We're coming in."

"She saved you, kid," Lucan grumbled. "Everyone in Cadence is dead because they found you there. Do the right thing."

Deimos spat at Lucan to shut him up. "Your holiness," he said. "Do not trust anyone with eyes like—"

The door swung back. Avery and Mackenzie poured through, the nurses flanking them.

"What happened?" Avery asked, looking like he was ready to cut off Deimos' and Lucan's heads.

"Nothing," Felix said. He pushed past his guards, past the nurses, his mind burning so hot it surely scorched them. "Take me back."

CHAPTER V

Knowledge is a sickness borne by right. What we learn, we believe we are entitled to share. We do this to enlighten, or we do it to burden. But not all minds accept knowledge equally. Some reject it, the same way a body may reject an infection. Some minds become fevered and irrational, offended and confrontational. While others harbor the knowledge and let it fester inside them, where it either changes them, or destroys them.

I, Victor Mors, have traveled the Membrane in-between, and there a sickness fell over me. I am contagious, you see, and though I know it to be false, only by sharing my sickness can I be free.

The Worms of the Earth. It is a name of my own creation, and yet I expect it has always been their name. They exist in a place parallel to our world, but as far as I can tell, they exist only because we do. Perhaps Parasites of the Earth would have been a more fitting name, but I am not yet convinced they are without merit.

But to truly begin, I must go back to the beginning, where on one dark night here in Eldrus, I found myself searching through the Archivist's relics. I was not looking for anything in particular, until, by happenstance, Deacon Wake's black chalice was in my hands. The research I had been conducting on the causes of the Trauma were leading nowhere. I had ideas. I had interpretations. But so did the gutter rats that clog the streets outside Ghostgrave. Ideas and interpretations weren't enough, and there wasn't enough evidence left on this earth, it seemed, to ascertain the truth of the matter. But then, on that dark night here in Eldrus, without trying, I stumbled upon the first ghoul's black chalice, the object by which he visited a place ostracized occultists have deemed the Membrane. We know this world was once densely packed with advancements and technologies beyond our current comprehension. For most of it to disappear, off the earth and from our minds, in such a haphazard fashion, led me to believe it had not vanished, but been moved elsewhere. And what better place for these things to have been relocated than a place of seemingly infinite space that runs alongside our own? Perhaps it makes me a deviant, but I smile when think that heaven may be there, and it is overflowing with all our ruin.

Using the black chalice was easier than I expected. Beneath it, there was a very small piece of parchment that had the instructions for its activation. This was too convenient to have been anything but deliberate, but I value my life too much to make accusations as to who may have been responsible for its placement there. After gathering the necessary ingredients, which took several days and several raids on the Archivist's stash, I retired to my chambers, locked the doors and windows, and proceeded to do the devil's work.

It took one hour of chanting and guzzling the contents of the black chalice. As the last drop of that infernal concoction touched my lips, the room began to spin. In a drunken haze, I fell to the ground. When I awoke, a portal loomed over me, the sinewy tendrils of light that wreathed it writhing and tasting the air. As I stumbled to my feet, I considered that it may close behind me, and that I would be trapped. I considered this, and then I went in, anyways.

It was as though I had walked through a door. On one side, my chambers, and on the other, the vertical sprawl of the Membrane. It felt as though I had shrunken down and wandered into the intestinal tract of some gargantuan creature. I could see the other side of the tunnel from the narrow ledge on which I stood, but the gaping pit between that point and mine prevented any attempt to cross. If there was a beginning or end to the place, I did not see it. Above and below, there was only darkness.

With nowhere to go but back, I turned around, thinking that a second ritual may place me somewhere else, where I could access additional parts of the Membrane. But that's when I saw it, something which may or may not have been there before. Behind the portal, a passageway had been carved out of the thick, tongue-like material of which the walls were comprised. In Deacon Wake's writings, he mentioned that his greatest mistake had been exiting this section of the Membrane, for this section was the barrier itself, and it was by this barrier he was safest. I knew that if I were to leave here, I would be exposing myself to that infectious knowledge I had spoken of earlier. But at the time, I considered myself inoculated by intelligence, so I went to that passageway, whose insides were made of roots and bones, and walked it.

First there was cold heat, followed by dark light, and then the passageway opened up to a pale desert that shimmered and shook beneath a sunless sky. I had come here alone, but when my feet touched the sand, I saw that I was expected. Humans, I thought at first, seeing the familiar and comforting shape of my fellow man dotting a nearby dune. Fellow travelers, I figured, watching as the shapes slinked down the dunes, their forms warped by mirage. But they were not humans, nor fellow travelers, I realized as they drew near, but something else, something empty, something hungry.

I tried to flee, but the sands held my feet. The creatures, the shadows, they swarmed over me in a black wave of silver fangs and burning eyes. At that moment, I expected death, and thought that I even deserved it. But much to my surprise, the shadows did not put me in the ground, but raised me from it. And on their midnight hands, emotionally vacant, I let them carry me across the sands, to that dune from whence they had emerged.

Up close, the dune was mountainous, and not entirely comprised of sand. As the bone-white grains shivered down *the sides of it, I saw an architecture within. It seemed like something our species would be capable of. In that moment, then, the alien desert that surrounded me suddenly became recognizable. I could not make sense of it, nor had I any memories to give credence to the claim, but like the word on the tip of one's tongue, it was simultaneously familiar and unfamiliar. Known and unknown.*

The shadows set me down, and when they did, I had a chance to consider them. Like dark shapes cast by light upon a wall, they were truly their name. The only difference was that they were not two dimensional, but three. They had a hazy transparency, and yet there was a weight to their actions, a strength in their voided forms. Looking at them, I became convinced they were truly human at some point. I still do not know what terrible thing they had endured to reduce to them to such a desolate state. But, at the time, I assumed they had brought me here to experience their fate.

The dune began to rumble, and the sands that covered the front of it began to part. A howling wind that sounded like sharpening knives sliced through my tenuous will. More shadows appeared at the crest of the dune. When the rumbling stopped, the sands had thinned away to a point where I could see a doorway beyond their ashen vale. I expected to be forced in against my will, but instead, the shadows merely outstretched their hands and pointed forwards. It was then that I realized I had been spared not to suffer, but to give witness to something secret inside.

I thought about running, but every step I took brought me closer to the dune, until, with sand having fallen into my eye, I stood upon that stony threshold. Beyond it, a steep staircase led downward into the desert, the light that illuminated it dim, its source invisible. This is what I wanted, I told myself, doubt setting in as I stared into that yawning abyss. I did not know at the time if I would find the answers I sought at the end of the staircase. But I knew I would have answers, even if they were answers to questions that had yet to be asked, let alone conceived.

I walked for what seemed like hours down those ancient

steps, until, at last, my feet found earth. The soil was wet and ruddy, and the stones that sat in it were pricks of light, like distant, dying stars. In that cavernous landing, I became convinced I had left the desert. Somewhere along the staircase, I had crossed another barrier—I felt this transition in my very bones—so where I stood now, mouth agape, goalless and grief-filled, I did not know. Despite the light around me, the shadows had stayed topside. I suspect each of them had seen this place once, and then never again.

I pressed forward, portal be damned. This was a binary situation I found myself in. Either I would escape, or I would not. But where was I to go? The strip of earth I navigated radiated outward in all directions, some doubling back the way of the staircase, the others going further still, deep into the even darker depths not even the invisible lights could penetrate. But as I wandered blindly, I noticed the Membrane once more, imposing itself into this realm. Here and there, those thick, muscular walls cordoned off areas so as to prevent passage. Though they were hard to look at, those disturbing murals of discarded organs and entrails were a welcome sign that I had not yet strayed too far.

Surrounded by inhuman things, I was reminded of my own humanity. Hunger, thirst, and sheer exhaustion were beginning to take a toll. When one plunges into a place such as that ancient temple beneath the sands, one does not expect to be done-in by dehydration or sleep deprivation. But then I saw something, something purposeful, something of intelligence and meaning, and I put aside my own mortality and donned immortal indifference.

The thin slice of earth came to an end, and beyond it, a red chasm of ruin. But I strayed from that sight, for it was too distant, and my eyes only saw what my imagination wanted them to see. Instead, I went to the nearest wall, where it was covered in strange, tubular growths, like veins that had been extracted from a body. Beyond the growths, I saw that the wall went further back, to another chamber, where, again, the strange architecture was present. There, large archways stood on islands in a sea of nothingness, and crowning each archway were gems of magnificent col-

or. White, red, and green on one side; gray, yellow, purple, and blue, the other. Each color had an archway and island all its own, and pressing my face through the veins, I saw that these islands were not made of stone or earth, but something else entirely. I could not reach the red chasm of ruin, but if I were careful enough, I could cross the vermillion veins and follow the causeway that ran under them and between those eldritch islands.

As I ducked and weaved through the vermillion veins, a part of me came to the conclusion that I would die here. I did not know where Deacon Wake had gone to contract ghoulism, but at that moment, I wished that I did and had gone there first. I had no doubt in my mind that I was close to stumbling upon ancient knowledge, and to think that I would be the only one of our world to carry it seemed cruel. In my selflessness, I became selfish, and perhaps that is why I sit here now and recount these recollections. Because the Worms of the Earth indulge selfishness, and they knew that, if I had done all of this for good alone, they would have had to let me perish in that otherworldly waste.

I do not know why I did it, but as I cleared the last of the vermillion veins, I turned around and took a bite out of it. A sour, invigorating fluid filled my mouth and, suddenly, I was no longer hungry, thirsty, or even exhausted. Bright, unfocused images flashed through my mind as I swallowed that red drink, but even to this day, I have yet to make sense of them.

I hurried across the causeway, towards the islands in their abyssal lake. On each of them, an idol was suspended between each archway, held there by silvery chains that looked like worms. For the red-gemmed island, the idol was a patch of skin. For the blue-gemmed island, a book made out of bones. On the green-gemmed island, it was a diseased skull. The idol of the grey-gemmed island was difficult to make out, but if I had to say it represented anything, it represented a firearm from the Old World. For the yellow-gemmed island, its idol was a shroud lined in gold. Suspended above the purple-gemmed island was the idol of two figures entwined, each one eating the other, in an unending circle of unfulfilled and everlasting appetites. On the white-gemmed island, the idol was simple, but poignant: a cross onto which millions of holy symbols had been etched.

Not all of the gems, however, shone as brightly as the others. For the green and white islands, the gems were lightless. I followed the causeway to these locations first and saw additional discrepancies between them and the others. Whereas the other islands had small stones identical to their gem's color littered about them, these did not. Leaning out from the causeway, I saw that the islands were not floating in the darkness, but were propped up there by grimy, almost glass-like, ribbed tubes. From the bottom of the island, where the tubes started, to as far as I could see in the dark through which they ran, they were clogged with a dormant, but twitching entity. But as I had mentioned earlier, there were discrepancies. The tubes of the green and white island were empty, as though whatever had been inside was already let loose. Looking at the blue island, I saw that the entity beneath it was nearing the surface of its island as well; it, too, appeared to be moving towards an awakening.

At that moment, a gigantic black shadow fell over me. Not a shadow like those above, but the shadow of an actual beast, snake-like in shape. In a million voices, it said, "They have fallen far, and are what they are. Nothing more. They do until they're done."

Without turning around, I whispered, "The Worms of the Earth."

The voices, pleased, said, "Through hell, we find heaven. Through them, they'll find It."

"It?" I felt my mortality returning to me. I felt the vermillion liquid bubbling in my stomach, eating away at its lining. "What is It?"

"Trauma, and rehabilitation. The One you did not look at, the One you meant to find all along."

"Are two of the Worms already summoned?" I asked, closing my eyes, trying desperately not to look at the horror behind me.

"Yes."

"Will more be summoned?"

"Yes."

"Will you... let us stop them?"

The voices laughed. "You will have to stop yourselves, first. They are so large, now. Time has shown us humans will never stop."

"How will they be summoned?"

"When they are known, and needed."

My eyes opened slightly and glanced at the shadow. But the shadow was no longer there.

"Go back, Victor Mors," it continued, voices echoing around me. "Your kind will see you out."

"My kind?" I backtracked across the causeway. "You mean the shadows?"

"Sure," the voices said.

I stopped, because I saw a little boy ahead, through the gaps in the vermillion barrier. He was standing there, half-formed, staring me down. "Hurry," he said. "They will think you have turned on them. And if they think that, your bones will become the sand your people choke on." The young boy giggled and then dropped off the side, into the red chasm.

I ran as hard as I could from that subterranean hell. When I emerged into the bright, lightless desert, the shadows swarmed once more and considered me. It was then that I realized they had not shown me the way so that I would learn of their masters below and give offerings to those secluded altars. No, these shadows, yours and my kind, these vessels, empty but for the hate and rage that fill them, showed me the way so that we could save them, and save ourselves from becoming them.

The Worms of the Earth. I think the phrase every moment of every hour, and of late, I have begun saying it aloud. And now that I am infected with this secret knowledge, I have started to see their presence in my daily life. Strange growths, strange people. Strange behaviors leading to even stranger occurrences. These supernatural entities are supernatural weapons that want desperately to be wielded.

This is but one of many entries I shall write. My

knowledge is spreading, but there are many who reject it. In Six Pillars, the prospect frightens them. I have received many death threats from the Lillian Quarter. Mother Abbess Priscilla is especially infuriated with my speeches.

Two Worms have already been summoned. Do they, too, move against me? They are what they are. But where are they? For the —, I have my suspicions. But it leads them not to death, but prosperity. They do until they are done. But is — ever truly over?

In my paranoid state, I sometimes wonder if I am a —. Too many questions remain. I — black chalice and try —.

Felix closed the ragged notebook, took a deep breath, and, for the first time since he'd started reading aloud from it, looked at Audra.

Winded from Victor Mors' account, he said, "I stole this from the Mother Abbess. Now do you believe I'm here to help you?"

Audra pursed her lips and pinched the bridge of her nose.

The scrappy remains of Victor Mors' journal hadn't actually been stolen. After Felix returned from Saint Priscilla's, he had found a small chest on his pillow. The journal had been inside it, past several layers of locks only the white key could undo. He read it once in his chambers. Abandoning his other duties, he hurried to this place, to share it with Pyra's captive.

"Alexander Blodworth read some of a copy of that to me," Audra said. She bit her thumb. To take her mind off things, she started to tend the plants inside her cell. "Some of it, but not all of it. He said I had a gift, but I thought he meant my gift for botany."

Felix's eyes went to the now much larger stalk at the back of the greenhouse. Its red markings no longer looked like teeth, but talons. Its roots were no longer in the soil, but bound around it, as though to stop it from spreading further. This time when he looked at it, not only did his veins bulge, but his heart began to pound, making him dizzy.

"Do you know what that is?" Audra asked, a spade in hand.

Felix closed his eyes to break the plant's spell over him.

"There's myths for everything, I guess." She took a deep breath, stabbed the spade into the ground. "In Eldrus, I created the Crossbreed, a plant which makes others susceptible to control. Before I realized what they were... going to do with it, I started working on that." She pointed to the stalk with the strange markings. "I had nothing else to do down here, and I thought Alexander Blodworth would let me go if I managed to... But I heard he's dead. I keep trying, anyways, though."

Felix, refusing to look at the plant, said, "What is it?"

"A Bloodless." She walked to the gate and sat down in front of it. "This one doesn't control. It just drains. Figured if I could make that, I'd either kill everyone in Pyra and get out that way, or it would just kill me and that would be that. But they know what I'm doing down here. They give me the ingredients. So I figure they're just waiting for it to turn on me, and then take it for themselves."

"Why don't you stop?"

Audra shrugged.

One of the artificial lights flickered on and off. In that moment, Felix saw a shadow standing beside Audra.

Crap, he thought, shaking his head. *Story's getting to me.* But then he remembered how Audra had used the shadows in Isla's room to speak to her. And how, when he first met her, she appeared to be talking to something on the wall.

Audra wrinkled her brow. "What?"

"Your friends... Do you speak to the shadows?"

Audra's back stiffened. "What?"

"Are they your friends? The ones that tell you things?"

She laughed at him. "You don't know what you're talking about."

"I just saw one standing right next to you. If they're the same, then—" Felix flipped open his own journal and began to write frantically.

Audra pressed herself up against the gate. "What are you doing? Hey!" She punched it, leaving a red mark on the glass. "Hey! Answer me!"

Alexander Blodworth took her before the murderer could get to her. But he didn't take her as a hostage, but for what she could do. Felix ignored Audra as she banged on the glass. He was pressing so hard with the pen that he wasn't writing words but scratching them into the paper. *Justine knew she was special, too.*

And Isla Taggart, she's with the Winnowers' Chapter. If the shadows are the same as from Victor Mors' journal, then she had to know about the Worms before Alexander Blodworth told her. What did he say? Felix opened the philosopher's journal again and reread the following passage: "No, these

479

shadows, yours and my kind, these vessels, empty but for the hate and rage that fill them, showed me the way so that we could save them, and save ourselves from becoming them."

Audra rumbled. "Holy Child, don't ignore me. I am tired of being ignored. I don't care who you are."

"I think I know why Alexander Blodworth took you." Felix closed both journals and jumped to his feet. He felt bad for feeling so giddy, but he couldn't help it. "But you have to tell me the truth. Are they the same shadows Victor Mors saw?"

Audra's lip quivered. "Why are you trying to help me?"

Felix heard something stir towards the entrance to this place. He looked back at the covered statues there; some of their sheets were moving slightly.

Because Justine told me to, he thought. But was that the case anymore? In the last three days, his entire life and what he thought about it had changed. And for some reason, this woman, Audra of Eldrus, was at the middle of it. But it wasn't just that.

"Alexander Blodworth took you from your home, your family." Felix tried to stop himself from talking, but it was too late. "He brought you here to make you something else. I think I can relate." He rubbed his eyes, so the tears wouldn't come. "Besides, god would want me to help you."

Audra nodded. "Yeah, the shadows are the same. I mean, what else could they be?" She sighed and rolled her eyes. "They've been with me since I was a little girl. I've never really had any friends, except for them. They were always there for me. Sometimes, they got me in trouble. Sometimes, they got me out of it. They lie a lot. But I don't think they can help it.

"I spent so much time trying to find out more about them, about others like me. Archivist Amon said that maybe I was a spellweaver, except that I could weave with shadows. He was really the only person I ever told. My twin brother Auster, and Edgar, found out later, but I don't want to talk about... that.

"Yeah, the shadows have taught me things. I already know what you're going to ask. They taught me how to use them. But I'm no good. It takes me so long to get it down. Once I figured out I was in Pyra, I used them to find Isla Taggart. And I spent months practicing how to communicate with her through them. I don't think us humans are meant to do what the shadows can do.

"But they never mentioned the Worms. And they never showed me that desert. But I think I've seen those archways, with the gems, in my dreams." Audra paused, swallowed hard. "The shadows always came to me. They were always there. They were a better family most of the time than my own." She took a deep breath and put her defenses up again. "Was that good enough for you, Holy Child? Am I pathetic enough to be freed?"

Audra was drenched in sweat; the slip she wore almost completely see-through because of it. Her muscles were so tight that he thought at any moment they would snap. She was panting, and her fingers were constantly fidgeting at her side. Anyone else might have thought she was sick or had lost her mind, but Felix knew better. She wasn't sick. She wasn't crazy. She had just bared a bit of her soul. Now, she was waiting to see what he would do with it. He had been in a similar situation once, that night when he finally told Justine what Samuel Turov had made him do in the South.

"I believe you," Felix finally said, smiling.

Audra let out a slow exhale and started to relax.

"I think Alexander Blodworth locked you up down here because he knew about the shadows." Felix read through his notes again. "Like Victor Mors said, the shadows don't want to help the Worms, they want to stop them. I think Alexander Blodworth brought you here because he thought a Worm would be summoned one day. He probably knew what your family was looking into—he was always at Eldrus—and realized you were in danger there.

"He didn't tell anyone, not even Justine, why you were here. If she knows what you can do, she will let you out herself, I know it. You're not the enemy, but a blessing from god!"

Audra's face darkened. She mumbled to herself and said, "Holy Child, I don't think you have all the right facts."

But at this point, Felix's mind was settled. "No, you're right, but I'm going to get them."

"That's not what I mean. I... never mind."

"I'm going to get you out of here. But if I do—" she would trust him better if the deal wasn't one-sided, "—will you help me?"

"Of course," Audra said. She started to suck on her greasy hair. "If you think that's really enough."

"I do," he said. "I have a... friend. I don't know what happened to her. But she's trapped somewhere, too. Somewhere in that Membrane, I bet. Could you try to find her with the shadows?"

"Yeah," Audra said. "I mean, I can try. Who is she?"

"Doesn't matter," Felix said. "This is just a big misunderstanding, Audra. I'll be back soon. I promise."

Felix ran as fast as he could to Mother Abbess Justine's chambers. Dinner had already started, so as long as he was quick enough, he would make it there before she sent a party out to find him. But as he crawled out of the hiding place and into the Ascent, he gasped and dropped the journals.

On the other side of the hall, one of the tall, humpbacked statues with the star-shaped heads stood. It was still covered, top to bottom, in the same kind of waxen sheet as the others, but the material looked looser, as though slowly but surely, it would melt from it.

"How? Who did this?" A cold chill ran like icy fingers down his spine. Not taking his eyes off the strange, shrouded sculpture, he picked up the journals and walked backwards down the Ascent, until it was out of sight.

There was a lot of noise coming from around the corner where Justine's chambers were. Voices, some shouting. He could hear the Mother Abbess herself barking orders. Did something happen? Was it about the Winnowers' Chapter? He didn't mention that part to Audra, but he had his own theory about them and her, too.

"We are not having a repeat of earlier," Justine shouted as Felix rounded the bend. He went to her doorway and saw not only her own personal guards inside the room, but Avery and Mackenzie as well. "If we have to tear Pyra apart—"

As soon as she saw him, Mother Abbess Justine told the guards to leave. They turned around, surprised looks of relief on their faces. The guards quickly filed out of the room, with Avery and Mackenzie being the last to leave, shutting the doors on their way out.

"I am so glad you are safe," Justine said. She nearly glided across the room and wrapped her arms around him. "I am a fool. Maybe I am not fit for my station."

Felix didn't know what she meant, but he did know that, if he didn't tell her what he had figured out right away, he might not get the chance to for a while. "We can trust her. We can trust Audra."

An almost fire-like heat exuded from Justine's chest to his. It made his skin itch; it was starting to hurt. She could sense it, too, so she let go of him, and said, "Felix—"

But he interrupted her, the first time he ever had in his entire life, and said, "Alexander Blodworth brought her here to use as a weapon against the Worms of the Earth! And I think the Winnowers' Chapter are the Cult of the Worm. I think Isla Taggart told them about her, after she told Isla everything she knew. I don't know if they are good or bad, but I think Audra is good." And then, to seal the deal, he added, "God thinks she is good, too. God's spoken to me and decreed it so."

Justine touched her chest, where the heat had been. She closed her fingers around what had to have been a piece of jewelry behind her shirt. "Felix, she's not good. I don't know why it took me so long to put this together. But she's not good. She's not even human."

"What?"

"Alexander Blodworth didn't bring her here to use as a weapon. He brought her here because she is a Worm. In Victor Mors' journal, he mentioned that the Green and White Worms were missing. Disease, and religion. I do not know which she is, but I am certain now she is one of them. She communicates with the shadow creatures. She is capable of growing deadly plants no one else can. And her brother, King Edgar, has started a new religion of his own. What if she was part of that? Its creation? And what if she's starting it here, here in Pyra, as well? Beginning with the Winnows' Chapter.

"Felix, she's been in that cell for years. We have not fed her once since Alexander Blodworth left for Geharra. And I'm sure she has mentioned the gas. That gas can kill a room full of men in five seconds. All it does to her is put her to sleep."

"But… why did Blodworth bring her here then?" Felix couldn't believe what he was hearing. She had to be wrong.

"I don't know. I think he thought we were safer if our enemy were in our hands. I think he thought we could learn from her. It's hard to say now, Felix. But I can say with absolute, infallible certainty that Audra of Eldrus is a Worm of the Earth."

Tears welled in his eyes. "What are we going to do?"

Justine smiled and touched his cheek. "We have to find out everywhere she's infiltrated, and then, with god's permission, we will destroy her."

CHAPTER VI

Felix didn't believe her. Not one bit. A Worm being kept as a prisoner in Pyra? No, he wasn't buying it. He didn't know what the creatures were capable of, but he doubted a greenhouse and a gate, regardless of what they were made out of, could stop one. Sometimes, Justine told him he was too trusting, that he wanted to make friends with everyone. But he hardly knew Audra. That couldn't be the case, could it? Maybe she really was a bad person. Heck, maybe she was the one who had killed her family. Felix wouldn't deny that if it were true, but he just wanted to know. And he didn't like that Justine thought she had to make up some crazy story to get him to turn on Audra. She was definitely testing him, but did she have other reasons for doing so? Did god speak to her, too? And if god did, did god share Felix's thoughts with her? He hoped not. That wouldn't be fair at all.

In the days that followed, Justine gave Felix more special missions. This time, she had him keeping tabs on several members of the Winnowers' Chapter, including Isla Taggart again, who, to no one's surprise, finally announced she was part of the extremist group. The Mother Abbess agreed that not only were the Winnowers' Chapter likely connected to the Disciples of the Deep, but this Cult of the Worm, too.

"They are probably one and the same," Justine said.

It was Saturday morning, breakfast time. Felix had just taken a seat after giving his prayer and announcements.

"Audra may even be using the shadows to communicate with

King Edgar."

Felix looked around the room. He couldn't believe she was talking about these things out in the open. The gathering hall was packed today. Ever since everyone found out about Geharra and the Red Worm, more and more people from Penance had been visiting Pyra.

"They can't hear us." Justine pushed around the food on her plate. He never saw her eat anything at breakfast, but somehow, it was always gone by the hour's end.

Felix whispered, "Do the exemplars know what we're doing?"

The Mother Abbess laughed and, with no subtlety whatsoever, glanced at the two tables where the exemplars sat. "No."

The exemplars smiled and nodded at her, oblivious.

"They are for the people, not for us."

"The Winnowers' call them idols, too," Felix said.

Justine covered her mouth, stifling a burp. She blushed, stuttered out an apology.

"Are you okay?" Felix asked, as he thought, *Holy crap, is she drunk?*

Justine ignored him. "I want you to follow Father Marshall Jones. The Winnowers' Chapter share leadership responsibilities. For now. He is one of those trusted few."

Father Marshall Jones. He was a priest who spent a lot of time in Penance, holding mass for the poorer parts of the city-state. He nodded—*Maybe I can go into the city after him. I could talk to Deimos and Lucan again*—and took a drink of his milk.

"So much has been happening lately that I forgot to ask about the survivors from Geharra."

Felix choked, spitting the milk into his cup. A splotchy, milk moustache ran across his lips. He wiped it off before someone noticed and said, "Brave men."

"I'm going to bring them into Pyra. We should celebrate their accomplishments. I think everyone will appreciate that."

"Did you—" he crunched into his apple, "—find out who they are?"

"Don't talk with your mouth full, your holiness."

She winked at him and hissed. Out of nowhere, he smelled burning wood. It made his eyes water.

"They're from Mistmarsh. It's a small town a few days out from the Divide. It's Alexander Blodworth's birthplace. He must have passed through on his way to Geharra and enlisted several of the men there who were part of Penance's reserve."

"Good way to keep what he was doing a secret," Felix said.

"Alexander Blodworth." Justine impaled a roll with her fork. "If ever there should have been an Exemplar of Secrets. You better visit Audra today. She will be suspicious, otherwise."

What is going on? Felix sat back in his chair and sank into the sounds of clinking silverware and sloshing cups around him.

She wants me to see her? He cringed as he heard every smacking lip, every gnashing mouth. *She wants me to go back and visit the Worm?* He could smell the candles and the congregation's hot, stale breath.

Why does she want to hurt me? The walls of the gathering hall darkened, and where there had been stone, there were trees, and where the congregation had been, there was only Samuel Turov, naked, in wait. *Oh, god, please tell me.* He didn't believe her about Audra, but what if she wasn't lying and was truly convinced the woman was a Worm?

God, tell me what she's doing to me.

"Your holiness?" Justine took his chin and turned his head towards her.

It made him feel like the eleven-year-old he was, so he jerked away. "She's a Worm."

"She is imprisoned. Each Worm seems to be powerful in one particular skill. Clearly, breaking out of jail isn't this one's." She stood up, signaling the end of breakfast for everyone, and added, "Just keep your distance from now on. You've got god on your side. I trust god to keep you safe. Don't you?" She sighed and bent down, putting her pale lips to his ear. "Did you forget? I want you to be our Holy Child forever. I know I am asking a lot, but if we can get through this together, we can get through anything."

Felix felt pretty badly for the rest of the day, because the truth was, he had forgotten Justine's offer. Eldrus' murder of Geharra. The Red Worm. The Disciples of the Deep. The Winnowers' Chapter. The Cult of the Worm. Night Terrors in his nightmares, and his city. Audra locked away, supposedly a Worm of the Earth herself. And then there was that niggling feeling that the Mother Abbess had let Samuel Turov take him away. That she had been behind all the disgusting things that man had… It was a lot. She expected a lot out of him. But it made sense. If he was going to be the last, true speaker of god, he had to prove himself. He couldn't crumble. He could question her, but he couldn't crumble.

After all the remodeling and additions to Pyra, to still call it an abbey was kind of a stretch. In this lower level of Pyra, the Lyceum, Felix now followed Father Marshall Jones through was a honeycomb of classrooms, sleeping quarters, and maintenance stations that sat beneath the main terminal. It was here that those wishing to join the Holy Order full-time began their training. But since it was Saturday, most of those students were in Penance, getting drunk with the maintenance workers.

When it came to special missions, the more corners, the better, and the Lyceum, being a literal honeycomb, had the best corners in all of Pyra. Felix had been down here about fifteen minutes. Right now, he was pressed up against a wall, fixing his wig. Further ahead, Father Marshall Jones was shuffling down the hall, his cane clicking with every other step down the hall.

Felix had put on his shabbiest dress, to look like one of the "tunnel rats" that assisted the maintenance workers. The problem was, he had grown out of it, so it kept riding up on him.

Father Marshall Jones was the definition of a geezer. He had white hair, long nails, bad breath, and a terrible temper. But he was observant, and if Felix ended up failing this special mission because he stopped at the wrong time to fish out a wedgie and Father Jones caught him, he might just give up this part-time spy business altogether.

Felix peeked around the corner. The priest had given up the turtle act and sprinted around the next corner. *Faker*, he thought. He took out his journal and scribbled on Father Marshall Jones' page: "He wants to look weak, so people won't know how strong he really is." He smiled, pleased with that little bit of insight, stowed the journal, and took off.

Where was Father Jones going? The Lyceum was basically a bland basement of cobblestone walls and identical rooms. But even Felix could tell they were going in circles. Did he know he was behind him? Felix sniffed himself. Could he smell his perfume? Why the heck did even put perfume on in the first place?

They were back at the beginning of the Lyceum, where the six descending staircases from the main terminal converged at a wide landing. Felix stayed back, in the shadows, flat against the wall. Father Marshall Jones hobbled to the center of the landing, spun around. Did he know he was being followed?

No, Felix thought, as the priest took off into another tunnel. *The geezer's just lost. Or he just forgot to stop acting.*

"Where's everyone?" Father Jones' voice echoed out of the tunnel he had disappeared down.

Felix scampered across the landing, to the edge of the tunnel. He saw the room that Father Jones was standing outside of. After he went in, Felix took out his journal and started towards the room, keeping to the shadows along the way.

"Where's everyone?" Father Jones cried.

"Keep your voice down! What's wrong with you?"

Isla Taggart. He could recognize that harpy's voice anywhere.

"I have to be in Penance in an hour," Father Jones shouted.

Isla groaned. Felix went flat against the wall. He heard her go to the doorway, saw her look out. Quietly, she shut the door.

"You need to… act together." Isla said, her voice muffled.

He had to get closer if he was going to make out what they were saying. He crouched down, slid across the wall. His dress snagged on a bit of brick and ripped. *No evidence*, he thought, grabbing the shred and stuffing it into his pocket. *No one can know I was here.*

Isla went on. "They're… everywhere… always listening."

Holding his breath, Felix went down on all fours, crawled in front of the door, and reared up. He put his eye to the keyhole. The room was a classroom with ten or so desks. On the chalkboard, a smeared map of Penance had been drawn, and there were arrows pointing to the poorer parts of the city. Isla was standing at the professor's podium, in a white burka that covered everything but her cleavage. Father Jones was slumped over one of the desks, looking at nothing but Isla's cleavage.

Annoyed, Isla blew at the mesh covering that hid her face. "What took you so long?"

Father Jones grumbled, "It all looks the same down here. Why are you dressed like that?"

"With the Disciples of the Deep, we have a chance to finally enact some real changes. What am I wearing? I modeled it after clothes from the Old World. Women who wear these outfits won't have to feel ashamed of their bodies if they don't meet society's standards of beauty."

Father Jones leaned back in his seat. "Did you run out of fabric when it came to your chest?"

Isla gripped the side of the podium. "Does my acceptance of my body and sexuality bother you, priest?"

"No, just your confused message and the fact that, not forty-eight hours after your initiation into the upper ranks of us Winnowers', you're already trying to convert everyone to your worldview."

"My worldview?" Isla scoffed. "I'm sorry, but is labeling not an abhorrent issue?"

"Ah, yes. But you're telling me it's okay to define others by their sex, gender, weight, eating habits, political views, and religious beliefs?"

Isla rolled her eyes as she said, "Don't twist my words. I'm saying we should appreciate everyone's unique and individual qualities, so we don't trample on them."

"Is that why you want the Disciples of the Deep to persecute homosexuals? And to have ugly women cover themselves? Or is it just ugly people in general?"

"I didn't say every unique and individual quality was okay." Isla bit her lip. "Don't get high and mighty with me, priest. The places where you preach in Penance keep getting poorer and poorer, and yet you keep getting richer and richer."

"I'm aware of my imperfections. I'm not so sure you are." Father Jones held up his hand as Isla tried to snap back. "Why did you call me down here? If you wanted to waste my time with your Old World regurgitations, you could have waited until next week."

"As I was saying," Isla said through her teeth. Felix could tell it was taking everything she had to stop from biting the old geezer's head off. "The Mother Abbess has eyes and ears everywhere. I invited a few others, but they didn't make it, because they were suddenly sent away on urgent matters in Penance. I don't think we're going to get any more support, so we have to act fast."

"What about those two survivors, those soldiers who came back from Geharra?"

Isla shook her head. "Untouchable. Word is the Mother Abbess is bringing them here, but that won't be enough time to see if Alexander Blodworth truly converted them to our cause."

Father Jones sighed and said, "Then we will have to be patient, and wait."

"No." Isla tore at the mesh that covered her face until she ripped a hole in it large enough she could slip her head through. "Stupid freaking dress. That's better. No, no waiting. That's all the Winnowers have been doing for years. Where has it gotten you?"

"Initiating you was a mistake." Father Jones stood up, the bones in his legs cracking, one after the other. "The Mother Abbess will leave the Winnowers' Chapter alone, like she always has, as long as she doesn't think we are a threat. And right now? We're not. No, Isla, we will wait. Alexander Blodworth murdered an entire city and let that pederast take the Holy Child into the South. Those terrible things will not have been for nothing. He bought us a lot of good will with King Edgar when he made those things happen. If we waste it, we are forsaken."

Felix covered his mouth. *Eldrus hired Alexander Blodworth to kill Geharra? And he's the one that got Samuel Turov to take me?* It all made sense, except for the part of how all this had happened behind Justine's back. Why he hadn't asked this earlier, he didn't know, but at that moment, he looked to heaven and thought: *Did Justine really not know what was going on?*

Much to his surprise, not one second later, there was a response. It was god. God spoke to him in his own voice, and said: *She did not know, my son. There are more devils than angels in this world, and most are indistinguishable from the other. This is why she needs you.*

"It's time to break her out," Isla said.

Felix tore himself away from the dialogue with his maker. A mixture of happiness and anxiety left him feeling like he had water in his ears.

"Audra?" Father Jones whispered. "How?"

"The Holy Child has been visiting her."

Father Jones gasped and said, "That's interesting."

"Someone gave him a key. I think we can all figure out who."

"If the Mother Abbess is sending him in to talk to her, there's a chance Audra's already turned on us. It might be wiser to leave her in there to rot."

"No. She's our connection to King Edgar. If we have her, we have all the support we need. She just wants to be free. She will side with anyone to make that happen."

Isla's eyes wandered over to the door.

Felix pulled away from the keyhole. *Did she see me?* He crept back to the keyhole and saw that she was looking at Father Jones again.

The priest said, "No, this needs to be decided upon by the other Winnowers before we make this decision. Once she's free, everything will change."

"It's too late," Isla said, smiling. "She's already putting the finishing touches on the potion to keep her awake when they gas her cell. We just have to make the Holy Child unlock the door to her prison."

"Isla," Father Jones said, raising his voice. "I swear to god, I will break your neck if you put a hand on that child."

"I'm getting her out of there, whether I'm part of your little group or not."

"We're finished here." Father Marshall Jones turned his back on Isla and headed for the door. "You're finished, too. I don't care if you're the niece of the Exemplar of Innocence. I want you out of the Winnowers' Chapter."

"My devotion is to the Disciples of the Deep. To the true God of the people."

Father Jones whipped around. "Your devotion is to yourself. You worship only that which will elevate you above others." He spat at her feet. "You're no better than the Hydra."

"I'm getting her out," Isla said, unrelenting. "I am the niece of the Exemplar of Innocence. You're just an old priest, like the rest of them, and that's all you and the Winnowers will ever be."

"And I thank god for that," Father Jones said. "Because when you ruin everything, the Mother Abbess is going to start with you first. And, yes, we may hang. But you, Isla Taggart? You're going to live a very long time. She'll make sure of it."

Father Marshall Jones hobbled quickly towards the door, leaving Isla speechless. Felix pulled away and hurried down the tunnel. The door flew open, cracking back against the wall. Father Jones and Isla had started arguing about something else, but as Felix rounded the corner at the tunnel's end, he wasn't listening.

Because there was a statue there. A tall, marble statue with a star-shaped head and a humpback, just like those outside Audra's cell. It was wandering around the Lyceum, one long arm holding the other. The statue started to suck on the waxen sheet that covered it, like a child would a blanket before going to sleep. It looked sad, as though it were lost, as though it knew it didn't belong here at all.

"It was a mistake calling you here!"

Felix peeked down the tunnel. Isla had gone one way, and Father Jones was coming his. He quickly turned around. Isla's shouting had to have given him away, and maybe it had. He couldn't be sure. Because in that second he had looked away, the statue had gone.

CHAPTER VII

By the time Felix had reached Audra's cell, his dress had split and his wig had fallen off somewhere back in the main terminal. Going to her, this supposed supporter of the Winnowers' Chapter and Worm of the Earth, should have been the last thing he did. But he had to know for himself what she was, and if there was any chance he could save her from what would happen if she were caught with the likes of Isla Taggart.

The abandoned part of the cloister smelled mildewed today. It was warmer than usual, too, as though a bunch of people had recently passed through. Felix ran to and unlocked the steel door. It gave him a quick shock, but at this point, he'd had worse shocks in his life.

"Come on, come on," he said.

Two thuds. One click. The key stopped turning, and the door popped open. The fluorescent light flickered in the passage beyond. Squinting, Felix shuffled in and shut and locked the door behind him. He crossed the passage and went to the circular door. There was a large bird feather on the ground in front of it.

"Vrana?" He picked it up. "Are you trying to get to Audra, too?" The feather could have been hers. There was a small piece of skin at the end of it, like it had been ripped out. *I have to help her*, he thought, pocketing the feather. *But when? It's too much.*

Felix slid the key into the circular door at the passage's end. There had been one of the strange statues in the Ascent, and the other that had been moving around in the Lyceum. That probably left about twenty on the other side, in Audra's prison. But when the door rattled open, he found that there weren't twenty on the other side. There weren't any at all. They were all missing. Every last one of them.

Felix slammed the circular door shut and ran to the greenhouse. "Audra! Audra!" He went to the gate and grabbed its bars. "Where are—" He pulled and, much to his surprise, the gate gave. "What the...?" He stepped back and looked around her cell. Cringing, he whispered, "Audra?"

She wasn't there. Not in the bed. Not at the worktable. He called out her name again. But this time, something else answered. From the back of the greenhouse, sounds came, leathery and low. And now that he was looking, he noticed that Audra's mythological plant, the Bloodless, was no longer just a stalk. It had fully bloomed.

Its roots had broken free of the bindings. They were splayed outward, running like greedy fingers across the greenhouse, in search of that special kind of sustenance. The Bloodless itself, however, was hard to find. He could only make out parts of it, because it had hidden itself behind the other plants and crops growing around it. It looked like it was almost eight feet tall now. And there were flower petals, too. Steely discs with razor edges. If he squinted hard enough, there appeared to be some sort of hole at the top of the plant, with hundreds of hair-like vines spilling out of it.

And just as he was about to, he heard Audra whisper, "Don't. Move."

With those two words, a clammy panic came over him. He turned on his heels and booked it.

"Holy Child! No!"

Felix didn't get five inches before something wrapped around his ankles and jerked his feet out from under him. Screaming, he hit the ground hard. A sharp, sinking feeling filled his stomach as he struggled to catch his breath. Already crying, he craned his neck around to see what had a hold on him.

The Bloodless' roots were wrapped around his ankles, dragging him towards it. The plant wasn't hiding anymore, either. Hunger had brought it out into the open. The monstrosity's body had changed completely. It was the color of raw meat, and looked like striated muscle. Pink sacs filled to the point of popping ballooned from its thick stalk. The razor petals he had noticed earlier started to click. From their dark red ovaries, a hissing liquid spewed.

"God help me," he screamed, pawing at the ground.

The Bloodless wasn't dragging him very fast. It was to be a slow death for Felix. One that he would experience several times over, in his head, before he finally reached the plant's gurgling gut.

"Shut up! Take this," Audra cried.

The tears in his eyes made the greenhouse nothing more than a stinging blur. But Audra was so close now that he couldn't help but find her. She was curled up in a patch of flowers, just a few feet from him. She looked bad, like the corpse of a corpse. In her hand, there was a vial. She was holding it out.

"Take it," she kept saying, over and over.

She's a Worm of the Earth, he heard Justine say to him. *You can't trust her.*

With a pathetic flick, she flung the vial at him. "It'll stop the Bloodless from eating you!" It bounced off his chest and rolled away. "Grab it!"

Felix's hand kept falling short of the vial. Suddenly, he couldn't breathe, let alone keep his eyes open. In a sluggish haze, he saw that the hair-like vines coming out of the Bloodless were rubbing against one another. And with every twist and curl, soft, lulling notes emerged. They were soothing, and they were weakening. Each movement they made pressed against his mind, cornering it, until it was capable of only the simplest functions.

First, he peed himself. Then, he started to drool, and as his tongue lolled outside his mouth, he apologized for all the sins he was guilty of.

"I'm sorry... for... doubting you." His eyelids shut, the soft sounds of the Bloodless' music closing them for him. "I'm sorry, god, for not... being better. I'm sorry for... jealousy. I'm... for letting him kiss me there. I... I'm sorry... I didn't mean to... like it."

The veins in his neck started to bulge. The Bloodless' roots tugged him harder, faster.

"I'm sorry I wasn't strong.... I tried to be good." With his last bit of strength, he forced open his eyes. He was right below the Bloodless. The razor petals were lowering towards him. And he could see bones in the pink sacs, floating through the liquid inside them. "I'm sorry I said... all those things. I just wanted to know... who Mom and Dad..."

The Bloodless' roots tried to yank him forward, but he wouldn't budge. There was something else holding him now. He glanced back and saw Audra behind him, her knee on his shoulder.

"Drink this!" In one hand, she had the vial, and with the other, she was prying open his lips.

Felix, dumb with delirium, said, "Stop. You're a Worm."

Audra ignored the accusation. She forced open his mouth and poured the potion down his throat.

"No," he cried in a slur.

Audra grabbed his chin and held his mouth and nose shut, until he swallowed. She sat down, wrapped her legs around his chest, and took both his arms. Between her and the Bloodless, Felix felt as though he were going to be torn in half.

"It hurts," he said, his stomach on fire.

The singing, hair-like vines extended further down the Bloodless' stalk. They crawled into Felix's dress and started to worm against his skin.

He tried to bite at Audra's hands. "You're killing me!"

"I know," she said. She held on tighter to him as the razor petals descended on them, determined to cut loose the boy from her grip. "It's the only way."

Felix bucked as the Bloodless leaned forward, the chomping hole at the top of it inches from his feet. "Oh god, please help me!"

Audra started to say something, but screamed instead. Something hot and wet splattered across Felix's face. *I'm sorry god*, he thought, eyes shutting for good. *Don't let it hurt.*

The Bloodless' mouth closed over his feet and started to suck them dry. *I don't want to hurt anymore. I just want to go home. I just—*

CHAPTER VIII

"The thing about hell," Samuel Turov had once said, "is that you won't know you're in it until you've gone too far. Until all doors close behind you, and every escape feels like a dead end."

These were the words going through Felix's head when he finally came to. Needless to say, he could have done without them. He looked like something that even the grave couldn't stomach. Sweat and soil clung to his goose-pimpled skin. He was groggy, his eyes large and their lids heavy. Swallowing all the spit in his mouth was hard, because he was pretty sure he might have swallowed a few knives hours before. His feet, bare now, were purple, inflamed by the thin cuts left there from the Bloodless. And try as he might, he could not seem to move himself much further from where he lay now. Whether it was the plant or the potion, he couldn't be sure, but something had sapped his strength.

"Well, all that was unexpected," Audra said.

Felix took his fingers and opened his eyes. It was the only way he was going to be able to see where he was. He was in Audra's prison, outside her cell, near the circular door, where the living statues should have been. The Bloodless was still confined to the greenhouse, its gate now shut and seemingly locked again.

"I know how you're feeling right now." Audra knelt down beside him. She was a bony blur of blotched skin and good intentions. "Take this."

Felix opened his mouth. With a bowl, she poured some water in, dousing the fires raging along his throat. He tried to get her to stop, but she kept going, until the bowl was empty, and his chest was drenched.

Audra sat down. Again, she wrapped her arms around him. But this time, she held his head against her chest. He sighed, smiled, as her fingers ran through his hair. No one had done this for him before, no one except for Justine.

"It will pass soon. I drank the same thing. It was a proxy potion called Vein Rot. I don't know who came up with these potion names, but sometimes, they are a little on the nose." She laughed. "I knew the Bloodless would bloom, eventually. Vein Rot tricks your body into thinking its infected with a blood disease. It's temporary, but as you can see, the Bloodless didn't want much to do with us once it was in our system. The problem is that it knocks you out. Makes you feel god awful. Not exactly the best defense."

Felix finally got a good look at her face. She had a long cut running across it, eye to nose to eye, from the razor petal. It looked like gory war paint.

"I made another potion to fight off the gas they use to put me to sleep. I'm kind of getting the feeling they wanted me to escape. I mean, they gave me all the ingredients, Holy Child." She touched his forehead, hummed to herself. "So I drank the potion, and then they gassed the chamber. At the same time, the Bloodless bloomed. When they came in to drop off food and supplies, the plant attacked. I overreacted and drank the Vein Rot. And because all they feed me are freaking leftover crumbs, it kicked in quickly. So the door was open, but that stupid plant had eaten the two guards with the key, and I was too sick to move."

"Then I came along," Felix whispered.

Audra laughed. "Yes, you did. I would have eventually gotten out of the cell, but not out of this prison, not without the key to open these doors."

"You could have left me," Felix mumbled. His hand found the white key, which was still in his pocket.

"I'm not that kind of woman," Audra said.

"What... do we do?"

"When you're ready to walk, we'll walk out of here together. You said you were going to help me. Do you have anything prepared yet?"

Felix shook his head. *Crap, this is going too far too fast.*

"That's okay. We will figure it out."

"You can... stay in my room," he offered, not really thinking about what he was saying.

"You really want a Worm of the Earth rooming with you?"

"Oh. Did I say that?"

Audra nodded.

Felix closed his eyes. In the emptiness there, he saw god's light, and god said to him, *You are doing the right thing.*

"I'm not a Worm. I guess I can see why you would think that. But look at me." She tilted his head back. "Do you really think I am one?"

Her face was gaunt, her cheekbones like the sides of a cliff. Her lips were chapped, chewed up. Her eyebrows were a mess and coming together in the middle. She had nice teeth, but they were dirtier than a used fork.

He peered into her emerald green and bloodshot eyes. When he had looked at Samuel Turov, Alexander Blodworth, and even the Demagogue, he always saw the dark inside them. It glinted in their pupils, like the scales of a fish swimming through placid waters. But when he looked at Audra, he didn't see anything evil. He just saw the woman who had lost almost everything, and who could have finally lost it all by saving him.

She wasn't a Worm of the Earth. She was something Mother Abbess Justine didn't understand, and because of that, she hated her for it.

"I think you're okay," Felix said. "Why not use the shadows to escape?"

"I wish it worked that way. Like I said, it takes a long time to understand them. Trying to get them to do anything for me is an exercise in futility. It rarely works." Laughing, she said, "Maybe if I were a Worm I could force them. But I'm only human, like you." She jerked her right arm. "Only Corrupted."

Felix hacked up some phlegm. He sat up, away from Audra. "What do you think they are?"

She smiled at his progress. "I think they're us."

"Like dead people?"

"I think so."

"From hell?"

"That would make sense. They're unhappy enough that it's certainly not heaven. But I try not to think about it, Holy Child. Being able to talk to the damned doesn't put me in a particularly good light."

If the Worms are from hell, I can see why Justine doesn't trust her. I just have to show her she's wrong. He asked, "Why do you think they are reaching out to you?"

"I think it's the same reason they reached out to Victor Mors. They want someone to listen, to help them, if they can. Maybe stop people from making the same mistakes. If I were stuck in hell, I would do the same."

Felix nodded towards the greenhouse. "What about the Blood-less?"

"I don't know." She stood up and held out her hand for him to take. "Maybe we can find a way to destroy it before I leave."

Quickly, Felix said, "Audra, do you know what happened to the statues that were here?"

She shook her head. "I guess they had someone better to go spy on."

It was dark outside. Felix had been gone for several hours. So he knew when Avery and Mackenzie finally spotted him, they would freak. Or, at least, he hoped they would. He was kind of counting on it.

Felix backed out of the hidden place, into the Ascent. Audra was further down the hidden place, shivering. He was dressed in his usual robes, to better hide the Bloodless' wounds.

"Stay here," he said, slurring his words, not yet fully recovered. "Do you remember where I told you to go?"

She nodded. He had given her the best directions that he could to his room. First, he would cause a distraction, running past this same place. Then, when she thought the coast was clear, Audra would go to his room and wait there until he came back later that night. If she decided to do something else, like escape Pyra on her own, then there was nothing he could do to stop her. The Third Commandment: God's followers are missionaries; it is their duty to save those who have strayed from god's grace. He was pretty sure she didn't believe in god, but he still had to help her all the same.

"Crap! Hang on," Felix said, remembering that, right outside this place, one of those living statues had been posted. *Crap, crap, crap,* he thought. *Big crap. I hope it didn't hear me talking to her.* He crawled from the hidden place, out from behind the bookshelf, and into the Ascent's hall.

But there was no statue. It was gone. He could see where it had been—there was dust around where it had stood—but as far as he could tell, it had been moved or moved itself.

I need to ask Justine what these are, he thought, looking both ways down the torch-lit hall. And then he froze, Isla Taggart's words from earlier today popping into his head: "The Mother Abbess has eyes and ears everywhere." Of course, she could have been talking about almost anyone or anything, but even Audra had called the statues spies.

He told himself to worry about that later. Returning to the hidden place, he bent down, said to Audra, "I'm going now," and went.

About halfway to his room, Felix felt as though he had swallowed a bottle full of quicksand. He stopped, propped himself up against the wall. Cold beads of sweat trickled down the back of his neck. For a second, he thought it was the potion, but deep down, he knew it wasn't. It was the realization that he was about to go directly against the orders of the Mother Abbess by letting the Holy Order's prisoner stay in his freaking room. What was he thinking? He banged his head against the cobblestones. Why would she want him to be the last Holy Child if he went and did something like that?

"This is what happens when you don't talk to me, god," Felix whispered, clenching his eyes shut. "I'm just a stupid little kid without you. I can't do anything right. I'm so—"

Footsteps. He opened his eyes and leaned away from the wall. There, a little down the hall, Avery and Mackenzie stood, jaws dropped, eyebrows raised.

Avery, red in the face, started first. "Where. Have. You. Been?"

Mackenzie threw up her hand. "It's not for us to know."

"But it is for us to keep him safe! I'm sorry, Mackenzie, but I care about our Holy Child, whether the Mother Abbess does or not."

"Hush!" She looked behind them. She slapped the back of his helmet. "Your holiness, please disregard what Avery said. We were worried sick. The Mother Abbess cares for you deeply. We do not always understand her decisions to send you out alone, but it is not our place—" She bared her teeth at Avery. "—It is not our place to."

Felix ignored her. "What time is it?"

"Late," Avery said. "Past your dinner with the Mother Abbess."

"Is she expecting me?"

Mackenzie nodded like she'd had too much coffee. "The Mother Abbess knows you've been busy these last few weeks. The Mother Abbess didn't request you until just now. And it was an urgent request. So, if you don't mind, please, come with us, your holiness."

"But you guys," Felix said, starting forward, "know about the white key. And the room in the abandoned part of the cloister."

"We do what we're told, your holiness," Avery said. He and Mackenzie parted for Felix to take the lead through the Ascent. "We do not ask questions, because we both know no one will guard you better than myself. And Mackenzie... I guess."

She smiled, pointed at him, and then her sword.

Avery moved to put his hand on Felix's shoulder, but stopped himself. "The Mother Abbess loves you greatly. If you trust her, we trust her."

He knew he shouldn't have said it, but he did, anyway. "And if I didn't?"

Mackenzie's mouth tightened. "Hurry, your holiness. She's been waiting. And people are starting to talk about how often you've been missing your duties. We don't want a repeat—"

"—Of when Samuel Turov took me?" Felix interrupted. The slashes on his ankles started to burn; so did the scars on his thigh.

"Yes," Avery said. This time, he did put his arm around him. "We do not want a repeat of any of... that."

They didn't go back the way towards the hiding place, but Felix figured Audra was a smart enough woman that she could handle a small change of plans. Instead, he and his guards headed into the cloister, where stalwart torches burned against the blizzard pouring through its open roof. Avery and Mackenzie bunched up against him, to protect him from winter's icy venom.

"Who the heck thought it would be a good idea not to a put a roof on this place?" Felix shouted over the unending wind.

Mackenzie put her weight against him. He took the hint, took the steps to the first floor of the cloister, and turned down the furthest arcade.

"Ever s-s-see it accumulate it though?" Avery chattered out.

"No more than a few inches," he said. He tried to curl the numbness from his toes, but it wasn't having any of that. "Always figured—" Avery nudged him down another arcade, which ran west to

Pyra's Tribunal, "—someone cleared it before people woke up."

"No one could clear this much snow," Mackenzie said. She blew on her hands and pressed them to Felix's neck to warm him. "It just melts faster than it can stick. Miracle from god, I suppose."

The Tribunal. Wait, why were they going to the Tribunal? Felix dug his heels into the ground and said, "Why are we going this way?"

"The Mother Abbess is holding Vehmic Court," Avery said. "She wants you there to pass judgment."

"What?" Felix threw out his hands. "Whoa, wait. On who? Why?" He looked ahead, where the cloister stopped and a second courtyard began. A great slab of stone loomed over it, like some sad silo where a human crop was kept. This was the Tribunal, and those that entered its massive steel doors to be judged seldom came out again. "I'm the Holy Child. I don't do that."

Voice choked, Mackenzie said, "You do now."

The cloister was empty, because everyone was here, in the Tribunal, roaming its halls in their nightwear, trying to figure out what was going on and how they could use it to their advantage. Because he had been with Audra not fifteen minutes earlier, Felix figured it either had to do with Winnowers' Chapter, Deimos and Lucan, or, heck, even the Cult of the Worm, whatever that was.

Avery had said Justine was holding a Vehmic Court, but the thing about Vehmic Courts was that they were supposed to be in secret, with only the Mother Abbess, the six exemplars, and the guilty present. These were final judgments, not trials, of individuals found undeniably guilty of crimes against the church, such as apostasy, treason, or murder. The fact that they were a secret was an old tradition meant to scare those from following in the offenders' footsteps. Maybe that was why all these people were here, Felix thought. Another old tradition she was slowly trying to do away with, like how she didn't want to train anymore Holy Children.

"Step aside," Avery bellowed.

Felix threw up his hands. Those gathered went silent and to their knees; another perk of being god's speaker, one which he didn't take advantage of enough.

"Part," Mackenzie cried. She drew her sword, which was unnecessary, but did the job well enough.

Several more guards emerged from amongst the people of Pyra

and they, too, made a path through the gossipmongers. They waved Felix onward, so with his two best friends, he moved onward.

Most of the people in the Tribunal tonight were what the Demagogue often called the "important people." Unlike the "unwashed masses" that strolled in to the abbey on a daily basis, they didn't try to touch Felix or beg him for guidance or prayers. So when he went past them, he did so without having to hear Avery and Mackenzie break bones behind him.

"Through here, your holiness," one of the guards said. He gestured to a small, wooden door with black metalwork. The door itself looked scorched. Most likely to remind the guilty who passed through it of the hell they were headed off to.

Felix took a deep breath and, with both hands and a little help from Mackenzie, pushed the door open. It budged about six or seven inches, but in the interest of saving face, Felix sucked it up and slipped into the courtroom on the other side.

There wasn't much to see, because there wasn't much to see. Except for the ten tiny candles laid out across the room, it was pitch-black inside. But at the back of the courtroom, there was something else: a white twinkle, like gems catching light.

"Is that you?" Justine asked. A flame appeared in the palm of a hand. There was her face, smiling above it. "I'm so happy you came. I think we both lost track of time today."

Felix, going forward, said, "What do you want me... to do?"

"Come up here with me." Justine took the flame in her hand and lit two candles. She placed one in front of her, at the top of the podium she stood at, and one on the podium beside her. "The Holy Child has never had a place at court before. I borrowed this other podium from another room. It will do until we have your own crafted."

Felix's stomach started to knot. "I can't see where I'm going."

"Here." Justine disappeared from the candlelight.

Out of nowhere, two warm hands wrapped around Felix's. "Ah," he shouted, pulling away.

"It's me." Justine's voice was still distant, still up there behind the podium, even though, apparently, she was right in front of him. "There are steps. Take it slow."

Felix squeezed the Mother Abbess' wrists. His toe hit with a loud thump the stairs she had mentioned. They were at the foot of the podium, which seemed several feet high now that he was under it.

Carefully, he went up the steps, turning as they turned around the podiums, until he was behind both and facing that infinite expanse of courtroom abyss.

"Why's it so dark in here?" he asked.

Justine let go of him. Before his hands were at his sides, she appeared back at the podium. Hovering over the candle, her thin skin looked how a leaf would if he held it up to the sun.

"I find it is easier to make hard decisions in the dark. There are less distractions. Come," she held out her hand to his podium, "take your place at my side."

"Okay," Felix said softly. He stepped up to his podium and rested his hands beneath the candle there. Hot wax dripped onto his skin, but he didn't flinch. There were good pains, and that was one of them.

"I cannot believe that it was just this morning I asked you to follow Father Marshall Jones."

"He met with Isla Taggart in the Lyceum," Felix said.

"I know." Justine smiled. She adjusted the strap on her black gown. The smell of burning wood came out of the fabric. "Isla was planning on releasing Audra. She was going to use her to make contact with King Edgar. Father Marshall Jones did not agree with Isla's idea."

"How do you know that?" Felix remembered the living statue with the star-shaped head he had seen in the Lyceum. *Eyes and ears everywhere.*

"Father Marshall Jones told me himself," Justine said, as though countering his thought. "After I interrogated him."

This time, Felix's hand did twitch when the hot wax dribbled onto it. "Interrogated him?"

Somewhere in the courtroom, someone coughed.

Justine clicked her tongue. The coughing stopped.

Felix leaned over the podium, saying, "What was—?"

"You've talked enough to Audra of Eldrus and several Winnowers by now to know Alexander Blodworth was a bad man, right?"

"Oh." He nodded. He did. He had forgotten, but he did. "Oh, yeah. But, I mean, I don't... There're so many questions, so many things I don't understand."

Justine took his wax-covered hand and started picking away the parts that had dried. "I know. I have asked you to grow up very quickly these last few weeks." She smiled, lifted his hand to her lips, and kissed it.

She had never done that before. It made him feel funny.

"Alexander Blodworth was a bad man. He had forged a secret alliance in Eldrus with King Edgar and Archivist Amon. Part of that alliance involved destroying Geharra, using Audra's Crossbreed and a Worm of the Earth."

"Why?" Felix asked.

Someone else coughed in the room.

Justine clicked her tongue again. "The Disciples of the Deep. It was a way in which Eldrus could slowly but surely propagate its new religion. They created a tragedy and an overwhelming threat with which only they had the tools to combat. King Edgar had tried to move into the Heartland years ago, but the Heartland rebelled. So he and Alexander Blodworth devised that insidious plan, instead.

"I do not know the full details, even now, but I do know Alexander Blodworth was the one who had Samuel Turov take you into the South. And I do know he did this to ensure that I would give him permission to travel to Geharra, to not only look for you, but help us make our way back into the city. I was desperate. He took advantage of that desperation. I figured that, even if you weren't there, it would buy us enough time to find you elsewhere."

Felix swallowed hard. "You really didn't know the exemplar was going to take me?"

Justine shook her head. "I really didn't, Felix." And then she continued. "The Winnowers' Chapter is Alexander Blodworth's pet. He put it together sometime after the royal family of Eldrus was murdered. My fault was assuming that they wanted to do our jobs better. What I didn't realize is that they were representing another religion entirely."

"The Disciples of the Deep," Felix whispered.

"Exactly. Because Alexander Blodworth died in Geharra, they have been trying to continue operations without him. He entrusted Audra's care to them. Isla Taggart is a colossal moron, Felix, do not get me wrong, but she is correct in assuming Audra is meant to be a connection to King Edgar. Alexander Blodworth brought her here for that reason, and for her abilities as a botanist. He wanted her to recreate her success with the Crossbreed, but instead, it seems she's outdone herself and created a Bloodless."

"You've seen it?" Felix covered his mouth, to hide the way his words shook.

"Not recently."

Again, someone coughed. And someone started to hyperventilate.

Justine made a fist and slammed it like a gavel against the podium. The candle jumped in place.

Felix's eyes darted back and forth across the courtroom. "Is there someone else in here?"

"Yes," Justine said. She took a deep breath and uncurled her fist. "The Winnowers' Chapter have converted those who guard and tend to Audra's cell. They have been supplying her with the means to create the mythological plant, the Bloodless. It is our belief they did this to orchestrate her escape and to launch an attack on Pyra itself, to better the Disciples of the Deep's position here. In doing so, they have graduated from being annoying elitists to dangerous terrorists. So they are here tonight, in this Vehmic Court, to receive the punishment for their heinous crimes."

"What?" Felix leaned over the podium. He looked at the ten candles that ran along the room. "They're here?"

"Vehmic Court is a stretch of the phrase," Justine went on, ignoring him. He noticed another white twinkle, somewhere near where she stood. "You saw the crowd. This is hardly a secret meeting. I made sure the Demagogue spread the word of what was going on here. But before we open the doors to our disposition, we have to come up with one. Are you ready?"

"Ready?" Felix put his hands together, as though to pray. "Ready for what?"

Justine smiled, fixed the strap on her dress again. "Lights, please."

Across the courtroom, a massive torch exploded in flames. Holding the torch was one of the living statues Felix had seen outside Audra's prison. Still covered in the waxen sheet that ran from its star-shaped head to its bare ankles, the walking marble monstrosity went about the room, lighting the sconces on the wall.

"What are they?" Without realizing it, he had stepped out from behind his podium and into Justine's. "What are—?"

A cone of light crossed the court from the first sconce. In it, Felix saw another living statue. It was standing behind one of the ten candles, and it was holding a man.

"M-Mother Abbess...?"

Another sconce flared, and another living statue was revealed, with yet another body in its grasp. As more light filled the room, he saw there were more living statues, and each one was holding a prisoner tightly against its unbreathing chest.

With the last sconce lit, the count was ten. Ten living statues with ten living captives. Felix's mouth had gone dry at the sight. The tiny candles were in front of them; and he had been so close. In the dark, he hadn't even noticed they were there.

"Father Marshall Jones," Felix said, recognizing the old man as he slowly awoke in the statue's clutches. "Father Peter Smith. Sister Mary Pascal. Father Conahan. Sister Beth Chambers." They were waking, too. They were all waking up, waking up to lie down with damnation. "These are all—" *Sister Zoe Mura, Sister Alexandra, Father Perrin Tribble, Father Davidian, Blessed Mother Lysandra,* "—the Winnowers' Chapter."

"Not all of them," Justine said. "They have about two hundred supporters. These are just the leaders." She leaned forward, her elbows on Felix's shoulders, and pointed to the torch-bearing living statue. "That one was meant for Isla Taggart. But the she-snake slipped our grip. Funny thing is, she went missing about the same time we lost track of the soldiers from Geharra."

Deimos and Lucan.

"Coincidence, or more double-crossing? Hard to say. But I guess there will not be a homecoming party for them." She stood upright. "Their punishment is death, though, these esteemed Winnowers, is it not, Felix?"

Was she asking him to put them to death? No, no, he couldn't, wouldn't, do that. He would do almost anything for Justine, but not this. He was god's speaker, not god's weapon.

"Felix." Justine bent over, looking him in the eyes as the Winnower leaders started to squirm and scream. "I will pass judgment. But you are the one who I have chosen to guide the Holy Order of Penance through these troublesome times. If the punishment is death, tell me it is so. If it is not, then what would you have us do with terrorists and their ilk?"

What do I do god? What do I do? He looked at the ten traitors, at the ten statues standing there, their grips slowly tightening around them. Their punishment was death, he knew that. But he didn't want to say it. If he said it, then his punishment would be death, too. Because if everything went right, then Audra was in his room right now, making him more of a traitor than those restrained here tonight.

"Felix," Justine said, breaking him out of his thoughts. "Do you want to know what happens to a Holy Child after another is chosen to take their place?"

"What?"

The Mother Abbess tilted her head at one of the living statues. "They are what happens."

He laughed. His eyes started to water. "I don't understand?"

"Those statues are the Holy Children that came before you. That's what god does to them when their service is finished. They continue to serve the church, and keep all their secrets to themselves. Do you see why I want this terrible tradition to end?"

The waxen sheets over their star-shaped heads. He understood now why they wore them. "But why would god make them look... look like that?"

"We are nothing more than clay to be molded as god sees fit, Felix. For the Holy Children god no longer needs, their form is what god saw fit. So tell me: the Winnowers here have committed terrible crimes. What is their punishment?"

Lip quivering, Felix closed his eyes. Images tore through his mind, of his body being ripped apart and put back together, of his head being chopped up and made pointed and severe.

His eyes snapped open and he said, with absolutely no conviction whatsoever, "The punishment is death."

Justine nodded. She rapped her fists six times upon the podium. The small, wooden courtroom door opened, the Demagogue and a crowd full of onlookers standing on the other side.

"Death!" Justine shouted to crowd funneling into the court. "These Disciples of the Deep have stripped their souls to appease their false god. They have turned on family and friend and shamed their creator to threaten the stability of our ancient order. You know them by name and face, and by involvement in the Winnowers' Chapter. I have been patient and open to their beliefs, but tonight, I have found them brewing death, trying to recreate the events of Geharra here in Pyra. The Holy Child and I have convened, and by the grace of god, we sentence these ten heretics to death."

The Holy Children wasted no time carrying out the judgment. They set down their fear-stricken prisoners. But before they could run away, the statues clapped their hands together. Pop, pop, pop, pop, pop. They clapped their hands together over the Winnowers' heads. Pop, pop, pop, pop, pop. Like melons, their skulls exploded, flinging pink mush and boney seeds across the courtroom audience.

And the courtroom audience accepted this new baptism with red-cheeked glee. They didn't scream out in terror or threaten revolt. They just looked at Felix and Justine and gave them silent thanks.

CHAPTER IX

Felix couldn't remember how he ended up back in the Ascent. He had long left his body before his body had left the Tribunal. His vision had become a tunnel of stretched smiles and marble limbs. His hearing had become a muffled cloud of small praises and whispered worries. In between the Tribunal and the Ascent, Avery, Mackenzie, and Justine had tried to get his attention and make sure that he was okay. But he hadn't been okay. In fact, he hadn't been anything at all. In that moment, he had been nothing more than the vessel he was supposed to be. And when he called on god to fill him, god was not there.

Back in the Ascent, seeing the door to his room, Felix thought of Audra and finally came out of it.

"I'll be fine," he said to the Mother Abbess and his guards. A few people skirted through the Ascent. They pointed at him and bowed. "I need to go to sleep."

"Your holiness," Mackenzie started.

Felix ignored her and pushed open his door.

"Your holiness, we have to check your room first," Avery said.

"What?" He stopped, the door barely open. He peered through the crack and thought he saw something on the other side. "Oh. No, it's fine."

"There may be more enemies in Pyra than we realize," Justine said. She lifted the hood attached to her gown and lowered it over her head. "Let your guards check your room. Let them do their jobs."

Mackenzie's face begged him to give them the chance to carry out their duties. He wanted to fight back, use god's demands against them, but he couldn't put Avery and Mackenzie in that situation. He didn't know what Justine would do to them if he did.

"Sure," he said. He peeked through the crack again, but this time, he didn't see anything. "I'm just really tired."

As Avery and Mackenzie went past him, Justine held out her arms. Felix waddled over to her and accepted the embrace.

"Why did you do that?" he whispered to her. He breathed in her gown, and it was like breathing in a campfire.

"Felix, you know that I have sentenced many, many prisoners to death."

"But you made me watch."

She touched the back of his head, pressed his face harder into her chest. "You are god's voice. A voice cannot speak without seeing the world and its inhabitants. Things are different now. Our words must have weight, or they will be swatted away, like flies."

Felix heard Avery mumble to Mackenzie. He craned his neck. Did they find her? Did they find Audra? Justine took his head and, again, pressed it hard against her chest.

"Those statues are really Holy Children?"

"Hush," Justine said. "That's our secret."

"Why were they in Audra's cell?"

Avery and Mackenzie stepped out of his room.

"So I could see and hear everything that was being done and said in there." Justine patted his head and turned him around. "Off to bed. We have more work to do tomorrow morning."

Avery and Mackenzie nodded at the Mother Abbess and took up their posts.

"See and hear everything?" Felix repeated.

"Yes. If people are going to call me the Hydra, I may as well play the part and put myself in everyone's business. You did a good job convincing her."

Felix froze. In that moment, he replayed every conversation he'd had with Audra. Did she know the woman was probably only a few feet away, in his bedchamber? His eyes darted back and forth, searching what he could of his room from the hall. Maybe this was the final test. Tonight, she had not only shown him what happens when someone goes against the Holy Order, but what happens to a Holy Child when god is finished with them.

Say it, he thought, hot pains twisting through his neck. *Say it. Tell her. Tell her she's in there. This has gone too far. She knows about Audra. Audra is nothing to me. Say it, say it!*

But he couldn't say it. He couldn't say anything at all. He just turned around, looked at Justine, and smiled. And as she said, "Goodnight," and started to walk away, god whispered: *You did the right thing. Audra is innocent. We will help the Mother Abbess see this. I give you my voice, but you must listen to what it says.*

Felix felt better after that. If it was good for god, it was good for him. He strolled into his room, shutting the door behind him. The door was thick, heavy, and he could lock it from the inside if he wanted. However, if Audra or her shadows said or did anything louder than a whisper, he knew Avery and Mackenzie would rip it off the hinges. But where was she?

Probably escaped while everyone was in the Tribunal, Felix thought. He lit several candles and drew back the curtain over the window. Trying to stick to routine, he sat on his bed and pretended to get undressed. Sitting there, he picked the room apart. Behind the mirror? He leaned over. No, not behind the mirror. Under the bed? He got down on all fours and hung over the edge. No, not under there, either.

He was supposed to go to the closet next, to change into his nightwear, so he jumped down and plodded across his room. There were piles of clothes on the floor. They weren't big enough to hide a woman, but he turned them over, just in case. The closet seemed about the most obvious of hiding places, but maybe Audra found some sort of secret compartment no one else knew was there.

Felix took a deep breath and pulled the closet open. Shirts and pants. Robes and shoes. Some old toys and couple copies of *Helminth's Way*. The closet was shallow, as most closets are, but in depth as well. He walked in, walked around. He felt up everything, cringing as he did so, just in case he accidentally felt up something he shouldn't. Shirts and pants. Robes and shoes. Some old toys and *Helminth's Way*. And some snacks he'd snuck out of the kitchen about two months ago. But no Audra. She wasn't here. She wasn't anywhere.

A mixture of sadness and relief washed over him as he stripped down and put on a breezy robe. He backed out of the closet and latched it shut. *What did you expect?* he thought, trotting into his personal bathroom. She wasn't in there, either. It was a sink, a toilet, and a bath. Unless she was in the floor or walls, she wasn't hiding in here. *She used you*, he thought, going to the sink and splashing water over his face. *It's good she didn't stay.* He dried his face, relieved himself for a good two minutes at the toilet. *I couldn't have done anything for her, anyway.*

On his way out of the bathroom, he grabbed a candle from the windowsill and did a tour of the room again. Shadows shot across the walls as he waved the candle back and forth, probing every patch of darkness for Audra.

"I don't blame you," he mumbled.

Again, Felix checked under the bed, behind the mirror, inside the closet. He searched the places where she couldn't fit, like his chest of drawers and a trunk filled with trinkets from special missions. But she wasn't there, either. He even opened his window, thinking she might have squeezed through and was hanging on for dear life on the other side. But all he got for his efforts was a blast of air that left his nose runny and his ears sore.

He sighed and shut the window. That was it. She was gone.

And then Audra whispered, "Holy Child."

Felix bit his tongue and dropped the candle. "Au-Audra?" he cried. He snatched the candle off the ground. "What… where?" He squinted, held the candle to the corner near the window. A web of shadows like a black cocoon clung to it. "Audra?"

One by one, the tenebrous strands fell, peeling away from the black husk. As the layers were stripped, the shadows became grayer, lighter. Besides their impossible thickness, there seemed to be a compartment within them, a deepness that betrayed their shallow dimensions. Inside it, several inches past where the corner itself should have been, Audra stood, stiller than the still-life she resembled.

The shadows, now pooled around her feet, began to take form. They spiraled upward, creating two gossamer torsos on both sides of Audra. The material then eroded across the creatures, bringing them definition and shape. Semi-translucent branches broke free of the trunks and tightened into long, gangling limbs. At the top of each torso, a dark swell of gloom ballooned into a neck and head.

"It's okay," Audra said, stepping out of the corner.

The shadows rose. Fangs, silver and dripping, pushed out of their black gums.

Audra swallowed hard. "He is a friend."

The creatures flexed their fingers. Each time that they did, their fingers grew longer, sharper, until they were like the blades of black scissors.

Heart pounding, Felix stumbled backward. Avery's and Mackenzie's names were in his throat. One shout and they would be in here, saving him, and damning him.

"Stop," Audra hissed. "I command you to stop!"

A light flickered in the shadows' eyeless sockets. Their shoulders slacked and their claws uncurled. Eerily, they took a step back to be at their dark mistress' side.

"It's okay," Audra said. She moved in front of them. "They're protective of me. But I promise they won't hurt you."

"You lied to me." Felix was practically tripping over his feet to reach the door. "You can control them."

She held out her hand, asking him to stop. "No, no, I can't. It doesn't always work. Only when I'm in dire need. And not even then. Listen, Holy Child, listen. You're safe. We're together. I waited. I heard you talking to the Hydra. Something bad happened. If she finds you here with me, how will you explain it? You're safe, Holy Child. Please, please." Tears poured down her face. "Please, don't tell them I'm here."

Felix sat at one end of the empty bathtub; Audra, the other. Knees to their chests, hearts in their throats, they mirrored one another not only physically, but most likely mentally. They kept quiet, kept twitching at every late-hour sound. They were like animals caught in a trap that had failed to be sprung. It was an uneasy tension that bound them, not the deeds they had done; they were their own prisoners.

It wasn't until the shadows faded from Audra's side that Felix finally broke the silence. Sinking down into the tub, he said, "I'm sorry I freaked out."

Audra shrugged. "Imagine how I felt the first time they visited me."

"How old were you?"

She raised her eyebrows. "Seven. I was in my room, making a new shadow puppet show for my twin, Auster. Out of nowhere, this strange feeling came over me. Like how you feel when you catch a cold?"

Felix nodded.

"Then the shadows started moving on their own. And I could move them, too, like they were there. I actually used a shadow to pick up a teacup next to the wall. Granted, I dropped it a few seconds later, but I wasn't able to do that again for… years. That's what I mean, Holy Child. I have these bursts of power, but I still don't know what I'm doing."

"You're a spellweaver." Felix sat up. He started to stretch out his legs, went all the way with them when it seemed she wouldn't mind. "So is it any shadow? Or just those creatures?"

"Any. The shadow creatures are different. I just think about how much I could do if I could use shadows around us. There's shadows everywhere. I could do a lot of good if I could just figure it all out. But I can't find anyone like me. Our Archivist Amon promised to teach me a thing or two, but that never happened."

Audra seemed to realize how much she was talking. She stopped abruptly and said, "Do you really hear the voice of god?"

"Yes, I do." Felix didn't hesitate to answer. It wasn't something you could hesitate to answer.

"What's god sound like?"

"Hard to say. Doesn't really sound like anything. God doesn't talk a lot. But I think it's because god wants us to make our own decisions. I think god is changing, too."

Audra grinned her yellow-toothed grin. "What does god think of me? The woman who spends more time with hell than anything else?"

"God told me to help you." Felix tapped his fingers on the edge of the bathtub. "I'm sorry I thought you were a Worm."

"I don't blame you." Audra nudged his legs with her toe. "I talk to the shadows. They're right there in Victor Mors' journal. I would have thought the same. When did you first hear god's voice?"

"I always did, I guess. That's what they told me. But the first thing I remember god saying to me was that I was—" Felix chewed on his lip, embarrassed, "—was that I was good. That there wasn't anything wrong with me."

"You thought there was something wrong with you?"

Felix's body went tense. He had walked into something he didn't want to talk about. But he really wanted to. Deep down. He was tired of secrets and keeping things to himself.

So he said, "I still do. Sometimes."

"Heh, me too," Audra said. "Funny we should meet. Wish the circumstances were different, Holy Child."

"Felix." He held out his hand and she shook it. "Name's Felix."

"Audra. Obviously. We're an odd pair, you and I. I talk to hell. You talk to heaven."

"I don't think… I don't think god is in heaven. I think god is somewhere else. I think god has big plans for the world. I think that's why we don't hear from god much. Are you a believer?"

"When I need to be. Don't think badly of me, Felix, but god wasn't there when my brother killed my family. I don't care if it was wrong of me to expect god to intervene, but I did. And god didn't."

Felix tried to hide his shock. "King Edgar k-killed your family? Are you sure? How… how?" Did Justine know? If what Audra had said were true, it may even be enough to destroy the Disciples of the Deep.

This time, it was Audra who was squirming to be out of the conversation. But like Felix, she swallowed her doubts and confessed. "He did. He came into my room that night. He stabbed me in my sleep." She lifted her filthy slip and bared her hip. There was a scar, a deep, albino gouge. "When I woke up, he stopped and walked out of my room. I didn't move. I didn't know what to do. If I had… if I had known that he was going to kill my mother and father, my brothers and sister, I might have done something. But instead, I lay there. I was so shocked, so betrayed. Edgar and I had plans. We were finally getting closer. We were going to do things for Eldrus. Together. I couldn't believe he would… It was paralyzing."

"I know what you mean," Felix said quietly. "It was the same way with Turov."

"I'm sorry I rubbed that in your face earlier, him taking you. I don't know much about it. I just wanted to hurt you."

Felix shrugged.

"Do you want to talk about it?"

Again, he shrugged. "You could tell everybody about what King Edgar did."

Audra's eyes went soft. It was too late. By mentioning his name alone, she had seen the hurt the exemplar had sown within him.

"I could, but what good would it do? It's been years. He's the king of Eldrus. If he knows I'm alive and I'm speaking out against him, all he has to say is that I'm a fake. Mmm, no. I don't know why he did it or if something forced him to, but I can't and won't forgive him. I know I'm too nice, too trusting. But not anymore. He could have come and saved me at any time, but he left me to rot here for two years.

"You know, it really makes me mad, Felix, that it's night right now. I haven't seen the sun in so long. It's still out there right?"

Felix grinned and said, "Yeah, it shows up, but it doesn't do much."

"Sounds like my father." Audra laughed at herself. "I'm sorry I keep talking. I'm probably giving us away. It's kind of been awhile, you know?"

Felix noticed a thin, brown layer had formed around Audra in the tub. It was all the dirt and grime that she had been carrying with her these last few years. At last, it seemed, it was starting to finally come off.

He was dirty, too, on the inside, where no one could see. Sometimes, he could taste it, smell it—a kind of bitter odor, sweet and revolting. When god spoke to him, it went away, but only for a while. He had to get clean, too, like Audra. He had to spit it out; otherwise, it was going to fill him up, and if it did, how could anything holy inhabit him anymore?

"How did you know Samuel Turov was going to kidnap me?" Felix asked. *Please don't laugh at me*, he thought, ready to share himself. *Please don't look at me funny.*

"Alexander Blodworth bragged about it on the ride from Eldrus to Pyra. He told me everything. What he was going to use the Crossbreed for. How he and my brother were working together. How he was going to have the Exemplar of Restraint hide you. That piece of... He didn't take me seriously. I was just a mirror to him. Something he could see and hear himself in. He knew I couldn't stop him. And he was right."

Weakly, Felix said, "Did he tell you what Samuel Turov was going to do with me?"

Audra shook her head. It only took a few seconds for her to put two and two together, and once she did, her face went dark and her eyes wide.

"Only god truly knows." Felix gathered himself. He called on the strength of heaven, but it was from that mire of hate inside him he found fortitude. "I think the Mother Abbess does, too, but I never told her everything."

Hands twitching like a broken clock's hour, he pulled up his robe, to his knees, where the scars started. "He kept me drugged in the beginning. I remember there were a few soldiers, but one day they were gone. It wasn't until we were in the South he stopped making me drink all those potions. I was so sick. Couldn't stop throwing up."

Keep going, god told him. *You are doing the right thing, my son.*

"I don't know if he meant to keep going, but we eventually stopped in a forest. He found a small house. There was a family living there and… I don't know what he did with them. But they didn't come back.

"He never really explained to me what we were doing. I trusted him, though, because he had always been nice to me. After a week or two, something went wrong. He stopped being nice. He told me I was a liar. That there was another voice of god."

Don't cry. Felix rubbed his eyes, but the tears were already coming. A cold chill crept up his spine and his jaw started to shake.

"It's okay," Audra said. She touched his leg. "You don't have—"

"He said I was a sinner!" Felix shouted. His voice dropped to a raspy whisper. "He said I was sinner who didn't know sin, and that he was going to show me what sin was."

Audra's forehead glistened with sweat. She covered her mouth, almost covered her ears. She knew what was coming.

"He made me do every sin he could think of." Large globs of spit gummed up Felix's mouth. When he breathed, he made choking sounds. Where he touched, wet patches of perspiration were left. "I did them to him. He did them to me. We hit each other. Cut each other. We, he, we cursed god. Sometimes, we stole from travelers. We ate our own…" Felix leaned over and pinched the bridge of his nose. He drooled hot spit all over himself. "He touched me. Made me touch him. Even when I was so sore. He would wake me up and make me… do things for him."

Wiping his mouth, he said, "I have to be a sinner, because sometimes I think I liked it."

"No, Felix," Audra said. This time, she didn't try to touch him. This time, he really wanted her to.

"No, you did absolutely nothing wrong. No, no, no."

"But I did like it. Sometimes, sometimes I think I miss it."

"No, Felix."

"There is something wrong with me. Normal people aren't like that."

"Felix, he took advantage of you. What you felt, what you did… Felix, he used you. And I'm so, so, sorry. He was just as insane as Alexander Blodworth."

"Are you sure?" he begged. "Why do I miss it? Why do I have these sinful feelings?" His eyes started to probe her slip. He quickly looked away. "I don't always, but sometimes, they sneak up on me."

"We all sin all the time," Audra said. "Felix, look at me."

He did.

"We are all sinners, and shadows of our sins. What Samuel Turov did to you was disgusting. But your feelings are not. They're just confused. That's all. We just have to make sense of them. Listen." She scooted forward, her legs outside his. She tightened them and took his wrists. "I created a plant that was responsible for killing thousands upon thousands. I wanted to use it for good, but someone used it for evil, instead. Does that make me evil?"

Felix shook his head. "You didn't know."

"You are good. You are a good kid. Our bodies are what they are. They don't read *Helminth's Way*. They are like my plants. Creatures of biology. Sometimes, they can tell when things are bad, yucky, but sometimes they get confused. What you felt was okay. What he did wasn't." She touched his cheeks, held his face. "You are good. There is nothing wrong with you. He showed you things you shouldn't have seen, and no one was there to make sense of them. You are good, Felix."

Swallowing hard, he nodded and said, "I wish you didn't have to leave Pyra."

She sniffled her nose. "How did you get away from Samuel Turov?"

"One day, we saw a Night Terror at the edge of the forest. He thought she was hunting us. He said he was going to kill her. He said we were going to eat her. It was a sin we hadn't tried yet." Felix's face brightened several shades of the sun. "The Night Terror killed him so fast. She tore out his heart. I was happy, but angry, too. Scared. I was getting used to him. I didn't know. I thought maybe the Night Terror would be worse. I had heard so many bad stories. Samuel Turov was awful, but he took care of me.

"The Night Terror was nice, though. Her name was… Vrana. She saved me from a monster and took me to Cadence. After that, I guess someone recognized me and soldiers brought me home."

"Now, that's a happy ending," Audra said. She nudged a laugh out of him. "You're good at turning it off and on, aren't you?"

Felix cocked his head, confused.

"The good and bad thoughts."

"Oh. Yeah." It was true; already, he could feel the filth inside him breaking free, breaking apart.

"Me, too. People like us, we have to be."

Felix didn't understand what she meant, so he just said, "I guess so."

Audra finally let go of his wrists and scooted back to her dirtied spot. It was time to change the subject. "You know, my brother, Vincent, was obsessed with Night Terrors."

Vrana, Felix thought. *Vrana, I'm so sorry I forgot about you.*

"Some of them wear the skulls or shells or whatever of animal lords. Vincent tried to catalogue them and figure out where they had come from."

"Uh, huh." Felix's thoughts had become twisted, a disturbing helix of the mutated Vrana and the last, depraved days of his time with Turov.

"He said there was an animal lord in the Ossuary, that great, big desert in the south. He said it was maggot lord with a kingdom of little maggots. Imagine the Night Terror who finally slays that..." Audra wiggled her leg until she had his attention. "What's the matter, Felix?"

"Will you still help me?" he blurted out.

"Help you?" Audra rested her elbows on the edge of the bathtub. "I have to be going soon. Help you with what?"

Gloomily, he said, "Never mind."

"No, wait." Audra stood and stepped out of the bath. Her nasty slip trailed behind her like the maggot lord she had mentioned. "I remember. You said you had a friend. You said you had a friend trapped in the Membrane. You wanted me to use the shadows to find her. I thought maybe you were... but you really do need my help."

A few lights dimmed in his bedroom. The candles were getting low, drowning in their own wax.

"It's the Night Terror. Vrana." Felix stood, too, and stepped out of the bath. "I don't know what's happened to her. But she's trapped somewhere. She came into my room, out of my dreams, one night, begging me to free her. She saved me from Samuel Turov. I just feel like I need to return the favor."

"You saved me, Felix," Audra said, nodding. "Whether or not I get caught or killed tonight, you still saved me. You have no idea how good it feels to be out of that cell. For that alone, I owe you. Her name's Vrana? I owe her, too, because without her, I wouldn't have met you. Night Terror or not, she deserves our help."

"I see her in my dreams. Do you think the shadows can... go into my dreams?"

"You were there when I talked to Isla Taggart through the shadows on the wall? That took a long time for me to pull off. But they can project themselves into different places. If you can dream about your friend, where she is, I think they'll be able to go there, through you, and tell us how we can get in, too."

"But you might be caught if you do this."

"If I do this for you, I'll happily be caught. This is Penance, and I've a lot of penance to do for the things I've done."

"But you said it. You said you're not evil."

Audra smiled a liar's smile and said, "Let's get started."

CHAPTER X

"I don't know if I want devils in my head," Felix said as he lay in bed, nursing a cup of Reprieve.

"We all have devils in our head," Audra said, sitting beside him. "At least you'll know where these devils came from."

Felix polished off the drink, cringed, and said, "Crap. I should have waited until the shadows came. This stuff makes me so tired."

"It'll be fine."

"But I have to help you get out!"

Audra patted his knee through the blankets. "Not so loud. Avery and... Mackenzie? They are probably still out there."

"They're supposed to be." His eyelids went up and down, one after the other. "I've—" he yawned into his pillow, "—I've sneaked out a few times around three in the morning. They're always gone by then."

"It's a little after midnight, now." Audra got off the bed. "What about the other guards?"

"There aren't a lot of guards in Pyra. The Mother Abbess said she didn't want this place to feel like prison."

Audra curled her lip and laughed.

"But there's usually always a few people running around. Everyone is supposed to keep an eye on everyone. Can you—" he rubbed his eyes and propped himself against the headboard, "—use the shadows to get around?"

"If they'll let me." Audra went through the room. She gathered up candle after candle, placed them all around Felix's bed. "The shadows are cold, though. Like that Vein Rot potion, being in them drains you. I could do it for a little bit. But I need a disguise, too. Something warm, preferably."

Felix pointed to his closet. "There's a bunch of girl stuff in there. Some of it is Mackenzie's."

Audra placed the last candle next to the headboard. "Oh?"

"They're for my special missions. I need disguises to do them. There're some coats, too. A lot of it is too big. I was saving it for later."

"Oh." Audra tongued her canines. "You dress up like a girl to get around Pyra unnoticed?"

Felix's nodded, and started to nod off.

"Anyone ever recognize you?"

"Huh? Yeah, but I think they just pretend not to."

Audra started moving the candles she'd set near Felix's bed, strategically creating shadows here and there. "Hey, Felix, you don't happen to have a weapon do you?"

Squinting, as though he were looking straight at the sun, he mumbled, "What?"

"A dagger. A sword."

She had created a trail of candles, running from the foot of the bed, to the center of the room. They seemed to form some sort of symbol, but Felix's vision was too blurry to make sense of it.

"To be honest, I don't know where I'm going to go," she continued. "But I need to be able to defend myself. I'll keep in contact, though, I promise. I'll get better at talking through the shadows, like with Isla."

"Okay," Felix chirped. His cheeks were too numb to smile. "There's, um." It took everything Felix had to move. He slumped over, dug under his mattress. This is where he kept his journal, and where he kept his knife. "Here." He slid it out and held it up. "I stole it from the sacristy."

The knife was a ceremonial tool used in baptism and contrition. Long and twisted, the blue blade had only one purpose: to cut Corruption, to symbolize the bleeding of sin from a new member's body. Felix had taken it after his ordeal with Samuel Turov, to protect himself. But the longer he had it, and the dirtier he felt on the inside, the more he used it. Not on his right arm, that would have been too obvious, but on his thighs—the true seat of his corruption.

Audra took the knife from Felix and said, "That'll do. Have you ever had to use it?"

He ignored her. "Go back to the hidden place. Come out in the cloister. Use the second floor sleeping quarters to get to the main terminal. The Lyceum is below that. There's maintenance tunnels down there. A few of them lead outside. It'll be really cold. Sometimes, they have food in the Lyceum for meetings. You could steal some. Maybe if we wait until the morning, I can go with you and—"

She cut him off. "You've done enough. Get comfortable, Holy Child." Audra's eyes rolled back in her head. "U'cha, ma'zil." Her body started to twitch. "Ih'ya, ih'ya."

Felix wasn't so tired anymore. Covers up to his chin, he said, "Is it... is it always like this?"

She took the knife, slashed her palm. "Fuh'zil. Ka'li'ya." And smeared the wound all over her face.

"The shadows are coming," she said, gripping her slip in her hand.

The candles flared and flickered, flared and flickered. On the ceiling, scabby holes opened. Out of them, shafts of sand poured, snuffing out the lights of each of the candles Audra had placed.

"The shadows are coming." She held out her hand and pointed her dripping finger at Felix. "Make him sleep." Her voice wasn't one but many; an agonizing chorus singing the only song they knew.

"Make him sleep," she said. Six shadows rose out of the ground around her, forming as the others had formed, one limb at a time. "Make him sleep, so we may see."

Fully completed, the shadows surged forwards and climbed onto the bed. Felix kicked off his blankets. Before he could sit up, the creatures piled onto him and held him in place. Their scissor-like fingers clamped down over his ankles, his knees; they wrapped around his wrists, pressed hard against his shoulders. The shadows put their weight into him, forcing the air out of his lungs, so he couldn't speak or scream. They were simultaneously as heavy as boulders and as ephemeral as ghosts. Sometimes, they slipped into him. When they did, it was like nails were being pounded into his bones. It hurt so bad it made him cry. But before the tears could leave his eyes, the shadows were already there, drinking them off his lids.

"Audra," he wheezed. Two shadows were hovering over him, running their claws across his face. "Please, I don't want to do this anymore!"

"Felix, please, be quiet," Audra said. "Tell them her name."

"V-Vrana," he stammered. "She's a—" A shadow drilled its claw directly into his forehead. "—A Night Terror!"

Agitated, Audra said, "Cover his mouth!"

As the shadow stirred the contents of Felix's skull, a second shadow covered his mouth and held his jaw shut. Audra started chanting again, but at this point, he had lost the ability to make sense of most anything. Consciousness came and went without concern for his safety. The shore of sleep wasn't far off now, either. He could hear it calling to him, promising a place to rest.

This is what I wanted. He closed his eyes and gave in to the pain his trust had bought him. *This is what I deserve.*

Felix may have been asleep for hours, but the dreams started immediately. Like a tapestry of memories, they came to him, one after the other, in quick succession. He dreamt of Audra, in his room, not as a friend, but as a sister. He dreamt of Justine and the Demagogue, his hand up her dress, her tongue in his mouth. He dreamt of the Bloodless, rising high above Penance, people lining up to feed themselves to it. He dreamt of the kindergarten he couldn't possibly remember attending. There were soldiers, and a woman, and someone was beating at the door, crying, screaming, begging, "Not him! Take the other, but not him!"

The dream was quickly dispelled, and others followed in its place. It was a dizzying display of experience and interpretations that left him disorientated. But as they came and went, he began to realize what was happening to him. The shadows. Like flipping through a book, they were turning the pages of his mind, searching for what they had been brought here to find.

Vrana. The Void. And the Witch who kept her there. Almost every night for the last month and a half, he'd had recurring nightmares of the place. And now that he actually wanted to go back, the doors were shut to him?

Vrana. The Void. And the Witch who kept her there. Felix focused as hard as he could on those three things.

He thought about Vrana, in the South, with that raven's head and ax of hers, and when they had sat beside the lake. Though he would be attacked moments later, it had been the first time since Samuel Turov had kidnapped him that he felt safe.

He thought about the Void, that dark and gray place, with the plummeting pits and whining winds. He remembered the unrelenting blackness that surrounded the wasteland, the greedy Abyss that gave no quarter when it came to light or life.

And finally, he thought about the Witch, of whom he knew little, and who terrified him on an almost instinctual level. That disgusting woman, with her pale, wet skin and ragged dress. That night she and Vrana had come to him, the Witch had crawled like a spider out of thin air and claimed the Raven. Who was she? What was she? How could anything do something like that?

Felix's eyes snapped open. He scraped the crust from their corners and wiped the drool from his mouth. *Crap*, he thought. He flung his legs over the side of his bed and stood up.

"Audra?" He stumbled forward blindly in the dark. "Where are you?"

There was something wrong with the floor. It didn't feel right. Still out of it, he bent over and closed his hands around a clump of grass. *What the heck?* He reared back and rubbed his eyes. With every pass, they worked a little better. Until, when they were good and ready, red and raw, he saw that he wasn't in his room at all.

"The Void," he whispered. His words rippled the air. "I'm here."

Standing on a hill, Felix could see most of the Void. The lowlands below him were a mess of narrow ravines and gaseous pits that fragmented the scaly stretch. The ground itself appeared as though it were liquid, not solid. Although the inky, rocky texture flowed in every direction, it never actually moved at all. There were dark masses that swept across the area, too; feathery whirlwinds of disease-wracked ravens that flew the lowlands in a constant patrol.

Felix backed up. He didn't want to be seen. Not by the birds. Not by anything that lived here, really. A clammy wind rolled off the peaks that loomed in the distance. Breathing it in, he quickly coughed it out, as it burned his lungs and turned his stomach.

Holding his breath, Felix turned around, to see what other sights sat behind him. At the furthest end of the hill, where the tall grass tapered off, there was a small house. Out of its chimney, thick, bruised-colored smoke poured. The front door to the house, or what was left of it, creaked open, stopped, and slammed shut. It did this over and over again.

"In the house."

Felix jumped and stumbled sideways. Beside him, one of Audra's shadows floated. Here, in the Void, the creature had more definition, more detail. There appeared to be bones inside it, a ghostly skeletal system that floated inside the hazy darkness the shadow was comprised of.

"So close to death," it said, flexing its claws. "Good place to hide."

Felix cleared his throat. "Can we g-get Vrana out?"

The shadow shrugged. "There are ways." It floated towards the house.

Felix ran after it. "What about the Witch?" After a few seconds, he was already out of breath. He stopped, buckled over, and gulped the vomit-flavored air. "Can you...? Oh, god." He retched. "Can you stop her?"

The shadow floated back to Felix and straightened him out. With its ice cold hands on his shoulders, it said, "No."

Looking into the creature's eyeless sockets, he whispered, "Can anything?"

The shadow nodded and pointed to the house, to the woman standing at the window, watching them from behind it. "She can."

Vrana? Felix wiped his mouth and broke into a sprint. The closer he got to the house, the more his body fought against him. His skin was on fire, and his muscles seizing. But he ignored it, all of it. This wasn't his body, anyway. Just a dream of his body. He was still back in Pyra, asleep, with Audra at his bedside and Avery and Mackenzie close by. He knew pain, and he knew it well. If Samuel Turov had taught him anything in their time together, it was that pain, much like money, had a value to it. It could buy a person, and it could be used to buy something with. Pain here, in the Void, was cheap, an inflated imitation. His time in the South had given him a wealth of suffering, real suffering, to spend. And now, at last, it was time to cash it all in.

Felix sprinted up the yard. The front door creaked open, paused, and slammed shut. As he reached for the handle, the shadow grabbed his arm from behind and said, "Wait."

"Wait?" a woman's voice cried inside the house. "Don't wait." The woman laughed cruelly. "No, no. Come in. We seldom have willing visitors."

The door slowly creaked open on its own. The shadow let go of Felix's arm and stood beside him. Blue light spilled over the threshold, across their feet.

The shadow leaned into Felix and whispered, "I can get her out. But we can't keep her out."

Felix noticed the drool that had started to fall from the shadow's fangs. "God will find a way," he said.

At that moment, the door slammed all the way back. It cracked against the house and flew off the hinges, just barely missing Felix and the shadow. Cringing, he gathered himself and stepped across the threshold.

The Witch was there, rocking back and forth in a chair made out of bones. She was rubbing her hands together over the fireplace, as though to get warm, yet there were no flames or logs inside it. Instead, there were tentacles—fat, blue, writhing tentacles that spewed the very same bruise-colored smoke he had seen coming out of the chimney. At the back of the fireplace, an object caught his eye. Squinting hard, he saw that it was the same silver, blue-gemmed necklace Vrana had been wearing the night she came into his room.

The Witch leaned back in the chair, her spinal column sinking into her skin. Lazily, she twisted her neck and looked at him, half-interested.

"Who's this?" another woman asked.

Felix's head snapped to his left, where another woman stood beside the windows. Unlike the Witch, who wore black, this woman wore white. She had a kinder face, too, with soft eyes and a small smile. She looked about as out of place here as he did. But then he saw the skinned bodies dangling from the rafters behind her and thought otherwise.

"That is the Holy Child of Penance," the Witch said, unenthused. She turned her head and went back to the fireplace. "She must have called him here."

The second woman nodded and put her finger to her lips. "You shouldn't let her do that."

The Witch waved off the woman's warning.

"My name's Joy," the second woman said, making a small curtsey. When she did, several dead fetuses fell out from in between her legs. They slid across the ground, like vaginal regurgitations. "I'm sorry." Her cheeks went red. "I'm so embarrassed."

Felix tried to cover his mouth, but he was already puking. He fell against the doorway, spitting up what little was left of what the dream thought was in his stomach.

The Witch howled with laughter. She fell back in her chair and pounded the armrests in grotesque delight. "Don't worry about it, Joy." The Witch came to her feet and clapped her hands together. "Vrana will clean it up."

Something rattled in the rafters above. As Felix looked up, Vrana dropped to the floor and scurried to where the fetuses had been spilt. She stopped short of Joy and reared back, stretching out her massive wings. With a look of disappointment, she nodded and turned away. In a ravenous fury, Vrana went down on all fours and started shoveling the abortions down her beak, swallowing them whole.

"I'm sorry to say," the Witch said, getting out of her chair, "but Vrana is grounded. She can't come out and play with you tonight."

"Please, don't," Felix begged, reaching out to Vrana. She was licking clean the floor. "God, please, make her—"

The Witch stomped her foot and shouted, "What is this? What is that behind you?"

Felix turned around. She was talking about the shadow, except it wasn't just one shadow anymore. There were several of them now. They were holding their hands in the air. Above them, a dark circle was forming, like they were etching it into reality itself.

"I told you she would be a problem," the Witch said to Joy. She spat at Felix and went to the fireplace. "I hope you've gotten right with the God, Holy Child. You're about to meet It very soon." The Witch clapped her hands and belted, "Vrana!"

"No, come with us," Felix cried as the Winged Horror scurried across the ground, talons clicking on the floorboards. "We're getting you out of here."

Vrana ignored him. She crawled up beside the Witch and lay her head at the woman's feet.

"Say the words," the Witch said. She grabbed Vrana by the feathers on her neck. "You know them. Say them!" She shoved Vrana's face into the tendrils. The silver necklace at the back of the fireplace glowed vibrantly. "Say them!"

"Penance, Pyra. The Holy Child. His quarters," Vrana croaked. Her feathers stood up across her body. The blue tendrils extended and stabbed into her skull. "Penance, Pyra! The Holy Child. His quarters!"

"What's going on?" He turned around to the shadows, but they were gone. "No, no!"

"Penance! Pyra! The Holy Child! His quarters!" Vrana clawed at the ground like a dog digging a hole. "Penance! Pyra! The Holy Child! His quarters!"

The Witch crossed her arms and grinned.

Felix, wake up! Wake up! It was Audra's voice. He backed out of the house. Where was she? His body started to shake. He felt hands on his shoulders, someone slapping him across the face. *Felix,* he heard Audra cry. *Felix, wake up!*

Joy stepped in front of him, frowning. "I'm sorry, but you really did do this to yourself. All of you. You and the whole world."

Felix! Audra screamed into his ear.

"Audra, where are—?"

Felix shot up, out of bed, and onto the floor. Onto the floor of his room. He knocked over the candles, burnt his arm on a few that had reignited. He was out of the dream. He was awake. He was awake and there was Audra. But she looked horrified; the way she had looked when the Bloodless had bloomed.

"Felix, Felix!" She shook him hard. "Felix, do you have any more weapons? Is there another way out?"

"What?" He heard screams and steel outside his room. Someone was beating on his door, trying to break it down. "Audra, what's going on?"

"She sent them. Her cult. Somehow, she—"

The door burst open. A flood of robed figures spilled into the room. They surrounded Audra and Felix with bloody daggers. Even though their eyes were glowing bright blue, he recognized them all. Patricia and Juda, doctors from the second floor clinic; Amanda, a cook, and Abram, her father; York, the quartermaster; Malachite, head of the kennels and stables. Even Grant was there, the man who was in charge of the main terminal, and the first person to mention to Felix the Cult of the Worm.

But Grant, unlike the others, wasn't holding a dagger. No, they were…. Felix covered his mouth and howled. In each of Grant's hands were heads. Severed heads. Avery's and Mackenzie's severed heads.

CHAPTER XI

"Kill the Holy Child," the cult chanted, Vrana's voice hidden behind their own. "Kill the Holy Child!"

Audra shielded Felix with her body. With his contrition knife, she spun around, slashing at every cult member that drew near.

"What do we do?" Felix clung to her slip. His nails tore through it and dug into her back.

"Kill the boy!" Juda grabbed Felix's robe and started to yank him away.

"Audra! Audra, help!"

Audra twisted back and stabbed the knife into Juda's arm. She ripped downward. His skin split open like overcooked meat.

Juda screamed in gut-wrenching pain. He toppled backward, severed veins and arteries dousing his robed brothers and sisters.

"Stay back," Audra threatened. Her hand was shaking so much she could barely keep hold of her weapon.

The cult members kept reaching for him, kept taunting him by stabbing the air. "God, please help us."

Patricia and Amanda stepped over Juda and filled in where he had been standing.

"Justine! Justine!" Felix wailed as Abram went for him.

Audra sliced across the quartermaster's collarbone. A red signature signed *Audra* dribbled down his chest.

"I'm so sorry," she said. She moved Felix in front of her. "Get back!"

Abram tried to stab her face, but Audra deflected the dagger.

"Don't listen to her, you morons!"

Juda twitched in the background, dying without any concern from those he'd come here with.

"We are going to kill him," Grant said, swinging the severed heads of Avery and Mackenzie back and forth by their hair. "Do you want to go first, shadow-weaver?"

Audra, holding him from behind, whispered, "Felix, pray to god."

Malachite, the head of the kennels, started to bark like the dogs he had so lovingly cared for. "Pray." He pricked his thumb on the dagger and flicked the blood in Felix's eyes. "Pray," he repeated, this time in Vrana's croaking drawl. "Pray you die quick!"

Felix dropped to the ground and curled into a ball. Audra shielded him.

Please god, make them stop. Please god, I won't ask you for anything else.

Audra shrieked. Felix looked back and saw Patricia's dagger in her shoulder blade. *Please! We need you now!*

"Wait." Grant was addressing Patricia, but the rest of the cult moved away from their victims. He took a seat on Felix's bed. Now the Witch spoke through him: "He sent a prayer. Let's see what happens."

Between Audra and Felix, a puddle of sweat had formed beneath them. His skin sliding across hers, he pulled her in and said, "Where are the shadows?"

"They abandoned me." Audra gripped the curved knife and put it to Felix's neck. "Do you want me to?"

Hearing that, Grant jumped to his feet and screamed, "Don't you dare!"

He threw the heads of Avery and Mackenzie at them. Avery's cracked on Audra's nose and sent her reeling to the ground. Mackenzie's slammed into the side of Felix's; everything went fuzzy and hot.

"Kill them," the cult started to chant.

Sitting there, stunned, Felix shouted, "No," as Malachite grabbed his leg and dragged him across the ground. "Get off! Get off!" He grabbed onto the bed posts, onto dead Juda's ankle. Patricia straddled Felix and punched his head into the floor.

Through his swelling eye, Felix watched Amanda, Abram, York, and Grant descend on Audra. He begged them to stop. Malachite smashed his face into the tile, so that each word he uttered caused his teeth to grind against the ground.

"I didn't want it to come to this," Abram said, both the Witch's voice and Vrana's tangled inside his own. He lowered his knife and pressed it to Audra's neck. "We had big plans for you, little boy."

"Audra, no!"

Suddenly, Patricia's lifeless body fell in front of him, blocking his view. The intensity of the blue light in her eyes blinded him. *What the...?* Crunch, snap. Something warm dribbled over his calf. Malachite's grip weakened.

"Deimos?" Grant cried.

Deimos? On wobbly arms, Felix pushed himself up and collapsed on Patricia's corpse. "Audra!" She had a dagger in her back, but she was breathing.

Out of nowhere, Deimos rushed past Felix, Abram at the end of his sword.

"Holy Child," he said, kicking Abram off his blade. "Lucan, get them!"

Grant, panicking, crawled backward, into the corner.

"Lucan?" Felix shifted on Patricia to look at the front of the room.

Lucan was there, by the door, his knee deep in Amanda's unhinged jaw. Grunting, he picked her up and hurled her through the mirror.

"Where's the other one?" Lucan said, panting.

Deimos pointed to a body on the ground. "Playing dead." He threw his sword to Lucan and closed in on Grant.

Lucan caught it and drove it through York's back. Eyes bleeding blue, he reared up, screaming. In one motion, Lucan tore out the sword and cleaved the cultist's head.

Felix fell backward onto his bed and used it to get to his feet. Pointing at Audra, he said, "Is she... she okay?"

Lucan hurtled across the room and scooped Felix into his arms. He tore some sheets off of the bed and started wrapping them around Felix's head. "She's not with them?"

"No, no." Felix's left eye had completely swollen shut. "She's good. She's... my friend."

Lucan nodded. He carried Felix to her side and laid him down beside her. "Hey, lady," Lucan said, nudging Audra. "We're going to get you out of here."

Grant screamed, in Vrana's voice, "Deimos... Deimos. Use her."

Brushing Audra's hair, Felix turned his attention to Grant in the corner.

"Vrana?" Deimos snapped his fingers. Lucan tossed him his sword. "Is that... you?"

"It is," Felix said. "It's her."

Audra stirred beside him. She grabbed his hand and pressed it to her lips. "Felix."

"Oh my god, Audra." He looked up at Lucan.

"Deimos, let's move," he said. "Help me with the woman."

"This is Vrana speaking through this man."

Deimos pointed the sword at Grant. "Holy Child, what is going on?"

"There's more," Grant screamed. "She won't stop until you've killed them all!" He plunged the dagger into his throat.

"Wait," Deimos cried. He dropped his sword and ripped the dagger away from Grant.

"Stupid girl," Grant said, his words bloody bubbles on his trembling lips. "This has been a..." Grant sputtered and slouched into the corner, "... learning experience." He looked up, eyes finally going dim. "We'll break her better... next time... Bat."

Deimos fell back on his haunches and didn't say anything else until Grant had finished dying.

"What are you...?" Felix's head was throbbing. His gums felt as though someone were running wire through them. "What are you doing here?"

"Hunting them." Lucan nodded at the dead cultists. Again, he picked up Felix, and added, "We've been here awhile now, trying to track them down."

Deimos sighed and walked over to Audra. He knelt down beside her, and whispered, "It's okay, I have you." Carefully, her arm around his shoulder, knife still protruding from her back, he helped her to her feet. "I'm sorry about your friends."

Avery and Mackenzie. Felix's good eye wandered over to the doorway, where a woman's arm lay across the threshold. It hurt too much to cry, so he closed his eye and waited for the feeling to pass.

"Do you know what happened here?" Deimos asked. He grabbed his sword and, with Audra, shuffled towards the door.

"The Witch made Vrana do it," Felix said. Lucan followed after them.

Deimos stepped over the corpses of Avery and Mackenzie. "Do you know how?"

Felix buried his face in Lucan's chest. "No," he babbled. He wished both his eyes were swollen shut, so he didn't have to see them like that.

They moved into the halls outside Felix's room. There were five more dead bodies staining the carpet, those of the gossipmongers who forever roamed Pyra's distinguished places. A few torches and candles burned along the walls, but elsewhere, further down in both directions, all lights were extinguished.

Felix's stomach grumbled nervously. "How many people did they kill?"

Lucan ignored him, said, "Where are the rest of the guards?"

"Not many guards," Audra rasped. "Don't want Pyra to look like a prison."

Deimos shook his head and raised his sword. "Where's the Mother Abbess? Isn't her quarters near?"

Felix nodded. He had one last look at the halos of gore that hovered where his best friends' heads should have been. Where was Justine? Or her guards? Why hadn't they come? He bit the side of his mouth to stop himself from cursing the Mother Abbess' name.

Audra raised her head. Chin quivering, she chattered, "Why's it so dark?"

Lucan let down Felix. He leaned against the wall and grabbed one of the two torches in the hall.

"It was not like this a few minutes ago," Deimos said, his breath puffs of fog on the air. "It is colder, too."

Felix brushed off Lucan's attempts to help him. He limped over to Audra, to share the torch's warmth with her. "Here," he said, smiling until she smiled.

Deimos lowered Audra from his shoulders. The dagger went deeper into her shoulder, but she held her composure.

"Leave it," Deimos said as she reached to rip it free. "You don't want to lose any more blood."

Audra scowled at him. She turned to Felix and said, "Thanks, but I'm really hot right now." It was true: her face was practically melting, and the slip was almost indistinguishable from her skin. "I'll be okay, though." She ruffled Felix's hair. "Do you smell that?"

Lucan crossed the hall and grabbed the other torch. "Smells like a toad," he said. He leaned forward, into the darkness that surrounded them. "Smells like a fat, rotted toad."

Felix listened closely. There was something else, something out there in the dark at both ends of the hall. It smelled awful, but it sounded... heavy. Thump. Skhhh. Thump. Skhhh. It sounded as though it were dragging a block of stone. Thump. Skhhh. Thump. Skhhh. But it was doing it as quietly as it could. Thinking, maybe, no one would hear.

Deimos took the torch out of Felix's hand. "Get ready to run," he whispered. "We're not alone."

Lucan nodded at Deimos and, together, both Night Terrors hurled their torches down the opposite ends of the hall. At first, as the torches lay there, singeing the carpet, there was nothing. But then the sounds started again. Thump. Skhhh. Thump. Skhhh. Thump. Skhhh.

"Is there any other way out?" Lucan grabbed Avery's sword off the ground. "Holy Child!" He shook Felix. "Is there any other way?"

But Felix wasn't paying him any attention. Ahead of them, a leg had stepped into the light. A pale, stone limb, with a waxen sheet that swayed around it. His head snapped back to the other end of the hall. There, a head floating above the torchlight, star-shaped and twitching. It looked like it was laughing.

"Run," Felix cried. He grabbed Audra's arm and pulled her back towards his room.

He didn't get a foot before the petrified Holy Children toppled him over and tore Audra away. Felix slammed into the wall and fell on top of Mackenzie's corpse. He grabbed her sword and struggled to his feet.

Deimos stabbed at one of the Holy Children. It caught the blade, and it broke it in its grip. With the shards in its palm, it punched them into Deimos' chest. He flew off his feet and into the open arms of the statue that had snuck up behind him.

Several more of the Holy Children ambled into the hall. Lucan hacked at their heads and sides, but the statues would not be stopped by the blows. They closed in until he couldn't move. One reached out and caught his arm, mid-swing. It snapped the bone in half and flung him across the hall. A smaller statue, jittery and giggling, quickly scooped him up and held him against its chest.

"Get out of here," Audra screamed.

537

Felix snapped out of it and saw her being hauled away by four statues, each one holding a limb.

He hurtled down the hall after her, tears and spit streaming down his face, belting, "Let her go, god damn you," when, as though out of thin air, Justine appeared before him.

Sword inches from her stomach, he dropped it and crashed into her. She wrapped her arms around him, stopped his momentum.

He pushed off her and screamed, "Make them stop!"

Justine sighed. "It's okay." She smiled. She couldn't have been calmer when she said, "They will not hurt them."

"What?" Felix laughed in disbelief. Deimos' chest. Lucan's arm. And Audra was on the verge of being split like a wishbone between the four statues that held her. "Are you kidding me?"

His pupils dilated with undiluted hatred. In that moment, he didn't care who she was, what she had done for him. In that moment, he could have killed her.

Justine was wearing a white dress tonight. A simple dress, but it was covered in ornate needlework that, even in the light, would be impossible to make sense of. It wasn't that the images were confusing; it was the fact that they were of symbols and shapes that simply didn't exist. Still smiling, she plucked a piece of thread from it and let it go. As soon as it touched the ground, it shriveled into diamond dust.

Through his teeth, Felix said, "What are you trying to be tonight?"

"Hmm?" Justine looked down and touched her dress. "Oh. Just myself, Felix. For once." She held out her hand. "Please, come with me."

He batted it away. "I'm not going anywhere." Deimos and Lucan struggled behind him. Audra had passed out. "Not until you let them go."

"Let go of Audra of Eldrus and the Night Terrors who broke into Pyra?" She shook her head. "That's not for me to decide, Felix."

"You're the Mother—"

"It's for you to decide." She held out her hand again. "If you want me to let them go, I will let them go. All I ask, your holiness, is that you listen to what I have to say."

"You're testing me." He looked at her fingers, so close to his, and thought about biting them off. "No, you're a liar! You have been tricking me this whole time. You don't care about me!"

Justine's hand returned to her side. "The test is over, Felix. I care about you more than anything else in this wretched world. That's why I am going to tell you everything. And you're going to tell me where we go from here." She went to her knees, her head at his feet. "Will you hear me out, your holiness? Do what you will with me afterward. No one will stop you, but don't you want to know why I've done this to you?"

CHAPTER XII

Felix stood at the furthest end of the Ascent, where an old, narrow staircase ran upward into a door built within the ceiling. Between him and the staircase was a wrought iron gate with more locks than Pyra itself. Though it had never been heavily manned, the Mother Abbess was known to be seen in the area on a daily basis, making sure the locks hadn't been tampered with. Surprisingly, Felix never had much interest in figuring out a way to get past the gates. To him, the gates were heaven's gates, and the staircase the bridge between this world and the next. It was a mystery that, unlike most things, was best left a mystery; because the less he understood of it, the longer it would last. He knew he would grow old, grow doubtful and different, and adulthood would corrode most of his childish fantasies. But if he kept heaven safe, deep down where his grimy soul squirmed, he could keep it forever.

But things were different now. With the Holy Children who had preceded him at his back, Felix watched as Justine undid the locks to heaven. She didn't need a key. Her hands were the key. One by one, the locks fell to the ground, thudding against the stone floor. Yesterday, he might have told her to stop, but tonight, all he wanted her to do was go faster. If god was at the top of those stairs, he would run to god. And if god was not, if heaven was as empty as he thought it might be, he would wait and do the best he could. Because anywhere was better than here.

Felix, staring over his shoulder at the Holy Children, said, "The stairs aren't wide enough for them to follow."

Justine removed the last lock. She held it in her hand. "They will have to wait down here, until we are finished."

Though nothing was holding it back, it took a moment for the gate to creak open. Locked up for so long, it had forgotten it could do such a thing.

Felix stayed rooted to his spot, arms crossed, his swollen eye now something he wore like a badge of honor.

Justine nodded at the Holy Children. "Deimos, Lucan, and Audra will be fine, I promise."

Fine? They were beaten and bruised and, in the arms of the Holy Children, appeared broken. Felix turned to Justine. "Where were you? Didn't you hear what was happening?"

"I went back to the Tribunal, to speak with the Demagogue about locating Isla Taggart. She was his star pupil, and a menace, if left to her own devices." Her eyes began to water, but it seemed as though she were forcing the tears out. "I came as fast as I could. I am very sorry about Avery and Mackenzie."

Felix shook his head. He didn't need to hear their names right now. Instead, he went forward, past Justine and through the gates. "Where are we going?" he asked, stopping at the foot of the staircase. A cold wind rolled down the steps, a chilling reminder that heaven, if it were up there, may not be what he expected.

"To get some fresh air," Justine said.

Felix looked at the Holy Children, at the Mother Abbess. He gritted his teeth in an unspoken threat that Justine registered with a nod. Taking a deep breath—it felt like a sin to walk into in heaven still living—he slowly started up the stairs. With each step he took, he grew colder and colder, until halfway up, he was shivering so badly he thought he might not walk into heaven alive after all.

"Here," Justine said, at his back. "Take this." She wrapped a blanket around his shoulders that she had seemingly conjured out of nowhere. It was white and featured the same intricate, impossible needlework found on her dress. "It'll keep you warm."

And it did. As soon as it touched his skin, a dull, liquid warmth washed over him and thawed the sudden frost. He pulled it down across his chest. He breathed in the fabric, and it smelled of burning wood. The scent, so strong and distinctly Justine's, caught him off-guard.

The Winnowers' Chapter often accused the people of Penance of worshiping the institution—the exemplars, the Mother Abbess, and the Holy Child himself—and, honestly, how could he blame them? Her scent and this private belonging had almost instantly made him forget his animosity towards her. Having heaven behind these gates was all well and good, but it was the touch, the tangibility, he and the rest of Penance cherished most. And who was he kidding? If he could grasp heaven, he wouldn't keep it deep down, where his grimy soul squirmed. He would take it out every day, look at it, and be proud of it. Yet, he didn't, because he couldn't touch it. It wasn't tangible. And maybe, not there at all.

Felix pulled the blanket closer and stomped his way to the top of the stairs. Besides the beatings he took, these grown-up thoughts were giving him a migraine.

I know it's you putting all this in my head, he said to god, completely disregarding the fact he had questioned heaven's existence moments ago. *Now's not a good time. Just help me get through tonight. Please. Help us all get through.*

"The door is open," Justine said behind him.

Felix stopped. He reached out to the ceiling, to a rectangular outline etched in the stone. It didn't look like a door so much as it did the front of a tomb.

"Give it a push, and it will give."

So he did. Cringing, because he didn't know what to expect, he threw his weight into the door. It fought him, not moving an inch from its place. But then Justine touched it. The door flung backward, as though a great force had wrenched it open.

Behind the door, there was only sky. The night sky. Moonlit and snow-speckled, the dark stretch was made brighter still by the bands of green light billowing across it. Auroras, an exemplar had told him once, that was their name. Felix had seen them here and there, but not like this, not so close. They were beautiful, breathtaking. They didn't seem a part of this world, but a glimpse of another. A place in-between. A portal, or a Membrane.

"Go on." Justine touched the small of his back. He flinched. "Go through."

Felix hurried up the steps, out and onto what was now obviously the roof of Pyra. The snow wasn't as deep here as it should have been, but with the abbey and the whole of Penance below and before him, he didn't care too much to consider such things.

"Beautiful, isn't it?" Justine chirped. She stepped onto the roof with him and stood beside him. "It's hard to appreciate the city when you've lived in it so long, but it is truly beautiful."

Justine had made a lot of bold statements over the last few weeks, especially regarding Audra being a Worm of the Earth. But saying Penance was beautiful? That was one sentiment Felix could get behind.

They were at the top of Pyra, which sat higher than the city itself. From here, for the first time in his life, he could view Penance in its glacial glory. He knew the city-state was huge, but to see it sprawled out for miles on end, from the frozen plains to the icy shore, was breathtaking. It had the quality of a crystal to it. There were large structures, angular and raw; crowded around them were smaller buildings, homes and local businesses. Penance didn't look like a place that had been built, but grown. A place where a hand far more capable than humanity's own had planted a seed and nurtured it for eons on end, to see it through the north's harsh climate. Felix could see god in it all, in every brick and stone, in every window and well. He still didn't know Justine's reason for bringing him up here, but if it had been to calm him physically, mentally, and spiritually, then she had succeeded.

"It won't look like this in the morning," Justine said. "In the light, you see all the city's flaws. Right now, most of those flaws are asleep—"

Felix cut her off by saying, "What did you want to tell me? Why are you stalling?"

Justine furrowed her brow. Her skin, so pale in the moonlight, left her veins on full display. "This is hard for me, too. I have to share something with you that I have only shared with a few."

Felix shrugged one shoulder, not nearly as disinterested as he was trying to appear.

Justine swallowed a mouthful of apprehension and said, "Have you decided if Audra of Eldrus is a Worm or not?"

The test. This was it. This was the moment where he either became the final Holy Child or one of those abominations below. What could he say? The truth? Or what she wanted to hear? In the last twenty minutes, he had already disrespected her more than he had during the whole time he had known her. And he had aided an enemy of the city and the Holy Order on more than one occasion.

Felix looked into Justine's eyes, which were like crystals them-selves—sparkling, lifeless, and cold—and said, "She is not a Worm of the Earth." He tightened his shoulders and braced for the fallout.

Justine hummed, nodded. "No, Felix, she's not. Because I am."

Taken aback, Felix said, "What?"

"I am a Worm of the Earth."

Felix shook his head. "Why are you doing this to me?"

Justine smiled. She reached back, undid her dress, and let it fall around her ankles. Underneath, she was naked, and looked like any other naked woman Felix had accidentally and purposefully seen in the past. Except, she didn't. Her breasts were without nipples, and between her legs she was sexless. And her chest, there was something wrong with her chest. She was wearing a necklace—he had always seen the chain, but never the piece itself. It was silver, with a white gem inside a tangle of worms. But behind the jewelry, there was a scorched hole that ran deep into her chest. Inside that, something was fixed, as though it had been lodged in there for safekeeping.

"I... I..." Felix covered his eyes. She took his hands away from his face and placed them at his sides. "I... I... you shouldn't say that about... about yourself."

A little bit of heat rushed to Justine's cheeks. "I am a Worm, Felix. Let me show you."

The Mother Abbess' stomach began to bubble and bulge, as though something were trying to break free. With a sickening tear, her stomach split open and tens of white, steaming tendrils spilt out. Fixed upon each one was a woman's face. In his horror, some of the faces even looked familiar to Felix. The tendrils snaked their way up Justine's body. As they did so, she continued to tear down the mid-dle, opening like a Venus flytrap. Her head sank down inside her and one of the tendrils took its place. Her body, wet and glistening, and twisted like a sheet, then began to relax, reform. Her skin took on different shades and her physique became thinner and heavier. At times, she had a penis, and others a vagina, and sometimes, between her legs, there was a gnashing mouth or long, flailing arms. The met-amorphosis went on for only a minute, but to Felix, it felt like hours.

The display did eventually come to an end. And when it did, Jus-tine's head worked its way out of her stomach and back onto her shoulders. The tendrils retreated into her gut, and her skin stitched itself back up. When she looked herself again, she slipped back into her dress and said, "I am the White Worm of the Earth. Do you doubt me still?"

He shook his head. At this moment, it was about all he could do.

"I am not going to hurt you. But I do have a lot to tell you." She took out the silver, white-gemmed necklace and let it lie over her dress. "May I share my secrets with you?"

Felix's thoughts had come to a standstill. He stared at her blankly, the transformation replaying over and over in his mind.

"I was testing you, Felix, but you already knew that. It wasn't a test of loyalty to me or the Holy Order, but a test of loyalty to yourself. As I did before and do now, I want you to be the last Holy Child. And I cannot lead Penance to greatness with someone who lacks the courage to do the right thing because it might hurt someone else's feelings.

"I had you follow Isla Taggart, because I wanted you to become aware of their schemes and alliance with the Disciples of the Deep. I had you speak with Audra, because I wanted you to challenge our system, to find humanity in those we consider enemies. And, yes, I did lie to you about her being a Worm of the Earth. I needed you to know that my brethren exist, and I needed to know how little effort it would take to sway you to my side, to my beliefs."

Felix covered his mouth. "Did I… f-fail?"

Justine let out a kind laugh. "No, you passed. You exceeded all my expectations. Felix—" she held his chin, ran her thumb along his cheek, "—you have convinced me. But now I must convince you."

Fear bringing him to a freeze, he pulled the blanket closer. "You're a Worm… You don't have to listen to me."

"But I want to."

Felix nodded. A tear slipped down his cheek. Justine caught it with her thumb. "Okay," he said. What else could he say? "Okay," he repeated, eyes going sideways, looking at the door, looking at his only escape. "Okay."

"Good." Justine let go of his chin, took a deep breath, and turned to face the city. "I am the White Worm of the Earth. There are many of us. We are all parts of a greater whole. Each of us, like the Red Worm or the Green Worm, have one purpose. It was from this purpose we are born. And when that purpose is fulfilled, we die. The Red Worm is violence incarnate. By violence, the Red Worm is born, and by the violence it provokes, it is destroyed. The Green Worm is disease, rot, and filth. I am the White Worm. I am humanity's need to understand those things it cannot. I am humanity's reassurance that all they do is not for nothing. I am religion. It is my purpose, and it should have been my downfall.

"I have lived many lives, Felix. You have seen them all, in the portraits in the Ascent, of every Mother Abbess that has come before me. Beginning as Mother Abbess Priscilla, I have worked effortlessly, for so many years now, creating and maintaining the Holy Order of Penance. To hide my identity, and to ensure our great city was not led to ruin, I created a line of successors, each being myself, of course. This is my purpose, you see. It is all I am supposed to know and do. And by my purpose, I will one day die. But there is a threat to my purpose lurking in the West, and I cannot let it destroy what I have spent so many, many years creating."

"The Disciples of the Deep," Felix whispered, enraptured. "King Edgar's new religion."

"Yes. And do you not agree our Holy Order is wonderful and necessary?"

Felix nodded.

"And though you may not realize it, the Disciples of the Deep are a threat. They may seem small. They may seem as though they have much catching up to do. But they have one thing we do not."

Felix shook his head. "What?"

"They have a God."

He looked pained as he said, "What? No, we have a god, too."

"No, we do not. We do not have a god. We have an idea of a god. We have everything a god could want, but we do not have a god ourselves."

"No!" Felix raised his fist, and then quickly put it back down. "No, we do. I hear god. I am god's speaker. You said it yourself! I hear god almost every day."

"You hear yourself, Felix, and what you think god would say to you, or what I would say to you. But I assure you, there is no god listening to our prayers—" she outstretched her hand to Penance, "—or to theirs. There is no god. Only us. And what we can do for them."

I don't believe it, he thought. He shouted, "I don't believe it!"

"There is a God, though, Felix." Justine touched the silver necklace, clutched in her pale grip. "There is a God. It is the Vermillion

God. It is the greater whole of which I and the other Worms are a part of. Liken the Worms to angels if you like. We are God's dutiful servants, meant to punish, empower, or pave the way."

"Then that's the God who has been speaking to me," Felix said. He chewed on his lip. "That's the voice I hear."

Justine sighed and said, "No, it is not. And you should be happy that it is not. Do you want to know why?"

Again, Felix shook his head. He crossed his arms and ground his heels into the snow.

"What we have here is better. What I have created, what you have created, is better. Its foundations are lies, but so are the foundations of all religions. There is a god out there, Felix, but the Vermillion God is not the god this world needs."

"You're confusing me." Felix held the sides of his head. He tried to hide inside himself, but the White Worm's gaze kept him anchored. "This doesn't make sense. No! This doesn't make any sense!"

"Yes, it does. You understand what I am saying completely. I do not fault you for not wanting to hear what I have to say, but you must listen."

Felix squeezed his eyes shut. He moaned, fell to his knees, and back on his legs.

"The Vermillion God is responsible for the Trauma. A woman named Lillian—yes, the same Lillian from which our Holy Order was created—and her followers, after so many, many years of preparation, were able to finally awaken It. You would think that humanity would be relieved to finally have some closure on whether there is a god or not. But it wasn't. Humanity tried to adapt, and the one true religion, the Lillians, was formed, but it wasn't enough. The humans still fought one another, destroyed one another, even over their clearly outdated and untrue beliefs. There was an even greater schism between the faiths than before. Eventually, humanity turned its ire towards the Vermillion God, which sat on Earth itself, and they tried to kill It.

"Gods are difficult to destroy. The Vermillion God is a god of great patience, but also incomprehensible cruelty. It gave humanity time to realize its mistake, to cease the attacks. But as millions of unbelievers sieged the Vermillion God, the world was tearing itself apart. To put it simply, humanity was not ready. So the Vermillion God made a decision.

"The Trauma was that decision. It would punish the humans for their attacks, for their refusal to commit to Its one, true religion. The Vermillion God stood and raised Its arms high, and over the course of unmeasurable time, stripped humanity bare. All creations were consumed. Cities were annihilated. The Earth was ripped apart, land masses shifted. Even ideas were eaten. The Vermillion God did not intend to destroy humanity completely. It only wanted to humiliate humanity, to traumatize it so deeply they would feel the effects of the Vermillion God's power for as long as their species existed.

"After that, the Vermillion God went back to sleep, back to the desert and the darkness, where we Worms reside as well. But you want to know the funny thing, Felix?"

He remained silent.

"The Vermillion God anticipated humanity would try to wake It once more. It is an inevitability. So what did It do? During the Trauma, the Vermillion God devoured the unbelievers and took them back to heaven, where it could feast on their suffering and, occasionally, send them to Earth to do minor tasks."

"Audra's shadows," Felix croaked.

Justine nodded. "And you, them—" she pointed to her right arm, at the fake Corruption there, "—are those that were left behind."

"But we are Corrupted." Felix rubbed the damning mark.

"No, you're not." Justine started to laugh uncontrollably. She covered her mouth, quickly gathered herself. "You're not Corrupted. You're Chosen. Humanity's Corruption has a kind of vermillion shade to it, does it not?"

Felix nodded.

"Not all, but most of those who were left behind by the Vermillion God were believers, Lillians. For their service and dedication, the Vermillion God gave them a boon: a coloration of their right arm that would be passed down, until the end of time, to signify their bloodlines' allegiance to God."

Felix dug his nails into his right arm. "But why is it called Corruption?"

Justine smirked. "Because humans are stupid. Because humans are forgetful. Because humans find flaws and turn them into the tools of persecution and control. It didn't happen immediately, but over time, what was once a blessing became known as a curse. All those things you hear about Corruption and it having to do with humanity's pre-disposition to violence is nothing more than a lie. A lie that started with the Night Terrors which, through humanity's own self-fulfilling prophecy, eventually took root and became truth. The Night Terrors used it as a means to separate themselves from the humans, to justify murdering them for their cultural reasons. Humanity fought this belief for a while, and then, with the help of the burgeoning religions of the time, they fell for it."

Felix struggled to his feet. "How... how do you know all this?"

"I have been alive since the Trauma. When the Vermillion God left, there was a need for religion. Untold numbers of people were slaughtered in an attempt to create some sort of spiritual order, and from their bloody, mutilated carcasses, I was born. I had watched from heaven all the Vermillion God had done, so I knew what to do when I was awoken. I met Lillian and tracked down her ragtag group of followers, and over time and across the continent, built back up that very religion which had almost killed the Earth.

"But something happened to me. When we settled Six Pillars, I realized I could do better. I could do better than the Lillian faith or the Vermillion God. I am religion, you see. It is all I know and am. And I realized I could do better. Because if I continued to work towards waking the Vermillion God, Trauma would come again, undoubtedly, and I would die. But if I created my own religion, one which could unify, one which could be reasonable and accepting of others, then I would have a religion that would persist, and I would live forever.

"I do not want to die, Felix. I have lived too long and worked too hard. I know that I am being selfish, but I am just being honest. But think on what I have told you. The Vermillion God. What It is capable of and what Its followers will do in Its name. Do you really want this world and your people to have to experience such an existential agony again?"

Felix didn't know what existential meant, but he shook his head all the same.

"Archivist Amon of Ghostgrave has been working very diligently for hundreds of years to bring the Vermillion God back. A few years ago, King Edgar began terraforming the Heartland to make it more agreeable to the Vermillion God's influence. Now, he has summoned the Red Worm and somehow had it defeated, to bolster the Disciples of the Deep's claims and demonstrate the existence of an entity that is more powerful than our non-existent god here in Penance. If left unchecked, King Edgar will get what he wants. Our world is much different now than it was in the Old World. There are less people. Information is not as readily available. Humanity has regressed. This time, if the Vermillion God is woken, it will stay awake. And Felix, this is something we cannot allow to happen. This is a God that revels in sacrifice and slaughter. Do you think that It will show benevolence when there is no one or nothing left to challenge It?"

Felix struggled to find his words, his sanity. He felt as though he were standing in hell, being tempted by a demon to betray everything he had ever believed in.

"We do not have a god on our side. But we are the single largest religion in the world. People believe in the Holy Order without even realizing it. We have the single largest city in the world. If we so wished it, we could have an army to destroy all armies. But I do not want that. I do not wish to secure our place in history by violence. I am the White Worm, not the Red. Religion is eternal. Our deeds must be eternal. The Disciples of the Deep have already begun the conversion. We must win back those we have lost. The imagination is a powerful weapon. King Edgar deals in tangibility, but we have what humanity's mind can conjure. Our promises are ethereal, but soothing. King Edgar's are harsh, and foul. We do not need a god. We only need each other. The Mother Abbess and the Holy Child. As it has always been, and as it should always be.

"So what say you, my love?" Justine went to one knee and bowed her head. "I am a monster, but I do not wish for monstrous things. I have gone beyond my purpose. Like the shadows, I was stripped, left to be one thing only, but somehow, I've become something more again. The decision is yours, Felix, but the decision must be made now."

Felix's hand was shaky as it reached out and touched Justine's soft hair. He ran his fingers across her scalp. He could feel ancient, eldritch things beneath it, squirming inside her skull. "I remember... you said there was the Anointed One. The Disciple's own Holy Child."

"Yes," Justine said. "Like myself, like Archivist Amon, he is just one part of the Vermillion God's whole. He did not have a choice. He is only what he is, and nothing more."

"If I said no, what... would happen?"

"We would clean up the bodies of those that attacked you, and you would go to bed. And we start tomorrow as we do all days."

"Even after everything you told me?"

"I can't take that back from you now."

"Would I be turned into a statue?"

"No, because you would not live to your eighteenth birthday. The Vermillion God and Its followers will make sure of that."

"What about Audra? And Deimos and Lucan?" He touched her face, touched her jawbone. She nudged his hand, as though comforted by it.

"Do what you like with them. Have them killed. Or let them go. They cannot stay, though."

"Aren't you afraid Audra will go back to King Edgar?"

Justine sighed. "If she goes back to her brother, it will be to kill him."

Felix crouched down, fingered the silver, white-gemmed necklace that Justine wore. "What is the Cult of the Worm? I saw a necklace like this, but it was blue."

"The Worms of the Earth are not aware of one another. They cannot track one another or contact one another. The Vermillion God made it so that they could not overthrow It or work together to create even greater chaos. But a blue necklace? That would be the Blue Worm, the Worm of knowledge, forbidden knowledge. I do not know why it is hunting you. I expect you have more to share on that matter. But if it has a cult of its own, then it, too, has overstepped its boundaries."

"Why are you hurt?" Felix moved the necklace aside, pulled down her dress to reveal the black hole in her chest. "It smells like a fire. You always smell like a fire."

"Here." Justine reached into the hole, her forearm deep in her chest, and removed what was inside. It was a small, white stone, with strange symbols like those of her dress burnt into it. "This is a sealing stone."

Felix took it. It bit his hand with invisible teeth, but he grinned through it. "What is it?"

"My death." She lifted the necklace, the white gem catching the moonlight. "To summon a Worm, a sacrifice and a necklace is required. This is my necklace. A Worm wears it while it is alive. When a Worm exists, a sealing stone is created. The stone is used to send the Worm back to sleep. That way, there is always a method by which to rid the world of Worms."

"I can kill you with this?" He turned the stone over in his hand. "You've been carrying it this whole time?"

"Day by day, I have lived in excruciating pain, keeping that object a secret, so that no one could use it again. But it is yours now. Offer it to me, and I have to accept it. And if I do, then I will be gone." Justine's eyes went wide, appealing to him. "I have given you everything, Felix. All that I am."

Felix ran his fingers across the stone. He felt a power unlike any other coursing through their tips. He didn't have to make a decision. All he had to do was give the White Worm the stone and send her back to the desert. Then, he could leave with Audra and the Night Terrors and be rid of this madness. He could be something other than the voice of god, something which he had apparently never been.

But instead, Felix set the stone in the snow and touched Justine's forehead gently. "I accept," he said. Her took her hand and helped her to her feet. "Give Audra and the Night Terrors safe passage and I will help you."

Justine threw her arms around him and pulled him close. He could feel the white tendrils inside her, moving behind her flesh, a hundred lives and lies at her beck and call. He should have feared her, but he didn't. He did, but not anymore. For the first time since he had met her, he knew exactly what she was and what she wanted. And if there was truth to what she wanted, he wanted it, too. But most of all, he didn't want to hurt anymore. He didn't want the grime, the guilt. God hadn't done anything for him he hadn't already done himself. Somewhere, there was probably some other little boy being taken into the South, being beaten and abused, and almost broken beyond repair. And what for? A heaven that only promised hell?

Felix let go of the White Worm. "The Cult took a friend of mine. A friend who saved me in the South from Samuel Turov. There's a Witch, the Maiden of Pain. Somehow, it's all connected. I tried to get her back."

"That makes sense now," Justine said, her cheeks rosy, her skin looking healthier than before. "Do you want to save her?"

Felix nodded. "I have to."

Justine took Felix's hand. "Then we will save her."

"How?"

"We are gods now, Felix. We will save her however we like."

YOU HAVE BEEN READING

"THE THREE HERETICS."

GLOSSARY

GLOSSARY

Terms in **bold** may contain spoilers for *The Three Heretics*

The Abyss: Where all who die are said to go.

Amon Ashcroft: The Archivist of Eldrus.

Arachne: Half-human, half-spider creatures from Atlach.

Alexander Blodworth: Understudy of Samuel Turov, an exemplar of Penance. He was given the task of going to Geharra to create a smokescreen for the disappearance of the Holy Child. Instead, he planted the Crossbreed in the city-state's sewer system and used it to control the entire populace. Along with the people of Alluvia, a neighboring Night Terror village to the city, Geharra's population was sacrificed by Alexander to birth the Red Worm.

Alluvia: The nearest Night Terror village to Geharra. It is the home of R'lyeh.

The Anointed One: Speaker for the Disciples of the Deep.

Ashen Man: His real name is Seth Barker. Partner of Herbert North. He was a supernatural investigator from the twentieth century who was investigating deaths and disappearances in the town Nachtla. There, he discovered the Witch, and fell in love with her. She took him into the Void and transformed him into one of her grotesque servants.

Audra: King Edgar's sister. She is a gifted botanist and appears to have an ability to speak with and manipulate shadows.

The Binding Road: A road, much like the Spine, that cuts through the Nameless Forest. It is one of the few places untouched by the Forest's chaos.

Black Hour: A temporal aberration that occurs at midnight and lasts for one hour. During this period of time, anything that has happened, will happen, or may never happen is possible.

Bloodless: A mythological plant, like the Crossbreed, that is said to be capable of draining an entire town's worth of blood in one night.

Blue Worm: A Worm of the Earth that was awoken on Lacuna by the Night Terrors to learn ancient knowledge. The Blue Worm taught the Night Terrors about magic, as well as how to procreate more effectively.

Cadence: The small southern village where Vrana leaves the little boy who she later learns was the Holy Child. Upon learning the Holy Child is there, Penance rides into the town, kills everyone, and returns the Holy Child to Penance.

Caldera: Vrana's home, and the southern-most Night Terror village. The village is built at the base of Kistvaen, a massive mountain.

Corrupted: A derogatory term used by the Night Terrors to identify humans. Humans are called this due to the crimson pigmentation in the skin of their right arms. The Night Terrors believe this defect is evidence of humanity's pre-disposition to violence; they use this as justification to murder the humans.

Crossbreed: A massive plant created from ingredients that are not supposed to work together. It secretes fluids that cause those who ingest them to become extremely susceptible to suggestion.

Dead City: An Old World city of skyscrapers and modern technology that is unreachable due to the poisonous fumes that cover the peninsula it sits upon.

Deimos: A Night Terror who wears a bat skull. He was a watcher of Geharra. His husband, Johannes, was killed by Corrupted. He hunted down Johannes' killers, but in doing so neglected his duties of keeping watch over Geharra. This allowed Penance to enter the city and take over its people.

Derleth: A Night Terror who wears an eel skull. R'lyeh had a crush on him. He is responsible for tricking R'lyeh into planting the Crossbreed's roots in Alluvia's water supply, thus giving Alexander Blodworth the ability to easily take over the village on his way to Penance.

The Disciples of the Deep: Eldrus' new religion.

The Divide: The massive river that cuts through the content, separating the snowy lands of Penance from the Heartland.

The Dread Clock: Rumored to be the origin of the Black Hour; a grandfather clock thought to be located in the Nameless Forest.

Edgar: The youngest of the royal family of Eldrus. He is the King of Eldrus, though his ascent to power is a mystery to most.

Eldrus: The northern city-state that sits above the Heartland. It is governed by a monarchy that is led by King Edgar.

Exemplars: Six individuals who are meant to be the embodiment of a certain skill or trait. They are meant to be examples for the people of Penance to follow.

Flesh fiends: Subterranean creatures with a conflicted mythology. They wear the flesh and body parts of their victims. When a Corrupted and a Night Terror mate, there is a chance a flesh fiend will be born. They were last spotted in the sacrificial pit of Geharra, as well as near the island of Lacuna.

Geharra: The western-most city-state. The Night Terrors favor this city due to its lack of interest in war and expansion. Now, due to Alexander Blodworth, the entire population is dead; they have become one with the Red Worm.

The Heartland: The lifeblood of Eldrus; many towns and villages exist here, including Gallows, Bedlam, Nyxis, Hrothas, Islaos, and Cathedra.

Herbert North: Seth Barker's (the Ashen Man) partner in supernatural investigations. Currently resides in the Membrane.

Holy Child: Believed to be the speaker for Penance's god. Only the Mother Abbess is higher than him in importance in the Holy Order of Penance.

Samuel Turov stole the Holy Child away into the South for unknown reasons, and kept him there until Vrana killed Samuel.

Johannes: A Night Terror who wears a fox skull. He was Deimos' husband.

Kistvaen: The massive mountain that sits behind Caldera. It may be a dormant or extinct volcano.

Lacuna: An island off the eastern coast. It sits within the Widening Gyre, and it is hidden from prying eyes by spellweavers. The Blue Worm was awakened on this island, and used by Mara and other Night Terrors to learn its secrets, as well as to discover a way to repopulate the Night Terror people.

Lotus: The mayor of Threadbare.

Lucan: A Night Terror who wears a beetle skull. He and Deimos were both last seen making contact with Penance outside of Geharra; this was after the Red Worm had been born.

The Maiden of Joy: Also known as Crestfallen, Joy, or Adelaide.

Mara: A Night Terror who wears a mask made out of centipedes. She was in control of Lacuna's fertility project. She has had run-ins with the Witch in the past.

The Membrane: A plane that exists between life and death; an area that may connect to additional planes and horrible dwellings. The dead pass through here.

Mother Abbess Justine: The ultimate authority of the Holy Order of Penance. Also known as the Hydra of Penance.

Nacthla: A small, abandoned town where it is believed a portal may exist into the Witch's Void.

The Nameless Forest: Like the Black Hour, anything is possible here; except the Nameless Forest is not bound by time, so the chaos it contains is constant. It is from here the vermillion veins are said to originate.

Night Terror: A race of humanoids whose entire culture and purpose is to understand and murder the Corrupted. They are believed to be supernatural creatures, though their origins are a mystery. The only actual observable difference between Night Terrors and Corrupted is that Night Terrors lack Corruption.

Old World: The world before the Trauma.

Ossuary: A massive desert located at the southern-most point of the continent. No one goes there, and nothing is said to thrive there.

Penance: The eastern-most city-state. It is the home of the Holy Order of Penance.

Pyra: The headquarters for the Holy Order of Penance.

Red Worm: A Worm of the Earth that was summoned from the ten thousand dead that had been raped and murdered in the bowels of Geharra. It is currently on the loose.

R'lyeh: A thirteen-year-old Night Terror who wears an octopus as a mask. One of the few survivors from the genocide of Geharra. Her hometown is Alluvia. She was Vrana's companion.

Samuel Turov: The Exemplar of Restraint. For unknown reasons, he stole the Holy Child and took him south.

Scavengers: A splinter group of the Lillians (who were an older incarnation of the Holy Order of Penance). They reside outside Geharra, where they worship a large, achromatic tower. They believe god lives inside the tower.

Shadows: Strange creatures that exist inside the Membrane. Audra of Eldrus has been known to speak with them.

Silver Necklaces with (colored) gems: Objects which are essential in the rituals used to summon the Worms of the Earth. When a Worm is summoned, it leaves behind a sealing stone, which is used to put the Worm back to sleep. When a Worm is put back to sleep, it leaves behind a silver necklace.

Six Pillars: An older name of Penance.

The Skeleton: A mysterious individual who Vrana sees twice in her journey. She meets him once in the Black Hour, and once again on the island of Lacuna. Mara tells Vrana the Skeleton was responsible for leading a rebellion against King Edgar.

Spellweavers: Individuals who are capable of magic.

The Spine: A massive highway system that once spanned the entire continent but has since fallen into disrepair.

The Trauma: A catastrophic event of unknown origin that has led the world to the state it is in now.

The Void: The home of the Witch.

The Woman in White Satin: A woman who lives inside the Nameless Forest and has charged Edgar with the task of killing the rulers of each village there.

The Worms of the Earth: Biological weapons of destruction brought about by ritualistic depravity and sacrifice. They are powerful creatures that have to be sustained by death. One Worm generally provokes the birth of another Worm.

Vermillion Veins: Growths thought to only exist in the Nameless Forest. They are sometimes known to appear elsewhere on the continent but for reasons unknown.

Victor Mors: A philosopher who was assassinated for his studies into the Membrane and the Worms of the Earth.

Vrana: A Night Terror who wears the mask of a raven. She was mutated by the Witch into a grotesque raven-like creature, and is now currently imprisoned in the Void.

Winnowers' Chapter: An elitist group of Holy Order members who disagree with the direction the Mother Abbess is taking the religion.

The Witch: Also known as the Maiden of Pain, the Witch has been responsible for countless deaths over untold years. She attacked Vrana's village of Caldera, and had been using Vrana as a way by which to spread her influence, so as to increase in power and relevance.

ABOUT THE AUTHOR

SCOTT HALE is the author of *The Bones of the Earth* series and screen-writer of *Entropy, Free to a Bad Home, and Effigies.* He is the co-owner of Halehouse Productions. He is a graduate from Northern Kentucky University with a Bachelors in Psychology and Masters in Social Work. He has completed *The Bones of the Earth* series, and has since begun working on a standalone novel entitled *In Sheep's Skin.* Scott Hale currently resides in Norwood, Ohio with his wife and frequent collaborator, Hannah Graff, and their three cats, Oona, Bashik, and Bellatrix.

Printed in Great Britain
by Amazon